D1029042

WIZARD FOR HIRE

Books by Jim Butcher

The Dresden Files
Storm Front
Fool Moon
Grave Peril
Summer Knight
Death Masks
Blood Rites
Dead Beat *(forthcoming)*

Codex Alera
Furies of Calderon
Academ's Fury *(forthcoming)*

WIZARD FOR HIRE

STORM FRONT
FOOL MOON
GRAVE PERIL

Jim Butcher

Publication History: Roc paperback, April 2000

Publication History: Roc paperback, January 2001

Publication History: Roc paperback, September 2001

First SFBC Science Fiction Printing: April 2005

Published by arrangement with:
New American Library
a division of Penguin Group (USA) Inc.
375 Hudson Street
New York, NY 10014

Visit The SFBC online at *http://www.sfbc.com*

ISBN 0-7394-5193-6

Printed in the United States of America.

CONTENTS

STORM FRONT

For Debbie Chester, who taught me everything I really needed to know about writing. And for my father, who taught me everything I really needed to know about living. I miss you dad.

ACKNOWLEDGMENTS

Special thanks go out to Caroline, Fred, Debra, Tara, and Corin: the original Harry Dresden fans. Without the perverse desire to make you guys scream at me to write the next chapter, Harry would never have gotten into so much trouble. More thanks are due to Ricia Mainhardt and to A. J. Janschewitz, great agents and good people, and to Chris Ely, who is just an all around neat person.

Super special thanks to my son, J. J., who believed his dada had written a good book even if he couldn't read it.

And thank you, Shannon, for too many things to list. You're my angel. One day, I will learn to turn my socks rightside out before throwing them on the bedroom floor.

Chapter 1

I heard the mailman approach my office door, half an hour earlier than usual. He didn't sound right. His footsteps fell more heavily, jauntily, and he whistled. A new guy. He whistled his way to my office door, then fell silent for a moment. Then he laughed.

Then he knocked.

I winced. My mail comes through the mail slot unless it's registered. I get a really limited selection of registered mail, and it's never good news. I got up out of my office chair and opened the door.

The new mailman, who looked like a basketball with arms and legs and a sunburned, balding head, was chuckling at the sign on the door glass. He glanced at me and hooked a thumb toward the sign. "You're kidding, right?"

I read the sign (people change it occasionally), and shook my head. "No, I'm serious. Can I have my mail, please."

"So, uh. Like parties, shows, stuff like that?" He looked past me, as though he expected to see a white tiger, or possibly some skimpily clad assistants prancing around my one-room office.

I sighed, not in the mood to get mocked again, and reached for the mail he held in his hand. "No, not like that. I don't do parties."

He held on to it, his head tilted curiously. "So what? Some kinda fortune-teller? Cards and crystal balls and things?"

"No," I told him. "I'm not a psychic." I tugged at the mail.

He held on to it. "What are you, then?"

"What's the sign on the door say?"

"It says 'Harry Dresden. Wizard.' "

"That's me," I confirmed.

"An actual wizard?" he asked, grinning, as though I should let him in on the joke. "Spells and potions? Demons and incantations? Subtle and quick to anger?"

"Not so subtle." I jerked the mail out of his hand and looked pointedly at his clipboard. "Can I sign for my mail please."

The new mailman's grin vanished, replaced with a scowl. He passed over the clipboard to let me sign for the mail (another late notice from my landlord), and said, "You're a nut. That's what you are." He took his clipboard back, and said, "You have a nice day, sir."

I watched him go.

"Typical," I muttered, and shut the door.

My name is Harry Blackstone Copperfield Dresden. Conjure by it at your own risk. I'm a wizard. I work out of an office in midtown Chicago. As far as I know, I'm the only openly practicing professional wizard in the country. You can find me in the yellow pages, under "Wizards." Believe it or not, I'm the only one there. My ad looks like this:

HARRY DRESDEN—WIZARD
Lost Items Found. Paranormal Investigations.
Consulting. Advice. Reasonable Rates.
No Love Potions, Endless Purses, Parties, or Other Entertainment

You'd be surprised how many people call just to ask me if I'm serious. But then, if you'd seen the things I'd seen, if you knew half of what I knew, you'd wonder how anyone could *not* think I was serious.

The end of the twentieth century and the dawn of the new millennium had seen something of a renaissance in the public awareness of the paranormal. Psychics, haunts, vampires—you name it. People still didn't take them seriously, but all the things Science had promised us hadn't come to pass. Disease was still a problem. Starvation was still a problem. Violence and crime and war were still problems. In spite of the advance of technology, things just hadn't changed the way everyone had hoped and thought they would.

Science, the largest religion of the twentieth century, had become somewhat tarnished by images of exploding space shuttles, crack babies, and a generation of complacent Americans who had allowed the television to raise their children. People were looking for something—I think they just didn't know what. And even though they were once again starting to open their eyes to the world of magic and the arcane that had been with them all the while, they still thought I must be some kind of joke.

Anyway, it had been a slow month. A slow pair of months, actually. My rent from February didn't get paid until the tenth of March, and it was looking like it might be even longer until I got caught up for this month.

My only job had been the previous week, when I'd gone down to Branson, Missouri, to investigate a country singer's possibly haunted house. It hadn't been. My client hadn't been happy with that answer, and had been even less happy when I suggested he lay off of any intoxicating substances and try to get some exercise and sleep, and see if that didn't help things more than an exorcism. I'd gotten travel expenses plus an hour's pay, and gone away feeling I had done the honest, righteous, and impractical thing. I heard later that he'd hired a shyster psychic to come in and perform a ceremony with a lot of incense and black lights. Some people.

I finished up my paperback and tossed it into the DONE box. There was a pile of read and discarded paperbacks in a cardboard box on one side of my desk, the spines bent and the pages mangled. I'm terribly hard on books. I was eyeing the pile of unread books, considering which to start next, given that I had no real work to do, when my phone rang.

I stared at it in a somewhat surly fashion. We wizards are terrific at brooding. After the third ring, when I thought I wouldn't sound a little too eager, I picked up the receiver and said, "Dresden."

"Oh. Is this, um, Harry Dresden? The, ah, wizard?" Her tone was apologetic, as though she were terribly afraid she would be insulting me.

No, I thought. It's Harry Dresden the, ah, lizard. Harry the wizard is one door down.

It is the prerogative of wizards to be grumpy. It is not, however, the prerogative of freelance consultants who are late on their rent, so instead of saying something smart, I told the woman on the phone, "Yes, ma'am. How can I help you today?"

"I, um," she said. "I'm not sure. I've lost something, and I think maybe you could help me."

"Finding lost articles is a specialty," I said. "What would I be looking for?"

There was a nervous pause. "My husband," she said. She had

a voice that was a little hoarse, like a cheerleader who'd been working a long tournament, but had enough weight of years in it to place her as an adult.

My eyebrows went up. "Ma'am, I'm not really a missing-persons specialist. Have you contacted the police or a private investigator?"

"No," she said, quickly. "No, they can't. That is, I haven't. Oh dear, this is all so complicated. Not something someone can talk about on the phone. I'm sorry to have taken up your time, Mr. Dresden."

"Hold on now," I said quickly. "I'm sorry, you didn't tell me your name."

There was that nervous pause again, as though she were checking a sheet of written notes before answering. "Call me Monica."

People who know diddly about wizards don't like to give us their names. They're convinced that if they give a wizard their name from their own lips it could be used against them. To be fair, they're right.

I had to be as polite and harmless as I could. She was about to hang up out of pure indecision, and I needed the job. I could probably turn hubby up, if I worked at it.

"Okay, Monica," I told her, trying to sound as melodious and friendly as I could. "If you feel your situation is of a sensitive nature, maybe you could come by my office and talk about it. If it turns out that I can help you best, I will, and if not, then I can direct you to someone I think can help you better." I gritted my teeth and pretended I was smiling. "No charge."

It must have been the no charge that did it. She agreed to come right out to the office, and told me that she would be there in an hour. That put her estimated arrival at about two-thirty. Plenty of time to go out and get some lunch, then get back to the office to meet her.

The phone rang again almost the instant I put it down, making me jump. I peered at it. I don't trust electronics. Anything manufactured after the forties is suspect—and doesn't seem to have much liking for me. You name it: cars, radios, telephones, TVs, VCRs—none of them seem to behave well for me. I don't even like to use automatic pencils.

I answered the phone with the same false cheer I had summoned up for Monica Husband-Missing. "This is Dresden, may I help you?"

"Harry, I need you at the Madison in the next ten minutes. Can you be there?" The voice on the other end of the line was also a woman's, cool, brisk, businesslike.

"Why, Lieutenant Murphy," I gushed, overflowing with saccharine, "It's good to hear from you, too. It's been so long. Oh, they're fine, fine. And your family?"

"Save it, Harry. I've got a couple of bodies here, and I need you to take a look around."

I sobered immediately. Karrin Murphy was the director of Special Investigations out of downtown Chicago, a de facto appointee of the Police Commissioner to investigate any crimes dubbed *unusual.* Vampire attacks, troll mauraudings, and faery abductions of children didn't fit in very neatly on a police report—but at the same time, people got attacked, infants got stolen, property was damaged or destroyed. And someone had to look into it.

In Chicago, or pretty much anywhere in Chicagoland, that person was Karrin Murphy. I was her library of the supernatural on legs, and a paid consultant for the police department. But two bodies? Two deaths by means unknown? I hadn't handled anything like that for her before.

"Where are you?" I asked her.

"Madison Hotel on Tenth, seventh floor."

"That's only a fifteen-minute walk from my office," I said.

"So you can be here in fifteen minutes. Good."

"Um," I said. I looked at the clock. Monica No-Last-Name would be here in a little more than forty-five minutes. "I've sort of got an appointment."

"Dresden, I've sort of got a pair of corpses with no leads and no suspects, and a killer walking around loose. Your appointment can wait."

My temper flared. It does that occasionally. "It can't, actually," I said. "But I'll tell you what. I'll stroll on over and take a look around, and be back here in time for it."

"Have you had lunch yet?" she asked.

"What?"

She repeated the question.

"No," I said.

"Don't." There was a pause, and when she spoke again, there was a sort of greenish tone to her words. "It's bad."

"How bad are we talking here, Murph?"

Her voice softened, and that scared me more than any images of gore or violent death could have. Murphy was the original tough girl, and she prided herself on never showing weakness. “It’s bad, Harry. Please don’t take too long. Special Crimes is itching to get their fingers on this one, and I know you don’t like people to touch the scene before you can look around.”

“I’m on the way,” I told her, already standing and pulling on my jacket.

“Seventh floor,” she reminded me. “See you there.”

“Okay.”

I turned off the lights to my office, went out the door, and locked up behind me, frowning. I wasn’t sure how long it was going to take to investigate Murphy’s scene, and I didn’t want to miss out on speaking with Monica Ask-Me-No-Questions. So I opened the door again, got out a piece of paper and a thumbtack, and wrote:

Out briefly. Back for appointment at 2:30. Dresden

That done, I started down the stairs. I rarely use the elevator, even though I’m on the fifth floor. Like I said, I don’t trust machines. They’re always breaking down on me just when I need them.

Besides which. If I were someone in this town using magic to kill people two at a time, and I didn’t want to get caught, I’d make sure that I removed the only practicing wizard the police department kept on retainer. I liked my odds on the stairwell a lot better than I did in the cramped confines of the elevator.

Paranoid? Probably. But just because you’re paranoid doesn’t mean that there isn’t an invisible demon about to eat your face.

Chapter 2

Karrin Murphy was waiting for me outside the Madison. Karrin and I are a study in contrasts. Where I am tall and lean, she's short and stocky. Where I have dark hair and dark eyes, she's got Shirley Temple blond locks and baby blues. Where my features are all lean and angular, with a hawkish nose and a sharp chin, hers are round and smooth, with the kind of cute nose you'd expect on a cheerleader.

It was cool and windy, like it usually is in March, and she wore a long coat that covered her pantsuit. Murphy never wore dresses, though I suspected she'd have muscular, well-shaped legs, like a gymnast. She was built for function, and had a pair of trophies in her office from aikido tournaments to prove it. Her hair was cut at shoulder length and whipped out wildly in the spring wind. She wasn't wearing earrings, and her makeup was of sufficient quality and quantity that it was tough to tell she had on any at all. She looked more like a favorite aunt or a cheerful mother than a hard-bitten homicide detective.

"Don't you have any other jackets, Dresden?" she asked, as I came within hailing distance. There were several police cars parked illegally in front of the building. She glanced at my eyes for a half second and then away, quickly. I had to give her credit. It was more than most people did. It wasn't really dangerous unless you did it for several seconds, but I was used to anyone who knew I was a wizard making it a point not to glance at my face.

I looked down at my black canvas duster, with its heavy mantling and waterproof lining and sleeves actually long enough for my arms. "What's wrong with this one?"

"It belongs on the set of *El Dorado*."

"And?"

She snorted, an indelicate sound from so small a woman, and spun on her heel to walk toward the hotel's front doors.

I caught up and walked a little ahead of her.

She sped her pace. So did I. We raced one another toward the front door, with increasing speed, through the puddles left over from last night's rain.

My legs were longer; I got there first. I opened the door for her and gallantly gestured for her to go in. It was an old contest of ours. Maybe my values are outdated, but I come from an old school of thought. I think that men ought to treat women like something other than just shorter, weaker men with breasts. Try and convict me if I'm a bad person for thinking so. I enjoy treating a woman like a lady, opening doors for her, paying for shared meals, giving flowers—all that sort of thing.

It irritates the hell out of Murphy, who had to fight and claw and play dirty with the hairiest men in Chicago to get as far as she has. She glared up at me while I stood there holding open the door, but there was a reassurance about the glare, a relaxation. She took an odd sort of comfort in our ritual, annoying as she usually found it.

How bad was it up on the seventh floor, anyway?

We rode the elevator in a sudden silence. We knew one another well enough, by this time, that the silences were not uncomfortable. I had a good sense of Murphy, an instinctual grasp for her moods and patterns of thought—something I develop whenever I'm around someone for any length of time. Whether it's a natural talent or a supernatural one I don't know.

My instincts told me that Murphy was tense, stretched as tight as piano wire. She kept it off her face, but there was something about the set of her shoulders and neck, the stiffness of her back, that made me aware of it.

Or maybe I was just projecting it onto her. The confines of the elevator made me a bit nervous. I licked my lips and looked around the interior of the car. My shadow and Murphy's fell on the floor, and almost looked as though they were sprawled there. There was something about it that bothered me, a nagging little instinct that I blew off as a case of nerves. Steady, Harry.

She let out a harsh breath just as the elevator slowed, then sucked in another one before the doors could open, as though she were planning on holding it for as long as we were on the floor and breathing only when she got back in the elevator again.

Blood smells a certain way, a kind of sticky, almost metallic odor, and the air was full of it when the elevator doors opened. My stomach quailed a little bit, but I swallowed manfully and followed Murphy out of the elevator and down the hall past a couple of uniform cops, who recognized me and waved me past without asking to see the little laminated card the city had given me. Granted, even in a big-city department like Chicago P.D., they didn't exactly call in a horde of consultants (I went down in the paperwork as a psychic consultant, I think), but still. Unprofessional of the boys in blue.

Murphy preceded me into the room. The smell of blood grew thicker, but there wasn't anything gruesome behind door number one. The outer room of the suite looked like some kind of a sitting room done in rich tones of red and gold, like a set from an old movie in the thirties—expensive-looking, but somehow faux, nonetheless. Dark, rich leather covered the chairs, and my feet sank into the thick, rust-colored shag of the carpet. The velvet velour curtains had been drawn, and though the lights were all on, the place still seemed a little too dark, a little too sensual in its textures and colors. It wasn't the kind of room where you sit and read a book. Voices came from a doorway to my right.

"Wait here a minute," Murphy told me. Then she went through the door to the right of the entryway and into what I supposed was the bedroom of the suite.

I wandered around the sitting room with my eyes mostly closed, noting things. Leather couch. Two leather chairs. Stereo and television in a black glossy entertainment center. Champagne bottle warming in a stand holding a brimming tub of what had been ice the night before, with two empty glasses set beside it. There was a red rose petal on the floor, clashing with the carpeting (but then, in that room, what didn't?).

A bit to one side, under the skirt of one of the leather recliners, was a little piece of satiny cloth. I bent at the waist and lifted the skirt with one hand, careful not to touch anything. A pair of black-satin panties, a tiny triangle with lace coming off the points, lay there, one strap snapped as though the thong had simply been torn off. Kinky.

The stereo system was state of the art, though not an expensive brand. I took a pencil from my pocket and pushed the PLAY button with the eraser. Gentle, sensual music filled the room, a low bass, a driving drumbeat, wordless vocals, the heavy breathing of a woman as background.

The music continued for a few seconds more, and then it began to skip over a section about two seconds long, repeating it over and over again.

I grimaced. Like I said, I have this effect on machinery. It has something to do with being a wizard, with working with magical forces. The more delicate and modern the machine is, the more likely it is that something will go wrong if I get close enough to it. I can kill a copier at fifty paces.

"The love suite," came a man's voice, drawing the word *love* out into *luuuuuuuv*. "What do you think, Mister Man?"

"Hello, Detective Carmichael," I said, without turning around. Carmichael's rather light, nasal voice had a distinctive quality. He was Murphy's partner and the resident skeptic, convinced that I was nothing more than a charlatan, scamming the city out of its hard-earned money. "Were you saving the panties to take home yourself, or did you just overlook them?" I turned and looked at him. He was short and overweight and balding, with beady, bloodshot eyes and a weak chin. His jacket was rumpled, and there were food stains on his tie, all of which served to conceal a razor intellect. He was a sharp cop, and absolutely ruthless at tracking down killers.

He walked over to the chair and looked down. "Not bad, Sherlock," he said. "But that's just foreplay. Wait'll you see the main attraction. I'll have a bucket waiting for you." He turned and killed the malfunctioning CD player with a jab from the eraser end of his own pencil.

I widened my eyes at him, to let him know how terrified I was, then walked past him and into the bedroom. And regretted it. I looked, noted details mechanically, and quietly shut the door on the part of my head that had started screaming the second I entered the room.

They must have died sometime the night before, as rigor mortis had already set in. They were on the bed; she was astride him, body leaned back, back bowed like a dancer's, the curves of her breasts making a lovely outline. He stretched beneath her, a lean and powerfully built man, arms reaching out and grasping at the satin sheets, gathering them in his fists. Had it been an erotic photograph, it would have made a striking tableau.

Except that the lovers' rib cages on the upper left side of their torsos had expanded outward, through their skin, the ribs jabbing out like ragged, snapped knives. Arterial blood had sprayed out of their bodies, all the way to the mirror on the ceiling, along with pulped, gelatinous masses of flesh that had to be what remained of their hearts. Standing over them, I could see into the upper cavity of the bodies. I noted the now greyish lining around the motionless left lungs and the edges of the ribs, which apparently were forced outward and snapped by some force within.

It definitely cut down on the erotic potential.

The bed was in the middle of the room, giving it a subtle emphasis. The bedroom followed the decor of the sitting room—a lot of red, a lot of plush fabrics, a little over the top unless viewed in candlelight. There were indeed candles in holders on the wall, now burned down to the nubs and extinguished.

I stepped closer to the bed and walked around it. The carpet squelched as I did. The little screaming part of my brain, safely locked up behind doors of self-control and strict training, continued gibbering. I tried to ignore it. Really I did. But if I didn't get out of that room in a hurry, I was going to start crying like a little girl.

So I took in the details fast. The woman was in her twenties, in fabulous condition. At least I thought she had been. It was hard to tell. She had hair the color of chestnuts, cut in a pageboy style, and it seemed dyed to me. Her eyes were only partly open, and I couldn't quite guess at their color beyond not-dark. Vaguely green?

The man was probably in his forties, and had the kind of fitness that comes from a lifetime of conditioning. There was a tattoo on his right bicep, a winged dagger, that the pull of the satin sheets half concealed. There were scars on his knuckles, layers deep, and across his lower abdomen was a vicious, narrow, puckered scar that I guessed must have come from a knife wound.

There were discarded clothes around—a tux for him, a little sheath of a black dress and a pair of pumps for her. There were a pair of overnight bags, unopened and set neatly aside, probably by a porter.

I looked up. Carmichael and Murphy were watching me in silence.

I shrugged at them.

"Well?" Murphy demanded. "Are we dealing with magic here, or aren't we?"

"Either that or it was really incredible sex," I told her.

Carmichael snorted.

I laughed a little, too—and that was all the screaming part of my brain needed to slam open the doors I'd shut on it. My stomach revolted and heaved, and I lurched out of the room. Carmichael, true to his word, had set a stainless-steel bucket outside the room, and I fell to my knees throwing up.

It only took me a few seconds to control myself again—but I didn't want to go back in that room. I didn't need to see what was there anymore. I didn't want to see the two dead people, whose hearts had literally exploded out of their chests.

And someone had used magic to do it. They had used magic to wreak harm on another, violating the First Law. The White Council was going to go into collective apoplexy. This hadn't been the act of a malign spirit or a malicious entity, or the attack of one of the many creatures of the Nevernever, like vampires or trolls. This had been the premeditated, deliberate act of a sorcerer, a wizard, a human being able to tap into the fundamental energies of creation and life itself.

It was worse than murder. It was twisted, wretched perversion, as though someone had bludgeoned another person to death with a Botticelli, turned something of beauty to an act of utter destruction.

If you've never touched it, it's hard to explain. Magic is created by life, and most of all by the awareness, intelligence, emotions of a human being. To end such a life with the same magic that was born from it was hideous, almost incestuous somehow.

I sat up again and was breathing hard, shaking and tasting the bile in my mouth, when Murphy came back out of the room with Carmichael.

"All right, Harry," Murphy said. "Let's have it. What do you see happening here?"

I took a moment to collect my thoughts before answering. "They came in. They had some champagne. They danced for a while, made out, over there by the stereo. Then went into the bedroom. They were in there for less than an hour. It hit them when they were getting to the high point."

"Less than an hour," Carmichael said. "How do you figure?"

"CD was only an hour and ten long. Figure a few minutes for dancing and drinking, and then they're in the room. Was the CD playing when they found them?"

"No," Murphy said.

"Then it hadn't been set on a loop. I figure they wanted music, just to make things perfect, given the room and all."

Carmichael grunted, sourly. "Nothing we hadn't already figured out for ourselves," he said to Murphy. "He'd better come up with more than this."

Murphy shot Carmichael a look that said "shut up," then said, softly, "I need more, Harry."

I ran one of my hands back over my hair. "There's only two ways anyone could have managed this. The first is by evocation. Evocation is the most direct, spectacular, and noisy form of expressed magic, or sorcery. Explosions, fire, that sort of thing. But I doubt it was an evocator who did this."

"Why?" Murphy demanded. I heard her pencil scritching on the notepad she always kept with her.

"Because you have to be able to see or touch where you want your effect to go," I told her. "Line of sight only. The man or woman would have had to be there in the room with them. Tough to hide forensic evidence with something like that, and anyone who was skilled enough to pull off a spell like that would have had the sense to use a gun instead. It's easier."

"What's the other option?" Murphy asked.

"Thaumaturgy," I said. "As above, so below. Make something happen on a small scale, and give it the energy to happen on a large scale."

Carmichael snorted. "What bullshit."

Murphy's voice sounded skeptical. "How would that work, Harry? Could it be done from somewhere else?"

I nodded. "The killer would need to have something to connect him or her to the victims. Hair, fingernails, blood samples. That sort of thing."

"Like a voodoo doll?"

"Exactly the same thing, yes."

"There's fresh dye in the woman's hair," Murphy said.

I nodded. "Maybe if you can find out where she got her hair styled, you could find something out. I don't know."

"Is there anything else you could tell me that would be of use?"

"Yes. The killer knew the victims. And I'm thinking it was a woman."

Carmichael snorted. "I don't believe we got to sit here and listen to this. Nine times out of ten the killer knows the victim."

"Shut up, Carmichael," Murphy said. "What makes you say that, Harry?"

I stood up, and rubbed at my face with my hands. "The way

magic works. Whenever you do something with it, it comes from inside of you. Wizards have to focus on what they're trying to do, visualize it, believe in it, to make it work. You can't make something happen that isn't a part of you, inside. The killer could have murdered them both and made it look like an accident, but she did it this way. To get it done this way, she would have had to want them dead for very personal reasons, to be willing to reach inside them like that. Revenge, maybe. Maybe you're looking for a lover or a spouse.

"Also because of when they died—in the middle of sex. It wasn't a coincidence. Emotions are a kind of channel for magic, a path that can be used to get to you. She picked a time when they'd be together and be charged up with lust. She got samples to use as a focus, and she planned it out in advance. You don't do that to strangers."

"Crap," Carmichael said, but this time it was more of an absentminded curse than anything directed at me.

Murphy glared at me. "You keep saying 'she,' " she challenged me. "Why the hell do you think that?"

I gestured toward the room. "Because you can't do something that bad without a whole lot of hate," I said. "Women are better at hating than men. They can focus it better, let it go better. Hell, witches are just plain *meaner* than wizards. This feels like feminine vengeance of some kind to me."

"But a man could have done it," Murphy said.

"Well," I hedged.

"Christ, you are a chauvinist pig, Dresden. Is it something that *only* a woman could have done?"

"Well. No. I don't think so."

"You don't *think* so?" Carmichael drawled. "Some expert."

I scowled at them both, angry. "I haven't really worked through the specifics of what I'd need to do to make somebody's heart explode, Murph. As soon as I have occasion to I'll be sure to let you know."

"When will you be able to tell me something?" Murphy asked.

"I don't know." I held up a hand, forestalling her next comment. "I can't put a timer on this stuff, Murph. It just can't be done. I don't even know if I can do it at all, much less how long it will take."

"At fifty bucks an hour, it better not be too long," Carmichael growled. Murphy glanced at him. She didn't exactly agree with him, but she didn't exactly slap him down, either.

I took the opportunity to take a few long breaths, calming myself down. I finally looked back at them. "Okay," I asked. "Who are they? The victims."

"You don't need to know that," Carmichael snapped.

"Ron," Murphy said. "I could really use some coffee."

Carmichael turned to her. He wasn't tall, but he all but loomed over Murphy. "Aw, come on, Murph. This guy's jerking your chain. You don't really think he's going to be able to tell you anything worth hearing, do you?"

Murphy regarded her partner's sweaty, beady-eyed face with a sort of frosty hauteur, tough to pull off on someone six inches taller than she. "No cream, two sugars."

"Dammit," Carmichael said. He shot me a cold glance (but didn't quite look at my eyes), then jammed his hands into his pants pockets and stalked out of the room.

Murphy followed him to the door, her feet silent, and shut it behind him. The sitting room immediately became darker, closer, with the grinning ghoul of its former chintzy intimacy dancing in the smell of the blood and the memory of the two bodies in the next room.

"The woman's name was Jennifer Stanton. She worked for the Velvet Room."

I whistled. The Velvet Room was a high-priced escort service run by a woman named Bianca. Bianca kept a flock of beautiful, charming, and witty women, pandering them to the richest men in the area for hundreds of dollars an hour. Bianca sold the kind of female company that most men only see on television and the movies. I also knew that she was a vampiress of considerable influence in the Nevernever. She had Power with a capital P.

I'd tried to explain the Nevernever to Murphy before. She didn't really comprehend it, but she understood that Bianca was a badass vampiress who sometimes squabbled for territory. We both knew that if one of Bianca's girls was involved, the vampiress must have been involved somehow, too.

Murphy cut right to the point. "Was this part of one of Bianca's territorial disputes?"

"No," I said. "Unless she's having it with a human sorcerer. A vampire, even a vamp sorcerer, couldn't have pulled off something like this outside of the Nevernever."

"Could she be at odds with a human sorcerer?" Murphy asked me.

"Possible. But it doesn't sound like her. She isn't that stupid."

What I didn't tell Murphy was that the White Council made sure that vampires who trifled with mortal practitioners never lived to brag about it. I don't talk to regular people about the White Council. It just isn't done. "Besides," I said, "If a human wanted to take a shot at Bianca by hitting her girls, he'd be better off to kill the girl and leave the customer healthy, to let him spread the tale and scare off business."

"Mmph," Murphy said. She wasn't convinced, but she made notes of what I had said.

"Who was the man?" I asked her.

Murphy looked up at me for a moment, and then said, evenly, "Tommy Tomm."

I blinked at her to let her know she hadn't revealed the mystery of the ages. "Who?"

"Tommy Tomm," she said. "Johnny Marcone's bodyguard."

Now it made sense. "Gentleman" Johnny Marcone had been the thug to emerge on top of the pile after the Vargassi family had dissolved into internal strife. The police department saw Marcone as a mixed blessing, after years of merciless struggle and bloody exchanges with the Vargassis. Gentleman Johnny tolerated no excesses in his organization, and he didn't like freelancers operating in his city. Muggers, bank robbers, and drug dealers who were not a part of his organization somehow always seemed to get ratted out and turned in, or else simply went missing and weren't heard from again.

Marcone was a civilizing influence on crime—and where he operated, it was more of a problem in terms of scale than ever before. An extremely shrewd businessman, he had a battery of lawyers working for him that kept him fenced in from the law behind a barricade of depositions and papers and tape recordings. The cops never said it, but sometimes it seemed like they were almost reluctant to chase him. Marcone was better than the alternative—anarchy in the underworld.

"I remember hearing he had an enforcer," I said. "I guess he doesn't anymore."

Murphy shrugged. "So it would seem."

"So what will you do next?"

"Run down this hairstylist angle, I guess. I'll talk to Bianca and to Marcone, but I can already tell you what they'll tell me." She flicked her notebook closed and shook her head, irritated.

I watched her for a minute. She looked tired. I told her so.

"I am tired," she replied. "Tired of being looked at like I'm some sort of nutcase. Even Carmichael, my own partner, thinks I've gone over the edge in all of this."

"The rest of the station think so too?" I asked her.

"Most of them just scowl and spin their index fingers around their temples when they think I'm not looking, and file my reports without ever reading them. The rest are the ones who have run into something spooky out there, and they're scared shitless. They don't want to believe in anything they didn't see on *Mister Science* when they were kids."

"How about you?"

"Me?" Murphy smiled, a curving of her lips that was a vibrantly feminine expression, making her look entirely too pretty to be such a hardass. "The world's falling apart at the seams, Harry. I guess I just think people are pretty arrogant to believe we've learned everything there is to know in the past century or so. What the hell. I can buy that we're just now starting to see the things around us in the dark again. It appeals to the cynic in me."

"I wish everyone thought like you do," I said. "It would cut down on my crank calls."

She continued to smile at me, impish. "But could you imagine a world where all the radio stations played ABBA?"

We shared a laugh. God, that room needed a laugh.

"Hey, Harry," Murphy said, grinning. I could see the wheels spinning in her head.

"Yeah?"

"What you said about being able to figure out how the killer did this. About how you're not sure you can do it."

"Yeah?"

"I know it's bullshit. Why did you lie to me about it?"

I stiffened. Christ, she was good. Or maybe I'm just not much of a liar. "Look, Murph," I said. "There's some things you just don't do."

"Sometimes I don't want to get into the head of the slime I go after, either. But you do what needs to be done to finish the job. I know what you mean, Harry."

"No," I said, shortly. "You don't know." And she didn't. She didn't know about my past, or the White Council, or the Doom of Damocles hanging over my head. Most days, I could pretend I didn't know about it, either.

All the Council needed now was an excuse, just an excuse, to find me guilty of violating one of the Seven Laws of Magic, and the Doom would drop. If I started putting together a recipe for a murder spell, and they found out about it, that might be all the excuse they needed.

"Murph," I told her. "I *can't* try figuring this spell out. I *can't* go putting together the things I'd need to do it. You just don't understand."

She glared at me, without looking at my eyes. I hadn't ever met anyone else who could pull that one off. "Oh, I understand. I understand that I've got a killer loose that I can't catch in the act. I understand that you know something that can help, or you can at least find out something. And I understand that if you dry up on me now, I'm tearing your card out of the department Rolodex and tossing it in the trash."

Son of a bitch. My consulting for the department paid a lot of my bills. Okay, most of my bills. I could sympathize with her, I supposed. If I was operating in the dark like she was, I'd be nervous as hell, too. Murphy didn't know anything about spells or rituals or talismans, but she knew human hatred and violence all too well.

It wasn't as though I was actually going to be doing any black magic, I told myself. I was just going to be figuring out how it was done. There was a difference. I was helping the police in an investigation, nothing more. Maybe the White Council would understand that.

Yeah, right. And maybe one of these days I'd go to an art museum and become well rounded.

Murphy set the hook a second later. She looked up at my eyes for a daring second before she turned away, her face tired and honest and proud. "I need to know everything you can tell me, Harry. Please."

Classic lady in distress. For one of those liberated, professional women, she knew exactly how to jerk my old-fashioned chains around.

I gritted my teeth. "Fine," I said. "Fine. I'll start on it tonight." Hoo boy. The White Council was going to love this one. I'd just have to make sure they didn't find out about it.

Murphy nodded and let out a breath without looking at me. Then she said, "Let's get out of here," and walked toward the door. I didn't try to beat her to it.

When we walked out, the uniform cops were still lazing around in the hall outside. Carmichael was nowhere to be seen. The guys from forensics were there, standing around impatiently, waiting for us to come out. Then they gathered up their plastic bags and tweezers and lights and things and filed past us into the room.

Murphy was brushing at her windblown hair with her hand while we waited for the ancient elevator to take its sweet time getting up to the seventh floor. She was wearing a gold watch, which reminded me. "Oh, hey," I asked her. "What time is it?"

She checked. "Two twenty-five. Why?"

I breathed out a curse, and turned for the stairs. "I'm late for my appointment."

I fairly flew down the stairs. I've had a lot of practice at them, after all, and I hit the lobby at a jog. I managed to dodge a porter coming through the front doors with an armload of luggage, and swung out onto the sidewalk at a lope. I have long legs that eat a lot of ground. I was running into the wind, my black duster billowing out behind me.

It was several blocks to my building, and after covering half of them I slowed to a walk. I didn't want to arrive at my appointment with Monica Missing-Man puffing like a bellows, with my hair windblown and my face streaming with sweat.

Blame it on being out of shape from an inactive winter season, but I was breathing hard. It occupied enough of my attention that I didn't see the dark blue Cadillac until it had pulled up beside me, and a rather large man had stepped out of it onto the sidewalk in front of me. He had bright red hair and a thick neck. His face looked like someone had smashed it flat with a board, repeatedly, when he was a baby—except for his jutting eyebrows. He had narrow little blue eyes that got narrower as I sized him up.

I stopped, and backed away, then turned around. Two more men, both of them as tall as me and a good deal heavier, were slowing down from their own jog. They had apparently been following me, and they looked annoyed. One was limping slightly, and the other wore a buzz cut that had been spiked up straight with some kind of styling gel. I felt like I was in high school again, surrounded by bullying members of the football team.

"Can I help you gentlemen?" I asked. I looked around for a cop, but they were all over at the Madison, I supposed. Everyone likes to gawk.

"Get in the car," the one in front of me said. One of the others opened the rear door.

"I like to walk. It's good for my heart."

"You don't get in the car, it isn't going to be good for your legs," the man growled.

A voice came from inside the car. "Mister Hendricks, please. Be more polite. Mister Dresden, would you join me for a moment? I'd hoped to give you a lift back to your office, but your abrupt exit made it somewhat problematic. Perhaps you will allow me to convey you the rest of the way."

I leaned down to look into the backseat. A man of handsome and unassuming features, dressed in a casual sports jacket and Levi's, regarded me with a smile. "And you would be?" I asked him.

His smile widened, and I swear it made his eyes twinkle.

"My name is John Marcone. I would like to discuss business with you."

I stared at him for a moment. And then my eyes slid aside to the very large and very overdeveloped Mister Hendricks. The man growled under his breath, and it sounded like Cujo just before he jumped at the woman in the car. I didn't feel like duking it out with Cujo and his two buddies.

So I got into the back of the Caddy with Gentleman Johnny Marcone.

It was turning out to be a very busy day. And I was still late for my appointment.

Chapter 3

Gentleman Johnny Marcone didn't look like the sort of man who would have my legs broken or my jaw wired shut. His salt-and-pepper hair was cut short, and there were lines from sun and smiling etched into the corners of his eyes. His eyes were the green of well-worn dollar bills. He seemed more like a college football coach: good-looking, tanned, athletic, and enthusiastic. The impression was reinforced by the men he kept with him. Cujo Hendricks hulked like an all-pro player who had been ousted for extreme unnecessary roughness.

Cujo got in the car again, glowered at me in the rearview mirror, then pulled out into the street, driving slowly toward my office. The steering wheel looked tiny and delicate in his huge hands. I made a mental note: Do not let Cujo put his hands around your throat. Or hand. It looked almost like one of them could manage it.

The radio was playing, but as I got in the car it fouled up, squealing feedback out over the speakers. Hendricks scowled and thought about it for a second. Maybe he had to relay the message through his second brain or something. Then he reached out and fiddled with the knobs before finally turning the radio off. At this rate I hoped the car would make it all the way to my office.

"Mister Dresden," Marcone said, smiling, "I understand that you work for the police department, from time to time."

"They throw the occasional tidbit my way," I agreed. "Hey, Hendricks. You should really wear your seat belt. Statistics say you're fifty or sixty percent safer."

Cujo growled at me in the rearview mirror again, and I

beamed at him. Smiling always seems to annoy people more than actually insulting them. Or maybe I just have an annoying smile.

Marcone seemed somewhat put off by my attitude. Maybe I was supposed to be holding my hat in my hand, but I had never really liked Francis Ford Coppola, and I didn't have a Godfather. (I *do* have a Godmother, and she is, inevitably perhaps, a faery. But that's another story.) "Mister Dresden," he said. "How much would it cost to retain your services?"

That made me wary. What would someone like Marcone want me for? "My standard fee is fifty dollars an hour plus travel expenses," I told him. "But it can vary, depending on what you need done."

Marcone nodded along with my sentences, as if encouraging me to speak. He wrinkled up his face as if carefully considering what he would say, and taking my well-being into account with grandfatherly concern. "How much would it set me back to have you not investigate something?"

"You want to pay me to not do something?"

"Let's say I pay you your standard fee. That comes out to fourteen hundred a day, right?"

"Twelve hundred, actually," I corrected him.

He beamed at me. "An honest man is a rare treasure. Twelve hundred a day. Let's say I pay you for two weeks worth of work, Mister Dresden, and you take some time off. Go catch a few movies, get some extra sleep, that sort of thing."

I eyed him. "And for more than a thousand dollars a day, you want me to . . . ?"

"Do nothing, Mister Dresden," Marcone smiled. "Nothing at all. Just relax, and put your feet up. And stay out of Detective Murphy's way."

Ah-hah. Marcone didn't want me looking into Tommy Tomm's murder. Interesting. I looked out the window and squinted my eyes, as though thinking about it.

"I've got the money with me," Marcone said. "Cash on the spot. I'll trust you to fulfill your end of the deal, Mister Dresden. You come highly recommended for your honesty."

"Mmmm. I don't know, John. I'm kind of busy to be accepting any more accounts right now." The car was almost to my office building. The car door was still unlocked. I hadn't worn my seat belt, either—just in case I needed to throw the door open and jump out. See how I think ahead? It's that wizardly intellect—and paranoia.

Marcone's smile faltered. His expression became earnest. "Mister Dresden, I am quite eager to establish a positive working relationship, here. If it's the money, I can offer you more. Let's say double your usual fee." He steepled his hands in front of him as he talked, half-turning toward me. My God, I kept expecting him to tell me to go out there and win one for the Gipper. He smiled. "How does that sound?"

"It isn't the money, John," I told him. I lazily locked my eyes onto his. "I just don't think it's going to work out."

To my surprise, he didn't look away.

Those who deal in magic learn to see the world in a slightly different light than everyone else. You gain a perspective you had never considered before, a way of thinking that would just never have occurred to you without exposure to the things a wizard sees and hears.

When you look into someone's eyes, you see them in that other light. And, for just a second, they see you in the same way. Marcone and I looked at one another.

He was a soldier, a warrior, behind that relaxed smile and fatherly manner. He was going to get what he wanted and he was going to get it in the most efficient way possible. He was a dedicated man—dedicated to his goals, dedicated to his people. He never let fear affect him. He made a living on human misery and suffering, peddling in drugs and flesh and stolen goods, but he took steps to minimize that suffering because it was simply the most efficient means of running his business. He was furious over Tommy Tomm's death—a cold and practical kind of fury that his rightful dominion had been invaded and challenged. He intended to find those responsible and deal with them in his own way—and he didn't want the police interfering. He had killed before, and would again, and it would all mean nothing more to him than a business transaction, than paying for groceries in the checkout line. It was a dry and cool place, inside Gentleman Johnny Marcone. Except for one dim corner. There, hidden away from his everyday thoughts, there lurked a secret shame. I couldn't quite see what it was. But I knew that, somewhere in the past there was something that he would give anything to undo, would spill blood to erase. It was from that dark place that he drew his resolve, his strength.

That was the way I saw him when I looked inside, past all his pretenses and defenses. And I was, on some instinctual level, certain that he had been aware of what I would see if I looked—that he had deliberately met my gaze, knowing what he would give away. That was his purpose in getting me alone. He wanted to take a peek at my soul. He wanted to see what sort of man I was.

When I look into someone's eyes, into their soul, their innermost being, they can see mine in return—the things I had done, the things I was willing to do, the things I was capable of doing. Most people who did that got really pale, at least. One woman had passed out entirely. I didn't know what they saw when they looked in there—it wasn't a place I poked around much, myself.

John Marcone wasn't like the other people who had seen my soul. He didn't even blink an eye. He just looked and assessed, and after the moment had passed, he nodded at me as though he understood something. I got the uncomfortable impression that he had duped me. That he had found out more about me than I had about him. The first thing I felt was anger, anger at being manipulated, anger that he should presume to soulgaze upon me.

Just a second later, I felt scared to death of this man. I had looked on his soul and it had been as solid and barren as a stainless-steel refrigerator. It was more than unsettling. He was strong, inside, savage and merciless without being cruel. He had a tiger's soul.

"All right, then," he said, smoothly, and as though nothing had happened. "I won't try to force my offer on you, Mister Dresden." The car was slowing down as it approached my building, and Hendricks pulled over in front of it. "But let me offer you some advice?" He had dropped the father-talking-to-son act, and spoke in a calm and patient voice.

"If you don't charge for it." Thank God for wisecracks. I was too rattled to have said anything intelligent.

Marcone almost smiled. "I think you'll be happier if you come down with the flu for a few days. This business that Detective Murphy has asked you to look into doesn't need to be dragged out into the light. You won't like what you see. It's on my side of the fence. Just let me deal with it, and it won't ever trouble you."

"Are you threatening me?" I asked him. I didn't think he was, but I didn't want him to know that. It would have helped if my voice hadn't been shaking.

"No," he said, frankly. "I have too much respect for you to resort to something like that. They say that you're the real thing, Mister Dresden. A real magus."

"They also say I'm nutty as a fruitcake."

"I choose which 'they' I listen to very carefully," Marcone

said. "Think about what I've said, Mister Dresden? I do not think our respective lines of work need overlap often. I would as soon not make an enemy of you over this matter."

I clenched my jaw over my fear, and spat words out at him quick and hard. "You don't want to make an enemy of me, Marcone. That wouldn't be smart. That wouldn't be smart at all."

He narrowed his eyes at me, lazy and relaxed. He could meet my eyes by then without fear. We had taken a measure of one another. It would not happen in such a way again. "You really should try to be more polite, Mister Dresden," he said. "It's good for business."

I didn't give him an answer to that: I didn't have one that wouldn't sound frightened or stupidly macho. Instead, I told him, "If you ever lose your car keys, give me a call. Don't try offering me money or threats again. Thanks for the ride."

He watched me, his expression never changing, as I got out of the car and shut the door. Hendricks pulled out and drove away, after giving me one last dirty look. I had soulgazed on several people before. It wasn't the sort of thing you forgot. I had never run into someone like that, someone so cool and controlled—even the other practitioners I had met gazes with had not been that way. None of them had simply assessed me like a column of numbers and filed it away for reference in future equations.

I stuck my hands in the pockets of my duster, and shivered as the wind hit me. I was a wizard, throwing around real magic, I reminded myself. I was not afraid of big men in big cars. I do not get rattled by corpses blasted from life by magic more intense than anything I could manage. Really. Honest.

But those dollar-bill-colored eyes, backed by that cool and nearly passionless soul, had me shaking as I took the stairs back up to my office. I had been stupid. He had surprised me, and the sudden intimacy of the soulgaze had startled and frightened me. All added together, it had caused me to fall apart, throwing threats at him like a frightened schoolkid. Marcone was a predator. He practically smelled my fear. If he got to thinking I was weak, I had a feeling that polite smile and fatherly facade would vanish as thoroughly and as quickly as it had appeared.

What a rotten first impression.

Oh, well. At least I was going to be on time for my appointment.

Chapter 4

Monica No-Last-Name was standing outside of my office when I got there, writing on the back of the note I had left taped to my office door.

I walked toward her, and she was too intent upon her writing to look up. She was a good-looking woman, in her mid-thirtysomethings. Ash blond hair that I thought must be natural, after a morbid and involuntary memory of the dead woman's dye job. Her makeup was tasteful and well applied, and her face was fair, friendly, with enough roundness of cheek to look fresh-faced and young, enough fullness of mouth to look very feminine. She was wearing a long, full skirt of palest yellow with brown riding boots, a crisp white blouse, and an expensive-looking green cardigan over it, to ward off the chill of early spring. She had to be in good shape to pull off a color combination like that, and she did it. Overall, it was a naggingly familiar look, something like Annette Funicello or Barbara Billingsley, maybe—wholesome and all-American.

"Monica?" I asked. I put on my most innocent and friendly smile.

She blinked at me as I approached. "Oh. Are you, um, Harry . . ."

I smiled and offered her my hand. "Harry Dresden, ma'am. That's me."

She took my hand after a tiny pause and kept her eyes firmly focused on my chest. At this point, I was just as glad to be dealing with someone who was too nervous to risk looking at my eyes. I gave her a firm, but gentle handshake, and let go of her, brushing past her to unlock the office door and open it up. "I apologize for being late. I got a call from the police that I had to look in on."

"You did?" she asked. "You mean, the police, um . . ." She waved her fingers instead of finishing the sentence and entered when I held the door open for her.

"Sometimes," I nodded. "They run into something and want my take on it."

"What sorts of things?"

I shrugged and swallowed. I thought of the corpses at the Madison, and felt green. When I looked up at Monica, she was studying my face, chewing on her lip nervously. She hurriedly averted her gaze.

"Can I get you some coffee?" I asked her. I shut the door behind us, flicked on the lights.

"Oh. No, thank you. I'm fine." She stood there, looking at my box of discarded paperbacks and holding her purse over her tummy with both hands. I thought she might scream if I said *boo* so I made sure to move carefully and slowly, making myself a cup of instant coffee. I breathed in and out, going through the familiar motions, until I had calmed down from my encounter with Marcone. By the time I was done, so was my coffee. I went to my desk, and invited her to have a seat in one of the two chairs across from me.

"Okay, Monica," I said. "What can I do for you today?"

"Well, um. I told you that my husband was . . . was . . ." She nodded at me, gesturing.

"Missing?" I supplied.

"Yes," she said with an exhalation of almost relief. "But he's not mysteriously missing or anything. Just gone." She flushed and stammered. "Like he just packed up a few things and left. But he didn't say anything to anyone. And he hasn't showed up again. I'm concerned about him."

"Uh-huh," I said. "How long has he been gone?"

"This is the third day," she said.

I nodded. "There must be some reason why you're coming to me, rather than a private investigator or the police."

She blushed again. She had a good face for blushing, fair skin that colored girlishly. It was quite fetching, really. "Yes, um. He had been interested in . . . In . . ."

"Magic?"

"Yes. He had been buying books on it in the religion section at the bookstore. Not like those Dungeons and Dragons games.

The real thing. He bought some of those tarot cards." She pronounced it like *carrot*. Amateurs.

"And you think his disappearance might have had something to do with this interest?"

"I'm not sure," she confessed. "But maybe. He was very upset. He had just lost his job and was under a lot of pressure. I'm worried about him. I thought whoever found him might need to be able to talk to him about all of this stuff." She took a deep breath, as if the effort of completing so many sentences without a single *um* had tired her.

"I'm still not clear on this. Why me? Why not the police?"

Her knuckles whitened on her purse. "He packed a bag, Mr. Dresden. I think the police will just assume he left his wife and his children. They won't really look. But he didn't. He's not like that. He only wants to make a good life for us, really, that's all he wants."

I frowned at her. Nervous that maybe hubby has run out on you after all, dear? "Even so," I said, "why come to me? Why not a private investigator? I know a reliable man if you need one."

"Because you know about . . ." She gestured, fitfully.

"About magic," I said.

Monica nodded. "I think it might be important. I mean, I don't know. But I think it might."

"Where did he work?" I asked her. While I spoke, I got a pad of paper out of my pocket and jotted down a few notes.

"SilverCo," she told me. "They're a trading company. They locate good markets for products and then advise companies where they can best spend their money."

"Uh-huh," I said. "What is his name, Monica?"

She swallowed, and I saw her twitching, trying to think of something to tell me other than his real name. "George," she supplied at last.

I looked up at her. She was staring furiously down at her hands.

"Monica," I said. "I know this must be really hard for you. Believe me, ma'am, there are plenty of people who are nervous when they come into my office. But please, hear me out. I am not out to hurt you or anyone else. What I do, I do to help people. It's true that someone with the right skills could use your names against you, but I'm not like that." I borrowed a line from Johnny Marcone. "It isn't good business."

She gave a nervous little laugh. "I feel so silly," she confessed. "But there's so many things that I've heard about . . ."

"Wizards. I see." I put my pencil down and steepled my fingers in wizardly fashion. The woman was nervous and had certain expectations. I might ease her fears a little if I fulfilled some of them. I tried not to look over her shoulder at the calendar I had hanging on the wall, and the red circle around the fifteenth of last month. Late rent. Need money. Even with the fee from today and what I would make in the future, it would take the city forever to pay up.

Besides. I could never resist going to the aid of a lady in distress. Even if she wasn't completely, one hundred percent sure that she wanted to be rescued by me.

"Monica," I told her. "There are powers in the universe that most people don't even know about. Powers that we still don't fully understand. The men and women who work with these powers see things in a different light than regular people. They come to understand things in a slightly different way. This sets them apart. Sometimes it breeds unwarranted suspicion and fear. I know you've read books and seen movies about how horrible people like me are, and that whole 'suffer not a witch to live' part of the Old Testament hasn't made things all roses. But we really aren't any different from anyone else." I gave her my best smile. "I want to help you. But if I'm going to do that, you're going to have to give me a little trust. I promise. I give you my word that I won't disappoint you."

I saw her take this in and chew on it for a while, while staring down at her hands.

"Victor," she said at last. "Victor Sells."

"All right," I said, picking up my pencil and duly noting it. "Is there anyplace he might have gone that you can think of, offhand?"

She nodded. "The lake house. We have a house down by . . ." She waved her hand.

"The lake?"

She beamed at me, and I reminded myself to be patient. "In Lake Providence, over the state line, around Lake Michigan. It's beautiful up there in the autumn."

"Okay, then. Are you aware of any friends he might have run off to see, family he might have visited, anything like that?"

"Oh, Victor wasn't on speaking terms with his family. I never knew why. He didn't talk about them, really. We've been married for ten years, and he never once spoke to them."

"Okay," I said, noting that down, too. "Friends, then?"

She fretted her lip, a gesture that seemed familiar to her. "Not really. He was friends with his boss, and some people at work, but after he was fired . . ."

"Uh-huh," I said. "I understand." I continued writing things down, drawing bold lines between thoughts to separate them. I spilled over onto the next page before I was finished writing down the facts and my observations about Monica. I like to be thorough about this kind of thing.

"Well, Mr. Dresden?" she asked. "Can you help me?"

I looked over the page and nodded. "I think so, Monica. If possible, I'd like to see these things your husband collected. Which books and so on. It would help if I had a picture of him, too. I might like to take a look around your house at Lake Providence. Would that be all right?"

"Of course," she said. She seemed relieved, but at the same time even more nervous than before. I noted down the address of the lake house and brief directions.

"You're aware of my fees?" I asked her. "I'm not cheap. It might be less costly for you to hire someone else."

"We've got quite a bit of savings, Mr. Dresden," she told me. "I'm not worried about the money." That seemed an odd statement from her, at the time—out of tune with her generally nervous manner.

"Well, then," I told her. "I charge fifty dollars an hour, plus expenses. I'll send you an itemized list of what I do, so you'll have a good idea what I'm working on. A retainer is customary. I'm not going to guarantee that I work exclusively on your case. I try to handle each of my customers with respect and courtesy, so I can't put any one of them before another."

She nodded to me, emphatically, and reached into her purse. She drew out a white envelope and passed it over to me. "There's five hundred inside," she told me. "Is that enough for now?"

Cha-ching. Five hundred dollars would take care of last month's rent and a good bit of this month's, too. I could get into this bit with nervous clients wanting to preserve the anonymity of their checking accounts from my supposed sorcerous might. Cash always spends.

"That will be fine, yes," I told her. I tried not to fondle the envelope. At least I wasn't crass enough to dump the money on my desk and count it out.

She drew out another envelope. "He took most of his things

with him," she said. "At least, I couldn't find them where he usually keeps them. But I did find this." There was something in the envelope, making it bulge, an amulet, ring, or charm of some kind, I was betting. A third envelope came out of her purse—the woman must be compulsively well organized. "There's a picture of him in here, and my phone number inside. Thank you, Mr. Dresden. When will you call?"

"As soon as I know something," I told her. "Probably by tomorrow afternoon or Saturday morning. Sound good?"

She almost looked at my eyes, caught herself, and smiled directly at my nose instead. "Yes. Yes, thank you so much for your help." She glanced up at the wall. "Oh, look at the time. I need to go. School's almost out." She closed her teeth over her words and flushed again, as though embarrassed that she had let such an important fact about her slip out.

"I'll do whatever I can, ma'am," I assured her, rising, and walking her to the door. "Thank you for your business. I'll be in touch soon."

She said her good-byes, never looking me in the face, and fled out the door. I shut it behind her and went back to the envelopes.

First, the money. It was all in fifties, which always look new even when they're years old because they get so little circulation. There were ten of them. I put them in my wallet, and trashed the envelope.

The envelope with the photo in it was next. I took it out and regarded a picture of Monica and a man of lean and handsome features, with a wide forehead and shaggy eyebrows that skewed his handsomeness off onto a rather eccentric angle. His smile was whiter-than-white, and his skin had the smooth, dark tan of someone who spends a lot of time in the sun, boating maybe. It was a sharp contrast against Monica's paleness. Victor Sells, I presume.

The phone number was written on a plain white index card that had been neatly trimmed down to fit inside the envelope. There was no name or area code, just a seven-digit number. I got out my cross-listing directory and looked it up.

I noted that down as well. I wondered what the woman had expected to accomplish by only giving out first names, when she had been going to hand me a dozen other ways of finding out in any case. It only goes to show that people are funny when they're nervous about something. They say screwy things, make odd choices which, in retrospect, they feel amazingly foolish for making. I would have to be careful not to say anything to rub that in when I spoke to her again.

I trashed the second envelope and opened the last one, turning it upside down over my desk.

The brown husk of a dead, dried scorpion, glistening with some sort of preservative glaze, clicked down onto my desk. A supple, braided leather cord led off from a ring set through the base of its tail, so that if it was worn, it would hang head down, tail up and curled over the dried body to point at the ground.

I shuddered. Scorpions were symbolically powerful in certain circles of belief. They weren't usually symbols of anything good or wholesome, either. A lot of petty, mean spells could be focused around a little talisman like that. If you wore it next to your skin, as such things are supposed to be worn, the prickly legs of the thing would be a constant poking and agitation at your chest, a continual reminder that it was there. The dried stinger at the tail's tip might actually pierce the skin of anyone who tried to give the wearer a hug. Its crablike pincers would catch in a man's chest hair, or scratch at the curves of a woman's breasts. Nasty, unpleasant thing. Not evil, as such—but you sure as hell weren't likely to do happy shiny things with magic with such an item around your neck.

Maybe Victor Sells had gotten involved in something real, something that had absorbed his attention. The Art could do that to a person—particularly the darker aspects of it. If he had turned to it in despair after losing his job, maybe that would explain his sudden absence from his home. A lot of sorcerers or wanna-be sorcerers secluded themselves in the belief that isolation would increase their ability to focus on their magic. It didn't—but it did make it easier for a weak or untrained mind to avoid distractions.

Or maybe it wasn't even a true talisman. Maybe it was just a curiosity, or a souvenir from some visit to the Southwest. There wasn't any way for me to tell if it was indeed a device used to improve the focus and direction of magical energies, short of actually using it to attempt a spell—and I really didn't want to be using such a dubious article, for a variety of good reasons.

I would have to keep this little un-beauty in mind as I tried to run this man down. It might well mean nothing. On the other hand, it might not. I looked up at the clock. A quarter after three. There was time to check with the local morgues to see if they had turned up any likely John Does—who knew, my search might be over before the day's end—and then to get to the bank to deposit my money and fire off a check to my landlord.

I got out my phone book and started calling up hospitals—not really my routine line of work, but not difficult, either, except for the standard problems I had using the telephone: static, line noise, other people's conversations being louder than mine. If something can go wrong, it will.

Once I thought I saw something out of the corner of my eye, a twitch of motion from the dried scorpion that sat on my desk. I blinked and stared at it. It didn't move. Cautiously, I extended my senses toward it like an invisible hand, feeling about for any traces of enchantment or magical energy.

Nothing. It was as dry of enchantment as it was of life.

Never let it be said that Harry Dresden is afraid of a dried, dead bug. Creepy or not, I wasn't going to let it ruin my concentration.

So I scooped it up with the corner of the phone book and popped it into the middle drawer of my desk. Out of sight, out of mind.

So I have a problem with creepy, dead, poisonous things. So sue me.

Chapter 5

McAnally's is a pub a few blocks from my office. I go there when I'm feeling stressed, or when I have a few extra bucks to spend on a nice dinner. A lot of us fringe types do. Mac, the pub's owner, is used to wizards and all the problems that come along with us. There aren't any video games at McAnally's. There are no televisions or expensive computer trivia games. There isn't even a jukebox. Mac keeps a player piano instead. It's less likely to go haywire around us.

I say *pub* in all the best senses of the word. When you walk in, you take several steps down into a room with a deadly combination of a low clearance and ceiling fans. If you're tall, like me, you walk carefully in McAnally's. There are thirteen stools at the bar and thirteen tables in the room. Thirteen windows, set up high in the wall in order to be above ground level, let some light from the street into the place. Thirteen mirrors on the walls cast back reflections of the patrons in dim detail, and give the illusion of more space. Thirteen wooden columns, carved with likenesses from folktales and legends of the Old World, make it difficult to walk around the place without weaving a circuitous route—they also quite intentionally break up the flow of random energies, dispelling to one degree or another the auras that gather around broody, grumpy wizards and keeping them from manifesting in unintentional and colorful ways. The colors are all muted, earth browns and sea greens. The first time I entered McAnally's, I felt like a wolf returning to an old, favorite den. Mac makes his own beer, ale really, and it's the best stuff in the city. His food is cooked on a wood-burning stove. And you can damn well walk your own self over to the bar to pick up your order when it's ready, according to Mac. It's my sort of place.

Since the calls to the morgues had turned up nothing, I kept a few bills out of Monica Sells's retainer and took myself to McAnally's. After the kind of day I'd had, I deserved some of Mac's ale and someone else's cooking. It was going to be a long night, too, once I went home and started trying to figure out how whoever it was had pulled off the death spell used on Johnny Marcone's hatchet man, Tommy Tomm, and his girlfriend, Jennifer Stanton.

"Dresden," Mac greeted me, when I sat down at the bar. The dim, comfortable room was empty, but for a pair of men I recognized by sight at a back table, playing chess. Mac is a tall, almost gangly man of indeterminate age, though there's a sense to him that speaks of enough wisdom and strength that I wouldn't venture that he was less than fifty. He has squinty eyes and a smile that is rare and mischievous when it manifests. Mac never says much, but when he does it's almost always worth listening to.

"Hey there, Mac," I hailed him. "Been one hell of a day. Give me a steak sandwich, fries, ale."

"Ungh," Mac said. He opened a bottle of his ale and began to pour it warm, staring past me, into the middle distance. He does that with everyone. Considering his clientele, I don't blame him. I wouldn't chance looking them in the face, either.

"You hear about what happened at the Madison?"

"Ungh," he confirmed.

"Nasty business."

Such an inane comment apparently didn't merit even a grunted reply. Mac set my drink out and turned to the stove behind the bar, checking the wood and raking it back and forth to provide even heating for it.

I picked up a prethumbed newspaper nearby and scanned the headlines. "Hey, look at this. Another ThreeEye rampage. Jesus, this stuff is worse than crack." The article detailed the virtual demolition of a neighborhood grocery store by a pair of ThreeEye junkies who were convinced that the place was destined to explode and wanted to beat destiny to the punch.

"Ungh."

"You ever seen anything like this?"

Mac shook his head.

"They say the stuff gives you the third sight," I said, reading the article. Both junkies had been admitted to the hospital and were in critical condition, after collapsing at the scene. "But you know what?"

Mac looked back at me from the stove, while he cooked.

"I don't think that's possible. What a bunch of crap. Trying to sell these poor kids on the idea that they can do magic."

Mac nodded at me.

"If it was serious stuff, the department would have already called me by now."

Mac shrugged, turning back to the stove. Then he squinted up and peered into the dim reflection of the mirror behind the bar.

"Harry," he said. "you were followed."

I had been too tense for too much of the day to avoid feeling my shoulders constrict in a sudden twinge. I put both hands around my mug and brought a few phrases of quasi-Latin to mind. It never hurt to be ready to defend myself, in case someone was intending to hurt me. I watched someone approach, a dim shape in the reflection cast by the ancient, worn mirror. Mac went on with cooking, unperturbed. Nothing much perturbed Mac.

I smelled her perfume before I turned around. "Why, Miss Rodriguez," I said. "It's always pleasant to see you."

She came to an abrupt stop a couple of paces from me, apparently disconcerted. One of the advantages of being a wizard is that people always attribute anything you do to magic, if no other immediate explanation leaps to mind. She probably wouldn't think about her perfume giving her identity away when she could assign my mysterious, blind identification of her to my mystical powers.

"Come on," I told her. "Sit down. I'll get you a drink while I refuse to tell you anything."

"Harry," she admonished me, "you don't know I'm here on business." She sat down on the barstool next to me. She was a woman of average height and striking, dark beauty, wearing a crisp business jacket and skirt, hose, pumps. Her dark, straight hair was trimmed in a neat cut that ended at the nape of her neck and was parted off of the dark skin of her forehead, emphasizing the lazy appeal of her dark eyes.

"Susan," I chided her, "you wouldn't be in this place if you weren't. Did you have a good time in Branson?"

Susan Rodriguez was a reporter for the Chicago *Arcane*, a yellow magazine that covered all sorts of supernatural and paranormal events throughout the Midwest. Usually, the events they covered weren't much better than: "Monkey Man Seen With

Elvis's Love Child," or "JFK's Mutant Ghost Abducts Shape-shifting Girl Scout." But once in a great, great while, the *Arcane* covered something that was real. Like the Unseelie Incursion of 1994, when the entire city of Milwaukee had simply vanished for two hours. Gone. Government satellite photos showed the river valley covered with trees and empty of life or human habitation. All communications ceased. Then, a few hours later, there it was, back again, and no one in the city itself the wiser.

She had also been hanging around my investigation in Branson the previous week. She had been tracking me ever since interviewing me for a feature story, right after I'd opened up my business. I had to hand it to her—she had instincts. And enough curiosity to get her into ten kinds of trouble. She had tricked me into meeting her eyes at the conclusion of our first interview, an eager young reporter investigating an angle on her interviewee. She was the one who had fainted after we'd soulgazed.

She smirked at me. I liked her smirk. It did interesting things to her lips, and hers were already attractive. "You should have stayed around for the show," she said. "It was pretty impressive." She put her purse on the bar and slid up onto the stool beside me.

"No thanks," I told her. "I'm pretty sure it wasn't for me."

"My editor loved the coverage. She's convinced it's going to win an award of some kind."

"I can see it now," I told her. " 'Mysterious Visions Haunt Drug-Using Country Star.' Real hard-hitting paranormal journalism, that." I glanced at her, and she met my eyes without fear. She didn't let me see if my jibe had ruffled her.

"I heard you got called in by the S.I. director today," she told me. She leaned toward me, enough that a glance down would have afforded an interesting angle to the V of her white shirt. "I'd love to hear you tell me about this one, Harry." She quirked a smile at me that promised things.

I almost smiled back at her. "Sorry," I told her. "I have a standard nondisclosure agreement with the city."

"Something off the record, then?" she asked. "Rumor has it that these killings were pretty sensational."

"Can't help you, Susan," I told her. "Wild horses couldn't drag it out of me, et cetera."

"Just a hint," she pressed. "A word of comment. Something shared between two people who are very attracted to one another."

"Which two people would that be?"

She put an elbow on the counter and propped her chin in her

hand, studying me through narrowed eyes and thick, long lashes. One of the things that appealed to me about her was that even though she used her charm and femininity relentlessly in pursuit of her stories, she had no concept of just how attractive she really was—I had seen that when I looked within her last year. "Harry Dresden," she said, "you are a thoroughly maddening man." Her eyes narrowed a bit further. "You didn't look down my blouse even once, did you," she accused.

I took a sip of my ale and beckoned Mac to pour her one as well. He did. "Guilty."

"Most men are off-balance by now," she complained. "What does it take with you, anyway, Dresden?"

"I am pure of heart and mind," I told her. "I cannot be corrupted."

She stared at me in frustration for a moment. Then she tilted back her head to laugh. She had a good laugh, too, throaty and rich. I *did* look down at her chest when she did that, just for a second. A pure heart and mind only takes you so far—sooner or later the hormones have their say, too. I mean, I'm not a teenager or anything, anymore, but I'm not exactly an expert in things like this, either. Call it an overwhelming interest in my professional career, but I've never had much time for dating or the fair sex in general. And when I have, it hasn't turned out too well.

Susan was a known quantity—she was attractive, bright, appealing, her motivations were clear and simple, and she was honest in pursuing them. She flirted with me because she wanted information as much as because she thought I was attractive. Sometimes she got it. Sometimes she didn't. This one was way too hot for Susan or the *Arcane* to touch, and if Murphy heard I'd tipped someone off about what had happened, she'd have my heart between two pieces of bread for lunch.

"I'll tell you what, Harry," she said. "How about if I ask some questions, and you just answer them with a yes or a no?"

"No," I said promptly. Dammit. I am a poor liar, and it didn't take a reporter with Susan's brains to tell it.

Her eyes glittered with cheerfully malicious ambition. "Was Tommy Tomm murdered by a paranormal being or means?"

"No," I said again, stubbornly.

"No he wasn't?" Susan asked, "Or no it wasn't a paranormal being."

I glanced at Mac as though to appeal for help. Mac ignored me. Mac doesn't take sides. Mac is wise.

"No, I'm not going to answer questions," I said.

"Do the police have any leads? Any suspects?"

"No."

"Are you a suspect yourself, Harry?"

Disturbing thought. "No," I said, exasperated. "Susan—"

"Would you mind having dinner with me Saturday night?"

"No! I—" I blinked at her. "What?"

She smiled at me, leaned over, and kissed me on the cheek. Her lips, that I'd admired so much, felt very, very nice. "Super," she said. "I'll pick you up at your place. Say around nine?"

"Did I just miss something?" I asked her.

She nodded, dark eyes sparkling with humor. "I'm going to take you to a fantastic dinner. Have you ever eaten at the Pump Room? At the Ambassador East?"

I shook my head.

"Steaks you wouldn't believe," she assured me. "And the most romantic atmosphere. Jackets and ties required. Can you manage?"

"Um. Yes?" I said, carefully. "This is the answer to the question of whether or not I'll go out with you, right?"

"No," Susan said, with a smile. "That was the answer I tricked out of you, so you're stuck, there. I just want to make sure you own something besides jeans and button-down Western shirts."

"Oh. Yes," I said.

"Super," she repeated, and kissed me on the cheek once more as she stood up and gathered her purse. "Saturday, then." She drew back and quirked her smirky little smile at me. It was a killer look, sultry and appealing. "I'll be there. With bells on."

She turned and walked out. I sort of turned to stare after her. My jaw slid off the bar as I did and landed on the floor.

Had I just agreed to a date? Or an interrogation session?

"Probably both," I muttered.

Mac slapped my steak sandwich and fries down in front of me. I put down some money, morosely, and he made change.

"She's going to do nothing but try to trick information out of me that I shouldn't be giving her, Mac," I said.

"Ungh," Mac agreed.

"Why did I say yes?"

Mac shrugged.

"She's pretty," I said. "Smart. Sexy."

"Ungh."

"Any red-blooded man would have done the same thing."

"Hngh," Mac snorted.

"Well. Maybe not you."

Mac smiled a bit, mollified.

"Still. It's going to make trouble for me. I must be crazy to go for someone like that." I picked up my sandwich, and sighed.

"Dumb," Mac said.

"I just said she was smart, Mac."

Mac's face flickered into that smile, and it made him look years younger, almost boyish. "Not her," he said. "You."

I ate my dinner. And had to admit that he was right.

This threw a wrench into my plans. My best idea for poking around the Sells lake house and getting information had to be carried out at night. And I already had tomorrow night slated for a talk with Bianca, since I had a feeling Murphy and Carmichael would fail to turn up any cooperation from the vampiress. That meant I would have to drive out to Lake Providence tonight, since Saturday night was now occupied by the date with Susan—or at least the premidnight portion was.

My mouth went dry when I considered that maybe the rest of the night might be occupied, too. One never knew. She had dizzied me and made me look like an idiot, and she was probably going to try every trick she knew to drag more information out of me for the Monday morning release of the *Arcane*. On the other hand, she was sexy, intelligent, and at least a little attracted to me. That indicated that more might happen than just talk and dinner. Didn't it?

The question was, did I really want that to happen?

I had been a miserable failure in relationships, ever since my first love went sour. I mean, a lot of teenage guys fail in their first relationships.

Not many of them murder the girl involved.

I shied away from that line of thought, lest it bring up too many old memories.

I left McAnally's, after Mac had handed me a doggy bag with a grunt of "Mister," by way of explanation. The chess game in the corner was still in progress, both players puffing up a sweet-smelling smog cloud from their pipes. I tried to figure out how to deal with Susan, while I walked out to my car. Did I need to clean up my apartment? Did I have all the ingredients for the spell I would cast at the lake house later tonight? Would Murphy go through the roof when I talked to Bianca?

I could still feel Susan's kiss lingering on my cheek as I got in the car.

I shook my head, bewildered. They say we wizards are subtle. But believe you me, we've got nothing, nothing at all, on *women*.

Chapter 6

Mister was nowhere to be seen when I got home, but I left the food in his dish anyway. He would eventually forgive me for getting home late. I collected the things I would need from my kitchen—fresh-baked bread with no preservatives, honey, milk, a fresh apple, a sharp silver penknife, and a tiny dinner set of a plate, bowl, and cup that I had carved myself from a block of teakwood.

I went back out to my car. The Beetle isn't really blue anymore, since both doors have been replaced, one with a green clone, one with a white one, and the hood of the storage trunk in front had to be replaced with a red duplicate, but the name stuck anyway. Mike is a super mechanic. He never asked questions about the burns that slagged a hole in the front hatch or the claw marks that ruined both the doors. You can't pay for service like that.

I revved up the Beetle and drove down I-94, around the shore of Lake Michigan, crossing through Indiana, briefly, and then crossing over the state line into Michigan itself. Lake Providence is an expensive, high-class community with big houses and sprawling estates. It isn't cheap to own land there. Victor Sells must have been doing well in his former position at SilverCo to afford a place out that way.

The lakeshore drive wound in and out among thick, tall trees and rolling hills down to the shore. The properties were well spread out, several hundred yards between them. Most of them were fenced in and had gates on the right side of the road, away from the lake as I drove north. The Sells house was the only one I saw on the lake side of the drive.

A smooth gravel lane, lined by trees, led back from the lakeshore drive to the Sells house. A peninsula jutted out into the lake, leaving enough room for the house and a small dock, at which no boats were moored. The house was not a large one, by the standards of the rest of the Lake Providence community. Built on two levels, it was a very modern dwelling—a lot of glass and wood that was made to look like something more synthetic than wood by the way it had been smoothed and cut and polished. The drive curved around to the back of the house, where a driveway big enough to host a five-on-five game of basketball around a backboard erected to one side was overlooked by a wooden deck leading off the second level of the house.

I drove the Blue Beetle around to the back of the house and parked there. My ingredients were in a black-nylon backpack, and I picked that up and brought it with me as I got out of the car and stretched my legs. The breeze coming up from the lake was cool enough to make me shiver a little, and I drew my mantled duster closed across my belly.

First impressions are important, and I wanted to listen to what my instincts said about the house. I stopped for a long moment and just stared up at it.

My instincts must have been holding out for another bottle of Mac's ale. They had little to say, other than that the place looked like a pricy little dwelling that had hosted a family through many a vacation weekend. Well, where instinct fails, intellect must venture. Almost everything was fairly new. The grass around the house had not grown long enough, this winter, to require a cutting. The basketball net was stretched out and loose enough to show that it had been used fairly often. The curtains were all drawn.

On the grass beneath the deck something red gleamed, and I went beneath the deck to retrieve it. It was a plastic film canister, red with a grey cap, the kind you keep a roll of film in when you send it in to the processors. Film canisters were good for holding various ingredients I used, sometimes. I tucked it in my duster's pocket and continued my inspection.

The place didn't look much like a family dwelling, really. It looked like a rich man's love nest, a secluded little getaway nestled back in the trees of the peninsula and safe from spying eyes. Or an ideal location for a novice sorcerer to come to try out his fledgling abilities, safe from interruptions. A good place for Victor Sells to set up shop and practice.

I made a quick circuit of the house, tried the front and rear doors, and even the door up on the deck that led, presumably, to a kitchen. All were locked. Locks really weren't an obstacle, but Monica Sells hadn't invited me actually to take a look inside the house, just around it. It's bad juju to go tromping into people's houses uninvited. One of the reasons vampires, as a rule, don't do it—they have enough trouble just holding themselves together, outside of the Nevernever. It isn't harmful to a human wizard, like me, but it can really impair anything you try to do with magic. Also, it just isn't polite. Like I said, I'm an old-fashioned sort of guy.

Of course, the TekTronic Securities control panel that I could see through the front window had some say in my decision—not that I couldn't hex it down to a useless bundle of plastic and wires, but a lot of security systems will cause an alarm with their contact company if they abruptly stop working without notice. It would be a useless exercise, in any case—the real information was to be had elsewhere.

Still, something nagged at me, a sense of not-quite-emptiness to the house. On a hunch, I knocked on the front door, several times. I even rang the bell. No one came to answer the door, and no lights were on, inside. I shrugged and walked back to the rear of the house, passing a number of empty trash cans as I did.

Now that was a bit odd. I mean, I would expect a little something in the trash, even if someone hadn't been there in a while. Did the garbage truck come all the way down the drive to pick up the trash cans? That didn't seem likely. If the Sellses came out to the house for the weekend and wanted the trash emptied, it would stand to reason that they'd have to leave it out by the drive near the road as they left. Which would seem to imply that the garbage men would leave the empty trash cans out by the road. Someone must have brought them back to the house.

Of course, it needn't have been Victor Sells. It could have been a neighbor, or something. Or maybe he tipped the garbagemen to carry the cans back away from the road. But it was something to go on, a little hint that maybe the house hadn't been empty all week.

I left the house behind me and walked out toward the lake. The night was breezy but clear, and a bit cool. The tall old trees creaked and groaned beneath the wind. It was still early for the mosquitoes to be too bad. The moon was waxing toward full overhead, with the occasional cloud slipping past her like a gauzy veil.

It was a perfect night for catching faeries.

I swept an area of dirt not far from the lakeshore clear of leaves and sticks, and took the silver knife from the backpack. Using the handle, I drew a circle in the earth, then covered it up with leaves and sticks again, marking the location of the circle's perimeter in my head. I was careful to focus in concentration on the circle, without actually letting any power slip into it and spoil the trap. Then, working carefully, I prepared the bait by setting out the little cup and bowl. I poured a thimbleful of milk into the cup and daubed the bowl full of honey from the little plastic bear in my backpack.

Then I tore a piece of bread from the loaf I had brought with me and pricked my thumb with the knife. In the silver light of the moon, a bit of dark blood welled up against the skin, and I touched it daintily to the underside of the coarse bread, letting it absorb the blood. Then I set the bread, bloody side down, on the tiny plate.

My trap was set. I gathered up my equipment and retreated to the cover of the trees.

There are two parts of magic you have to understand to catch a faery. One of them is the concept of true names. Everything in the whole world has its own name. Names are unique sounds and cadences of words that are attached to one specific individual—sort of like a kind of theme music. If you know something's name, you can associate yourself with it in a magical sense, almost in the same way a wizard can reach out and touch someone if he possesses a lock of their hair, or fingernail clippings, or blood. If you know something's name, you can create a magical link to it, just as you can call someone up and talk to them if you know their phone number. Just knowing the name isn't good enough, though: You have to know exactly how to say it. Ask two John Franklin Smiths to say their names for you, and you'll get subtle differences in tone and pronunciation, each one unique to its owner. Wizards tend to collect names of creatures, spirits, and people like some kind of huge Rolodex. You never know when it will come in handy.

The other part of magic you need to know is magic-circle theory. Most magic involves a circle of one kind or another. Drawing a circle sets a local limit on what a wizard is trying to do. It helps him refine his magic, focus and direct it more clearly. It does this by creating a sort of screen, defined by the perimeter of the circle, that keeps random magical energy from going past it, containing it within the circle so that it can be used. To make a circle, you draw it out on the ground, or close hands with a bunch of people, or walk about spreading incense, or any of a number of other methods, while focusing on your purpose in drawing it. Then, you invest it with a little spark of energy to close the circuit, and it's ready.

One other thing such a circle does: It keeps magical creatures, like faeries, or even demons, from getting past it. Neat, huh? Usually, this is used to keep them out. It's a bit trickier to set up a circle to keep them *in*. That's where the blood comes into play. With blood comes power. If you take in some of someone else's blood, there is a metaphysical significance to it, a sort of energy. It's minuscule if you aren't really trying to get energy that way (the way vampires do), but it's enough to close a circle.

Now you know how it's done. But I don't recommend that you try it at home. You don't know what to do when something goes wrong.

I retreated to the trees and called the name of the particular faery I wanted. It was a rolling series of syllables, quite beautiful, really—especially since the faery went by the name of Toot-toot every time I'd encountered him before. I pushed my will out along with the name, just made it a call, something that would be subtle enough to make him wander this way of his own accord. Or at least, that was the theory.

What was his name? Please, do you think wizards just *give* information like that away? You don't know what I went through to get it.

About ten minutes later, Toot came flickering in over the water of Lake Michigan. At first I mistook him for a reflection of the moon on the side of the softly rolling waves of the lake. Toot was maybe six inches tall. He had silver dragonfly's wings sprouting from his back and the pale, beautiful, tiny humanoid form that echoed the splendor of the fae lords. A silver nimbus of ambient light surrounded him. His hair was a shaggy, silken little mane, like a bird of paradise's plumes, and was a pale magenta.

Toot loved bread and milk and honey—a common vice of the lesser fae. They aren't usually willing to take on a nest of bees to get to the honey, and there's been a real dearth of milk in the Nevernever since hi-tech dairy farms took over most of the industry. Needless to say, they don't grow their own wheat, harvest it, thresh it, and then mill it into flour to make bread, either.

Toot alighted on the ground with caution, scanning around the trees. He didn't see me. I saw him wipe at his mouth and walk in a slow circle around the miniature dining set, one hand rubbing greedily at his stomach. Once he took the bread and closed the circle, I'd be able to bargain information for his release. Toot was a lesser spirit in the area, sort of a dockworker of the Nevernever. If anyone had seen anything of Victor Sells, Toot would have, or would know someone who had.

Toot dithered for a while, fluttering back and forth around the meal, but slowly getting closer. Faeries and honey. Moths and flame. Toot had fallen for this several times before, and it wasn't in the nature of the fae to keep memories for very long, or to change their essential natures. All the same, I held my breath.

The faery finally hunkered down, picked up the bread, dipped it in the honey, then greedily gobbled it down. The circle closed with a little *snap* that occurred just at the edge of my hearing.

Its effect on Toot was immediate. He screamed a shrill little scream, like a trapped rabbit, and took off toward the lake in a buzzing flurry of wings. At the perimeter of the circle, he smacked into something as solid as a brick wall, and a little puff of silver motes exploded out from him in a cloud. Toot grunted and fell onto his little faery ass on the earth.

"I should have known!" he exclaimed, as I approached from the trees. His voice was high-pitched, but more like a little kid's than the exaggerated kind of faery voices I'd heard in cartoons. "Now I remember where I've seen those plates before! You ugly, sneaky, hamhanded, big-nosed, flat-footed mortal worm!"

"Hiya, Toot," I told him. "Do you remember our deal from last time, or do we need to go over it again?"

Toot glared defiantly up at me and stomped his foot on the ground. More silver faery dust puffed out from the impact. "Release me!" he demanded. "Or I will tell the Queen!"

"If I don't release you," I pointed out, "you *can't* tell the Queen. And you know just as well as I do what she would say about any dewdrop faery who was silly enough to get himself caught with a lure of bread and milk and honey."

Toot crossed his arms defiantly over his chest. "I warn you, mortal. Release me now, or you will feel the awful, terrible, irresistible might of the faery magic! I will rot your teeth from your head! Take your eyes from their sockets! Fill your mouth with dung and your ears with worms!"

"Hit me with your best shot," I told him. "After that, we can talk about what you need to do to get out of the circle."

I had called his bluff. I always did, but he probably wouldn't remember the details very well. If you live a few hundred years, you tend to forget the little things. Toot sulked and kicked up a little spray of dirt with one tiny foot. "You could at least *pretend* to be afraid, Harry."

"Sorry, Toot. I don't have the time."

"Time, time," Toot complained. "Is that all you mortals can ever think about? Everyone's complaining about *time*! The whole city rushes left and right screaming about being late and honking horns! You people *used* to have it right, you know."

I bore the lecture with good nature. Toot could never keep his mind on the same subject long enough to be really trying, in any case.

"Why, I remember the folk who lived here before you pale, wheezy guys came in. And they *never* complained about ulcers or—" Toot's eyes wandered to the bread and milk and honey again, and glinted. He sauntered that way, then snatched the remaining bread, sopping up all the honey with it and eating it with greedy, birdlike motions.

"This is good stuff, Harry. None of that funny stuff in it that we get sometimes."

"Preservatives," I said.

"Whatever." Toot drank down the milk, too, in a long pull, then promptly fell down on his back, patting at his rounded tummy. "All right," he said. "Now, let me out."

"Not yet, Toot. I need something first."

Toot scowled up at me. "You wizards. Always needing something. I really could do the thing with the dung, you know." He stood up and folded his arms haughtily over his chest, looking up at me as though I weren't a dozen times taller than he. "Very well," he said, his tone lofty. "I have deigned to grant you a single request of some small nature, for the generous gift of your cuisine."

I worked to keep a straight face. "That's very kind of you."

Toot sniffed and somehow managed to look down his little pug nose at me. "It is my nature to be both benevolent and wise."

I nodded, as though this were a very great wisdom. "Uh-huh. Look, Toot. I need to know if you were around this place for the past few nights, or know someone who was. I'm looking for someone, and maybe he came here."

"And if I tell you," Toot said, "I take it you will disassemble this circle which has, by some odd coincidence no doubt, made its way around me?"

"It would be only reasonable," I said, all seriousness.

Toot seemed to consider it, as though he might be inclined not to cooperate, then nodded. "Very well. You will have the information you wish. Release me."

I narrowed my eyes. "Are you sure? Do you promise?"

Toot stamped his foot again, scattering more silver dust motes. "Harry! You're ruining the drama!"

I folded my arms. "I want to hear you promise."

Toot threw up his hands. "Fine, fine, *fine*! I promise, I promise, I promise! I'll dig up what you want to know!" He started to buzz about the circle in great agitation, wings lifting him easily into the air. "Let me out! Let me out!"

A promise thrice made is as close to absolute truth as you can get from a faery. I went quickly to the circle and scuffed over the line drawn in the dirt with my foot, willing the circle to part. It did, with a little hiss of released energy.

Toot streaked out over Lake Michigan's waters again, a miniature silver comet, and vanished in a twinkling, just like Santa Claus. Though I should say that Santa is a *much* bigger and more powerful faery than Toot, and I don't know his true name anyway. You'd never see me trying to nab Saint Nick in a magic circle, even if I did. I don't think anyone has stones that big.

I waited around, walking about to keep from falling asleep. If I did that, Toot would be perfectly within his rights as a faery to fulfill his promise by telling me the information while I was sleeping. And, given that I had just now captured and humiliated him, he'd probably do something to even the scales—two weeks from now he wouldn't even remember it, but if I let him have a free shot at me tonight, I might wake up with an ass's head, and I didn't think that would be good for business.

So I paced, and I waited. Toot usually took about half an hour to round up whatever it was I wanted to know.

Sure enough, half an hour later he came sparkling back in and buzzed around my head, drizzling faery dust from his blurring wings at my eyes. "Hah, Harry!" he said. "I did it!"

"What did you find out, Toot?"

"Guess!"

I snorted. "No."

"Aw, come on. Just a little guess?"

I scowled, tired and irritated, but tried not to let it show. Toot couldn't help being what he was. "Toot, it's late. You promised to tell me."

"No fun at *all*," he complained. "No wonder you can't get a date unless someone wants to know something from you."

I blinked at him, and he chortled in glee. "Hah! I love it! We're watching you, Harry Dresden!"

Now that was disconcerting. I had a sudden image of a dozen faery voyeurs lingering around my apartment's windows and peering inside. I'd have to take precautions to make sure they couldn't do that. Not that I was afraid of them, or anything. Just in case.

"Just tell me, Toot," I sighed.

"Incoming!" he shrilled, and I held out my hand, fingers flat and palm up. He alighted in the center of my palm. I could barely feel his weight, but the sense, the aura of him ran through my skin like a tiny electric current. He stared fearlessly at my eyes—the fae have no souls to gaze upon, and they could not fathom a mortal's soul, even if they could see it.

"Okay!" Toot said. "I talked to Blueblossom, who talked to Rednose, who talked to Meg O' Aspens, who said that Goldeneyes said that he was riding the pizza car when it came here last night!" Toot thrust out his chest proudly.

"Pizza car?" I asked, bewildered.

"Pizza!" Toot cried, jubilant. "Pizza! Pizza! Pizza!" His wings fluttered again, and I tried to blink the damned faery dust out of my eyes before I started sneezing.

"Faeries like pizza?" I asked.

"Oh, Harry," Toot said breathlessly. "Haven't you ever had pizza before?"

"Of course I have," I said.

Toot looked wounded. "And you didn't share?"

I sighed. "Look. Maybe I can bring you guys some pizza sometime soon, to thank you for your help."

Toot leapt about in glee, hopping from one fingertip to the other. "Yes! Yes! Wait until I tell them! We'll *see* who laughs at Toot-toot next time!"

"Toot," I said, trying to calm him, "did he see anything else?"

Toot tittered, his expression sly and suggestive. "He said that there were mortals sporting and that they needed pizza to regain their strength!"

"Which delivery place, Toot?"

The faery blinked and stared at me as though I were hopelessly stupid. "Harry. *The* pizza truck." And then he darted off skyward, vanishing into the trees above.

I sighed and nodded. Toot wouldn't know the difference between Domino's and Pizza Hut. He had no frame of reference, and couldn't read—most faeries were studiously averse to print.

So, I had two pieces of information. One, someone had ordered a pizza to be delivered here. That meant two things. First, that someone was here last night. Second, that someone had seen them and talked to them. Maybe I could track down the pizza driver, and ask if he had seen Victor Sells.

The second piece of information had been Toot's reference to sporting. Faeries didn't think too much of mortals' idea of "sporting" unless there was a lot of nudity and lust involved. They had a penchant for shadowing necking teenagers and playing tricks on them. So Victor had been here with a lover of some kind, for there to be any "sport" going on.

I was beginning to think that Monica Sells was in denial. Her husband wasn't wandering around learning to be a sorcerer, spooky scorpion talismans notwithstanding. He was lurking about his love nest with a girlfriend, like any other husband bored with a timid and domestic wife might do under pressure. It wasn't admirable, but I guess I could understand the motivations that could cause it.

The only problem was going to be telling Monica. I had a feeling that she wasn't going to want to listen to what I had found out.

I picked up the little plate and bowl and cup and put them back into my black-nylon backpack, along with the silver knife. My legs ached from too much walking and standing about. I was looking forward to getting home and getting some sleep.

The man with the naked sword in his hands appeared out of the darkness without a warning rustle of sound or whiff of magic to announce his presence. He was tall, like me, but broad and heavy-chested, and he carried his weight with a ponderous sort of dignity. Perhaps fifty years old, his listless brown hair going grey in uneven patches, he wore a long, black coat, a lot like mine but without the mantle, and his jacket and pants, too, were done in dark colors—charcoal and a deep blue. His shirt was crisp, pure white, the color that you usually only see with tuxedos. His eyes were grey, touched with crow's-feet at the corners, and dangerous. Moonlight glinted off those eyes in the same shade it did from the brighter silver of the sword's blade. He began to walk deliberately toward me, speaking in a quiet voice as he did.

"Harry Blackstone Copperfield Dresden. Irresponsible use of true names for summoning and binding others to your will violates the Fourth Law of Magic," the man intoned. "I remind you that you are under the Doom of Damocles. No further violations of the Laws will be tolerated. The sentence for further violation is death, by the sword, to be carried out at once."

Chapter 7

Have you ever been approached by a grim-looking man, carrying a naked sword with a blade about ten miles long in his hand, in the middle of the night, beneath the stars on the shores of Lake Michigan? If you have, seek professional help. If you have not, then believe you me, it can scare the bejeezus out of you.

I took in a quick breath, and had to work not to put it into a quasi-Latin phrase on the exhale, one that would set the man's body on fire and reduce him to a mound of ashes. I react badly to fear. I don't usually have the good sense to run, or hide—I just try to smash whatever it is that is making me afraid. It's a primitive sort of thing, and one I don't question too much.

But reflex-based murder seemed a tad extreme, so rather than setting him on fire, I nodded instead. "Evening, Morgan. You know as well as I do that those laws apply to mortals. Not faeries. Especially for something as trivial as I just did. And I didn't break the Fourth Law. He had the choice whether to take my deal or not."

Morgan's sour, leathery face turned a bit more sour, the lines at the corners of his mouth stretching and becoming deeper. "That's a technicality, Dresden. A pair of them." His hands, broad and strong, resettled their grip upon the sword he held. His unevenly greying hair was tied into a ponytail in the back, like Sean Connery's in some of his movies, except that Morgan's face was too pinched and thin to pull off the look.

"Your point being?" I did my best to keep from looking nervous or impressed. Truth be told, I was both. Morgan was my Warden, assigned to me by the White Council to make sure I didn't bend or break any of the Laws of Magic. He hung about and spied on me, mostly, and usually came sniffing around after I'd cast a spell of some kind. I would be damned if I was going to let the White Council's guard dog see any fear out of me. Besides, he would take it as a sign of guilt, in the true spirit of paranoid fanatics everywhere. So, all I had to do was keep a straight face and get out before my weariness made me slip up and do or say something he could use against me.

Morgan was one of the deadliest evocators in the world. He wasn't bright enough to question his loyalties to the Council, and he could do quick-and-dirty magic like few others could.

Quick and dirty enough to rip the hearts out of Tommy Tomm and Jennifer Stanton's chests, in fact, if he wanted to.

"My point," he said, scowling, "is that it is my assigned duty to monitor your use of your power, and to see to it that you do not abuse it."

"I'm on a missing-persons case," I said. "All I did was call up a dewdrop faery to get some information. Come on, Morgan. Everybody calls up faeries now and then. There's no harm in it. It's not as though I'm mind-controlling the things. Just leaning on them a little."

"Technicality," Morgan growled.

I stuck out my chin at him belligerently. We were of a height, though he outweighed me by about a hundred pounds. I could pick better people to antagonize, but he'd really gotten under my skin. "A technicality I'm prepared to hide wildly behind. So, unless you want to convene a meeting of the Council to call me on it, we can just drop the discussion right here. I'm pretty sure it will only take them about two days to cancel all their plans, make travel arrangements, and then get here. I can put you up until then. I mean, you'd be dragging a bunch of really crotchety old men away from their experiments and things for nothing, but if you really think it's necessary . . ."

Morgan scowled at me. "No. It isn't worth it." He opened his dark trench coat and slid the sword away into its scabbard. I relaxed a little. The sword wasn't the most dangerous thing about him, not by a long shot, but it was his symbol of the authority given to him by the White Council, and if rumors were true, it was enchanted to cut through the magical spells of anyone resisting him. I didn't want things ever to go far enough for me to find out if the rumors were true.

"I'm glad we agree about something," I said. "Nice seeing you again." I started to walk past him.

Morgan put one of those big hands on my arm as I went by, and his fingers closed around it. "I'm not finished with you, Dresden."

I didn't dare mess around with Morgan when he was acting in his role as a Warden of the White Council. But he wasn't wearing that hat, now. Once he'd put the sword away, he was acting on his own, without any more official authority than any other man—or at least, that was the technical truth. Morgan was big on technicalities. He had scared the heck out of me and annoyed the heck out of me, in rapid succession. Now he was trying to bully me. I hate bullies.

So I took a calculated risk, used my free hand, and hit him as hard as I could in the mouth.

I think the blow startled him more than anything. He took a step back, letting go of my arm in surprise, and just blinked at me. He put one hand to his mouth, and when he drew his fingers away, there was blood on them.

I planted my feet and faced him, without meeting his eyes. "Don't touch me."

Morgan continued to stare at me. And then I saw anger creep over his face, set his jaw, make the veins at his temple stand out.

"How dare you," he said. "How dare you strike me."

"It wasn't so hard," I said. "If you've got Council business with me, I'm willing to give you whatever respect is your due. When you come on strong to me on personal business, I don't have to put up with it."

I saw the steam coming out of his ears as he mulled it over. He looked for a reason to come after me, and realized that he didn't have one, according to the Laws. He wasn't too bright—did I mention that already?—and he was a big one for following the Laws. "You're a fool, Dresden," he sputtered finally. "An arrogant little fool."

"Probably," I told him. I tensed myself to move quickly if necessary. I may not like to run away from what scares me, but I try not to fight hopeless battles, either, and Morgan had me by years of experience and a hundred pounds, at least. There was no Law of Magic that protected *me* from *him* and his fists, either, and if that occurred to him, he might decide to do something about it. That punch I'd landed had been lucky, coming out of the blue. I wouldn't get away with it again.

"Someone killed two people with sorcery last night, Dresden. I think it was you. And when I find how you did it and can trace it back to you, don't think you're going to live long enough to cast the same spell at me." Morgan swiped at the blood with one big fist.

It was my turn to blink. I tried to shift mental gears, to keep up with the change in subject. Morgan thought I was the killer. And since Morgan didn't do too much of his own thinking, that meant that the White Council thought I was the killer. Holy shit.

Of course, it made sense, from Morgan's narrow and single-minded point of view. A wizard had killed someone. I was a wizard who had already been convicted of killing another with magic, even if the self-defense clause had kept me from being executed. Cops looked for people who had already committed crimes before they started looking for other culprits. Morgan was just another kind of cop, as far as I was concerned.

And, as far as he was concerned, I was just one more dangerous con.

"You're not serious," I told him. "You think I did it?"

He sneered at me. His voice was contemptuous, confident, and seethed with absolute conviction. "Don't try to hide it, Dresden. I'm sure you think you're clever enough to come up with something innovative that we hidebound old men won't be able to trace. But you're wrong. We'll determine how you did it, and we'll follow it back to you. And when we do, I'll be there to make sure you never hurt anyone again."

"Knock yourself out," I told him. It was hard, really hard, to keep my voice as blithe as I wanted it to sound. "I didn't do it. But I'm helping the police find the man who did."

"The police?" Morgan asked. He narrowed his eyes, as though gauging my expression. "As if they could have any authority on this matter. They won't do you any good. Even if you do set someone up to take the fall for you under mortal law, the White Council will still see that justice is done." His eyes glittered, fanatic-bright underneath the stars.

"Whatever. Look, if you find something out about the killer, anything that could help the cops out, would you give me a call?"

Morgan looked at me with profound distaste. "You ask me to warn you when we are closing in on you, Dresden? You are young, but I never thought you stupid."

I bit back the obvious comment that leapt to mind. Morgan was on the edge of outrage already. If I'd realized how rabid he was to catch me slipping, I wouldn't have added more fuel to his fire by hitting him in the mouth.

Okay. I probably still would have hit him in the mouth. But I wouldn't have done it quite so hard.

"Good night, Morgan," I told him. I started to walk away again, before I could let my mouth get me into more trouble.

He moved faster than I would have given a man his age credit for. His fist went across my jaw at approximately a million miles an hour, and I spun down to the dirt like a string-cut puppet. For several long moments, I was unable to do anything at all, even breathe. Morgan loomed over me.

"We'll be watching you, Dresden." He turned and started walking away, the shadows of the evening quickly swallowing up his black coat. His voice drifted back to me. "We'll find out what really happened."

I didn't dare spout out a snappy comeback. I felt my jaw with my fingers, and made sure it wasn't broken, before I stood up and walked back to the Beetle, my legs feeling loose and watery. I fervently hoped that Morgan would find out what had really happened. It would keep the White Council from executing me for breaking the First Law, for one thing.

I could feel his eyes on my back, all the way to the Beetle. Damn that Morgan. He didn't have to take quite so much pleasure in being assigned to spy on me. I had a sinking feeling that anywhere I went over the next few days, he would be likely to turn up, watching. He was like this big, cartoon tomcat waiting outside the mousehole for the little mouse to stick its nose out so he could smash it flat with one big paw. I was feeling a lot like that little mouse.

I let that analogy cheer me up a bit. The cartoon cats always seemed to get the short end of the stick, in the final analysis. Maybe Morgan would, too.

Part of the problem was that seeing Morgan always brought up too many memories of my angsty teenage days. That was when I'd started to learn magic, when my mentor had tried to seduce me into Black wizardry, and when he had attempted to kill me when he failed. I killed him instead, mostly by luck—but he was just as dead, and I'd done it with sorcery. I broke the First Law of Magic: *Thou Shalt Not Kill*. There is only one sentence, if someone is found guilty, and one sword that they use to carry it out.

The White Council commuted the death sentence, because tradition demands that a wizard can resort to the use of deadly force if he is defending his own life, or the lives of the defenseless, and my claim that I had been attacked first could not be contested by my master's corpse. So instead, they'd stuck me on a kind of accelerated probation: One strike and I was out. There were some wizards who thought that the judgment against me was a ludicrous injustice (I happened to be one of them, but my vote didn't really count), and others who thought that I should have been executed regardless of extenuating circumstances. Morgan belonged to that latter group. Just my luck.

I was feeling more than a bit surly at the entire White Council, benevolent intentions aside. I guess it only made sense that they'd suspect me, and God knows I'd been a thorn in their side, flying in the face of tradition by practicing my art openly. There were plenty of people on the Council who might well want me dead. I would have to start being more careful.

I rolled down the Beetle's windows on the way back to Chicago to help me stay awake. I was exhausted, but my mind was racing around like a hamster on an exercise wheel, working furiously, getting nowhere.

The irony was thick enough to make my tongue curl. The White Council suspected me of the killings, and if no other suspect came forward, I was going to take the rap. Murphy's investigation had just become very, very important to me. But to pursue the investigation, I would have to try to figure out how the killer had pulled off that spell, and to do *that*, I would have to indulge in highly questionable research that would probably be enough to get me a death sentence all by itself. Catch twenty-two. If I had any respect at all for Morgan's intelligence, I would have suspected him of pulling off the killings himself and setting me up to take the blame.

But that just didn't track. Morgan might twist and bend the rules, to get what he saw as justice, but he'd never blatantly violate them. But if not Morgan, then who could have done it? There just weren't all that many people who could get enough power into that kind of spell to make it work—unless there was some flaw in the quasiphysics that governed magic that let hearts explode more easily than other things; and I wouldn't know that until I had pursued the forbidden research.

Bianca would have more information on who might have done it—she had to. I had already planned on talking to the vampiress, but Morgan's visit had made it a necessity, rather than merely a priority. Murphy was not going to be thrilled that I was thrusting myself into her side of this investigation. And, better and better, because White Council business was all hush-hush to nonwizards, I wouldn't be able to explain to her why I was doing it. Further joy.

You know, sometimes I think Someone up there really hates me.

Chapter 8

By the time I got home, it was after two o'clock in the morning. The clock in the Beetle didn't work (of course), but I made a pretty good guess from the position of the stars and the moon. I was strung out, weary, and my nerves were stretched as tight as guitar strings.

I didn't think sleep was likely, so I decided to do a little alchemy to help me unwind.

I've often wished that I had some suave and socially acceptable hobby that I could fall back on in times like this. You know, play the violin (or was it the viola?) like Sherlock Holmes, or maybe twiddle away on the pipe organ like the Disney version of Captain Nemo. But I don't. I'm sort of the arcane equivalent of a classic computer geek. I do magic, in one form or another, and that's pretty much it. I really need to get a life, one of these days.

I live in a basement apartment beneath a big, roomy old house that has been divided up into lots of different apartments. The basement and the subbasement below it are both mine, which is sort of neat. I'm the only tenant living on two floors, and my rent is cheaper than all the people who have whole windows.

The house is full of creaks and sighs and settling boards, and time and lives have worn their impressions into the wood and the brick. I can hear all the sounds, all the character of the place, above and around me all through the night. It's an old place, but it sings in the darkness and is, in its own quirky little way, alive. It's home.

Mister was waiting for me at the bottom of the stairs that led down to the apartment's front door. Mister is an enormous grey cat. I mean, enormous. There are dogs smaller than Mister. He weighs in at just over thirty pounds, and there isn't an undue amount of fat on his frame. I think maybe his father was a wildcat or a lynx or something. I had found Mister in a garbage can about three years before, a mewling kitten, with his tail torn off by a dog or a car—I was never sure which, but Mister hated both, and would either attack or flee from them on sight.

Mister had recovered his dignity over the next few months, and shortly came to believe that he was the apartment's tenant, and I was someone he barely tolerated to share the space with him. Right now he looked up and mrowed at me in an annoyed tone.

"I thought you had a hot date," I told him.

He sauntered over to me and rammed one shoulder playfully against my knee. I wavered, recovered my balance, and unlocked the door. Mister, as was his just due, entered before I did.

My apartment is a studio, one not-too-large room with a kitchenette in the corner and a fireplace to one side. There's a door that leads to the other room, my bedroom and bathroom, and then there's the hinged door in the floor that goes down to the subbasement, where I keep my lab. I've got things pretty heavily textured—there are multiple carpets on the floor, tapestries on the walls, a collection of knickknacks and oddities on every available surface, my staff and my sword cane in the corner, and several bulging bookshelves which I really will organize one day.

Mister went to his spot before the fireplace and demanded that it be made warm. I obliged him with a fire and lit a lamp as well. Oh, I have lights and so on, but they foul up so often it almost isn't worth turning them on. And I'm not even about to take chances with the gas heater. I stick with the simple things, the fireplace and my candles and lamps. I have a special charcoal stove and a vent to take most of the smoke out, though the whole place smells a little of woodsmoke and charcoal, no matter what I do.

I took off my duster and got out my heavy flannel robe before I went down into the lab. That's why wizards wear robes, I swear to you. It's just too damned cold in the lab to go without one. I clambered down the ladder to the lab, carrying my candle with me, and lit a few lamps, a pair of burners, and a kerosene heater in the corner.

The lights came up and revealed a long table in the center of the room, other tables against three of the walls around it, and a clear space at one end of the room where a brass circle had been laid out on the floor and fastened into the cement with U-shaped bolts. Shelves over the tables were crowded with empty cages, boxes, Tupperware, jars, cans, containers of all descriptions, a pair of unusual antlers, a couple of fur pelts, several musty old books, a long row of notebooks filled with my own cramped writing, and a bleached white human skull.

"Bob," I said. I started clearing space off of the center table, dumping boxes and grocery sacks and plastic tubs over the brass circle on the floor. I needed room to work. "Bob, wake up."

There was a moment of silence, while I started getting some things down from the shelves. "Bob!" I said, louder. "Come on, lazybones."

A pair of lights came up in the empty sockets of the skull, orangish, flickering like candle flames. "It isn't enough," the skull said, "that I have to wake up. I have to wake up to bad puns. What is it about you that you have to make the bad puns?"

"Quit whining," I told him, cheerfully. "We've got work to do."

Bob the Skull grumbled something in Old French, I think, though I got lost when he got to the anatomical improbabilities of bullfrogs. He yawned, and his bony teeth rattled when his mouth clicked closed again. Bob wasn't really a human skull. He was a spirit of air—sort of like a faery, but different. He made his residence inside the skull that had been prepared for him several hundred years ago, and it was his job to remember things. For obvious reasons, I can't use a computer to store information and keep track of the slowly changing laws of quasiphysics. That's why I had Bob. He had worked with dozens of wizards over the years, and it had given him a vast repertoire of knowledge—that, and a really cocky attitude. "Blasted wizards," he mumbled.

"I can't sleep, so we're going to make a couple of potions. Sound good?"

"Like I have a choice," Bob said. "What's the occasion?"

I brought Bob up to speed on what had happened that day. He whistled (no easy trick without lips), and said, "Sounds sticky."

"Pretty sticky," I agreed.

"Tell you what," he said. "Let me out for a ride, and I'll tell you how to get out of it."

That made me wary. "Bob, I let you out once. Remember?"

He nodded dreamily, scraping bone on wood. "The sorority house. I remember."

I snorted, and started some water to boiling over one of the burners. "You're supposed to be a spirit of intellect. I don't understand why you're obsessed with sex."

Bob's voice got defensive. "It's an academic interest, Harry."

"Oh yeah? Well maybe I don't think it's fair to let your academia go peeping in other people's houses."

"Wait a minute. My academia doesn't *just* peep—"

I held up a hand. "Save it. I don't want to hear it."

He grunted. "You're trivializing what getting out for a bit means to me, Harry. You're insulting my masculinity."

"Bob," I said, "you're a *skull*. You don't *have* any masculinity to insult."

"Oh yeah?" Bob challenged me. "Pot kettle black, Harry! Have you gotten a date yet? Huh? Most men have something better to do in the middle of the night than play with their chemistry sets."

"As a matter of fact," I told him, "I'm set up for Saturday night."

Bob's eyes fluttered from orange to red. "Oooooo," he leered. "Is she pretty?"

"Dark skin," I said. "Dark hair, dark eyes. Legs to die for. Smart, sexy as hell."

Bob chortled. "Think she'd like to see the lab?"

"Get your mind out of the gutter."

"No, seriously," Bob said. "If she's so great, what's she doing with you? You aren't exactly Sir Gawain, you know."

It was my turn to get defensive. "She likes me," I said. "Is that such a shock?"

"Harry," Bob drawled, his eye lights flickering smugly, "what you know about women, I could juggle."

I stared at Bob for a moment, and realized with a somewhat sinking feeling that the skull was probably right. Not that I would admit that to him, not in a million years, but he was.

"We're going to make an escape potion," I told him. "I don't want to be all night, so can we get to work? Huh? I can only remember about half the recipe."

"There's always room to make two if you're making one, Harry. You know that."

That much was true. The process of mixing up an alchemical potion is largely stirring, simmering, and waiting. You can always get another one going and alternate between them. Sometimes you can even do three, though that's pushing it. "Okay, so, we'll make a copy."

"Oh, come on," Bob chided me. "That's dull. You should stretch yourself. Try something new."

"Like what?"

Bob's eye sockets twinkled cheerfully. "A love potion, Harry! If you won't let me out, at least let me do that! Spirits know you could use it, and—"

"No," I said, firmly. "No way. No love potion."

"Fine," he said. "No love potion, no escape potion either."

"Bob," I said, warningly.

Bob's eye lights winked out.

I growled. I was tired and cranky, and under the best of circumstances I am not exactly a type A personality. I stalked over, picked up Bob by the jaws and shook him. "Hey!" I shouted. "Bob! You come out of there! Or I'm going to take this skull and throw it down the deepest well I can find! I swear to you, I'll put you somewhere where no one can ever let you out ever again!"

Bob's eyes winked on for a moment. "No you won't. I'm far too valuable." Then they winked out again.

I gritted my teeth and tried not to smash the skull to little pieces on the floor. I took deep breaths, summoning years of wizardly training and control to not throw a tantrum and break the nice spirit to little pieces. Instead, I put the skull back on the shelf and counted slowly to thirty.

Could I make the potion by myself? I probably could. But I had the sinking feeling that it might not have precisely the effect I wanted. Potions were a tricky business, and a lot more relied upon precise details than upon intent, like in spells. And just because I made a love potion didn't mean I had to use it. Right? It would only be good for a couple of days, in any case—surely not through the weekend. How much trouble could it cause?

I struggled to rationalize the action. It would appease Bob, and give him some kind of vicarious thrill. Love potions were about the cheapest things in the world to make, so it wouldn't cost me too much. And, I thought, if Susan should ask me for some kind of demonstration of magic (as she always did), I could always—

No. That would be too much. That would be like admitting I couldn't get a woman to like me on my own, and it would be unfair, taking advantage of the woman. What I wanted was the escape potion. I might need it at Bianca's place, and I could always use it, if worse came to worst, to make a getaway from Morgan and the White Council. I would feel a lot better if I had the escape potion.

"Okay, Bob. Fine. You win. We'll do them both. All right?"

Bob's eye lights came up warily. "You're sure? You'll do the love potion, just like I say?"

"Don't I always make the potions like you say, Bob?"

"What about that diet potion you tried?"

"Okay. That one was a mistake."

"And the antigravity potion, remember that?"

"We *fixed* the floor! It was no big deal!"

"And the—"

"Fine, fine," I growled. "You don't have to rub it in. Now cough up the recipes."

Bob did so, in fine humor, and for the next two hours we made potions. Potions are all made pretty much the same way. First you need a base to form the essential liquid content; then something to engage each of the senses, and then something for the mind and something else for the spirit. Eight ingredients, all in all, and they're different for each and every potion, and for each person who makes them. Bob had centuries of experience, and he could extrapolate the most successful components for a given person to make into a potion. He was right about being an invaluable resource—I had never even heard of a spirit with Bob's experience, and I was lucky to have him.

That didn't mean I didn't want to crack that skull of his from time to time, though.

The escape potion was made in a base of eight ounces of Jolt cola. We added a drop of motor oil, for the smell of it, and cut a bird's feather into tiny shavings for the tactile value. Three ounces of chocolate-covered espresso beans, ground into powder, went in next. Then a shredded bus ticket I'd never used, for the mind, and a small chain which I broke and then dropped in, for the heart. I unfolded a clean white cloth where I'd had a flickering shadow stored for just such an occasion, and tossed it into the brew, then opened up a glass jar where I kept my mouse scampers and tapped the sound out into the beaker where the potion was brewing.

"You're sure this is going to work, Bob?" I said.

"Always. That's a super recipe, there."

"Smells terrible."

Bob's lights twinkled. "They usually do."

"What's it doing? Is this the superspeed one, or the teleportation version?"

Bob coughed. "A little of both, actually. Drink it, and you'll be the wind for a few minutes."

"The wind?" I eyed him. "I haven't heard of that one before, Bob."

"I am an air spirit, after all," Bob told me. "This'll work fine. Trust me."

I grumbled, and set the first potion to simmering, then started on the next one. I hesitated, after Bob told me the first ingredient.

"Tequila?" I asked him, skeptically. "Are you sure on that one? I thought the base for a love potion was supposed to be champagne."

"Champagne, tequila, what's the difference, so long as it'll lower her inhibitions?" Bob said.

"Uh. I'm thinking it's going to get us a, um, sleazier result."

"Hey!" Bob protested, "Who's the memory spirit here! Me or you?"

"Well—"

"Who's got all the experience with women here? Me or you?"

"Bob—"

"Harry," Bob lectured me, "I was seducing shepherdesses when you weren't a twinkle in your great-grandcestor's eyes. I think I know what I'm doing."

I sighed, too tired to argue with him. "Okay, okay. Sheesh. Tequila." I got down the bottle, measured eight ounces into the beaker, and glanced up at the skull.

"Right. Now, three ounces of dark chocolate."

"Chocolate?" I demanded.

"Chicks are into chocolate, Harry."

I muttered, more interested in finishing than anything else, and measured out the ingredients. I did the same with a drop of perfume (some name-brand imitation that I liked), an ounce of shredded lace, and the last sigh at the bottom of the glass jar. I added some candlelight to the mix, and it took on a rosy golden glow.

"Great," Bob said. "That's just right. Okay, now we add the ashes of a passionate love letter."

I blinked at the skull. "Uh, Bob. I'm fresh out of those."

Bob snorted. "How did I guess. Look on the shelf behind me."

I did, and found a pair of romance novels, their covers filled with impossibly delightful flesh. "Hey! Where did you get these?"

"My last trip out," Bob answered blithely. "Page one seventy-four, the paragraph that starts with, 'Her milky-white breasts.' Tear that page out and burn it and add those ashes in."

I choked. "That will work?"

"Hey, women eat these things up. Trust me."

"Fine," I sighed. "This is the spirit ingredient?"

"Uh-huh," Bob said. He was rocking back and forth on his jawbones in excitement. "Now, just a teaspoon of powdered diamond, and we're done."

I rubbed at my eyes. "Diamond. I don't have any diamonds, Bob."

"I figured. You're cheap, that's why women don't like you. Look, just tear up a fifty into real little pieces and put that in there."

"A fifty-dollar bill?" I demanded.

"Money," Bob opined, "Very sexy."

I muttered and got the remaining fifty out of my pocket, shredding it and tossing it in to complete the potion.

The next step was where the effort came in. Once all the ingredients are mixed together, you have to force enough energy through them to activate them. It isn't the actual physical ingredients that are important—it's the meaning that they carry, too, the significance that they have for the person making the potion, and for those who will be using it.

The energy from magic comes from a lot of places. It can come from a special place (usually some spectacular natural site, like Mount St. Helens, or Old Faithful), from a focus of some kind (like Stonehenge is, on a large scale), or from inside of people. The best magic comes from the inside. Sometimes it's just pure mental effort, raw willpower. Sometimes it's emotions and feelings. All of them are viable tinder to be used for the proverbial fire.

I had a lot of worry to use to fuel the magic, and a lot of annoyance and one hell of a lot of stubbornness. I murmured the requisite quasi-Latin litany over the potions, over and over, feeling a kind of resistance building, just out of the range of the physical senses, but there, nonetheless. I gathered up all my worry and anger and stubbornness and threw them all at the resistance in one big ball, shaping them with the strength and tone of my words. The magic left me in a sudden wave, like a pitcher abruptly emptied out.

"I love this part," Bob said, just as both potions exploded into puffs of greenish smoke and began to froth up over the lips of the beakers.

I sagged onto a stool, and waited for the potions to fizz down, all the strength gone out of me, the weariness building up like a load of bricks on my shoulders. Once the frothing had settled, I leaned over and poured each potion into its own individual sports bottle with a squeeze-top, then labeled the containers with a permanent Magic Marker—very clearly. I don't take chances in getting potions mixed up anymore, ever since the invisibility/hair tonic incident, from when I was trying to grow out a decent beard.

"You won't regret this, Harry," Bob assured me. "That's the best potion I've ever made."

"I made it, not you," I growled. I really was exhausted, now—way too tired to let petty concerns like possible execution keep me from bed.

"Sure, sure," Bob agreed. "Whatever, Harry."

I went around the room putting out all the fires and the kerosene heater, then climbed the ladder back to the basement without saying good night. Bob was chortling happily to himself as I did.

I stumbled to my bed and fell into it. Mister always climbs in and goes to sleep draped over my legs. I waited for him, and a few seconds later he showed up, settling down and purring like a miniature outboard motor.

I struggled to put together an itinerary for the next couple of days through the haze of exhaustion. Talk to the vampire. Locate missing husband. Avoid the wrath of the White Council. Find the killer.

Before he found me.

An unpleasant thought—but I decided that I wasn't going to let that bother me, either, and curled up to go to sleep.

Chapter 9

Friday night, I went to see Bianca, the vampiress.

I didn't just leap out of bed and go see her, of course. You don't go walking into the proverbial lion's den lightly. You start with a good breakfast.

My breakfast took place around three in the afternoon, when I woke up to hear my phone ringing. I had to get out of bed and pad into the main room to answer it.

"Mmmrrmmph," I grumbled.

"Dresden," Murphy said, "what can you tell me?"

Murphy sounded stressed. Her voice had that distinct edge that she got whenever she was nervous, and it rankled me, like fingernails scraping on bones. The investigation into Tommy Tomm's murder must not be going well "Nothing yet," I said. Then I lied to her, a little. "I was up most of the night working, but nothing to show yet."

She answered me with a swear word. "That's not good enough, Harry. I need answers, and I need them yesterday."

"I'll get to it as quick as I can."

"Get to it faster," she snarled. She was angry. Not that this was unusual for Murphy, but it told me that something else was going on. Some people panic when things get rough, harried. Some people fall apart. Murphy got pissed.

"Commissioner riding your back again?" City Police Commissioner Howard Fairweather used Murphy and her team as scapegoats for all sorts of unsolvable crimes that he had dumped in her lap. Fairweather was always lurking around, trying for an opportunity to make Murphy look bad, as though by doing so he could avoid being crucified himself.

"Like a winged monkey from *The Wizard of Oz*. Kind of makes you wonder who's leaning on *him* to get things done." Her voice was sour as ripe lemons. I heard her drop an Alka-Seltzer into a glass of liquid. "I'm serious, Harry. You get me those answers I need, and you get them to me fast. I need to know if this was sorcery, and, if so, how it was done and who could have done it. Names, places—I need to know everything."

"It isn't that simple, Mur—"

"Then *make* it simple. How long before you can tell me? I need an estimate for the Commissioner's investigative committee in fifteen minutes or I might as well turn in my badge today."

I grimaced. If I was able to get something out of Bianca, I might be able to help Murph on the investigation—but if it proved fruitless, I was going to have spent the entire evening doing nothing productive, and Murphy needed her answers now. Maybe I should have made a stay-awake potion. "Does the committee work weekends?"

Murphy snorted. "Are you kidding?"

"We'll have something by Monday, then."

"You can have it figured out by then?" she asked.

"I don't know how much good it will do you, even if I can puzzle it out. I hope you've got more to go on than this."

I heard her sigh into the phone and drink the fizzy drink. "Don't let me down, Harry."

Time to change the subject, before she pinned me down and smelled me lying. I had no intention of doing the forbidden research if I could find a way out of doing it. "No luck with Bianca?"

Another swear word. "That bitch won't talk to us. Just smiles and nods and blows smoke, makes small talk, and crosses her legs. You should have seen Carmichael drooling."

"Well. Tough to blame him, maybe. I hear she's cute. Listen, Murph. What if I just—"

"No, Harry. Absolutely not. You will not go over to the Velvet Room, you will *not* talk to that woman, and you will not get involved in this."

"Lieutenant Murphy," I drawled. "A little jealous, are we?"

"Don't flatter yourself. You're a civilian, Dresden, even if you do have your investigator's license. If you get your ass laid out in the hospital or the morgue, it'll be me that suffers for it."

"Murph, I'm touched."

"I'll touch your head to a brick wall a few times if you cross me on this, Harry." Her voice was sharp, vehement.

"Hey, wind down, Murph. If you don't want me to go, no problem." Whups. A lie. She'd be all over that like a troll on a billy goat.

"You're a lousy liar, Harry. Godammit, I ought to take you down to lockup just to keep you from—"

"What?" I said, loudly, into the receiver. "Murph, you're breaking up. I can't hear you. Damn phone again. Call me back." Then I hung up on her.

Mister padded over to me and batted at my leg. He watched me with serious green eyes as I leaned down and unplugged the phone as it started to ring again.

"Okay, Mister. You hungry?"

I got us breakfast. Leftover steak sandwich for him, SpaghettiOs heated up on the wood stove for me. I rationed out my last can of Coke, which Mister craves at least as badly as I do, and by the time I was done eating and drinking and petting, I was awake and thinking again—and getting ready for sundown.

Daylight savings time hadn't cut in yet, and dark would fall around six. I had about two hours to get set to go.

You might think you know a thing or two about vampires. Maybe some of the stuff you've heard is accurate. Likely, it's not. Either way, I wasn't looking forward to the prospect of going into Bianca's lair to demand information from her. I was going to assume that things were going to get ugly before all was said and done, just to make sure I didn't get caught with my staff down.

Wizardry is all about thinking ahead, about being prepared. Wizards aren't really superhuman. We just have a leg up on seeing things more clearly than other people, and being able to use the extra information we have for our benefit. Hell, the word *wizard* comes from the same root as *wise*. We know things. We aren't any stronger or faster than anyone else. We don't even have all that much more going in the mental department. But we're godawful sneaky, and if we get the chance to get set for something, we can do some impressive things.

As a wizard, if you're ready to address a problem, then it's likely that you'll be able to come up with something that will let you deal with it. So, I got together all the things I thought I might need: I made sure my cane was polished and ready. I put my silver knife in a sheath that hung just under my left arm. I put the escape potion in its plastic squeeze-bottle into my duster's pocket. I put on my favorite talisman, a silver pentacle on a silver chain—it had been my mother's. My father had passed it down to me. And I put a small, folded piece of white cloth into my pocket.

I had several enchanted items around—or half-enchanted items, anyway. Carrying out a full enchantment is expensive and time-consuming, and I just couldn't afford to do it very much. We blue-collar wizards just have to sling a few spells out where we can and hope they don't go stale at the wrong time. I would have been a lot more comfortable if I had been carrying my blasting rod or my staff, but that would be like showing up at Bianca's door in a tank, walking in carrying a machine gun and a flamethrower, while announcing my intention to fight.

I had to maintain a fine balance between going in ready for trouble and going in asking for trouble.

Not that I was afraid, mind you. I didn't think Bianca would be willing to cause problems for a mortal wizard. Bianca wouldn't want to piss off the White Council by messing with me.

On the other hand, I wasn't exactly the White Council's favorite guy. They might even look the other way if Bianca decided to take me quietly out of the picture.

Careful, Harry, I warned myself. Don't get entirely paranoid. If you get like that, you'll be building your little apartment into a Basement of Solitude.

"What do you think?" I asked Mister, once I was decked out in what paraphernalia I was willing to carry.

Mister went to the door and batted at it insistently.

"Everyone's a critic. Fine, fine." I sighed. I let him out, then I went out, got into my car and drove down to the Velvet Room in its expensive lakeside location.

Bianca runs her business out of a huge old mansion from the early days of the Roaring Twenties. Rumor has it that the infamous Al Capone had it built for one of his mistresses.

There was a gate with an iron fence and a security guard. I pulled the Beetle up into the little swath of driveway that began at the street and ended at the fence. There was a hiccoughing rattle from back in the engine as I brought the machine to a halt. I rolled down the window and stuck my head out, peering back. Something went *whoomph*, and then black smoke poured out from the bottom of the car and scuttled down the slope of the drive and into the street.

I winced. The engine gave an almost apologetic rattle and

shuddered to its death. Great. Now I had no ride home. I got out of the Beetle, and stood mourning it for a moment.

The security guard on the other side of the gate was a blocky man, not overly tall but overly muscled and hiding it under an expensive suit. He studied me with attack-dog eyes, and then said, through the gate, "Do you have an appointment?"

"No," I told him. "But I think Bianca will want to see me."

He looked unimpressed. "I'm sorry," he said. "Bianca is out for the evening."

Things are never simple anymore. I shrugged at him, folded my arms, and leaned on the hood of the Beetle. "Suit yourself. I'll just stay until a tow truck comes by, then, until I can get this thing out of the drive for you."

He stared at me, his eyes narrowed down to tiny slits with the effort of thinking. Eventually, the thoughts got to his brain, got processed, and sent back out with a message to "pass the buck." "I'll call your name in," he said.

"Good man," I approved. "You won't be sorry."

"Name," he growled.

"Harry Dresden."

If he recognized my name, it didn't show on his face. He glared at me and the Beetle then walked a few paces off, lifting a cellular phone from his pocket and to his ear.

I listened. Listening isn't hard to do. No one has practice at it, nowadays, but you can train yourself to pay attention to your senses if you work at it long enough.

"I've got a guy down here says that Bianca will want to talk to him," the guard said. "Says his name is Harry Dresden." He was silent for a moment. I couldn't quite make out the buzz of the other voice, other than that it was female. "Uh-huh," he said. He glanced back at me. "Uh-huh," he said again. "Sure. Sure, I will. Of course, ma'am."

I reached in through the window of the Beetle and got out my cane. I rested it on the concrete beside my boots and tapped it a few times, as though impatient.

The guard turned back to me, leaned over to one side, and pushed a button somewhere. The gate buzzed and clicked open.

"Come on in, Mr. Dresden," he said. "I can have someone come tow your car, if you like."

"Super," I told him. I gave him the name of the wrecker Mike has a deal with and told him to tell the guy that it was Harry's car again. Fido the Guard dutifully noted this down, writing on a small notebook he drew from a pocket. While he did, I walked past him toward the house, clicking my cane on the concrete with every pace.

"Stop," he told me, his voice calm and confident. People don't speak with that kind of absolute authority unless they have a gun in their hands. I stopped.

"Put the cane down," he told me, "And put your arms up. You are to be searched before you are allowed inside."

I sighed, did what he said, and let him pat me down. I didn't turn around to face him, but I could smell the metal of his gun. He found the knife and took it. His fingers brushed the nape of my neck, felt the chain there.

"What's this?" he said.

"Pentacle," I told him.

"Let me see it. Use one hand."

I used my left to draw it out of my shirt and show it to him, a silver five-pointed star within a circle, all smooth geometry. He grunted, and said, "Fine." The search went on, and he found the plastic squeeze-bottle. He took it out of my pocket, opened it, and sniffed at it.

"What's this?"

"A health cola," I told him.

"Smells like shit," he said, capped it, and put it back in my pocket.

"What about my cane?"

"Returned when you leave," he said.

Damn. My knife and my cane had been my only physical lines of defense. Anything else I did would have to rely wholly upon magic and that could be dicey on the best of days. It was enough to rattle me.

Of course, Fido the Guard had missed a couple of things. First, he'd overlooked the clean white handkerchief in my pocket. Second, he'd passed me on with my pentacle still upon my neck. He probably figured that since it wasn't a crucifix or a cross, that I couldn't use it to keep Bianca away from me.

Which wasn't true. Vampires (and other such creatures) don't respond to symbols as such. They respond to the power that accompanies an act of faith. I couldn't ward off a vampire mosquito with my faith in the Almighty—He and I have just never seemed to connect. But the pentacle was a symbol of magic itself, and I had plenty of faith in that.

And, of course, Fido had overlooked my getaway potion.

Bianca really ought to trust her guards with more awareness of the supernatural and what sort of things to look for.

The house itself was elegant, very roomy, with the high ceilings and the broad floors that they just don't make anymore. A well-groomed young woman with a short, straight haircut greeted me in the enormous entry hall. I was passing polite to her, and she showed me to a library, its walls lined with old books in leather bindings, similar to the leather-cushioned chairs around the enormous old dogfoot table in the room's center.

I took a seat and waited. And waited. And waited. More than half an hour went by before Bianca finally arrived.

She came into the room like a candle burning with a cold, clear flame. Her hair was a burnished shade of auburn that was too dark to cast back any ruddy highlights, but did anyway. Her eyes were dark, clear, her complexion flawlessly smooth and elegantly graced with cosmetics. She was not a tall woman, but shapely, wearing a black dress with a plunging neckline and a slash in one side that showed off a generous portion of pale thigh. Black gloves covered her hands to above the elbows, and her three-hundred-dollar shoes were a study in high-heeled torture devices. She looked too good to be true.

"Mister Dresden," she greeted me. "This is an unexpected pleasure."

I rose when she entered the room. "Madame Bianca," I replied, nodding to her. "We meet at last. Hearsay neglected to mention how lovely you are."

She laughed, lips shaping the sounds, head falling back just enough to show a flash of pale throat. "A gentleman, they said. I see that they were correct. It is a charmingly passé thing to be a gentleman in this country."

"You and I are of another world," I said.

She approached me and extended her hand, a motion oozing feminine grace. I bowed over her hand briefly, taking it and brushing my lips against the back of her glove. "Do you really think I'm beautiful, Mister Dresden?" she asked me.

"As lovely as a star, Madame."

"Polite and a pretty one, too," she murmured. Her eyes flickered over me, from head to toe, but even she avoided meeting gazes with me, whether from a desire to avoid inadvertently directing her power at me, or being on the receiving end of mine, I couldn't tell. She continued into the room, and stopped beside one of the comfortable chairs. As a matter of course, I stepped around the table, and drew out the chair for her, seating her. She crossed her legs, in that dress, in those shoes, and made it look good. I blinked for just a moment, then returned to my own seat.

"So, Mister Dresden. What brings you to my humble house? Care for an evening of entertainment? I quite assure you that you will never have another experience like it." She placed her hands in her lap, smiling at me.

I smiled at her, and put one hand into my pocket, onto the white handkerchief. "No, thank you. I came to talk."

Her lips parted in a silent, *ah*. "I see. About what, if I might ask?"

"About Jennifer Stanton. And her murder."

I had all of a second's warning. Bianca's eyes narrowed, then widened, like those of a cat about to spring. Then she was coming at me over the table, faster than a breath, her arms extended toward my throat.

I toppled over backward in my chair. Even though I'd started to move first, it almost wasn't enough to get away from her reaching nails in time. One grazed my throat with a hot sensation of pain, and she kept coming, following me down to the floor, those rich lips drawn back from sharp fangs.

I jerked my hand out of my pocket, and flapped open my white hanky at her, releasing the image of sunlight I'd been storing for use in potions. It lit up the room for a moment, brilliant.

The light smashed into Bianca, hurled her back across the old table into one of the shelves, and tore pieces of flesh away from her like bits of rotten meat being peeled off a carcass by a sandblaster. She screamed, and the flesh around her mouth sloughed and peeled away like a snake's scales.

I had never seen a real vampire before. I would have time to be terrified later. I took in the details as I tugged my talisman off over my neck. It had a batlike face, horrid and ugly, the head too big for its body. Gaping, hungry jaws. Its shoulders were hunched and powerful. Membranous wings stretched between the joints of its almost skeletal arms. Flabby black breasts hung before it, spilling out of the black dress that no longer looked feminine. Its eyes were wide, black, and staring, and a kind of leathery, slimy hide covered its flesh, like an inner tube lathered with Vaseline, though there were tiny holes corroded in it by the sunlight I had brought with me.

It recovered quickly, crouching and spreading long arms that ended in claw-tipped fingers to either side with a hiss of rage.

I drew my pentacle into my fist, raised it like every vampire slayer you ever saw does it, and said, "Jesus Christ, lady. I just came here to talk."

The vampire hissed and started toward me with a gangling, weirdly graceful step. Its clawed feet were still wearing the three-hundred-dollar black pumps.

"Back," I said, taking a step towards it, myself. The pentacle began to burn with the cold, clear light of applied will and belief—my faith, if you will, that it could turn such a monster aside.

It hissed, and turned its face aside, lifting its membranous arms to shield its eyes from the light. It took one step back, and then another, until its hunched back was pressed against a wall of books.

Now what did I do? I wasn't going to go try to put a stake through her heart. But if I lowered my will, she might come at me again—and I didn't think I had anything, even the quickest evocations, that I could get out of my mouth before she tore it off of my head. And even if I got past her, she probably had mortal lackies, like the security guard at the gate, who would be happy to kill me if they saw me trashing their mistress.

"You killed her," the vampire snarled, and its voice was exactly the same, sultry and feminine, even though twisted by rage and coming from that horrid mouth. It was unsettling. "You killed Jennifer. She was *mine*, mageling."

"Look," I told her. "I didn't come here for any of this. And the police know I'm here. Save yourself a lot of trouble. Sit down, talk with me, and then we'll both go away happy. Christ, Bianca, do you think that if I'd killed Jennifer and Tommy Tomm that I'd just be waltzing in here like this?"

"You expect me to believe that you didn't? You will never leave this house alive."

I was feeling angry myself, and frightened. Christ, even the *vampire* thought I was the bad guy. "What'll it take to convince you that I didn't do it?"

Black, bottomless eyes stared at me through the burning fire of my faith. I could feel some sort of power there, trying to get at me, and held off by the force of my will, just as the creature itself was. The vampire snarled, "Lower the amulet, wizard."

"If I do, are you going to come at my throat again?"

"If you do not, I most certainly will."

Shaky logic, that. I tried to work through the situation from her point of view. She had been scared when I showed up. She'd had me searched and divested of weapons as best she could. If she thought that I was Jennifer Stanton's murderer, would the mere mention of that name have brought that sudden violence out of her? I began to get that sinking feeling you get when you realize that not everything is as it appears.

"If I put this down," I told her, "I want your word that you'll sit down and talk to me. I swear to you, by fire and wind, that I had nothing to do with her death."

The vampire hissed at me, shielding its eyes from the light with one taloned hand. "Why should I believe you?"

"Why should I believe *you*?" I countered.

Yellowed fangs showed in its mouth. "If you do not trust my word, wizard, then how can I trust yours?"

"Then you give it?"

The vampire stiffened, and though its voice was still harsh with rage and pain, still sexy as a silk shirt without any buttons, I thought I heard the ring of truth in its words. "You have my promise. Lower your talisman, and we will talk."

Time for another calculated risk. I tossed the pentacle onto the table. The cold light drained away, leaving the room lit by mere electricity once more.

The vampire slowly lowered its arms, blinking its too-big eyes at me and then at the pentacle upon the table. A long, pink tongue flickered out nervously over its jaws and lower face, then slipped back into its mouth. It was surprised, I realized. Surprised that I had done it.

My heart was racing, but I forced my fear back down out of my forebrain and into the background. Vampires are like demons, like wolves, like sharks. You don't let them think that you are potential food and get their respect at the same time. The vampire's true appearance was grotesque—but it wasn't as bad as some of the things I had seen in my day. Some demons were a lot worse, and some of the Elder Things could rip your mind apart just by letting you look at them. I regarded the creature with a level gaze.

"How about it?" I said. "Let's talk. The longer we sit around staring at one another, the longer Jennifer's killer stays free."

The vampire stared at me for a moment more. Then it shuddered, drawing its wing membranes about itself. Black slime turned into patches of pale, perfect flesh that spread over the vampire's dark skin like a growth of fungus. The flabby black breasts swelled into softly rounded, rosy-tipped perfection once more.

Bianca stood before me a moment later, settling her dress back into modesty again, her arms crossed over her as though she was cold, her back stiff and her eyes angry. She was no less beautiful than she had been a few moments before, not a line or a curve any different. But for me, the glamour had been ruined. She still had the same eyes, dark and fathomless and alien. I would always remember what she truly looked like, beneath her flesh mask.

I stooped and picked up my chair, righting it. Then I went around the table, turned my back on her, and stood hers up as well. Then I held it out for her, just as I had when I had entered the room.

She stared at me for a long minute. Some expression flickered across her face. She was disconcerted by my apparent lack of concern about the way she looked, and it told. Then she lifted her chin, proud, and settled gracefully into the chair again, regal as any queen, every line stiff with anger. The Old World rules of courtesy and hospitality were holding—but for how long?

I returned to my seat and leaned over to pick up my white handkerchief, toying with it. Bianca's angry eyes flickered down to it, and once again she repeated the nervous gesture of licking her teeth and lips, though this time her tongue looked human.

"So. Tell me about Jennifer and Tommy Tomm," I said.

She shook her head, almost sneering. "I can tell you what I told the police. I don't know who could have killed them."

"Come on, Bianca. We don't have to hide things from one another. We're not a part of the mortal world."

Her eyebrows slanted down, revealing more anger. "No. You're the only one in the city with the kind of skill required to cast that sort of spell. If you didn't do it, I have no idea who else could have."

"You don't have any enemies? Anyone who might have been wanting to make an impression on you?"

A bitter little line appeared at the corner of her lips, something that was not quite a smile. "Of course. But none of them could have managed what happened to Tommy and Jenny." She drummed her fingernails over the tabletop, leaving little score marks in the wood. "I don't let any enemies that dangerous run around alive. At least, not for long."

I settled back in my chair, frowning, and did my damnedest

not to let her see how scared I was. "How did you know Tommy Tomm?"

She shrugged, her shoulders gleaming like porcelain, and just as brittle. "You may have thought he was just a bruiser for Johnny Marcone, Mister Dresden. But Tommy was a very gentle and considerate man, underneath. He was always good to his women. He treated them like real people." Her gaze shifted from side to side, not lifting. "Like human beings. I wouldn't take on a client if I thought he wouldn't be a gentleman, but Tommy was better than most. I met him years ago, elsewhere. I always made sure he had someone to take care of him when he wanted an evening of company."

"You sent Jennifer out to him that night?"

She nodded, her expression bleak. Her nails drummed the tabletop again, gouging out more wood.

"Was there anyone else he saw on a regular basis? Maybe someone who would have talked to him, known what was going on in his life?"

Bianca shook her head. "No," she said. But then she frowned.

I just watched her, and absently tossed the handkerchief on the tabletop. Her eyes flicked to it, then up to mine.

I didn't flinch. I met her bottomless gaze and quirked my mouth up in a little smile, as though I had something more, and worse, to pull out of my hat if she wanted to come after me again. I saw her anger, her rage, and for just a moment I got a peek inside, saw the source of it. She was furious that I had seen her true form, horrified and embarrassed that I had stripped her disguise away and seen the creature beneath. And she was afraid that I could take away even her mask, forever, with my power.

More than anything else, Bianca wanted to be beautiful. And tonight, I had destroyed her illusion. I had rattled her gilded little world. She sure as hell wasn't going to let me forget that.

She shuddered and jerked her eyes away, furious and frightened at the same time, before I could see any deeper into her—or she into me. "If I had not given you my word, Dresden," she whispered, "I would kill you this instant."

"That would be unfortunate," I said. I kept my voice hard. "You should know the risks in a wizard's death curse. You've got something to lose, Bianca. And even if you could take me out, you can bet your pretty ass I'd be dragging you into hell with me."

She stiffened, then turned her head to one side, and let her fingers go limp. It was a silent, bitter surrender. She didn't move quickly enough for me to miss seeing a tear streak down one cheek.

I'd made the vampire cry. Great. I felt like a real superhero. Harry Dresden, breaker of monsters' hearts.

"There may be one person who might know something," she said, her lovely voice dull, flat, lifeless. "I had a woman who worked for me. Linda Randall. She and Jennifer went out on calls together, when customers wanted that sort of thing. They were close."

"Where is she now?" I asked.

"She's working as a driver for someone. Some rich couple who wanted a servant that would do more than windows. She wasn't the type I usually keep around in any case. I think Jennifer had her phone number. I can have someone fetch it for you, Mister Dresden." She said my name as though it were something bitter and poisonous that she wanted to spit out.

"Thank you. That would be very kind." I kept my tone carefully formal, neutral. Formality and a good bluff were all that was keeping her from my throat.

She remained quiet, controlling her evident emotions, before she started to look up again, at last. Her eyes froze, then widened when they came to my throat. Her expression went perfectly, inhumanly still.

I grew tense. Not just tense, but steel-tight, wirebound, spring-coiled. I was out of tricks and weapons. If she came after me now, I wasn't going to get the chance to defend myself. There was no way I would be able to drink the potion before she tore me apart. I gripped the arms of my chair hard, to keep myself from bolting. Do not show fear. Do not run away. It would only make her chase me, snap her instincts into the reaction of pursing the prey.

"You're bleeding, Mister Dresden," she whispered.

I lifted my hand, slowly, to my throat, where her nails had scored me, earlier. My fingertips came away slick with my own blood.

Bianca kept on staring. Her tongue flickered around her mouth again. "Cover it," she whispered. A strange, mewling sound came out of her mouth. "*Cover* it, Dresden."

I picked up my handkerchief, and pressed it over my throat. Bianca blinked her eyes closed, slowly, and then turned away, half-hunched over her stomach. She didn't stand up.

"Go," she told me. "Go now. Paula's coming. I'll send her down to the gate with the phone number in a little while."

I walked toward the door, but then stopped, glancing back at her. There was a sort of horrid fascination to it, to knowing what was beneath the alluring exterior, the flesh mask, but seeing it twist and writhe with need.

"Go," Bianca whimpered. Fury, hunger, and some emotion I couldn't even begin to fathom made her voice stretched out, thinner. "Go. And do not think that I will not remember this night. Do not think that I will not make you regret it."

The door to the library opened, and the straight-haired young woman who had greeted me earlier entered the room. She gave me a passing glance, then walked past me, kneeling at Bianca's side. Paula, I presumed.

Paula murmured something too soft to hear, gently brushing Bianca's hair back from her face with one hand. Then she unbuttoned the sleeve of her blouse, rolled it up past her elbow, and pressed her wrist to Bianca's mouth.

I had a good view of what happened. Bianca's tongue flashed out, long and pink and sticky, smearing Paula's wrist with shining saliva. Paula shuddered at the touch, her breath coming quicker. Her nipples stiffened beneath the thin fabric of the blouse, and she let her head fall slowly backwards. Her eyes were glazed over with a narcotic langour, like a junkie who had just shot up.

Bianca's fangs extended and slashed open Paula's pale, pretty skin. Blood welled. Bianca's tongue began to flash in and out, faster than could really be seen, lapping the blood up as quickly as it appeared. Her dark eyes were narrowed, distant. Paula was gasping and moaning in pleasure, her entire body shivering.

I felt a little sick and withdrew step by step, not turning my back on the scene. Paula toppled slowly to the floor, writhing her way toward unconsciousness with an evident glee. Bianca followed her down, unladylike now, a creature of beastial hunger. She crouched over the supine woman, and in the hunch of her pale shoulders I could see the batlike thing beneath the flesh mask, lapping up Paula's blood.

I got out of there, fast, shutting the door behind me. My heart was hammering, too quickly. The scene with Paula might have aroused me, if I hadn't seen what was underneath Bianca's mask. Instead, it only made me sick to my stomach, afraid. The woman had given herself to that thing, as quickly and as willingly as any woman to her lover.

The saliva, some part of me rationalized, desperate to latch on to something cold and logical and detached. The saliva was probably narcotic, perhaps even addictive. It would explain Paula's behavior, the need to have more of her drug. But I wondered if Paula would have been so eager, had she known Bianca's true face.

Now I understood why the White Council was so hard-nosed with vampires. If they could get that kind of control over a mortal, what would happen if they could get their hooks into a wizard? If they could addict a wizard to them as thoroughly as Bianca had the girl I'd just seen? Surely, it wasn't possible.

But if it wasn't, why would the Council be so nervous about them?

Do not think I will not make you regret it, she had said.

I felt cold as I hurried down the dark driveway toward the gate.

Fido the security guard was waiting for me at the front gate, and passed back my knife and my cane without a word. A tow truck was out front, latching itself to the Beetle. I put one hand on the cold metal of the gate and kept the other, with its handkerchief, pressed to my throat, as I watched George the tow-truck guy work. He recognized me and waved, flashing a grin that showed the white teeth in his dark face. I nodded back. I wasn't up to answering the smile.

A few minutes later, the guard's cellular phone beeped at him. He withdrew several paces, repeated several affirmatives, then took a notebook from his pocket, writing something down. He put the phone away and walked back over to me, offering me the piece of paper.

"What's this?" I said.

"The phone number you were looking for. And a message."

I glanced at the paper, but avoided reading it just then. "I thought Bianca was going to send Paula down with it."

He didn't say anything. But his jaw tightened, and I saw his eyes flick toward the house, where his mistress was. He swallowed. Paula wasn't coming out of the house, and Fido was afraid.

I took the paper. I kept my hand from shaking as I looked at it.

On it was a phone number. And a single word: *Regret.*

I folded the piece of paper in half and put it away into the pocket of my duster. Another enemy. Super. At least with my hands in my pockets, Fido couldn't see them shaking. Maybe I should have listened to Murphy. Maybe I should have stayed home and played with some nice, safe, forbidden black magic instead.

Chapter 10

I departed Bianca's place in George's loaner, a wood-panel Studebaker that grumbled and growled and squealed everywhere it went. I stopped at a pay phone, a short distance from the house, and called Linda Randall's number.

The phone rang several times before a quiet, dusky contralto answered, "Beckitts', this is Linda."

"Linda Randall?" I asked.

"Mmmm," she answered. She had a furry, velvety voice, something tactile. "Who's this?"

"My name is Harry Dresden. I was wondering if I could talk to you."

"Harry who?" she asked.

"Dresden. I'm a private investigator."

She laughed, the sound rich enough to roll around naked in. "Investigating my privates, Mr. Dresden? I like you already."

I coughed. "Ah, yes. Ms. Randall—"

"Miss," she said, cutting in. "Miss Randall. I'm not occupied. At the moment."

"Miss Randall," I amended. "I'd like to ask you some questions about Jennifer Stanton, if I could."

Silence on the other end of the line. I could hear some sounds in the background, a radio playing, perhaps, and a recorded voice talking about white zones and red zones and loading and unloading of vehicles.

"Miss Randall?"

"No," she said.

"It won't take long. And I assure you that you aren't the subject of anything I'm doing. If you could just give me a few moments of your time."

"No," she told me. "I'm on duty, and will be the rest of the night. I don't have time for this."

"Jennifer Stanton was a friend of yours. She's been murdered. If there's anything you could tell me that might help—"

She cut me off again. "There isn't," she said. "Good-bye, Mr. Dresden."

The line went dead.

I scowled at the phone, frustrated. That was it, then. I had gone through all the preparation, the face-off with Bianca, and possible future trouble for nothing.

No way, I thought. No way in hell.

Bianca had said that Linda Randall was working as a driver for someone, the Beckitts, I presumed, whoever they were. I'd recognized the voice in the background as a recorded message that played outside the concourses at O'Hare airport. So she was in a car at the airport, maybe waiting to pick up the Beckitts, and definitely not there for long.

With no time to lose, I kicked the wheezing old Studebaker into gear and drove to O'Hare. It was far easier to blow off someone over the phone than it was to do it in person. There were several concourses, but I had to trust to luck—luck to guide me to the right one, and luck to get me there before *Miss* I-am-not-occupied Randall had the opportunity to pick up her employers and leave. And a little more luck to keep the Studebaker running all the way to O'Hare.

The Studebaker did make it all the way there, and on the second concourse I came across a silver baby limo, idling in a parking zone. The interior was darkened, so I couldn't see inside very well. It was a Friday evening, and the place was busy, business folk in their sober suits returning home from long trips about the country. Cars continually purred in and out of the semicircular drive. A uniformed cop was directing traffic, keeping people from doing brainless things like parking in the middle of one of the traffic lanes in order to load up the car.

I swerved the old Studebaker into a parking place, racing a Volvo for it and winning by dint of driving the older and heavier vehicle and having the more suicidal attitude. I kept an eye on the silver limo as I got out of the car and strode over to a bank of pay phones. I plopped my quarter in, and once more dialed the number provided by Bianca.

The phone rang. In the silver limo, someone stirred.

"Beckitts', this is Linda," she purred.

"Hello, Linda," I said. "This is Harry Dresden again."

I could almost hear her smirk. There was a flicker of light from inside the car, the silhouette of a woman's face, then the orange glow of a cigarette being lit. "I thought I told you I didn't want to talk to you, Mr. Dresden."

"I like women who play hard to get."

She laughed that delicious laugh. I could see her head move in the darkened car when she did. "I'm getting harder to get by the second. Good-bye again." She hung up on me.

I smiled, hung up the phone, walked over to the limo, and rapped on the window.

It buzzed down, and a woman in her mid-twenties arched an eyebrow at me. She had beautiful eyes the color of rain clouds, a little too much eye shadow, and brilliant scarlet lipstick on her cupid's-bow lips. Her hair was a medium brown, drawn back into a tight braid that made her cheeks look almost sharp, severe, except for her forelocks, which hung down close to her eyes in insolent disarray. She had a predatory look to her, harsh, sharp. She wore a crisp white shirt, grey slacks, and held a lit cigarette in one hand. The smoke curled up around my nose, and I exhaled, trying to push it away.

She looked me up and down, frankly assessing. "Don't tell me. Harry Dresden."

"I really need to talk to you, Miss Randall. It won't take long."

She glanced at her watch and then at the terminal doors. Then back up at me. "Well. You've got me cornered, don't you? I'm at your mercy." Her lips quirked. She took a drag of her cigarette. "And I like a man who just won't stop."

I cleared my throat again. The woman was attractive, but not unduly so. Yet there was something about her that revved my engines, something about the way she held her head or shaped her words that bypassed my brain and went straight to my hormones. Best to head directly to the point and minimize my chances of looking moronic. "How did you know Jennifer Stanton?"

She looked up at me through long lashes. "Intimately."

Ahem. "You, uh. Worked for Bianca with her."

Linda blew more smoke. "That prissy little bitch. Yes, I worked with Jen. We were even roommates for a while. Shared a bed." She wrapped her lips around the last word, drawing it out with a little tremor that dripped wicked, secret laughter.

"Did you know Tommy Tomm?" I asked.

"Oh, sure. Fantastic in bed." She lowered her eyes and shifted on the car's seat, lowering one of her hands out of sight, and making me wonder where it had gone. "He was a regular customer. Maybe twice a month Jen and I would go over to his place, have a little party." She leaned toward mc. "He could do things to a woman that would turn her into a real animal, Harry Dresden. You know what I mean? Growling and snarling. In heat."

She was driving me crazy. That voice of hers inspired the kinds of dreams you wish you could remember more clearly in the morning. Her expression promised to show me things that you don't talk about with other people, if I would give her half a chance. Your job, Harry. Think about your job.

Some days I really hate my job.

"When was the last time you talked to her?"

She took another drag, and this time I saw a small shake to her fingers, one she quickly hid. Just not quickly enough. She was nervous. Nervous enough to be shaking, and now I could see what she was up to. She was wearing the alley-cat mask, appealing to my glands instead of my brain, and trying to distract me with it, trying to keep me from finding something out.

I'm not inhuman. I can be distracted by a pretty face, or body, like any other youngish man. Linda Randall was damned good at playing the part. But I do not like to be made the fool.

So, Miss Sex Goddess. What are you hiding?

I cleared my throat, and asked, mildly, "When was the last time you spoke to Jennifer Stanton, Miss Randall?"

She narrowed her eyes at me. She wasn't dumb, whatever else she was. She'd seen me reading her, seeing through her pretense. The flirting manner vanished. "Are you a cop?" she demanded.

I shook my head. "Scout's honor. I'm just trying to find out what happened to her."

"Dammit," she said, softly. She flicked the butt of the cigarette out onto the concrete and blew out a mouthful of smoke. "Look. I tell you anything and see a cop coming around, I never saw you before. Got it?"

I nodded.

"I talked to Jen on Wednesday evening. She called me. It was Tommy's birthday. She wanted to get together again." Her mouth twisted. "Sort of a reunion."

I glanced about and leaned down closer to her. "Did you?"

Her eyes were roving about now, nervous, like a cat who has

found herself shut into a small room. "No," she said. "I had to work. I wanted to, but—"

"Did she say anything unusual? Anything that might have made you suspect she was in danger?"

She shook her head again. "No, nothing. We hadn't talked much for a while. I didn't see her as much after I split from the Velvet Room."

I frowned at her. "Do you know what else she was doing? Anything she might have been involved with that could have gotten her hurt?"

She shook her head. "No, no. Nothing like that. That wasn't her style. She was sweet. A lot of girls get like—They get pretty jaded, Mr. Dresden. But it never really touched her. She made people feel better about themselves somehow." She looked away. "I could never do that. All I did was get them off."

"There's nothing you can tell me? Nothing you can think of?"

She pressed her lips together and shook her head. She shook her head, and she lied to me as she did it. I was just sure of it. She was closing in, tightening up, and if there was nothing to tell me, she wouldn't be trying to hide it. She must know something—unless she was just shutting down because I'd stomped all over her feelings, as I had Bianca's. Either way, she wasn't telling me anything else.

I tightened my fist, frustrated. If Linda Randall had no information for me, I was at a dead end. And I'd romped all over another woman's feelings—two in one night. You are on a roll, Dresden. Even if one of them had been something not-human.

"Why," I asked her, the words slipping out before I thought about them. "Why the slut act?"

She looked up at me again, and smirked. I saw the subtle shifting in her, magnifying that sort of animal appeal she had, once more, as she had been doing when I first approached her—but it didn't hide the self-loathing in her eyes. I looked away, quickly, before I had to see any more of it. I got the feeling that I didn't want to see Linda Randall's soul. "Because it's what I do, Mr. Dresden. For some people it's drugs. Booze. For me, orgasms. Sex. Passion. Just another addict. City's full of them." She glanced aside. "Next best thing to love. And it keeps me in work. Excuse me."

She swung open the door. I took a quick step back and out of her way as she moved to the back of the limo, long legs taking long steps, and opened the trunk.

A tall couple, both wearing glasses and dressed in stylish grey business clothes emerged from the terminal and approached the limo. They had the look of lifestyle professionals, the kind that have a career and no kids, with enough money and time to spend on making themselves look good—a NordicTrack couple. He was carrying an overnight bag over his shoulder and a small suitcase in one hand, while she bore only a briefcase. They wore no jewelry, not even watches or wedding rings. Odd.

The man slung the luggage items into the limo's trunk and looked from Linda to me. Linda avoided his eyes. He tried to speak quietly enough not to be heard, but I have good ears.

"Who's this?" he asked. His voice had a strained note to it.

"Just a friend, Mr. Beckitt. A guy I used to see," she answered him.

More lies. More interesting.

I looked across the limo to the woman, presumably Mrs. Beckitt. She regarded me with a calm face, entirely void of emotion. It was a little spooky. She had the look I'd seen in films, on the faces of prisoners released from the German *stalags* at the end of World War II. Empty. Numb. Dead, and just didn't know it yet.

Linda opened the back door and let Mr. and Mrs. Beckitt into the car. Mrs. Beckitt briefly put a hand on Linda's waist in passing, a gesture that was too intimate and possessive for the hired help. I saw Linda shiver, then close the door. She walked back around the car to me.

"Get out of here," she said, quietly. "I don't want to get in any trouble with my boss."

I reached for her hand, grabbed it, and held it between both of mine, as an old lover might, I supposed. My business card was pressed between our palms. "My card. If you think of anything else, give me a call. Okay?"

She turned away from me without answering, but the card vanished into a pocket before she got back into the limo.

Mrs. Beckitt's dead eyes watched me through the side window as the limo went by me. It was my turn to shiver. Like I said, spooky.

I went on into the airport. The monitors displaying flight times flickered to fuzz when I walked by. I went to one of the cafés inside, sat down, and ordered myself a cup of coffee. I had to pay for it with change. Most of my money had gone into paying off last month's rent and into the love potion I'd let Bob talk me into making. Money. I needed to get to work on Monica Sells's case, finding her husband. I didn't want to get out of hot water with the White Council only to lose my office and apartment because I couldn't pay the bills.

I sipped coffee and tried to organize my thoughts. I had two areas of concern. The most important was finding who had killed Tommy Tomm and Jennifer Stanton. Not only to catch the killer before any more corpses turned up, but because if I didn't, the White Council would probably use the opportunity to have me put to death.

And, while tracking down killers and avoiding execution squads, I had to do some work for someone who would pay me. Tonight's excursion wasn't something I could charge Murphy for—she'd have my ass in a sling if she knew I was running around asking questions, poking my nose in where it shouldn't be. So, if I wanted money from Chicago P.D., I would have to spend time doing the research Murphy wanted—the black-magic research that could get me killed all by itself.

Or, I could work on Monica Sells's missing husband case. I thought I had that one pretty well pegged down, but it wouldn't hurt to get it fleshed out fully. I could spend time working on it, fill out the hours on the retainer, maybe even get a few more added on. That appealed to me a lot more than trying to work out some black magic.

So, I could follow up on the lead Toot-toot had given me. There'd been pizza delivered out to the Lake Providence home that night. Time to talk to the deliveryman, if possible.

I left the café, went out to the pay phones, and dialed directory assistance. There was only one place near the Lake Providence address that delivered pizza. I got the number and dialed through.

"Pizza 'Spress," someone with his mouth full said. "What'll it be tonight?"

"Hey there," I said. "I wonder if you can help me out. I'm looking for the driver who took an order out to an address on Wednesday night." I told him the address, and asked if I could speak to the driver.

"Another one," he snorted. "Sure, hang on. Jack just got in from a run." The voice on the other end of the line called out to someone, and a minute later the high baritone of a young man spoke tentatively into my ear.

"H-hello?"

"Hello," I answered. "Are you the driver who took pizza to—"

"*Look*," he said, his voice exasperated and nervous. "I *said* I was sorry already. It won't happen again."

I blinked for a minute, off balance. "Sorry for what?"

"Jeezus," he said. I heard him move across a room, with a lot of music and loud talk in the background, and then the background noise cut off, as though he had stepped into another room and shut the door behind him. "Look," he said in a half whine. "I told you I'm not gonna say anything to anyone. I was only looking. You can't blame me, right? No one answered the door, what was I supposed to do?" His voice cracked in the middle of his sentences. "Hell of a party, but hey. That's your business. Right?"

I struggled to keep up with the kid. "What, exactly, did you see, Jack?" I asked him.

"No one's face," he assured me, his voice growing more nervous. He gave a jittery little laugh and tried to joke. "Better things to look at than faces, right? I mean, I don't give a damn what you do in your own house. Or your friends, or whoever. Don't worry about me. Never going to say a thing. Next time I'll just leave the pizza and run a tab, right?"

Friends, plural. Interesting. The kid was awfully nervous. He must have gotten an eyeful. But I had a gut instinct that he was hiding something else, keeping it back.

"What else?" I asked him. I kept my voice calm and neutral. "You saw something else. What was it?"

"None of my business," he said, instantly. "None of my business. Look, I gotta get off this line. We have to keep it open for orders. It's Friday night, we're busy as hell."

"What," I said, separating my words, keeping them clipped, "else?"

"Oh, shit," he breathed, his voice shaking. "Look, I wasn't with that guy. Didn't know anything about him. I didn't tell him you were having an orgy out there. Honest. Jeezus, mister, I don't want any trouble."

Victor Sells seemed to have a real good idea of how to party—and of how to frighten teenagers. "One more question, and I'll let this go," I told him. "Who was it you saw? Tell me about him."

"I don't know. I don't know him, didn't recognize him. Some guy, with a camera, that's all. I went around the back of the house to try the back door, got up on your deck, and just saw inside. I didn't keep on looking. But he was up there, all in black, with this camera, taking pictures." He paused as someone pounded on the door he had closed earlier. "Oh, God, I have to go, mister. I don't know you. I don't know nothing." And then there was a scrambling of feet, and he hung up the phone.

I hung up the phone myself and ambled back to George's loaner. I worked out the details I had just learned on the way back to my apartment.

Someone else had called Pizza 'Spress, evidently just before I had. Someone else had gone asking after the pizza boy. Who?

Why, Victor Sells, of course. Tracing down people who might have information about him, his possible presence in the lake house. Victor Sells, who had been having some sort of get-together out there that night. Maybe he'd been drunk, or one of his guests had, and ordered the pizza—and now Victor was trying to cover his tracks.

Which implied that Victor knew someone was looking for him. Hell, as far as I knew, he'd been *in* the house when I'd gone out there last night. This made things a lot more interesting. A missing man who doesn't want to be found could get dangerous if someone came snooping after him.

And a photographer? Someone lurking around outside of windows and taking pictures? I rummaged in my duster pocket and felt the round plastic film canister. That explained where the canister had come from, at any rate. But why would someone be out there at the house, taking pictures of Victor and his friends? Maybe because Monica had hired someone else, a PI, without telling me. Maybe just a neighbor with the hots for taking dirty pictures. No way to tell, really. More mysteries.

I pulled the Studebaker into my drive and killed the engine. I tallied the score for the evening. Enigmas: lots. Harry: zero.

My investigation for Monica Sells had netted me one husband throwing wild parties in his beach house after losing his job, and working hard not to be found. Probably an advanced case of male menopause. Monica didn't seem to be the kind of woman who would take such a thing with good grace—more like the kind who would close her eyes and call me a liar if I told her the truth. But at least it merited a little more looking into—I could log a few more hours in on the case, maybe earn some more money out of it before I gave her the bill. But I still didn't really *know* anything.

The angle with Bianca had come to a dead end at Linda Randall. All I had were more questions for Miss Randall, and she was as closed as a bank on Sunday. I didn't have anything solid enough to hand to Murphy to let her pursue the matter. Dammit. I was going to have to do that research after all. Maybe it *would* turn up something helpful, some kind of clue to help lead me and the police to the murderer.

And maybe dragons would fly out my butt. But I had to try.

So I got out of the car to go inside and get to work.

He was waiting for me behind the trash cans that stood next to the stairs leading down to my front door. The baseball bat he swung at me took me behind the ear and pitched me to the bottom of the stairs in a near-senseless heap. I could hear his footsteps, but couldn't quite move, as he came down the stairs toward me.

It figured. It was just the kind of day I was having.

I felt his foot on the back of my neck. Felt him lift the baseball bat. And then it came whistling down toward my skull with a mighty crack of impact.

Except that it missed my motionless head, and whacked into the concrete next to my face, right by my eyes, instead.

"Listen up, Dresden," my attacker said. His voice was rough, low, purposefully hoarse. "You got a big nose. Stop sticking it where it doesn't belong. You got a big mouth. Stop talking to people you don't need to talk to. Or we're going to shut that mouth of yours." He waited a melodramatically appropriate moment, and then added, "Permanently."

His footsteps retreated up the stairs and vanished.

I just lay there watching the stars in front of my eyes for a while. Mister appeared from somewhere, probably drawn by the groaning noises, and started licking at my nose.

I eventually regained my mobility and sat up. My head was spinning, and I felt sick to my stomach. Mister rubbed up against me, as though he sensed something was wrong, purring in a low rumble. I managed to stand up long enough to unlock my apartment door, let Mister and myself in, and lock it behind me. I staggered over to my easy chair in the darkness and sat down with a *whuff* of expelled breath.

I sat motionless until the spinning slowed down enough to allow me to open my eyes again, and until the pounding of my head calmed down. Pounding head. Someone could have been pounding on my head with a baseball bat just then, pounding my head into new and interesting shapes that were inconducive to carrying on businesslike pursuits. Someone could have been pounding Harry Dresden right into the hereafter.

I cut off that line of thought. "You are not some poor rabbit, Dresden!" I reminded myself, sternly. "You are a wizard of the old school, a spellslinger of the highest caliber. You're not going to roll over for some schmuck with a baseball bat because he tells you to!"

Galvanized by the sound of my own voice, or maybe only by the somewhat unsettling realization that I had begun talking to myself, I stood up and built up the fire in the fireplace, then walked unsteadily back and forth in front of it, trying to think, to work out the details.

Had this evening's visits triggered the warning? Who had reason to threaten me? What were they trying to keep me from finding? And, most importantly, what was I going to do about it?

Someone had seen me talking to Linda Randall, maybe. Or, more likely, someone had seen me showing up at Bianca's place, asking questions. The Blue Beetle may not be glitzy, but it is sort of difficult to mistake for anyone else's car. Who would have reason to have me watched?

Why, hadn't Gentleman Johnny Marcone followed me so that he could have a word with me? So he could ask me to keep out of this business with Tommy Tomm's murder? Yes he had. Maybe this had been another reminder from the mob boss. It had that kind of mafioso feel to it.

I staggered to my kitchenette and fixed myself a tisane tea for the headache, then added in some aspirin. Herbal remedies are well and good, but I don't like to take chances.

Working on that same principle, I got my Smith & Wesson .38 Chief's Special out of its drawer, took the cloth covering off of it, and made sure it was loaded. Then I stuck the revolver in my jacket pocket.

Wizardry aside, it's tough to beat a gun for discouraging men with baseball bats. And I sure as hell wasn't going to roll over for the tiger-souled Johnny Marcone, let him push me around, let him know that it was all right to walk all over me whenever he felt like it. No way in hell or on earth, either.

My head was throbbing, and my hands were shaking, but I went down the ladder to my workroom—and started figuring out how to rip someone's heart out of his chest from fifty miles away.

Who says I never do anything fun on a Friday night?

Chapter 11

It took me the rest of the night and part of the morning, but I worked out how I could murder someone in the same manner that Tommy Tomm and Jennifer Stanton had been killed. After the fifth or sixth time I'd checked the figures, I stared at my calculations.

It didn't make any *sense*. It was *impossible*.

Or maybe we were all underestimating just how dangerous this killer was.

I grabbed my duster, and headed out without bothering to check my looks. I don't keep any mirrors in my home. Too many things can use mirrors as windows—or doors—but I was pretty sure I looked like a wreck. The Studebaker's rearview mirror confirmed this. My face was haggard, with a shadow of a beard, deep circles under bloodshot eyes, and hair that looked as though it had been riding a speeding motorcycle through a cloud of greasy smoke. Smoothing your hair back with sweaty palms as a study habit will do that to you. Especially if you do it for twelve or fourteen hours straight.

It didn't matter. Murphy wanted this information, and she needed to have it. Things were bad. They were very, very bad.

I made quick time down to the station, knowing Murphy would want to hear this from me face-to-face. The police station Murphy worked in was one in an aged complex of buildings that housed the metro police department. It was run-down, sagging in places like an old soldier who nonetheless stood at attention and struggled to hold in his gut. There was graffiti along one wall that the janitor wouldn't come to scrub off until Monday morning.

I parked in the visitors' parking—easy to do on a Saturday

morning—and headed up the steps and into the building. The desk sergeant wasn't the usual mustached old warhorse who I had run into before, but a greying matron with steely eyes who disapproved of me and my lifestyle in a single glance, then made me wait while she called up Murphy.

While I waited, a pair of officers came in, dragging a handcuffed man between them. He wasn't resisting them—just the opposite, in fact. His head was down, and he was moaning in an almost musical way. He was on the thin side, and I got the impression that he was young. His denim jeans and jacket were battered, unkempt, as was his hair. The officers dragged him past the desk, and one of them said, "That DUI we called in. We're going to take him up to holding until he can see straight."

The desk sergeant passed a clipboard over, and one of the officers took it under his arm, before the two of them dragged the young man up the stairs. I waited, rubbing at my tired eyes, until the sergeant managed to get through to someone upstairs. She gave a rather surprised "Hmph," and then said, "All right, Lieutenant. I'll send him on up." She waved a hand at me to go on past. I could feel her eyes on me as I went by, and I smoothed my palm self-consciously over my head and jaw.

Special Investigations kept a little waiting area just within the door at the top of the staircase. It consisted of four wooden chairs and a sagging old couch that would probably kill your back if you tried to sleep on it. Murphy's office was at the end of a double row of cubicles.

Murphy stood just inside her office with a phone pressed to her ear, wearing a martyred expression. She looked like a teenager having a fight with an out-of-town boyfriend, though she'd tear my head off if she heard me saying any such thing. I waved my hand, and she nodded back at me. She pointed at the waiting area, then shut her office door.

I took a seat in one of the chairs and leaned my head back against a wall. I had just closed my eyes when I heard a scream from behind me in the hallway. There was a struggling sound, and a few startled exclamations, before the scream repeated itself, closer this time.

I acted without thinking—I was too tired to think. I rose and went into the hall, towards the source of the sound. To my left was the staircase, and to my right the hallway stretched ahead of me.

A figure appeared, the silhouette of a running man, moving toward me with long strides. It was the man who had hung so limply between the two officers, humming, a few minutes before. He was the one screaming. I heard a scrabbling sound, and then the pair of officers I had seen downstairs a few moments before came around the corner. Neither of them was a young man anymore, and they both ran with their bellies out, puffing for breath, holding their gun belts against their hips with one hand.

"Stop!" one of the officers shouted, panting. "Stop that man!"

The hair on the back of my neck prickled. The man running toward me kept on screaming, high and terrified, his voice a long and uninterrupted peal of . . . something. Terror, panic, lust, rage, all rolled up into a ball and sent spewing out into the air through his vocal cords.

I had a quick impression of wide, staring eyes, a dirty face, a denim jacket, and old jeans as he came down the shadowy hallway. His hands were behind his back, presumably held there by cuffs. He wasn't seeing the hall he was running through. I don't know what he *was* looking at, but I got the impression that I didn't want to know. He came hurtling toward me and the stairs, blind and dangerous to himself.

It wasn't any of my business, but I couldn't let him break himself apart in a tumble down the stairs. I threw myself toward him as hard as I could, attempting to put my shoulder into his stomach and drive him backward in a football-style tackle.

There is a reason I got cut every year during high school. I rammed into him, but he just *whuffed* out a breath and spun to one side, into a wall. It was as though he hadn't seen me coming and had no realization that I was there. He just kept staring blindly and screaming, careening off the wall and continuing on his way, toward the stairs. I went down to the floor, my head abruptly throbbing again where the unknown tough had rapped me with a baseball bat last night.

One good thing about being as tall as I am—I have long arms. I rolled back toward him and lashed out with one hand, fingers clutching. I caught his jeans at the cuff and gave his leg a solid sideways tug.

That did it. He spun, off-balance, and went down to the tile floor. The scream stopped as the fall took the wind from him. He slid to the top of the stairs and stopped, feebly struggling. The officers pounded past me toward him, one going to either side.

And then something strange happened.

The young man looked up at me, and his eyes rounded and dilated, until I thought they had turned into huge black coins dotted onto his bloodshot eyeballs. His eyes rolled back into his head until he could hardly have been able to see, and he started to shout in a clarion voice.

"Wizard!" he trumpeted. "Wizard! I see you! I see you, wizard! I see the things that follow, those who walk before and He Who Walks Behind! They come, they come for you!"

"Jesus Christ on a crutch," the shorter, rounder officer said, as they took the man by his arms and started dragging him back down the hall. "Junkies. Thanks for the assist, buddy."

I stared at the man, stunned. I caught the sleeve of the taller officer. "What's going on, sir?" I asked him.

He stopped, letting the prisoner hang between him and his partner. The prisoner's head was bowed forward, and his eyes were still rolled back, but he had his head turned toward me and was grinning a horrible, toothy grin. His forehead was wrinkled oddly, almost as though he were somehow focusing on me through the bones of his browridges and the frontal lobes of his brain.

"Junkie," the taller officer said. "One of those new ThreeEye punks. Caught him down by the lake in his car with nearly four grams of the stuff. Probably more in him." He shook his head. "You okay?"

"Fine, fine," I assured him. "ThreeEye? That new drug?"

The shorter officer snorted. "One that's supposed to make them see the spirit world, that kind of crap."

The taller one nodded. "Stuff hooks harder than crack. Thanks for the help. Didn't know you were a civilian, though. Didn't expect anyone but police down here this time of day."

"No problem," I assured him. "I'm fine."

"Hey," the stouter one said. He squinted at me and shook his finger. "Aren't you the guy? That psychic consultant Carmichael told me about?"

"I'll take the fifth," I said to him with a grin that I didn't feel. The two officers chuckled and turned back to their business, quickly shouldering me aside as they dragged their prisoner away.

He whispered in a mad little voice, all the way down the hall. "See you, see you, wizard. See He Who Walks Behind."

I returned to my chair in the waiting area at the end of the row of cubicles and sat down, my head throbbing, my stomach rolling uncomfortably. He Who Walks Behind. I had never seen the junkie before. Never been close to him. I hadn't sensed the subtle tension of power in the air around him that signified the presence of a magical practitioner.

So how the hell had he seen the shadow of He Who Walks Behind flowing in my wake?

For reasons I don't have time to go into now, I am marked, indelibly, with the remnants of the presence of a hunter-spirit, a sort of spectral hit man known as He Who Walks Behind. I had beaten long odds in surviving the enemy of mine who had called up He Who Walks Behind and sent him after me—but even though the hunter-spirit had never gotten to me, the mark could still be seen upon me by those who knew how, by using the Third Sight, stretching out behind me like a long and horribly shaped shadow. Sort of a spiritual scar to remind me of the encounter.

But only a wizard had that kind of vision, the ability to sense the auras and manifestations of magical phenomena. And that junkie had been no wizard.

Was it possible that I had been wrong in my initial assessment of ThreeEye? Could the drug genuinely grant to its users the visions of the Third Sight?

I shuddered at the thought. The kind of things you see when you learn how to open your Third Eye could be blindingly beautiful, bring tears to your eyes—or they could be horrible, things that made your worst nightmares seem ordinary and comforting. Visions of the past, the future, of the true natures of things. Psychic stains, troubled shades, spirit-folk of all description, the shivering power of the Nevernever in all its brilliant and subtle hues—and all going straight into your brain: unforgettable, permanent. Wizards quickly learn how to control the Third Eye, to keep it closed except in times of great need, or else they go mad within a few weeks.

I shivered. If the drug was real, if it really did open the Third Eye in mortals instead of just inflicting ordinary hallucinations upon its users, then it was far more dangerous than it seemed, even with the deleterious effects demonstrated by the junkie I had tackled. Even if a user didn't go mad from seeing too many horrible or otherworldly things, he might see through the illusions and disguises of any of a number of beings that passed among mankind regularly, unseen—which could compel such creatures to act in defense, for fear of being revealed. Double jeopardy.

"Dresden," Murphy snapped, "wake up."

I blinked. "Not asleep," I slurred. "Just resting my eyes."

She snorted. "Save it, Harry," and pushed a Styrofoam cup into my hands. She'd made me coffee with a ton of sugar in it, just the way I like, and even though it was a little stale, it smelled like heaven.

"You're an angel," I muttered. I took a sip, then nodded down the row of cubicles. "You want to hear this one in your office."

I could feel her eyes on me as I drank. "All right," she said. "Let's go. And the coffee's fifty cents, Harry."

I followed her to her office, a hastily assembled thing with cheap plywood walls and a door that wasn't hung quite straight. The door had a paper sign taped to it, neatly lettered in black Magic Marker with LT. KARRIN MURPHY. There was a rectangle of lighter wood where a plaque had once held some other hapless policeman's name. That the office never bothered to put up a fresh plaque was a not-so-subtle reminder of the precarious position of the Special Investigations director.

Her office furniture, the entire interior of the office, in fact, was a contrast with the outside. Her desk and chair were sleek, dark, and new. Her PC was always on and running on its own desk set immediately to her left. A bulletin board covered most of one little wall, and current cases were neatly organized on it. Her college diploma, the aikido trophies, and her marksman's awards were on the wall to one's immediate right as you entered the office, and sitting there right next to your face if you were standing before her desk or sitting in the chair in front of it. That was Murphy—organized, direct, determined, and just a little bit belligerent.

"Hold it," Murphy told me. I stopped outside of her office, as I always did, while she went inside and turned off, then unplugged her computer and the small radio on her desk. Murphy is used to the kind of mayhem that happens whenever I get around machinery. After she was done, I went on in.

I sat down and slurped more coffee. She slid up onto the edge of her desk, looking down at me, her blue eyes narrowed. She was dressed no less casually on a Saturday than she was on a workday—dark slacks, a dark blouse, set off by her golden hair, and bright silver necklace and earrings. Very stylish. I, in my rumpled sweats and T-shirt, black duster, and mussed hair, felt very slouchy.

"All right, Harry," she said. "What have you got for me."

I took one last drink of coffee, stifled a yawn, and put the cup down on her desk. She slipped a coaster under it as I started speaking. "I was up all night working on it," I said, keeping my voice soft. "I had a hell of a time figuring out the spell. And as near as I can figure it, it's almost impossible to do it to one person, let alone two at once."

She glared at me. "Don't tell me almost impossible. I've got two corpses that say otherwise."

"Keep your shirt on," I growled at her. "I'm just getting started. You've got to understand the whole thing if you're going to understand any of it."

Her glare intensified. She put her hands on the edge of her desk, and said in a deadly, reasonable tone, "All right. Why don't you explain it to me."

I rubbed at my eyes again. "Look. Whoever did this did it with a thaumaturgic spell. That much I'm sure of. He or she used some of Tommy Tomm and Jennifer Stanton's hair or fingernails or something to create a link to them. Then they ripped out a symbolic heart from some kind of ritual doll or sacrificial animal and used a whale of an amount of energy to make the same thing happen to the victims."

"This doesn't tell me anything new, Harry."

"I'm getting there, I'm getting there," I said. "The amount of energy you need to do this is staggering. It would be a lot easier to manage a small earthquake than to affect a living being like that. Best-case scenario, I might be able to do it without killing myself. To one person who had really, really pissed me off."

"You're naming yourself as a suspect?" Murphy's mouth quirked at the corner.

I snorted. "I said I was strong enough to do it to one person. I think it would kill me to try two."

"You're saying that some sort of wizard version of Arnold Schwarzenegger pulled this off?"

I shrugged. "It's possible, I suppose. More likely, someone who's just really good pulled it off. Raw power doesn't determine all that you can do with magic. Focus matters, too. The better your focus is, the better you are at putting your power in one place at the same time, the more you can get done. Sort of like when you see some ancient little Chinese martial-arts master shatter a tree trunk with his hands. He couldn't lift a puppy over his head, but he can focus what power he does have with incredible effect."

Murphy glanced at her aikido trophies and nodded. "Okay," she said, "I can understand that, I think. So we're looking for the wizard version of Mister Miyagi."

"Or," I said, lifting a finger, "more than one wizard worked on this at the same time. Pooled their power together and used it all at once." My pounding head, combined with the queasy stomach and the caffeine, was making me a little woozy. "Teamwork, teamwork, that's what counts."

"Multiple killers," Murphy drawled. "I don't have one, and you're telling me there might be fifty."

"Thirteen," I corrected her. "You can never use more than thirteen. But I don't think that's very likely. It's a bitch to do. Everyone in the circle has to be committed to the spell, have no doubts, no reservations. And they have to trust one another implicitly. You don't see that kind of thing from your average gang of killers. It just isn't something that's going to happen, outside of some kind of fanaticism. A cult or political organization."

"A *cult*," Murphy said. She rubbed at her eyes. "The *Arcane* is going to have a field day with this one, if it gets out. So Bianca is involved in this, after all. Surely she's got enough enemies out there who could do this. She could inspire that kind of effort to get rid of her."

I shook my head. The pain was getting worse, heavier, but pieces were falling into place. "No. You're thinking the wrong angle here. The killer wasn't taking out the hooker and Tommy Tomm to get at Bianca."

"How do you know?"

"I went to see her," I responded.

"Dammit, Harry!"

I didn't react to her anger. "You know she wasn't going to talk to you, Murph. She's an old-fashioned monster girl. No cooperation with the authorities."

"But she *did* talk to you?" Murphy demanded.

"I said pretty please."

"I would beat you to crap if you didn't already look like it," Murphy said. "What did you find out?"

"Bianca wasn't in on it. She didn't have a clue who it could have been. She was nervous, scared." I didn't mention that she'd been scared enough to try to take me to pieces.

"So someone was sending a message—but not to Bianca?"

"To Johnny Marcone," I confirmed.

"Gang war in the streets," Murphy said. "And now the outfit is bringing sorcery into it as well. Mafioso magic spells. Jesus Christ." She drummed her heels on the edge of the desk.

"Gang war. ThreeEye suppliers versus conventional narcotics. Right?"

She stared at me for a minute. "Yeah," Murphy said. "Yeah, it is. How did you know? We've been holding out details from the papers."

"I just ran into this guy who was stoned out of his mind on ThreeEye. Something he said makes me think that stuff isn't a bunch of crap. It's for real. And you would have to be one very, very badass wizard to manufacture a large quantity of this kind of drug."

Murphy's blue eyes glittered. "So, whoever is the one supplying the streets with ThreeEye—"

"—is the one who murdered Jennifer Stanton and Tommy Tomm. I'm pretty sure of it. It feels right."

"I'd tend to agree," Murphy said, nodding. "All right, then. How many people do you know of who could manage the killing spell?"

"Christ, Murphy," I said, "you can't ask me to just hand you a list of names of people to drag downtown for questioning."

She leaned down closer to me, blue eyes fierce. "Wrong, Harry. I can ask you. I can *tell* you to give them to me. And if you don't, I can haul you in for obstruction and complicity so quick it will make your head spin."

"My head's already spinning," I told her. A little giggle slipped out. Throbbing head, pound, pound, pound. "You wouldn't do that, Murph. I know you. You know damned well that if I had anything you could use, I would give it to you. If you'd just let me in on the investigation, give me the chance to—"

"No, Harry," she said, her voice flat. "Not a chance. I am ass deep in alligators already without you getting difficult on me. You're already hurt, and don't ask me to buy some line about falling down the stairs. I don't want to have to scrape you off the concrete. Whoever did Tommy Tomm is going to get nasty when someone comes poking around, and it isn't your job to do it. It's mine."

"Suit yourself," I told her. "You're the one with the deadline."

Her face went pale, and her eyes blazed. "You're such an incredible shit, Harry."

I started to answer her, I really did—but my skull got loose and shaky on my neck, and things spun around, and my chair sort of wobbled up onto its back legs and whirled about precariously. I thought it was probably safest to slide my way along to the floor, rubbery as a snake. The tiles were nice and cool underneath my cheek and felt sort of comforting. My head went boom, boom, boom, the whole time I was down there, spoiling what would have otherwise been a pleasant little nap.

Chapter 12

I woke up on the floor of Murphy's office. The clock on the wall said that it was about twenty minutes later. Something soft was underneath my head, and my feet were propped up with several phone books. Murphy was pressing a cool cloth against my forehead and throat.

I felt terrible. Exhausted, achy, nauseous, my head throbbing. I wanted to do nothing so much as curl up and whimper myself to sleep. Given that I would never live *that* down, I made a wisecrack instead. "Do you have a little white dress? I've had this deep-seated nurse fantasy about you, Murphy."

"A pervert like you would. Who hit your head?" she demanded.

"No one," I mumbled. "Fell down the stairs to my apartment."

"Bullshit, Harry," she said, her voice hard. Her hands were no less gentle with the cool cloth, though. "You've been running around on this case. That's where you got the bump on the head. Isn't it?"

I started to protest.

"Oh, save it," she said, letting out a breath. "If you didn't already have a concussion, I'd tie your heels to my car and drive through traffic." She held up two fingers. "How many fingers am I holding up?"

"Fifty," I said, and held up two of my own. "It's not a concussion. Just a little bump on the head. I'll be fine." I started to sit up. I needed to get home, get some sleep.

Murphy put her hand on my neck and pressed me back down on the pillow beneath my head, which was, apparently, her jacket, because she wasn't wearing it. "Stay down," she growled. "How did you get here? Not in that heap of a car, I hope."

"The Beetle is doing its phoenix impression," I told her. "I've got a loaner. Look, I'll be fine. Just let me out of here, and I'll go home and get some sleep."

"You aren't in any shape to drive," Murphy said. "You're a menace. I'd have to arrest myself if I let you behind a wheel in your condition."

"Murph," I said, annoyed, "unless you can pay up what you owe me already, right now, I can't exactly afford a cab."

"Dream on, Harry," Murphy said. "And save your breath. I'll give you a ride home."

"I don't need a—" I began, but she got up from her knees and stalked out of her office.

Foolishness, I thought. Stupidity. I was perfectly capable of moving myself around. So I sat up and heaved myself to my feet.

Or tried to. I actually managed to half sit up. And then I just heaved.

Murphy came back in to find me curled on my side, her office stinking from where I'd thrown up. She didn't, for a change, say anything. She just knelt by me again, cleaned off my mouth, and put another cool cloth over the back of my neck.

I remember her helping me out to her car. I remember little pieces of the drive back to my apartment. I remember giving her the keys to the loaner, and mumbling something about Mike and the tow-truck driver.

But mostly I remember the way her hand felt on mine—cold with a little bit of nervousness to the soft fingers, small beneath my great gawking digits, and strong. She scolded and threatened me the entire way back to the apartment, I think. But I remember the way she made sure she held my hand, as though to assure herself that I was still there. Or to assure me that she was, that she wasn't going anywhere.

There's a reason I'll go out on a limb to help Murphy. She's good people. One of the best.

We got back to my apartment sometime before noon. Murphy helped me down the stairs and unlocked the door for me. Mister came running up and hurled himself against her legs in greeting. Maybe being short gives her better leverage or something, since she didn't really wobble when Mister rammed her, like I do. Or maybe it's the aikido.

"Christ, Harry," she muttered. "This place is dark." She tried the light switch, but the bulbs had burnt out last week, and I hadn't had the cash to replace them. So she sat me down on the couch and lit some candles off of the glowing coals in the fireplace. "All right," she said. "I'm putting you in bed."

"Well. If you insist."

The phone rang. It was in arm's reach so I picked it up. "Dresden," I mumbled.

"Mister Dresden, this is Linda. Linda Randall. Do you remember me?"

Heh. Do men remember the scene in the movie with Marilyn standing over the subway grating? I found myself remembering Linda Randall's eyes and wondering things a gentleman shouldn't.

"Are you naked?" I said. It took me a minute to register what I'd said. Whoops.

Murphy gave me an arch look. She stood up and walked into my bedroom, and busied herself straightening the covers and giving me a modicum of privacy. I felt cheered. My slip had thrown Murphy off better than any lie I could have managed. Maybe a woozy Harry was not necessarily a bad Harry.

Linda purred laughter into the phone. "I'm in the car right now, honey. Maybe later. Look, I've come up with a few things that might help you. Can you meet me tonight?"

I rubbed at my eyes. It was Saturday. Tonight was Saturday night. Wasn't there something I was supposed to do tonight?

To hell with it, I thought. It couldn't have been all that important if I couldn't even remember it. "Sure," I told her. "Fine."

She mmmmed into the phone. "You're such a gentleman. I like that, once in a while. I get off at seven. All right? Do you want to meet me? Say at eight?"

"My car exploded," I said. My tongue felt fuzzy. "I can meet you at the 7-Eleven down the street from my apartment."

She poured that rich, creamy laughter into my ear again. "Tell you what. Give me an extra hour or so to go home, get a nice hot bath, make myself all pretty, and then I'll be there in your arms. Sound good to you?"

"Well. Okay."

She laughed again, and didn't say good-bye before disconnecting.

Murphy appeared again as soon as I hung up the phone. "Tell me you didn't just make a date, Dresden."

"You're just jealous."

Murphy snorted. "Please. I need more of a man than you to keep me happy." She started to get an arm beneath me to help me up. "You'd break like a dry stick, Dresden. You'd better get to bed before you get any more delusions."

I put a hand against her shoulder to push her back. I didn't have that kind of strength, but she backed off, frowning. "What?"

"Something," I said. I rubbed at my eyes. Something was bothering me. I was forgetting something, I was sure of it. Something I said I would do on Saturday. I struggled to push thoughts of drug wars and people driven mad by the Third Sight visions given them by the ThreeEye drug, and tried to concentrate.

It didn't take long to click. Monica. I had told her I would get in contact with her. I patted at my duster pockets until I found my notepad, and took it out. Fumbled it open, and waved at Murphy. "Candle. Need to read something."

"Christ, Dresden. I swear you're at least as bad as my first husband. He was stubborn enough to kill himself, too." She sighed, and brought a candle over. The light hurt my eyes for a moment. I made out Monica's number and I dialed her up.

"Hello?" a male child's voice asked.

"Hi," I said. "I need to speak to Monica, please."

"Who's this?"

I remembered I was working for her on the sly and answered, "Her fourth cousin, Harry, from Vermont."

"'Kay," the kid said. "Hold on." Then he screamed, without lowering the mouthpiece of the phone from his lips, "MOM! YOUR COUSIN HARRY FROM VERMONT IS ON THE PHONE LONG-DISTANCE!"

Kids. You gotta love them. I adore children. A little salt, a squeeze of lemon—perfect.

I waited for the pounding in my head to resolve into mere agony as the kid dropped the phone and ran off, feet thumping on a hardwood floor.

A moment later, there was the rattle of the phone being picked up, and Monica's quiet, somewhat nervous voice said, "Um. Hello?"

"It's Harry Dresden," I told her. "I just wanted to call to let you know what I'd been able to find out for y—"

"I'm sorry," she interrupted me. "I don't, um . . . need any of those."

I blinked. "Uh, Monica Sells?" I read her the phone number.

"Yes, yes," she said, her voice hurried, impatient. "We don't need any help, thank you."

"Is this a bad time?"

"No. No, it's not that. I just wanted to cancel my order. Discontinue the service. Don't worry about me." There was an odd quality to her voice, as though she were forcing a housewife's good cheer into it.

"Cancel? You don't want me looking for your husband anymore? But ma'am, the money—" The phone began to buzz and static made the line fuzzy. I thought I heard a voice in the background, somewhere, and then the sound went dead except for the static. For a moment, I thought I'd lost the connection entirely. Blasted unreliable phones. Usually, they messed up on my end, not on the receiving end. You can't even trust them to foul up dependably.

"Hello? Hello?" I said, cross and grumpy.

Monica's voice returned. "Don't worry about that. Thank you *so* much for all of your help. Good day, bye-bye, thank you." Then she hung up on me.

I took the phone away from my ear and stared at it. "Bizarre," I said.

"Come on, Harry," Murphy said. She took the phone from my hand and planted it firmly in its cradle.

"Aww, mom. It's not even dark yet." I made the lame joke to try to think about something besides how terribly my head was going to hurt when Murphy helped me up. She did. It did. We hobbled into the bedroom and when I stretched out on the cool sheets I was reasonably certain I was going to set down roots.

Murphy took my temperature and felt my scalp with her fingers, careful around the goose egg on the back of my skull. She shined a penlight into my eyes, which I did not like. She also got me a drink of water, which I did like, and had me swallow a couple of aspirin or Tylenol or something.

I only remember two more things about that morning. One was Murphy stripping me out of my shirt, boots, and socks, and leaning down to kiss my forehead and ruffle my hair. Then she covered me up with blankets and put out the lights. Mister crawled up and lay down across my legs, purring like a small diesel engine, comforting.

The second thing I remember was the phone ringing again. Murphy was just about to leave, her car keys rattling in her hand.

I heard her turn back to pick up the phone, and say, "Harry Dresden's residence."

There was a silence.

"Hello?" Murphy said.

After another pause Murphy appeared in the doorway, a small shadow, looking down at me. "Wrong number. Get some rest, Harry."

"Thanks, Karrin." I smiled at her, or tried to. It must have looked ghastly. She smiled back, and I'm sure hers was nicer than mine.

She left then. The apartment got dark and quiet. Mister continued to rumble soothingly in the dark.

It kept nagging at me, even as I fell asleep. What had I forgotten? And another, less sensible question—who had been on the line who hadn't wanted to speak to Murphy? Had Monica Sells tried to call me back? Why would she call me off the case and tell me to keep the money?

I pondered that, and baseball bats and other matters until Mister's purring put me to sleep.

Chapter 13

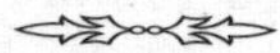

I woke up when thunder rattled the old house above me.

True dark had fallen. I had no idea of what time it was. I lay in bed for a moment, confused and a little dizzy. There was a warm spot on my legs, where Mister must have been until a few moments before, but the big grey cat was nowhere to be seen. He was a chicken about thunderstorms.

Rain was coming down in sheets. I could hear it, on the concrete outside and on the old building above me. It creaked and swayed in the spring thunderstorm and the wind, timbers gently flexing, wise enough with age to give a little, rather than put up stubborn resistance until they broke. I could probably stand to learn something from that.

My stomach was growling. I got out of bed, wobbled a little, and rooted about for my robe. I couldn't find it in the dark, but came across my duster where Murphy had left it on a chair, neatly folded. Laying on top of it was a scattering of cash, along with a napkin bearing the words "You will pay me back.—Murphy." I scowled at the money and tried to ignore the flash of gratitude I felt. I picked up my duster and tugged it on over my bare chest. Then I padded on naked feet out into the living room.

Thunder rumbled again, growling outside. I could feel the storm, in a way that a lot of people can't, and that most of those who can put down to nerves. It was raw energy up there, naked and pulsing through the clouds. I could feel the water in the rain and clouds, the moving air blowing the droplets in gusts against the walls of the house above. I could sense, waiting, the fire of the deadly lightning, leaping from cloud to cloud above and seeking a path of least resistance to the patient, timeless earth that bore the brunt of the storm's attack. All four elements, interacting, moving, energy flashing from place to place in each of its forms. There was a lot of potential in storms, that a sorcerer could tap into if he was desperate or stupid enough. A lot of energy to be used, up there, where the forces of ancient nature brawled and tumbled.

I frowned, thinking about that. It hadn't occurred to me before. Had there been a storm on Wednesday night? Yes, there had. I remember thunder waking me for a few moments in the hours before dawn. Could our killer have tapped into it to fuel his spells? Possibly. It bore looking into. Such tapped magic was often too unstable or volatile to use in such a carefully directed fashion.

Lightning flashed again, and I counted three or four seconds before the rumble reached me. If the killer *was* using the storms, it would make sense that if he or she were to strike again, it would happen tonight. I shivered.

My stomach growled, and more mundane matters took my attention. My head was feeling somewhat better. I wasn't dizzy anymore. My stomach was furious with me—like a lot of tall, skinny men, I eat endlessly, but it never stays on. I have no idea why. I shambled into the kitchen and started building up the grill.

"Mister?" I called. "You hungry, bud? I'm gonna fry up some burgers, mmm, mmm, mmm."

Lightning flashed again, closer this time, the thunder following right on its heels. The flash was bright enough to sear through my half-sunken windows and make me wince against it. But, in the flash of light, I caught sight of Mister.

The cat was up on the top of my bookshelf, in the far corner of the apartment—as far as it was possible to get away from my front door. He was watching it, his eyes luminous in the half dark, and though he had the cat-lazy look of any lounging feline, his ears were tilted forward, and his gaze focused unwaveringly upon the door. If he'd had a tail, it would have been twitching.

There came a knocking, a rapping, at my chamber door.

Maybe it was the storm making me nervous, but I quested out with my senses, feeling for any threat that might have been there. The storm made a mess of things, and all of that noise, both physical and spiritual, kept me from being able to tell anything more than that there was someone outside my door.

I felt in the pocket of my duster for the gun—but I remembered that I had set it aside in the lab last night and not taken it with me down to the police station. Police don't take kindly to anyone but police toting firearms inside the station, don't ask me why. In any case, it was out of easy reach now.

And then I remembered that Linda Randall was supposed to be showing up. I berated myself for getting spooked so easily, and then again for sleeping so long, and then again for looking and smelling like I hadn't showered in a couple of days or combed my hair or shaved or anything else that might have made me marginally less unappealing. Ah, well. I got the impression that with Linda, that sort of thing didn't seem to matter too much. Maybe she was into *eau des hommes*.

I walked over to the door and opened it, smoothing back my hair with one hand and trying to keep a sheepish grin off of my face.

Susan Rodriguez waited outside in the rain, her black umbrella held above her. She wore a khaki trench coat and an expensive black dress beneath it, with heels. Pearls shone at her throat and ears. She blinked at me when I appeared in the door. "Harry?"

I stared at her. Oh my gosh. I had forgotten my date with Susan. How in the world could I have forgotten that? I mean, the White Council, the police, vampires, concussions, junkies, mob bosses, and baseball-bat-swinging thugs notwithstanding—

Well, no. There probably weren't any women incredible enough to make me keep my mind on them through all of that. But all the same, it seemed a little rude of me.

"Hi, Susan," I said, lamely. I peered past her. When had Susan said she was going to show up? Nine? And when had Linda said? Eight—no, wait. She'd said eight o'clock at first, and then said she'd be by in another hour after that. At nine. Hooboy. This was not going to be pretty.

Susan read me like a book and glanced back behind her in the rain, before looking back up at me. "Expecting someone, Harry?"

"Not exactly," I told her. "Uh, well. Maybe. Look, come on in. You're getting drenched." Which wasn't exactly true. *I* was getting drenched, my bare feet soaked, standing there in the open door, the wind blowing rain down the stairway at me.

Susan's mouth quirked in a malicious, predatory little smile, and she came in, folding down her umbrella and brushing past me. "This is your apartment?"

"Nah," I told her. "This is my summer home in Zurich." She eyed me as I closed the door, took her coat, and hung it up on a tall old wooden hat stand near the doorway.

Susan turned away from me as I hung up her coat. Her dress showed her back, the long curve of her spine, all the way down to her waist. It had a fairly tame hemline, and long, tight sleeves. I liked it. A lot. She let me see her back for a while as she walked away from me, toward the fireplace, then slowly turned to face me, smirking, leaning one smooth hip on the couch. Her midnight hair was bound up on top of her head, displaying a long and slender neck, her skin an advertisement for something smooth and wonderful. Her lips quirked up at the corners, and she narrowed her dark, flashing eyes at me. "The police having you put in overtime, Harry?" she drawled. "The killings must be sensational. Major crime figure, murdered with magic. Care to make a statement?"

I winced. She was still hunting for an angle for the *Arcane*. "Sure," I told her. Her eyes widened in surprise. "I need a shower," I said. "I'll be right back. Mister, keep an eye on the lady, eh?"

Susan gave me a little roll of her eyes, then glanced up and studied Mister on his perch on the bookcase. Mister, for his part, flicked an ear and continued staring at the door.

More thunder rumbled overhead.

I lit a few candles for her, then took one with me into the bathroom. Think, Harry. Get awake, and get your head clear. What to do?

Get clean, I told myself. You smell like a horse. Get some cool water over your head and work this out. Linda Randall is going to be here in a minute, and you need to figure out how to keep Susan from prying her nose into the murders.

So advised, I agreed with myself and hurriedly got undressed and into the shower. I don't use a water heater, and consequently I am more than used to cold showers. Actually, given how often I, and wizards in general, get to date actual real women, maybe that's just as well.

I was just lathering up with shampoo when the lightning got a lot worse, the thunder a lot louder, the rain a lot harder. The height of the storm had hit the old house and hit it hard. It was almost possible to see clearly in the violent electrical discharge. Almost impossible to hear over the thunder. But I caught a flicker of motion out of the corner of my eye, a shadow that moved across the sunken window (covered by modest curtains) in the bathroom. Someone was moving toward the stairs down to my apartment.

Did I mention how I haven't had a ton of success with women? Nights like this are one reason why. I panicked, hard. I leapt out of the shower, my head all a-sudsy, wrapped a towel around my waist, and headed out into the front room.

I couldn't let Linda just come to the door and have Susan answer it. *That* would be the cattiest thing you've ever seen, and I would be the one to get all the scratches and bites, too.

I rounded the corner from my bedroom into the main room and saw Susan reaching for the doorknob. Lightning flashed again, and thunder kept me from hearing the knob's *click-clack.* I heard something else, though, a snarling, spitting sound, and saw Mister, on his feet now, his back arched up and all his fur fluffed out, teeth bared, his no-longer-sleepy eyes fastened on the door.

The thunder passed as Susan swung the door open. I could see her face in profile. One hand was on her hip, and there was an amused, dangerous little smile on her pretty mouth.

As the door opened, I felt it, the cloud of energies that accompanies a spirit-being when it comes into the mortal world, disguised until now by the background clutter of the storm. A figure stood in the doorway, rather squat, less than five feet tall, dressed in a plain brown trench coat, illuminated by blue lightning overhead. There was something *wrong* to the shape, something that just wasn't a part of good old Mother Earth. It's "head" turned to look at me, and sudden twin points of fire, as blue as the lightning dancing above, flared up, illuminating the leathery, inhuman curves of a face that most closely resembled that of a large and warty toad.

Susan got a good look at the demon's eyes and face from two feet away and screamed.

"Susan!" I shouted, already moving toward the couch. "Get out of the way!" I threw myself to the floor behind the couch, landed with a *whumph* of hard floor hitting my ribs.

The demon's jaws parted in a silent hiss, and its throat constricted weirdly as I vanished behind the couch. There was a hissing sound, and a heart-sized section of the couch just *dissolved* in a cloud of mist and foul stench. Droplets of liquid spattered through, onto the floor near me, and where they touched little holes corroded outward in the space of two seconds. I rolled away from the couch and the demon's acid.

"Susan!" I shouted. "Get back toward the kitchen! Don't get between it and me!"

"What is it?" she screamed back at me.

"A bad guy." I poked my head up and peered through the smoking hole in the couch, ready to duck back down at a moment's notice. The demon, squat and bulkier than a human, was standing in the doorway, both long-fingered, pad-tipped hands leaning forward toward the inside of the house. It paused as though resting against a light screen.

"Why isn't it coming in?" Susan asked from the far corner, near the door. Her back was pressed to the wall, and her eyes were wide and terrified. My God, I thought, just don't pass out on me, Susan.

"Homestead laws," I said. "It isn't a mortal creature. It has to gather its energy to push through the barrier around a home."

"Can it get in?" she said. Her voice was thin, reedy. She was asking questions, gathering information, data, falling back on her ingrained career instincts—because, I suspected, her rational brain had short-circuited. That happens to people who get a good hard look at a demon for the first time.

I hurried over to her and grabbed her arm, dragging her back toward the door leading down to my lab. "Get down there," I shouted, jerking the door up and revealing the folding ladder-staircase.

"It's *dark*," Susan protested. "Oh, God." She blinked down at my waist. "Harry? Why are you naked?"

I looked down. And blushed. The towel must have fallen off while I was dancing around. Looking down made the shampoo suds still in my hair runnel down into my eyes, making them sting and burn. Could this evening get any worse?

There was a tearing sound from the doorway, and the toad-demon sort of surged forward a stumbling step. It was now in my house. Lightning still danced in the sky behind it, and I could only see it in ugly, hunchbacked outline, except for the electric light of its wide, round, googly eyes as it came toward me. Its throat was working in little, undulating motions.

"Crap," I said. I'm quite eloquent in times of crisis. I shoved Susan toward the stairs, and turned toward the demon, tips of my thumbs touching, fingers spread, palms out toward it.

The demon's mouth opened again, and it made a slick, spittooning sound.

"*Vento Riflittum,*" I shouted, willing my fear and anxiety into a tangible shape, throwing it down from my pounding heart through my shoulders and arms, directed at the foe. The globule of demonacid sped toward my face.

My terror and adrenaline roared out of my fingertips in the form of wind, gathering up speed enough to tear the hair from a man's head. It caught the blob of acid and flung it back at the demon in a fine spray, stopped the thing dead in its tracks, and even drove it back several feet, its claw-tipped feet sliding on my smooth floor, catching on the rugs.

The acid sizzled and spat little electric blue sparks on its skin, but it didn't seem to harm the demon. It did, however, dissolve the trench coat to shreds in less time than it takes to draw a breath and wreaked havoc on my rugs and furniture.

The demon shook its head, gathering its wits. I turned to the far corner, near the door, and extended my hand, trumpeting, *"Vento servitas!"* The pale, smooth wood of my wizard's staff all but glowed in the darkness as it flew toward me, driven by a gentler, finer blast of the same wind. I caught it in my hand and spun it toward the demon, calling on the lines of power and force deep within the long, unbroken grains of wood in the staff. I extended the staff toward it, horizontally like a bar, and shouted, "Out! Out! Out! You are not welcome here!" A touch dramatic in any other circumstance, maybe—but when you've got a demon in your living room, nothing seems too extreme.

The toad-demon hunched its shoulders, planted its broad feet, and grunted as a wave of unseen force swept out from my staff like a broom whisking along the floor. I could feel the demon resist me, pressing against the strength of the staff, as though I were leaning the wood against a vertical steel bar and attempting to snap it across that length.

We strained silently for several seconds until I realized that this thing was just too strong for me. I wasn't going to be able to brush it off like a minor imp or a niggling poltergeist. It wouldn't take me long to exhaust myself, and once the demon could move again it was either going to dissolve me with its acid or else just waddle up to me and rip me into pieces. It would be stronger than a mortal, a hell of a lot faster, and it was not going to stop until I was dead or the sun had come up or one of any of a number of other unlikely conditions were met.

"Susan!" I shouted, my chest heaving. "Are you down there?"

"Yes," she said. "Is it gone?"

"Not exactly, no." I felt my palms get sweaty, the smooth wood of the staff begin to slip. The burning of the soap suds in my eyes increased, and the lights of the demon's eyes brightened.

"Why don't you set it on fire? Shoot it! Blow it up!" Her voice had a searching quality to it, as though she were looking around, down there in the lab.

"I *can't,*" I said to her. "I can't pump enough juice into it to *hurt* the thing without blowing us up along with it. You've got to get out of there." My mind was racing along, calculating possibilities, numbers, my reserves of energy, cold and rational. The thing was here for me. If I drew it off to one side, into my bedroom and bathroom, Susan might be able to escape. On the other hand, it might be under orders to kill me and any witnesses, in which case after it had finished me it would simply go after her as well. There had to be another way to get her out of here. And then I remembered it.

"Susan!" I shouted. "There's a sports bottle on my table down there. Drink what's in it, and think about being away from here. Okay? Think about being far away."

"I found it," she called up a second later. "It smells bad."

"Dammit, it's a potion. It'll get you out of here. Drink it!"

There was a gagging noise, and then a moment later she said, "Now what?"

I blinked and looked at the stairs going down. "It should have work—" I broke off as the toad thing leaned forward, reached out a clawed foot, and in that stride gained three feet of ground toward me. I was able to stop it again, barely, but I knew that it was going to be coming for my throat in a few more seconds.

"Nothing happened," she said. "Dammit, Harry, we have to do something." And then she came pounding up the ladder, dark eyes flashing, my .38 revolver in her hand.

"No!" I told her. "Don't!" I felt the staff slip more. The demon was getting ready to come through all my defenses.

Susan raised the gun, face pale, her hands shaking, and started shooting. A .38 Chief's Special carries six rounds, and I use a medium-speed load, rather than armor-piercing or explosive bullets or anything fancy like that. Fewer chances that something will go wrong in the presence of a lot of magic.

A gun is a pretty simple machine. A revolver approaches *very* simple. Wheels, gears, and a simple lever impact to ignite the powder. It's tough for magic to argue with physics, most of the time.

The revolver roared six times.

The first two shots must have gone wide and hit somewhere else. The next two struck the demon's hide and made deep dents in it before springing off and rebounding wildly around the room, as I had feared they would, more of a threat to us than to it. Fortunately, neither of us was injured or killed by the ricochets. The fifth shot went between its long, oddly shaped legs and past it.

The sixth hit the thing square between its lightning-lantern eyes, knocked it off-balance, and sent it tumbling over with a toady hiss of frustration.

I gasped and grabbed at Susan's wrist. "Basement," I wheezed, as she dropped the gun. We both scrambled down the ladder. I didn't bother to shut it behind me. The thing could just tear its way through the floor, if it needed to. This way, I would at least know where it would come down, rather than have it tunnel through the floor and come out on top of my head.

At my will, the tip of the staff I still held burst into light, illuminating the room.

"Harry?" Bob's voice came from the shelf. The skull's eyelights came on, and he swiveled around to face me. "What the hell is going on? Woo woo, who is the babe?"

Susan jumped. "What is *that*?"

"Ignore him," I said, and followed my own advice. I went to the far end of my lab table and started kicking boxes, bags, notebooks, and old paperbacks off the floor. "Help me clear this floor space. Hurry!"

She did, and I cursed the lack of cleaning skills that had left this end of the lab such a mess. I was struggling to get to the circle I had laid in the floor, a perfect ring of copper, an unbroken loop in the concrete that could be empowered to hold a demon in—or out.

"Harry!" Bob gulped as we worked. "There's, a, um. A seriously badass toad-demon coming down the ladder."

"I *know* that, Bob." I heaved a bunch of empty cardboard boxes aside as Susan frantically tossed some papers away, exposing the entirety of the copper ring, about three feet across. I took her hand and stepped into the circle, drawing her close to me.

"What's happening?" Susan asked, her expression bewildered and terrified.

"Just stay close," I told her. She clung tightly to me.

"It sees you, Harry," Bob reported. "It's going to spit something at you, I think."

I didn't have time to see if Bob was right. I leaned down, touched the circle with the tip of my staff, and willed power into it, to shut the creature out. The circle sprang up around us, a silent and invisible tension in the air.

Something splattered and hissed against the air a few inches from my face. I looked up to see dark, sputtering acid slithering off the invisible shield the circle's power provided us. Half a second earlier and it would have eaten my face off. Cheery thought.

I tried to catch my breath, stand straight, and not let any part of me extend outside the circle, which would break its circuit and negate its power. My arms were shaking and my legs felt weak. Susan, too, was visibly trembling.

The demon stalked over to us. I could see it clearly in the light of my staff, and I wished that I couldn't. It was horribly ugly, misshapen, foul, heavily muscled, and I compared it to a toad only because I knew of nothing else that even remotely approached a description of it. It glared at us and drove a fist at the circle's shield. It rebounded in a shower of blue sparks, and the thing hissed, a horrible and windy sound.

Outside, the storm continued to rumble and growl, muffled by the thick walls of the subbasement.

Susan was holding close to me, and almost crying. "Why isn't it killing us? Why isn't it getting us?"

"It can't," I said, gently. "It can't get through, and it can't do anything to break the circle. So long as neither of us crosses that line, we'll be safe."

"Oh, God," Susan said. "How long do we have to stand here?"

"Dawn," I said. "Until dawn. When the sun rises, it has to go."

"There's no sun down here," she said.

"Doesn't work that way. It's got a sort of power cord stretching back to whoever summoned it. A fuel line. As soon as the sun comes up, that line gets cut, and he goes away, like a balloon with no air."

"When does the sun come up?" she asked.

"Oh, well. About ten more hours."

"Oh," she said. She laid her head against my bare chest and closed her eyes.

The toad-demon paced in a slow circuit around the circle, searching for a weakness in the shield. It would find none. I closed my eyes and tried to think.

"Uh, Harry," Bob began.

"Not now, Bob."

"But Harry—" Bob tried again.

"Dammit, Bob. I'm trying to think. If you want to be really useful, you could try to figure out why that escape potion you were so confident of didn't work for Susan."

"*Harry,*" Bob protested, "that's what I'm trying to tell you."

Susan murmured, against my chest, "Is it getting warm in here? Or is it just me?"

A terrible suspicion struck me. I looked down at Susan and got a sinking feeling. Surely not. No. It couldn't be.

She looked up at me, her dark eyes smoky. "We're going to

die, aren't we Harry? Have you ever thought you'd want to die making love?"

She kissed my chest, almost absently.

It felt nice. Really, really nice. I tried not to notice all the bare, lovely back that was naked underneath my hand.

"I've thought that, many times," she said, against my skin.

"Bob," I began, my voice getting furious.

"I *tried* to tell you," Bob wailed. "I did! She grabbed the wrong potion and just chugged it down." Bob's skull turned toward me a bit, and the lights brightened. "You've got to admit, though. The love potion works *great*."

Susan was kissing my chest and rubbing her body up against me in a fashion that was unladylike and extremely pleasant and distracting. "Bob, I swear, I am going to lock you in a wall safe for the next two hundred years."

"It's not my *fault*!" Bob protested.

The demon watched what was happening in the circle with froggy eyes and kicked a section of floor clear enough of debris for it to squat down on its haunches and stare, restless and ready as a cat waiting for a mouse to stick its head out of its hole. Susan stared up at me with sultry eyes and tried to wrench me to the floor, and consequently out of the circle's protective power. Bob continued to wail his innocence.

Who says I don't know how to show a lady a good time?

Chapter 14

Susan tugged at my neck and jerked my head down to hers for a kiss. As kisses went, well. It was, um, extremely interesting. Perfectly passionate, abandoned, not a trace of self-consciousness or hesitation to it. Or at any rate not from her. I came up for air a minute later, my lips itching with the intensity of it, and she stared up at me with burning eyes. "Take me, Harry. I need you."

"Uh, Susan. That's not really a good idea right now," I said. The potion had taken hold of her hard. No wonder she had recovered from her terror enough to come back up the stairs and fire my gun at the demon. It had lowered her inhibitions to a sufficient degree that it must also have dulled her fears.

Susan's fingers wandered, and her eyes sparkled. "Your mouth says no," she purred, "but *this* says yes."

I went up on my toes, and swallowed, trying to keep my balance and get her hand off me at the same time. "That thing is *always* saying something stupid," I told her. She was beyond reason. The potion had kicked her libido into suicidal overdrive. "Bob, help me out here!"

"I'm stuck in the skull," Bob said. "If you don't let me out, I can't do much of anything, Harry."

Susan stood up on tiptoe to gnaw at my ear, wrapped her shapely thigh around one of mine, and started whimpering and pulling me toward the floor. My balance wavered. A three-foot circle was not enough to perform wrestling or gymnastics or . . . anything else in, without leaving something sticking out for the waiting demon to chew on.

"Is the other potion still there?" I asked.

"Sure," Bob said. "I can see it where it fell on the floor. Could throw it to you, too."

"Okay," I said, growing excited—well. More excited. I might yet get out of this basement alive. "I'm going to let you out for five minutes. I want you to help me by throwing me the potion."

"No, boss," Bob said, his voice maddeningly cheerful.

"No? No?!"

"I get a twenty-four-hour leave, or nothing."

"Dammit, Bob! I'm responsible for what you do if I let you out! You know that!"

Susan whispered, into my ear, "I'm not wearing any underwear," and tried something approximating a pro-wrestling takedown to drop me to the floor. I wavered in balance and barely managed to stave her off. The demon's frog-eyes narrowed, and it came to its feet, ready to leap on us.

"Bob!" I yelled. "You slimy jerk!"

"You try living in a bony old skull for a few hundred years, Harry! You'd want to get a night off once in a while, too!"

"Fine!" I shouted, my heart leaping into my throat as my balance wavered again. "Fine! Just make sure you get me the potion! You have twenty-four hours."

"Just make sure you catch it," Bob replied. And then a flood of orangish light flowed out of both of the skull's eye sockets and into the room. The lights swooped down in an elongated cloud over the potion bottle that lay on the floor at the far side of the lab, gathered it up, and hurled it through the air toward me. I reached up with my spare hand and caught it, bobbled it for a minute, and then secured it again.

The orange lights that were Bob's spirit-form danced a little jig, then whizzed up the ladder and out of the lab, vanishing.

"What's that?" Susan murmured, eyes dazed.

"Another drink," I said. "Drink this with me. I think I can cover us both in the focus department, get us out of here."

"Harry," she said. "I'm not *thirsty*." Her eyes smoldered. "I'm *hungry*."

I hit upon an idea. "Once we drink this, I'll be ready, and we can go to bed."

She looked up at me hazily and smiled, wicked and delighted. "Oh, Harry. Bottoms up."Her hands made a sort of silent commentary on her words, and I jumped, almost dropping the bottle. More shampoo from my hair trailed down my already burning eyes, and I squeezed them closed.

I slugged away about half the potion, trying to ignore the flat-cola taste, and quickly passed the rest to Susan. She smiled lazily and drank it down, licking her lips.

It started in my guts—a sort of fluttery, wobbly feeling that moved out, up through my lungs and out along my shoulders, down my arms. It also went down, over my hips and into my legs. I began to shake and quiver uncontrollably.

And then I just flew apart into a cloud of a million billion tiny pieces of Harry, each one with its own perspective and view. The room wasn't just a square, cluttered basement to me, but a pattern of energies, grouped into specific shapes and uses. Even the demon was only a cloud of particles, slow and dense. I flowed around that cloud, up through the opening in the ceiling pattern, and outside of the apartment and into the raging nonpattern of the storm.

It took maybe five seconds, and then the power of the potion faded. I felt all the little pieces of me abruptly rush back together and slam into one another at unthinkable speed. It hurt, and made me nauseous, a sort of heavy-duty thump of impact that didn't come from any one direction, but from every direction at once. I staggered, planted my staff on the ground, and felt the rain wash down over me.

Susan appeared next to me a heartbeat later, and promptly sat down on her butt on the ground, in the rain. "Oh, God. I feel terrible."

Inside the apartment, the demon screamed, a raging, voiceless hiss. I could hear it madly rampaging around inside. "Come on," I told her. "We've got to get out of here before it gets smart and starts looking outside for us."

"I'm sick," she said. "I'm not sure I can walk."

"The mixed potions," I said. "They can do that to you. But we have to go now. Come on, Susan. Up and at 'em." I bent down and got her up on her feet and moving away from my apartment.

"Where are we going?" she asked.

"Do you have your car keys?"

She patted the dress, as if looking for pockets, and then shook her head dazedly. "They were in my coat pocket."

"We walk, then."

"Walk where?"

"Over to Reading Road. It always floods when there's this much rain. It'll be enough water to ground that thing if it tries to follow us." It was only a couple of blocks away. The cold rain came down in buckets. I was shaking, shivering, and naked, and more soap was getting into my eyes. But hey. At least I was clean.

"Wha?" she mumbled. "What will the rain do to it?"

"Not rain. Running water. It kills him if he tries to go over it after us," I explained to her, patiently. I hoped the potions mixing together in her stomach hadn't done anything irreversible. There had been accidents before. We were moving at good speed, all things considered, and had covered maybe forty yards in the pouring rain. Not much farther to go.

"Oh. Oh, that's good," she said. And then she convulsed and pitched to the ground. I tried to hold her, but I was just too tired, my arms too weak. I nearly went down with her. She rolled to her side and lay that way, retching horribly, vomiting herself empty.

Thunder and lightning raged around us again, and I heard the sharp crack of the storm's power touching a tree nearby. I saw a bright flash of contact and then the subdued glow of burning branches. I looked in the direction we had been heading. The flooding Reading Road, safety from the demon, was still thirty yards away.

"I didn't think you'd last this long," someone said.

I almost jumped out of my skin. I picked my staff up in both hands and turned in a slow circle, searching for the source of the voice. "Who's there?" There, to one side, a spot of cold—not physical cold, but something deeper and darker that my other senses detected. A pooling of shadows, an illusion in the darkness between lights, gone when lightning flashed and back again when it had passed.

"Do you expect me to give you my name?" the shadows scorned. "Suffice to say that I am the one who has killed you."

"You're an underachiever," I shot back, still turning, eyes searching. "The job's not done."

In the darkness underneath a broken streetlight, then, maybe twenty feet away, I could make out the shape of a person. Man or woman, I couldn't tell, nor could I distinguish from the voice. "Soon," the shape said. "You can't last much longer. My demon will finish you before another ten minutes have passed." The voice was supremely confident.

"You called that demon here?"

"Indeed," the shadowy shape confirmed.

"Are you *crazy*?" I demanded, stunned. "Don't you know what could happen to you if that thing gets loose?"

"It won't," the shape assured me. "It is mine to control."

I extended my senses toward the shape, and found that what I had suspected was true. It wasn't a real person, or an illusion masking a real person. It was only the seeming of one, a phantasm of shape and sound, a hologram that could see and hear and speak for its creator, wherever he or she was.

"What are you doing?" it demanded. It must have sensed me feeling it out.

"Checking your credentials," I said, and sent some of my remaining will toward it, the sorcerous equivalent of a slap in the face.

The image cried out in surprise and reeled back. "How did you *do* that?" it snarled.

"I went to school."

The hologram growled, then raised up its voice, calling out in rolling syllables. I tried to hear what had been said, but another peal of thunder blocked out the middle half of what was undoubtedly the demon's name.

From within my apartment, the distant, faint sound of the demon's smashing ruckus came to an abrupt halt.

"Now," the image said, a sneer to its voice. "Now you will pay."

"Why are you doing this?" I demanded.

"You're in my way."

"Let the woman go."

"Sorry," the image said. "She's seen too much. She's in the way, too, now. My demon will kill you both."

"You bastard," I snarled.

It laughed at me.

I looked over my shoulder, back toward the apartment. Through the rain I heard a dry and raspy hiss, underlaid with a sort of clicking growl. Blue frog-eyes, reflecting the storm's lightning, came up the stairs from my basement apartment. It focused on me immediately and started forward. The back fender of Susan's car, which she had parked outside my apartment, got in its way, and with the pad-tipped fingers of one skinny, soft-looking hand, it picked up the back end of the car and tossed it to one side, where it landed with a heavy crunch.

I tried not to think about those fingers around my throat.

"You see?" the image said. "Mine to call. Time for you to die, Mr. Dresden."

Another flash of lightning showed the demon falling to all fours and scrambling toward me like an overweight lizard scuttling across hot sand to shade, in an exaggerated wagging motion that looked ridiculous but brought it closer and closer at deceptive speed.

"Deposit another quarter to continue your call, asshole," I said. I thrust my staff toward the shadowy image, this time, focusing my will into a full-fledged attack. *"Stregallum finitas."*

Scarlet light abruptly flooded over it, devouring its edges and moving inward.

The image snarled, then gasped in pain. "Dresden! My demon will roll in your bones!" And then it broke off into a scream of anguish as my counterspell began to tear the image-sending apart. I was better than whoever had made the image, and they couldn't hold the spell in the face of my counter. The image and the scream alike faded slowly into the distance until both were gone. I allowed myself the smallest touch of satisfaction, and then turned to the woman on the ground.

"Susan," I said, crouching by her, keeping my eyes on the onrushing demon. "Susan, get up. We have to go."

"I can't," she sobbed. "Oh, God," and she threw up some more. She tried to rise but collapsed back to the ground, moaning piteously.

I looked back at the water, gauging the thing's speed. It was coming, fast, but not quite as fast as a man could run. I could still escape it, if I ran, full out. I could get across the water. I could be safe.

But I couldn't carry Susan there. I'd never make it, with her slowing me down. But if I didn't go, both of us would die. Wouldn't it be better for one of us, at least, to live?

I looked back at the demon. I was exhausted, and it had caught me unprepared. The heavy rain would keep fire, man's ancient weapon against the darkness and the things it hid, from being effective in holding it back. And I didn't have enough left in me to do anything else. It would be as good as suicide to stand against it.

Susan sobbed on the ground, helpless in the rain, sick from my potions, unable to rise.

I leaned my head back and let the rain wash the last traces of shampoo from my eyes, my hair. Then I turned, took a step toward the oncoming demon. I couldn't leave Susan to that thing. Not even if it meant dying. I'd never be able to live with myself afterward.

The demon squalled something at me in its hissing, toady voice, and raised both its hands toward me, coming up onto its hind legs. Lightning flashed overhead, blinding bright. Thunder came hard on its heels, deep enough to shake the street beneath my bare feet.

Thunder.

Lightning.

The storm.

I looked up at the boiling clouds overhead, lit by the dancing lightning moving among them, deadly beautiful and luminous. Power seethed and danced in the storm, mystic energies as old as time, enough power to shatter stones, superheat air, boil water to steam, burn anything it touched to ashes.

At this point, I think it is safe to say, I was desperate enough to try anything.

The demon howled and waddled forward, clumsy and quick. I raised my staff to the sky with one hand, and with the other pointed a finger at the demon. This was dangerous work, tapping the storm. There was no ritual to give it shape, no circle to protect me, not even words to shield my mind from the way the energies of magic would course through it. I sent my senses coursing upward, toward the storm, taking hold of the formless powers and drawing them into patterns of raw energy that began to surge toward me, toward the tip of my staff.

"Harry?" Susan said. "What are you doing?" She huddled on the ground in her evening dress, shuddering. Her voice was weak, thready.

"You ever form a line of people holding hands when you were a kid, and scuff your feet across the carpeting together, and then have the last person in the line touch someone on the ear to zap them?"

"Yeah," she said, confused.

"I'm doing that. Only bigger."

The demon squalled again and drove itself into the air with its powerful toad-legs, hurtling toward me, sailing through the air with a frightening and unnatural grace.

I focused what little I had left of my will on the staff, and the clouds and raging power above. *"Ventas!"* I shouted, *"Ventas fulmino!"*

At my will, a spark leapt up from the tip of my staff toward the clouds above. It touched the rolling, restless belly of the storm.

Hell roared down in response.

Lightning, white-hot fury, with a torrent of wind and rain, all fell upon me, centered around the staff. I felt the power hit the end of the soaking wet wood with a jolt like a sledgehammer. It coursed down the staff and into my hand, making my muscles convulse, bowing my naked body with the strain. It took everything I had to hold the image of what I wanted in my mind, to keep my hand pointed at the demon as it came for me, to keep the energy surging through me to wreak its havoc on flesh less tender than mine.

The demon was maybe six inches away when the storm's fury boiled down my body and out through my arm, out of my pointing finger, and took it in the heart. The force of it threw the thing back, back and up, into the air, and held it there, wreathed in a corona of blinding energy.

The demon struggled, screamed, toad-hands flailing, toad-legs kicking.

And then it exploded in a wash of blue flame. The night was lit once more, bright as day. I had to shield my eyes against it. Susan cried out in fear, and I think I must have been screaming along with her.

Then the night grew quiet again. Flaming bits of something that I didn't want to think about were raining down around us, landing with little, wet, plopping sounds upon the road, the sidewalk, the yards of the houses around me, burning quickly to little briquettes of charcoal and then hissing into sputtering coolness. The wind abruptly died down. The rain slowed to a gentle patter, the storm's fury spent.

My legs gave out, and I sat down shakily on the street, stunned. My hair was dry, and standing on end. There was smoke curling up from the blackened ends of my toenails. I just sat there, happy to be alive, to be breathing in and out again. I felt like I could crawl back in bed and go to sleep for a few days, even though I'd gotten up not half an hour ago.

Susan sat up, blinking, her face blank. She stared at me.

"What are you doing next Saturday?" I asked her.

She just kept on staring for a minute. And then quietly lay down again on her side.

I heard the footsteps approach from the darkness off to one side. "Summoning demons," the sour voice said, disgusted. "In addition to the atrocities you have already committed. I knew I smelled black magic on the winds tonight. You are a blight, Dresden."

I sort of rolled my head over to one side to regard Morgan, my warden, tall and massive in his black trench coat. The rain had plastered his greying hair down to his head, and coursed down the lines of his face like channels in a slab of stone.

"I didn't call that thing," I said. My voice was slurred with fatigue. "But I damn well sent it back to where it belongs. Didn't you see?"

"I saw you defend yourself against it," Morgan said. "But I didn't see anyone else summon it. You probably called it up yourself and lost control of it. It couldn't have taken me anyway, Dresden. It wouldn't have done you any good."

I laughed, weakly. "You're flattering yourself," I said. "I sure as hell wouldn't risk calling up a demon just to get to *you*, Morgan."

He narrowed his already-narrow eyes. "I have convened the Council," he said. "They will be here two dawns hence. They will hear my testimony, Dresden, and the evidence I have to present to them against you." There was another, more subdued flash of lightning, and it gave his eyes a wild, madman's gleam. "And then they will order you put to death."

I just stared at him for a moment, dully. "The Council," I said. "They're coming here. To Chicago."

Morgan smiled at me, the kind of smile sharks reserve for baby seals. "Dawn, on Monday, you will be brought before them. I don't usually enjoy my position as executioner, Harry Blackstone Copperfield Dresden. But in your case, I am proud to fulfill that role."

I shuddered when he pronounced my full name. He did it almost exactly right—maybe by accident, and maybe not, too. There were those on the White Council who knew my name, knew how to say it. To run from the Council convened, to avoid them, would be to admit guilt and invite disaster. And because they knew my name, they could find me. They could get to me. Anywhere.

Susan moaned and stirred. "H-H-Harry?" she mumbled. "What happened?"

I turned to her, to make sure she was all right. When I glanced back over my shoulder, Morgan was gone. Susan sneezed and huddled against me. I put an arm around her, to share what little warmth I had.

Monday morning.

Monday morning, Morgan would bring his suspicions and level his accusations, and it would likely be enough to get me voted dead. Whoever Mister or Miss Shadows was, I had to find him, her, it, or them before Monday morning, or I was as good as dead.

I was reflecting on what a miserable date I was, when the squad car pulled up, turned its spotlights on us, and the officer said, over the loudspeaker, "Set the stick down and put your hands up. Don't make any sudden moves."

Perfectly natural, I thought, embracing a sort of exhausted stoicism, for the officer to arrest a naked man and a woman dressed in an evening gown, sitting on a sidewalk in the pouring rain like a couple of drunks fresh off a bender.

Susan shielded her eyes and then looked at the spotlight. All the throwing up she'd done must have gotten rid of the potion in her, ended its amorous effects. "This," she said, in a calm and dispassionate voice, "is the worst night of my life." The officers got out of the car and started toward us.

I grunted. "That's what you get for trying to go out with a wizard."

She glanced aside at me, and her eyes glittered darkly for a moment. She almost smiled, and there was a sort of vindictive satisfaction to her tone when she spoke.

"But it's going to make a *fantastic* story."

Chapter 15

As it turned out, Linda Randall had a darn good reason for skipping out on our appointment Saturday night.

Linda Randall was dead.

I sneezed as I ducked under the yellow police tape in the sweatpants and T-shirt I had been allowed to pluck from the mess of my place before the police car had brought me across town to Linda Randall's apartment. And cowboy boots. Mister had dragged one of my sneakers off, and I hadn't had time to find it, so I wore what I had. Freaking cat.

Linda had died a bit earlier that evening. After getting to the scene, Murphy had tried to phone me, failed to get through, and then sent a squad car down to pick me up and bring me in to do my consultant bit. The dutiful patrolmen sent to collect me had stopped to check out the crazy naked guy a block away from my apartment, and had been surprised and more than a little suspicious when I turned out to be the very same man they were supposed to pick up and bring to the crime scene.

Dear Susan had come to my rescue, explaining away what had happened as "Just one of those things, tee-hee," and assuring the officers that she was all right and would be fine to drive home. She got a little pale around the edges when she saw once more the ruins of my apartment and the enormous dent the demon had put in the side of her car, but she made a bold face of it and eventually left the scene with that "I have a story to write" gleam in her eye. She stopped and gave me a kiss on the cheek on her way out, and whispered, "Not bad, Harry," in my ear. Then she patted my bare ass and got in her car.

I blushed. I don't think the cops noticed it, in the rain and the dark. The patrolmen had looked at me askance, but were more than happy to let me go put on some fresh clothes. The only things I had clean were more sweats and another T-shirt, this one proclaiming in bold letters over a little cartoon graveyard, "EASTER HAS BEEN CANCELED—THEY FOUND THE BODY."

I put those on, and my duster, which had somehow survived the demon attack, and my utterly inappropriate cowboy boots, and then I had gotten in the patrol car and been driven across town. I clipped my little ID card to my coat's lapel and followed the uniforms in. One of them led me to Murphy.

On the way, I took in little details. There were a lot of people standing around gawking. It was still fairly early, after all. The rain came down in a fine mist and softened the contours of the scene. There were several police cars parked in the apartment building's parking lots, and one on the lawn by the door leading out to the little concrete patio from the apartment in question. Someone had left his bulbs on, and blue lights flashed over the scene in alternating swaths of shadow and cold light. There was a lot of yellow police tape around.

And right in the middle of it all was Murphy.

She looked terrible, like she hadn't eaten anything that didn't come out of a vending machine or drunk anything but stale coffee since I had seen her last. Her blue eyes were tired, and bloodshot, but still sharp. "Dresden," she said. She peered up at me. "You planning on having King Kong climb your hair?"

I tried to smile at her. "We still need to cast our screaming damsel. Interested?"

Murphy snorted. She snorts really well for someone with such a cute nose. "Come on." She spun on one heel and walked up to the apartment, as though she wasn't exhausted and at the end of her rope.

The forensics team was already there, so we got some nifty plastic booties to put over our shoes and loose plastic gloves for our hands from an officer standing beside the door. "I tried to call earlier," Murphy said, "but your phone was out of service. Again, Harry."

"Bad night for it," I responded, wobbling as I slipped the booties on. "What's the story?"

"Another victim," she said. "Same M.O. as Tommy Tomm and the Stanton woman."

"Jesus," I said. "They're using the storms."

"What?" Murphy turned and fixed her eyes on me.

"The storm," I repeated. "You can tap storms and other natural phenomena to get things done. All natural fuel for the mojo."

"You didn't say anything about that before," Murphy accused.

"I hadn't thought of it until tonight." I rubbed at my face. It made sense. Hell's bells, that was how the Shadowman had been able to do all of that in one night. He'd called the demon and been able to send it after me, as well as appearing in the shadow he'd projected. And he'd been able to kill again.

"Have you got an ID on the victim?" I asked.

Murphy turned to go inside as she answered. "Linda Randall. Chauffeur. Age twenty-nine."

It was a good thing Murphy had turned away, or the way my jaw dropped would have told her that I knew the deceased, and she would have had all sorts of uncomfortable questions. I stared after Murphy for a second, then hurriedly veiled my expression and followed her inside the apartment.

Linda Randall's one-room apartment looked like the trailer of a rock band that did little besides play concerts, host parties, and fall into a stupor afterward. Dirty clothes were strewn on one side of a king-size bed. There was a disproportionate amount of clothing that looked as though it had been purchased from a Frederick's of Hollywood catalog—lacy and silky and satiny colors, all bright, designed to attract the eye. There were many candles around the bed, on shelves and dressers and a night table, most burned halfway down. The drawer of the night table was partly open, revealing a number of personal amusements—Linda Randall had, apparently, liked her toys.

The kitchenette, off to one side, looked largely unused, except for the coffeepot, the microwave, and the trash can, in which several pizza boxes were crammed. Maybe it was the pizza boxes that did it, that gave me a sudden pang of understanding and empathy for Linda. My own kitchen looked the same, a lot of the time, minus the microwave. Here had lived someone else who knew that the only thing waiting at home was a sense of loneliness. Sometimes it is comforting. Most often, it isn't. I'll bet Linda would have understood that.

But I'd never have the chance to know. The forensics team was gathered around the bed, concealing whatever was there, like a cluster of buzzards around the exposed head of the outlaws they used to bury up to their necks in the Old West. They spoke among themselves in low, calm voices, dispassionate as skilled dinner chatter, calling little details to the attention of their companions, complimenting one another on their observations.

"Harry?" Murphy said, quietly. Her tone of voice suggested that it wasn't the first time she'd said it. "Are you sure you're all right for this?"

My mouth twitched. Of course I wasn't all right for this. No one should ever be all right for this sort of thing. But instead of saying that, I told her, "My head's just aching. Sorry. Let's just get it over with."

She nodded and led me over toward the bed. Murphy was a lot shorter than most of the men and women working around the bed, but I had almost a head of height on all of them. So I didn't have to ask anyone to move, just stepped up close to the bed and looked.

Linda had been on the phone when she died. She was naked. Even this early in the year, she had tan lines around her hips. She must have gone to a tanning booth during the winter. Her hair was still damp. She lay on her back, her eyes half-closed, her expression tranquil as it hadn't been any time I'd seen her.

Her heart had been torn out. It was lying on the king-size bed about a foot and a half from her, pulped and squashed and slippery, sort of a scarlet and grey color. There was a hole in her chest, too, showing where bone had been splintered outward by the force that had removed her heart.

I just stared for a few moments, noting details in a sort of detached way. Again. Again someone had used magic to end a life.

I had to think of her as she sounded on the phone. Joking, a quick wit. A sort of sly sensuality, in the way she said her words and phrased her sentences. A little hint of insecurity around the edges, vulnerability that magnified the other parts of her personality. Her hair was damp because she'd been taking a bath before she came to see me. Whatever anyone said of her, she had been passionately, vitally alive. Had been.

Eventually, I realized how quiet the room was.

The men and women of the forensics team, all five of them, were looking up at me. Waiting. As I looked around, they all averted their gazes, but you didn't have to be a wizard to see what was in their faces. Fear, pure and simple. They had been faced with something that science couldn't explain. It rattled them, shook them to their cores, this sudden, violent, and bloody evidence that three hundred years of science and research was no match for the things that were still, even after all this time, lurking in the dark.

And I was the one who was supposed to have the answers.

I didn't have any for them, and I felt like shit for remaining silent as I stepped back and turned away from Linda's body, then walked across the room to the small bathroom. The tub was still full of water. A bracelet and earrings were laid out on the counter in front of a mirror, plus a little makeup, a bottle of perfume.

Murphy appeared beside me and stood with me, looking at the bathroom. She seemed a lot smaller than she usually does.

"She called us," Murphy said. "Nine one one has the call recorded. That's how we knew to come out here. She called and said that she knew who had killed Jennifer Stanton and Tommy Tomm and that now they were coming for her. Then she started screaming."

"That's when the spell hit her. The phone probably went out right after."

Murphy frowned up at me and nodded. "Yeah. It did. But it was working fine when we got here."

"Magic disrupts technology sometimes. You know that." I rubbed at one eye. "Have you talked to any relatives, anything like that?"

Murphy shook her head. "There aren't any relatives in town. We're looking, now, but it might take some time. We tried to reach her boss, but he wasn't available. A Mr. Beckitt?" She studied my face, waiting for me to say something. "You ever heard of him?" she asked, after a moment.

I didn't look back at Murphy. I shrugged.

Murphy's jaw tensed, little motions at the corners of her face. Then she said, "Greg and Helen Beckitt. Three years ago, their daughter, Amanda, was killed in a cross fire. Johnny Marcone's thugs were shooting it out with some of the Jamaican gang that was trying to muscle in on the territory back then. One of them shot the little girl. She lived for three weeks in intensive care and died when they took her off life support."

I didn't say anything. But I thought of Mrs. Beckitt's numb face and dead eyes.

"The Beckitts attempted to lodge a wrongful death suit against Johnny Marcone, but Marcone's lawyers were too good. They got it thrown out before it even went to court. And they never found the man who shot the little girl. Word has it that Marcone offered to pay them blood money. Make reparation. But they turned him down."

I didn't say anything. Behind us, they were putting Linda in a body bag, sealing her in. I heard men count to three and lift her, put her onto a gurney of some kind, and wheel her out. One of the forensics guys told Murphy they were going to take a break and would be back in ten minutes. She nodded and sent them out. The room got even more quiet.

"Well, Harry," she said. Her voice was hushed, like she didn't want to disturb the apartment's new stillness. "What can you tell me?" There was a subtle weight to the question. She might as well have asked me what I wasn't telling her. That's what she meant. She took her hand out of her jacket pocket and handed me a plastic bag.

I took it. Inside was my business card, the one I'd given to Linda. It was still curled a little, where I'd had to palm it. It was also speckled with what I presumed was Linda's blood. I looked at the part of the bag where you write the case number and the identification of the piece of evidence. It was blank. It wasn't on the records. It wasn't official. Yet.

Murphy was waiting for my answer. She wanted me to tell her something. I just wasn't sure if she was waiting for me to tell her that a lot of people have my card, and that I didn't know how it had gotten here, or if she wanted me to say how I had known the victim, how I had been involved with her. Then she would have to ask me questions. The kinds of questions you ask suspects.

"If I tell you," I said, "that I was having a psychic premonition, would you take me seriously?"

"What kind of premonition?" she said. She didn't look up at me.

"I sense . . ." I paused, thinking of my words. I wanted them to be very clear. "I sense that this woman will have a police record, probably for possession of narcotics and solicitation. I sense that she used to work at the Velvet Room for Madame Bianca. I sense that she used to be close friends and lovers with Jennifer Stanton. I sense that if she had been approached, yesterday, and asked about those deaths, that she would have claimed to know nothing."

Murphy mulled over my words for a moment. "You know, Dresden," she said, and her voice was tight, cool, furious, "if you'd *sensed* these things yesterday, or maybe even this morning, it's possible that we could have talked to her. It's possible that we could have found out something from her. It's even *possible*"—and she turned to me and slammed me against the doorway with one forearm and the weight of her body, suddenly and shockingly hard—"it's even possible," she snarled, "that she'd still be *alive*." She stared up at my face, and she didn't look at all like a cutesy cheerleader, now. She looked like a mother wolf standing over the body of one of her cubs and getting ready to make someone pay for it.

This time I was the one to look away. "A lot of people have my card," I said. "I put them up all over the place. I don't know how she got it."

"Godammit, Dresden," she said. She stepped back from me and walked away, toward the bloodstained sheets. "You're holding out on me. I know you are. I can get a warrant for your arrest. I can have you brought in for questioning." She turned back to me. "Someone's killed three people already. It's my *job* to stop them. It's what I do."

I didn't say anything. I could smell the soap and shampoo from Linda Randall's bath.

"Don't make me choose, Harry." Her voice softened, if not her eyes or her face. "Please."

I thought about it. I could bring everything to her. That's what she was asking—not half the story, not part of the information. She wanted it all. She wanted all the pieces in front of her so she could puzzle them together and bring the bad guys in. She didn't want to work the puzzle knowing that I was keeping some of the pieces in my pocket.

What could it hurt? Linda Randall had called me earlier that evening. She had planned on coming to me, to talk to me. She was going to give me some information and someone had shut her up before she could.

I saw two problems with telling Murphy that. One, she would start thinking like a cop. It would not be hard to find out that Linda wasn't exactly a high-fidelity piece of equipment. That she had numerous lovers on both sides of the fence. What if she and I were closer than I was admitting? What if I'd used magic to kill her lovers in a fit of jealous rage and then waited for another storm to kill her, too? It sounded plausible, workable, a crime of passion—Murphy had to know that the DA would have a hell of a time proving magic as a murder weapon, but if it had been a gun instead, it would have flown.

The second problem, and the one that worried me a lot more, was that there were already three people dead. And if I hadn't gotten lucky and creative, there would have been two more dead people, back at my apartment. I still didn't know who the bad guy was. Telling Murphy what little more I knew wouldn't give her any helpful information. It would only make her ask more questions, and she wanted answers.

If the voice in the shadows knew that Murphy was heading the investigation to find him, and was on the right track, he would have no qualms about killing her, too. And there was nothing she could do to protect herself against it. She might have been formidable to your average criminal, but all the aikido in the world wouldn't do her any good against a demon.

Then, too, there was the White Council. Men like Morgan and his superiors, secure in their own power, arrogant and considering themselves above the authority of any laws but their own, wouldn't hesitate to remove one police lieutenant who had discovered the secret world of the White Council.

I looked at the bloodstained sheets and thought of Linda's corpse. I thought of Murphy's office, and what it would look like with her sprawled on the floor, her heart torn from her chest, or her throat torn out by some creeping thing from beyond.

"Sorry, Murph," I said. My voice came out in a rasping whisper. "I wish I could help you. I don't know anything useful." I didn't try to look up at her, and I didn't try to hide that I was lying.

I sensed, more than saw, the hardening around her eyes, the little lines of hurt and anger. I'm not sure if a tear fell, or if she really just raised a hand to brush back some of her hair. Then she turned to the front door, and shouted, "Carmichael! Get your ass in here!"

Carmichael looked equally as slobbish as he had a few days ago, as though the passage of time hadn't changed him—it certainly hadn't changed his jacket, only the food stains on his tie and the particular pattern of rumplement to his hair. There had to be something comforting, I reflected, in that kind of stability. No matter how bad things got, no matter how horrible or sickening the scene, you could count on Carmichael to look like the same quality of crap. He glared at me as he came in. "Yeah?"

She tossed the plastic bag to him, and he caught it. "Mark that and log it," she said. "Hang around for a minute. I want a witness."

Carmichael looked down at the bag and saw my card. His beady eyes widened. He looked back up at me, and I saw the shift in gears in his head, reclassifying me from *annoying ally* to *suspect.*

"Mr. Dresden," Murphy said. She kept her tone frosty, polite. "There are some questions we'd like to ask you. Do you think you could come down to the station and make a statement?"

Questions to be asked. The White Council would convene and execute me in a little more than thirty hours. I didn't have time for questions. "I'm sorry, Lieutenant. I've got to comb my hair tonight."

"Tomorrow morning, then," she said.

"We'll see," I said.

"If you aren't there in the morning," Murphy said, "I'm going to ask for a warrant. We'll come and find you and by God, Harry, I'll get some answers to this."

"Suit yourself," I told her, and I started for the door. Carmichael took a step forward and stood in my way. I stopped and looked at him, and he kept his eyes focused on the center of my chest. "If I'm not under arrest," I told her, "then I presume I'm free to go."

"Let him go, Ron," Murphy said. Her tone of voice was disgusted, but I could hear the hurt underneath it. "I'll talk to you again soon, Mr. Dresden." She stepped closer and said, in a perfectly even tone, "And if it turns out that you're the one behind all this, rest assured. Whatever you can do and whatever you can pull, I will find you and I will bring you down. Do you understand me?"

I did understand, really. I understood the pressure she was under, her frustration, her anger, and her determination to stop the killing from happening again. If I was some kind of hero from a romance novel, I'd have said something brief and eloquent and heartrending. But I'm just me, so I said, "I do understand, Karrin."

Carmichael stepped out of my way.

And I walked away from Murphy, who I couldn't talk to, and from Linda, who I couldn't protect, my head aching, weary to my bones, and feeling like a total piece of shit.

Chapter 16

I walked down the block from Linda Randall's apartment building, my thoughts and emotions a far more furious thunderstorm than the one now rolling away from the city, out over the vastness of the lake. I called a cab from the pay phone outside a gas station and stood about with my back resting against the wall of the building in the misting rain, scowling and waiting.

I had lost Murphy's trust. It didn't matter that I had done what I had to protect both her and myself. Noble intentions meant nothing. It was the results that counted. And the results of my actions had been telling a bald-faced lie to one of the only people I could come close to calling a friend. And I wasn't sure that, even if I found the person or persons responsible, even if I worked out how to bring them down, even if I did Murphy's job for her, that what had happened between us could ever be smoothed over.

My thoughts were on that topic and similar issues of doom and gloom when a man with a hat pulled low over his face began to walk past me, stopped halfway, then turned and drove his fist into my belly.

I had time to think, *Not again,* and then he struck me a second, and third time. Each blow drove into my guts, thrust me back against the unyielding wall, made me sick. My breath flew out of my mouth in a little, strangling gasp, and even if I'd had a spell already in mind, I wouldn't have had the breath to speak it.

I sort of sagged when he stopped hitting me, and he threw me to the ground. We were at a well-lit gas station, just before midnight on a Friday night, and anything he did was in full view of any cars going by. Surely, God, he didn't plan on killing me. Though at the moment, I was too tired and achy to care.

I lay there for a moment, dazed. I could smell my attacker's sweat and cologne. I could tell it was the same person who had jumped me the night before. He grabbed my hair, jerked my head up, and, with an audible snip of steel scissors, cut off a big lock of my hair. Then let me go.

My blood went cold.

My hair. The man had cut off my hair. It could be used in almost any kind of magic, any kind of deadly spell, and there wouldn't be a damned thing I could do to stop it.

The man turned away, walking quickly, but not running. In a flood of panic and desperation, I leapt at his leg, got him around the knee, and yanked hard. I heard a distinctive little *pop,* and then the man screamed, "Son of a bitch!" and fell heavily to earth. One fist, one very large and knob-knuckled fist, was clutched around my hair. I tried to suck in a breath, and leapt for that hand.

My attacker's hat had fallen off, and I recognized him—one of Johnny Marcone's men who had followed me from the hotel on Thursday afternoon, the one who had begun limping after jogging after me for several blocks. Apparently, Gimpy had a trick knee, and I had just made it jump through its hoop.

I grabbed his wrist and held on with both hands. I'm not a particularly strong man, but I'm made out of wire, and stubborn as hell. I curled up around his wrist and hung on, trying to pry at his thick fingers. Gimpy tried to jerk his arm away. He was carrying a lot of muscle on that arm, but it wasn't enough to move the weight of my whole body. He shoved at me with his other arm, trying to push me off of him, then started pounding at me with one fist.

"Let go of me, dammit," Gimpy shouted. "Get off of me!"

I hunched my head down, my shoulders up, and hung on. If I could dig my thumbs into his tendons for long enough, his hand would have to open, no matter how strong he was. I tried to imagine his wrist as Play-Doh and my thumbs as solid steel, pushing into him, and held on for everything I was worth. I felt his fingers start to loosen. I could see the dark, thin strands of my hair.

"Jesus Christ," someone shouted. "Hey, Mike, come on!"

There were running footsteps.

And then a couple of young guys dressed in jogging suits and sneakers came over and dragged me off Gimpy. I screamed, incoherently, as my hands slipped from Gimpy's wrist. Some of my hair spilled out, onto the wet concrete, but more stayed in his grip as his fingers closed over it again.

"Easy, easy man," one of the guys was saying as they dragged me off. "Take it easy."

There wasn't any use struggling against the pair of them. Instead, I dragged in a breath and managed to gasp, "Wallet. He's got my wallet."

Considering the way I was dressed, compared to Gimpy's suit and coat, that was one lie that was never going to get off the ground. Or at least, it wouldn't have, if Gimpy hadn't turned and started hurrying away. The two men let me go, confused. Then, taking the cautious route, they started away, walking hurriedly back to their car.

I struggled to my feet and after Gimpy, wheezing like a leaky accordion. Gimpy headed across the street to a car, and was already in it and leaving by the time I got there. I shambled to a halt in a cloud of his exhaust, and stared dully after his taillights as he drove off into the misting rain.

My heart pounded in my chest and didn't slow down even after I recovered my breath. My hair. Johnny Marcone now had a lock of my hair. He could give it to someone who used magic, and use it to do whatever they damn well pleased to me.

They could use my hair to tear my heart from my chest, rip it right out, like they had done to Jennifer Stanton, Tommy Tomm, and poor Linda Randall. Marcone had warned me to stop, twice, and now he was going to take me out once and for all.

My weariness, fear, and fatigue were abruptly burned away by anger. "Like hell," I snarled. "Like hell you will!"

All I had to do was to find them, find Johnny Marcone, find Gimpy, and find Marcone's wizard, whoever he or she was. Find them, get my hair back, lay them out like ninepins, and send in Murphy to round them up.

By God, I wasn't going to take this lying down. These assholes were serious. They'd already tried to kill me once, and they were coming after me again. Marcone and his boys—

No, I thought. Not Marcone. That didn't make any sense, unless it had been Marcone's gang dealing the ThreeEye from the very beginning. If Marcone had a wizard in residence, why would he have tried to bribe me away? Why not just swipe a lock of hair from me when he'd sent the thug with the bat, and then kill me when I didn't pay attention?

Could it be Marcone? Or could his thug be playing two sides of the street?

I decided that ultimately it didn't matter. One thing was clear: Someone had a lock of my hair. Some wizard, somewhere, meant to kill me.

Whoever this wizard was, he wasn't much good—I'd seen that when I'd wiped out his shadow-sending spell. He couldn't stand up to me if I could force him into a direct confrontation—he might have a lot of moxie, and a lot of raw power, to harness the storms as he had and to slap a demon into servitude. But he was like a big, gawky teenager, new to his strength. I had more than just strength, more than just moxie. I had training, experience, and savvy on my side.

Besides. At the moment I was mad enough to chew up nails and spit out paper clips.

The Shadowman couldn't take a shot at me yet. He didn't have that kind of strength. He needed to wait for the storms that came each spring, and to use them to kill me. I had time. I had time to work. If I could just find out where they were, where Gimpy had taken my hair, I could go after him.

The answer came to me in a flash, and it seemed simple. If the hair could be used as a link to the rest of me, I should be able to reverse it—to create a link from me back to the hair. Hell, maybe I could just set it on fire, burn it all up from my apartment. The formula for a spell like that would be screwy as hell, though. I needed Bob. Bob could help me work out a spell, figure out a formula like that in minutes instead of hours or days.

I grimaced. Bob was gone, and would be for almost another twenty-four hours. There was no way I could work out that formula in less than ten or twelve hours by myself, and I didn't think my brain was coherent enough to come up with solid calculations at the moment, anyway.

I could have called Murphy. Murphy would have known where Marcone was lurking, and Gimpy would probably be nearby. She could have given me an idea, at least, of how to find Gentleman Johnny, Gimpy, and the Shadowman. But she never would, now. And even if she did, she'd demand to know the whole story, and after I'd told it to her, she'd try to take me into protective custody or something ridiculous like that.

I clenched my fists, hard, and my nails dug into my palms. I should trim them sometime—

I looked down at my nails. Then hurriedly crossed the street to stand under the gas station's lights, and stared at my hands.

There was blood under my fingernails, where they'd bitten

into Gimpy's wrists. I threw back my head and laughed. I had everything I needed.

I moved back out of the misting rain and squatted down on the concrete sidewalk. I used a bit of chalk I keep in my duster pocket to sketch out a circle on the concrete, surrounding me. Then I scraped the blood out from under my nails and put it onto the concrete between my feet. It glistened in the fine, misty fall of rain.

The next part took me a moment to figure out, but I settled for using the tracking spell I already knew rather than trying to modify it to something a little more dignified. I plucked out a couple of nose hairs and put them in the circle, too, on top of the bits of Gimpy's skin and blood. Then I touched a finger to the chalk circle and willed energy into it, closing it off.

I gathered up my energy, from my anger, my renewed fear, my aching head and queasy stomach, and hurled it into the spell. *"Segui votro testatum."*

There was a rush of energy that focused on my nostrils and made me sneeze several times in a row. And then it came to me, quite strongly, the scent of Gimpy's cologne. I stood up, opened the circle again with a swipe of my foot, and walked out of it. I turned in a slow circle, all the way around. Gimpy's scent came to me strongly from the southwest, out toward some of the richer suburbs of Chicago.

I started laughing again. I had the son of a bitch. I could follow him back to Marcone, or whoever he was working for, but I had to do it now. I hadn't had enough blood to make it last long.

"Hey, buddy!" The cabby leaned out the window and glared at me, the engine running at an idle, the end of his cheroot glowing orange.

I stared at him for a second. "What?"

He scowled. "What, are you deaf? Did someone call for a cab?"

I grinned at him, still angry, still a little light-headed, still eager to go kick Gimpy and the Shadowman's teeth in. "I did."

"Why do I get all the nuts?" he said. "Get in."

I did, closing the door behind me. He eyed me suspiciously in the mirror and said, "Where to?"

"Two stops," I told him. I gave him my apartment's address, and sat back in the seat, my head automatically drawn toward the southwest, toward where the men who wanted to kill me were.

"That's one," he said. "Where's number two?"

I narrowed my eyes. I needed a few things from my apartment.

My talismans, my blasting rod, my staff, a fetish that should still be vital. And after that, I was going to have a serious talk with one of Chicago's biggest gangsters.

"I'll tell you when we get there."

Chapter 17

We ended up at the Varsity, a club Marcone owned in a Chicago suburb. It was a busy place, catering to much of the college-age crowd to be found on this side of the city, and even at one-thirty in the morning it was still fairly crowded for someplace so isolated, alone in a strip mall, the only business open at this time of the evening, the only lit windows in sight.

"Loony," the cabby muttered as he drove away, and I had to pause for a moment and agree with him. I had directed him about in a meandering line, the spell I'd cast letting me literally follow my nose along Gimpy's trail. The spell had begun fading almost the moment I'd cast it—I didn't have enough blood to make a more lasting enchantment—but it had held long enough for me to zero in on the Varsity, and to identify Gimpy's car in the parking lot. I walked past the windows and, sure enough, in a large, circular booth in the back I saw Johnny Marcone, the bull-necked Mr. Hendricks, Gimpy, and Spike, sitting together and talking. I ducked out of sight in a hurry, before one of them noticed me. Then walked back into the parking lot to consider exactly what I had at my disposal.

A bracelet on each wrist. A ring. My blasting rod. My staff.

I thought of all the subtle and devious means by which I might tilt the situation in my favor—clever illusions, convenient faltering of electricity or water, a sudden invasion of rats or cockroaches. I could have managed any of them. Not many people who use magic are that versatile, but very few have the kind of experience and training it takes to put such spells together on the fly.

I shook my head, irritated. I didn't have time to bother with subtlety.

Power into the talismans, then. Power into the ring. I reached for the power in both the staff and rod, cool strength of wood and seething anger of fire, and stepped up to the front door of the Varsity.

Then I blew it off its hinges.

I blew it out, rather than in. Pieces flew toward me and bounced off the shield of air I held in front of me, while others rained back behind me, into the parking lot. It wouldn't do to injure a bunch of innocent diners on the other side. You only get one chance to make a first impression.

Once the door was off, I pointed my blasting rod inside and spoke a command. The jukebox slammed back against the wall as though a cannonball had impacted it, and then melted into a puddle of liquid-plastic goo. The music squealed out the speakers and stopped. I stepped into the doorway and released a pent-up wave of energy from my ring. Starting at the door and then circling throughout the room, the lightbulbs began to explode with sharp little detonations and showers of powdered glass and glowing bits of filament. People at the bar and at all the wooden tables scattered around the room reacted as people tend to do in this sort of situation. They started screaming and shouting, rising to their feet or ducking beneath their tables in confusion. A few ducked out the fire door at the back of one side of the room. Then there was an abrupt and profound silence. Everyone stood stock-still and stared at the doorway—they stared at me.

At the back table, Johnny Marcone regarded the doorway with his passionless, money-colored eyes. He was not smiling. Mr. Hendricks, beside him, was glaring at me, his single eyebrow lowered far enough to threaten him with blinding. Spike was tight-lipped and pale. Gimpy stared at me in pure horror. None of them made any moves or any sound. I guess seeing a wizard cut loose can do that to you.

"Little pig, little pig, let me in," I said, into the silence. I planted my staff on the ground and narrowed my eyes at Marcone. "I'd really like to talk to you for a minute, John."

Marcone stared at me for a moment, then his lips twitched up at the corners. "You have a singular manner of persuasion, Mr. Dresden." He stood up and spoke aloud to the room without ever taking his eyes off me. He must have been angry, but the icy exterior concealed it. "Ladies and gentlemen, the Varsity is closing early, it would seem. Please make an orderly exit through the door nearest you. Don't worry about your bills. Mr. Dresden, if you would step out of the doorway and allow my customers to leave?"

I stepped out of the doorway. The place cleared out fast, customers and staff alike, leaving me alone in the room with Marcone, Hendricks, Spike, and Gimpy. None of them moved as they waited for the customers, the witnesses, to leave. Gimpy started sweating. Hendricks's expression never changed. The big man was as patient as a mountain lion, ready to leap out on the unsuspecting deer.

"I want my hair back," I said, as soon as the last college-age couple had hustled out the door.

"Beg pardon?" Marcone said. His head tilted to one side, and he seemed genuinely puzzled.

"You heard me," I said. "This piece of trash of yours"—I swung my blasting rod up and pointed it at Gimpy—"just jumped me outside a gas station across town and cut off some of my hair. I want it back. I'm not going to go out like Tommy Tomm did."

Marcone's eyes abruptly shone with a terrible, cold, money-colored anger. He turned his head, deliberately, to Gimpy.

Gimpy's broad face went a bit more pasty. He blinked a trickle of sweat out of his eyes. "I don't know what he's talking about, boss."

Marcone's gaze never wavered. "I presume, Mr. Dresden," he said, "that you have some kind of proof?"

"Look at his left wrist," I said. "He's got several fingernail marks on his skin where I grabbed him."

Marcone nodded, those cold, tiger's eyes on Gimpy's, and said, almost gently, "Well?"

"He's lying, boss," Gimpy protested. He licked at his lips. "Hell, I got some fingernail marks from my girl. He knew that. You know what you said, he's for real, he knows things."

The pieces of the puzzle fell into place. "Whoever killed Tommy Tomm knows that I'm on his trail," I said. "Your rival, whoever it is selling the ThreeEye. Gimpy here must have gotten a sweet deal from him to turn on you. He's been providing your rival with information all along, running errands for him."

Gimpy couldn't have played a game of poker to save his life. He stared at me in horror, shook his head in protest.

"There's an easy way to settle this," Marcone said, his voice smooth and even. "Lawrence. Show me your wrist."

"He's lying, boss," Gimpy Lawrence said again, but his voice was shaking. "He's just trying to mess with your head."

"Lawrence," Marcone said, his tone the gentle reproof of parent to child.

Gimpy Lawrence knew it was over. I saw the desperate decision in his face before he actually moved. "Liar!" he howled at me. He got up, lifting his hand from underneath the table. I had time to realize he held a revolver, virtually a twin to my own .38, in his fist, before he started shooting.

Several things happened at the same time. I lifted my hand, focusing my will on the bracelet of tiny medieval-style shields around my left wrist, and hardened the protective energies around me. Bullets hammered against it with whining noises, striking sparks in the near dark of the restaurant.

Spike leapt clear of the table, staying low, a small Uzi-style automatic now in his hand. Hendricks was more ruthless and direct, reacting with the mindlessly violent instincts of a savage. With one hand, the big bodyguard hauled Marcone back, putting his own bulk between the mob boss and Gimpy Lawrence. With the other hand, he produced a compact semiautomatic.

Gimpy Lawrence turned his head and saw Hendricks and his gun. He panicked, turning his own weapon toward the larger man.

Hendricks shot him with a ruthless efficiency, three sharp claps of sound, three flashes of muzzle light. The first two shots hit Gimpy in the middle of his chest, driving him back a pair of steps. The third hit him over the right eyebrow, jerked his head back, and toppled him to the ground.

Gimpy Lawrence had dark eyes, like mine. I could see them. His head turned toward me as he lay there on the floor. I saw him blink, once. Then the lights went out of them, and he was gone.

I stood there for a moment, stunned. Grand entrance or not, this wasn't what I had wanted to happen. I didn't want to kill anyone. Hell, I didn't want anyone to die, not me and not them. I felt sick. It had been a sort of game, a macho contest of showmanship I had been determined to win. All of a sudden, it wasn't a game anymore, and I just wanted to walk away from it alive.

We all stood there, no one moving. Then Marcone said, from beneath Hendricks, "I wanted him alive. He could have answered several questions, first."

Hendricks frowned and got up off of Marcone. "Sorry, boss."

"That's all right, Mr. Hendricks. Better to err on the side of caution, I suppose." Marcone stood up, straightened his tie, then went and knelt by the body. He felt the man's throat, then wrist, and shook his head. "Lawrence, Lawrence. I would have paid you twice what they offered you, if you'd come to me with it. You never were very smart, were you?" Then, his face showing no more emotion than it had the entire evening, Marcone peeled back Gimpy Lawrence's left sleeve, and studied the man's wrist. He frowned, and lowered the arm again, his expression pensive.

"It would seem, Mr. Dresden," he said, "that we have a common enemy." He turned to focus his gaze on me. "Who is it?"

I shook my head. "I don't know. If I did, I wouldn't be here. I thought maybe it was you."

Marcone lifted his eyebrows. "You should have known me better than that, Mr. Dresden."

It was my turn to frown. "You're right. I should have." The killings had been more vicious, savage than Marcone would have cared to use. Competitors might have to be removed, but there would be no sense in making a production of it. Certainly, there was no reason to murder bystanders, like Linda, like Jennifer Stanton. It was inefficient, bad for business.

"If he has something of yours, you are welcome to take it, Mr. Dresden," Marcone said. He looked around the room and sighed. "Better hurry. I think the Varsity has seen its last crowd. A shame."

It was hard, but I walked over to Gimpy Lawrence's body. I had to set aside my staff, my rod, to rifle the corpse's pockets. I felt like a ghoul, crouched over the body of a dead man, picking what was valuable to me off of it, out of his pockets.

I didn't find my hair anywhere. I looked up at Marcone, and he regarded me, my eyes, without any readable emotion.

"Nothing," I told him.

"Interesting. He must have passed the material in question to someone else before he came here," Marcone said.

"Someone after he got here, maybe?"

Marcone shook his head. "I am quite sure he did not do that. I would have noticed."

"I believe you," I told him, and I did. "But who?"

"Our enemy," Marcone said. "Obviously."

I closed my eyes, suddenly sagging with weariness. "Dammit."

Marcone said nothing. He stood up, and issued a few quiet orders to Hendricks and Spike. Hendricks wiped down his gun with a napkin, then left it lying on the floor. Spike went over behind the bar and started to do something involving a power cord and a bottle of whiskey.

I gathered up my staff and rod, stood up, and turned to Marcone. "Tell me what else you know. I need everything you have if I'm going to catch this guy."

Marcone considered that, and nodded. "Yes, you do. Unfortunately, you chose a public forum for this discussion. You have set yourself up in the eyes of anyone who cared to watch as my enemy. As understandable as your reasons might have been, the fact that you have publically defied me remains. I cannot let that go without response, regardless of my personal feelings, without inviting more of the same. I must maintain control. It isn't personal, Mr. Dresden. It's business."

I tightened my jaw, and my grip on my blasting rod, and made sure my shield was still there, ready to go. "So what are you going to do about it?"

"Nothing," he said. "I need do nothing. Either our enemy will kill you, in which case I need not risk myself or my people in removing you, or you will find him in time and bring him down. If you do defeat him, I will let it be understood to any who ask that you did so at my behest, after which I will be inclined to forget this evening. Either way, it profits me best to wait and see."

"If he kills me," I pointed out, "if I'm the next one to have my heart ripped out, you still won't know where he is. You won't be any closer to removing him and protecting your business."

"True," Marcone said. Then he smiled, an expression that lasted for only a fraction of a second. "But I think you will not be such easy prey. I think that even if he kills you, he will reveal himself in some way. And since our encounter the other day, I think I have a better feel for what sorts of things to look for."

I scowled at him and turned to go, moving briskly toward the door.

"Harry," he said. I stopped and turned back around.

"On a personal note—I know nothing that would profit you in any case. All of his people we managed to take revealed nothing. They were that afraid of him. No one seems to know just where the drug comes from, from what it is made, or where this person does business. Shadows, they say. That he is always in the shadows. That is all that I have learned."

I regarded Johnny Marcone for a moment, and then nodded, once. "Thank you."

He shrugged. "Good luck. I think it would be best if you and I did not encounter one another in the future. I cannot tolerate any more interference in my affairs."

"I think that's a good idea, too," I said.

"Excellent. It is good to have someone who understands." And then he turned back toward his remaining two men, leaving the corpse of Gimpy Lawrence on the floor behind him.

I turned and trudged out of the place, into the night and the cold and the misty rain. I still felt sick, could still see Gimpy Lawrence's eyes as he died. I could still hear Linda Randall's husky laughter in my head. I still regretted lying to Murphy, and I still had no intentions of telling her any more than I already had. I still didn't know who was trying to kill me. I still had no defense to present to the White Council.

"Let's face it, Harry," I told myself. "You're still screwed."

Chapter 18

Have you ever felt despair? Absolute hopelessness? Have you ever stood in the darkness and known, deep in your heart, in your spirit, that it was never, ever going to get better? That something had been lost, forever, and that it wasn't coming back?

That's what it felt like, walking out of the Varsity, walking out into the rain. When I'm in turmoil, when I can't think, when I'm exhausted and afraid and feeling very, very alone, I go for walks. It's just one of those things I do. I walk and I walk and sooner or later something comes to me, something to make me feel less like jumping off a building.

So I walked. It was pretty stupid, in retrospect, walking around Chicago late on a Saturday night. I didn't look up very often. I walked and let things roll around in my head, my hands in the pockets of my duster, which flapped around my long legs while the light rain gradually plastered my hair to my head.

I thought about my father. I usually do, when I get that low. He was a good man, a generous man, a hopeless loser. A stage magician at a time when technology was producing more magic than magic, he had never had much to give his family. He was on the road most of the time, playing run-down houses, trying to scratch out a living for my mother. He wasn't there when I was born.

He wasn't there when she died.

He showed up more than a day after I'd been born. He gave me the names of three magicians, then took me with him, on the road, entertaining children and retirees, performing in school gymnasiums and grocery stores. He was always generous, kind—more kind and more generous than we could afford, really. And he was always a little bit sad. He would show me pictures of my mother, and talk about her, every night. It got to where I almost felt that I knew her, myself.

As I got older, the feeling increased. I saw my father, I think, as she must have—as a dear, sweet, gentle man. A little naive, but honest and kind. Someone who cared for others, and who didn't value material gain over all else. I can see why she would have loved him.

I never got to be old enough to be his assistant, as he had promised me. He died in his sleep one night. An aneurism, the doctors said. I found him, cold, smiling. Maybe he'd been dreaming of Mother when he went. And as I looked at him, I suddenly felt, for the very first time in my life, utterly, entirely alone. That something was gone that would never return, that a little hole had been hollowed out inside of me that wasn't ever going to be filled again.

And that was how I felt, that rainy spring night in Chicago, walking along the streets, my breath pluming into steam, my right boot creaking with every step, dead people occupying all of my thoughts.

I shouldn't have been surprised, I suppose, when after hours of walking, my steps carried me back to Linda Randall's apartment. The police were all gone, now, the lights all off, all the gawking neighbors cozy in their beds. It was quiet in the apartment complex. Dawn wasn't yet brushing the sky, but somewhere, on a window ledge or in a rooftop nest, a bird was twittering.

I was at the end of my strength, my resources. I hadn't thought of anything, hadn't come up with any brilliant ideas. The killer was going to get a spell together to kill me the next time he had a storm to draw on, and from the way the air felt that could be anytime. If he didn't kill me, Morgan would certainly have the White Council set to execute me at dawn on Monday. The bastard was probably out lobbying votes, already. If the matter came before the Council, I wouldn't stand a chance.

I leaned against the door to Linda's apartment. It was striped with POLICE LINE—DO NOT CROSS yellow-and-black tape. I didn't really realize what I was doing until I had already worked a spell that opened the door, unfastened the lowest strip of yellow tape, and walked into her apartment.

"This is stupid, Harry," I told myself. I guess I wasn't in the mood to listen. I walked around Linda's apartment, smelling her perfume and her blood. They hadn't come to clean up the blood, yet. The apartment manager would probably have to handle that, later. They never really show you details like that at the movies.

I eventually found myself lying on the floor, on the carpeting next to Linda Randall's large bed. I was curled on my side, my back to her bed, my face toward the sliding glass doors that led out to her little concrete patio. I didn't feel like moving, like going anywhere, like doing anything. Useless. It had all been useless. I was going to die in the next two days.

The worst part was that I wasn't sure that I cared. I was just so tired, exhausted from all the magic I'd had to use, from the walking, from the bruises and punches and lack of sleep. It was dark. Everything was dark.

I think I must have fallen asleep. I needed it, after everything that had happened. I don't remember anything else, until the sun was too bright in my eyes.

I blinked and lifted a hand against the light, keeping my eyes closed. Mornings had never been my best time, and the sun had risen above the tops of the buildings across the street, cheerful springtime sunshine that dashed down through Linda Randall's curtains, through my eyelids and into my brain. I grumbled something, and rolled over, face to the cool darkness under Linda's bed, back to the warm sunlight.

But I didn't go back to sleep. Instead, I started to get disgusted with myself.

"What the hell are you doing, Harry?" I demanded, out loud.

"Lying down to die," I told myself, petulantly.

"Like hell," my wiser part said. "Get off the floor and get to work."

"Don't wanna. Tired. Go away."

"You're not too tired to talk to yourself. So you're not too tired to bail your ass out of the alligators, either. Open your eyes," I told myself, firmly.

I hunched my shoulders, not wanting to obey, but against my better judgment, I did open my eyes. The sunlight had turned Linda Randall's apartment into an almost cheerful place, overlaid with a patina of gold—empty still, to be sure, but warm with a few good memories. I saw a high-school yearbook lying nearby, underneath the bed, several photographs serving as bookmarks. There was also a framed picture of a much-younger Linda Randall, smiling brightly, none of the jaded weariness I had seen in her in evidence, standing in her graduation robes between a kind-looking couple in their late fifties. Her parents, I presumed. She looked happy.

And, lying just in the edge of a stray little beam of sunlight, one that was already retreating as the sun rose above the edge of the buildings, was a small, red plastic cylinder with a grey cap.

My salvation.

I snatched it out from under the bed. I was shaking. I shook the canister, and it rattled. A roll of film was inside. I opened up the canister and dumped the film into my hand. The plastic leader had been retracted into the case—there were pictures on the film, but they hadn't been developed yet. I closed the film up again and reached into the pocket of my duster and drew out another canister, the one I'd found at Victor Sells's lake house. The two were a match.

My mind spun around, taking off down a whole new track. An entirely new realm of possibility had opened up to me, and somewhere in it might be my opportunity, my chance to get out of this alive, to catch the killer, to salvage everything that had started going to hell.

But it still wasn't clear. I couldn't be sure what was going on, but I had a possible link now, a link between the murder investigation and Monica Sells's aborted inquiry into the disappearance of her husband, Victor. I had another lead to follow, but there wasn't much time to follow it. I had to get up, to get on my feet, and get going, fast. You can't keep a good wizard down.

I stood up, grabbed my staff and rod, and started toward the door. The last thing I needed was to get caught trespassing on a crime scene. It could get me arrested and stuck in holding, and I'd be dead before I could get bail. My mind was already rolling ahead, working out the next step, trying to find this photographer who had been at Victor's beach house, and getting these pictures developed and seeing if there was anything in them that was worth Linda Randall's death.

It was then that I heard a sound, and stopped. It came again, a quiet scraping.

Someone turned the key in the dead bolt of the apartment's front door and swung it open.

Chapter 19

There was no time to flee beneath the bed, or into the bathroom, and I didn't want to be limited in mobility in any case. I leapt forward and stood behind the door as it opened, keeping very still.

A man entered—slim, short, harried-looking. His hair, a listless shade of brown, was drawn back into a ponytail. He wore dark cotton pants, a dark jacket, and carried a pouch on a strap at his side. He shut the door, most of the way, and looked around with great agitation. But, like most people who are too nervous to be thinking clearly, he was seeing less than he should have been, and though his head swept over where I would have been in his peripheral vision, he didn't notice me. He was a good-looking man, or so it seemed, with strong lines to his jaw and cheekbones.

He crossed the room and stopped short when he saw the bloodstained bed. I saw him clench his hands into fists. He made a strange, cawing little sound, then hurried forward, to throw himself down on the floor by the bed and start pawing underneath it. After a few seconds, his pawing grew more frantic, and I heard him curse out loud.

I slid my fingers over the smooth surface of the film canister in my pocket. So. The mysterious photographer lurking outside of Victor Sells's lake house was here looking for the film. I had a feeling in my stomach like I get when I finish a particularly difficult jigsaw puzzle—a peculiar satisfaction mingled with a touch of smugness.

I settled my staff and rod silently into the corner by the door and flipped my official police consultant's badge, complete with my photograph on it, out of my duster, so that it showed against the black canvas. I covered my ratty old T-shirt with the coat and hoped that the man would be too rattled and nervous to notice that I was wearing sweatpants and cowboy boots beneath the duster.

I kept my hands in my pockets, pushed the door shut with a little nudge of my boot, and just as it closed, said, "So. Returning to the scene of the crime. I knew we'd catch you if I just waited."

The man's reaction would have had me rolling in laughter on any other day. He jerked, slammed his head against the bottom of the bed, yelped, drew himself back from the bed, turned to look at me, and all but leapt back over the bed in surprise when he saw me. I revised my opinion of his looks—his mouth was too pinched, his eyes too small and too close together, giving him the intent, predatory look of a ferret.

I narrowed my eyes and stalked toward him one slow pace at a time. "Just couldn't stay away, could you?"

"No!" he said, "Oh, God! You don't understand. I'm a photographer. See? See?" He fumbled with the case at his side and produced a camera from it. "Taking pictures. For the papers. That's what I'm doing here, just trying to get a good look around."

"Save it," I told him. "We both know you aren't here to take pictures. You were looking for this." And I pulled the film canister out of my pocket, held it up, and showed it to him.

His babbling stopped, and he stood stock-still, staring at me. Then at the canister. He licked his lips and started trying to say something.

"Who are you?" I asked. I kept my voice gruff, demanding. I tried to think of what Murphy would sound like, if I was downtown with her right now, waiting for her to ask me questions.

"Uh, Wise. Donny Wise." He swallowed, staring at me. "Am I in some kind of trouble?"

I narrowed my eyes at him and sneered, "We'll see about that. Do you have identification?"

"Sure, yeah."

"Let me see it." I speared him with a glance, and added, "Slowly."

He goggled at me and reached for his hip pocket with exaggerated slowness. With one hand, he drew out his wallet and flipped it open to his driver's license. I stalked toward him, snatched it, and studied it. His license and picture agreed with the name he'd given me.

"Well, Mr. Wise," I began, "this is an ongoing investigation. So long as you give me your cooperation, I don't think that we—"

I looked up to see him peering at my name badge, and my voice trailed off. He jerked his wallet back, and accused, "You're not a cop!"

I tilted my head back at an arrogant angle. "Okay. Maybe not. But I work with the cops. And I've got your film."

He cursed again and started stuffing his camera back into his bag, clearly meaning to leave. "No. You got nothing. Nothing that connects any of this to me. I'm out of here."

I watched him start past me, toward the door. "Don't be so hasty, Mr. Wise. I really think you and I have things to discuss. Like a dropped film canister underneath the deck of a house in Lake Providence, last Wednesday night."

He flicked a quick glance up at me. "I have nothing to say to you," he mumbled, "whoever the hell you are." He reached for the door and started to open it.

I gestured curtly to my staff in the corner, and hissed, in my best dramatic voice, "*Vento servitas,*" jerking my hand at the doorway. My staff, driven by tightly controlled channels of air moving in response to my evocation, leapt across the room and slammed the door shut in front of Donny Wise's nose. He went stiff as a board. He turned to face me, his eyes wide.

"My God. You're one of them. Don't kill me," he said. "Oh, God. You've got the pictures. I don't know anything. Nothing. I'm no danger to you." He tried to keep his voice calm, but it was shaking. I saw him tilt his eyes at the glass sliding doors to the little patio, as though calculating his chances of making it there before I could stop him.

"Relax, Mr. Wise," I told him. "I'm not here to hurt you. I'm after the man who killed Linda. Help me. Tell me what you know. I'll take care of the rest."

He let out a harsh little laugh, and eased a half step toward the glass windows. "And get myself killed? Like Linda, like those other people? No way."

"No, Mr. Wise. Tell me what you know. I'll put a stop to the killings. I'll bring Linda's murderer to justice." I tried to keep my voice soothing, even, fighting against the frustration I felt. Hell, I'd wanted to rattle him, but I hadn't meant to scare him so badly that he wanted to jump through a plate-glass sliding door. "I want these people stopped just as badly as you do."

"Why?" he demanded. I saw a little contempt in his eyes, now. "What was she to you? Were you sleeping with her, too?"

I shook my head. "No. No, she's just one more dead person who shouldn't be."

"You're not a cop. Why risk your ass to do this? Why go up against these people? Haven't you seen what they can do?"

I shrugged. "Who else is going to?" He didn't answer me, so I held up the film canister. "What are these pictures, Mr. Wise? What is on this film that was worth killing Linda Randall for?"

Donny Wise rubbed his palms over his thighs. His ponytail twitched as he looked about the room. "I'll make you a deal. Give me the film, and I'll tell you what I know."

I shook my head. "I might need what's on here."

"What's there isn't any good to you if you don't know what you're looking at," he pointed out. "I don't know you from Adam. I don't want any trouble. All I want is to get my ass out of this alive and in one piece."

I stared at him for a moment. If I traded him, I'd lose the film, and whatever was on it. If I didn't, and if he was telling me the truth, the film wouldn't do me any good. The trail had led me here, to him. If I didn't dig up a lead to somewhere else, I was dead.

So I snapped my fingers, letting my staff rattle to the floor. Then I tossed him the film, underhand. He dropped it, and stooped to recover it, studying me warily.

"After I get out of here," he said, "we're quits. I've never seen you before."

I nodded. "Fine. Let's have it."

Donny swallowed and ran a hand back over his hair, giving his ponytail a nervous little tug at the end of the motion. "I knew Linda from around. I'd taken some pictures of her, for a portfolio. I do shoots for some of the girls around town. They want to make it into magazines, most of them."

"Adult magazines?" I asked.

"No," he snapped, nervous still, "Uncle Abner's magazine for children. Of course adult mags. Nothing really classy, but you can make some good money even if you're not Hugh Hefner's type.

"So on Wednesday, Linda comes to me. She says she's got a deal for me. I shoot some pictures for her and give her the film, and I get—and she's real nice to me. All I have to do is show up where she says, shoot a roll through the windows, and go. Deliver to her the next day. So I did it. And now she's dead."

"Out in Lake Providence," I said.

"Yeah."

"What did you see there?" I asked.

Donny Wise shook his head, his eyes drawn past me to the bed again. "Linda. Some other people. No one I knew. They were having some kind of party. All candles and stuff. It was storming like hell, a lot of thunder and lightning, so I couldn't really hear them. I worried for a while about someone looking up and seeing me in the lightning, but I guess they were too busy."

"They were having sex," I said.

"No," he snapped. "They was playing canasta. Yeah, sex. The real thing, not fake stuff on a set. The real thing don't look as good. Linda, some other woman, three men. I shot my roll and got out."

I grinned, but he didn't seem to have noticed the double entendre. You just don't get quality lowlife often enough anymore. "Can you describe any of these other people?"

He shook his head. "I wasn't looking. But they wasn't being too particular, if you take my meaning. Turned my stomach."

"Did you know what Linda wanted with the pictures?"

He looked at me and then snickered, as though I were extremely simple. "Jesus, buddy. What do you think someone wants with pictures like that? She wanted to get leverage on somebody. Hell, it wouldn't hurt her reputation any if pictures of her in the middle of an orgy got out. But it might have, some of the people with her. What kind of simp, wanna-be cop are you?"

I ignored the question. "What are you going to do with the film, Donny?"

He shrugged. "Trash it, probably." I saw his eyes flick from side to side, and I knew that he was lying to me. He'd keep the film, find out who was in the pictures, and if he thought he could get away with it, he'd try to weasel whatever profit he could out of it. He seemed the type, and I trusted my instincts.

"Allow me," I said, and snapped my fingers. "*Fuego.*"

The canister's grey lid flew off in a little whoosh of flame, and Donny Wise yelped, drawing his hand back sharply. The red canister burst into flame on its way to the ground and landed there in a crumpled, smoking lump.

He stared at the film, then up at me, his mouth gaping.

"I hope I don't find out you've lied to me, Donny," I told him. He went white as a sheet, assured me that he hadn't, then turned and fled out of the apartment, knocking loose two bits of police tape on the way out. He didn't close the door behind him.

I let him go. I believed him. He didn't seem bright enough to make up a story on the fly, as rattled as he'd been. I felt a ferocious surge of triumph, of anger, and of the desire to find this person, whoever it was, who was taking the raw forces of life and creation and turning them to the ends of destruction, and to put him in the trash with the rest of the garbage. Whoever he was, murdering with magic and killing people by degrees with the ThreeEye drug, he was someone I wanted to put down. My brain lurched into gear, now that there was something to work with, some other possibility for tomorrow morning than me dying in a variety of gruesome ways.

Linda Randall had been planning on blackmailing someone. I took a staggering mental leap and figured it was Victor, or someone out at his house during the party. But why? I didn't have any pictures now, only the information I'd gotten from Donny Wise. I couldn't afford to wait around. I *had* to pursue the lead he'd given me if I was to get to the bottom of this, and find out who had killed Linda.

How had I managed to get into all of this trouble in only a few days? And how in the world had I managed to stumble across what appeared to be a complex and treacherous little plot by chance, out at the house in Lake Providence, on a separate investigation entirely?

Simple answer—it hadn't been an accident. It had all been by design. I had been directed there. Someone had wanted me out at the lake house, had wanted me to get involved and to find out what was going on out there. Someone who was nervous as hell around wizards, who refused to give out her name, who had carefully dropped phrases that would make me believe her ignorance, who had to rush out quickly from her appointment and who was willing to let five hundred dollars go, just to get me off the phone a few seconds faster. Someone had drawn me out and forced me into the open, where I had attracted all sorts of hostile attention.

That was the key.

I gathered up my staff and rod and stalked out the door.

It was time to talk to Monica Sells.

Chapter 20

The cabby dropped me off a block away from Monica Sells's house in the suburbs. I was running out of time, out of Murphy's loan, and out of patience, so I didn't waste any daylight in walking down the street toward her place.

It was a cute little house, two stories, a couple of young trees in the front yard, just now starting to rival the house for height. There was a minivan in the driveway, and a basketball goal, well used. The lawn was grown rather long, but all the recent rains left a good excuse for that. The street was a quiet one, and it took me a moment to realize that most of the houses on it were not occupied. FOR SALE signs stood in many of the yards. Sparse curtains draped over empty, gaping windows, like cobwebs. There wasn't a lot of birdsong, for a street with so many trees, and I couldn't hear any dogs barking as I walked along the sidewalk. Overhead, clouds were thickening, building up for another thunderstorm.

Taken all together, it had the feel of someplace blighted, a place where a black wizard had set up shop. I swung up through the Sells yard and to the front door.

I rang the bell, and waited.

There was no answer.

I knocked. I leaned on the doorbell.

Still no answer.

I tightened my jaw and looked around. I didn't see anyone, so I turned back to the door, preparing to use a spell to open it.

Instead, the door swung open, maybe six inches. Monica Sells stood inside, peering out at me with her green eyes. She was dressed in jeans, a plain flannel shirt with the sleeves rolled up, and her hair was covered by a bandana. She wore no makeup. She looked both older and more appealing that way—I think maybe because it was a more natural look for her, something that was closer to the sort of person she really was, rather than the nicer clothes and jewelry she'd worn when she visited my office. Her face went pale, her lips bloodless.

"I don't have anything to say to you, Mr. Dresden," she said. "Go away."

"I can't do that," I said. She started to swing the door shut, but I jammed the end of my staff into the doorway, keeping it from closing.

"I'll call the police," she said, voice strained. She leaned against the door, trying to keep me from coming in.

"Do it," I growled, and then I played a hunch, "and I'll tell them about you and your husband." I was taking a shot in the dark, but what the hell. She didn't know that I didn't know what the hell was going on.

My instincts paid off. I heard her suck in a breath and felt her resistance on the door sag a little. I put my shoulder to the door, leaned into it hard, and she stepped back from me in surprise. I don't think she'd expected me to physically force my way into her house. Hell, I hadn't expected me to do that. I hadn't realized how angry I was until I saw the look of panic on her face when she looked up at me. I don't know what I looked like, but it must not have been friendly.

I stopped. I closed my eyes. I took a deep breath, and tried to get a handle on my anger. It wouldn't profit me anything to lose control.

That was when she went for the stunner.

I heard her move, opened my eyes in time to see her snatch a black-plastic case the size of a cellular phone from the piano and lunge toward me. Her face was pale, frightened. Blue lightning danced between the two tines of the stunner as she shoved it at my stomach.

I swept my staff, upright, from right to left, and the buzzing device went past me, along with her lunge, striking the doorframe behind me. I slipped past her, into the living room, turning to face her as she recovered and turned around.

"I won't let you hurt them," she snarled. "Not you, not anyone. I'll *kill* you before I let you touch them, wizard." And then she was coming at me again, fury replacing the terror in her eyes, a grim determination to succeed that made me think of Murphy for a second. For the first time, she was looking me in the face. For the first time she forgot to keep her eyes averted from mine, and in that second, I saw inside of her.

Things seemed to slow down for a moment. I had time to see the color of her eyes, the structure of her face. To recognize where I had seen them before, why she had looked familiar to me. I had time to see, behind her eyes, the fear and the love that motivated every move she made, every step she took. I saw what had moved her to come to me, why she was afraid. I saw her grief, and I saw her pain.

And the pieces all fell into place. Knowing the emotions that drove her, the terrible love that she was showing even now, it all seemed perfectly obvious, and I felt stupid for not figuring it out days ago.

"Stop," I said, or tried to say, before she thrust the stunner at my chest. I dropped staff and rod alike in a clatter of falling wood, and caught her wrist in both of my hands. She pushed the stunner up at my face, and I let her do it.

It got to within about three inches of me, the light bright in my eyes. Then I drew in a breath and puffed it out onto the stunner, along with an effort of will. There was a spark, a little puff of smoke, and then it went dead in her hands, like every other electronic gizmo seemed to do whenever I came around. Hell, I was surprised it had taken as long as it did to stop working. And even if it hadn't, it wasn't any trouble for me to hex it into uselessness.

I continued holding her wrist, but the driving tension behind her arm had eased away to nothing. She was staring at my face, her eyes wide with shock from the meeting of our gazes. She started shaking and dropped the useless stunner from limp fingers. It clattered to the floor. I let go of her, and she just stared at me.

I was shaking, too. A soulgaze is never something pleasant or simple. God, sometimes I hated that I had to live with that. I hadn't wanted to know that she had been abused as a child. That she'd married a man who provided her with more of the same, as an adult. That the only hope or light that she saw in her life was in her two children. There hadn't been time to see all of her reasons, all of her logic. I still didn't know why she had drawn me into this entire business—but I knew that it was, ultimately, because she loved her two kids.

And that was all I really needed, that and one other connection, the nagging resemblance to someone that I had noticed in her at my office. The rest fell into place from there.

It took Monica Sells a moment to recover herself. She did it with remarkable speed, as though she were a woman used to drawing on a mask again after having it knocked off. "I . . . I'm sorry, Mr. Dresden." She lifted her chin, and regarded me with a fragile, wounded pride. "What do you want here?"

"A couple of things," I told her. I stooped down to recover my staff, my rod. "I want my lock of hair back. I want to know why you came to me last Thursday, why you dragged me into this mess. And I want to know who killed Tommy Tomm and Jennifer Stanton and Linda Randall."

Monica's eyes grew even duller, and her face paled. "Linda's dead?"

"Last night," I told her. "And someone's planning on taking me out the same way, the next chance they get."

Outside, in the far distance, thunder rumbled. Another storm was in the works, slowly building. When it got to town, I was a dead man. It was as simple as that.

I looked back to Monica Sells, and it was all over her face—she knew about the storm just as well as I did. She knew about it, and there was a sort of sad and weary frustration in her eyes.

"You have to go, Mr. Dresden," she said. "You can't be here when . . . You've got to go, before it's too late."

I stepped toward her. "You're the only chance I have, Monica. I asked you once before to trust me. You've got to do it again. You've got to know that I'm not here to hurt you or your—"

A door opened, in the hallway behind Monica. A girl, on the gawky end of preadolescence, with hair the color of her mother's, leaned out into the hallway. "Mom?" she said in a quavering voice. "Mom, are you okay? Do you want me to call the police?" A boy, perhaps a year or two younger than his sister, poked his head out, too. He was carrying a well-used basketball in his hands, turning it in nervous little gestures.

I looked back to Monica. Her eyes were closed. There were tears coming, trailing down her cheeks. It took her a moment, but she drew in a breath and spoke to the girl in a clear, calm voice, without turning around. "I'm fine," she told them. "Jenny, Billy, get back into the room and lock the door. I mean it."

"But Mom—" the boy began.

"Now," Monica said. Her voice was strained.

Jenny put a hand on her brother's shoulder. "C'mon, Billy." She looked at me for just a moment. Her eyes were too old and too knowing for a child her age. “C’mon.” The two vanished back into the room, closed the door, and locked it behind them.

Monica waited until they were gone, and then broke down into more tears. “Please. Please, Mr. Dresden. You have to go. If you’re here when the storm comes, if he knows . . .” She buried her face in her hands and made a quiet, croaking sound.

I stepped closer to her. I had to have her help. No matter how much pain she was in, no matter what kind of agony she was going through, I had to have her help. And I thought I knew the names to invoke to get it.

I can be such a bastard sometimes.

“Monica. Please. I’m up against a wall. I’m out of options. Everything I have leads here. To you. And I don’t have time to wait. I need your help, before I wind up just like Jennifer and Tommy and Linda.” I sought her eyes, and she looked up at me without turning her gaze away. “Please. Help me.” I watched her eyes, saw the fear and the grief and the weariness there. I saw her look at me as I leaned on her, and demanded more out of her than she could afford to give.

“All right,” she whispered. She turned away and walked toward the kitchen. “All right. I’ll tell you what I know, wizard. But there’s nothing I can do to help you.” She paused at the doorway and looked back at me. Her words fell with the weight of conviction, simple truth. “There’s nothing anyone can do, now.”

Chapter 21

Monica Sells had a cheerful, brightly colored kitchen. She collected painted cartoon cows, and they ranged over the walls and cabinet doors of the room in a cheerful, bovine sort of indolence. The refrigerator was covered with crayon drawings and report cards. There was a row of colored glass bottles on the windowsill. I could hear wind chimes outside, restlessly stirred by a cool, rising wind. A big, friendly cow clock on the wall swung its tail back and forth, *tick, tick, tick.*

Monica sat down at the kitchen table. She drew up her legs beneath her, and seemed to relax by a few degrees. Her kitchen, I sensed, was her sanctuary, the place where she retreated when she was upset. It was lovingly maintained, sparkling clean.

I let her relax for as long as I could, which wasn't long. I could almost feel the air building up to greater tension, the storm brewing in the distance. I couldn't afford to play with kid gloves. I was just about to open my mouth, to start pushing, when she said, "Ask questions, wizard. I'll answer them. I wouldn't even know where to start, myself." She didn't look at me. She didn't look at anything.

"All right," I said. I leaned against the kitchen counter. "You know Jennifer Stanton, don't you. You're related to her."

Her expression didn't change. "We have our mother's eyes," she confirmed. "My little sister was always the rebel. She ran away to become an actress, but became a whore instead. It suited her, in her own way. I always wanted her to stop, but I don't think she wanted to. I'm not sure she knew how."

"Have the police contacted you yet, about her death?"

"No. They called my parents, down in St. Louis. They haven't realized, yet, that I live in town. Someone will notice soon, I'm sure."

I frowned. "Why didn't you go to them? Why did you come to me?"

She looked over at me. "The police can't help me, Mr. Dresden. Do you think they would believe me? They'd look at me like I was some kind of lunatic, if I went to them babbling about magic spells and rituals." She grimaced. "Maybe they'd be right. Sometimes I wonder if I'm going crazy."

"So you came to me," I said. "Why didn't you just tell me the truth?"

"How could I?" she asked. "How could I walk into the office of someone I didn't even know, and tell him—" She swallowed, and squeezed her eyes shut over more tears.

"And tell me what, Monica?" I asked. I kept my voice soft. "Who killed your sister?"

Wind chimes tinkled outside. The friendly cow clock went *tick, tick, tick.* Monica Sells drew in a long, shuddering breath and closed her eyes. I saw her gathering up the frayed threads of her courage, knotting them up as tightly as she could. I knew the answer, already, but I needed to hear it from her. I needed to be sure. I tried to tell myself that it would be good for her to face such a thing, just to say it out loud. I wasn't sure I bought that—like I said, I'm not a very good liar.

Monica squeezed her hands into tight fists, and said, "God help me. God help me. It was my husband, Mr. Dresden. It was Victor." I thought she would dissolve into tears, but instead she just hunched tighter into her little defensive ball, as though she expected someone to start hitting her.

"That's why you wanted me to find him," I heard myself say. "That's why you sent me out to the lake house, to look for him. You knew he was there. You knew that if you sent me out there, he would see me." My voice was quiet, not quite angry, but the words pounded around Monica Sells like sledgehammers throwing up chips of concrete. She flinched from each of them.

"I had to," she moaned. "God, Mr. Dresden. You don't know what it was like. And he was getting worse. He didn't start as a bad man, really, but he kept getting worse and worse, and I was afraid."

"For your kids," I said.

She nodded, and rested her forehead on her knees. And then

the words started spilling out of her, slowly at first, and then in a greater and greater rush, as if she couldn't hold back the immense weight of them any longer. I listened. I owed it to her, for walking all over her feelings, for forcing her to talk to me.

"He was never a bad man, Mr. Dresden. You have to understand. He worked hard. He worked so hard for us, to give us something better. I think it was because he knew that my parents had been so wealthy. He wanted to give me just as much as they could have, and he couldn't. It would make him so frustrated, so angry. Sometimes he would lose his temper. But it wasn't always so bad. And he could be so kind, sometimes, too. I thought that maybe the children would help him to stabilize.

"It was when Billy was about four that Victor found the magic. I don't know where. But he started getting obsessed with it. He brought home books and books. Strange things. He put a lock on the door to the attic, and after dinner he'd vanish up there. Some nights, he wouldn't come to bed. Some nights, I thought I could hear things, up there. Voices. Or things that weren't voices." She shuddered.

"He started to get worse. He'd get angry, and things would happen. Little things. The drapes would catch on fire at one edge. Or things would fly off the walls and break." She turned her haunted gaze toward her cute, tacky cows for a moment, as though assuring herself that they were still there.

"He'd scream at us for no reason. Or burst out laughing for no reason. He . . . He saw things. Things I couldn't see. I thought he was going crazy."

"But you never confronted him," I said, quietly.

She shook her head. "No. God forgive me. I couldn't. I had gotten used to being quiet, Mr. Dresden. To not making a fuss." She took a deep breath and continued. "Then, one night, he came to me and woke me up. He made me drink something. He told me that it would make me see, make me understand him. That if I drank, I would see the things he saw. That he wanted me to understand him, that I was his wife." This time, she did start crying, tears that coursed silently down her cheeks, the corners of her mouth.

Something else clicked solidly into place, where I'd already thought it would go. "The ThreeEye," I said.

She nodded. "And . . . I saw things, Mr. Dresden. I saw *him*." Her face screwed up, and I thought she was going to vomit. I could sympathize. To have the Third Sight suddenly opened to you like that, not knowing what it was, what was happening to you; to look on the man you had wed, who had given you children, and to see him for what he truly was, obsessed with power, consumed by greed—it had to have been hell. And it would remain with her. Always. She would never find the memory fading, never find the comfort and solace of years putting a comfortable padding between her and the image of her husband as a monster.

She continued, speaking in a low, hurried rush. "I wanted more. Even when it was over, even though it was horrible, I wanted more. I tried not to let it show, but he could tell. He looked into my eyes and he *knew*, Mr. Dresden. Like you did just now. And he started to laugh. Like he'd just won the lottery. He kissed me, he was so happy. And it made me sick.

"He started making more of the drug. But he could never make enough. It drove him berserk, furious. And then he started to realize that when he was angry, he could do more. He'd look for excuses to be angry. He'd drive himself into rages. But it still wasn't enough." She swallowed. "That's when . . . when."

I thought of frightened pizza drivers and faerie commentary on human "sporting." "That's when he realized that he could touch other people's emotions, too," I said. "Use them to help power his magic."

She nodded, and curled tighter in on herself. "It was only me, at first. He'd frighten me. And afterward I would be so exhausted. Then he found out that for what he was doing, lust worked better. So he started looking around. For backers. Investors, he called them." She looked up at me, her eyes pleading. "Please, Mr. Dresden. You have to understand. It wasn't always so bad. There were moments that I could almost see him again. That I thought he was going to come back to us."

I tried to look on her with compassion. But I wasn't sure I felt anything but fury, that someone, *anyone* should treat his family that way—or anyone else, for that matter. My feelings must have showed on my face, because Monica quickly averted her eyes, and huddled down in fear. She spoke in a hurried voice, as though to put off my rage, in the voice of a woman who has put off rage with desperate words more than once.

"He found the Beckitts. They had money. And he told them that if they would help him, he would help them get their vengeance on Johnny Marcone. For their daughter. They put their trust in him. They gave him all the money he needed."

I thought of the Beckitts, and their lean, hungry faces. I thought of Mrs. Beckitt's dead eyes.

"And he started the rituals. The ceremony. He said he needed our lust." Her eyes shifted left and right, and the sickened look on her face grew deeper. "It wasn't so bad. He would close the circle, and all of a sudden, nothing mattered. Nothing but flesh. I could lose myself for a while. It was almost like an escape." She rubbed her hand on the leg of her jeans, as if trying to wipe something foul off of it. "But it wasn't enough. That's when he started talking to Jennifer. He knew what she did. That she would know the right kind of people. Like her, like Linda. Linda introduced him to Marcone's man. I don't know his name, but Victor promised him something that was enough to bring him into the circle.

"I didn't have to go all the time, then. Either Jenny or I would stay with the children. Victor made the drug. We started to make money. Things got better for a little while. As long as I didn't think too much." Monica took a deep breath. "That's when Victor started getting darker. He called demons. I saw them. And he said he needed more power. He was hungry for it. It was horrible, like watching a starving animal, forever pacing. And I saw him start . . . start *looking* at the children, Mr. Dresden. It made me afraid. The way he looked at them, sometimes, I knew—" This time she buckled and doubled toward the floor with a groan. She shuddered and wept, out of control. "Oh, God. My babies. My babies."

I wanted to go over to her. To offer her my hand to hold, to put an arm over her shoulders and to tell her that it would be all right. But I knew her, now. I had looked inside. It would make her scream. God, Harry, I thought. Haven't you tortured this poor woman enough?

I rummaged in cabinets until I found a glass. I ran cold water from the sink, poured it into the glass, then went over and put it down by her. She straightened in her chair and took the glass between shaking hands. She took a sip, and spilled a little onto her chin.

"I'm sorry," I said. It was all I could think of to say.

If she heard me, it didn't show. She sipped water, then continued, as if desperate to finish, to get the taste of the words out of her mouth. "I wanted to leave him. I knew he'd be furious, but I couldn't let the children stay close to him. I tried to talk to Jenny about it. And she took matters into her own hands. My little sister, trying to protect me. She went to Victor and told him that if he didn't let me leave, she'd go to the police and to Johnny Marcone. She'd tell them all about him. And he . . . He . . ."

"He killed her," I said. Hell. Victor hadn't needed any of Jennifer Stanton's hair to kill her. Any kind of sample of bodily fluids would have worked. With the ceremonies of lust that he'd been holding, he'd have had ample opportunity to collect from poor Jennifer Stanton. Maybe he'd even had her bring him a sample from Tommy Tomm. Or maybe Jennifer and Tommy Tomm had just been too close, as they were making love, for the spell to affect just one of them when he killed them.

"He killed her," Monica confirmed. Her shoulders slumped with a sudden weariness. "That's when I came to you. Because I thought you might be able to see. Be able to do something, before he hurt my babies. Before he killed someone else. And now Linda's dead, too. And soon you, Mr. Dresden. You can't stop him. No one can."

"Monica," I said.

She shook her head and curled up in a miserable little ball. "Go," she said. "Oh, God. Please go, Mr. Dresden. I don't want to see it when he kills you, too."

My heart felt like a lump of cold wax in my chest. I wanted so badly to tell her that everything would be all right. I wanted to dry her tears and tell her that there was still joy in the world, that there was still light and happiness. But I didn't think she would hear me. Where she was, there was nothing but an endless, hopeless darkness full of fear, pain, and defeat.

So I did the only thing I could. I withdrew in silence and left her to her weeping. Perhaps it would help her start to heal.

To me, it only sounded like pieces of glass falling from a shattered window.

As I walked toward the front door, a little motion to the left caught my eye. Jenny Sells stood in the hallway, a silent wraith. She regarded me with luminous green eyes, like her mother's, like the dead aunt whose namesake she was. I stopped and faced her. I'm not sure why.

"You're the wizard," she said, quietly. "You're Harry Dresden. I saw your picture in the newspaper, once. The *Arcane*."

I nodded.

She studied my face for a long minute. "Are you going to help my mom?"

It was a simple question. But how do you tell a child that things just aren't that simple, that some questions don't have simple answers—or any answer at all?

I looked back into her too-knowing eyes, and then quickly away. I didn't want her to see what sort of person I was, the things I had done. She didn't need that. "I'm going to do everything I can to help your mom."

She nodded. "Do you promise?"

I promised her.

She thought that over for a moment, studying me. Then she nodded. "My daddy used to be one of the good guys, Mr. Dresden. But I don't think that he is anymore." Her face looked sad. It was a sweet, unaffected expression. "Are you going to kill him?"

Another simple question.

"I don't want to," I told her. "But he's trying to kill me. I might not have any choice."

She swallowed and lifted her chin. "I loved my Aunt Jenny," she said. Her eyes brightened with tears. "Momma won't say, and Billy's too little to figure it out, but I know what happened." She turned, with more grace and dignity than I could have managed, and started to leave. Then said, quietly, "I hope you're one of the good guys, Mr. Dresden. We really need a good guy. I hope you'll be all right." Then she vanished down the hall on bare, silent feet.

I left the house in the suburbs as quickly as I could. My legs drove me down the oddly silent sidewalk, and back to the corner where the cabby was waiting, meter ticking away.

I got in the cab and told the cabby to drive me to the nearest pay phone. Then I closed my eyes and struggled to think. It was hard, through all the pain I felt. Maybe I'm stupid or something, but I hate to see people like Monica, like little Jenny, hurting like that. There shouldn't be pain like that in the world, and every time I run into it, it makes me furious. Furious and sad. I didn't know if I wanted to scream or to cry. I wanted to pound Victor Sells's face in, and I wanted to crawl into bed and hide under the covers. I wanted to give Jenny Sells a hug, and to tell her that everything would be all right. And I was still afraid, all tight and burning in my gut. Victor Sells, of the shadows and demons, was going to kill me as soon as the storm rolled in.

"Think, Harry," I told myself. "*Think*, dammit." The cabby gave me an odd look in the rearview mirror.

I stuffed down all the feelings, all the fear, all the anger into a tight little ball. I didn't have time to let those feelings blind me now. I needed clarity, focus, purpose. I needed a plan.

Murphy. Murphy might be able to help me. I could tip her off about the lake house and send in the cavalry. They might find a stockpile of ThreeEye there. They could then arrest Victor like any other dealer.

But there were too many holes in that plan. What if Victor wasn't keeping his stores at the lake house? What if he eluded the police? Monica and her children would be in danger, if he did. Not only that, what if Murphy didn't listen to me? Hell, the judge might not issue a warrant to search private property on the word of a man who probably had a warrant out for his own arrest, now. Not only that, but the bureaucracy involved in working with the authorities in Lake Providence, on a Sunday, no less, would slow things down. It might not happen in time to save me from having my heart torn out. No, I couldn't rely on the police.

If this was any other time, if I was held in less suspicion by the White Council, I would report Victor Sells to them and let them handle the whole thing. They're not exactly soft on people using magic like Victor used it, to call up demons, to kill, to produce drugs. He had probably broken every Law of Magic. The White Council would waste no time in sending someone like Morgan to wipe Victor out.

But I couldn't do that, either. I was already under suspicion, thanks to Morgan's narrow-minded blindness. The Council was already meeting at sunrise on Monday. Some of the other members of the Council might listen to me, but they would be traveling, now. I had no way of reaching any of those who were sympathetic to me, no way of asking for help. There wasn't time, in fact, to try to round up any of my usual allies.

So, I concluded. It was up to me. Alone.

It was a sobering thought.

I had to confront Victor Sells, as strong a practitioner as I had ever gone up against, in his own place of power—the lake house. Not only that, but I had to do it without breaking any of the laws of magic. I couldn't kill him with sorcery—but somehow, I had to stop him.

Odds seemed really good that I was going to get killed, whether I tried to face him or not. To hell with it, then. If I was going to go out, it wasn't going to be while I was lying around moaning and bitching about how useless it all was. If Victor Sells wanted to take out Harry Blackstone Copperfield Dresden, he was going to have to shove his magic right down my throat.

This decision cheered me somewhat. At least I knew what I was doing now, where I was going. What I needed was an edge, I decided. Something to pull on Victor, something he wouldn't expect.

Now that I knew who he was, I understood the magic I had run into outside of my apartment a little bit better. It had been potent, deadly, but not sophisticated, not well controlled. Victor was powerful, strong, a natural mage—but he wasn't practiced. He didn't have any training If only I had something of his, something like his own hair, that I could use against him. Maybe I should have checked the bathroom at Monica's, but I had the feeling that he wouldn't have been that careless. Anyone who spends time thinking about how to use that sort of thing against people is going to be doubly paranoid that no one have the opportunity to use it against him.

And then it struck me—I did have something of Victor's. I had his scorpion talisman, back in the drawer of my desk at the office. It was one of his own devices, something close and familiar. I could use it to create a bond to him, to sort of judo his own power back against him and beat him with it, hands down, no questions asked.

I might have a chance, yet. I wasn't finished, not by a long shot.

The cabby pulled into a gas station and parked next to the pay phone. I told him to wait for me a minute and got out, fumbling a quarter from my pocket to make the call. If it did turn out that I wouldn't live to see tomorrow, I wanted to make damn sure that the hounds of Hell would be growling at Victor Sells's heels.

I dialed Murphy's number, down at the station.

It rang several times, and finally someone answered. The line was scratchy, noisy, and I could barely make out who it was. "Murphy's desk, this is Carmichael."

"Carmichael," I said loudly into the phone. "It's Harry Dresden. I need to talk to Murphy."

"What?" Carmichael said. There was a squeal of static. Dammit, the phones go to hell on me at the worst times. "I can't hear you. Murphy? You want Murphy? Who is this? Anderson, is that you?"

"It's Harry Dresden," I shouted. "I need to talk to Murphy."

"Eh," Carmichael grunted. "I can't hear you, Andy. Look, Murphy's out. She took that warrant down to Harry Dresden's office to take a look around."

"She *what*?" I said.

"Harry Dresden's office," Carmichael said. "She said she'd be back soon. Look, this connection is awful, try to call back." He hung up on me.

I fumbled for another quarter, my hands shaking, and dialed my own office number. The last thing I needed was for Murphy to go poking around in my office, maybe impounding things. If she stuck the scorpion in evidence, I was done for. I'd never be able to explain it to her in time. And if she saw me face-to-face, she might be furious enough with me to just have me slapped into holding and left there overnight. If that happened, I'd be dead by morning.

My phone rang a couple of times, then Murphy answered. The line was blissfully clear. "Harry Dresden's office."

"Murph," I said. "Thank God. Look, I need to talk to you."

I could practically feel her anger. "Too late for that now, Harry. You should have come to talk to me this morning." I heard her moving around. She started opening drawers.

"Dammit, Murph," I said, frustrated. "I know who the killer is. Look, you've got to keep out of that desk. It could be dangerous." I thought I had been going to tell her a lie, but I realized as I said it that I was telling the truth. I remembered seeing, or thinking I had seen, movement from the talisman when I had examined it before. Maybe I hadn't been imagining things.

"Dangerous," Murphy growled. I heard her scattering pens out of the top drawer of my desk, moving things around. The talisman was in the drawer beneath. "I'll tell you what's dangerous. Fucking with me is dangerous, Dresden. I'm not playing some kind of game here. And I can't trust what you say anymore."

"Murphy," I said, trying to keep my voice even, "you've got to trust me, one more time. Stay out of my desk. Please."

There was silence for a moment. I heard her draw in a breath, and let it out through her mouth. Then Murphy said, her voice hard, professional, "Why, Dresden? What are you hiding?"

I heard her open the middle drawer.

There was a clicking sound, and a startled oath from Murphy. The receiver clattered to the floor. I heard gunshots, shockingly loud, whining ricochets, and then a scream.

"Dammit!" I shouted at the phone. "Murphy!" I slammed the phone down and sprinted back to the cab.

The cabby blinked at me. "Hey, buddy. Where's the fire?"

I slammed the door shut, and gave him the address to my

office. Then I thrust all of my remaining cash at him, and said, “Get me there five minutes ago.”

The cabby blinked at the money, shrugged, and said, “Crazies. Cabbies get all the crazies.” Then he tore out into the street, leaving a cloud of smoke behind us.

Chapter 22

The building was locked on Sunday. I jammed my key in the lock, twisted it hard to open it, and jerked the keys out again. I didn't bother with the elevator, just hurtled up the stairs as quickly as I could.

Five stories' worth of stairs. It took me less than a minute, but I begrudged every second of it. My lungs were burning and my mouth was dry as sand as I reached the fifth floor and sprinted down the hallway to my office. The halls were quiet, empty, dim. The only light came from the exit signs and from the overcast day outside. Shadows stretched and settled in the closed doorways.

The door to my office was ajar. I could hear my ceiling fan squeaking on its mounting, underneath the labored wheezing of my own breath. The overhead light wasn't on, but the reading light on my desk must have been, because yellow light outlined the doorway and laid a swath of gold across the floor of the hall. I stopped at the threshold. My hands were shaking so much I could hardly hold my staff and rod.

"Murphy?" I called out. "Murphy, can you hear me?" My voice was hoarse, breathless.

I closed my eyes, and listened. I thought I heard two things.

The first was a labored breath, with a faint moan on the exhale. Murphy.

The second was a dry, scuttling sound.

I could smell gunpowder on the air.

I clenched my jaw in sudden anger. Victor Sells's little beastie, whatever it was, had hurt my friend. Like hell I was going to stand out here and give it the run of my office.

I shoved the door open with my staff and stalked into the office, my blasting rod extended before me and words of power upon my lips.

Directly in front of my office door is a table arranged with a series of pamphlets with titles like *Real Witches Don't Float So Good*, and *Magic in the Twenty-first Century*. I had written some of them myself. They were meant for the curious, for people who just wanted to know about witches and magic. I squatted for a moment, blasting rod aimed beneath the table, but saw nothing. I rose again, looking back and forth, rod still ready.

To the right of the door is a wall lined with filing cabinets and a couple of easy chairs. The cabinets were shut, but something could have been hiding beneath one of the chairs. I slid to my left, checked behind the door to the office, and pressed my shoulders to the wall, keeping my eyes on the room.

My desk is in the back corner, to the right as you come in the door, diagonal from it. It's a corner office. There are windows on either of the outside walls. My shades were, as usual, drawn. The overhead fan, in the center of the room, spun around with a tired little groan on every rotation.

I kept my eyes moving, my senses alert. I choked down my anger, ferociously, and made myself remain cautious. Whatever had happened to Murphy, I wouldn't do her any good by letting it happen to me, too. I moved slowly, carefully, my blasting rod held ready.

I could see Murphy's tennis shoes behind my desk. She looked like she was curled on her side, from the way her feet were angled, but I couldn't see the rest of her. I pushed forward, striding to the center of the back wall, keeping my blasting rod leveled like a gun at the floor behind the desk as it became visible.

Murphy lay there, curled on her side, her golden hair in an artless sprawl about her head, her eyes open and staring blindly. She was dressed in jeans, a button-down shirt, and a Cubs satin jacket. Her left shoulder was stained with a blot of blood. Her gun lay next to her, a couple of feet away. My heart stepped up into my throat. I heard her take a little breath and groan when she let it out.

"Murphy," I said. Then, louder, "Murphy."

I saw her stir, a fitful little motion that was in response to my voice. "Easy, easy," I told her. "Relax. Don't try to move. I'm going to try to help you."

I knelt next to her, very slowly, watching the room all around. I didn't see anything. I set my staff aside, and felt her throat. Her pulse was racing, thready. There was not enough blood for it to be a serious injury, but I touched her shoulder. Even through the jacket, I could feel the swelling.

"Harry?" Murphy rasped. "Is that you?"

"It's me, Murph," I told her, setting my blasting rod aside and slowly reaching for the phone. The middle drawer of my desk, where the scorpion talisman had been, was open and empty. "Just hang on. I'm going to call an ambulance to help you."

"Can't believe it. You bastard," Murphy wheezed. I felt her stir around a little. "You set me up."

I drew the phone down and dialed 911. "Hush, Murph. You've been poisoned. You need help, fast."

The 911 operator came on and took my name and address. I told her to send an ambulance prepared to treat someone for poisoning, and she told me to stay on the line. I didn't have time to stay on the line. Whatever had done this to Murphy, it was still around, somewhere. I had to get her out of there, and then I had to recover Victor's talisman, to be able to use it against him when I went out to the lake house.

Murphy stirred again, and then I felt something hard and cool flick around my wrist and *clicker-clack* shut. I blinked and looked down at her. Murphy's jaw was set in a stubborn line as she clicked the other end of the handcuffs shut around her own wrist.

"You're under arrest," she wheezed. "You son of a bitch. Wait till I get you in an interrogation room. You aren't going anywhere."

I stared at her, stunned. "Murph," I stammered. "My God. You don't know what you're doing."

"Like hell," she said, her lip lifting in a ghost of its usual snarl. She twisted her head around, grimacing in pain, and squinted at me. "You should have talked to me this morning. Got you now, Dresden." She broke off in a panting gasp, and added, "You jerk."

"You stubborn bitch from hell." I felt at a loss for a second, then shook my head. "I've got to get you out of here before it comes back," I said, and I stooped forward to try to gather her up.

That was when the scorpion exploded toward me from the shadows beneath my desk, a harsh burst of dry, scuttling motion. It wasn't a bug I could squash with my fingers, anymore. It was the size of a large terrier, all brown and glinting, and it was almost too fast to see coming.

I convulsed away from it, and saw the flash of its tail, saw its stinger whip forward and miss my eye by a hair breadth.

Something cool and wet speckled my cheek, and my skin started to burn. Venom.

My startled motion made my leg jerk, and kicked my staff and rod away from me. I rolled after the latter desperately. Murphy's handcuffs brought me up short, and both of us made sounds of discomfort as the steel bands cut at the base of our hands. I stretched for the rod, felt the smooth roundness of it on my fingertips, and then there was another scuttling sound and the scorpion came at my back. The rod squirted out from beneath my grasping fingers and rolled away, out of reach.

I didn't have time for a spell, but I grabbed at the middle drawer of my desk, jerked it all the way out of its frame and barely managed to shove it between the scorpion and myself. There was a hiss of air and a smacking sound of breaking wood. The scorpion's stinger plunged through the bottom of the desk drawer and stuck fast. A crab-claw pincer gouged a hole through my sweatpants and into my leg.

I screamed and hurled the drawer away. The scorpion, its tail still stuck, went with it, and they both landed in a heap a few feet away.

"Won't do you any good, Dresden," Murphy moaned incoherently. She must have been too far gone from the poison to understand what was going on. "I've got you. Stop fighting it. Get some answers from you, now."

"Sometimes, Murph," I panted, "you make things just a little harder than they need to be. Anyone ever tell you that?" I bent down to her, and slipped my cuffed wrist beneath her arm and around her back, drawing her own arm back with me, my right arm and her left bound by the handcuff.

"My ex-husbands," she moaned. I strained and lifted us both up off the ground, then started hobbling toward the door. I could feel the blood on my leg, the pain where the scorpion had ripped it, hot and hateful. "What's happening?" Confusion and fear trembled in Murphy's voice. "Harry, I can't see."

Shit. The poison was getting to her. The poison of the common brown scorpion found all over most of the United States isn't much more venomous than the sting of a bumblebee. Of course, most bumblebees aren't the size of the family dog, either. And Murphy wasn't a big person. If a lot of poison had been introduced into her system, the odds were against her. She needed medical attention, and she needed it immediately.

If my hands had been free, I would have taken up my staff and rod and done battle, but I didn't like my odds tied to Murphy—even if I could keep the thing off of me, it might land on her, sting her again, and put an end to her. I was at a bad angle to search for her keys, and I didn't have time to go down the ring trying them on the handcuffs one by one. Any magic that I could work fast enough to shatter the cuffs in time would probably kill me with flying shrapnel, and there wasn't time to work out a gentler escape spell. *Dammit, Dad,* I thought, *I wish you'd lived long enough to show me how to slip out of a pair of handcuffs.*

"Harry," Murphy repeated, her voice thready, "what's happening? I can't see."

I saved my breath and lugged Murphy toward the door without answering her. Behind me, there was a furious scraping and clicking. I looked back over my shoulder. The scorpion's stinger was stuck fast in the drawer, but the thing was rapidly ripping the wood to shreds with its pincers and legs.

I gulped, turned, and hobbled out of my office and down the hall with Murphy. I managed to swing the door to my office shut with one foot. Murphy's legs did little to support her, and the difference in our heights made the trip awkward as hell. I was straining to keep her upright and moving.

I reached the end of the hall, the door to the stairway on my right, the elevator on my left.

I stopped for a moment, panting, trying not to let the sounds of splintering wood down the hall rattle my judgment. Murphy sagged against me, speechless now, and if she was breathing, I couldn't tell. There was no way I was going to be able to carry her down the stairs. Neither one of us had enough left to manage that. The ambulance would be arriving in minutes, and if I didn't have Murphy down there when it arrived, I might as well just leave her on the floor to die.

I grimaced. I hated elevators. But I pushed the button and waited. Round lights over the elevator doors began counting up to five.

Down the hall from me, the splintering sounds stopped, and something crashed into my office door, rattling it on its frame.

"Hell's bells, Harry," I said aloud. I looked up at the lights. Two. A pause approximately ten centuries long. Three. "Hurry *up*," I snarled, and jabbed the button a hundred more times.

Then I remembered the bracelet of shields around my left wrist. I tried to focus on it but couldn't, with it twisted awkwardly beneath Murphy, supporting her. So I laid her down as gently and quickly as I could, then lifted my left hand and focused on the bracelet.

The lower third of my office door exploded outward, and the brown, gleaming form of the scorpion bounded across the hallway and into the wall. It was bigger, now. The damn thing was growing. It bounced off of the wall with a scrabbling, horrible agility, oriented on me, and hurtled down the hall toward me as fast as a man can run, its legs clicking and scuttling furiously over the floor. It leapt at me, claws extended, stinger flashing. I focused my will on the defensive shield the bracelet helped me form and maintain, struggling to get it together before the scorpion hit me.

I did it, barely. The invisible shield of air met the scorpion a handsbreadth from my body and sent it rebounding back onto its back. There it struggled for a second, awkward and flailing.

Behind me, the elevator dinged, and the doors swooped graciously open.

Without time to be delicate, I grabbed Murphy's wrist and hauled her into the elevator with me, jabbing at the button for the lobby. In the hall, the scorpion thrashed its tail and righted itself, oriented on me again with an uncanny intelligence, and flew toward me. There wasn't time to get my shield together again. I screamed.

The elevator doors swooped shut. There was a sharp thud, and the car rattled, as the scorpion smashed into them.

The car started down, and I tried to regain my breath. What the hell *was* that thing?

It wasn't just an insect. It was too fast, too damn smart for that. It had ambushed me, waiting until I had set my weapons aside to come after me. It had to be something else, some kind of power construct, built small, but designed to draw in energy, to get bigger and stronger, an arthropod version of Frankenstein's monster. It wasn't really alive, just a golem, a robot, a programmed thing with a mission. Victor must have figured out where his talisman had gotten to, and set a spell on it to attack anyone it came in contact with, the crazy bastard. Murphy had stumbled right into it.

It was still growing, getting faster and stronger and more vicious. Getting Murphy out of danger wasn't enough. I had to find a way to deal with the scorpion. I didn't want to, but I was the only one on the block who could. There was too much potential danger involved. What if it didn't stop growing? I had to kill it before it got out of control.

The lights on the elevator panel kept counting down, four to three to two. And then the elevator shuddered and ground to a stop. The lights flickered and went out.

"Oh, crap," I said. "Not now. Not *now*." Elevators hate me. I jabbed at the buttons, but nothing happened, and a second later there was a cough of smoke, and the lights behind the buttons went out, too, leaving me in darkness. The emergency lighting came on for just a second, but then there was the pop of a burning filament, and it went away too. Murphy and I were left huddling in the darkness on the floor.

Overhead, outside in the elevator shaft, there was the sound of shrieking metal. I looked up at the invisible roof of the elevator car in the darkness. "You have got to be kidding me," I muttered.

Then there was a rattling bang, and something the weight of a small gorilla landed on the roof of the elevator. There was a second's silence, and then something started a deafening tearing at the roof.

"You have got to be kidding me!" I shouted. But the scorpion wasn't. It was wrenching back the roof of the elevator, rattling the bolts and supports, making it groan. Dust rattled down in the darkness, unseen grit for my unseeing eyes. We were sardines in a can, waiting to be torn up and eaten. I got the feeling that if the thing stung me now, the poison would be redundant—I would bleed to death before it became an issue.

"Think, Harry," I shouted at myself. "Think, think, think!" I was stuck in a frozen elevator, handcuffed to my unconscious friend who was dying of poison while a magical scorpion the size of some French cars tried to tear its way into me and rip me apart. I didn't have my blasting rod or my staff, the other gizmos I'd brought with me to the Varsity were drained and useless, and my shield bracelet would only prolong the inevitable.

A long strip of metal ripped away in the roof, letting in a strip of dim light, and I looked up at the scorpion's underbelly, saw it wedge a claw into the breach and start to tear it open wider.

I should have smashed it when it was just a bug. I should have taken off my shoe and smashed it right there on my desk. My heart leapt into my throat as the thing tilted up, drove an exploratory pincer down into the upper third of the elevator, then started tearing the hole even larger.

I gritted my teeth and started drawing in every ounce of power that I had. I knew it was useless. I could direct a firestorm up at the thing, but it would slag the metal it was on and that would come raining back down on us and kill us, make the elevator shaft too hot for us to survive. But I wasn't just going to let the thing have me, either, by God. Maybe, if I did it just right, I could catch it as it leapt, minimize the damage that I did to the surrounding scenery. That was the problem with not being too great at evocation. Plenty of speed, plenty of power, not much refinement. That's what the staff did, and the blasting rod—they were designed to help me focus my power, give me pinpoint control. Without them I might as well have been a suicide soldier carrying a dozen grenades strapped to his belt and ready to jerk out the pin.

And then it occurred to me. I was thinking in the wrong direction.

I swung my eyes down from the ceiling, to the elevator's floor, pressed my palms against it. Bits of something rained down on my head and shoulders, and the clicking and scuttling of the scorpion got louder. I took all the power I'd drawn in and focused it beneath my palms. There was airspace beneath the elevator, in the elevator shaft, and that was what I reached for—air, instead of fire.

This was a simple spell, one I'd done hundreds of times, I told myself. It wasn't any different from calling my staff to my hand. Just . . . a little bigger.

"Vento servitas!" I shouted, pouring every bit of strength, every ounce of anger, every shred of fear I had into the spell.

And, beneath the elevator, the winds rose up at my call, a solid column of air that caught the bottom of the elevator like a giant's palm and hurled it upward, through the darkness of the elevator shaft. The brakes squealed, threw off sparks, and fell to pieces that dropped through the hole the scorpion had torn, to land next to me. The force of it pressed me down to the floor with a groan. There was a long and rising whine as the car accelerated up the elevator shaft.

I hadn't meant for there to be quite *that* much wind, I thought, and prayed that I hadn't just killed me and Murphy both.

The elevator hurtled up and up and up, and I could feel my face sagging down with the speed of it. My office building is twelve stories high. We'd started at the second floor, so assuming an average of nine feet per story, it was almost a hundred feet to the building's roof.

The car shot up it in less than a half dozen of my frantic heartbeats, slammed past the blocks at the top of the line, and hammered into the roof of the shaft like the bell on the strongman's sledgehammer game at the amusement park. The impact crushed the scorpion into the concrete with a series of sharp popping sounds as chitinous plates cracked and splintered, flattening it into a shapeless brown splotch. Colorless goo, the ectoplasm of magically created mass, spattered out between the crushed plates and hide and down into the car.

At the same time, Murphy and I were hurled *up,* meeting the goo halfway. I kept Murphy in the shelter of my body, trying to stay between her and the roof, and my back hit it hard enough to make me see stars. We tumbled loosely back down to the elevator's floor in a sprawl of limbs, and Murphy groaned beneath me when I landed on her.

I lay still for a moment, stunned. The scorpion was dead. I'd killed it, crushed it between the elevator and the roof of the shaft, and drenched myself and Murphy in ichor, doing it. I'd saved our lives from the murderous device, against the odds.

But I just couldn't shake the nagging impression that I was forgetting something.

There was a little groan from the elevator, and then it shuddered, and started sliding back down the shaft, no longer supported by the powerful but short-lived pillar of wind that had driven it up there. We were falling back down the way we had come, and I had the feeling that we weren't going to have a much better time of it at the bottom than the scorpion had at the top.

Now was the time for the bracelet, and I didn't waste a heartbeat grabbing Murphy close to me, and bringing the shield into being around us. I only had a couple of seconds to focus, to think—I couldn't make the globe around us too brittle, too strong, or we'd just smash ourselves against the inside of it in the same way we would if we just rode the elevator down. There had to be some give to it, some flexibility, to distribute the tremendous force of the abrupt stop at the first floor.

It was dark, and there wasn't much time. Murphy and I rose up to the center of the space of the elevator while I pushed the shield out all around us, filled up the space with layer after layer of flexible shielding, semicohesive molecules of air, patterns of force meant to spread the impact around. There was a sense of pressure all around me, as though I had been abruptly stuffed in Styrofoam packing peanuts.

We fell, faster and faster. I sensed the bottom of the shaft coming. There was an enormous sound, and I held on to the shield with all of my might.

When I opened my eyes again, I was sitting on the floor of the shattered, devastated elevator, holding a sagging, unconscious Murphy. The elevator doors gave a warped, gasping little ding, then shuddered open.

A pair of EMTs with emergency kits in hand stood staring at the elevator, at Murphy and me, their jaws hanging open to their knees. Dust billowed everywhere.

I was alive.

I blinked at that, somewhat stunned. I was alive. I looked down at myself, at my arms and legs, and they were all there. Then I let my head fall back and howled out a defiant laugh, a great, gawping whoop of primal joy.

"Take *that*, Victor Shadowman!" I shouted. "Hah! *Hah*! Give me your best shot, you murderous bastard! I'm going to take my staff and shove it down your *throat*!"

I was still laughing when the EMTs gathered me up and helped me and Murphy toward the ambulance, too stunned to ask any questions. I saw them both give me wary looks, though, and then trade a glance with one another that said they were going to sedate me with something as soon as they got the chance.

"The champion!" I howled, still on an adrenaline rush the size of the Colorado River, as they helped me out toward the ambulance. I thrust my fist into the air, scarcely noting or caring that my bracelet of silver shields had turned into a blackened ring of curled and wilted links, burned to uselessness by the energies I had forced through it. "I am the *man*! Shadowman, you'd better put your head between your legs and kiss your—"

The EMTs helped me outside. Into the rain. The wet slaps of raindrops on my face shut me up, made me cold sober faster than anything else in the world could have done. I was suddenly acutely aware of the handcuffs around my wrist, still, of the fact that I did not have Victor's talisman to use to turn his own power against him. Victor was still out there, out at his lake house, he still had a hank of my hair, and he was still planning on ripping my heart out as soon as he possibly could, when the storm gave him the strength he needed.

I was alive, and Murphy was alive, but my elation was premature. I didn't have anything to be celebrating, yet. I lifted my face to the sky.

Thunder growled, near at hand. Lightning danced overhead, somewhere in the clouds, casting odd light and spectral shadows through the roiling overcast.

The storm had arrived.

Chapter 23

Raindrops pelted down around me, the big, splashy kind you only really see in the spring. The air grew thicker, hotter, even with the rain falling. I had to think fast, use my head, be calm, hurry up. Murphy's handcuffs still held me fastened to her wrist. Both of us were coated in dust that was stuck to the stinking, colorless goo, the ectoplasm that magic called from somewhere else whenever generic mass was called for in a spell. The goo wouldn't last long—within a few more minutes, it would simply dissipate, vanish into thin air, return to wherever it had come from in the first place. For the moment, it was just a rather disgusting, slimy annoyance.

But maybe one that I could put to use.

My own hands were too broad, but Murphy had delicate little lady's hands, except where practice with her gun and her martial arts staff routines had left calluses. If she had heard me thinking that, and had been conscious, she would have punched me in the mouth for being a chauvinist pig.

One of the EMTs was babbling into a handset, while the other was on Murphy's other side, supporting her along with me. It was the only chance I was going to get. I hunched over beside Murphy's diminutive form and tried to shroud what I was doing with the dark folds of my black duster. I worked at her hand, squeezing her limp, slimy fingers together and trying to slip the steel loop of the handcuffs over her hand.

I took some skin off of her, and she groaned a lot, but I managed to get the cuffs off of her wrist just as the EMT and I sat her down on the curb next to the ambulance. The other EMT ran to the back of the ambulance and swung it open, rummaging around inside of it. I could hear sirens, both police cars and fire engines, approaching from all directions.

Nothing's ever simple when I'm around.

"She's been poisoned," I told the EMT. "The wound site is on her right upper arm or shoulder. Check for a massive dose of brown scorpion venom. There should be some antivenin available somewhere. She'll need a tourniquet and—"

"Buddy," the EMT said, annoyed, "I know my job. What the hell happened in there?"

"Don't ask," I said, glancing back at the building. The rain came down more heavily by slow degrees. Was I too late? Would I be dead before I could get to the lake house?

"You're bleeding," the EMT told me, without looking up from Murphy. I looked down at my leg, but it didn't start hurting until I actually saw the injury and remembered I had it. The scorpion's claw had ripped me pretty good, opening a six-inch tear in the leg of my sweats and a comparable gash in the leg beneath, ragged and painful. "Sit down," the EMT said. "I'll take care of it in a second." He wrinkled up his face. "What the hell *is* this stinking shit all over you?"

I wiped rain from my hair, slicking it back. The other EMT came running with a bottle of oxygen and a stretcher, and they both bent over their work with Murphy. Her face had discolored, pale in parts, too brightly red in others. She was as limp as a wet dollar, except for the occasional shudder or flinch, quivers of her muscles that came from nowhere, pained her for a moment, and then apparently vanished.

It was my fault Murphy was there. It had been my decision to hold information away from her that had compelled her to take direct action, to search my office. If I'd just been more open, more honest, maybe she wouldn't be lying there right now, dying. I didn't want to walk away from her. I didn't want to turn my back on her again and leave her behind me, alone.

But I did. Before the support units arrived, before police started asking questions, before the EMTs began looking around for me and giving my description to police officers, I turned on my heel and walked away.

I hated myself every step. I hated leaving before I knew if Murphy would survive the scorpion's venomous sting. I hated that my apartment and my office building had been trashed, torn to pieces by demons and giant insects and my own clumsy power. I hated to close my eyes and see the twisted, mangled bodies of Jennifer Stanton and Tommy Tomm, and Linda Randall. I hated the sick twisting of fear in my guts when I imagined my own spare frame torn asunder by the same forces.

And, most of all, I hated the one responsible for all of it. Victor Sells. Victor, who was going to kill me as soon as this storm grew. I could be dead in another five minutes.

No. I couldn't. I got a little more excited as I thought about the problem and looked up at the clouds. The storm had come in from the west, and was only now going over the city. It wasn't moving fast; it was a ponderous roller of a thunderstorm that would hammer at the area for hours. The Sells's lake house was to the east, around the shore of Lake Michigan, maybe thirty or forty miles away, as the crow flies. I could beat the storm to the lake house, if I was fast enough, if I could get a car. I could get out to the lake house and challenge Victor directly.

My rod and staff were gone, dropped when the scorpion attacked. I might have been able to call them down from my office with winds, but as worked up as I was, I might accidentally blow out the wall if I tried. I didn't care to be crushed by hundreds of pounds of flying brick, called to my outstretched hand by the strength of my magic and my fury. My shield bracelet was gone, too, burned out by countering the tremendous force of the impact of the falling elevator.

I still had my mother's pentacle talisman at my throat, the symbol of order, of the controlled patterns of power that were at the heart of white magic. I still had the advantage of years of formal training. I still had the edge in experience, in sorcerous confrontations. I still had my faith.

But that was about all. I was weary, battered, tired, hurt, and I had already pulled more magic out of the hat in one day than most wizards could in a week. I was pushing the edge already, in both mystic and physical terms. But that just didn't matter to me.

The pain in my leg didn't make me weaker, didn't discourage me, didn't distract me as I walked. It was like a fire in my thoughts, my concentration, burning ever more brightly, more pure, refining my anger, my hate, into something steel-hard, steel-sharp. I could feel it burning, and reached for it eagerly, shoving the pain inside to fuel my incandescent anger.

Victor Shadowman was going to pay for what he'd done to all

those people, to me and to my friends. Dammit all, I was not going out before I'd caught up to that man and shown him what a real wizard could do.

It didn't take me long to walk to McAnally's. I came through the door in a storm of long legs, rain, wind, flapping duster, and angry eyes.

The place was packed, people sitting at every one of the thirteen stools at the bar, at every one of the thirteen tables, leaning against most of the thirteen columns. Pipe smoke drifted through the air in a haze, stirred by the languidly spinning blades of the ceiling fans. The light was dim, candles burning at the tables and in sconces on the walls, plus a little grey storm light sliding in through the windows. The light made the carvings on the columns vague and mysterious, the shadows changing them in a subtle fashion. All of Mac's chessboards were out on the tables, but my sense of it was that those playing and watching the games were trying to keep their minds off of something that was disturbing them.

They all turned to stare at me as I came in the door and down the steps, dripping rainwater and a little blood onto the floor. The room got really quiet.

They were the have-nots of the magical community. Hedge magi without enough innate talent, motivation, or strength to be true wizards. Innately gifted people who knew what they were and tried to make as little of it as possible. Dabblers, herbalists, holistic healers, kitchen witches, troubled youngsters just touching their abilities and wondering what to do about it. Older men and women, younger people, faces impassive or concerned or fearful, they were all there. I knew them all by sight, if not by name.

I swept my gaze around the room. Every one of the people I looked at dropped their eyes, but I didn't need to look deep to see what was happening. Word has a way of getting around between practitioners of magic, and the arcane party line was working as it usually did. Word was out. There was a mark on my head, and they all knew it. Trouble was brewing between two wizards, white and black, and they had all come here, to the shelter offered by McAnally's winding spaces and disruptive configurations of tables and columns. They'd come here to shelter until it was over.

It didn't offer any shelter to me, though. McAnally's couldn't protect me against a sharply directed spell. It was an umbrella, not a bomb shelter. I couldn't get away from what Victor would do to me, unless I cared to flee to the Nevernever itself, and for me that was more dangerous, in some ways, than staying at Mac's.

I stood there in the silence for a moment, but said nothing. These people were associates, friends of a casual sort, but I couldn't ask them to stand beside me. Whatever Victor thought he was, he had the power of a real wizard, and he could crush any of these people like a boot could a cockroach. They weren't prepared to deal with this sort of thing.

"Mac," I said, finally. My voice fell on the silence like a hammer on glass. "I need to borrow your car."

Mac hadn't quit polishing the bar with a clean white cloth when I entered, his spare frame gaunt in a white shirt and dark breeches. He hadn't stopped when the room had grown still. And he didn't stop when he pulled the keys out of his pocket and tossed them to me with one hand. I caught them, and said, "Thanks, Mac."

"Ungh," Mac said. He glanced up at me, and then behind me. I took the gesture for the warning it was, and turned.

Lightning flashed outside. Morgan stood silhouetted in the doorway at the top of the little flight of stairs, his broad frame black against the grey sky. He came down the stairs toward me, and the thunder came in on his heels. Rain had made little difference in the lay of his dull brown and grey hair, except for changing the texture of curl in his warrior's ponytail. I could see the hilt of the sword he wore, beneath his black overcoat. He had a muscular, scarred hand on it.

"Harry Dresden," he said. "I finally figured it out. Using the storms to kill those people is insanely dangerous, but you are just the sort of ambitious fool who would do it." He set his jaw in a hard line. "Have a seat," he said, gesturing at a table. The people sitting at it cleared away, fast. "We're going to stay here, both of us. And I'm going to make sure that you don't have the chance to use this storm to hurt anyone else. I'm going to make sure you don't get to try your cowardly tricks until the Council decides your fate." His grey eyes glittered with grim determination and certainty.

I stared at him. I swallowed my anger, the words I wanted to throw back at him, the spell I wanted to use to blast him out of my way, and spoke gently. "Morgan, I know who the killer is. And he's after me, next. If I don't get to him and stop him, I'm as good as dead."

His eyes hardened, a fanatic's gleam. He spoke in two sharp little explosions of single syllables. "Sit. Down." He drew the sword out from its scabbard by a couple of inches.

I let my shoulders sag. I turned toward the table. I leaned against the back of one of the chairs for a moment, taking a little weight off of my injured leg, and drew the chair out from the table.

Then I picked it up, spun in a half circle with it to gather momentum, and smashed it into the Warden's stomach. Morgan tried to recoil, but I'd caught him off guard, and the blow struck home, hard and heavy with the weight of Mac's handmade wooden chair. In real life, the chair doesn't break when you slug somebody with it, the way it does in the movies. The person you hit is the one who breaks.

Morgan doubled forward, dropping to one hand and one knee. I didn't wait for him to recover. Instead, as the chair bounced off his ribs, I used the momentum of it to spin all the way around in a complete circle in the other direction, lifting the chair high, and brought it smiting down over the other man's back. The blow drove him hard into the floor, where he lay unmoving.

I sat the chair back at the table and looked around the room. Everyone was staring, pale. They knew who Morgan was, what his relationship to me was. They knew about the Council, and my precarious stance with it. They knew that I had just assaulted a duly appointed representative of the Council in pursuit of the execution of his duty. I'd rolled the stone over my own grave. There wasn't a prayer that I could convince the Council that I wasn't a rogue wizard fleeing justice, now.

"Hell with him," I said aloud, to no one in particular. "I haven't got time for this."

Mac came out from behind the bar, not moving in a hurry, but not with his usual laconic lack of concern, either. He knelt by Morgan and felt at his throat, then peeled back an eyelid and peered at the man. Mac squinted up at me and said, expressionless, "Alive."

I nodded, feeling some slight relief. However much of an ass Morgan was, he had good intentions. He and I wanted the same thing, really. He just didn't realize that. I didn't want to kill him.

But, I had to admit in some gleeful little corner of my soul, that the look of shocked surprise on his arrogant face as I hit him with the chair was a sight worth remembering.

Mac stooped and picked up the keys, where I'd dropped them

on the floor as I swung the chair. I hadn't noticed that I had. Mac handed them back to me and said, "Council will be pissed."

"Let me worry about that."

He nodded. "Luck, Harry." Mac offered me his hand, and I took it. The room was still silent. Fearful, worried eyes watched me.

I took the keys and walked up, out of the light and shelter of McAnally's and into the storm, my bridges burning behind me.

Chapter 24

I drove for my life.

Mac's car was an '89 TransAm, pure white, with a big eight-cylinder engine. The speedometer goes to 130 miles an hour. In places, I went past that. The falling rain made the roads dangerous at the speed I was driving, but I had plenty of incentive to keep the car moving as quickly as possible. I was still riding the steel-hard edge of anger that had carried me away from the ruins of my office and through Morgan.

The sky grew darker, a combination of building banks of storm clouds and the approaching dusk. The lighting was strange, greenish, the leaves of the trees as I left the city standing out too sharply, too harshly, the yellows of the lines in the road too dim. Most of the cars I saw had their headlights on, and streetlights were clicking alight as I barreled down the highway.

Fortunately, Sunday evening isn't a busy one, as far as traffic goes. I'd have been dead any other night. I must also have been driving during the watch rotation for the highway patrol, because not one of them tried to pull me over.

I tried to tune in the weather station, on the radio, but gave it up. The storm, plus my own agitation, was creating a cloud of squealing feedback on the radio's speakers, but nothing intelligible about the storm. I could only pray that I was going to get over to Lake Providence before it did.

I won. The curtains of rain parted for me as I whipped past the city-limits sign for Lake Providence. I hit the brakes to slow for the turn onto the lakefront road that led to the Sells house, started hydroplaning, turned into the slide with more composure and ability than I really should have had, and got the vehicle back under control in time to slide onto the correct road.

I pulled into the Sells gravel drive, on the swampy little peninsula that stretched out into Lake Michigan. The TransAm slid to a halt in a shower of gravel and a roar of mighty engine, then sputtered and gasped into silence. I felt, for a giddy second and a half, like Magnum, P.I. Blue Beetle aside, I could get into this sports-car thing. At least it had lasted long enough for me to get to the Sells place. "Thanks, Mac," I grunted, and got out of the car.

The gravel driveway leading back to the lake house was half-sunk in water from the recent storms. My leg hurt me too much to run very fast, but I set off down the drive at a long-legged lope, rapidly eating the distance to the house. The storm loomed before me, rolling across the lake toward the shore—I could see columns of rain, dimly lit by the fading light, falling into its waters.

I raced the storm to the house, and as I did I drew in every bit of power and alertness that I could, keyed myself to a tighter level, tuned my senses to their sharpest pitch. I came to a halt twenty yards shy of the house and closed my eyes, panting. There could be magical traps or alarms strewn about, or spiritual or shrouded guardians invisible to the naked eye. There could be spells waiting, illusions meant to hide Victor Sells from anyone who came looking. I needed to be able to see past all that. I needed to have every scrap of knowledge I could get.

So I opened my Third Eye.

How can I explain what a wizard sees? It isn't something that lends itself readily to description. Describing something helps to define it, to give it limits, to set guardrails of understanding around it. Wizards have had the Sight since time began, and they still don't understand how it works, why it does what it does.

The only thing I can say is that I felt as though a veil of thick cloth had been lifted away from me as I opened my eyes again—and not only from my eyes, but from all of my senses. I could abruptly smell the mud and fish odor of the lake, the trees around the house, the fresh scent of the coming rain preceding the storm on the smoke-stained wind. I looked at the trees. Saw them, not just in the first green coat of spring, but in the full bloom of summer, the splendor of the fall, and the barren desolation of winter, all at the same time. I Saw the house, and each separate part of it as its own component, the timbers as parts of spectral trees, the windows as pieces of distant sandy shores. I could feel the heat of summer and the cold of winter in the wind coming off the lake. I

Saw the house wreathed in ghostly flames, and knew that those were part of its possible future, that fire lay down several of the many paths of possibility that lay ahead in the next hour.

The house itself was a place of power. Dark emotions—greed, lust, hatred—all hung over it as visible things, molds and slimes that were strewn over it like Spanish moss with malevolent eyes. Ghostly things, restless spirits, moved around the place, drawn to the sense of fear, despair, and anger that hung over it, mindless shades that were always to be found in such places, like rats in granaries.

The other thing that I Saw over the house was a grinning, empty skull. Skulls were everywhere, wherever I looked, just at the edge of my vision, silent and still and bleach white, as solid and real as though a fetishist had scattered them around in anticipation of some bizarre holiday. Death. Death lay in the house's future, tangible, solid, unavoidable.

Maybe mine.

I shuddered and shoved the feeling away. No matter how strong the vision, how powerful the image gained with the Sight, the future was always mutable, always something that could be changed. No one had to die tonight. It didn't have to come to that, not for them and not for me.

But a sick feeling had settled into me, as I looked on this darkling house, with all of its stinking lust and fear, all of its horrid hate worn openly upon it to my Sight, like a mantle of flayed human skin on the shoulders of a pretty girl with gorgeous hair, luscious lips, sunken eyes, and rotting teeth. It repulsed me and it made me afraid.

And something about it, intangible, something I couldn't name, called to me. Beckoned. Here was power, power I had thrust aside once before, in the past. I had thrown away the only family I had ever known to turn away power exactly like this. This was the sort of strength that could reach out and change the world to my will, bend it and shape it to my desiring, could cut through all the petty trivialities of law and civilization and impose order where there was none, guarantee my security, my position, my future.

And what had been my reward for turning that power aside thus far? Suspicion and contempt from the very wizards I had acted to support and protect, condemnation from the White Council whose Law I had clung to when all the world had been laid at my feet.

I could kill the Shadowman, now, before he knew I was here. I could call down fury and flame on the house and kill everyone in it, not leave one stone upon another. I could reach out and embrace the dark energy he had gathered in this place, draw it in and use it for whatever I wanted, and the consequences be damned.

Why not kill him now? Violet light, visible to my Sight, throbbed and pulsed inside the windows, power being gathered and prepared and shaped. The Shadowman was inside, and he was gathering his might, preparing to unleash the spell that would kill me. What reason had I to let him go on breathing?

I clenched my fists in fury, and I could feel the air crackle with tension as I prepared to destroy the lake house, the Shadowman, and any of the pathetic underlings he had with him. With such power, I could cast my defiance at the Council itself, the gathering of white-bearded old fools without foresight, without imagination, without vision. The Council, and that pathetic watchdog, Morgan, had no idea of the true depths of my strength. The energy was all there, gleeful within my anger, ready to reach out and reduce to ashes all that I hated and feared.

The silver pentacle that had been my mother's burned cold on my chest, a sudden weight that made me gasp. I sagged forward a little, and lifted a hand. My fingers were so tightly crushed into fists that it hurt to try to open them. My hand shook, wavered, and began to fall again.

Then something strange happened. Another hand took mine. The hand was slim, the fingers long and delicate. Feminine. The hand gently covered mine, and lifted it, like a small child's, until I held my mother's pentacle in my grasp.

I held it in my hand, felt its cool strength, its ordered and rational geometry. The five-pointed star within the circle was the ancient sign of white wizardry, the only remembrance of my mother. The cold strength of the pentacle gave me a chance, a moment to think again, to clear my head.

I took deep breaths, struggling to see clear of the anger, the hate, the deep lust that burned within me for vengeance and retribution. That wasn't what magic was for. That wasn't what magic did. Magic came from life itself, from the interaction of nature and the elements, from the energy of all living beings, and especially of people. A man's magic demonstrates what sort of person he is, what is held most deeply inside of him. There is no truer gauge of a man's character than the way in which he employs his strength, his power.

I was not a murderer. I was not like Victor Sells. I was Harry Blackstone Copperfield Dresden. I was a wizard. Wizards control their power. They don't let it control them. And wizards don't use magic to kill people. They use it to discover, to protect, to mend, to help. Not to destroy.

The anger abruptly evaporated. The burning hate subsided, leaving my head clear enough to think again. The pain in my leg settled into a dull ache, and I shivered in the wind and the first droplets of rain. I didn't have my staff, and I didn't have my rod. The trinkets I did have with me were either expended or burned to uselessness. All I had was what was inside me.

I looked up, suddenly feeling smaller and very alone. There was no one near me. No hand was touching mine. No one stood close by. For just a moment, I thought I smelled a whiff of perfume, familiar and haunting. Then it was gone. And the only one I had to help me was myself.

I blew out a breath. "Well, Harry," I told myself, "that's just going to have to be enough."

And so, I walked through a spectral landscape littered with skulls, into the teeth of the coming storm, to a house covered in malevolent power, throbbing with savage and feral mystic strength. I walked forward to face a murderous opponent who had all the advantages, and who stood prepared and willing to kill me from where he stood within the heart of his own destructive power, while I was armed with nothing more than my own skill and wit and experience.

Do I have a great job or what?

Chapter 25

The Sight of Victor's lake house will always be with me. It was an abomination. It looked innocuous enough, physically. But on a deeper level, it was foul, rotten. It seethed with negative energy, anger and pride and lust. Especially lust. Lust for wealth, lust for power, more than physical desire.

Shadowy spirit-beings that weren't wholly real, only manifestations of the negative energy of the place, clung to the walls, the rain gutters, the porch, the windowsills, glutting themselves on the negative energy left over from Victor's spellcasting. I was guessing that there was a lot of it. He didn't strike me as someone who would be able to make sure that his spells were energy-efficient.

I limped up the front steps. My Sight revealed no alarms, no sorcerous trip wires. I might be giving Victor Shadowman too much credit. He was as powerful as a full-blown wizard, but he didn't have the education. Muscle, not brains, that was Victor Shadowman. I had to keep that in mind.

I tried the front door, just for the hell of it.

It opened.

I blinked. But I didn't question the good fortune, or the overconfidence that had seen to it that Victor left his front door standing unlocked. Instead, I took a breath, gathered up what will I had, and pressed inside.

I forget how the house was furnished or decorated. All I remember is what the Sight showed me. More of the same as the outside, but more concentrated, more noxious. *Things* clung everywhere, things with silent, glittering eyes and hungry expressions. Some reptilian, some more like rats, some insectoid. All of them were unpleasant, hostile, and shied away from me as I came in, as the aura of energy I held in readiness around me touched them. They made quiet noises, things I would never have heard with my ears—but the Sight encompasses all of that.

There was a long, dark hallway coated with the things. I advanced slowly, quietly, and they oozed and crept and slithered from my path. The dark purple light of magic, that I had seen from the outside, was ahead of me, and growing brighter. I could hear music playing, and recognized it as the same piece that had been playing on the CD player at the Madison in Tommy Tomm's suite when Murphy had asked me there on Thursday. Slow, sensuous music, steady rhythm.

I closed my eyes for a moment, listening. I heard sounds. A quiet whisper, being repeated over and over, a man's voice repeating an incantation, holding a spell in readiness for release. That would be Victor. I heard soft sighs of pleasure from a woman. The Beckitts? I could only assume so.

And, in a rumble that I could feel through the soles of my boots, I heard thunder over the lake. The low, chanting voice took on an edge of vicious, spiteful satisfaction, and continued the incantation.

I gathered up what energy I had and stepped around the corner, out of the hallway, into a spacious room that stretched up to the full height of the house without interruption, yards of open air. The room below was a living room. A spiral staircase wound its way up to what looked like a kitchen and dining room on a sort of platform or balcony above the rest of the room. The elevated deck on the back of the house must be accessible from the platform.

There was no one in the main room. The chanting, and the occasional sigh, came from the platform above. The CD player was down in the room beneath, music flowing from speakers that were covered with an image of fire and dozens of bloated, disgusting creature forms, feeding on the music as it came out. I could see the influence of the music as a faint, violet mist, in tune with the light coming from the platform above. This was a complex ritual spell, then, involving many base elements coordinated by the central wizard, Victor. Tricky. No wonder it was so effective. It must have taken Victor a lot of trial and error to figure it out.

I glanced up at the platform, then crossed the room, keeping as far away as I could from the CD player. I slipped under the platform without making any noise, and dozens upon dozens of slimy not-physical spirit things oozed from my path. Rain increased to a dull, steady rhythm outside, on the roof and on the wooden deck and against the windows.

There were boxes stacked all around me, plastic cases and cartons and cardboard boxes and wooden crates. I opened the nearest one, and saw, inside, at least a hundred slender vials like the ones I had seen before, full of the liquid ThreeEye. Beneath the vision of my Sight, it looked different, thick and cloudy with possibility, potential disaster lurking in every vial. Faces, twisted in horror and torment, swam through the liquid, ghostly images of what might be.

I looked at the other boxes. In one, ancient liquor bottles full of an almost luminescent green liquid. Absinthe? I leaned closer, sniffing, and could almost taste the madness that swam latent in the liquid. I leaned back from the boxes, stomach churning. I checked the other boxes, quickly. Ammonia, reminiscent of hospitals and mental wards. Peyote mushrooms in plastic Tupperware—I was familiar with them. Alum, white and powdery. Antifreeze. Glitter in a hundred metallic shades in a huge plastic bag. Other things, deeper in the shadows, that I didn't take the time to look at. I had already figured out what all the articles were for.

Potions.

Ingredients for potions. This was how Victor was making the ThreeEye. He was doing the same thing I did when I made my little potions, but on a grander scale, using energy hc stole from other places, other people. He used absinthe as the base, and moved out from there. Victor was mass-producing what amounted to a magical poison, one that probably remained inert until it was inside someone, interacting with their emotions and desires. That would explain why I hadn't noticed anything about it, before. It wouldn't have been obvious to a cursory examination, or to anything short of fully opening up my Sight, and that wasn't something I did very often.

I closed my eyes, shaking. The Sight was showing me too much. That was always the problem with it. I could look at these ingredients, the cases of the finished drug, and catch flash images of exactly how much suffering could be caused. There was too much. I was starting to get disoriented.

Thunder came again, more sharply, and above me, Victor's voice rose in pitch, to something audible. He was chanting in an ancient language. Egyptian? Babylonian? It didn't really matter. I could understand the sense of the words clearly enough. They were words of hate, malevolence. They were words that were meant to kill.

My shaking was becoming more pronounced. Was it only the effects of the Sight? The presence of so much negative energy, reacting with me?

No. I was simply afraid. Terrified to come out of my hiding place under the platform and to meet the master of the slithering horde that was draped over everything in sight. I could feel his strength from here, his confidence, the force of his will infusing the very air with a sort of hateful certainty. I was afraid with the same fear that a child feels when confronted with a large, angry dog, or with the neighborhood bully, the kind of fear that paralyzes, makes you want to make excuses and hide.

But there was no time for hiding. No time for excuses. I had to act. So I forced my Sight closed and gathered my courage as best I could.

Thunder roared outside and there was a flash of lightning, the two happening close together. The lights flickered, and the music skipped a track. Victor screamed out the incantation in a kind of ecstasy above me. The woman's voice, presumably Mrs. Beckitt's, rose to a fevered pitch.

"You pays your money, you takes your chances," I muttered to myself.

I focused my will, extended my right arm and open palm to the stereo system, and shouted, *"Fuego!"* A rush of heat from my hand exploded into flame on the far side of the room and engulfed the stereo, which began to emit a sound more like a long, tortured scream than music. Murphy's handcuffs still dangled from my wrist, one loop swinging free.

Then I turned, extended my arms and roared, *"Veni che!"* Wind swept up beneath me, making my duster billow like Batman's cloak, lifting me directly up to the platform above and over its low railing into the suspended room.

Even expecting the sight, it rattled me. Victor was dressed in black slacks, a black shirt, black shoes—very stylish, especially compared to my sweatpants and cowboy boots. His shaggy eyebrows and lean features were highlighted eerily by the dark light flowing up from the circle around him, where the implements of his ritual spell were ready to complete the ceremony that would kill me. He had what looked like a spoon, its edges sharpened to razor keenness, a pair of candles, black and white, and a white rabbit, its feet bound with red cord. One of its legs was bleeding from a small tear, staining the white fur. And tied against its head with a cord was the lock of my own dark, straight hair. Over to one side was another circle, laid out in chalk upon the carpeting, maybe fifteen feet across. The Beckitts were inside, writhing together in mindless, sweating desire, generating energy for Victor's spell.

Victor stared at me in shock as I landed upon the balcony, wind whipping around me, roaring inside the small room like a miniature cyclone, knocking over potted plants and knickknacks.

"You!" he shouted.

"Me," I confirmed. "There's something I've been meaning to talk to you about, Vic."

His shock transformed into snarling anger in a heartbeat. He snatched up the sharpened spoon, raised it in his right hand, and screamed out words of the incantation. He dragged the rabbit in front of him, the ceremonial representation of me, and prepared to gouge out its, and therefore my, heart.

I didn't give him the chance to finish. I reached into a pocket and hurled the empty plastic film canister at Victor Shadowman.

As a weapon, it wasn't much. But it was real, and it had been hurled by a real person, a mortal. It could shatter the integrity of a magic circle.

The canister went through the air above Victor's circle and broke it, just as he completed the incantation and drove the spoon's blade down at the poor rabbit. The energy of the storm came whipping down the cylinder of focus created by Victor's now-flawed circle.

Power shattered out into the room, wild, undirected, and unfocused, naked color and raw sound spewing everywhere with hurricane force. It sent objects flying, including Victor and me, and shattered the secondary circle the Beckitts were in, sending them rolling and bumping across the floor and into one wall.

I braced myself against the guardrail and held on as the power raged around me, charging the air with raw, dangerous magic, surging about like water under pressure, seeking an outlet.

"You bastard!" Victor screamed into the gale. "Why don't you just die!" He lifted a hand and screamed something at me, and fire washed across the space between us, instant and hot.

I tapped some of the ample power now available in the room and formed a hard, high wall in front of me, squeezing my eyes shut in concentration. It was a dozen times harder to shield without my bracelet, but I blocked the flame, sent it swirling high and over me, huddling under a little quarter dome of hardened air that would not let Victor's magic past it. I opened my eyes in time to see the flames touch the ceiling beams and set them alight.

The air still thrummed with energy as the wash of flame passed. Victor snarled when he saw me rise, lifted a hand to one side, and snarled out words of summoning. A crooked stick that looked like it might be some kind of bone soared through the air toward him, and he caught it in one hand, turning to me with the attitude of a man holding a gun.

The problem with most wizards is that they get too used to thinking in terms of one venue: Magic. I don't think Victor expected me to rise, lurch across the trembling floor toward him, and drive my shoulder into his chest, slamming him back into the wall with a satisfying thud. I leaned back a little and drove a knee toward his gut, missed, and got him square between the legs instead. The breath went out of him in a rush, and he doubled over to the ground. By this time, I was screaming at him, senseless and incoherent. I started kicking at his head.

I heard a metallic, ratcheting sound behind me and spun my head in time to see Beckitt, naked, point an automatic weapon at me. I threw myself to one side, and heard a brief explosion of gunfire. Something hot tore at my hip, spinning me into a roll, and I kept going, into the kitchen. I heard Beckitt snarl a curse. There were a number of sharp clicking sounds. The automatic had jammed. Hell, with this much magic flying around the room, we were all lucky the thing hadn't just exploded.

Victor, meanwhile, shook the end of the bone tube he held, and a half dozen dried, brown scorpion husks fell out onto the carpeting. His whiter-than-white teeth flashed in his boater brown face, and he snarled, *"Scorpis, scorpis, scorpis!"* His eyes gleamed with lust and fury.

One of my legs wasn't answering my calls to action, so I crab-walked backward into the kitchen on the heels of my hands and one leg. Out on the dining section of the balcony, the scorpions shuddered to life and started to grow. First one, and then the others, oriented on the kitchen and started toward me in scuttling bursts of speed, getting larger as they came.

Victor howled his glee. The Beckitts rose, both naked, lean and savage-looking, both sporting guns, their eyes empty of everything but a wild sort of bloodlust.

I felt my shoulders press against a counter. There was a rattle, and then a broom fell down against me, its handle bouncing off of my head and landing on the tile floor beside me. I grabbed at it, my heart pounding somewhere around my throat.

A roomful of deadly drug. One evil sorcerer on his home turf. Two crazies with guns. One storm of wild magic looking for something to set it into explosive motion. And half a dozen scorpions like the one I had barely survived earlier, rapidly growing to movie-monster size. Less than a minute on the clock and no time-outs remaining for the quarterback.

All in all, it was looking like a bad evening for the home team.

Chapter 26

I was so dead. There was no way out of the kitchen, no time to use an explosive evocation in close quarters, and the deadly scorpions would rip me to pieces well before Victor could blow me up with explosive magic or one of the blood-maddened Beckitts could get their guns working long enough to put a few more bullets in me. My hip was beginning to scream with pain, which I supposed was better than the deadly dull numbness of more serious injuries and shock, but at the moment it was the least of my worries. I clutched the broom to me, my only pitiful weapon. I didn't even have the mobility to use it.

And then something occurred to me, something so childish that I almost laughed. I plucked a straw from the broomstick and began a low and steady chant, a bobbing about in the air with the fingers that held the straw. I reached out and took hold of the immense amounts of untapped energy running rampant in the air and drew them into the spell. *"Pulitas!"* I shouted, bringing the chant to a crescendo. *"Pulitas, pulitas!"*

The broom twitched. It quivered. It jerked upright in my hands. And then it took off across the kitchen floor, its brush waving menacingly, to meet the scorpions' advance. The last thing I had expected to use that cleaning spell for when I had laboriously been forced to learn it was a tide of poisonous scorpion monsters, but any port in a storm. The broom swept into them with ferocious energy and started flicking them across the kitchen toward the rest of the balcony with tidy, efficient motions. Each time one of the scorpions would try to dodge around it, the broom would tilt out and catch the beastie before it could, flick it neatly onto its back and continue about its job.

I'm pretty sure it got all the dirt on the way, too. When I do a spell, I do it right.

Victor screeched in anger when he saw his pets, still too small to carry much mass, being so neatly corralled and ushered off the balcony. The Beckitts lifted their guns and opened fire on the broom, while I hunkered down behind the counter. They must have been using revolvers, now, because they fired smoothly and in an ordered rhythm. Bullets smacked into the walls and the counters at the back of the kitchen, but none of them came through the counter that sheltered me.

I caught my breath, pressing my hand against the blood on my hip. It hurt like bloody hell. I thought the bullet was stuck, somewhere by the bone. I couldn't move my leg. There was a lot of blood, but not so much that I was sitting in a puddle. Out on the balcony, the fire was beginning to catch, spreading over the roof. The entire place was going to come crashing down before much longer.

"Stop shooting, stop shooting, damn you!" Victor screamed, as the gunfire came to a halt. I risked a peek over the counter. My broom had swept the scorpions off the edge of the balcony and to the floor of the room below. As I watched, Victor caught the broom by its handle and broke it over the balcony railing with a snarl. The straw I still held in my fingers broke with a sharp little *twang,* and I felt the energy fade from the spell.

Victor Shadowman snarled. "A cute trick, Dresden," he said, "but pathetic. There's no way you can survive this. Give up. I'll be willing to let you walk away."

The Beckitts were reloading. I ducked my head back down before they got any funny ideas, and hoped that they didn't have heavier rounds that could penetrate the counters I hid behind and whatever contents they contained, to kill me.

"Sure, Vic," I replied, keeping my voice as calm as I could. "You're known for your mercy and sense of fair play, right?"

"All I have to do is keep you in there until the fire spreads enough to kill you," Victor said.

"Sure. Let's all die together, Vic. Too bad about all your inventory down there, though, eh?"

Victor snarled and pitched another burst of flame into the kitchen. This time, it was much easier to cover myself, half-shielded as I already was by the counters. "Oh, cute," I said, my voice dripping scorn. "Fire's the simplest thing you can do. All the real wizards learn that in the first couple of weeks and move on up from there." I looked around the kitchen. There had to be something I could use, some way I could escape, but nothing presented itself.

"Shut up!" Victor snarled. "Who's the real wizard here, huh? Who's the one with all the cards and who's the one bleeding on the kitchen floor? You're nothing, Dresden, *nothing*. You're a *loser*. And do you know why?"

"Gee," I said. "Let me think."

He laughed, harshly. "Because you're an idiot. You're an idealist. Open your eyes, man. You're in the jungle, now. It's survival of the fittest, and you've proved yourself unfit. The strong do as they wish, and the weak get trampled. When this is over, I'm going to wipe you off my shoe and keep going like you never existed."

"Too late for that," I told him. I was in the mood to tell a white lie. "The police know all about you, Vic. I told them myself. And I told the White Council, too. You've never even heard of them, have you, Vic? They're like the Superfriends and the Inquisition all rolled up into one. You'll love them. They'll take you out like yesterday's garbage. God, you really *are* an ignorant bastard."

There was a moment's silence. Then, "No," he said. "You're lying. You're lying to me, Dresden."

"If I'm lying I'm dying," I told him. Hell, as far as I knew, I was. "Oh. And Johnny Marcone, too. I made sure that he knew who and where you were."

"Son of a bitch," Victor said. "You stupid son of a bitch. Who put you up to this, huh? Marcone? Is that why he pulled you off the street."

I had to laugh, weakly. A bit of flaming cabinet fell off an upper shelf onto the tiles next to me. It was getting hot in there. The fire was spreading. "You never figured it out, did you, Vic?"

"Who?" Victor screamed at me. "Who was it, damn you? That whore, Linda? Her whore friend Jennifer?"

"Strike two, strike three, the other side gets a chance to steal," I said back. Hell. At least if I could keep him talking, I might keep him in the house long enough to go down with me. And if I could make him mad enough, he might make a mistake.

"Stop talking to him," Beckitt said. "He's not armed. Let's kill him and get out of here before we all die."

"Go ahead," I said in a cheerful tone. "Hell, I've got nothing to lose. I'll send this whole house up in a fireball that'll make Hiroshima look like a hibachi. Make my day."

"Shut up," Victor shouted. "Who was it, Dresden? Who, damn you?"

If I gave him Monica, he might still be able to get to her if he got away. There was no sense in risking that. So all I said was, "Go to hell, Vic."

"Get the car started," Victor snarled. "Go out through the deck doors. The scorpions will kill anything on the first floor."

I heard motion in the room, someone moving out the doors onto the elevated deck at the back of the house. The fire continued to spread. Smoke rode the air in a thick haze.

"I've got to go, Dresden," Victor told me. His voice was gentle, almost a purr, "but there's someone I want you to meet, first."

I got a sick, twisty little feeling in the pit of my stomach.

"Kalshazzak," Victor whispered.

Power thrummed. The air shimmered and shone, began to twist and spiral.

"Kalshazzak," Victor whispered again, louder, more demanding. I heard something, a warbling hiss that seemed to come from a great distance, rushing closer. The black wizard called the name for the third and final time, his voice rising to a screech, "Kalshazzak!"

There was a thundercrack in the house, a dull and sulfurous stench, and I craned my neck to see over the counter, risking a glance.

Victor stood by the sliding glass doors that led out onto the wooden deck. Red-orange flames wreathed the ceiling on that side of the house, and smoke was filling the room below, casting the whole place in a hellish glow.

Crouched down on the floor in front of Victor was the toad-demon I had banished the night before. I had known that I hadn't killed it. You can't kill demons, as such, only destroy the physical vessels they create for themselves when they come to the mortal world. If called again, they can create a new vessel without difficulty.

I watched in fascination, stunned. I had seen only one person call a demon before—and I had killed my old master shortly after. The thing crouched in front of Victor, its lightning blue eyes whirling with shades of scarlet hate, staring up at the black-clad wizard, trembling with the need to tear into him, to rend and destroy the mortal being who had dared summon it forth.

Victor's eyes grew wider and more mad, glittering with fevered intensity. Sweat ran down his face, and he tilted his head slowly to one side, as though his vision were skewing along the horizontal and by the motion he would compensate for it. I gave silent thanks that I had closed my Third Eye when I did. I did not want to see what that thing really looked like—and I didn't want to get a good look at the real Victor Sells, either.

The demon finally gave a hiss of frustration and turned toward me with a croaking growl. Victor dropped his head back and laughed, his will triumphant over that of the being he had called from beyond. "There, Dresden. Do you see? The strong survive, and the weak are torn to little pieces." He flapped his hand at me and said, to the demon, "Kill him."

I struggled to my feet, supporting my weight on the counter, to face the demon as it rose and began its slow stalk toward me.

"My God, Victor," I said. "I can't get over how clumsy you are."

Victor's smile immediately became a snarling sneer once again. I saw fear touch the corners of his eyes, uncertainty even though he was on top, and I felt a little smile quirk my lips. I moved my gaze to the demon's.

"You really shouldn't just hand someone else a demon's name," I told him. Then I drew in a breath, and shouted out in a voice of command, "Kalshazzak!"

The demon stopped in its tracks and gave a whistling howl of agony and rage as I called its name and drew my will up to hurl against it.

"Kalshazzak," I snarled again. The demon's presence was suddenly *there*, in my head, raging slippery and slimy and wriggling like a venomous tadpole. It was a pressure, a horrible pressure on my temples that made me see stars and threatened to steal enough of my balance to send me falling to the floor.

I tried to speak again and the words stuck in my throat. The demon hissed in anticipation, and the pressure on my head redoubled, trying to force me down, to make me give up the struggle, at which point the demon would be free to act. The lightning blue of its eyes became glaringly bright, painful to look upon.

I thought of little Jenny Sells, oddly enough, and of Murphy, lying pale and unconscious on a stretcher in the rain, of Susan, crouched next to me, sick and unable to run.

I had beaten this frog once. I could do it again.

I cried out the demon's name for the third and final time, my throat burning and raw. The word came out garbled and imperfect, and for a sinking moment I feared the worst, but Kalshazzak howled again, and hurled itself furiously to the floor, thrashing its limbs about like a poisoned bug, raging and tearing great swaths out of the carpet. I sagged, the weariness that came over me threatening to make me black out.

"What are you doing?" Victor said, his voice rising to a high-pitched shriek. "What are you doing?" He was staring at the demon in horror. "Kill him! I am your master! Kill him, kill him!" The demon howled in rage, turned its burning glare to me and then Victor, as though trying to decide who to devour first. Its eyes settled on Victor, who went pale and ran for the doors.

"Oh no you don't," I muttered, and I uttered the last spell I could manage. One final time, on the last gasps of my power, the winds rose and lifted me from the earth. I hurtled into Victor like an ungainly cannonball, driving him away from the doors, past the demon as it made an awkward lunge at us, and toward the railing of the balcony.

We fell in a confused heap at the edge of the balcony that overlooked the room beneath, full of dark smoke and the red glow of flame. The air had grown almost too hot to breathe. Pain jolted through my hip, more bright and blinding than anything I had ever imagined, and I sucked in a breath. The smoky air burned, made me choke and gasp.

I looked up. Fire was spreading everywhere. The demon was crouched between us and the only way out. Over the edge of the balcony was only chaos and flame and smoke—strange, dark smoke that should have been rising, but instead was mostly settled along the floor like London fog. The pain was too great. I simply couldn't move. I couldn't even take in enough breath to scream.

"Damn you," Victor screamed. He regained his feet and hauled me up toward his face with berserk strength. "Damn you," he repeated. "What happened? What did you do?"

"The Fourth Law of Magic forbids the binding of any being against its will," I grated out. Pain was tight around my throat, making me fight to speak the words. "So I stepped in and cut your control over it. And didn't establish any of my own."

Victor's eyes widened, "You mean . . ."

"It's free," I confirmed. I glanced at the demon. "Looks hungry."

"What do we do," Victor said. His voice was shaking, and he started shaking me, too. "What do we do?"

"We die," I said. "Hell, I was going to do that anyway. But at least this way, I take you out with me."

I saw him glance at the demon, then back to me, eyes terrified and calculating. "Work with me," he said. "You stopped it before. You can stop it again. We can beat it, together, and leave."

I studied him for a moment. I couldn't kill him with magic. I didn't want to. And it would only have brought a death sentence on my head in any case. But I could stand by and do nothing. And that's exactly what I did. I smiled at him, closed my eyes, and did nothing.

"Fuck you, then, Dresden," Victor snarled. "It can only eat one of us at a time. And I'm not going to be the one to get eaten today." And he picked me up to hurl me toward the demon.

I objected with fragile tenacity. We grappled. Fire raged. Smoke billowed. The demon came closer, lightning eyes gleaming through the hell-lit gloom. Victor was shorter than me, stockier, better at wrestling, and he hadn't been shot in the hip. He levered me up and almost threw me, but I moved quicker, whipping my right arm at his head and catching him with the flailing free end of Murphy's handcuffs, breaking his motion. He tried to break away, but I held on to him, dragged him in a circle to slam against the guardrail of the balcony, and we both toppled over.

Desperation gives a man extraordinary resources. I flailed at the balcony railing and caught it at the base, keeping myself from going over into the roiling smoke below. I shot a glance below, and saw the glistening brown hide of one of the scorpions, its stinging tail held up like the mast of a ship cutting through smoke at least four feet deep. The room was filled with angry clicking, scuttling sounds. Even in a single desperate glance, I saw a couch torn to pieces by a pair of scorpions in less time than it took to take a breath. They loomed over it, their tails waving in the air like flags from the back of golf carts. Hell's bells.

Victor had grabbed on to the railing a little above me and to the left, and he stared at the oncoming demon with a face twisted with hatred. I saw him draw in a breath, and try to plant a foot firmly enough to free one hand to point at the oncoming demon in some sort of magical attack or defense.

I couldn't allow Victor to get out of this. He was still whole. If he could knock the demon down, he might still slip out. So I had to tell him something that would make him mad enough to try to take my head off. "Hey, Vic," I shouted. "It was your wife. It was Monica that ratted on you."

The words hit him like a physical blow, and his head whipped around toward me, his face contorting in fury. He started to say something to me, the words of a spell meant to blow me to bits, maybe, but the toad-demon interrupted him by rearing up with an angry hiss and snapping its jaws down over Victor's collarbone and throat. Bone broke with audible snaps, and Victor squealed in pain, his arms and legs shuddering. He tried to push his way *down*, away from the demon, and the creature's balance wobbled.

I gritted my teeth and tried to hold on. A scorpion leapt at me, brown and gleaming, and I drew my legs up out of reach of its pincers, just barely.

"Bastard," Victor cried, struggling uselessly in the demon's jaws. There was blood running down his body, fast and hot. The demon had hit an artery, and it was simply holding on, wavering at the edge of the balcony as Victor struggled and started kicking at my near hand. He hit me once, twice, and my balance wavered, my grip slipping. A quick glance below me showed me another scorpion, getting ready to jump at me, this one closer.

Murphy, I thought. *I should have listened to you.* If the scorpions didn't kill me, the demon would, and if the demon didn't, the fire was going to kill me. I was going to die.

There was a certain peace in thinking that, in knowing that it was all about to be over. I was going to die. It was as simple as that. I had fought as hard as I could, done everything I could think of, and it was over. I found myself, in my final seconds, idly wishing that I could have had time to apologize to Murphy, that I could apologize to Jenny Sells for killing her daddy, that I could apologize to Linda Randall for not figuring things out fast enough and saving her life. Murphy's handcuffs lay tight and cold against my forearm as monsters and demons and black wizards and smoke closed in all around me. I closed my eyes.

Murphy's handcuffs.

My eyes snapped open.

Murphy's handcuffs.

Victor swung his foot at my left hand again. I kicked with my legs and hauled with my shoulders to give me a second of lift, and grabbed Victor Sells's pant leg in my left hand. With my right, I flicked the free end of the handcuffs around one of the bars of the guardrail. The ring of metal cycled around on its hinge and locked into place.

Then, as I started to fall back down, I hauled hard on Victor's leg. He screamed, a horrible, high-pitched squeal, as he started to fall. Kalshazzak, finally overbalanced by the additional weight and leverage I had added to Victor's struggles, pitched over the balcony guardrail and into the smoke below, crashing down to the floor, carrying Victor with him.

There was a rush of scuttling, clicking sounds, a piercing whistle-hiss from the demon. Victor's screams rose to something high-pitched and horrible, until he sounded more like an animal, a pig squealing at slaughter, than a man.

I swung from the balcony, my feet several feet above the fray, held suspended in an acutely painful fashion by Murphy's handcuffs, one loop around my wrist, the other locked around the balcony railing. I looked down as my vision started to fade. I saw a sea of brown, gleaming plates of segmented, chitinous armor. I saw the scorpions' stinging tails flashing down, over and over again. I saw the lightning eyes of Kalshazzak's physical vessel, and I saw one of them pierced and put out by the flashing sting of one of the scorpions.

And I saw Victor Sells, struck over and over again by stingers the size of ice picks, the wounds foaming with poison. The demon ignored the pincers and the stingers of the scorpions to begin tearing him apart. His face contorted in the final agony of rage and fear.

The strong survive, and the weak get eaten. I guess Victor had invested in the wrong kind of strength.

I didn't want to watch what was happening below me. The fires consuming the ceiling above were rather beautiful, actually, rolling waves of flame, cherry red, sunset orange. I was too weak to try to get out of this mess, and the entire thing had become far to annoying and painful to even consider anymore. I just watched the flames, and waited and noticed, oddly, that I was simply *starving*. And no wonder. I hadn't eaten a decent meal since . . . Friday? Friday. You notice odd things in those final moments, they say.

And then you start seeing things. For instance, I saw Morgan come through the sliding glass doors leading in from the outside deck, the silver sword of the White Council's justice in his hands. I saw one of the scorpions, now the size of a German shepherd, figure out the stairs, scuttle up them, and hurtle at Morgan. I saw Morgan's silver sword slash, *snickersnack,* and leave the scorpion in writhing pieces on the floor.

Then I saw Morgan, his expression grim, his weight making the fire-chewed balcony shudder, come for me. His eyes narrowed when he saw me, and he lifted the sword, leaning far over the balcony railing. The blade flashed bright silver in the firelight as it started to come down.

Typical, was my last thought. *How perfectly typical, to survive everything the bad guys could do, and get taken down by the people for whose cause I had been fighting*.

Chapter 27

I awoke somewhere cool and dark, in tremendous pain, coughing my lungs out. Rain was falling on my face, and it was the greatest feeling I'd ever known. Morgan's face was over mine, and I realized he'd been giving me CPR. Eww.

I coughed and spluttered and sat up, wheezing for breath. Morgan watched me for a moment, then scowled and stood up, eyes flickering around.

I managed to get enough wind to speak, and said, numbly, "You saved me."

He grimaced. "Yes."

"But why?"

He looked at me again, then stooped to pick up his sword and slip it into the scabbard at his side. "Because I saw what happened in there. I saw you risk your life to stop the Shadowman. Without breaking any of the Laws. You weren't the killer."

I coughed some more, and said, "That doesn't mean you had to save me."

He turned and blinked at me, as though puzzled. "What do you mean?"

"You could have let me die."

His hard expression never changed, but he said, "You weren't guilty. You're a part of the White Council." His mouth twisted as though the words were fresh lemons. "Technically. I had an obligation to preserve your life. It was my duty."

"I wasn't the killer," I said.

"No."

"So," I wheezed, "that would make me right. And then that would make *you*—"

Morgan scowled. "More than ready to carry out the Doom if you cross the line, Dresden. Don't think this has gotten you off the hook, as far as I'm concerned."

"So. If I remember correctly, as a Warden, it is your duty to report on my conduct to the Council, isn't it?"

His scowl darkened.

"So you're going to have to go to them on Monday and tell them all about what really happened. The whole truth and nothing but the truth."

"Yes," he snarled. "It is even possible they will lift the Doom."

I started laughing, weakly.

"You haven't won, Dresden. There are many on the Council who know full well that you have consorted with the powers of darkness. *We*, at least, will not relax our vigil on you. We will watch you day and night, we will *prove* that you are a danger who must be stopped."

I kept laughing. I fell over on my side, I laughed so much.

Morgan arched an eyebrow and simply stared at me. "Are you all right?"

"Give me about a gallon of Listerine," I choked, "and I'll be just fine."

Morgan just stared at me, and I laughed harder. He rolled his eyes and growled something about the police being here any moment to provide medical care. Then he turned and stomped off into the woods, muttering to himself the whole way.

The police arrived in time to catch the Beckitts trying to leave and arrested them for, of all things, being naked. Later, they were implicated in the ThreeEye drug ring, and prosecuted on distribution charges. Just as well for them that they're in the Michigan justice system. They wouldn't have come out of a cell alive if they'd been in Chicago. It wouldn't have been good for Johnny Marcone's business.

The Varsity suffered a mysterious fire the night of my visit. I hear Marcone didn't have any trouble collecting the insurance money, in spite of all the odd rumors going around. Word hit the street that Marcone had hired Harry Dresden to take out the head of the ThreeEye gang, one of those rumors that you can't trace back to any one person. I didn't try to deny it. It was a cheap enough price to not have to worry about anyone bombing my car.

I was too hospitalized to show up at the meeting of the White Council, but it turned out that they decided to lift the Doom of Damocles (which I had always thought a rather pretentious name in any case) from me, due to "valorous action above and beyond the call of duty." I don't think Morgan ever forgave me for being a good guy. He had to eat crow in front of the whole Council, relentlessly driven by his anal-retentive sense of duty and honor. There's no love lost between us. But the guy was honest. I'll give him credit for that.

And hell. At least I don't have to look forward to him popping out from nowhere every time I cast a spell. I hope.

Murphy was in critical condition for nearly seventy-two hours, but she pulled through. They gave her a room right down the hall from me, in fact. I sent flowers to her hospital room, along with the surviving ring of her handcuffs. I told her, in a note, not to ask how the chain between the rings had been so neatly severed. I didn't think she'd buy that someone cut it with a magic sword. The flowers must have helped. The first time she got out of bed was to totter down the hall to my room, throw them in my face, and leave without saying a word.

She professed to have no memory of what had happened at my office, and maybe she didn't. But in any case, she got the warrant for my arrest rescinded, and a couple weeks later, when she went back to work, she called me in for advice the next day. And she sent a big check to cover my expenses in the murder investigations. I guess that means we're friends again, in a professional sense. But we don't joke anymore. Some wounds don't heal very quickly.

The police found the remains of the huge ThreeEye stash in what was left of the lake house, and Victor Sells eventually came up as the bad guy. Monica Sells and her children vanished into Witness Protection. I hope they've got a better life now than they had before. I suppose it couldn't be much worse.

Bob eventually came home again, more or less within the twenty-four-hour time limit, I suppose. I turned a deaf ear to rumors of a particularly wild party at the University of Chicago which lasted from Saturday night to Sunday night, and Bob wisely never mentioned it.

DATE WITH A DEMON was a headliner for the *Arcane* when it came out the following Monday, and Susan came by my hospital room to bring me a copy and to talk to me about it. She seemed greatly amused by the cast that held my hips immobilized until the docs could be sure that there wasn't too much fracturing (the X-ray machine kept fouling whenever they tried to use it on me, for some reason), and commented that it was a pity I wasn't more mobile. I used the sympathy factor to badger another date out of her, and she didn't seem to mind too much.

That time, we were *not* interrupted by a demon. And I didn't need any of Bob's love potions or advice, thank you very much.

Mac got his TransAm back. I got the Blue Beetle back. That didn't seem exactly equitable, but at least the Beetle still runs. Most of the time.

I made sure to send pizza out to Toot-toot and his faerie buddies every night for a week, and once a week ever since. I'm pretty sure the kid from Pizza 'Spress thought I was a loony, having him drop off pizza by the roadside. Heck with him. I make good on my promises.

Mister got a little shortchanged on the whole deal, but it is well beneath his dignity to notice such things.

And me? What did I get out of it? I'm not really sure. I escaped from something that had been following me for a long time. I'm just not sure what. I'm not sure who was more certain that I was a walking Antichrist waiting to happen—the conservative branch of the White Council, the men like Morgan, or me. For them, at least, the question has been partly laid to rest. For myself, though, I'm not so sure. The power is there. The temptation is there. That's just the way it's going to be.

I can live with that.

The world is getting weirder. Darker every single day. Things are spinning around faster and faster, and threatening to go completely awry. Falcons and falconers. The center cannot hold.

But in my corner of the country, I'm trying to nail things down. I don't want to live in Victor's jungle, even if it did eventually devour him. I don't want to live in a world where the strong rule and the weak cower. I'd rather make a place where things are a little quieter. Where trolls stay the hell under their bridges and where elves don't come swooping out to snatch children from their cradles. Where vampires respect the limits, and where the faeries mind their *p*'s and *q*'s.

My name is Harry Blackstone Copperfield Dresden. Conjure by it at your own risk. When things get strange, when what goes bump in the night flicks on the lights, when no one else can help you, give me a call.

I'm in the book.

FOOL MOON

Chapter 1

I never used to keep close track of the phases of the moon. So I didn't know that it was one night shy of being full when a young woman sat down across from me in McAnally's pub and asked me to tell her all about something that could get her killed.

"No," I said. "Absolutely not." I folded the piece of paper, with its drawings of three concentric rings of spidery symbols, and slid it back over the polished oak-wood table.

Kim Delaney frowned at me, and brushed some of her dark, shining hair back from her forehead. She was a tall woman, buxom and lovely in an old-world way, with pale, pretty skin and round cheeks well used to smiling. She wasn't smiling now.

"Oh, come on, Harry," she told me. "You're Chicago's only practicing professional wizard, and you're the only one who can help me." She leaned across the table toward me, her eyes intent. "I can't find the references for all of these symbols. No one in local circles recognizes them either. You're the only real wizard I've ever even heard of, much less know. I just want to know what these others are."

"No," I told her. "You don't want to know. You're better off forgetting this circle and concentrating on something else."

"But—"

Mac caught my attention from behind the bar by waving a hand at me, and slid a couple of plates of steaming food onto the polished surface of the crooked oak bar. He added a couple of bottles of his homemade brown ale, and my mouth started watering.

My stomach made an unhappy noise. It was almost as empty as my wallet. I would never have been able to afford dinner tonight, except that Kim had offered to buy, if I'd talk to her about something during the meal. A steak dinner was less than my usual rate, but she was pleasant company, and a sometime apprentice of mine. I knew she didn't have much money, and I had even less.

Despite my rumbling stomach, I didn't rise immediately to pick up the food. (In McAnally's pub and grill, there aren't any service people. According to Mac, if you can't get up and walk over to pick up your own order, you don't need to be there at all.) I looked around the room for a moment, with its annoying combination of low ceilings and lazily spinning fans, its thirteen carved wooden columns and its thirteen windows, plus thirteen tables arranged haphazardly to defray and scatter the residual magical effects that sometimes surrounded hungry (in other words, angry) wizards. McAnally's was a haven in a town where no one believed in magic. A lot of the crowd ate there.

"Look, Harry," Kim said. "I'm not using this for anything serious, I promise. I'm not trying any summoning or binding. It's an academic interest only. Something that's been bothering me for a while." She leaned forward and put her hand over mine, looking me in the face without looking me in the eyes, a trick that few non-practitioners of the Art could master. She grinned and showed me the deep dimples in her cheeks.

My stomach growled again, and I glanced over at the food on the bar, waiting for me. "You're sure?" I asked her. "This is just you trying to scratch an itch? You're not using it for any anything?"

"Cross my heart," she said, doing so.

I frowned. "I don't know . . ."

She laughed at me. "Oh, come *on,* Harry. It's no big deal. Look, if you don't want to tell me, never mind. I'll buy you dinner anyway. I know you're tight for money lately. Since that thing last spring, I mean."

I glowered, but not at Kim. It wasn't her fault that my main employer, Karrin Murphy, the director of Special Investigations at the Chicago Police Department, hadn't called me in for consulting work in more than a month. Most of my living for the past few years had come from serving as a special consultant to SI, but after a fracas last spring involving a dark wizard fighting a gang war for control of Chicago's drug trade, work with SI had slowly tapered off—and with it, my income.

I didn't know why Murphy hadn't been calling me in as often. I had my suspicions, but I hadn't gotten the chance to confront her about them yet. Maybe it wasn't anything I'd done. Maybe the monsters had gone on strike. Yeah, right.

They bottom line was I was strapped for cash. I'd been eating ramen noodles and soup for too many weeks. The steaks Mac had prepared smelled like heaven, even from across the room. My belly protested again, growling its neolithic craving for charred meat.

But I couldn't just go and eat the dinner without giving Kim the information she wanted. It's not that I've never welshed on a deal, but I've never done it with anyone human—and definitely not with someone who looked up to me.

Sometimes I hate having a conscience, and a stupidly thorough sense of honor.

"All right, all right," I sighed. "Let me get the dinner and I'll tell you what I know."

Kim's round cheeks dimpled again. "Thanks, Harry. This means a lot to me."

"Yeah, yeah," I told her, and got up to weave my way toward the bar, through columns and tables and so on. McAnally's had more people than usual tonight, and though Mac rarely smiled, there was a contentment to his manner that indicated that he was happy with the crowd. I snatched up the plates and bottles with a somewhat petulant attitude. It's hard to take much joy in a friend's prosperity when your own business is about to go under.

I took the food, steaks and potatoes and green beans, back to the table and sat down again, placing Kim's plate in front of her. We ate for a while, myself in sullen silence and she in hearty hunger.

"So," Kim said, finally. "What can you tell me about that?" She gestured toward the piece of paper with her fork.

I swallowed my food, took a sip of the rich ale, and picked up the paper again. "All right. This is a figure of High magic. Three of them, really, one inside the other, like layered walls. Remember what I told you about magical circles?"

Kim nodded. "They either hold something out or keep it in. Most work on magic energies or creatures of the Nevernever, but mortal creatures can cross the circles and break them."

"Right," I said. "That's what this outermost circle of symbols is. It's a barrier against creatures of spirit and magical forces. These symbols here, here, here, are the key ones." I pointed out the squiggles in question.

Kim nodded eagerly. "I got the outer one. What's the next?"

"The second circle is more of a spell barrier to *mortal* flesh. It wouldn't work if all you used was a ring of symbols. You'd need something else, stones or gems or something, spaced between the drawings." I took another bite of steak.

Kim frowned at the paper, and then at me. "And then what would that do?"

"Invisible wall," I told her. "Like bricks. Spirits, magic, could go right through it, but mortal flesh couldn't. Neither could a thrown rock, bullets, anything purely physical."

"I see," she said, excited. "Sort of a force field."

I nodded. "Something like that."

Her cheeks glowed with excitement, and her eyes shone. "I *knew* it. And what's this last one?"

I squinted at the innermost ring of symbols, frowning. "A mistake."

"What do you mean?"

"I mean that it's just gobbledygook. It doesn't mean anything useful. Are you sure you copied this correctly?"

Kim's mouth twisted into a frown. "I'm sure, I'm sure. I was careful."

I studied her face for a moment. "If I read the symbols correctly, it's a third wall. Built to withhold creatures of flesh *and* spirit. Neither mortal nor spirit but somewhere in between."

She frowned. "What kind of creatures are like that?"

I shrugged. "None," I said, and officially, it was true. The White Council of wizards did not allow the discussion of demons that could be called to earth, beings of spirit that could gather flesh to themselves. Usually, a spirit-circle was enough to stop all but the most powerful demons or Elder Things of the outer reaches of the Nevernever. But this third circle was built to stop things that could transcend those kinds of boundaries. It was a cage for demonic demigods and archangels.

Kim wasn't buying my answer. "I don't see why anyone would make a circle like this to contain nothing, Harry."

I shrugged. "People don't always do reasonable, sensible things. They're like that."

She rolled her eyes at me. "Come on, Harry. I'm not a baby. You don't have to shelter me."

"And you," I told her, "don't need to know what kind of thing that third circle was built to contain. You don't want to know. Trust me."

She glowered at me for a long moment, then sipped at her ale and shrugged. "All right. Circles have to be empowered, right? You have to know how to switch them on, like lights?"

"Something like that. Sure."

"How would a person turn this one on?"

I stared at her for a long time.

"Harry?" she asked.

"You don't need to know that, either. Not for an academic interest. I don't know what you've got in mind, Kim, but leave it alone. Forget it. Walk away, before you get hurt."

"Harry, I am not—"

"Save it," I told her. "You're sitting on a tiger cage, Kim." I thumped a finger on the paper for emphasis. "And you wouldn't need it if you weren't planning on trying to stick a tiger in there."

Her eyes glittered, and she lifted her chin. "You don't think I'm strong enough."

"Your strength's got nothing to do with it," I said. "You don't have the training. You don't have the knowledge. I wouldn't expect a kid in grade school to be able to sit down and figure out college calculus. And I don't expect it of you, either." I leaned forward. "You don't know enough yet to be toying with this sort of thing, Kim. And even if you did, even if you did manage to become a full-fledged wizard, I'd still tell you not to do it. You mess this up and you could get a lot of people hurt."

"*If* I was planning to do that, it's my business, Harry." Her eyes were bright with anger. "You don't have the right to choose for me."

"No," I told her. "I've got the responsibility to help you make the right choice." I curled the paper in my fingers and crushed it, then tossed it aside, to the floor. She stabbed her fork into a cut of steak, a sharp, vicious gesture. "Look, Kim," I said. "Give it some time. When you're older, when you've had more experience . . ."

"You aren't so much older than me," Kim said.

I shifted uncomfortably in my seat. "I've had a lot of training. And I started young." My own ability with magic, far in excess of my years and education, wasn't a subject I wanted to explore. So I tried to shift the direction of the conversation. "How is this fall's fund-raiser going?"

"It's not," she said. She leaned back wearily in her seat. "I'm tired of trying to pry money out of people to save the planet they're poisoning or the animals they're killing. I'm tired of writing letters and doing marches for causes no one believes in anymore." She rubbed at her eyes. "I'm just tired."

"Look, Kim. Try to get some rest. And please, please don't play with that circle. Promise me."

She tossed her napkin down, left a few bills on the table, and stood up. "Enjoy your meal, Harry," she said. "And thanks for nothing."

I stood up as well. "Kim," I said. "Wait a minute."

But she ignored me. She stalked off toward the door, her skirt swaying along with her long hair. She cut an impressive, statuesque figure. I could feel the anger bubbling off her. One of the ceiling fans shuddered and let out a puff of smoke as she walked under it, then whirled down to a halt. She raced up the short flight of stairs and exited the bar, banging the door shut behind her. People watched her leave, then glanced back to me, speculation on their faces.

I sat back down, frustrated. Dammit. Kim was one of several people I had coached through the difficult period surrounding the discovery of their innate magical talents. It made me feel like crap to withhold information from her, but she had been playing with fire. I couldn't let her do that. It was my responsibility to help protect her from such things, until she knew enough to realize how dangerous they were.

To say nothing of what the White Council would think of a nonwizard toying with major summoning circles. The White Council didn't take chances with things like that. They just acted, decisively, and they weren't always particular about people's lives and safety when they did it.

I had done the right thing. Keeping that kind of information out of Kim's hands had been the right decision. I had been protecting her from danger she didn't, couldn't, fully appreciate.

I had done the right thing—even if she had trusted me to provide answers for her, as I had in the past, when teaching her to contain and control her modest magical talents. Even if she had trusted me to show her the answers she needed, to be her guide through the darkness.

I'd done the right thing.

Dammit.

My stomach was soured. I didn't want any more of Mac's delicious meal, steak or no steak. I didn't feel like I'd earned it.

I was sipping ale and thinking dark thoughts when the door opened again. I didn't look up, occupied as I was with brooding, a famous pastime of wizards everywhere. And then a shadow fell over me.

"Sitting here pouting," Murphy said. She bent over and absently picked up the wadded scrap of paper I had tossed aside earlier, tucking it tidily into her coat pocket rather than letting it lie about as clutter on the floor. "That's not much like you, Harry."

I glanced up at Murphy. I didn't have far to look. Karrin Murphy wasn't much more than five feet tall. She'd gotten her golden hair cut, from shoulder length to something far shorter, and a little longer in front than in back. It was a punky sort of look, and very appealing with her blue eyes and upturned nose. She was dressed for the weather in what must have been her at-home clothes: dark jeans, a flannel shirt, hiking boots, and a heavy woodsman's jacket. She was wearing her badge on her belt.

Murphy was extremely cute, for a grown adult who also held a black belt in aikido, and had several marksmanship awards from Chicago PD. She was a real professional, one who had fought and clawed her way up the ranks to become full lieutenant. She'd made enemies along the way, and one of them had seen to it that she was put in charge of Special Investigations soon after.

"Hello there, Murphy," I told her. I took a swig of ale and said, "Long time, no see." I tried to keep my voice even, but I'm pretty sure she heard the anger in it.

"Look Harry—"

"Did you read the editorial in the *Tribune*? The one criticizing you for wasting the city's money hiring a 'charlatan psychic named Harry Dresden'? I guess you must have, since I haven't heard from you since it came out."

She rubbed at the bridge of her nose. "I don't have time for this."

I ignored her. "Not that I blame you. I mean, not many of the good taxpayers of Chicago believe in magic, or wizards. Of course, not many of them have seen what you and I have. You know. When we worked together. Or when I was saving your life."

Her eyes tightened at the edges. "I need you. We've got a situation."

"You need me? We haven't talked for more than a month, and you need me all of a sudden? I've got an office and a telephone and everything, Lieutenant. You don't need to track me down here while I'm having dinner."

"I'll tell the killer to be sure to operate during business hours next time," Murphy said. "But I need you to help me find him."

I straightened in my chair, frowning. "There's been a murder? Something in my field?"

Murphy flashed a hard smile at me. "I hope you didn't have anything more important to do."

I felt my jaw grow tense. "No. I'm ready." I stood up.

"Well then," she said, turning and walking away. "Shall we go?"

Chapter 2

Murphy declined to ride in the Blue Beetle, my old Volkswagen bug.

The Beetle wasn't really blue, not anymore. One of the doors had been replaced with a green duplicate, the other one with white, when something with claws had shredded the originals. The hood had been slagged by fire, and my mechanic, Mike, had replaced it with the hood from a red vehicle. The important thing is that the Beetle runs, even if it doesn't do it very fast, and I'm comfortable with the car. Mike has declared that the VW bug is the easiest car in the world to repair, and so that's what I drive. He keeps it running eight or nine days in ten. That's phenomenal.

Technology tends to foul up around wizards—flip on a light switch, and it'll be the time the bulb burns out. Drive past a streetlight, and it'll pick just then to flicker and die. Whatever can go wrong will, automobiles included.

I didn't think it made much sense for Murphy to risk her vehicle when she could have taken mine, but she said she'd take her chances.

She didn't speak as she drove her Saturn down the JFK, out toward Rosemont. I watched her, uncomfortable, as we went. She was in a hurry, taking a few too many chances cutting in and out of traffic, and I put on my seat belt. At least we weren't on her motorcycle.

"Murph," I asked her, "where's the fire?"

She glanced aside at me. "I want you out there before some other people show up."

"Press?" I couldn't quite keep a nasty slur out of the word.

She shrugged. "Whoever."

I frowned at her, but she didn't say anything else—which seemed typical. Murphy didn't speak much to me anymore. We rode the rest of the way in silence, exited the JFK, and pulled into the parking lot of a half-completed little strip mall. We got out of the car.

A jet came in, low, heading for O'Hare International Airport, only a few miles to the west. I squinted at it for a moment, and then frowned at Murphy as a uniformed officer led us toward a building surrounded by police tape. There was an abundance of light, the moon overhead bright silver and almost a completely round circle. I cast an enormous, gangly shadow as I walked, my duster flapping around my legs. It towered beside Murphy's far smaller shadow ahead of me.

"Murphy?" I said, "Aren't we outside Chicago city limits?"

"Yeah," Murphy said shortly.

"Uh. Then aren't we out of your jurisdiction, technically?"

"People need help wherever they can get it, Dresden. And the last several killings happened in Chicago, so we want to look at this firsthand. I already worked things out with the local force. It's not really an issue."

"Several killings?" I said. "Several? As in more than one? Murphy, slow down."

But she didn't. Instead, she led me into a roomy building that proved to be under construction, though all the exterior work was finished. Some of the windows were still covered with board. I didn't see the sign on the building's front doors until I got close.

"The Varsity?" I said, reading it. "I thought Marcone burned it down last spring."

"Mmm-hmm," Murphy said, glancing at me over her shoulder. "Relocated and rebuilding."

Chicago's resident crime lord, Gentleman Johnny Marcone, was the robber baron of the mean streets. He kept all the rough business inside the city proper, leaving his legitimate interests out in the suburbs, like here in Rosemont. Last spring, when I had confronted him in his club, a previous incarnation of the Varsity, about a deadly new drug on the streets, the place had wound up burning to the ground.

After the whole mess was over, word got out that the drug dealer I'd taken out had been Marcone's enemy, and that I had nuked him at the crime lord's request. I hadn't refuted the rumor.

It was easier to let people talk than to force Marcone to make an issue of things.

Inside the building, the floors were rough, unfinished. Someone had turned on a couple of halogen work lights, and they cast the interior into brilliant, clear white light. There was drywall dust everywhere. There were a few card tables set up, with workmen's tools left out on them in places. Plastic buckets of paint, tarps, and a sack of new paintbrushes waited for use off to one side. I didn't notice the blood until Murphy put her arm out in front of me to keep me from walking into it.

"Wake up, Dresden," she said. Her voice was grim.

I stopped, and looked down. Blood. A lot of blood. It began near my feet, where a long splatter had reached out like an arm from a drowning man, staining the dusty floor with scarlet. My eyes followed the path of the long bloodstain back to a pool, maybe an eighth of an inch deep, surrounding a mound of ripped cloth and torn meat that must have been the corpse.

My stomach quailed, threatening to eject the bites of steak I'd taken earlier that evening, but I forced it down. I walked in a circle around the body, keeping my distance. The corpse was, I guessed, that of a male in his thirties. He had been a large man, with a short, spiky haircut. He had fallen onto his side, facing away from me, his arms curled up toward his head, his legs up toward his vitals. A weapon, a little automatic pistol, lay seven or eight feet away, uselessly out of the victim's reach.

I walked around the corpse until I could see the face.

Whatever had killed him, it hadn't been human. His face was gone, simply torn away. Something had ripped his lips off. I could see his bloodstained teeth. His nose had been torn all the way up one side, and part of it dangled toward the floor. His head was misshapen, as though some enormous pressure had been put upon his temples, warping his skull in.

His eyes were gone. Torn out of his head. Bitten out. There were the ragged slash marks of fangs all around the edges of the sockets.

I closed my eyes, tightly. I took a deep breath. Another. A third. That didn't help. The body stank, a sickly sewer-smell that rose up from the torn innards. My stomach wanted to roll up my throat, out my mouth, and onto the floor.

I could remember the other details, even with my eyes closed, and catalogued them neatly for later reference. The victim's jacket and shirt had been torn to bloody ribbons along his forearms, in defensive wounds. His hands and arms were a mass of pulped, ripped meat, the palms and fingers slashed to ragged lumps. The curl of his body hid his abdomen from me, but that was where the blood was pooling from, spreading out like ink from a spilled bottle. The stench only confirmed that he had been eviscerated.

I turned away from the corpse and opened my eyes, staring down at the floor.

"Harry?" Murphy said, from the far side of the body. The note of hardness that had been in her voice all evening was absent. She hadn't moved while I had done my cursory examination.

"I recognize him," I said. "At least, I think I do. You'll need to check dental records or something, to be sure."

I could hear her frown in her words. "Yeah? Who was he?"

"I don't know his name. I always called him Spike. For the haircut. He was one of Johnny Marcone's bodyguards."

Murphy was quiet for a moment, then said, succinctly, "Shit."

"What, Murph?" I looked back at her, without looking down at Spike's mangled remains.

Murphy's face was set in concern, for me, her blue eyes gentle. I saw her wipe the expression away, as quickly as a shadow crosses the floor, a smoothing of lines that left her features neutral. I guess she hadn't expected me to turn to her. "Take a look around a little more," she said. "Then we'll talk."

"What am I looking for?" I asked her.

"You'll know it," she said. Then added, in a whisper that I think she didn't intend me to hear, "I hope."

I turned back to my work, and looked around the room. Off to one side, one of the windows was broken. Near it was a table, lying askew on the floor, its legs warped and bent. I walked over to it.

Broken glass littered the ground around the collapsed table. Since the glass was on the inside of the building, something must have come in through the window. There was blood on several of the broken pieces of glass. I picked up one of the larger ones and frowned at it. The blood was dark red, and not yet wholly dried. I took a white handkerchief from my pocket, folded the shard of glass into it, and then slipped it into the pocket of my duster.

I rose and paced over the floor, my eyes downcast, studying the dust. In one spot, it was rubbed almost clean off the floor, as though a struggle had taken place there without blood being spilled. In another spot, where the halogen lamps didn't quite reach, there was a pool of silver moonlight below a window. I knelt down beside it.

In the center of the pool was a paw print, in the dust, a paw print almost as big as my spread hand. Canine. Dots at the tips of the paw spoke of heavy nails, almost claws.

I looked up through the window at the rounded silver shape of the almost-full moon.

"Oh, hell," I breathed. "Oh, hell."

Murphy came toward me and watched me silently for a moment, waiting. I licked my lips, stood up, and turned to her. "You've got problems."

"No kidding. Talk to me, Dresden."

I nodded, then pointed at the window. "The attacker probably came in there. He went after the victim, attacked him, got the gun away from him, and killed him. It's the attacker's blood on the window. They struggled a while, over there by that clean spot, maybe, and Spike made a break for the door. He didn't make it there. He got torn to pieces first."

I turned toward Murphy, looking down at her solemnly. "You've had other murders happen in the same way. Probably about four weeks ago, when the moon was last full. Those were the other killings you were talking about."

Murphy glanced at my face for a moment, keeping her eyes off mine, and nodded her head. "Yeah. Four weeks ago, almost exactly. But no one else picked up the full moon angle. Just me."

"Uh-huh. Then you should see this, too," I said. I led her over to the window and showed her the paw print in the dust beneath it. She regarded it in silence.

"Harry," she said after a minute. "Are there such things as werewolves?" She brushed a strand of hair back from her cheek, a small and oddly vulnerable gesture. She folded her arms over her stomach, as though she were cold.

I nodded. "Yeah. Not like you see in the movies, but yeah. I figure that's what you got going here."

She drew in a deep breath. "All right, then. All right. What can you tell me? What do I need to know?"

I opened my mouth to speak, but I didn't get a chance to say anything. There was a brief bout of shouting outside, and then the front doors of the building banged open. Murphy tensed, and I saw her mouth set in a hard little line. Her back straightened, and she stopped hugging herself, putting her fists on her hips.

"Godammit," she said. "How do those assholes get everywhere so fast?"

I stepped forward, so that I could see. A quartet of people in suits came through the door, fanned out in an almost military diamond formation. The man in front was not quite as tall as me, but still very tall, six feet and three or four inches. His hair was jet black, as were his eyebrows, while his eyes were a shade of grey as pale as wood smoke. His dark blue suit fit him well, and I had the impression that it concealed an athletic build, in spite of the fact that he had obviously seen more than four decades. A blue identification badge reading "FBI" in huge, obnoxious letters dangled from one lapel.

"Secure the scene," he said, his voice deep, tense. "Lieutenant Murphy, what the hell are you doing on a crime scene out of your jurisdiction?"

"Nice to see you, too, Agent Denton," Murphy said in a flat tone. "You get around fast."

"I told you that you weren't welcome on this investigation," Denton said, his words crisp. His grey eyes flashed, and I saw a vein bulge rhythmically on his forehead. His gaze shifted to me. "Who is this?"

"Har—" I started to say, but Murphy's snort cut over my words.

"No one," she said. She flashed me a look that said, very clearly, to shut up. That annoyed the hell out of me.

"Harry Dresden," I said, making the words loud and clear. Murphy and I exchanged a glare.

"Ah," Denton said. "The charlatan. I've read about you in the *Tribune*." His clear, tense gaze returned to Murphy. "You and your psychic friend might want to step out of the way. There's police work being done here. The real kind, where we worry about fingerprints, fibers, genetic matches—silly things like that."

Murphy's eyes narrowed, along with mine, but if the twin glares affected Denton, it didn't show in his face. Murphy and Denton had a brief staring match, her fury against his steely intensity.

"Agent Benn!" Denton called.

A woman, not quite into her thirties, with a shoulder-length mane of hair gone prematurely grey, turned toward us from her intent contemplation of the corpse. She had olive skin, deep, green eyes, and a thin, severe mouth. She walked toward us with a sort of hard-muscled sensuality, moving like someone who is capable of being fast and dangerous when necessary. Of the four FBI agents who had entered the room, she was the only one obviously sporting a weapon. Her jacket was unbuttoned, and I could see the straps of her shoulder rig against the white of her shirt.

"Yes, sir," Benn said. Her voice was very quiet. Her eyes took up a position midway between Murphy and me, looking at neither of us while watching us both.

"Please escort these two *civilians*," Denton stressed the word, "from the crime scene."

Benn nodded once, but didn't say anything in reply. Just waited. I gathered myself to go, but paused. Murphy planted her feet and lowered her arms casually to her sides. I recognized the stubborn out-thrust angle of her jaw. She had that look she got when she was behind on points in one of her martial-arts tournaments. Murphy was ready to fight. Damn. I had to get her cooled off before we could accomplish anything.

"Murphy," I said, quietly. "Can we talk outside?"

"Like hell," Murphy said. "Whoever this killer is, he's knocked off half a dozen people in the last month. I'm here, and I'm after this man. The Rosemont department has given their consent for me to be here." Murphy glared up at Benn. The FBI agent had her by a considerable margin of reach and muscle. I saw Benn's eyes narrow, her shoulders grow tenser.

"Do you have that in writing?" Denton demanded. The vein in his head throbbed more angrily. "And do you really think you want me reporting this to your superiors, Lieutenant?"

"Don't push me, Denton," Murphy said, her voice hot. I winced.

"Look, Murphy," I said. I put a hand on her shoulder. "Let's just go outside for a minute." I squeezed, just a little.

Murphy turned back toward me. She chanced a brief glance up at my eyes, and then relaxed a little, a flicker of uncertainty crossing her features. She started to ease down, and I let my breath out. I definitely didn't want this dissolving into violence. It wouldn't accomplish anything.

"Get them out of here," Denton said, and there was a note to his voice that I didn't like.

Benn didn't give us any warning. She just moved, fast and hard, stepping toward Murphy and flicking some sort of martial-arts blow I wasn't familiar with toward her temple. There was a quick blur of motion. Murphy's hands got there before the blow landed, and she turned, somehow levering Benn's weight off from her legs and slamming the grey-maned woman hard into a wall.

Benn's expression went from shocked and surprised to furious in the space of half a second. Her hand dipped into her jacket, hesitated for half a second, and then resumed motion. She drew her gun with an expert's precision, smooth and quick without seeming hurried. Her green eyes blazed. I threw myself at Murphy, colliding with her and driving her over and down as the gun went off, louder than a close clap of thunder in the interior of the half-finished restaurant. We landed in a heap on the dusty floor.

"Benn!" Denton shouted. He lunged for her, heedless of the gun, and got between the armed woman and us. I could hear him talking to her in a low, urgent voice.

"You crazy bitch!" I shouted. "What is the matter with you?"

The two other FBI guys and several patrol officers from outside came running. Murphy grunted and elbowed me in the gut, urgently. I grunted back and moved off of her. Both of us climbed to our feet unhurt.

"What the hell happened?" demanded one of the officers, an older man with thinning grey hair.

Denton turned to the officer, calm and cool. "Misfire. There was a misunderstanding and Agent Benn's weapon accidentally discharged."

The officer rubbed at his scalp and eyed Murphy. "Is that true, Lieutenant?"

"Like hell!" I said. I pointed a finger at Benn. "This crazy bi—"

Murphy jammed an elbow into my stomach and glared at me. "That's true," Murphy said, while I rubbed at my gut. "It happened just like Agent Denton said. An accident."

I stared at her. "Murph, give me a break. This woman—"

"Had an accident with her weapon," Murphy said, voice hard. "Could have happened to anyone." Murphy turned her glare on the aging officer, and he blinked mildly at her, then shrugged.

Denton turned back to us and studied Murphy intently for a second. Then he nodded. "Roj, George. Why don't you two make sure the Lieutenant is all right and help her to her car?"

"Sure, sure, Phil," said a skinny kid with red hair, big ears, and freckles. "Uh, Mr. Dresden, Lieutenant Murphy. Why don't we go outside and get some air? I'm Roger Harris, and this is Agent Wilson."

The other FBI guy, a bulky, overweight man in his late forties, his hair receding and his gut overhanging his belt, just beckoned us to follow him and walked toward the door. Murphy glared at

Denton for a moment, then spun on her heel and stalked after the bulky Wilson. I followed her.

"I can't believe that. You all right? Why the hell didn't you tell them what she did?" I asked Murphy, sotto voce.

"That bitch," Murphy said back, not nearly as quiet. "She tried to sucker punch me."

"She tried to *ventilate* you, Murph," I countered.

Murphy let out a breath between her teeth, but kept walking. I glanced back at the room behind us and saw Spike's torn and mangled body being surrounded by more police tape. Forensics had arrived, and the team was getting set to sweep the room. Denton was kneeling down beside Benn, who had her face in her hands, and looked as though she were weeping. Denton was watching me, his grey eyes calculating and expressionless, filing me away under "tall, slender, dark hair, dark eyes, hawkish features, no visible scars."

I stared at him for a minute and got a hunch, a solid intuition of which I was completely sure. Denton was hiding something. He knew something, and he wasn't talking. Don't ask me how I knew it, but something about him, about the way the veins bulged in his forehead, or the way he held his neck so stiffly, made me think so.

"Um," the kid, Harris, said. I blinked and turned to him. He opened the door for Murphy and me, and we walked outside. "Maybe give Deborah some slack. She's really stressed out about these Lobo killings. She hasn't slept much the past month. She knew one of the guys who got killed. She's been tense ever since."

"Shut up, Harris," the overweight Agent Wilson said, his tone disgusted. "Just shut up." He turned to the two of us and said in a calm voice, "Get the hell out of here. I don't want to see either of you around a scene that isn't on your turf, Lieutenant Murphy. Internal Affairs has enough to do, don't you think?"

He turned and went back into the building. The redheaded kid gave us an apologetic, awkward smile, and then hurried to catch up with the overweight agent. I saw him shoot a glance back at me, his expression thoughtful. Then he was gone. The door shut, leaving Murphy and me on the outside, away from the investigation and the evidence at the crime scene.

I looked up through the clear night at the almost-full moon. Werewolves jumping through windows at gangster's lackeys in unfinished restaurants. A mangled corpse in the middle of a blood-drenched floor. Berserk FBI field agents drawing guns and shooting to kill. A little kung fu, a little John Wayne, and a few casual threats.

So far, I thought, my nerves jangling, just one more night on the job.

Chapter 3

My stomach roiled around with disgust at the macabre sights inside the building, and with tension at what had nearly happened. One of my ears was still ringing from the sound of the gunshot. I was starting to shake all over now, the adrenaline rush fading and leaving me jumpy and wired. I stuck my hands in my duster's pockets, careful of the bloodstained shard of glass wrapped in my handkerchief, and turned my face into the wind, closing my eyes.

Relax, Harry, I told myself. Calm down. Breathe in and out, and just keep doing it. See? You aren't dead. Dead people don't breathe like that. You aren't Spike, all torn to pieces on the floor. You don't have any bullet holes in you, either. You're alive, and Murphy's all right, and you don't have to look at that eyeless face anymore.

But I could see the torn body, still, behind my eyelids. I could smell the ghastly stench of his opened innards. I could remember the blood, sticky on the dusty floor, congealing, thick with tiny flecks of drywall. I tasted bile in my throat, and fought to keep from throwing up.

I wanted to scream, to run, to wave my arms and kick something until I felt better. I could understand Agent Benn's reaction, almost, if she had been working a string of killings like the one I'd just seen. You can't stare at that much blood for very long without starting to see more of it everywhere else.

I just kept taking deep breaths, in and out. The wind was cool and fresh in my face, sharp with the smells of the coming autumn. October evenings in Chicago are chilly, breezy, but I love them anyway. It's my favorite time of year to be outside. I eventually calmed down. Murphy must have been doing the same thing beside me, making herself relax. We both started walking back toward the car at the same time, no words needing to be passed between us.

"I . . ." Murphy began, and fell silent again. I didn't look at her, didn't speak. "I'm sorry, Harry. I lost control. Agent Denton is an asshole, but he does his job, and he was right. Technically speaking, I didn't have any right to be on the scene. I didn't mean to drag you into all this."

She unlocked the doors and got in the car. I got in the passenger side, then reached out and plucked the keys from her hand as she began to start the engine. She quirked her head at me, narrowing her eyes.

I closed my hands around the keys. "Just sit down and relax for a while, Murph. We need to talk."

"I don't think that's a good idea, Harry," she said.

"This is the thanks I get for saving your life. Twice, now. You're going to hold out on me."

"You should know how it works," she said, scowling. But she settled back in her seat and looked out the windshield of the car. We could see the police, forensics, and the FBI suits moving back and forth inside the building. We were both quiet for a long time.

The funny thing was that the problems between Murphy and me came from the same source as the problems with Kim Delaney earlier tonight. Murphy had needed to know something to pursue an investigation. I could have given her the information—but it would have put her in danger to do so. I'd refused to say anything, and when I'd pursued the trail by myself all the way to its end, there had been some burning buildings and a corpse or two. There wasn't enough evidence to bring any charges against me, and the killer we'd been after had been dealt with. But Murphy hadn't ever really forgiven me for cutting her out of the loop.

In the intervening months, she'd called me in for work several times, and I'd given the best service I could. But it had been cool between us. Professional. Maybe it was time to try to bridge that gap again.

"Look, Murph," I said. "We've never really talked about what happened, last spring."

"We didn't talk about it while it was happening," she said, her tone crisp as autumn leaves. "Why should we start now? That was last spring. It's October."

"Give me a break, Murphy. I wanted to tell you more, but I couldn't."

"Let me guess. Cat had your tongue?" she said sweetly.

"You know I wasn't one of the bad guys. You have to know that by now. Hell's bells, I risked my neck to save you."

Murphy shook her head, staring straight forward. "That's not the point."

"No? Then what is?"

"The point, Dresden, is that you lied to me. You refused to give me information that I needed to do my job. When I bring you in on one of my investigations, I am *trusting* you. I don't just go around trusting people. Never have." She took a grip on the steering wheel, her knuckles whitening. "Less than ever, now."

I winced. That stung. What's worse, she was in the right. "Some of what I knew . . . It was dangerous, Murph. It could have gotten you killed."

Her blue eyes fixed on me with a glare that made me lean back against the car door. "I am *not* your daughter, Dresden," she said, in a very soft, calm voice. "I am not some porcelain doll on a shelf. I'm a police officer. I catch the bad guys and I put their asses away, and if it comes down to it, I take a bullet so that some poor housewife or CPA doesn't have to." She got her gun out of its shoulder holster, checked the ammo and the safety, and replaced it. "I don't need your protection."

"Murphy, wait," I said hastily. "I didn't do it to piss you off. I'm your friend. Always have been."

She looked away from me as an officer with a flashlight walked past the car, shining the light about on the ground as he looked for exterior evidence. "You were my friend, Dresden. Now . . ." Murphy shook her head once and set her jaw. "Now, I don't know."

There wasn't much I could say to that. But I couldn't just leave things there. In spite of all the time that had gone by, I hadn't tried to look at things from her point of view. Murphy wasn't a wizard. She had almost no knowledge of the world of the supernatural, the world that the great religion of Science had been failing to banish since the Renaissance. She had nothing to use against some of the things she encountered, no weapon but the knowledge that I was able to give her—and last spring I had taken that weapon away from her, left her defenseless and unprepared. It must have been hell for Murphy, to daily place herself at odds with things that didn't make any sense, things that made forensics teams just shake their heads.

That's what Special Investigations did. They were the team specially appointed by the mayor of Chicago to investigate all the "unusual crimes" that happened in the city. Public opinion, the Church, and official policy still frowned at any references to magic, the supernatural, vampires, or wizards; but the creatures of the spirit world still lurked about, trolls under bridges, cradle-robbing faeries, ghosts and spooks and boogers of every kind. They still terrorized and hurt people, and some of the statistics I'd put together indicated that things were only getting worse, not better. Someone had to try to stop it. In Chicago or any of its sprawling suburbs, that person was Karrin Murphy, and her SI team.

She had held the position longer than any of her many predecessors—because she had been open to the idea that there might be more than was dreamt of in Horatio's books. Because she used the services of the country's only wizard for hire.

I didn't know what to say, so my mouth just started acting on its own. "Karrin. I'm sorry."

Silence lay between us for a long, long time.

She gave a little shiver, finally, and shook her head. "All right," she said, "but if I bring you in on this, Harry, I want your word. No secrets, this time. Not to protect me. Not for anything." She stared out the window, her features softened in the light of the moon and distant streetlights, more gentle.

"Murphy," I said, "I can't promise that. How can you ask me to—"

Her face flashed with anger and she reached for my hand. She did something to one of my fingers that made a quick pain shoot up my arm, and I jerked my hand back by reflex, dropping the keys. She caught them, and jammed one of them in the ignition.

I winced, shaking my stinging fingers for a moment. Then I covered her hand with mine.

"Okay," I said. "All right. I promise. No secrets."

She glanced at me, at my eyes for a breath, and then looked away. She started the car and drove from the parking lot. "All right," she said. "I'll tell you. I'll tell you because I need every bit of help I can get. Because if we don't nail this thing, this werewolf, we're going to have another truckload of corpses on our hands this month. And," she sighed, "because if we don't, I'm going to be out of a job. And you'll probably end up in jail."

Chapter 4

"Jail?" I said. "*Jail?* Hell, Murphy. Were you planning on mentioning this to me anytime soon?"

She shot me an irritated scowl, headlights of cars going the opposite way on the highway flaring across her face. "Don't even start with me, Harry. I've had a long month."

A dozen questions tried to fight their way out of my mouth. The one that ended up winning was, "Why didn't you call me in on the other killings, last month?"

Murphy turned her eyes back to the road. "I wanted to. Believe me. But I couldn't. Internal Affairs started riding me about what happened with Marcone and Victor Sells last spring. Someone got the idea that I was in cahoots with Marcone. That I helped to murder one of his competitors and took out the ThreeEye drug ring. And so they were poking around pretty hard."

I felt an abrupt twinge of guilt. "Because I was on the scene. You had that warrant out for me and then had it rescinded. And then there were all those rumors about me and Marcone, after the whole thing was over . . ."

Murphy's lips compressed, and she nodded. "Yeah."

"And if you'd have tried to tell me about it, it would have been throwing gasoline on the fire." I rubbed at my forehead. And it would have gotten me looked at harder, too, by whoever was investigating Murphy. She had been protecting me. I hadn't even considered what those rumors Marcone had spread might do to anyone besides myself. Way to go, Harry.

"One thing you're not is stupid, Dresden," she confirmed. "A little naive, sometimes, but never stupid. IA couldn't turn anything up, but there are enough people who are certain I'm dirty that, along with the people who already don't like me, they can screw me over pretty hard, given the chance."

"That's why you didn't make an issue out of what Agent Benn did," I guessed. "You're trying to keep everything quiet."

"Right," Murphy said. "I'd get ripped open from ass to ears if IA got word of me so much as bending the rules, much less tussling with one of the bureau's agents. Believe me, Denton might look like a jerk, but at least he isn't convinced that I'm dirty. He'll play fair."

"And this is where the killings come in. Right?"

Instead of answering, she cut into the slow lane and slowed to a leisurely pace. I half turned toward her in my seat, to watch her. It was while I did this that I noticed the headlights of another car drift across a couple lanes of traffic to drop into the slow lane behind us. I didn't say anything about it to Murphy, but kept a corner of my eye on the car.

"Right," Murphy said. "The Lobo killings. They started last month, one night before the full moon. We had a couple of gangbangers torn to pieces down at Rainbow Beach. At first, everyone figured it for an animal attack. Bizarre, but who knew, right? Anyway, it was weird, so they handed the investigation to me."

"All right," I said. "What happened then?"

"The next night, it was a little old lady walking past Washington Park. Killed the same way. And it just wasn't *right,* you know? Our forensics guys hadn't turned up anything useful, so I asked in the FBI. They've got access to resources I can't always get to. High-tech forensics labs, that kind of thing."

"And you let the djinni out of the bottle," I guessed.

"Something like that. FBI forensics, that redheaded kid with them, turned up some irregularities in the apparent dentition of the attackers. Said that the tooth marks didn't match genuine wolves or dogs. Said that the paw prints we found were off, too. Didn't match real wolves." She gave a little shudder and said, "That's when I started thinking it might be something else. You know? They figured that someone was trying to make it *look* like a wolf attack. With this whole wolf motif, someone started calling the perpetrator the Lobo killer."

I nodded, frowning. The headlights were still behind us. "Just a crazy thought: Have you considered telling them the truth? That we might be dealing with a werewolf here?"

Murphy sneered. "Not a chance. They hire conservatives for jobs at the bureau. People who don't believe in ghosts and goblins and all that crap out there that I come to you about. They said that the murders must have been done by some sort of cult or pack of psychos. That they must have furnished themselves with weapons made out of wolf teeth and nails. Left symbolic paw prints around. That's why all the marks and tracks were off. I got Carmichael to check up on you, but your answering service said you were in Minnesota on a call."

"Yeah. Someone saw something in a lake," I confirmed. "What happened after that?"

"All hell broke loose. Three bums in Burnham Park, the next night, and they weren't just dead, they were *shredded*. Worse than that guy tonight. And on the last night of the full moon, an old man outside a liquor store. Then the night after that, we had a businessman and his driver torn up in a parking garage. IA was right there breathing down my neck the whole time, too. Observing everything." She shook her head with a grimace.

"That last victim. All the others were outside, and in a bad part of town. Businessman in a parking garage doesn't fit that pattern."

"Yeah," Murphy said. "James Harding III. One of the last of the red-hot industrialists. He and John Marcone are business partners in some development projects up in the Northwest."

"And tonight, we have another victim linked to Marcone."

"Yeah." Murphy nodded. "I'm not sure what's scarier. Thinking that these are just regular animal attacks, that they're being done by a bunch of psychos with knives edged with wolf teeth, or that they're organized werewolves." She let out a strained little laugh. "That still sounds crazy, even to me. Yes, Your Honor, the victim was killed by a werewolf."

"Let me guess. After the full moon it got quiet."

Murphy nodded. "IA wrapped up with inconclusive findings, and nothing much else happened. No one else died. Until tonight. And we've got four more nights of bright moonlight left, if whoever they are sticks to their pattern."

"You sure there's more than one?" I asked.

"Yeah," Murphy said. "There's bite marks, or bitelike marks, according to Agent Denton, from at least three different weapons. As far as all the lab guys are concerned, it could be multiple perpetrators, but there's no way for forensics to be sure."

"Unless it's real werewolves we're dealing with. In which case each set of marks goes with a different set of teeth, and we're looking at a pack."

Murphy nodded. "But there's no way I'm going to just come out and tell them that. That would put the nails in my career's coffin."

"Uh-huh," I said. "This is the part where you tell me about your job being in danger."

She grimaced. "They only need a good reason to get rid of me, now. If I don't catch these guys, whoever they are, politics will hang me out to dry. After that, it'll be simple for them to get some charges going on me for complicity or obstruction. And they'll probably try to get to you, too. Harry, we've got to catch the killer, or killers. Or I'm history."

"You ever get any blood or hair from the scenes?" I asked.

"Yeah, some," Murphy said.

"What about saliva?"

Murph frowned at me.

"Saliva. It would be in the bite wounds."

She shook her head. "If they've found it, no one has said anything. Besides, all the samples won't do us a lot of good without a suspect to match them against."

"It won't do *you* a lot of good," I corrected her. "Something left blood on the window when it came through. Maybe that'll turn something up."

Murphy nodded. "That would be great. Okay, Harry. So you know what's going on now. What can you tell me about werewolves?"

I pursed my lips for a minute. "Not much. They weren't ever anything I studied too hard. I can tell you what they're not, mostly. Give me until morning, though, and I'll put together a full report on them." I glanced out the back window as Murphy pulled off the JFK Expressway. The car that I thought had been following us exited as we did.

Murphy frowned. "Morning? Can you do it any sooner?"

"I can have it on your desk by eight. Earlier, if you tell the night sergeant to let me in."

Murphy sighed and rubbed at her eyes. "Okay. Fine." We got back to McAnally's, and she pulled in next to the Blue Beetle. Behind us, the car that had been following us also came into the parking lot. "Jesus, Harry. I can't believe I'm sitting here talking to you about werewolves killing people in downtown Chicago."

She turned her face to me, her eyes anxious. "Tell me I'm not going nuts."

I got out of the car, but leaned down to the window. "I don't think you're going nuts, Murph. I don't know. Maybe the FBI is right. Maybe it's not werewolves. Crazy things happen sometimes." I gave her half of a smile, which she answered with a faint snort.

"I'll probably be in my office, Dresden," she said. "Have that report on my desk by morning."

And then she pulled out of the parking lot, turning quickly out onto the street. I didn't get into the Beetle. Instead, I watched the car that had followed us into the parking lot. It cruised around the far side of the lot, then started down the row, toward me, and kept on going.

The driver, a striking woman with shaggy, dark brown hair, peppered with grey, did not turn to look at me as she went past.

I watched the car go, frowning. It left the lot, turning the opposite way Murphy had, and vanished from sight. Had that been the same vehicle that had followed us down the JFK? Or had it only been my imagination? My gut told me that the woman in the car had been following me, but then again, my instincts had cried wolf before.

I got into the Blue Beetle and thought for a minute. I was feeling guilty and a little queasy still. It was my fault Murphy had gotten in trouble. I had put her in the middle of extremely questionable circumstances by not telling her what was going on last spring. The pressure she was under now was my responsibility.

I have what might be considered a very out-of-date and chauvinist attitude about women. I like to treat women like ladies. I like to open doors for them, pay for the meal when I'm on a date, bring flowers, draw out their seat for them—all that sort of thing. I guess I could call it an attitude of chivalry, if I thought more of myself. Whatever you called it, Murphy was a lady in distress. And since I had put her there, it only seemed right that I should get her out of trouble, too.

That wasn't the only reason I wanted to stop the killings. Seeing Spike torn up like that had scared the hell out of me. I was still shaking a little, a pure and primitive reaction to a very primal fear. I did not want to get eaten by an animal, chewed up by something with a lot of sharp teeth. The very thought of that made me curl up on my car's seat and hug my knees to my chest, an awkward position considering my height and the comparatively cramped confines of the Beetle.

What had happened to Spike was as brutal and violent a death as anyone could possibly have. Maybe the thug had deserved it. Maybe not. Either way, he was only one victim of many that had been torn apart by something that regular people shouldn't have to face. I couldn't just stand aside and do nothing.

I'm a wizard. That means I have power, and power and responsibility go hand in hand. I have a responsibility to use the power I've been given, when there is a need for it. The FBI was not in any sense prepared to deal with a pack of ravening werewolves stalking down victims in the midst of a Chicago autumn. That was more my department.

I let out a long breath and sat up again. I reached into my duster's pocket for car keys, and found the shard of glass wrapped up in my white handkerchief.

I unwrapped it slowly and found the blood-smeared glass still there.

Blood has a kind of power. I could use the blood, cast a spell that would let me follow the blood back to the person who had spilled it. I could find the killer tonight, simply let my magic lead me to him, or them. But it would have to be now. The blood was almost dry, and once it was, I would have a hell of a lot more trouble using it.

Murphy would be royally pissed if I took off without her. She would probably assume that I had intended to follow the trail tonight, purposely leaving her out of the loop. But if I didn't follow the trail, I'd lose the chance to stop the killer before another night fell.

It didn't take me long to make up my mind. In the end, saving lives was more important than keeping Murphy from being pissed off at me.

So I got out of the Beetle and opened the storage trunk at the front of the VW. I took out a few wizardly implements: my blasting rod, the replacement for my shield bracelet, and one other thing that no wizard should be without. A Smith and Wesson .38 Chief's Special.

I carried all of these back to the front of the car with me and got out the shard of glass with smeared blood.

Then I made with the magic.

Chapter 5

I got out the lump of chalk I always keep in my duster pocket, and the circular plastic dome compass that rides a strip of velcro on my dashboard, then squatted down, my voluminous coat spreading out over my legs and ankles. I drew a rough circle upon the asphalt around me with the chalk. The markings were bright against the dark surface and almost glowed beneath the light of the nearly full moon.

I added an effort of will, a tiny investment of energy, to close the circle, and immediately felt the ambient magic in the air around me crowd inward, trapped within the confines of the design. The hairs at the nape of my neck prickled and stood on end. I shivered, and took the shard of glass with its swiftly drying bloodstain and laid it down in the circle between the toes of my boots.

I began a low little chant of nonsense syllables, relaxing, focusing my mind on the effect I wanted. *"Interessari, interressarium,"* I murmured, and touched the plastic dome of the compass to the damp blood. Energy rushed out of me, swirled within the focusing confines of the circle I had drawn, and then rushed downward into the compass with a visible shimmer of silver, dust-like motes.

The compass needle shuddered, spun wildly, and then swung to the bloodstain on the dome like a hound picking up a scent. Then it whirled about and pointed to the southeast, whipping around the circle to hover steadily in that direction.

I grinned in anticipation and smudged the chalk with my boot, releasing the remaining stray energy back into the air, then took up the compass and returned to the Blue Beetle.

The problem with this particular spell was that the compass needle would point unerringly at whomever the blood had come from until the sun rose the next morning and disrupted the simple magical energies I had used to make the spell; but it didn't point out the swiftest way to get to the target, only the direct direction in which he, she, or it lay.

Traffic in Chicago isn't ever what any sane person would call friendly or simple, but I had lived there for a while and had learned to survive. I drove past Cook County Hospital, a virtual city of its own inside Chicago, and down past Douglas Park, then turned south on Kedzie. The compass needle slowly aligned to point hard to the east as I traveled south, and I wound up turning east on Fifty-fifth, toward the University of Chicago and Lake Michigan.

It wasn't exactly a good part of town. In fact, as far as neighborhoods go in Chicago, it was pretty bad. There was a high crime rate, and a lot of the buildings were run-down, abandoned, or only infrequently used. Streetlights were out in a lot of places, so when night closed in, it was darker than most areas. It's always been a favorite haunt for some of the darker things that come crawling out of the Nevernever for a night on the town. Trolls lurked about like muggers some nights, and any new vampire that came through the city always ended up in this neighborhood or one like it, searching for prey until he could make contact with Bianca or one of the lesser vampire figures of the city.

I pulled over as the compass swung to point at what looked like an abandoned department store, and I killed the engine. The faithful Beetle rattled to a grateful halt. I got the map of the city out of the glove box and squinted at it for a moment. Washington Park and Burnham Park, where four of last month's deaths had taken place, were less than a mile away on either side of me.

I felt a little shiver run through me. This sure as hell looked like the place to find Murphy's Lobo killer.

I got out of the car. I kept the blasting rod in my right hand, the dashboard compass in my left. My shield bracelet dangled on my left wrist. My gun was in the left pocket of my duster, within easy reach. I took a moment to take a deep breath, to clear my mind, and to clarify what I wanted to do.

I wasn't here to bring the killer down, whoever he was. I was just locating him for Murphy. Murphy could put the guy under surveillance and nail him the next time he tried to move. Even if I did capture him, Murphy couldn't exactly bring him up on charges, based on the word of a professional *wizard*. Municipal judges would love having a cop appear before them and start spouting such crazy talk.

I spun my blasting rod around in my fingers, grinned, and started forward. That was all right. I didn't need the justice system to recognize my power to be able to use it.

There were boards over the front windows of the once department store. I tested each one as I went past and found one that swung in easily. I stopped and examined it carefully, wary of any alarms that might be attached to it.

Such as the string tied across the bottom, lined with little jingle bells. If I had pushed the wooden sheet any further inward, I would have set it to jangling. Instead, I slipped the string off the head of one of the nails it hung by, lowered the bells carefully, and slipped inside the dim confines of the abandoned store.

It was a skeletal place. There were still the bones of shelves, forming long aisles, but now barren of merchandise. Empty fluorescent light fixtures dangled in forlorn rows from the ceiling, and the powdered glass of shattered, tubular bulbs dusted the floor beneath them. Light seeped in from the street, mostly moonlight, but more light came from the back of the store. I checked my bloodstained compass. The needle was pointing firmly toward the light. I closed my eyes, and Listened, a skill that isn't hard to pick up, but that most people don't know how to do anymore. I heard voices, at least a pair of them, talking in hushed, urgent tones.

I crept toward the back of the store, using the barren shelves to keep myself from being seen. Then I held my breath and peeked up over the top of the last row of shelves.

Gathered around an old Coleman lantern were several people, all young, of various shapes and sizes and both genders. They were dressed in all shades of black, and most wore jackets and bracelets and collars of dark leather. Some had earrings and nose rings; one had a tattoo showing on his throat. If they had been tall, muscular folk, they would have looked intimidating, but they weren't. They looked like college students, or younger, some still with acne, or too-oily hair, beards that wouldn't quite grow all the way in, and the thinness of youth. They looked awkward and out of place.

Four or five of them were gathered behind and around a stout young man less than five and a half feet tall. He had thick glasses and pudgy fingers, and would have looked more at home with a pocket protector than with the spiked leather gloves on his fingers. He stood with his hands on his hips, glaring up at a rail-thin blonde girl at least a head taller than he, the lines of her willowy body all awkward, her long, sad face set in an expression of anger. Her hair fell about her face and head in a ragged mane, but her eyes sparkled with contained wrath. Another five or six of the young people were gathered behind her, and everyone seemed tense.

"And I'm telling you," the young man snarled in a muted voice, "that we should be out there right now. We can't allow ourselves to rest until we've found them all and torn them apart." There was a murmur of agreement from the people behind him.

"I swear, Billy," the blonde said. "You're such a testosterone-laden idiot. If we were out there right now, they might catch on to us."

"Use your head, Georgia," Billy snapped back. "You think they haven't figured it out by now? They could take all of us out right this minute if they hit us."

"They haven't," Georgia pointed out. "*She* told us not to move again tonight, and I'm not moving. And if you try it, so help me, I'm going to tie your ankles to your ears."

Billy growled, actually growled, though it sounded posed and forced, and stepped forward. "You think you can handle me, bitch?" he said. "Bring it on."

Georgia's eyes narrowed. "I didn't sign on to this wolf thing to fight hapless losers like you, Billy. Don't make me start now." She glared at the young people standing behind Billy. "You know what *she* told us. Are you going to start going up against her word?"

"Listen, Alphas," Billy said, turning to look at those behind him, and then at those backing his opponent. "I've led you for all this time. I've done what I've promised to do. Are you going to stop trusting *me*?"

I peered at the discussion and then lowered my head again, back into the shadows. Holy I-Was-a-Teenage-Werewolf, Batman. I checked my compass, and it pointed firmly at the lit room, the group gathered around the lantern. Were these the killers? They looked more like a group of computer nerds geared up for Leather Night.

This was a start at least. I could clear out now, and let Murphy know what I had seen. I'd need to check around the building outside first, see if any of the group had any cars parked nearby, to be able to give Murphy the license plate numbers. Hell, we weren't far from the university. Maybe some of them would have parking passes.

"What is the meaning of this?" came a clear, strident woman's voice.

I craned my neck up to the edge of the shelf again. A dark-complected woman, as tall as the long-faced blonde, but older, solid with muscle and moving with an animal surety, had come into the room from a back door. Her brown hair was peppered with grey, and it took me only a second to recognize the woman from the car in the parking lot outside of McAnally's. My heart started to pound a little more quickly with excitement. She had been following Murphy and me, after all. She glared at the two groups of young people, her eyes an almost eerie shade of amber that could barely be construed as brown. "Have I taught you no better?" the woman demanded.

Billy and Georgia were both looking down at the floor uncomfortably. The other young people had assumed similar postures, like a group of children caught planning to go out after curfew.

"This isn't a game. Someone followed me here. They're on to us. If you start making mistakes now, you'll pay for them with your life," the woman said, stalking back and forth around the group. I checked my compass.

The needle swung back and forth as she walked, pointing solidly at her. My heart leapt into my throat. I considered this woman, with her almost animal vitality, her commanding presence and force of will. This woman, I thought, might be a killer. And she knew she had been followed. How? How in the hell had she known I was after her?

I looked up at her again, excited, only to find her staring intently at the thick patch of shadows around the shelves I hid behind. One of the young people started to say something, and the woman raised her hand for silence. I saw her nostrils flare as she breathed in through her nose, and she took a step in my direction. I held my breath, not daring to duck back down behind the shelves, lest the motion give me away.

"Join hands," snapped the woman. "Now." And then she turned to the Coleman lantern on the floor and snuffed it out, plunging the room into blackness.

There was a moment of confused murmuring, a commanding hiss from the woman, and then there was nothing but silence and the sound of shoes and boots moving over the tiles, toward the back of the store. They were getting away. I rose, blind, and headed around the shelves toward them as quickly as I could, trying to follow.

In retrospect, it wasn't the smartest decision, but I knew that I couldn't afford to let them get away. The spell I'd wrought on my compass wouldn't last long, not long enough to find the woman again, much less any of her pack of young people. I wanted to follow them out, to get the license plates on their cars, anything that would let me help Murphy locate them after they'd run.

I miscalculated the length of my stride and bounced into the wall at the end of the aisle. I sucked in a hiss of pain and reoriented myself, following them, using the darkness to conceal me as much as they did. I could have made some light for myself—but as long as no one could see, no one would start shooting, either, I reasoned. I moved out carefully, Listening, and following the sounds.

I had only a second's warning, the sound of claws sliding on the old tile, and then something large and furry slammed into my legs below the knee, taking them out from under me and sending me heavily to the floor. I let out a shout and swung my blasting rod like a baseball bat, feeling it crack down solidly on something hard and bony. There was a snarl, a deep, animal sound, and something tore the rod from my hand and sent it flying away. It clattered hollowly on the tile floor. I dropped my compass, scrabbled for my gun, and got my feet underneath me, backpedaling, yelling my fear out into a wordless challenge.

I stood still for a moment, staring at nothing, breathing hard, my gun heavy in my hand. Fear made my heart pound, and as always, anger followed hard on the heels of fear. I was furious that I had been attacked. I'd half expected something to try to stop me, but in the dark whatever had been snarling had scared me a lot more than I'd thought it would.

Nothing happened after a minute, and I couldn't hear anything. I reached into my shirt and drew out the silver pentacle that had been my mother's, the five-pointed star upright within a circle, the symbol of order, symmetry, balance of power. I focused my will on it, concentrating, and the pentacle began to glow with a faint, gentle light—hardly the blinding luminescence that came as the result of focusing power against a being of the Nevernever, but adequate enough to navigate by, at least. I moved toward the back room, blue-white light like moonlight pooled around me.

It was definitely stupid to keep going forward, but I was angry, furious enough to bumble my way through the back room of the department store, until I saw the dark blue outline of an open doorway. I headed for it, tripping over a few more things along the way that I couldn't quite make out in the werelight of my amulet, angrily kicking a few things from the path of my feet, until I emerged into an alley behind the old building, breathing open air, able to see again in dim shapes and colors.

Something hit me heavily from behind, driving me to the ground, gravel digging into my ribs through my shirt. My concentration vanished, and with it the light of my amulet. I felt something hard and metallic shoved against the back of my skull, a knee pressed into the small of my back, and a woman's voice snarled, "Drop the gun, or I blow your head off."

Chapter 6

Call me crazy, but I'm not big on defiance when I've got a gun rammed against my skull. I carefully set the .38 in my left hand down and moved my fingers away from it.

"Hands behind your back. Do it," snarled the woman. I did it. I felt the cold metal of the handcuffs around my wrists, heard the ratcheting sound of the cuffs closing around them. The knee lifted off of my back, and my attacker shoved me over with one leg, snapped on a flashlight, and shone it in my eyes.

"Harry?" she said.

I blinked and squinted against the light. I recognized the voice now. "Hi, Murphy. This is going to be one of those conversations, isn't it?"

"You jerk," Murphy said, her voice harsh. She was still only a shadow behind the flashlight, but I recognized the contours now. "You found a lead and followed it, and you didn't contact me."

"Those who live in glass houses, Lieutenant," I said, and sat up, my hands still held tightly behind my back. "There wasn't time. It was hot and I couldn't afford to wait or I might have lost it."

Murphy grunted. "How did you find this place?"

"I'm a wizard," I told her, and waggled my arms as best I could. "Magic. What else?" Murphy growled, but hunkered down behind me and unlocked the cuffs. I rubbed at my wrists after they were freed. "How about you?"

"I'm a cop," she said. "A car tailed us back to McAnally's from the murder scene. I waited until it was gone and followed it back here." She stood up again. "You were inside. Did anyone go out the front?"

"No. I don't think so. But I couldn't see."

"Dammit," Murphy said. She put her gun away in her coat. "They didn't come out the back. There must be some way up to the roof." She stood up and peered around at the closely packed buildings, shining her flashlight around the roof's edge. "They're long gone by now."

"Win some, lose some." I got to my feet.

"Like hell," she said and turned and started into the building.

I hurried to catch up with her. "Where are you going?"

"Inside. To look for stairs, a ladder, whatever."

"You can't follow them," I said, falling into step beside her as she went into the darkened building. "You can't take them on, not with just you and me."

"Them?" Murphy said. "I only saw one." She stopped and looked at me, and I explained to her in terse terms what had happened since we parted in the parking lot. Murphy listened, the lines at the corners of her blue eyes serious.

"What do you think happened?" she asked when I was finished.

"We found werewolves," I said. "The woman, the dark one with the grey in her hair, was their leader."

"Group killers?" Murphy said.

"Pack," I corrected her. "But I'm not so sure that they were the killers. They didn't seem . . . I don't know. Cold enough. Mean enough."

Murphy shook her head and turned to walk outside. "Can you give me a good description?"

I kept up with her. "Good enough, I guess. But what do you want it for?"

"I'm going to put out an APB for the woman we saw, and I want you to describe the kids you heard talking."

"What do you need that for? Don't you have the plates off the car she was driving?"

"I already called them in," Murphy said. "Rental. Probably taken out under a false ID."

"I think you've got the wrong people, Murph," I said. "Don't put out that APB."

"Why shouldn't I?" Murphy asked. "Someone follows me back to town from the scene of a murder. Not only that, but you can confirm to me that they were the killer from the scene. Not in a court of law, I know, but you can give it to me, and that's enough. Standard investigation will turn up the rest if we know where to look."

I held up my hand. "Hold on, hold on. My spell didn't tell me that the woman was the killer. Only that it was her blood at the scene."

Murphy folded her arms and glared up at me. "Whose side are you on, anyway?"

"You still don't get it, Murphy," I said, my own temper rising a little. "You don't start something with the kind of people who live in boogety-land unless you're willing to take it all the way, right there, right then. If you start harassing a pack of werewolves, setting the police after them, you've just declared war. You'd better be ready to fight it."

Murphy thrust her jaw out. "Don't worry about me. I can handle it."

"I'm not saying you can't," I said. "But whatever it was that tore apart Spike back at Marcone's club wasn't the same thing that was with me in the dark back there." I jerked my head at the main room of the department store.

"Oh yeah?" Murphy said. "Why not?"

"Because it could have killed me and it didn't."

"You don't think you could have taken care of yourself against a wolf, Harry?"

"In the dark?" I said. "Murphy, it's been nearly a hundred years since the wolf went extinct in most of the United States. You've got no idea, none at all, of how dangerous they can be. A wolf can run faster than you can drive a car through most of Chicago. His jaws can snap your thighbones with one jerk. A wolf can see the heat of your body in the complete dark, and can count the hairs on your head from a hundred yards off by starlight. He can hear your heart beating thirty or forty yards away. The wolf that was there in the dark with me could have killed me, easy. It didn't. It disarmed me, even after I'd hit it, and then it left."

"That doesn't mean anything," Murphy said—but she folded her arms over her stomach and glanced at the shadows around us with a little shiver. "Maybe the killer knows you. Maybe it didn't want to risk killing a wizard. Maybe, just maybe, the wolf did it to throw you off. Maybe it spared you just so you would react in this way, just to avoid suspicion."

"Maybe," I admitted. "But I don't think so. The kids I saw . . ." I shook my head. "Don't put out the APB, yet. Hold off on it, until I can get you some more information. Look, you pay me to give you my advice, to be your consultant on the supernatural. I'm your expert, right? Listen to me. Trust me."

She stared up at my face, her expression intent, looking away quickly when her eyes met mine. Murphy had known me for a while. You don't go looking into a wizard's eyes without a darned good reason. Wizards see too much.

"All right," she said finally. "I'll hold off on it—but only until tomorrow morning, when I have that report. If you can't show me anything by then, I'm going ahead after the people we saw tonight." Her mouth quirked in a fierce little grin. "I'd have a hell of a time explaining what I was doing out at the crime scene in Rosemont, anyway." The grin vanished, leaving only ferocity. "But you *will* have that information for me, Dresden, bright and early. Make no mistake. I will catch the killer before anyone else dies."

I nodded to Murphy. "In the morning," I said. "You got it."

Murphy's flashlight flickered and then went out as the filament burst with an audible pop.

Murphy sighed in the darkness. "Nothing ever works right when you're here. Sometimes, Harry," she said, "I really hate hanging out with you."

Chapter 7

I entered my apartment, tossed my blasting rod, which I had recovered from the abandoned department store, into the corner next to my wizard's staff and my sword cane, and locked the door behind me. It was one of those steel-frame doors, the antiburglar kind. I bought it after a demon had come stomping into my apartment six months ago and wrecked my place.

My apartment is in the basement of a huge old rooming house that somehow managed to survive all the Chicago fires. It's made almost entirely of wood, and it creaks and groans when the wind blows, which is all the time in this city, and makes gentle, soothing music. It's a place with a history, the neighbors are quiet, and my rent is cheap—though less so than it was before the demon trashed my place.

The apartment itself is devoid of electrical devices, for reasons that should be evident by now. There is a fireplace, and a kitchenette off the main room, a little bedroom adjacent to that, and a bathroom inside the bedroom. Sunken windows are high on each of the four walls, and one is on the wall of the bathroom.

I decorate in textures more than I do in colors; there were thick rugs all over the bare stone floors, layered on top of one another in most places. Demon acid had burned away most of my furniture, and I had been obliged to scavenge secondhand stores for replacements. I like furniture with a lot of old wood and soft cloth, and I had made my purchases accordingly. Tapestries hung from my walls, the oldest tapestries that I could find, covering the bare stone. In the ruddy firelight, the oranges and browns and reds that constituted the primary colors of the decor didn't look half bad.

I went over to the fireplace and built up the fire. October in Chicago is a cold, breezy month, and my dank little haven is usually chilly until I get a fire going. I dropped a few logs on the fire, and Mister made an appearance, rubbing up against my leg and purring fondly, staggering my balance off to one side.

"Been getting into the steaks again, eh, Mister?" I said, and rubbed the big, grey cat's ears. Mister is larger than a lot of dogs. Maybe one of his parents was part wildcat. I found him in a dumpster one day when he was a kitten and he promptly adopted me. Despite my struggles, Mister had been an understanding soul, and I eventually came to realize that I was a part of his little family, and by his gracious consent was allowed to remain in his apartment. Cats. Go figure.

I fired up the wood-burning stove and prepared a quick meal of Spaghettios, grilled chicken, and toast. Mister shared in my meal, and split a can of Coke with me, as usual, and I tossed the dishes in the sink to soak before I went to my bedroom and put on my robe.

Let the wizardry commence.

I went to a spot in the far corner and moved the rug there, then lifted up the door in the floor beneath it, revealing the steep stepladder that led down to the subbasement, where I kept my lab.

I teetered down the stairs, holding a lit candle that cast a golden glow on the cheerful havoc that is my laboratory. Tables lined the walls, and the longest table filled most of the center of the room, leaving a cramped walk space around it, except for an area at the far side of the lab that I kept completely clear for my summoning circle, a ring of bright copper set into the floor. Books, notebooks, defunct ballpoint pens, broken pencils, boxes, plastic containers, old butter bowls, empty jelly jars, and plastic Baggies lay next to other containers of every size and shape that held the spices, rare stones, bones, fur, blood, oddments, jewelry, and other ingredients useful to wizardly pursuits and studies.

I reached the bottom of the ladder, stepped over a precariously balanced stack of comic books (don't ask), and started lighting the other candles that lay on dishes around the chilly room, finally bending to light up the kerosene heater that I keep down in the lab in an effort to at least blunt the cold. "Bob," I said then. "Wake up, sleepyhead."

Up on one of the shelves, huddled in the midst of a thick stack of hardbacks, was the bleached, smooth form of a human skull, its empty eye sockets gaping. Deep in those eye sockets, there was a flickering of orange light, which grew and solidified into twin points of lambent illumination. "Sleepyhead. Oh, that's rich, Harry. With a sense of humor like that, you could make a living as a garbage man anywhere in the country." The skull's mouth gaped open in the parody of a yawn, though I knew the spirit within, Bob, didn't feel fatigue in the same way that living beings did. I put up with his lip, so to speak—Bob had worked for several wizards over the course of a dozen mortal lifetimes, and he knew more about the nuts and bolts of magic than I ever would.

"What are we doing, now?" Bob sniggered. "More weight-loss potions?"

"Look, Bob," I said. "That was only to get me through a rough month. Someone's got to pay the rent around here."

"All right," Bob said smugly. "You going to get into breast enhancement, then? I'm telling you, that's where the money is."

"That isn't what magic is for, Bob. How petty can you get?"

"Ah," Bob said, his eye lights flickering. "The question is, how *pretty* can you get *them*? You aren't a half-bad wizard, Dresden. You should think about how grateful all those beautiful women will be."

I snorted and started cleaning off a space on the center table, stacking things up to one side. "You know, Bob, some of us aren't obsessed with sex."

Bob snorted, no easy feat for a guy with no nose or lips. "Some of us don't take a real, working body and all five senses for granted, either, Harry. When's the last time you saw Susan?"

"I don't know," I responded. "Couple weeks ago. We're both pretty busy with work."

Bob heaved a sigh. "A gorgeous woman like that, and here you are, down in your musty old lab, getting ready to do more ridiculous nonsense."

"Precisely," I said. "Now, shut up and let's get to work."

Bob grumbled something in Latin, but rattled a few times to shake the dust off of the skull. "Sure, what do I know? I'm just a pathetic little spirit, right?"

"With a photographic memory, three or four hundred years' worth of research experience, and more deduction capacity than a computer, Bob, yeah."

Bob almost seemed to smile. "Just for that, you get my best effort tonight, Harry. Maybe you're not such an idiot after all."

"Great," I said. "I want to work up a couple of potions, and I want to know everything you know about werewolves."

"What kind of potions, and what kind of werewolves?" Bob said promptly.

I blinked. "There's more than one?"

"Hell, Harry. We've made at least three dozen different kinds of potions down here ourselves, and I don't see why you wouldn't—"

"No, no, no," I growled at Bob. "Werewolves. There's more than one kind of werewolf?"

"Eh? More than one kind of what?" Bob tilted his skull over to one side, as though cocking an invisible hand to his ear bones.

"Werewolf, werewolf."

"*There* wolf," Bob replied solemnly, his voice seething with a hokey accent. "*There* castle."

I blinked at him. "Uh. What the heck are you talking about?"

"It's a *joke,* Harry. Stars almighty, you *never* get out, do you?"

I eyed the grinning skull and growled in frustration. "Don't make me come up there."

"Okay, okay. Sheesh. Aren't we grumpy tonight?" Bob's jaws stretched in a yawn again.

"I'm working another murder case, Bob, and I don't have time to goof around."

"Murder. Mortal business is so complicated. You never hear about murder charges in the Nevernever."

"That's because everything there is immortal. Bob, just shut up and tell me what you know about werewolves. If there's a bunch of different flavors, tell me what they are." I got out a notebook and a fresh pencil, then a couple of clean beakers with alcohol-flame burners to heat whatever liquid I put in them.

"All right," Bob said. "How much do you know?"

"Exactly nothing about werewolves. My teacher never covered that with me."

Bob barked out a harsh little laugh. "Old Justin had a lousy sense of just about everything. He got what was coming to him, Harry, and don't let anyone on the White Council tell you any different."

I stopped for a moment. A sudden rush of mixed feelings, anger and fear and mostly regret, washed through me. I closed my eyes. I could still see him, my teacher, dying in flames born of my will and anger. "I don't want to talk about it."

"Hell, the Council even suspended the sentence on you. You were vindicated. Say, I wonder what ever happened to Elaine. Now *there* was a sweet piece of—"

"Werewolves, Bob," I said, in a very quiet, very angry voice. One hand started to hurt, and I saw that my fingers had clenched into a fist, the knuckles turning white. I turned my eyes to him, glaring.

I heard the skull make a gulping sound. And then he said, "Right. Okay. Werewolves. And, uh, which potions did you want?"

"I want a pick-me-up potion. A night's rest in a bottle. And I want something that will make me imperceptible to a werewolf." I reached for the notebook and my pencil.

"First one's tough to do. There's nothing quite like a decent night's sleep. But we can make some super-coffee, no problem." He spouted out the formula to me, and I noted it down as he went, my handwriting too dark and angular. I was still angry from the mere mention of my old master's name. And the welter of emotions that rushed up with my memories of Elaine wouldn't subside for an hour.

We all have our demons.

"What about the second one?" I asked the skull.

"Can't really be done," Bob said. "Wolves have just got way too much on the ball to hide from every one of their senses without doing some major work. I'm talking, like, a greater Ring of Invisibility, not just a Shadowcape or something."

"Do I look like I'm made of money? I can't afford that. What about a partial-hiding potion, then?"

"Oh, like a blending brew? Look like an unobtrusive part of the background, something like that? I would think that would be the most useful, really. Keep you from being noticed to begin with."

"Sure," I said. "I'll take what I can get."

"No problem," Bob assured me, and rattled off another formula, which I jotted down. I checked the ingredients list, and thought that I had them all in stock among the countless containers on my shelves.

"Fine. I can get started on these. How much do you know about werewolves, Bob?"

"Plenty. I was in France during the Inquisition." Bob's voice was dry (but that is to be expected, considering).

I started on the first potion, the stimulant. Every potion has eight parts. One part is a base liquid to hold the others and provide a medium for mixing. Five parts are symbolically linked to each of the five senses. One is similarly linked to the mind, and another to the spirit. The basic ingredient to the stimulant potion was coffee, while the base for the scent-masking potion was water. I got them both to boiling. "Lot of werewolfery going on then?"

"Are you kidding?" Bob said. "It was werewolf central. We had every kind of werewolf you could think of. Hexenwolves, werewolves, lycanthropes, and loup-garou to boot. Every kind of lupine theriomorph you could think of."

"Therro-what?" I said.

"Theriomorph," Bob said. "Anything that shapeshifts from a human being into an animal form. Werewolves are theriomorphs. So are werebears, weretigers, werebuffaloes . . ."

"Buffaloes?" I asked.

"Sure. Some Native American shamans could do a buffalo. But almost everyone does predators, and until pretty recently, wolves were the scariest predator anyone around Europe could think of."

"Uh, okay," I said. "And there's a difference between types of werewolves?"

"Right," Bob confirmed. "Mostly it depends on how you go from human form to wolf form, and how much of your humanity you retain. Don't burn the coffee."

I turned down the flame beneath the beaker of coffee, annoyed. "I know, I know. Okay, then. How do you get to be a wolf?"

"The classic werewolf," Bob said, "is simply a human being who uses magic to shift himself into a wolf."

"Magic? Like a wizard?"

"No," Bob said. "Well. Sort of. He's like a wizard who only knows how to cast the one spell, the one to turn him into a wolf, and knows how to get back out of it again. Most people who learn to be werewolves aren't very good at it for a while, because they keep all of their own humanity."

"What do you mean?"

"Well," Bob said, "they can reshape themselves into the form of a wolf, but it's pretty much just topology. They rearrange their physical body, but their mind remains the same. They can think and reason, and their personality doesn't change—but they don't have a wolf's instincts or reflexes. They're used to being sight-oriented bipeds, not smell-oriented quadrupeds. They would have to learn everything from scratch."

"Why would someone do something like that?" I said. "Just learn to turn into a wolf, I mean."

"You've never been a peasant in medieval France, Harry," Bob said. "Life was hard for those people. Never enough food, shelter, medicine. If you could give yourself a fur coat and the ability to go out and hunt your own meat, you would have jumped at the chance, too."

"Okay, I think I've got it," I said. "Do you need silver bullets or anything? Do you turn into a werewolf if you get bitten?"

"Bah," Bob said. "No. Hollywood stole that from vampires. And the silver-bullet thing is only in special cases. Werewolves are just like regular wolves. You can hurt them with weapons just like you can a real wolf."

"That's good news," I said, stirring the potion. "What other kinds are there?"

"There's another version of a werewolf—when someone *else* uses magic to change you into a wolf."

I glanced up at him. "Transmogrification? That's illegal, Bob. It's one of the Laws of Magic. If you transform someone into an animal, it destroys their personality. You *can't* transform someone else without wiping out their mind. It's practically murder."

"Yeah. Neat, huh? But actually, most personalities can survive the transformation. For a little while at least. Really strong wills might manage to keep their human memories and personality locked away for several years. But sooner or later, they're irretrievably gone, and you're left with nothing but a wolf."

I turned from the potions to scribble in my notebook. "Okay. What else makes a werewolf?"

"The most common way, back in France, was to make a deal with a demon or a devil or a powerful sorcerer. You get a wolf-hide belt, put it on, say the magic words, and whammy, you're a wolf. A *Hexenwolf*."

"Isn't that just like the first kind?"

"No, not at all. You don't use your own magic to become a wolf. You use someone else's."

I frowned. "Isn't that the second kind, then?"

"Stop being obtuse," Bob chided me. "It's different because you're employing a talisman. Sometimes it's a ring or amulet, but usually it's a belt. The talisman provides an anchor for a spirit of bestial rage. Nasty thing from the bad side of the Nevernever. That spirit wraps around a human personality to keep it from being destroyed."

"A kind of insulation," I said.

"Exactly. It leaves you with your own intellect and reason, but the spirit handles everything else."

I frowned. "Sounds a little easy."

"Oh, sure," Bob said. "It's really easy. And when you use a talisman to turn into a wolf, you lose all of your human inhibitions and so on, and just run on your unconscious desires, with the talisman-spirit in charge of the way the body moves. It's really efficient. A huge wolf with human-level intelligence and animal-level ferocity."

I eyed Bob, and gathered up the other ingredients for the stimulant potion: a morning donut, for taste; a cock's crow, for hearing; fresh soap, for smell; bits of a washcloth, for touch; and a beam of dawn sunshine for sight; a to-do list, for the mind; and a bit of bright, cheerful music, for the spirit; and the potion was simmering along nicely.

Bob said nothing while I added the ingredients, and when I was finished I said, "Most people don't have the strength to control a spirit like that, I'd think. It would influence their actions. Maybe even control them. Suppress their conscience."

"Yeah. So?"

"So it sounds more like you'd be creating a monster."

"It's effective," Bob said. "I don't know about the good or the evil of the thing. That's something that only you mortals worry about."

"What did you call this flavor again?"

"Hexenwolf," Bob said, with a strong Germanic accent. "Spell wolf. The Church declared war on anyone who chose to become a Hexenwolf, and burned a huge number of people at the stake."

"Silver bullets?" I asked. "Bitten and turn into a werewolf?"

"Would you get off this 'bitten and turn into a werewolf' kick, Harry?" Bob said. "It doesn't work that way. Not ever. Or you'd have werewolves overrunning the entire planet in a couple of years."

"Fine, fine," I sighed. "What about the silver bullets?"

"Don't need them."

"All right," I said, and continued jotting down information to put together for Murphy in a report. "*Hexenwolf*. Got it. What else?"

"Lycanthropes," Bob said.

"Isn't that a psychological condition?"

"It might *also* be a psychological condition," Bob said. "But it was a reality first. A lycanthrope is a natural channel for a spirit of rage. A lycanthrope turns into a beast, but only inside his head. The spirit takes over. It affects the way he acts and thinks, makes him more aggressive, stronger. They also tend to be very resistant to pain or injury, sickness; they heal rapidly—all sorts of things."

"But they don't actually shapeshift into a wolf?"

"Give that boy a Kewpie," Bob said. "They're just people, too, but they're awfully fierce. Ever heard of the Norse berserkers? Those guys were lycanthropes, I think. And they're born, not made."

I stirred the stimulant potion, and made sure it was at an even simmer. "And what was the last one? Loop what?"

"Loup-garou," Bob said. "Or that was the name Etienne the Enchanter used for them, before he got burned at the stake. The loup-garou are the major monsters, Harry. Someone has cursed them to become a wolflike demon, and usually at the full moon. That someone's got to be really powerful, too, like a major heavyweight sorcerer or a demon lord or one of the Faerie Queens. When the full moon comes, they transform into a monster, go on a killing spree, and slaughter everything they come across until the moon sets or the sun rises."

A sudden little chill went over me, and I shivered. "What else?"

"Supernatural speed and power. Supernatural ferocity. They recover from injuries almost instantly, if they become hurt at all. They're immune to poison and to any kind of sorcery that goes for their brain. Killing machines."

"Sounds great. I guess this hasn't happened all that often? I'd have heard something by now."

"Right," Bob said. "Not often. Usually, the poor cursed bastard knows enough to shut himself away somewhere, or to head out into the wilderness. The last major loup-garou rampage happened around Gevaudan, France, back in the sixteenth century. More than two hundred people were killed in a little more than a year."

"Holy shit," I said. "How did they stop it?"

"They killed it," Bob said. "Here's where the silver bullets finally come in, Harry. Only a silver weapon can hurt a loup-garou, and not only that, the silver has to be inherited from a family member. Inherited silver bullets."

"Really? Why would that work and not regular silver?"

"I don't make the laws of magic, Harry. I just know what they are and have an idea of when they're changing. That one hasn't changed. I think maybe it has something to do with the element of sacrifice."

"Inherited silver," I mumbled. "Well. We'll just have to hope that this wasn't a loup-garou, I guess."

"If it was a louper, you'd know," Bob said wisely. "In the middle of this town, you'd have a dozen people dead every time the full moon came around. What's going on?"

"A dozen people are dying every time the full moon comes around." I filled Bob in on the Lobo killings, giving him all the information Murphy had given to me, and started on the next potion. Into the water went the ingredients: plastic wrap for sight; a bit of plain white cotton, for touch; a little deodorant for smell; a rustle of wind for hearing; a leaf of plain old lettuce, for taste; and finally I threw in a blank piece of paper, for the mind, and some elevator music for the spirit. The ingredients were boring. The potion looked and smelled boring. Perfect.

"Lot of dead people," Bob commented. "I'll let you know if I think of anything good. I wish I knew something else."

"I want you to learn more," I told him. "Go out and see what else you can round up on werewolves."

Bob snorted. "Fat chance, Harry. I'm a spirit of intellect, not an errand boy." But when I said the word "out," Bob's eyes glittered.

"I'll pick you up some new romance novels, Bob," I offered.

Bob's teeth clicked a couple of times. "Give me a twenty-four-hour pass," he said.

I shook my head. "Forget it. The last time I let you out, you invaded a party over at Loyola and set off an orgy."

Bob sniffed. "I didn't do anything to anyone that a keg wouldn't have done."

"But those people didn't *ask* for you to get into their systems, Bob. No way. You had your fun, and I'm not letting you out again for a while."

"Oh, come on, Harry."

"No," I said flatly.

"It would only be one little night o—"

"No," I said again.

Bob glowered at me and demanded, "New romances. None of those tatty used ones. I want something off the bestseller list."

"I want you back by sunrise," I countered.

"Fine," Bob snapped. "I can't believe how ungrateful you are, after everything I've done for you. I'll see if I can get someone's name. There might be a spirit or two who could get you some juicy information." The orange lights that were his eyes glittered and then flowed out of the skull in a misty cloud of lambent illumination. The cloud flowed up the ladder and out of my laboratory.

I sighed and set the second potion to simmering. It would take another hour or two to cook the potions, and then to shove the magic into them, so I sat down with my notebook and started writing up my report. I tried to ignore the headache that was creeping up the back of my neck toward the crown of my head, but it did little good.

I had to help Murphy nail the killer, whoever it was, while avoiding any trouble with the FBI. Otherwise, she was out of a job, and even if I didn't end up in jail, I would be out of a living myself. Johnny Marcone's man had been killed, and I would be a fool to think he would stand idly by and do nothing in response. I was sure the gangster would rear his head sooner or later.

Aside from all of that, there was a monster of one kind or another lurking in the dark, and the police and the FBI had been helpless to stop it. That left only me, Harry Dresden, your friendly neighborhood wizard, to step in and do something about it. And, if the killer figured out that I was getting involved, he would doubtless start gunning for me next. My troubles were multiplying.

Hexenwolves. Werewolves. Lycanthropes. Loup-garou.

What will they think of next?

Chapter 8

The police headquarters downtown consists of a sprawling collection of buildings that have sprung up over the years as the need for law enforcement has increased. They don't match, and they come from a wildly varying selection of styles and designs, but they have somehow adapted themselves into a cohesive whole—much like the force itself. Special Investigations operates out of a big, run-down old building, a huge cube that has managed to hold up solidly in spite of the years, the grime, the smog, and the graffiti sprayed on its walls. It has bars over the windows and the doors and sits hunkered amidst buildings much taller than it, like a faithful old bulldog amidst a crowd of unruly children, struggling to maintain peace and order.

The inside of the building is plain, even dingy, but they keep it clean. The old warhorse of a desk sergeant eyed me as I entered the station, his grey mustache bristling over an impressive jaw. "Hiya, Bill," I told him, and held up the manila envelope I had under one arm. "Bringing something up to Murphy in SI."

"Dresden," he said warily and jerked a thumb toward the stairs behind him, giving me permission to go.

I hadn't gotten much sleep the night before, but I had showered and dressed nicely before I left the house, in neat business clothes, for once, instead of my usual western shirt and blue jeans. I kept the battered old duster, though, with my blasting rod dangling from a thong inside of it. I took the stairs two at a time and passed a few cops along the way. Several recognized me, and one or two even nodded, but I thought I could detect a sense of uneasiness from each of them. Apparently, I was carrying a distinct odor with the law at the moment.

I wrinkled up my nose. The police had always known me as something of a nut, the crazy guy who claimed to be a wizard, but a useful nut, who could provide good information and whose apparent "psychic abilities" had helped them on a number of occasions. I was used to being seen as one of the good guys, but now the cops were giving me the neutral, professional glances that they would give to a potential criminal, rather than the casual greetings one would give to a comrade in arms. It was to be expected, maybe, since rumor had associated my name with Johnny Marcone's, but it was still disturbing.

I was muttering to myself and deep in my own sleep-deprived thoughts when I bumped into a tall, lovely woman, dark of hair and eye, full of mouth, long of leg. She was wearing a tan skirt and jacket with a crisp white blouse. Her raven brows furrowed in consternation until she looked up at me, and then her eyes glowed with a sort of friendly avarice. "Harry," she said, her lips curving into a smile. She stood up on her tiptoes and kissed my cheek. "Fancy seeing you here."

I cleared my throat. "Hi, Susan," I said. "Did that syndication deal go through?"

She shook her head. "Not yet, but I'm hoping. After those stories you gave me last spring, people started taking me a little more seriously." She paused, drawing in a little breath. It made her chest rise and fall most attractively. "You know, Harry. If you're working with the police again, and if you should happen to be able to let me in on whatever is going on . . ."

I shook my head and tried to scowl at her. "I thought we agreed. I won't poke into your business deals and you won't poke into mine."

She smiled up at me and touched a finger to my chest. "That was whenever we were out on a date, Harry." She let her eyes wander down the length of my body, and then back up. "Or staying in on one."

"Susan Rodriguez, I never knew you were a lawyer as well as a journalist."

"Now you're getting nasty," she said, grinning. "Seriously, Harry. Another exposé like last spring could make my career."

"Yeah, well after last spring, the city made me sign about two tons of nondisclosure agreements. I can't tell you anything about the case."

"So don't tell me about the case, Harry—but if you could mention, say, a nice spot in the street where I might stand and get some good pictures, I would be very," she leaned up and kissed my neck. "Very"—the kiss traveled to my earlobe—"grateful."

I swallowed and cleared my throat. Then took a step back down the stairs, away from her. I closed my eyes for a second and listened to the thunder of my suddenly pounding heart. "I'm sorry. I can't do that."

"Oh, Harry. You're no fun." She reached out and ran a hand over my hair, then smiled to let me know that there were no hard feelings. "But let's get together soon, all right? Dinner?"

"Sure," I said. "Hey. What are you doing down here this early?"

She tilted her head, considering me. "Trade me? I'll show you mine if you'll show me yours. Off the record, even."

I snorted. "Susan, give me a break."

She let out a little sigh and shook her head. "I'll call you about dinner, all right?" She started down the stairs past me.

"All right," I said. "All right. I'm bringing a report on werewolves to Murphy."

"Werewolves," she said, her eyes lighting. "Is that who's behind the Lobo murders?"

I frowned. "No comment. I thought the FBI was keeping that under wraps."

"You can't kill a dozen people and expect no one to notice," Susan said, her voice sly. "I keep track of the city morgues."

"God, you're so romantic. All right, your turn. Give."

"I was trying to talk to the investigator from the department's Internal Affairs. Word is that they're putting pressure on Murphy, trying to clear her out of Special Investigations."

I grimaced. "Yeah. I heard that, too. Why does it concern you and the *Arcane*?"

"The most successful preternatural investigator the police department has gets hung out to dry? Even if people don't believe it, Murphy does a lot of good. If Murphy gets fired, and I can show how the numbers of mysterious crimes and unexplained deaths go up after she leaves, maybe I can get people to listen to papers like the *Arcane*. And to people like you."

I shook my head. "People don't want to believe in magic anymore. Or things that go bump in the dark. For the most part, they're happier not knowing."

"And when not knowing gets someone killed?"

I shrugged. "That's where people like me and Murphy come in."

Susan eyed me doubtfully. "All I need is something solid, Harry. An eyewitness account, a photograph, something."

"You can't photograph anything really supernatural," I pointed out. "The energies around things like that will mess up cameras. Besides, the stuff I'm dealing with right now is too dangerous. You could get hurt."

"What if I shot from a long way off?" she pressed. "Used a telephoto lens?"

I shook my head. "No, Susan. I'm not going to tell you anything. It's for your own good as much as for mine."

She pressed her lips together. "Fine," she said, her tone crisp, and went on down the stairs. I watched her go, dismayed. It seemed I was making a habit of excluding people from certain brands of information. Not only were my job and my freedom on the line, and Murphy's job, too—now it seemed that my love life, or what passed for it, was in danger as well.

I took a moment to try to sort through my thoughts and feelings on Susan, and gave it up as hopeless. Susan was a reporter for the Midwestern *Arcane,* a tabloid circulated widely from Chicago. It usually ran headlines about Elvis and JFK singing duets in Atlantic City, or on similar topics, but once in a while Susan managed to slip in something about the real world of the supernatural, the one that people had forgotten about in favor of Science. She was damned good at her job, absolutely relentless.

She was also charming, gorgeous, funny, and sexy as hell. Our dates often ended in long, passionate evenings at my place or hers. It was an odd relationship, and neither one of us had tried to define it. I think maybe we were worried that if we did, we would change our minds and write it off as a bad idea.

I continued up the stairs, my mind a tired muddle of blood-spattered corpses, savage beasts, angry ex-apprentices, and sultry, dark eyes. There are times when my work is hard on my love life. But one thing I'm not is a boring date.

The doors to the SI office swung open just before I reached for them, and I drew up short. Agent Denton of the FBI was there, tall and immaculate in his grey suit. He stopped, too, and looked at me, holding open the door with one arm. There were bags under his grey eyes, but they were still calculating, assessing, and the veins in his forehead bulged with hypertension.

"Mr. Dresden," he said, and nodded to me.

"Agent Denton," I replied, keeping my tone polite, even

friendly. "Excuse me. I need to get something to Lieutenant Murphy."

Denton frowned a little, and then glanced at the room behind him, before coming all the way out into the hall and letting the door swing shut. "Maybe now isn't the best time for you to see her, Mr. Dresden."

I glanced up at the clock on the wall. It was five minutes before eight. "She wanted it early." I stepped to one side, to go around him.

Denton put a hand on my chest—just that. But he was strong. He might have been shorter than me, but he was carrying a lot more muscle. He didn't look at my eyes, and when he spoke, his voice was very quiet. "Look, Dresden. I know what happened last night didn't look good, but believe me when I say that I've got nothing against Lieutenant Murphy. She's a good cop, and she does her job. But she's got to follow the rules, just like everyone else."

"I'll keep that in mind," I told him and started to move again.

He kept up the pressure against my chest. "There's an agent from Internal Affairs in there with her right now. He's already in a bad mood from being hassled by some reporter. Do you really want to go in there and make him start asking all sorts of questions?"

I glanced at him, frowning. He lowered his hand from my chest. I didn't go around him, yet. "You know about the investigation she's under?"

Denton shrugged a shoulder. "It's to be expected, all things considered. Too much of what has happened in the past looks suspicious."

"You really don't believe, do you?" I asked him. "You don't believe that I'm a real wizard. You don't believe in the supernatural."

Denton straightened his tie. "What I believe doesn't matter, Mr. Dresden. What is important is that a lot of the scum out there believe in it. It affects the way they think and operate. If I could make use of your advice to solve this case, I would, the same as any other law officer." He glanced at me and added, "Personally, I think you are either slightly unstable or a very intelligent charlatan. No offense."

"None taken," I said, my voice wry. I nodded to the door. "How long will Murphy be busy?"

Denton shrugged. "If you like, I'll take the report in to her, drop it on her desk. You can go down the hall and call her. It doesn't matter to me, but I don't mind helping out a straight cop."

I thought it over for a second, and then passed the folder to him. "I appreciate it, Agent Denton."

"Phil," he said. For a second, he almost smiled, but then his face resumed its usual tense expression. "Do you mind if I take a look at it?"

I shook my head. "But I hope you like fiction, Phil."

He flicked the folder open and studied the first page for a moment, expressionless. He looked up at me. "You can't possibly be serious."

It was my turn to shrug. "Don't knock it. I've helped Murphy out before."

He glanced over the rest of the report, the look of skepticism on his face growing more secure. "I'll . . . give this to Murphy for you, Mr. Dresden," he said, then nodded to me and turned to walk toward the SI office.

"Oh, hey," I said casually. "Phil."

He turned to me and lifted his eyebrows.

"We're both on the same team here, right? Both of us looking for the killer?"

He nodded.

I nodded back. "What is it that you're not telling me?"

He stared for a long moment, and then blinked slowly. The lack of reaction gave him away. "I don't know what you're talking about, Mr. Dresden," he said.

"Sure you do," I told him. "You know something you can't or won't tell me, right? So why not just put it out on the table, now?"

Denton glanced up and down the hall and repeated, in precisely the same tone of voice, "I don't know what you're talking about, Mr. Dresden. Do you understand?"

I didn't understand, but I didn't want him to know that. So I just nodded again. Denton nodded back, turned, and went into the SI office.

I frowned, puzzling over Denton's behavior. His expression and reaction had conveyed more than his words, but I wasn't sure exactly what. Except for that one flash of insight the night before, I was having trouble reading him. Some people were just like that, very good at keeping secrets with their bodies and motions as well as with their mouths.

I shook my head, went to the pay phone down the hall, dropped in my quarter, and dialed Murphy's number.

"Murphy," she said.

"Denton's dropping off my report. I didn't want to wander in on you with Internal Affairs hanging around."

There was a note of relief in Murphy's voice, subtle but there. "Thank you. I understand."

"The investigator is in your office now, isn't he?"

"Right," Murphy said, her tone neutral, polite, professional, and disinterested. Murphy keeps a great poker face when it's necessary, too.

"If you have any questions, I should be at my office," I said. "Hang in there, Murph. We'll nail this guy." There was the sound of a deeper voice, Denton's, and then the slap of a folder hitting the surface of Murphy's desk. Murphy thanked Denton, and then spoke to me again.

"Thank you very much. I'll be right on it." Then she hung up on me.

I hung up the phone myself, and realized that I was vaguely disappointed that I hadn't gotten to really speak to Murphy, that we hadn't had the chance to exchange our usual banter. It bothered me that I couldn't just walk into her office anymore, made me feel a little queasy and tense inside. I hate politics, but it was there, and as long as I was being held in any amount of suspicion, I could get Murphy in trouble just by being around.

Brooding all the while, I stomped down the stairs and out the front door of the station, toward the visitor parking, where the Blue Beetle waited for me.

I had gotten in and was preparing to coax it to life when I heard footsteps. I squinted up into the morning sunshine at the skinny form and big ears of the redheaded young FBI agent from the scene in Rosemont last night. I rolled down the window as he stepped up to my car. He glanced around, his face anxious, and then knelt down beside the window so that he could not be easily observed.

"Hi there, Agent . . ."

"Harris," he said. "Roger Harris."

"Right," I said. "Can I help you, Agent Harris?"

"I need to know, Mr. Dresden. I mean, I wanted to ask you last night, but I couldn't. But I need to ask you now." He glanced around again, restless as a rabbit when a fox goes by, and said, "Are you for real?"

"A lot of people ask me that, Agent Harris," I said. "I'll tell you what I tell them. Try me and see."

He chewed on his lip and looked at me for a minute. Then nodded a jerky little nod, his head bobbing. "All right," he said. "All right. Can I hire you?"

My eyebrows went up in surprise. "Hire me? What for?"

"I think . . . I think I know something. About the Lobo killings. I tried to get Denton to let us check it out, but he said that there wasn't enough evidence. We'd never be able to get a surveillance put on them."

"On who?" I asked, wary. The last thing I needed was to be getting involved in any more shady goings-on. On the other hand, as an independent operator, I could sometimes go poking my nose where the police couldn't. If there was a chance that I could turn up something for Murphy, or find the killer and stop him outside of legal channels entirely, I couldn't afford to pass it up.

"There's a gang in Chicago," Harris began.

"No kidding?" I asked, affecting puzzlement.

It was lost on the kid. "Yeah. They call themselves the Streetwolves. They've got a really rough reputation, even for this town. A spooky reputation. Even the criminals won't go near them. They say that the gang has strange powers. Streetwolf territory is down by the Forty-ninth Street Beach." He stared at me intently.

"Down by the university," I filled in. "And by the parks where last month's murders took place."

He nodded, eager as a puppy. "Yeah, right, down there. You see what I'm getting at?"

"I see, kid, I see," I told him and rubbed at my eye. "Denton couldn't go there and look around, so he sent you down here to get me to do it."

The kid flushed, his skin turning bright red, until his freckles vanished. "I . . . Uh . . ."

"Don't worry about it," I told him. "You didn't do a bad job with the act, but you've got to get up pretty early in the morning, et cetera."

Harris chewed on his lip and nodded. "Yeah, well. Will you do it?"

I sighed. "I guess you can't go on record as paying my fee, can you?" It wasn't really a question.

"Well. No. Officially, you are a suspect source, as a consultant."

I nodded. "I thought so."

"Can you do it, Mr. Dresden? Will you?"

I was regretting it even before I spoke. "All right," I said. "I'll check it out. But in exchange, tell Denton I want any of the information that the FBI or the Chicago police has on me."

Harris paled. "You want us to copy your files?"

"Yeah," I said. "I could get them through the Freedom of Information Act, anyway. I just don't want to spend the time and postage. Do we have a deal or not?"

"Oh, God. Denton would *kill* me if he found out. He doesn't like it when someone bends the rules." He chewed his lip until I thought it would fall off.

"You mean like he's doing by sending you here to me?" I shrugged. "Suit yourself, kid. That's my price. You can find my number if you change your mind." I coaxed the Beetle to life, and it rattled and coughed and started running.

"All right," he said. "All right. Deal." He offered me his hand.

I shook it, sealing the bargain, and got an uneasy feeling as I did. Harris walked away from the Beetle as quickly as he could, still looking around nervously.

"That was stupid, Harry," I told myself. "You shouldn't be getting yourself into anything more complicated than you already have."

I was right. But the potential gains made the risk worth it. I could possibly find the killers, stop them, and additionally find out why the cops had a bug up their collective ass about me. It might help me to work things out with Murphy. It might even help me get her out of the trouble she was having.

"Cheer up, Harry," I told myself. "You're just going to go poke around a biker gang's lair. Ask them if they happen to have killed some people lately. What could possibly go wrong?"

Chapter 9

A block from the Forty-ninth Street Beach there was a run-down garage, the sort of place you only find in the worst sections of big cities. The building consisted of corrugated metal on a steel frame, oxidating in the rain and the mist rising off the lake so that gobbets of rust ran down the walls in streaks and pooled on the sidewalks in uneven puddles. On one side of the garage was a vacant lot; on the other, what looked like the sort of pawn shop where crooks traded in their spare guns and knives for a few extra dollars when things were tight. A faded sign hung askew over one of the garage doors, reading FULL MOON GARAGE. I pulled the Beetle into the gravel parking lot, and parked a few feet from the building.

"Thank God it's not too obvious or anything," I muttered, and killed the engine. It died with a new, moaning note to its usual rattle. I got out of the car, squinted at the building, and headed toward it. I didn't have my gun with me, but I did have my blasting rod, my shield bracelet, and a ring on my right hand in which I had stored up about as much energy as someone twice my size could put into a solid punch. Gravel crunched under my shoes as I walked, and rare autumn sunshine glared in my eyes and cast a long shadow behind me.

I wasn't sure who to expect inside, if anyone. The people I'd seen with the dark-haired woman the night before, the rather nerdy bunch of young people clad in imitation biker-leathers, didn't seem to be the sort of folk to inspire fear in other criminal toughs as the Streetwolves apparently had. But maybe there was a connection. Maybe the dark-haired woman from last night was linked with the Streetwolves, somehow, as well as with the young people I had seen. What had the stout young man, Billy, called them? The Alphas.

What, then, had the Alphas been? Biker thugs in training? That sounded ridiculous, even to me. But what if those young people had been lycanthropes, like the ones Bob had told me about? What if they were being trained, somehow, as junior members of the Streetwolves until they could be brought in as full werewolves? Presuming the Streetwolves themselves were lycanthropes or werewolves, that is. Sometimes, a biker gang is just a biker gang. There might be no connection to the Alphas at all. My head spun a little, trying to sort out the possibilities.

All in all, it was far better to hope that the building was empty, and that I wouldn't have to deal with anyone, werewolves or otherwise. I would much rather just poke around and find something incriminating inside, something that I could bring back to Murphy and Denton that would point them in the correct direction.

There was a regular door beside the pair of big, roll-up garage doors. Both of them were closed. I tried the regular door, and it opened easily enough, so I went on inside. There were no windows, and the only light in the garage fell into it from the open door behind me.

"Hello?" I called into the darkness. I tried to peer around, but saw nothing other than dim shapes and outlines, what might have been a car with the hood up, a couple of those rolling tool-cabinets. There was a dull reflection of glass windows off to one side, where there might have been an office. I stepped to one side of the doorway, squinting, and waited for my eyes to adjust.

There was a quiet sound, a dull rustle of clothing.

Dammit. I reached a hand into my duster, wrapping my fingers around my blasting rod, and Listened. I could hear the sound of breathing in the room, from multiple sources in a variety of directions. There was a scuffling sound, shoes on the concrete floor.

"I'm not a cop," I said into the darkness. I had the feeling that might be important for them to know. "My name is Harry Dresden. I just want to speak to the Streetwolves."

The room dropped into dead silence. No moving. No breathing. Nothing.

I waited, tense and ready to run.

"Take your hand out of your jacket," a male voice said. "And keep your hands where I can see them. We've heard of your kind, wizard. We've heard of you. You're with the cops."

"You're late on the gossip," I said wryly. "I'm playing doubles with Johnny Marcone now. Didn't you know?"

There was a snort from the dark. "Like hell. That's just Marcone's story. We know the real deal with you, wizard."

Christ. I wished the police were as savvy as these ne'er-do-wells. "I've heard a few things about you all, too," I said. "Not much of it is too friendly. Some of it might even be considered a little weird."

There was a rough laugh. "What do you think they say about you, Dresden? Get your hands where I can see them. Now." There was the click-clack of a pump shotgun's action.

I swallowed and took my hand slowly off my blasting rod, then held both of my hands innocuously out in front of me, palms up. I willed strength through my shield bracelet as I did, drawing its protective energies about me. "All right," I said. "Come up where I can see you."

"You don't give the orders here," the male voice snarled. "I do."

I pressed my lips together and drew in a breath through my nose. "I just want to talk to you."

"About what?" said the voice.

I tried to come up with something, something believable—but I'm not much of a liar. So I told them the truth. "Some dead people last month. More dead last night."

The voice didn't answer me for a moment. I licked my lips and kept going.

"There were fake wolf tracks around the murder scenes. And the feds think someone used a weapon lined with wolf teeth to tear the victims up. You wouldn't know anything about that, would you?"

There was a flurry of mutters around the room, low voices in hushed tones all around me. A dozen, maybe. More. I got a sudden, sinking feeling in the pit of my stomach. If these people were the murderers, if they were responsible for last month's deaths, I was in big trouble.

And if they were real werewolves, if they could shapeshift and come after me before I could clear out of there, I was as good as dead, shield bracelet or no. I choked down a surge of panic and forced myself not to turn and run for the door.

"Kill him," someone said from the darkness, off to my left, a female voice with a deep, growling tone to it. There was an answering chorus of mewling sounds from the dark around me, repetitions of "Kill him, kill him, kill him."

My eyes were starting to adjust to the lack of light. I could see them now, the shapes of people restlessly pacing. Their eyes glowed like dogs' eyes in the glare of headlights. Both men and women moved around me, though I couldn't tell their ages. There were blankets and pillows made into pallets on the floor, thrown aside while their occupants had risen. The female voice I had heard continued to chant, "Kill him, kill him, kill him," while the others followed her lead. The air grew tight and heavy with a kind of energy I had never sensed before, a power that was gaining momentum as they chanted, a feral, raging current.

Directly in front of me, not fifteen feet away, stood the large shape of a man holding a shotgun. "Stop it," he snarled, turning his head toward the others in the room. I could see his body responding as the energy grew, growing tenser, more ready. "Fight it. Hold it in, dammit. You can't let it loose here. There will be cops all over us."

When his head turned, I darted toward the doorway. I kept my left palm up and turned out toward the leader, the one with the shotgun, and held on to my shield as hard as I could.

My motion triggered a frenzied howl from the others in the room and they came surging toward me like a dozen creatures with one controlling mind. The shotgun roared and threw a flash of white light over the room, showing me a frieze of half-dressed or naked men and women hurtling toward me, their faces twisted with grimaces of berserk anger. The force of the blast slammed into my shield. It wasn't quite enough to shatter the protective field, but it made my bracelet grow warm and shoved my opposite shoulder hard against the wall.

I stumbled, thrown off balance. One of the men, a heavy-set fellow with his shoulders covered in tattoos, got between me and the door. I ran at him, and he spread his arms to grab me, assuming I would try to go past him.

Instead, I drove my fist at his nose as hard as I could. I don't carry a lot of power on my own when I punch. But when I added in the kinetic energy stored in the ring, my fist became a battering ram of bone and flesh, flattening the man's nose in a gout of blood, and sending him sprawling to the ground six feet away.

I was through the door in a flash and felt the sun's welcome heat on my back. I pelted toward the Beetle, my long legs covering the ground quickly.

"Stop! Stop!" the leader shouted, and I cast a glance over my shoulder to see him, an older man with greasy hair beginning to go grey. He planted his feet in the doorway, facing inside, holding the shotgun across his body and shoving at the people trying to get past him.

I threw myself into the Beetle and jammed my key in the ignition.

The car wheezed and rattled, but didn't start. Dammit.

My hands were trembling, but I kept trying to get the car going, using every trick I knew to coax the engine to life, while watching the door. The leader of the Streetwolves was still there, fighting to hold the frenzied group inside. They were screaming and howling, but he shoved them away, clubbed them down with the shotgun like wild dogs, the muscles in his shoulders and back straining. "Parker!" screamed one of them, the woman who had begun the killing chant, "Let me through!" He swatted her down with the butt of the shotgun without hesitation.

Then Parker turned his head toward me, and I met his eyes. There was a swimming moment, and then I was past his eyes, to what lay behind them.

Fury overwhelmed me, naked lust for meat, for the hunt. I needed to run, to kill. I was invincible, unstoppable. I could feel the power in my arms and hands, feel the raw energy of the wild coursing through me, sharpening my senses to animal keenness.

I felt his emotions like they were my own. Fury beneath rigid control, the ocean beating at a tide wall. The fury was directed at me, Dresden, at the man who had invaded his territory, challenged his authority, and driven his people out of control, endangering them. I saw that he was the leader of the lycanthropes called the Streetwolves, men and women with the minds and souls of beasts, and that he was aging, was not as strong as he once had been. Others, like the woman earlier, were beginning to challenge his authority. Today's events might tear him from leadership, and he would never live through it.

If Parker was to live, I had to die. He had to kill me, pure and simple, and he had to do it alone to prove his strength to the pack. That was the only thing that kept him from coming at my throat that very second.

Worse, he didn't know a damned thing about the last month's killings.

And then the moment was past, the soulgaze over. Parker's face was stunned. He had seen me in much the same way I had seen him. I don't know what he saw when he looked upon my soul. I didn't want to know what was down there.

I recovered from it before he did and fumbled at the keys again. The Beetle coughed to life, and I pulled out and onto the street, swerving wildly before gathering speed and heading back uptown as quickly as I could.

I shook the entire way, my shoulders so tight with fear and reaction that I could hear my collarbones creaking with strain. I could still hear the mewling chants of "Kill him, kill him," in my head. Those things in that garage had not been people. They had looked like people, but they weren't. And they scared the hell out of me.

While sitting at an intersection, I slammed my hand on the steering wheel, abruptly angry. "Stupid, Harry," I said. "How could you have been so stupid? Why in the hell did you go wandering in there like that? Do you realize how close those Neanderthal freaks came to tearing you apart?" I glared ferociously out my side window, at an old lady in a business suit who was staring at me as though I were a ranting madman. Which, I suppose, was what I looked like.

I stopped myself from glaring at her, took a deep breath, and tried to calm down. A couple of blocks later, I was able to start thinking straight again.

Parker and the Streetwolves were not responsible for the murders last month. That didn't make them any less dangerous. They were lycanthropes, the kind Bob had told me about, and I could see now why they had been feared. People with the souls of beasts, possessed of a ferocity so great that it could transform them into something inhuman without altering a single cell of their bodies.

They lived in a pack, and Parker was their leader. I had challenged his dominance in my clueless, bumbling way, and now he couldn't afford to let me live, or he would be killed himself. So now I had to worry about someone else coming after me, trying to kill me. Not only that, all of this trouble had come gratis, without giving me any lead on the true culprit of the Lobo killings.

Maybe it was a good time to leave town for a while.

I brooded over that for a block or so, and then shook my head. I wouldn't run. I had made this trouble for myself, and I would get out of it myself. I had to stay, to help Murphy find the killer, and to help save lives before the full moon rose again. And if Parker wanted to kill me, well—he'd find that doing in a full-fledged wizard is no easy task.

I gripped the steering wheel grimly. If it came to it, I would kill him. I knew I could do that. Technically, I suppose, Parker and his lycanthropes weren't human. The First Law of Magic, Thou Shalt Not Kill, wouldn't necessarily apply to them. Legally, I might be able to make a case for the use of lethal magic to the White Council.

I just wouldn't be safe from myself. I wouldn't be safe from the loathing I would feel, using a tool made of life's essence, its energy, to bring an end to life. Magic was more than just an energy source, like electricity or petroleum. It was power, true, but it was a lot of other things as well. It was all that was deepest and most powerful in nature, in the human heart and soul. The ways in which I applied it were crude and clumsy in comparison to magic in its pure form. There's more magic in a baby's first giggle than in any firestorm a wizard can conjure up, and don't let anyone tell you any different.

Magic comes from what is inside you. It is a part of you. You can't weave together a spell that you don't believe in.

I didn't want to believe that killing was deep inside of me. I didn't want to think about the part of me that took a dark joy in gathering all the power it could and using it as I saw fit, everything else be damned. There was power to be had in hatred, too, in anger and in lust, in selfishness and in pride. And I knew that there was some dark corner of me that would enjoy using magic for killing—and then long for more. That was black magic, and it was easy to use. Easy and fun. Like Legos.

I parked the Beetle in the lot of my office building and rubbed at my eyes. I didn't want to kill anybody, but Parker and his gang might not give me any choice. I might have to do a lot of killing, if I was going to live.

I tried not to think too much about what sort of person it might be who survived. I would burn that bridge when I came to it.

I would go up to my office and hold business hours for the rest of the day. I would wait for Murphy to call me, and give her any aid that I could. I would keep my eyes and ears open in case Parker or any of his gang came after me. There wasn't much more I could do, and it was frustrating as hell.

I went up to my office, unlocked it, and flipped on the lights. Gentleman Johnny Marcone was seated at my desk in a dark blue business suit, and his hulking bodyguard, Mr. Hendricks, was standing behind him.

Marcone smiled at me, but it didn't touch the corners of his eyes. "Ah, Mr. Dresden. Good. We need to talk."

Chapter 10

Marcone had eyes the color of old, faded dollar bills. His skin was weatherworn, with an outdoorsman's deep tan. Creases showed at the corners of his eyes and mouth, as though from smiling, but those smiles were rarely sincere. His suit must have cost him at least a thousand dollars. He sat at ease in my chair, *my* chair, mind you, and regarded me with professional calm.

From behind him, Mr. Hendricks looked like an all-star collegiate lineman who hadn't been smart enough to go into the pros. Hendricks's neck was as big around as my waist, and his hands were big enough to cover my face—and strong enough to crush it. His red hair was buzz cut, and he wore his ill-fitting suit like something that he planned to rip his way out of when he turned into the Hulk. I couldn't see his gun, but I knew he was carrying one.

I stood in the doorway and stared at Marcone for a minute, but my gaze did nothing to stir him. Marcone had met it already, and taken my measure more than I had taken his. My eyes held no more fear for him.

"Get out of my office," I said. I stepped inside and closed the door.

"Now, now, Mr. Dresden," Marcone said, a father's reproof in his tone. "Is that any way to talk to a business partner?"

I scowled. "I'm not your partner. I think you're scum. The worst criminal this city has. One of these days the cops will nail you, but until then, I don't have to put up with you here in my own office. Get out."

"The police," Marcone said, a hint of correction in his voice, "would be best off run by private agencies, rather than public institutions. Better pay, better benefits—"

"Easier to bribe, corrupt, manipulate," I injected.

Marcone smiled.

I took off my duster and dropped it over the table in front of the door, the one covered in pamphlets with titles like "Witches and You," and "Want to Do Magic? Ask Me How!" I untied my blasting rod from its thong and set it calmly on the table in front of me. I had the satisfaction of seeing Hendricks tense up when he saw the rod. He remembered what I had done to the Varsity last spring.

I glanced up. "Are you still here?"

Marcone folded his hands in front of him. "I have an offer to make you, Mr. Dresden."

"No," I said.

Marcone chuckled. "I think you should hear me out."

I looked him in the eyes and smiled faintly. "No. Get out."

His fatherly manner vanished, and his eyes became cold. "I have neither the time nor the tolerance for your childishness, Mr. Dresden. People are dying. You are now working on the case. I have information for you, and I will give it to you. For a price."

I felt my back stiffen. I stared at him for a long minute, and then said, "All right. Let's hear your price."

Marcone held out his hand and Hendricks handed him a folder. Marcone put the folder down on the battered surface of my old wooden desk and flipped it open. "This is a contract, Mr. Dresden. It hires you as a consultant for my firm, in personal security. The terms are quite generous. You get to name your own hours, with a minimum of five per month. You can fill in your salary right now. I simply want to formalize our working relationship."

I walked over to my desk. I saw Hendricks's weight shift, as though he were about to jump over the desk at me, but I ignored him. I picked up the folder and looked over the contract. I'm not a legal expert, but I was familiar with the forms for this kind of deal. Marcone was on the up and up. He was offering me a dream job, with virtually no commitment, and as much money as I could want. There was even a clause that specified that I would not be asked or expected to perform any unlawful acts.

With that kind of money, I could live the life I wanted. I could stop scraping for every dollar, running my legs off working for every paranoid looney who wanted to hire me to investigate his great-aunt's possessed cow. I could catch up on reading, finally, do the magical research I'd been itching to do for the past few years. I wouldn't live forever, and every hour that I wasted looking for UFOs in Joliet was one more hour I couldn't spend doing something I wanted to do.

It was a pretty damned tempting deal.

It was a very comfortable collar.

"Do you think I'm an idiot?" I said, and tossed the folder down on my desk.

Marcone's eyebrows went up, his mouth opening a little. "Is it the hours? Shall I lower the minimum to one hour per week? Per month?"

"It isn't the hours," I said.

He spread his hands. "What, then?"

"It's the company. It's the thought of a drug-dealing murderer having a claim on my loyalty. I don't like where your money comes from. It's got blood on it."

Marcone's cold eyes narrowed again. "Think carefully, Mr. Dresden. I won't make this offer twice."

"Let me make you an offer, John," I said. I saw the corner of his cheek twitch when I used his first name. "Tell me what you know, and I'll do my best to nail the killer before he comes for you."

"What makes you think I'm worried, Mr. Dresden?" Marcone said. He let a fine sneer color his words.

I shrugged. "Your business partner and his pet bodyguard get gutted last month. Spike gets torn to bits last night. And then you crawl out from under your rock to dangle information in my face to help me catch the killer and try to strong-arm me into becoming your bodyguard." I bent down and rested my elbows on the surface of the desk, then lowered my head until my eyes were a few inches from his. "Worried, John?"

His face twitched again, and I could smell him lying. "Of course not, Mr. Dresden. But you don't get where I have in life by being reckless."

"Just by being soulless, right?"

Marcone slammed his palms down on the desktop and stood. I rose with him, enough to stand over him, and to keep my eyes on his. "I am a man of business, Mr. Dresden. Would you prefer anarchy in the streets? Wars between rival crime lords? I bring *order* to that chaos."

"No. You just make the chaos more efficient and organized," I shot back. "Stick whatever pretty words you want onto it, but that doesn't change the fact that you're a thug, a fucking animal that should be in a cage. Nothing more."

Marcone's normally passionless face went white. His jaw clenched over words of rage. I pressed him, hard, my own anger spilling out with a passion gone out of control. I poured all of my recent frustration and fear into venomous words and hurled them at him like a handful of scrap metal.

"What's out there, John? What could it possibly be? Did you see Spike? Did you see how they'd torn his face off? Did you see the way they'd ripped his guts open? I did. I could smell what he had for dinner. Can you just imagine it happening to you next, John?"

"Don't call me that," Marcone said, his voice so quiet and cold that it set my momentum back on its heels. "If we were in public, Mr. Dresden, I'd have you killed for speaking that way to me."

"If we were in public," I told him, "you'd try." I drew myself up and glared down my nose at him, ignoring Hendricks's looming presence. "Now. Get the hell out of my office."

Marcone straightened his jacket and his tie. "I presume, Mr. Dresden, that you are going to continue your investigation with the police department."

"Of course."

Marcone walked around my desk, past me, and toward my door. Hendricks followed in his wake, huge and quiet. "Then in my own interests, I must accept your offer and aid the investigation however I might. Look up the name Harley MacFinn. Ask about the Northwest Passage Project. See where they lead you." He opened the door.

"Why should I believe you?" I asked him.

He looked back at me. "You have seen the deepest reaches of my soul, Mr. Dresden. You know me in a way so profound and intimate that I cannot yet fathom its significance. Just as I know you. You should know that I have every reason to help you, and that the information is good." He smiled again, wintry. "Just as you should know that it was unwise to make an enemy of me. It need not have been this way."

I narrowed my eyes. "If you know me so well, you should know that there's no other way it could be."

He pursed his lips for a moment, and did not try to refute me. "Pity," he said. "A true pity." And then he left. Hendricks gave me a pig-eyed little glare, and then he was gone, too. The door shut behind them.

I let out a long, shaking breath, and slumped against my desk. I covered my face with my hands, noticing as I did that they were shaking, too. I hadn't realized the depth of the disgust in me for Marcone and what he stood for. I hadn't realized how much it had sickened me to have my name associated with his. I hadn't realized how much I wanted to launch myself at the man and smash him in the nose with my fists.

I stayed that way for a few minutes, letting my heart beat hard, catching my breath. Marcone could have killed me. He could have had Hendricks tear me apart, or put a bullet in me right there—but he hadn't. That wasn't Marcone's way. He couldn't eliminate me now, not after working so hard to spread the word throughout the underworld that he and I had some sort of alliance. He would have to be more indirect, more subtle. Having Hendricks scatter my brains out on the floor wasn't the way to do it.

I thought over what he had said, and the implications of his acceptance of the deal I'd offered. He was in danger. Something had him scared, something that he didn't understand and didn't know how to fight. That was why he had wanted to hire me. As a wizard, I take the unknown and I turn it into something that can be measured. I take that cloak of terror off of things, make people able, somehow, to deal with them. Marcone wanted me to stand by him, to help him not be afraid of those things lurking in the dark.

Hell. It was only human.

I winced. I wanted to hate the man, but disgust, maybe anger, was as far as I could go. Too much of what he said was true. Marcone was a businessman. He had reduced violence in the streets—while sending the number of dollars made by criminals in this town soaring. He had protected the city's flesh while siphoning away its blood, poisoning its soul. It changed nothing, nothing at all.

But to know that the man I knew, the tiger-souled predator, the businessman killer—to know that he was frightened of what I was about to go up against: That scared the hell out of me, and added an element of intimidation to the work I was doing that hadn't been present before.

That didn't change anything, either. It's all right to be afraid. You just don't let it stop you from doing your job.

I sat down on the desk, forced thoughts of blood and fangs and agonizing death from my mind, and started looking for the name Harley MacFinn and the Northwest Passage Project.

Chapter 11

The demon trapped in the summoning circle screamed, slamming its crablike pincers against the unseen barrier, hurling its chitinous shoulders from side to side in an effort to escape the confinement. It couldn't. I kept my will on the circle, kept the demon from bursting free.

"Satisfied, Chauncy?" I asked it.

The demon straightened its hideous form and said, in a perfect Oxford accent, "Quite. You understand, I must observe the formalities." Then it took a pair of wholly incongruous wire-frame spectacles from beneath a scale and perched them upon the beaklike extremity of its nose. "You have questions?"

I let out a sigh of relief, and sat down on the edge of the worktable in my lab. I had cleared away all the clutter from around the summoning ring in the floor, and I'd have to move it before I could clamber up out of my lab, but I didn't like to take chances. No matter how comfortable Chaunzaggoroth and I were with our working relationship, there was always a chance that I could have messed up the summoning. There were rules of protocol that demonic beings were obliged to follow—one of them was offering resistance to any mortal wizard who called them. Another was doing their best to end the life of the same wizard, should they be able to escape the confines of the circle.

All in all, squeezing information from faeries and spirits of the elements was a lot easier and safer—but Bob had turned up nothing in his search among the local spirits. They weren't always up on information to be had in the city, and Bob now resided in his skull again, exhausted and unable to help any further.

So I'd gone to the underworld for assistance. They know when you've been bad or good, and they make Santa Claus look like an amateur.

"I need information about a man named Harley MacFinn, Chauncy. And about something he was working on called the Northwest Passage Project."

Chauncy clacked his pincers pensively. "I see. Presuming I have this information, what is it worth to you?"

"Not my soul," I snorted. "So don't even start with that. Look, I could dig this up myself in a few days."

Chauncy tilted his head, birdlike. "Ah. But time is of the essence, yes? Come now, Harry Dresden. You do not call upon me lightly. The possible dangers, both from myself and from your own White Council, are far too great."

I scowled at him. "Technically," I said, "I'm not breaking any of the Laws of Magic. I'm not robbing you of your will, so I'm clear of the Fourth Law. And you didn't get loose, so I'm clear of the Seventh Law. The Council can bite me."

The bone ridges above Chauncy's eyes twitched. "Surely, that is merely a colorful euphemism, rather than a statement of desire."

"It is."

Chauncy pushed the glasses a bit higher up on his nose. "The moral and ethical ramifications of your attitudes are quite fascinating, Harry Dresden. I am continually amazed that you remain in the Council's good graces. Knowing full well that most of the Council would look the other way while their enforcers killed you, should they learn that you have willfully brought a demon into this world, you still summon me not once, but a half-dozen times. Your attitudes are much more contiguous with those of many of my brethren in the World Below—"

"And I should throw in with your side, accept the dark powers, et cetera, et cetera," I finished for him, with a sigh. "Hell's bells, Chauncy. Why do you keep on trying to sucker me into signing on with Downbelow, eh?"

Chauncy shrugged his bulky shoulders. "I admit that it would give me no small amount of status to gather a soul of your caliber into our legions," he said. "Additionally, it would free me from the onerous duties which make even these excruciating visits to your world seem pleasant by comparison."

"Well, you aren't getting my soul today," I told him. "So make me a counteroffer, or we can call a close to the negotiations and I can send you back."

The demon shuddered. "Yes, very well. Let us not be hasty, Harry Dresden. I have the information you need. Additionally, I have more information of which you are not aware, and which would be of great interest to you, and which I judge, additionally, may help to preserve your life and the lives of others. Given the situation, I do not think the price I will ask inappropriate: I wish another of your names."

I frowned. The demon had two of my names already. If he gained my whole name, from my own lips, he could use it in any number of magical applications against me. That didn't particularly disturb me—demons and their ilk had great difficulty in reaching out from the Nevernever, the spirit world beyond the physical one we inhabited, with sorcery.

But Chaunzaggoroth was a popular source of information among wizards who went to the underworld in need of it. What bothered me was the possibility that one of them would get it. Chauncy was correct—there were a lot of people on the White Council who would be happy to see me dead. If one of them got my name, there was the chance that they would use it against me, either to kill me or to magically force me to do something that would openly violate one of the Seven Laws and have me brought to trial and killed.

On the other hand, Chauncy never lied to me. If he said he had information that could save people's lives, he had it, and that's all there was to it. Hell, he might even know who the killer was, though a demon's grasp of individual human identity was somewhat shaky.

I decided to gamble.

"Done," I said. "All pertinent information on the subject of my inquiry in exchange for another of my names."

Chauncy nodded once. "Agreed."

"All right," I said. "Let's have the information on MacFinn and the Northwest Passage Project."

"Very well," Chauncy said. "Harley MacFinn is an heir to a considerable fortune made in coal mining and railroads at the turn of the twentieth century. He is one of the ten richest men in the country known as the United States. He served during the police action in Vietnam, and when he returned to this country he began divesting himself of business interests, merely accruing capital. His favorite color is red, his shoe size is—"

"We can skip the little details unless you think they will be really relevant," I said. "I could hear about his favorite food and his problems in middle school all day and it wouldn't help anything." I got out my notebook and started taking notes.

"As you wish," Chauncy assented. "The object of his endeavors for the past several years has been the Northwest Passage Project. The project is an effort to buy enormous tracts of land, beginning in the central Rocky Mountains of the American Southwest, and moving northwest into Canada, to provide for an enormous, migratory-sized preserve for North American wildlife."

"He wants to make his own private playground out of the Rocky Mountains?" I blurted.

"No, Harry Dresden. He wishes to acquire the lands that are not already owned by the government, then donate them, provided the government guarantees that they will be used as a part of the Northwest Passage Project. He has considerable backing from environmentalist groups throughout the country, and support in your capital, as well, provided he can get the land."

"Wow," I said, impressed. "You said he has a lot of support. Who wants to stop him?"

"Industrial interests still looking to expand into the Northwest," Chauncy said.

"Let me guess. James Harding III was one of them," I said, already writing it down.

"How did you know?" Chauncy asked.

"He was killed by a werewolf last month, along with his bodyguard. Several other people died as well."

Chauncy beamed. "You are a clever man, Harry Dresden. Yes. James Douglas Harding III was exceptionally interested in blocking MacFinn's efforts to acquire property. He came to Chicago to have negotiations with MacFinn, but died before they were complete."

I closed my eyes for a minute, thinking. "Okay. Harding comes to town to talk to MacFinn. Harding's in cahoots with Marcone, so maybe Marcone is hosting the talks. Harding and his bodyguard get et-all-up by a werewolf. So . . . MacFinn is the werewolf in question?"

Chauncy smiled, a rather intimidating expression. "MacFinn is a member of an ancient family line from an island known as Ireland. His family has a notable history. Sometime in the murky past, legend would have it, the man known as Saint Patrick cursed his ancestor to become a ravening beast at every full moon. The curse came with two addenda. First, that it would be hereditary, passing down to someone new each and every generation. And second, that the cursed line of the family would never, ever die out, lasting until the end of days."

I wrote that down as well. "A Catholic saint did that?"

Chauncy made a sound of distaste. "I am not responsible for the sorts of people the Other Side employs, wizard. Or the tactics they use."

"Considering the source, I think I'll note it as a biased opinion. Your folk have done a thousand times worse," I said.

"Well. True," Chauncy admitted. "But we tend to be quite honest about the sort of beings we are and the sorts of things we stand for, at least."

I snorted. "All right. This is making a lot more sense now. MacFinn is a loup-garou, one of the legendary monsters. He's trying to do some good in his spare time, make the big park for all the furry critters, but Harding puts himself in the way. MacFinn goes on a killing spree and wipes him out." I frowned. "Except that Harding was the last person to be murdered last month. You would have thought that if MacFinn was going to lose it, Harding would be the first to go." I peered at Chauncy. "Is MacFinn the murderer?"

"MacFinn is a murderer," Chauncy said. "But among humankind, he is one of many, and not the most monstrous."

"Is he the one who killed Marcone's bodyguard? The other people last month?"

"My information on that point is inconclusive, Harry Dresden," Chauncy said. His black eyes gleamed. "Perhaps for the price of another name, I could inquire of my brethren and give you a more precise answer."

I scowled. "Not a chance. Do you know who murdered the other people, last month?"

"I do," Chauncy said. "Murder is one of the foremost sins, and we keep close track of sins."

I leaned forward intently. "Who was it?"

Chauncy laughed, a grating sound. "Really, Harry Dresden. In the first place, our bargain was for information regarding MacFinn and the Northwest Passage Project. In the second, I could not tell you the answer to such a direct question, and you know it. There is a limit to how much I may involve myself in mortal affairs."

I let out a breath of frustration and rubbed at my eyes. "Yeah, yeah. All right, Chauncy. What else can you tell me?"

"Only that Harley MacFinn was planning to meet with J[illegible] Marcone tomorrow night, to continue the talks."

"Wait a minute. Is Marcone the major opponent to the proje[illegible] now?"

"Correct," Chauncy said. "He assumed control of a majority of the business interests shared with Harding upon Harding's death."

"So . . . Marcone had a fantastic motive to have Harding killed. It broadened his financial empire, and put him in a position to gouge MacFinn for as much money as he possibly could."

Chauncy adjusted his wire-frame spectacles. "Your reasoning would seem to be sound."

I thumped my pencil on my notebook, staring at what I had written. "Yeah. But it doesn't explain why everyone else got killed. Or who did it. Unless Marcone's got a pack of werewolves in his pocket, that is." I chewed on my lip, and thought about my encounter at the Full Moon Garage. "Or Streetwolves."

"Is there anything else?" Chauncy asked, his manner solicitous.

"Yes," I said. "Where can I find MacFinn?"

"Eight eighty-eight Ralston Place."

I wrote it down. "But that's right here in Chicago. In the Gold Coast."

"Where did you expect a billionaire to live when he was in Chicago, Harry Dresden? Now, I seem to have lived up to all of my obligations. I expect my payment now." Chauncy took a few restless steps back and forth within the circle. His time on earth was beginning to wear on him.

I nodded. "My name," I said, "is Harry Blackstone Dresden." I carefully omitted "Copperfield" from the words, while leaving the tones and pronunciation the same.

"Harry. Blackstone. Dresden," Chauncy repeated carefully. "Harry as in Harry Houdini? Blackstone, the stage illusionist?"

I nodded. "My dad was a stage musician. When I was born, he gave me those names. They were always his heroes. I think if my mother had survived the birth, she would have slapped him for it." I made a few more notes on my page, getting ideas down on paper before they fled from memory.

"Indeed," Chauncy agreed. "Your mother was a most direct and willful woman. Her loss was a great sadness to all of us."

I blinked, startled, and the pencil fell from my fingers. I stared at the demon for a moment. "You . . . you knew my mother? You knew Margaret Gwendolyn Dresden?"

Chauncy regarded me without expression or emotion. "Many the underworld were . . . familiar with her, Harry Blackstone Dresden, though under a different name. Her coming was awaited with great anticipation, but the Dark Prince lost her, in the end."

"What do you mean? What are you talking about?"

Chauncy's eyes gleamed with avarice. "Didn't you know about your mother's past, Mr. Dresden? A pity that we didn't have this conversation sooner. You might have added it into the bargain we made. Of course, if you would like to forfeit another name, to know all about your mother's past, her . . ." his voice twisted with distaste, "redemption, and the unnatural deaths of both mother and father, I am certain we can work something out."

I gritted my teeth in a sudden rush of childlike frustration. My heart pounded in my ears. My mother's dark past? I had expected that she was a wizardess, but I had never been able to prove anything, one way or another. Unnatural deaths? My father had perished in his sleep, of an aneurism, when I was young. My mother had died in childbirth.

Or had they?

A sudden, burning desire to know filled me, starting at my gut and rolling outward through my body—to know who my mother was, what she had known. She had left me her silver pentacle, but I knew nothing of the sort of person she was, other than what my gentle and too-generous father had told me before his death. What were my parents like? How had they perished and why? Had they been killed? Did they have enemies lurking out there, somewhere? If so, had I inherited them?

My mother's dark past. Did that explain my own fascination with the darker powers, my somewhat-less-than-sterling adherence to the rules of the White Council that I considered foolish or inconvenient?

I looked up at the demon, and felt like a sucker. I had been set up. He had intended, all along, to dangle this information in front of me as bait. He wanted to get my whole name, if he could, or more.

"I can show them to you, Harry Blackstone Dresden, as they really are," Chaunzaggoroth assured me, his voice dulcet. "You've never seen your mother's face. I can give that to you. You've never heard her voice. I can let you hear that as well. You know nothing of what sort of people your parents were—or if you have any other family out there. Family, Harry Blackstone Dresden. Blood. Every bit as tormented and alone as you are . . ."

I stared at the demon's hideous form and listened to his soothing, relaxing voice. Family. Was it possible that I had a family? Aunts? Uncles? Cousins? Others, like me, perhaps, moving through the secret societies of the wizards, hidden from the view of the mortal world?

"The price is comparatively low. What need have you for your immortal soul when your body is finished with it? What harm to pass on to me only one more name? This is not information easily gained, even by my kind. You may not have the chance to garner it again." The demon pressed his pincers against the barrier of the conjuring circle. His beaklike maw fairly trembled with eagerness.

"Forget it," I said quietly. "No deal."

Chaunzaggoroth's jaw dropped open. "But, Harry Blackstone Dresden—" he began.

I didn't realize that I was shouting until I saw him flinch. "I said forget it! You think I'm some kind of simp for you to sucker in, darkspawn? Take what you have gained and go, and feel lucky that I do not send you home with your bones torn from your body or your beak ground into dust."

Chaunzaggoroth's eyes flashed with rage and he hurled himself against the barrier again, howling with blood lust and fury. I extended my hand and snarled, "Oh no you don't, you slimy little shit head." The demon's will strained against mine, and though sweat burst out on my forehead, I came out ahead once more.

Chaunzaggoroth began to grow smaller and smaller, howling out his frustrated rage. "We are watching you, wizard!" he screamed. "You walk through shadows and one night you will slip and fall. And when you do, we will be there. We will be waiting to bring you down to us. You will be ours in the end."

He went on like that until he shrank to the size of a pinpoint and vanished with a little, imploding sound. I let my hand drop and lowered my head, breathing hard. I was shaking all over, and not only with the cold of my laboratory. I had badly misjudged Chaunzaggoroth, thought him a somewhat reliable, if dangerous, source of information, willing to do reasonable business. But the rage, the fury, the frustrated malice that had been in his final offer, those last words, had shown his true colors. He had lied to me, deceived me about his true nature, played me along like a sucker and then tried to set the hook, hard. I felt like such an idiot.

The phone began to ring upstairs. I stirred into sudden motion, shoving stacks of things out of my way, pushing past them and over them, to reach the stepladder stairs that led up to my apartment. I hurried up them, my notebook in one hand, and caught the phone on its fifth ring. My apartment was dark. Night had fallen while I had interviewed the demon.

"Dresden," I said, puffing.

"Harry," Murphy said, her voice weak. "We've got another one."

"Son of a bitch," I said. "I'm coming. Give me the address." I set down the notebook and held my pencil ready to write.

Murphy's tone was numb. "Eight eighty-eight Ralston Place. Up in the Gold Coast."

I froze, staring at the address I had written down on the notebook. The address the demon had given me.

"Harry?" Murphy said. "Did you hear me?"

"I heard," I told her. "I'm coming, Murph." I hung up the phone and headed out into the light of the full moon overhead.

Chapter 12

Eight eighty-eight Ralston was a townhouse in the Gold Coast, the richest area of Chicago. It was set on its own little plot, surrounded by trees that hid the house from view almost entirely. High hedges, worked around the house in a small garden, added to the concealment as I drove up the white pebble drive, and parked the Beetle at the rear of a small fleet of police cars and emergency vehicles.

The strobing blue lights were almost comforting, by now. I'd seen them so many times that it felt, in an unsettling way, like a homecoming. Murphy had called me in early—I didn't see the forensics van yet, and only now were officers putting up yellow tape around the property.

I got out of my car, dressed in my jeans, button-down shirt, and boots again, my old black duster flapping around my calves. The wind was brisk, cold. The moon was riding high overhead, barely visible through the city's haze of pollution.

A chill ran down my neck, and I stopped, looking at the rows and rows of elegantly illuminated hedge sculptures, flower beds, and rows of shrubbery around me. I was abruptly certain that someone was out in the darkness; I could feel eyes on me.

I stared out at the night, sweeping my gaze slowly around. I could see nothing, but I would have bet money that there was someone out there. After a moment, the sense of being watched faded, and I shivered. I shoved my hands in my pockets and walked quickly toward the townhouse.

"Dresden," someone called, and I looked up to see Carmichael coming down the front stairs of the townhouse toward me.

Carmichael was Murphy's right hand in Special Investigations. Shorter than average, rounder than average, slobbier than average, and with piggier eyes than average, Carmichael was a skeptic, a doubter, and a razor-sharp cop. He came down the stairs in his soup-stained old tie and shirtsleeves. "It's about fucking time. Jesus Christ, Dresden." He wiped a hand over his sweating brow.

I frowned down at Carmichael as we went up the stairs side by side. "That's the nicest greeting you've ever given me, I think," I said. "You change your mind about me being a fake?"

Carmichael shook his head. "No. I still think you're full of shit with this wizard-magic business. But Christ almighty, there are times when I wish you weren't."

"You never can tell," I said, my voice dry. "Where's Murphy?"

"Inside," Carmichael said, his mouth twisting with distaste. "You go on up the stairs. The whole place belongs to this guy. Murphy figures you might know something. I'm going to stay here and bog down the Feds when they show."

I glanced at him. "She still worried about looking bad for Internal Affairs?"

Carmichael grimaced. "Those assholes in IA would be all over her if she kicked the Feds out. Christ almighty, I get sick of city politics sometimes."

I nodded agreement and started up the stairs.

"Hey, Dresden," Carmichael said.

I looked over my shoulder at him, expecting the familiar jeers and insults. He was studying me with bright, narrow eyes. "I hear things about you and John Marcone. What's the deal?"

I shook my head. "No deal. He's lying scum."

Carmichael studied me intently, and then nodded. "You ain't much of a liar, Dresden. I don't think you could keep a straight face about something like this. I believe you."

"But you don't believe me when I say I'm a wizard?" I asked.

Carmichael grimaced and looked away. "Do I look like a fucking moron to you? Huh? You better get upstairs. I'll make some noise when Denton and the Stepford agents get here."

I turned to go and saw Murphy standing at the head of the stairs in a crisp grey business jacket and slacks, with sensible low heels and jewelry the color of steel. Her earrings seemed to be little more than bright beads of silver in her ears, which I had never really noticed when she had worn her golden hair long. Murphy's earlobes were cute. She'd kill me, just for thinking it.

"About time, Dresden. Get up here." Her voice was hard,

angry. She vanished from the top of the stairway, and I took the rest of the stairs two at a time to catch up with her.

The apartment (though it was too big for the word to really apply) was brightly lit, and smelled, very faintly, of blood. Blood has a sweet sort of metallic odor. It makes the hairs on the back of your neck stand up, and mine snapped to attention at once. There was another smell as well, maybe incense of some kind, and the fresh scent of the wind. I turned down a short hall at the top of the stairs, and followed Murphy into what was apparently a master bedroom, where I found the source of all the scents.

There was no furniture inside the master bedroom—and it was huge, large enough to make you wince at how far you'd have to go to get to the bathroom in the middle of the night. There was no carpeting. There were no decorations on the walls. There was no glass in the huge, single-pane window, letting in the October wind. The full moon shone down through it like a picture in a frame.

What the room did have was blood. There was blood all over, scattered in droplets and splashed in spurts against one wall. The scarlet footprints of something like a large wolf led in a straight line toward the shattered window. In the center of the room were the remains of a greater circle of summoning, its three rings of symbols carefully wrought in white chalk upon the wooden floor, burning sticks of incense interspersed among the symbols of the second ring.

What was left of Kim Delaney lay naked and supine on the bloodstained floor a few feet from the circle. The expression of shock and surprise on her face wouldn't change until rigor set in. Her dark, once-glittering eyes stared up at the ceiling, and her lips were parted, as though in the middle of an apology.

A large, wheel section of flesh beneath her chin was missing, and with it Kim's larynx and trachea. Bloody red meat was showing, the ragged ends of arteries and torn sections of muscle, and pale white bones gleamed at the bottom of the wound. Long rakes down her body had opened her like a Ziploc bag, leaving her covered in scarlet.

Something went "click" in my head. Someone threw some kind of switch that just turned off my emotions entirely and immersed me in a surreal haze. I couldn't be seeing this. It simply couldn't be real. It had to be some sort of game or hoax, in which the actors would start giggling in a few moments, unable to contain the mirth of their prank.

I waited. But no one started giggling. I wiped at my forehead with my hand and found cold sweat there. My fingers began to shake.

Murphy said, her voice still tight with anger, "Apparently, the incense set off the fire alarm in the hall. When the fire department got here, no one answered, so they came on in. They found her up here, around eight o'clock. She was still warm."

Eight o'clock. When I had been talking to the demon. Moonrise?

Behind me, Murphy closed the door to the bedroom. I turned to her, away from the grisly corpse. There was anger in every inch of her, in the way she glared at me.

"Murph," I said. "I don't know if I can do this."

"What's there to figure?" Murphy said. "There's a monster in the middle of the circle. I figure it's one of those loup-garou from your report. I figure it's Harley MacFinn, the owner of this house. Someone who knows he's going to go nuts when the moon rises. The girl tries to hold the monster inside the magic circle, right? Something goes wrong when MacFinn goes furry; he gets out of the circle, wastes her, then leaves."

"Uh-huh," I said, without turning around to look at Kim's body again. "It makes sense." And I told her what I had learned from the demon about Harley MacFinn, the Northwest Passage Project, and his antagonism with Marcone's business interests. Murphy listened to me in utter silence. When I was finished, she nodded, and turned to leave the room.

"Follow," she said shortly.

I followed, almost on her heels. I didn't turn around to see the room again before I left.

She led me down the hall, into another bedroom, this one furnished and neatly kept. "Come here," she said, moving to a dresser. I did, and she handed me a photograph of a middle-aged, starkly handsome man, his skin deeply tanned, the bones of his face gaunt and sharp. He was smiling.

Beside him in the picture was the amber-eyed woman from the department store where I'd run across the Alphas. She was also smiling. Her teeth were very white, very even, and her dark skin and silver-peppered hair went well with the man beside her. I chewed on my lip for a second, trying to think.

"That's Harley MacFinn," Murphy said. "Matches the picture on his driver's license. I didn't turn up any ID on the woman next to him, though." She studied my face critically. "She matches the description of the woman you said you saw in the department store, though. The one who followed us back from the scene in Rosemont. Is that her?"

I nodded. "Yeah. That's her."

Murphy nodded, took the picture from me, and set it back on the dresser. "Follow," she said again and walked out. I stared after her. What was wrong with Murphy? Had the scene unsettled her so much? I shook my head, still stunned from what I had seen, from too many facts coming together all at once, slam-bang in my brain.

"Murph, wait," I said. "Stop a minute. What's going on?"

She didn't answer me, just shot me a glare over her shoulder and continued walking. I hurried to catch up with her.

We went down what looked like a servant's narrow spiral staircase, down into the basement. She led me to the back of a storage room and pushed open a heavy, steel door there that opened onto a small, stark chamber, all of concrete, with no other exits. In the center of the chamber was another three-ring summoning circle, but this one's symbols had been made from silver and set into the concrete of the floor. Short bars of what looked like a mixture of silver and obsidian were interspersed around the second circle, creating what would, if the circle was functional, be a very formidable barrier.

But the symbols had been marred, torn, broken. Several from the critical inner ring had been pried up from the floor and were simply missing. Some of the bars had been broken. The circle, as it was, was nonfunctional and worthless—but whole, it would have served to contain Harley MacFinn when he shifted into his beast form. The room was a prison he had created for himself, something to contain the fury of the beast inside of him.

But someone had intentionally marred the circle, made the prison useless.

And I abruptly understood Kim Delaney's request. She had to have known Harley MacFinn, maybe through her environmental activism. She must have learned of his curse, and wanted to help him. When I had refused to help her, she had attempted to recreate the greater summoning circle upstairs in the bedroom, to hold in MacFinn once the moon rose. As I had warned her would happen, she had failed. She hadn't had the knowledge necessary to understand how such a construct would function, and consequently, she hadn't been able to make it work.

MacFinn had killed her. Kim was dead because I had refused

to share my knowledge with her, because I hadn't given her my help. I had been so secure in my knowledge and wisdom; withholding such secrets from her had been the action of a concerned and reasoned adult speaking to an overeager child. I couldn't believe my own arrogance, the utter confidence with which I had condemned her to death.

I started to shake, harder, too many things pressing against my head, my heart. I could feel the pressure, somewhere inside of me, that switch on the inside of my head quivering, getting ready to flick back beneath a tide of raging anger, fury, regret, self-hatred. I took deep breaths and closed my eyes, trying not to let it happen.

I opened my eyes and looked up at Murphy. God, I needed to talk to her. I needed a friend. I needed someone to listen, to tell me it would be all right whether it was the truth or not. I needed someone to let me unload on them, to keep me from flying apart.

She regarded me with cold, angry eyes.

"Karrin," I whispered.

She drew from her pocket a crumpled piece of paper. She unfolded it, and held it up to me, so that I could see Kim Delaney's graceful handwriting, the sketch of the summoning circle that she had brought to me in McAnally's. The sketch I had refused to tell Kim about. The sketch I had crumpled into a little ball and tossed on the floor, and which Murphy had picked up, absently, just to get the trash out of people's way.

And I realized why there was so much anger in Murphy's eyes.

I stared at the sketch. "Karrin," I began again. "Stars above, you've got to listen to me." I took the sketch from her hands, my fingers trembling.

"Harry," she said, in a calm tone. "You lying *bastard,*" and on the word she drove her fist into my stomach, hard, doubling me over. The motion put my head within easy reach, and her fist took me across the jaw in a right cross that sent me to the floor like a lump of wet pasta, stars dancing in my vision.

I was only dimly aware of her taking the sketch back from me. She twisted my arms painfully behind my back, and snapped her handcuffs around my wrists. "You promised me," she said, her voice furious. "You *promised*. No secrets. You lied to me all along. You played me like a sucker the entire while. Godammit, Dresden, you're involved in this and people are dying."

"Murph," I mumbled. "Wait."

She grabbed my hair, jerked my head back, and slammed me

across the jaw again, near-berserk anger lending her strength. My head swam, and blackness closed over my vision for several seconds.

"No more talking. No more *lies,*" I heard her say, and she dragged me to my feet, shoved my face and chest against a wall, and began searching me for weapons. "No more people torn up like meat on a block. You have the right to remain silent. Anything you say can and will be used against you in a court of law."

She took my blasting rod. My shield bracelet. The energy ring. Even my lump of chalk. Her voice went on, hard, cold, and professional, letting me know my rights.

I closed my eyes and leaned against the stone wall. Next to my head, it was the softest thing in the room. I didn't try to fight or to explain.

What was the point?

Chapter 13

Walking down stairs with your hands fastened behind your back is more difficult than you would think. You depend upon your arms for balance, whether you realize it or not. With my hands cuffed at the small of my back, and Murphy walking me up the narrow servant's staircase, and then down the front stairs of MacFinn's building in front of a gaggle of staring police officers, my balance was gone.

As we came down, I could hear arguing voices. "You want to get in my face about this?" Carmichael demanded. "Look. I'm doing my job. My boss said no one was to go up, so no one goes up. Do I need to use shorter words or what?"

I looked up to see Denton towering over Carmichael, the veins in his forehead athrob, his three associates spread out in a fan behind him. "You are interfering with a duly appointed officer executing his duties," Denton snarled. "Get out of my way, Detective Carmichael. Or do you want to get added to Internal Affairs' to-do list along with your boss?"

"It's all right, Ron," Murphy said. "I'm done with my business up there, anyway."

Carmichael looked up at me and stared, his mouth opening. Denton and his crew looked, too. I saw Denton's face twist in surprise, and then close again, hedging out any emotion from his expression. Roger, the redheaded kid who worked for Denton, was staring at me openly, his jaw dropped. Benn, the woman who had attacked Murphy last night, regarded me with an almost bored expression, and Wilson, the overweight one, let out a satisfied snort.

"Lieutenant," Carmichael said. "You sure about this?"

"He was arguing with the most recently deceased last night. I can connect him to at least one resident of the house, as well as some of the . . . decorations there. I'm taking him in for obstructing and for conspiracy to commit murder. Put him in the car, Carmichael, and then get your ass upstairs." Murphy gave me a sharp push toward Carmichael, and I stumbled. Carmichael caught me.

"So let's go, Denton," Murphy said, and turned and stalked away. Denton gave me an expressionless glance, and stepped after Murphy, beckoning his companions to follow.

Carmichael shook his head and walked me to one of the police cars. "Fuck, Dresden. And here I was getting ready to throw in on your side. Guess I'm just a sucker for the underdog."

Carmichael unlocked the back of the car and put his hand on the back of my head as I bent down to get into it. "Watch your head. Christ, what happened to your jaw?"

I sat down in the back of the car and looked straight ahead. I didn't answer him. Carmichael stared at me for a while, and then shook his head. "We'll have someone drive you downtown as soon as the scene is secure. You can get in touch with your lawyer, then."

I kept my eyes forward and still didn't answer him.

Carmichael studied me some more, then stood and shut me into the car.

I closed my eyes.

I have felt low before in my life, have experienced events that left me broken and groveling and wishing I was dead. That was pretty much how I felt now, too. It wasn't that I hadn't found the killer—I've been beaten before, taken the blow on the chin, and come out fighting the next round. I can roll with the punches as well as anyone. But I hated feeling that I had betrayed a friend.

I had promised Murphy that I would keep no secrets from her—and I hadn't. Not really. But I had been stupid. I should have been putting pieces together more quickly, more instinctively. Perhaps I had some excuse in that I had been distracted by nearly having my head blown off at the Full Moon Garage, that I had been distracted by my soulgaze upon the Streetwolves' leader, and the knowledge that he wanted to kill me. But it wasn't a good enough excuse to clear things with Murphy. I wasn't sure anything would have been. I felt alone. I felt frustrated. I felt like shit.

And I felt worse, a moment later, when I looked out the car

window at the full moon and realized something that I should have put together an hour before—the real killer or killers were still out there.

MacFinn couldn't have been responsible for all of the deaths the previous month. Two of the murders had occurred on the nights before and after the full moon. If MacFinn's curse was indeed to become a ravening beast during the full moon, he could not have murdered either of last month's victims, or Spike at the Varsity last night.

Which begged the question: Who *had* done the killings?

I didn't have any answers. If the dark-haired woman who had led the Alphas was indeed connected with MacFinn, could she have been responsible? Something wolflike had attacked me in the abandoned department store when all the lights had been out—had it been her? One of the Alphas? Perhaps that would explain how the other murders happened.

But if it had been true, why hadn't the killer finished me off while I was floundering in the dark, virtually helpless?

More and more questions, and no answers.

Not that it mattered to me now. A nice, quiet jail cell didn't sound too bad, once I thought about it. At least it would keep the criminal element off of my back. Provided they didn't shut me up with a four-hundred-pound con named "Hump" or anything.

And then an odd feeling crept over me, derailing my train of thought. Once more, the hairs on my neck were standing up. Someone was watching me.

I looked around. There was no one in sight. All of the police were inside the house. I was alone in the back of the patrol car, with my hands bound. I was helpless and alone, and I suddenly became very aware of the fact that Harley MacFinn had yet to be found or apprehended. He was still lurking in the night, unable to keep from tearing apart anyone he saw.

I thought of Spike's torn corpse. Of poor Kim Delaney, covered in her own blood upstairs in the townhouse. I added imaginary (and far more horrible) images of half a dozen other victims, stacking scene upon scene of blood and death in my mind within a few seconds.

I broke out in a cold sweat and looked out the other window.

Directly into a pair of brilliant, feral, amber eyes.

I yelled and flinched away, lifting my legs to kick should something come rushing through the vehicle's window. Instead, the door opened, and the dark-haired, amber-eyed woman from the department store said, "Be quiet, Mr. Dresden, or I will not be able to rescue you."

I blinked at her, over my upraised knees. "Huh?"

"Rescue you, Mr. Dresden. Get out of the car and come with me. And quickly, before the police return." She peered past me, toward the house. "There is not much time."

"Are you crazy?" I demanded. "I don't even know who the hell you are."

"I am Harley MacFinn's fiancée, Miss West," she said. "I am called Tera."

I shook my head. "I can't leave. I'd be buying more trouble than you could imagine."

Her amber eyes glinted. "You are the only one who can stop my fiancée, Mr. Dresden. You cannot do that from a jail cell."

"I'm not the Lone Ranger," I snapped in reply. "I'm a hired consultant. And I don't think the city is going to foot the bill for this sort of thing."

Tera West's teeth showed. "If money is your concern, I assure you that it is not a problem, Mr. Dresden. Time presses. Will you come, or not?"

I studied her face. She had clean, striking features, exceptional more than attractive. There were crow's-feet at the edges of her eyes, though they were the only sign of age on her that I could see. There was, along the edge of her forehead, at the hairline, a long, slender, purpling bruise.

"You," I said. "It was you who attacked me in the department store. I hit you, and you took my rod away from me."

She glared at me. "Yes," she said.

"You're a werewolf."

"And you," she said, "are a wizard. And we have no more time." She crouched a bit lower, staring past me. I looked in that direction, and saw Denton and his cronies exiting the townhouse, engaged in an animated discussion. "Your friend," she said, "the police detective, is close to finding my fiancée. Do you really want her to be the one to face him? Is she prepared to deal with what she will find? Or will she die, as the others did?"

Dammit. The bitch (no pun intended) was right. I was the one who was capable of actually doing something about MacFinn. If Murphy was the one to catch up to him first, people would get killed. She was a fantastic cop, and was becoming more adept at dealing with the supernatural, but she wasn't able to handle a major werewolf berserker. I turned back to Tera. "If I go with you, you'll take me to MacFinn."

She stopped in the midst of turning to leave. "When I can. At dawn. If you think you can create the circle, hold him in when the moon again rises. If you can help him."

I nodded once. My decision was made. "I can. I will."

"She who was called Kim Delaney said the same thing," Tera West said, and spun on her heels to head away from me, crouched low to the ground.

I rolled out of the backseat and followed Tera West out into the shrubberies and garden shadows around the building, away from the police cars and the lights.

Someone shouted in surprise, somewhere behind me. Then there was a cry of "Stop!" I just stood and ran, as fast as I could, to get out of the lights and the line of sight of any possible shooters.

Apparently, the one shout was all the warning I was going to get. Gunfire erupted behind me as I ran. Bullets tore up the dirt next to my feet. I think I started screaming without slowing down, hunching my shoulders and ducking my head as best I could.

I was maybe five feet away from the sheltering shadows behind the hedges when something slammed into my shoulder and threw me *through* the hedge and out the other side. I landed in a roll and stumbled halfway back to my feet. There was a second of screaming, confused input from my shoulder, as though my joints could suddenly hear a welter of sound, feel a broad variety of sensation and texture beneath my skin. And then my shoulder went numb entirely, and my vision started spinning. I reached out a hand to support myself as I started to fall—and remembered that my wrists were still cuffed behind me. I went into the turf, felt the grass against my cheek.

"He's down, he's down!" came a cold, female voice—Agent Benn's, I thought. "Take him!"

There was no warning of presence, just the feeling of someone jerking me up to my feet by my duster. I felt Tera's hand slide beneath my jacket, then vanish as she pressed it to the numbed area of my arm.

"You are not bleeding badly," Tera said, her voice calm. "You were shot in the shoulder. Not the leg. Run or die." Then she turned and started making her way through the hedges.

Some encouragement—but I had a hunch I would be feeling a

lot worse a few minutes from now. So I swallowed the sickly taste of fear and loped after Tera West as best I could.

We started a game of shadow-haunted hide-and-seek in the little garden, Tera and me against the agents behind us. She moved like a wraith, in utter silence, smooth and steady in the black shadows and silver light of the moon overhead. She immediately cut into the hedges, taking lefts and rights every few paces. She did not slow down for me, and I was somehow very certain that MacFinn's fiancée would not stop and wait for me should I fall. She wouldn't hesitate to leave me behind if I could not keep the pace.

I did it for a while. It wasn't even too hard. Oh, I felt a little out of breath, a little hampered by the handcuffs, but other than that, it was almost as though I hadn't been shot, aside from the trickling warmth I could feel sliding down my ribs and over my belly. Endorphins—what a rush.

Our pursuers plunged into the maze of hedges, shrubs, and statuary, but my guide seemed to have an uncanny knack for avoiding them. She kept to the darkest parts of the garden as we went, checking behind her to make sure I was keeping the pace.

I wasn't sure how much time passed that way, ghosting through the darkness while our pursuers struggled to coordinate their efforts and remain quiet at the same time, but it couldn't have been long. I've read somewhere that the initial shock of gunshot injuries always wears off after a few moments—besides, I was out of shape. I couldn't have kept up with Tera West for long. She was that fast, that good.

My shoulder began to pound double time to my laboring heart as we emerged from the last of the hedges to the street outside—and the eight-foot wrought iron fence that surrounded the property. I slid to a halt and stumbled against the fence, wheezing.

Tera looked over her shoulder, her amber eyes bright beneath the moon. She was breathing through her nose silently, the crouched run having not tired her in the least, it seemed.

"I can't climb the fence," I said. The pain from my shoulder was starting to become very real now—it felt like a runner's cramp, only higher up. "There's no way. Not with my hands cuffed."

Tera nodded once. "I will lift you," she said.

I stared at her, through a growing haze of pain. Then sighed. "You'd better hurry, then," I said. "I'm about to pass out."

She took the words in stride and said, “Lean against the fence. Keep your body stiff.” Then she seized my ankles. I did my best to follow her directions, and she heaved, straining with effort.

For a second, nothing happened. And then she started, very slowly, to move me up, my good shoulder against the fence. She kept pressing my ankles higher, until I bent forward at the waist, scrabbled with my legs for a second—and then tumbled gracelessly to the ground on the far side of the fence. I hit the ground, and as I did a nuclear weapon went off in my shoulder, white fire, blinding heat.

I sucked in a breath and tried not to scream, but some sound must have escaped. There was a shout from somewhere behind me, and the sound of voices converging on our position.

Tera grimaced and turned to face the oncoming voices.

“Hurry up,” I gasped. “Climb it and let’s go.”

She shook her head, a stirring of dark hair. “No time. They are here.”

I gritted my teeth until they creaked and got my feet underneath me. She was right. The oncoming voices were close. Someone, Benn again, I thought, shouted out orders not to move. If Tera tried to clamber over the fence now, she’d be a perfect target at the top. The pursuers were too close. Tera didn’t stand much chance of escaping, and if she didn’t, I wouldn’t make it far. I’d be caught, and in more trouble than ever—and MacFinn would be on a rampage, with no one to oppose him.

I blinked sweat out of my eyes and knelt down as my blood pattered to the sidewalk. Little curls of steam came up where it hit the cold concrete.

I took a breath and drew in every bit of will I could summon, drew in the pain and my fear and sick frustration and shoved it all into a hard little ball of energy.

“Ventas veloche,” I murmured. *“Ubrium, ubrium.”* I repeated the words in a breathless chant, curling my fingers in toward my palm as I did.

The curls of steam from my blood began to thicken and gather into dense tendrils of mist and fog. Back along our trail, where more of my blood had spilled, more fog arose. For a few seconds, it was nothing, just a low and slithering movement along the ground—and then it erupted forth, billows of fog rising to cover the ground as the energy rushed out of me, covering Tera from my sight and causing shouts of confusion and consternation to come from the law officials pursuing us.

I dropped to my side, overwhelmed by pain and fatigue.

There was a whisper of sound, a creak of wrought metal, and then a light thump as Tera West landed beside me, invisible in the fog though she was only a few feet away. She moved toward me, and then I saw her expression, her eyes wide with wonder, the first emotion I had seen on her face.

"Wizard," she whispered.

"Don't wear it out," I mumbled. And then everything went black.

Chapter 14

I woke up someplace dark and warm. But then I opened my eyes, and it wasn't dark anymore. Just dim.

I was in a hotel room, a cheap one, lying on my back in a double bed. Heavy curtains were drawn, but cheap curtain rods sagged in the middle and let light in from outside. I felt that I had been lying there for a while. I took a deep breath and it made my shoulder begin a dull, pounding throb. I moaned, before I could think to keep quiet. I'm not a wimp; it just hurt that bad. My throat was parched, my lips chapped.

I turned my head, which made my jaw ache where Murphy had socked me. My left shoulder was covered in thick, white bandages and wrapped firmly in tape. It looked clean and neat, except for the bruises that I could see spreading out toward my chest and down my arm from beneath the bandages. As a side note, I noticed that I was naked, and the list of candidates for who could have undressed me was awfully short.

Beyond my shoulder, on the nightstand beside the bed, was a pile of miscellany. A book entitled *SAS Survival Manual* lay open to a page with several black and white illustrations of bandaging techniques. Beside it were some empty cardboard boxes whose labels declared them to have once contained cotton gauze wrapping, medical tape, that sort of thing. A brown bottle of hydrogen peroxide lay on its side atop a hacksaw with a nicked blade. A paper sack sat on the floor beside the bed, its top folded closed.

I moved my right hand up to rub at my aching head. One bracelet of Murphy's handcuffs hung around my wrist, the chain swinging from the base of the bracelet, where it had apparently been severed by the hacksaw. The other bracelet was down on my left wrist. I could feel it as a dull, throbbing band around the lower part of my arm.

I did my best not to move too much, but the pain didn't go away. After a few minutes, I decided that my wound wasn't going to start hurting any less, so I sat up. Slowly. Rising wasn't too much more trouble, though my legs shook a little. I made it to the bathroom and made use of the facilities, then splashed water on my face with my right hand.

This time, she didn't surprise me. I heard her move out of the darkness of the back corner of the room. I glanced up into Tera West's amber-colored eyes in the mirror and said, "Tell me I didn't get lucky last night."

Her expression never blinked, as though the insinuation had flown past her. She was still dressed in the same clothes and still held herself with the same relaxed composure she had always displayed. "You were very lucky," she said. "The bullet went through the muscle and missed the bone and the artery. You will live."

I scowled. "I don't feel so lucky."

Tera shrugged. "Pain is to be endured. It ends or it does not." I saw her consider my back, and then lower portions. "You are in reasonably good condition. You should be able to withstand it."

I felt a hot rush of blood to my face, and I fumbled for a towel and awkwardly slung it around my hips. "Are you the one who bandaged me? And, uh . . ." I made a vague gesture with the fingers of the hand that was holding the towel and preserving my modesty.

She nodded. "I am. And I have procured clothing for you that is not soaked in blood. You must dress, so that we may help my fiancée."

I turned to face her, and tried out my best glower. She didn't twitch an eyebrow. "What time is it?"

She shrugged. "Late afternoon. The sun will set soon, and the moon will rise soon after. We have no time to waste if we are to reach him before the change."

"Do you know where he is?"

She shrugged again. "I know him."

I let out a breath and slowly walked past her. I went to the paper bag on the floor next to the bed. Inside it, I found a pair of enormous purplish sweatpants and a white T-shirt with Old Glory flying on it in rippling, metallic colors, subtitled: INVEST IN AMERICA—BUY A CONGRESSMAN. I wrinkled up my nose at the sweatpants, liked the shirt, and fumbled myself into the clothing, ripping off price tags as I went.

"Where are we?" I asked.

"A hotel in East Chicago," she said.

I nodded. "How did you pay for it?"

"I used cash. MacFinn told me that the police can track the plastic cards."

I squinted at her. "Yeah. They can." I rubbed a hand over my head and went to the mirror again to study myself. I was walking more easily now—the pain wasn't any less, but I was beginning to get more used to it. "Do you have any ibuprofen, anything like that?"

"Drugs," she said. "No." She picked up a set of rental-car keys and turned toward the door.

"Stop," I told her. She turned to me, her eyes narrowed.

"We are going now," she said.

"We are not going," I replied, "until I have a few answers."

Her eyebrows furrowed, and she glared at me. Then she turned and walked out of the room, letting in a brief flood of orange-tinted sunlight before the door slammed behind her.

I considered the door for a moment. Then I sat down on the bed and waited.

Perhaps three minutes passed. Then she reappeared. "Now," she said, "we will leave."

I shook my head. "I told you *no*. Not until I get some answers."

"MacFinn will answer your questions," Tera told me. "Now, you must leave this place."

I snorted and folded my arms over my chest. My shoulder took fire and I wobbled on the bed before I lowered my left arm again. I left the right one folded across my chest, but it just didn't have the same effect. "Where is MacFinn? Why did he kill Marcone's business partner and his bodyguard? Or did he kill them at all?"

"You will leave this pl—" Tera began.

"Who are you? Why did the pair of you mess up the first circle, the one in your basement? How did you know Kim Delaney?"

Tera West snarled and seized me by the front of my shirt. "You will leave this place *now,*" she said, glaring into my eyes.

"Why should I?" I snarled, and for once I didn't avert my eyes. I stared into her gleaming amber eyes and braced myself for the impact of looking into her soul, and for her to peer into mine.

Instead, nothing happened.

That, in itself, was enough to make my jaw drop incredulously. I continued the stare, and she didn't blink, didn't turn away—and didn't fall into soulgaze with me. I shuddered in reaction. What was going on? Why didn't the 'gaze begin? There were only two kinds of people whose eyes I could meet for more than a second or two: the people who had already met my eyes in a soulgaze were one kind; inhuman beings from the Nevernever were the other.

I had never looked upon Tera West's soul before. I remembered a soulgaze, every time it happened. The experience wasn't the sort of thing you could forget. That only left one conclusion.

Whoever she was—whatever she was, Tera West wasn't human.

"We will leave now," she growled.

I felt a surge of defiant grumpiness course through me. "Why *should* I?" I whispered back.

"Because I have called the police and told them that you are here, that you are acting irrational and dangerous, and that you possess a weapon. They will be here momentarily. I think that the police might be feeling threatened, given all the recent deaths. They will be likely to shoot you rather than take chances." She let go of my shirt with a little push, and stalked out of the room.

I sat on the bed for about five seconds. Then I rose and hobbled after her, taking time to snatch my duster from where it was draped over a chair. There were holes in the upper left arm, one in the front of the sleeve, one in the back, and it was crusty with dried blood that didn't much show against the black canvas. It was disgusting, but hey, it was mine. The boots and socks I had been wearing last night were next to it, and I snagged them, too.

Outside, it was late afternoon. The streets and highways would soon be crowded with commuters going home from work. Tera had rented a beat-up old car, probably from an independent rental business, rather than from one of the major chains—good move on her part. It would draw things out while the police methodically went through agency after agency, looking for someone of her description, and they always started with the big places first.

I studied her as she got in the car. She was tall and lean and pretty in a knife-edge sort of way. Her eyes moved around constantly—not nervously or randomly, but with the cool precision of someone making herself aware of everything surrounding her at all times. Her hands were scarred, long-fingered, and strong. The bruise on her head, where I had smacked her with my blasting rod the night before (no, *two* nights before; I had lost a day sleeping in the hotel room) was probably hurting like hell, but she didn't seem to notice it.

She drove us out onto the streets of East Chicago, one of the distant suburbs of the big city, down at the south end of Lake Michigan, finally turning off into a quiet drive beside a sign that read WOLF LAKE PARK.

Tera West made me nervous. She had appeared from nowhere to save me from the back of a police car, true, but what were her intentions? Was she really trying to help her fiancée keep from falling victim to his family curse again? Or were the two of them working together to remove anyone who could rebuild the magical circle that could contain MacFinn and render him harmless? That would make sense, given that once Kim Delaney was dead, they came after me.

On the other hand, that didn't fit with a lot of the other facts. MacFinn, if he was truly a loup-garou, changed into a beast only during the nights of the full moon. At least half a dozen people had been killed when the moon was waxing full, but not yet all the way there, or after it had been full for three nights already and was waning back toward half full again.

And Tera West wasn't a werewolf. A werewolf was a human being who used magic to turn into a wolf. She had looked upon my eyes and not been drawn in. Therefore, she wasn't a human being.

Could she be some kind of shapeshifter from the Nevernever? MacFinn's partner in crime, killing on the off nights to keep suspicion from falling on him? Some sort of being with which I was unfamiliar? Most of my background on the paranormal was Western European in origin. I should have been reading more books on Native American beliefs, South American spooks and haunts, African legend, East Asian folklore—but it was a little late for such regrets. If Tera West was a monster, and wanted me dead, she could have killed me already—and she surely would not have bothered to clean and dress my injury.

Of course, that begged the question: What *did* she really want?

And that question led the way to many more. Who were the young people I had seen her with that first evening? What was she doing with them? Did she have some kind of cult of followers, like vampires sometimes built up? Or was it something else entirely?

Tera pulled over onto a little gravel lane, drove a quarter mile up it, and pulled off into the weeds. "Get out," she said. "He will be here, somewhere."

The bouncing car ride had come to an end, mercifully, and the sun was still solidly above the horizon, with moonrise not for at least an hour after sunset. So I ignored the pain and pushed my way out of the car, to follow her into the woods.

It was darker underneath the ancient oaks and sycamores, and quiet. Birdsong came to us, but from far away, as though the birds were choosing the better part of valor in remaining where the sun could still touch the tree branches. The wind sighed through the woods, sending leaves spinning down in all shades of gold and orange and russet, adding to the thick, crunchy carpeting under our feet. Our steps sounded out distinctly as we moved ahead through the leaves, and the cool wind made me grateful that I had thought to drape my duster over my shoulders.

I studied the usually quiet Tera. She was walking with exaggerated motions, planting her feet down solidly with each step, as though intentionally trying to make noise. Once or twice, she stepped out of her way to tread on a branch, snapping it with a dry popping sound. I was too tired and sore to go to any such effort. I just walked, and it made more noise than she did. Who says I can't do anything right?

We hadn't gone more than a few hundred yards when Tera abruptly tensed, crouching, her eyes scanning all around. There was a whistling sound, and then a bent sapling jerked upright, dragging a noose around Tera's ankles and hauling her across the rock- and leaf-covered floor of the woods with a yelp of surprise.

I blinked at her, and then something came up out of the leaves, rose right up like Hamlet's dad from the stage floor. But instead of bemoaning his fate and charging me with avenging him, he slugged me across the jaw (on the same side of my face that already sported dark purple bruises) and sent me spinning to the ground, stunned.

I landed badly, but on my unwounded side, and rolled out of the way as a muddy, naked foot stomped down at my head. I grabbed on to it and jerked with more desperation than strength, and the foot's owner fell down beside me. Instead of being slowed, he slapped his arms at the ground as he hit it, in much the same way Murphy did when practicing falls. Then he rolled as I struggled to my hands and knees, and slid a hard, strong forearm beneath my throat, locking it there with the other hand and pressing back against my windpipe.

"Got you. I *got* you," snarled my attacker. I struggled against him, but he was bigger than me, stronger than me. He had me down, and he hadn't been shot or beaten up anywhere near as often as I had in the last fifteen hours or so.

I didn't stand a chance.

Chapter 15

So there I was being strangled by a ranting, half-naked madman in the middle of the woods, with a she-werewolf dangling from a rope snare somewhere nearby. My gunshot wound hurt horribly, and my jaw throbbed from where my buddy the cop had brutalized it the night before. I've had worse days. That's the great thing about being a wizard. I can always tell myself, honestly, that things could be worse.

I stopped trying to struggle against the man who was choking me. Instead, I grabbed his wrist and prepared to do something foolish.

Magic is a kind of energy. It is given shape by human thoughts and emotions, by imagination. Thoughts define that shape—and words help to define those thoughts. That's why wizards usually use words to help them with their spells. Words provide a sort of insulation as the energy of magic burns through a spell caster's mind. If you use words that you're too familiar with, words that are so close to your thoughts that you have trouble separating thought from word, that insulation is very thin. So most wizards use words from ancient languages they don't know very well, or else they make up nonsense words and mentally attach their meanings to a particular effect. That way, a wizard's mind has an extra layer of protection against magical energies coursing through it.

But you can work magic without words, without insulation for your mind. If you're not afraid of it hurting a little.

I drew in my will, my exhausted fear, and focused on what I wanted. My vision swam with dots of color. The man on my back snarled and growled incoherently, and spittle or foam dribbled onto the side of my face. Dried leaves and mud pressed against the other side of my face. Things started going black.

Then I ground my teeth together and released my will with a burst of sudden energy.

Two things happened. First, a rush of blinding thought, brilliant and wild and jangling, went through my head. My eyes swam with color, my ears with phantom sound. My senses were assaulted with a myriad of impressions: the sharp scent of the earth and dry leaves, the rippling scratch of a centipede's legs fluttering up the skin of my forearms, the sensation of warm sunlight against my scalp, dozens of others I couldn't identify—things with no basis in reality. They were a side effect of the energy rushing through my head.

The second thing that happened was a surge of electricity gathered from the air around me to my fingertips, gripped on my attacker's wrist, and surged up through his arm and into his body. He convulsed against my back, out of control, and the strength of his own reaction threw him off of me and to his back on the leaves, jerking and flopping, his face stretched in a tight-lipped expression of shock and fear.

I wheezed in a breath, stunned and shaking, then scrambled back to my feet, only to stagger against a tree. I huddled there, watching my attacker's convulsions fade into a numb paralysis. Finally, he just stared at the sky, his lips open, his chest heaving in and out.

I studied the man a little more closely. He was big. He was really big, at least as tall as me and twice as broad. He was dressed only in a pair of cutoff blue jeans, and those looked like they were ill fit. He was in a condition best described as "overwhelmingly masculine," hairy-chested and muscled like a professional wrestler. There was grey in his hair and beard, and there were lines on his face, putting his age at well into maturity. It was his eyes that showed me the most about him. They burned green, wild and haunted, fastened on the distant sky now, but heavy with the weight of too much terrible knowledge. It couldn't have been easy to live with a curse like his.

There was a scrambling sound, a muffled thump, and I looked up to see MacFinn's noose trap hanging empty, the rope swinging back and forth. My eyes tracked down to earth to find an indistinct shape stir in the leaves, and then resolve itself into Tera West's long limbs and practical clothes. She gathered her legs beneath her and crossed at once to MacFinn, her chest heaving, her eyes vague and distant.

"MacFinn," she said. "MacFinn! You've killed him," she snarled, and her eyes snapped up to mine, bright and burning with amber anger. I could have sworn I saw her face start to change, her bared teeth begin to grow into fangs. Maybe that was just the effect of the magic on my perceptions, though, or a primitive, lizard-brain sort of reaction to Tera rising to her feet and charging toward me with a howl. There was murder in her eyes.

I hadn't gotten beaten up twice, shot, and nearly strangled to get taken out by a misguided werewolf bitch. I gathered in my dizzy, spinning will and extended my good hand toward the charging woman, flicking my wrist in a circle. *"Vento giostrus!"* I trumpeted.

The winds howled down from the trees and whipped into a savage circle of moving air, lifting up dried leaves, sticks, and small stones. The miniature cyclone picked the charging Tera up off the ground and hurled her a good twenty feet through the air, into the branches of a pine tree. It also hurled out a cloud of rocks and small debris, forcing me to seek shelter behind a tree trunk.

How embarrassing. It was a little more wind than I had wanted. That's the danger of evocation, of that instantaneous, ka-blowie sort of magic. Control can be somewhat tricky. All I had wanted was something to spin Tera around and then to plop her down on her ass.

Instead, rocks hammered against the tree trunk and zipped by, rattling against the trees all around in an almost deafening clatter. The wind shook the trees, tore branches from them, and cast half a ton of dirt and dust into the air in a choking cloud.

The wind died after about half a minute, leaving me choking and coughing on dust and dirt. I peered around the edge of my tree, to see what I could see.

The trees had been cleaned of their autumn colors in a fifty-foot-wide circle, leaving only stark branches behind. Where the bark had been brittle or dry, the cyclone had torn it from the trees, leaving pale, gleaming wood flesh visible. The leaves on the ground were gone as well, as were six or eight inches of topsoil—wind erosion gone berserk. A few stones, newly naked, could be seen in the torn earth, as could the roots of some of the trees and a number of startled worms.

MacFinn was sitting up, evidently recovered from the jolt I'd given him. His face was pasty and stunned as he looked around him. His chest rose and fell in uneven jerks.

There was a rustle, and then I caught sight of Tera West tumbling to the ground from the branches of the pine tree. She landed with a thump and sat there coughing and staring, her mouth hanging open in surprise. She blinked at me and nervously scooted a few inches backward over the ground.

"See there?" I wheezed, raising a hand and pointing at MacFinn. "He's breathing. He'll be all right." My mind was still spinning from my unshielded magic attack on MacFinn. I caught the strong scent of wildflowers and stagnant water, and felt what I was sure were the scales of a snake slithering across the palms of my hands, while something with wings and glittering, multifaceted eyes hovered at the edge of my vision, vanishing whenever I tried to look at it. I tried to shove everything that didn't make sense out of my way, to ignore it, but it was difficult to sort the false impressions from the ones that were in front of me.

Tera rose, and made her way toward the fallen man. She knelt down over MacFinn and wrapped her arms around him. I closed my eyes and wheezed until my head began to slow down a little. I focused on all the pain that was lurking in the midst of the confusion. Pain in my shoulder, my throat, my jaw, gave me a concrete foundation, a place that I knew was stable, if unpleasant. I fastened on it, concentrated, until I began to get less woozy. Once the pain returned in force, I wasn't sure I wanted to be less woozy, but I opened my eyes anyway.

MacFinn had his arms around Tera's shoulders, and she was kissing him as if she were trying to inhale him. I felt vaguely voyeuristic.

"Ahem," I said. "Maybe we should get somewhere out of the open?"

They disengaged, slowly, and Tera helped MacFinn to rise to his full, impressive height. He made her look like a slip of a girl, but he leaned against her a little as he stood. He studied me, and I kept my eyes away from his. I didn't want to see what was inside of him.

"Kim's dead," MacFinn said. "Isn't she?"

It wasn't a question, but I nodded. "Yeah. Last night."

The big man shuddered and closed his eyes. "Dammit," he whispered. "Dammit all."

"There was nothing you could do," Tera said, her voice low. "She knew the risks."

"And you must be Harry Dresden," MacFinn said. He glanced at the burns on his wrist, where my magic had taken him. "Sorry about that. I didn't see Tera with you. I didn't know who you were."

I shrugged. "Don't worry about it. But can we get out of the open? Last thing we need is a couple of runners or bikers to come back and report us to the police."

MacFinn nodded at me. "All right. Let's go." Tera gave me a last, wary look, and then turned with MacFinn to help him farther back into the woods. I followed them.

MacFinn's camp turned out to be hidden in the overhang of a bank of earth, heavily laced with the roots of the ancient trees above it that held it in place and kept it from simply spilling into a mound of mud. There was a small fire built at the back of the shelter the bank afforded, well shielded from sight. MacFinn made his way to the fire and settled down before it. Twilight would cast the sheltered camp into deep darkness, but for now it was only shady and out of the wind. The fire had made the place warm, comfortable. It didn't feel like we were within fifteen miles of the third largest city in the country.

Tera settled down beside MacFinn, her manner restless. I remained standing, though the throbbing in my arm made me wish I was lying down in a bed somewhere, instead of huddling in the middle of a small but genuine forest.

"All right, MacFinn," I said. "You want my help. And I want to keep more people from being hurt. But I need some things from you."

He peered up at me, his green eyes calculating. "I am hardly in a position to bargain, Mr. Dresden. What you need, I will give you."

I nodded. "Answers. I've got about a million questions."

"Dark will come in less than two hours. Moonrise is only slightly more than an hour after that. We don't have much time for questions."

"Time enough," I assured him. "Why did you come here?"

"I woke up about five miles from here this morning," MacFinn said, looking away from me as he did, staring at the fire. "I've got several stashes hidden around the city. Just in case. This is one of the older ones. The damp had gotten to the clothes, and all I had was these." He gestured at the jean shorts.

"Do you remember what you did?" The words had an edge to them, but at least I didn't say, "Do you remember murdering Kim Delaney?" Who says I can't be diplomatic?

MacFinn shuddered. "Pieces," he said. "Just pieces." He looked at me and said, "I didn't mean to hurt her. I swear to you."

"Then why is she dead?" The words came out flat, cool. Tera glared at me, but I watched MacFinn for his answer.

"The curse," he said quietly. "When it happens, when I change—have you ever been angry, Mr. Dresden? So angry that you lost control? That nothing else mattered to you but acting on your anger?"

"Once," I said.

"Maybe you can understand part of it then," MacFinn said. "It comes on me, and there's nothing left but the need to hurt something. To act on the rage. I tried to tell Kim that the circle wasn't working, that she had to get out, but she wouldn't *listen*." I heard the frustration in his voice, and his hands clenched into fists. "She wouldn't listen to me."

"It frustrated you," I said. "And when you changed . . ."

He nodded. "It's how I came back from 'Nam. Everyone else in my platoon died but me. I knew the full moon was coming. And I knew that I hated them, hated the soldiers who had killed my friends. When I changed, I started killing until there wasn't anyone left alive within maybe two miles."

I stared at MacFinn for a long moment. I believed that he was telling me the truth. That he didn't have much control, if any, over his actions when he transformed. Though it occurred to me that if he *wanted* someone dead, he could probably point his monster-self in the right direction before he lost control.

Note to self: Do not cut MacFinn off in traffic.

"All right," I said. "Why come here? Why to 'Wolf Woods'? Why not to one of the other stashes?"

He smirked at the flames. "Where else would a werewolf run, Mr. Dresden?"

"Someplace a little less freaking obvious," I shot back.

MacFinn shook his head. "The FBI doesn't believe in werewolves. They aren't going to make the connection."

"Maybe," I conceded. "But there are smarter people than the FBI looking for you now. I don't think we should stay here for long."

MacFinn glanced at me, and then around him, as though listening for pursuers. "You might be right," he admitted. "But I'm not going anywhere until my head stops spinning. You don't look so good, either."

"I'll make it," I said. "All right, then. How did you know Kim Delaney? From her activist functions, I assume."

MacFinn's face went pale at the mention of her name, but he

nodded. "Originally. We came to know of her talents about a year ago. She told us how you were helping her control her abilities. She was helping me, indirectly, with the Northwest Passage Project. Then, last month, I asked her for her help."

"Why did you do that?"

MacFinn glanced warily at Tera, and then back at me. "Someone broke my circle."

I hunkered down on my heels, resting my aching arm on my knees. "Someone broke your circle? The one in the basement?"

"Yes," MacFinn said. "I don't know who. I'm not at home a lot. We found it broken when we went downstairs before moonrise, last month."

"And you asked Kim to fix it?"

MacFinn closed his eyes and nodded. "She said she could. She told us she would be able to make a new circle, one that would keep me from . . ."

I chewed on my lip as his voice trailed off. "Last month, you were meeting with Marcone's business partner, right? Negotiations over the Project?"

"I didn't kill him," MacFinn said quickly. "He died the night after the full moon. I couldn't have made the change and done it then. And the other two nights, I made sure I was well away from human beings. I didn't kill anyone the second two nights, either. I was alone."

"Your fiancée could have done those killings," I said, and flicked a glance at Tera West. She glared at my eyes for a moment, and then looked away.

"She didn't," MacFinn said, his tone cool.

"Let's go back a bit," I said. "Someone messed up your circle. To do that, they would have had to know about your curse, right? And they would have had to get into your house. So, the question is, who could do those things? And then the question is, who would have done it, and why?"

MacFinn shook his head. "I don't know," he said. "I just don't. I don't have much contact with the supernatural, Mr. Dresden. I keep my head down. I don't know anyone else who can make the change, except for her." He put his hand over that of the woman beside him.

A suspicion took root in my mind, someplace dark and sneaky. I studied Tera as I spoke to MacFinn. "You want to hear a theory?" I said. I didn't wait for him to answer. "Presuming you're telling the truth, I figure someone else did the killings the night before the full moon, last month. Some gangsters in town. Then they made sure that you would be the one going berserk the next three nights by fucking up your circle."

"Why would they do that?" MacFinn asked.

"To set you up. They kill some people, maybe just for kicks, maybe for a good reason, and then they lay the blame at your feet. Someone like me, or the White Council, comes poking around, and they go straight to you. You're notorious. Like a convicted felon. They find you over the body with a bloody knife, metaphorically speaking, and you're the one to burn at the stake. Literally."

MacFinn studied my face for a moment. "Or you think that there might be another reason."

I shrugged. "Maybe you *are* the killer. You could be trying to make it look like someone is setting you up to me and the Council. The police can't prove shit against you under the mundane justice system, and using this deception clears you with the supernatural community. So you moan and pose and say 'Woe is me, I am only the poor cursed guy,' and meanwhile a bunch of people end up dead. People who were standing in the way of your completing the Northwest Passage Project."

MacFinn showed me his teeth. "You think the world wouldn't be better off without people like Marcone and his lickspittles?"

"Good word, lickspittles," I replied, keeping my voice bland. "That doesn't really concern me right now, MacFinn. Men like Marcone know the risks and take their chances. What bothers me is that a bunch of other people are getting dead, and they don't really deserve it."

"Why would I be killing innocents?" MacFinn demanded, his voice growing tight, clipped.

"Innocents like Kim?" I said. I'm a wizard, not a saint. I'm allowed to be vindictive.

MacFinn went pale and looked down.

"Maybe you're doing it as a smoke screen. Maybe you can't help it. Or hell, maybe you really are just a poor cursed guy, and someone's using you like a puppet. There's no way for me to tell right now."

"Assuming I'm not lying," MacFinn grated, "who would have an interest in setting me up?"

I shook my head. "That's the million-dollar question. I'd say that it was Johnny Marcone—he stands to benefit if you can't oppose his business interests in the Northwest. As I understand it, the Northwest Passage would pretty much put nails in the coffin of a lot of industry up in that direction."

MacFinn nodded grimly. "It would."

"So that gives him a good motive. But how did he know about your curse? And how did he pull off ruining the circle? It doesn't sound like him. He would just have your brakes fail, or maybe arrange for you to meet a couple of big men in a dark alley. It's just his way." I shrugged. "Who else would be doing it? Can you think of anyone?"

MacFinn shook his head. "I've always been lucky. Been able to hold myself in, lock myself up. Or been able to go far away, out into the wilds where no one would find me. So that when I changed, no one would be killed."

"That's why you were backing the Northwest Passage," I guessed. "A place for you to go in safety when the full moon comes—a really big no-people zone."

MacFinn glanced aside at Tera, who was staring stoically into the distance. "That and other reasons." His jaw tightened, and he looked back to the fire. "You don't know what it's like, Mr. Dresden. To live with yourself."

I rubbed at my mouth and chin with my good hand. I needed a shave. I studied MacFinn and Tera for a moment, trying to make up my mind.

Was MacFinn telling me the truth? Was he just a victim, someone being used by a faceless villain still at large? Or was he lying to me?

If he was lying, if all of this had been his design, what purpose would he have had in luring me out here? Killing me, of course, getting rid of the only wizard who could pen up his monstrous form. That was, after all, exactly what he would have done if I hadn't have been able to shock him silly. But did that even make sense? What would he gain by removing me if I never stood in his way in the first place?

Careful, Harry. Don't get *too* paranoid. Not everyone is planning and plotting and lying. But I had to wonder about Tera West. A nasty scenario was laying itself out in my mind. What if the dear, sweet fiancée was tired of hubby? What if she had done the before- and after-moon killings, then set up her sweetiekins to take the fall for her? She could get rid of MacFinn and Marcone's partner all in one fell swoop.

Leaving her and Marcone alive. Marcone could have found

out about MacFinn from Tera, and about the weakness of his circle from Tera as well. Tera wasn't human, not even a little. She was something else, maybe a being of the Nevernever. Who knew how her mind worked?

And then there was the group of young people Tera seemed to be in charge of. How did they fit into this? What was she using them for?

I went fishing. "How are Georgia and Billy, Tera?" I asked, my tone conversational.

She blinked. Her mouth worked for a second, and then she answered, "Fine. They are well." She pressed her lips together, clearly desiring the conversation to end.

I watched MacFinn. His face registered confusion, and then he looked between Tera and me uneasily. He didn't know who the hell I was talking about, and she didn't seem to want to let MacFinn in on what was apparently a secret.

Aha, little miss werewolf-shapeshifter-thing. What are you plotting?

I was going to press her harder, when MacFinn and Tera both looked up at exactly the same time, out toward the woods. I stared at them like a moron for a couple of seconds, my mind still running along trails of thought, tracing potential lies, possibilities. Then I shook that out of my brain and Listened.

"Both of you along that way," Murphy said from somewhere in the distance downslope. "Ron, take your three and fan out until we're even with the feds. Then we sweep west, up the hill."

"Christ, Murphy," Carmichael said. "We don't owe the feds shit. If they'd have showed up on time, we'd have been out here hours ago. If we hadn't got that report about the West woman in the hotel room, we still wouldn't be here."

"Can it, Carmichael," Murphy snapped. "Pictures of MacFinn and the woman have been passed out. And you all know what Dresden looks like. Spread out and nab them."

"You don't even know if they're here," Carmichael protested.

"I'll bet you sex to donuts that they are, Carmichael," Murphy said, her voice dripping sweet venom. "And that should tell you how certain I am."

Carmichael muttered something under his breath, and then growled orders to his men to fan out as Murphy had indicated.

"Dammit," MacFinn snarled. "How did they know I was here?"

"Where else would a werewolf go to hide?" I sniped. "Shit. How do we get out?"

"Wind," Tera said. She and MacFinn both came to their feet. "Or fog. Can you do one of those again?"

I grimaced and shook my head. "I don't think so. I'm worn out. I'd probably make a mistake and that could kill someone."

"If you don't," Tera said, "we will all be captured or killed."

"You can't solve all your problems by magic," I snapped.

"He's right," MacFinn said quietly. "We split up. The first one discovered makes a lot of noise, puts up a fight, and gives the others a chance to get away."

"No," I said. "MacFinn, you've got to stay with me. I can make the circle with some sticks and dirt, if necessary, but if I'm not there, I can't hold you in when the curse takes hold later tonight."

MacFinn's teeth showed again. "No time to argue, Mr. Dresden," he said.

"Indeed there is not," said Tera, and then she took off at a dead run. MacFinn hissed a curse and grabbed for her as she ran, but missed. Tera flew on into the woods, rushing silently down the slope on an angle that would take her past the edge of the pursuers' line. She was noticed after only a few steps, shouts going up from three or four throats.

"Bitch," MacFinn cursed, and he started after her. I seized his arm, my fingers clamping on his bicep hard enough to make him stop and stare at me, his green eyes fierce and wild.

"Split up," I said, looking back down the hill. "If we're lucky, they won't even know that we were here."

"But Tera—"

"Knows what she's doing," I said. "If the police nail us, there's no way you're going to be able to hold it in tonight. We go, now, and we meet at the nearest gas station to the park. All right?"

From down slope came the sounds of running men, a warning call, and then a gunshot. For Tera's sake, I hoped that Agent Benn wasn't down there. MacFinn clenched his jaw, and then ran up the slope, on an angle. Down below us, there were more shouts, more shots fired, and a short, sharp cry of pain.

Call me crazy, but those sounds, added to all the other things that had happened that day, were just too much for me to handle. I turned, cradling my wounded arm against me, and stumbled up the hill into a long, loping run. I kept my head down, watching my feet, only looking up often enough to make sure that I didn't run into a tree, and fled.

Chapter 16

I made it out of the park, exhausted and barely able to keep from screaming with pain. I stopped at the first gas station I could find, so I could take off my boots. Old and comfortable as they were, cowboy boots were not meant for running cross-country. I leaned against the side of the building by the pay phones, away from the street, and sat down on the sidewalk. My body throbbed with pain, slowing as my heart and breathing did.

I gave MacFinn an hour, but he didn't show up. No one did.

I got restless, fast. Could both MacFinn and Tera West have been captured? Murphy's cops may not have looked like much, but I knew they were tough and smart. It wasn't out of the realm of possibility.

I rummaged in my duster's pockets, came up with enough change to make a phone call, then made my painful way to the phone.

"Midwestern *Arcane,* this is Ms. Rodriguez," Susan said, when she picked up the phone. Her voice sounded tired, stressed.

"Hi, Susan," I said. My shoulder twinged, and I gritted my teeth, pulling my duster around me a little more tightly. The evening was bringing a cold wind and grey clouds, and the sweats and cotton T-shirt Tera West had given me weren't enough to keep out the chill.

"Harry?" she said disbelievingly. "My God. Where are you? The police are looking for you. They keep calling here. Something about a murder."

"Misunderstanding," I said and leaned against the wall. The pain was getting worse as chills soaked in and I started to shiver.

"You sound terrible," Susan said. "Are you all right?"

"Can you help me?"

There was a pause on the other end of the line. "I don't know, Harry. I don't know what's going on. I don't want to get into any trouble."

"I could explain it," I offered, struggling to keep my words clear through the pain. "But it's sort of a long story." I dropped a subtle emphasis on that last word. Sometimes it scares me how easy it is to get people to do what you want them to do, if you know something about them.

"Story, eh?" Susan said. I could hear the sudden twinge of interest in her voice.

"Sure. Murder, violence, blood, monsters. Give you the whole scoop if you can give me a ride."

"You bastard," she breathed, but I thought she was smiling. "I would have come to get you anyway."

"Sure you would have," I said, but I felt a smile on my own lips. I told her the address of the gas station and hoped that the feds hadn't taken the time to get a wiretap for Susan's phone.

"Give me half an hour," Susan said. "Maybe more, depending on traffic."

I squinted up at the sky, which was rapidly darkening, both with oncoming dusk and heavy, brooding clouds. "Time's important. Hurry if you can."

"Just take care of yourself, Harry," she said, worry in her voice. Then she hung up the phone.

I did, too, and leaned back against the wall. I hated to draw Susan into this. It made me feel cheap, somehow. Weak. It was that whole problem with chivalry that I had. I didn't want a girl to be riding to my rescue, protecting me. It just didn't seem right. And I didn't want to endanger Susan, either. I was a murder suspect, and the police were looking for me. She could get in trouble, for aiding and abetting, or something like that.

On the other hand, I didn't have much choice. I didn't have any money for a cab, even if I could get one this far from the city. I didn't have a car. I was in no shape to walk anywhere. My contacts, in the persons of MacFinn and Tera West, were gone. I had to have help, and Susan was the only one I thought I could trust to do it. If there was a story involved, she'd go to hell itself to get it.

And I had used that against her, to lever her into helping me. I didn't like it that I had. I'd thought better of myself. I ducked my head against the cold, and shivered, and wondered if I'd done the right thing.

It was while I was leaning against the wall, waiting, that I heard a scrabbling sound around the corner of the gas station. I tensed and waited. The sound repeated itself, a definite pattern of three short movements. A signal.

Warily, I made my way to the back of the building, ready to turn and run as best I could. Tera West was there, behind the building, crouched down between several empty cardboard boxes that smelled of beer and the garbage bin. She was naked, her body a uniform shade of brown, without an ounce of excess fat on her. Her hair was mussed and had leaves and bits of twig caught in it. Her amber eyes looked even more alien and wild than usual.

She rose and came toward me, evidently unconscious of the cold. She moved with a feral sort of grace that made me all too aware of her legs, and her hips, even though I was battered, fatigued, and brooding.

"Wizard," she greeted me. "Give me your coat."

I snapped my eyes back up to hers, then slipped out of my duster, though my shoulder screamed with pain as I pulled the coat off of it, and my body sent up an entirely different round of complaints as the cold wind gleefully cut through the thin clothes I wore beneath the duster. Tera took the coat and slid into it, wrapping it around her and buttoning it closed. The sleeves were too long, and the coat dangled to her ankles, but it covered her lean, strong body well enough. I found myself faintly regretful that I'd had it with me.

"What happened?" I asked her.

She shook her head. "The police do not know how game runs, or how to chase it. One grabbed me. I made him let go." She glanced around us warily, and raked her fingers through her hair, trying to comb out leaves and sticks. "I led them away from you and MacFinn, changed, and made my way back to the camp. I followed MacFinn's trail."

"Where is he?"

She bared her teeth. "The federal people caught him. They took him away."

"Hell's bells," I breathed. "Do you know where?"

"Into a car," she responded.

"No," I said, growing frustrated. "Do you know where the car went?"

She shook her head. "But they had an argument with the one

called Murphy. Murphy had more people with her, more guns. MacFinn went where Murphy wanted him to go."

"Downtown," I said. "Murphy would want him in holding down at the station. Hell, it's on the same floor as Special Investigations."

Tera shrugged, her expression hard. "As you say."

"We don't have much time," I said.

"For what? There is nothing more to be done. We cannot reach him now. MacFinn will change when the moon rises. Murphy and the police people will die."

"Like hell," I said. "I've got to get to the station before it happens."

Tera studied me with narrowed eyes. "The police are hunting for you as well, wizard. If you go there, you too will be locked in a cage. You will not be allowed to go to MacFinn."

"I wasn't planning on asking permission," I said. "But I think I can get inside. I just have to get to my apartment."

"The police will be watching it," Tera said. "They will be waiting for you there. And in any case, we have no car and no money. How will you reach Chicago before moonrise? There is nothing more to be done, wizard."

There came the crunch of tires around the side of the gas station, and I peeked around the corner. Susan's car was just coming to a halt. Raindrops were starting to come down and to make little impact circles on her Taurus's windshield. I felt a little surge of defiant energy.

"There's our ride," I said. "Follow." I relished throwing the terse command at Tera, and she stared at me. I turned my back on her and stalked over to the car.

Susan leaned across and threw open the passenger door, then blinked at me in surprise. She blinked again when Tera slipped in front of me, threw the passenger seat forward, and slid into the backseat with a flash of long, lean legs, then regarded Susan with unreadable, distant eyes.

I pushed the seat back and settled into place. It was a real effort to shut the door, and a small sound of discomfort escaped my mouth. When I looked at Susan, she was staring at me, and at my arm. I looked down and found that the bandage, and a part of the T-shirt's sleeve were soaked through with blood. The purple bruises had spread a few inches, it seemed, and showed beneath the shirt's sleeve.

"Good Lord," Susan gasped. "What happened?"

"I got shot," I said.

"Doesn't it hurt?" Susan stammered, still stunned.

"Is this female always so stupid?" Tera asked. I winced. Susan turned in the seat and glowered at Tera, and I looked back to see Tera narrow her eyes and bare her teeth in what one could hardly say was a smile.

"It hurts," I confirmed. "Susan, take us to my place, but don't stop when you get there. Just drive past slowly. I'll tell you everything on the way."

Susan gave Tera one last, skeptical glance, particularly taking in my bullet-torn duster and Tera's bare limbs. "This better be good, Dresden," she said. Then she slapped the car into gear and started driving with irritated haste back toward the city.

I wanted to collapse into sleep, but I made myself explain most of what had happened over the past couple of days to Susan, editing out mentions of the White Council, demons, that sort of thing. Susan listened, and drove, and asked intent questions, fastening gleefully on to the information concerning the Northwest Passage Project, and Johnny Marcone's links to the businesses opposing it. Rain started coming down in a steady, murky veil, and she flicked on the windshield wipers.

"So you've got to get to MacFinn," Susan said, when I was finished, "before the moon comes up and he transforms."

"You've got it," I said.

"Why don't you call Murphy? Tell her what's going on?"

I shook my head. "Murphy isn't going to be in the mood to listen. She busted me and I fled arrest. She'd have me in a cell before I could say abracadabra."

"But it's raining," Susan protested. "We won't be able to see the moon tonight. Won't that stop MacFinn from changing?"

I blinked at the question and glanced back at Tera. She was watching the buildings pass out the side window as the streetlights started flickering on. She didn't look at me, but shook her head.

"No such luck," I told Susan. "And with these clouds, I can't even tell if the sun has gone down yet, much less how much time we have before moonrise."

Susan breathed out slowly. "How are you going to get to MacFinn, then?"

"I've got a couple things at my apartment," I said. "Drive on by. Let's see if there's anyone watching the old place."

Susan turned the car down my street, and we rolled slowly through the rain. The old boarding house huddled stoically beneath the downpour, its gutters gurgling and spouting streams of water. The streetlights glowed with silver haloes as the rain came down. A bit down from my building, a plain brown sedan was parked, and a couple of shadowy forms could be seen inside it when Susan drove past.

"That's them," I said. "I recognize one of them from Murphy's unit."

Susan let out another breath and drew the car around the corner, parking it along the street. "Is there any way to sneak into your place? A back door?"

I shook my head. "No. There's only the one door in, and you can see the windows from here. I just need the police to not be looking for a few minutes."

"You need a distraction," Tera said. "I will do it."

I looked over my shoulder. "I don't want any violence."

She tilted her head to one side, her expression never changing. "Very well," she said. "For MacFinn's sake, I will do as you say. Open the door."

I stared at her fathomless eyes for a second, searching for any signs of deception or betrayal. What if Tera was the killer? She had known about MacFinn, and was able to transform in one fashion or another. She could have committed the murders last month, as well as the one two nights past. But if so, why had she seemingly sacrificed herself so that MacFinn and I could escape? Why had she come to find me?

Then again, MacFinn had been captured. And her words at the gas station may have been calculated to make me give up trying to help him, if one looked at them from a certain point of view. What if she was trying to take care of both MacFinn and me by throwing us to the mundane legal system?

My head spun with pain and weariness. Paranoid, Harry, I told myself. You've got to trust someone, somewhere—or else MacFinn goes furry and Murphy and a lot of other good people die tonight. There wasn't much choice.

I opened the door, and we both got out of the car. "What are you going to do?" I asked Tera.

Instead of answering, the amber-eyed woman stripped off my duster and handed it back to me, leaving herself nude and lovely under the rain. "Do you like to look at my body?" she demanded of me.

"Careful how you answer this one, buster," Susan growled from the car.

I coughed, and glanced back at Susan, keeping my eyes off of the other woman. "Yeah, Tera. That will work fine, I guess."

"Wait for twenty slow breaths," she said. There was a note of amusement in her voice. "Pick me up at the far end of this block." Then she turned on a bare heel and glided into the darkness between streetlights in a graceful lope. I frowned after her for a moment, and then drew my duster back on.

"You don't have to look quite so hard," Susan said. "Is she the human-interest angle for this story?"

I winced, holding my wounded arm close to my side, and leaned down to meet Susan's eyes. "I don't think she's human," I said. Then I stood and started walking down the street, slowing my steps so that I didn't round the corner until Tera's prescribed time limit had elapsed. Even when I did, I walked quickly, like someone hurrying home out of the rain, my hands in my pockets, keeping my head down against the grey downpour.

I crossed the street toward my apartment building, glancing at the sedan as I did.

The cops weren't watching me. They were staring at the pool of light beneath the streetlight behind them, where Tera spun gracefully through the steps of some sort of gliding dance, moving to a rhythm and a music I could not hear. There was a primal sort of intensity to her motions, raw sexuality, feminine power coursing through her movements. Her back arched as she spun and whirled, offering out her breasts to the chill rain, and her skin was slick and gleaming with water.

I tripped over the curb on the far side of the street and felt my cheeks start to flame as I hurried down the steps to my apartment. I unlocked the door and went inside, shutting it behind me. I didn't light any candles, relying upon my knowledge of the house to move around.

The two potions were in their plastic sports bottles on the counter where I had left them. I grabbed up my black nylon backpack from the floor and threw the bottles into it. Then I went into my bedroom and grabbed the blue coveralls with the little red patch over one breast pocket stenciled with **MIKE** in bold letters. My mechanic had accidentally left them in the trunk of the Blue Beetle the last time the Beetle was in the shop. I added a baseball cap, a first aid kit, a roll of duct tape, a box of chalk, seven smooth stones from a collection of them I keep in my closet, a white T-shirt and a pair of blue jeans, and a huge bottle of Tylenol, zipped up the backpack, and headed back out again. At the last moment, I took up my wizard's staff from the corner by the door.

Something flashed past my legs, moving out into the night, and I almost jumped out of my skin. Mister paused at the top of the stairs to look back at me, his cat eyes enigmatic and irritated, and then vanished into the darkness. I muttered something under my breath and locked the door behind me, then headed out once more, my heart rattling along too quickly to be comfortable.

Tera was on her hands and knees in the middle of the pool of light behind the sedan, her damp hair fallen all around her face, her lips parted, facing the two plainclothes officers, who had gotten out of the car and were speaking to her from several feet away. Her chest was heaving in and out, but having seen her in action, I doubted that it was merely from the exertion of her dancing. Looked nice, though. The policemen were sure as hell staring.

I gripped my staff in hand, along with the backpack, and walked away down the street again. It didn't take long to make it back to Susan's car, and she immediately wheeled the vehicle around the block without comment. Susan hardly had begun to slow down when Tera appeared from between a couple of buildings and loped over to the car. I leaned forward, opened the door, and she got into the backseat. I threw her the extra clothes I had picked up, and she began to dress without comment.

"It worked," I said. "We did it."

"Of course it worked," Tera said. "Men are foolish. They will stare at anything female and naked."

"She's got that right," Susan said, under her breath, and jerked the car into motion again. "Oh, we are going to talk about this one, mister. Next stop, Special Investigations."

Outside the battered old police-building downtown, I pulled the baseball cap a little lower over my eyes, and drank the blending potion. It didn't really have any taste to it at all, but it twitched and bubbled all the way down my gullet until it hit my stomach.

I gave the potion a few seconds to work and shifted my hands on the handle of my wizard's staff. Even though the end of it was shoved into a wheeled bucket, it still didn't look much like the handle of a mop. And even though I was dressed in the dark blue coveralls, they were ridiculously short on me. I did not look much like a janitor.

That's where the magic came in. If the potion worked, I would look like background to any casual observers, a part of the scenery that they wouldn't glance at twice. So long as they didn't give me an intense scrutiny, the potion's power should be able to keep me from being noticed, which would let me get close to MacFinn, which would let me put the containment circle around him and keep his transformed self from going on a rampage.

Of course, if it didn't work, I might just end up studying the inside of a jail cell for a few years—provided the transformed MacFinn didn't tear me apart first.

I tried to ignore the pain in my shoulder, the nervous tension in my stomach. I was rebandaged, Tylenoled, and as reasonably refreshed as I could possibly have been without drinking the potion I had brewed just for that purpose.

If I could have had both potions going in my system without them making me too ill to move, I would have downed the refresher potion the moment I got my hands on it, but without the blending potion, there was no way I could get inside to MacFinn. I could only hope that I'd find a use for it eventually. I'd hate the effort to go to waste.

I waited impatiently in the rain, sure for a moment that I had messed something up when making the potion, that it wasn't going to have any effect at all.

And then I felt it start to work.

A sort of grey feeling came over me, and I realized with a start that the colors were fading from my vision. A sort of listless feeling came over me, a lassitude that advised me to sit down somewhere and watch the world go by, but at the same time the hairs on the back of my neck prickled up as the potion's magic took effect.

I took a deep breath and walked up the stairs of the building with my bucket and my "mop," pulled open the doors, and went inside. Shadows shifted and changed oddly, all greys and blacks and whites, and for a second I felt like an extra on the set of *Casablanca* or *The Maltese Falcon*.

The solid old matron of a sergeant sat at the front desk, thumbing through a glossy magazine, a portrait done in colorless hues. She glanced up at me for a second, and tinges of color returned to her uniform, her cheeks, and her eyes. She looked me over casually, sniffed, and lowered her face to her magazine again. As her attention faded, so did the colors from her clothing and skin. My perceptions of her changed as she paid attention to me or did not.

I felt my face stretch in a victorious smile. The potion had worked. I was inside. I had to suppress an urge to break into a soft-shoe routine. Sometimes, being able to use magic was so *cool*. I almost stopped hurting for a few seconds, from sheer enjoyment of the special effects. I would have to remember to tell Bob how much I liked the way this potion worked.

I kept my head down and moved past the desk sergeant, just one more janitor coming in to clean up the police station after hours. I picked up the bucket and my "mop" and went up the stairs, toward the holding cells and the Special Investigations offices on the fifth floor. One cop passed me on the stairs and didn't so much as look at me. His uniform and skin remained entirely devoid of color. I grew more confident and moved with more speed. I was effectively invisible.

Now all I had to do was find MacFinn, trick my way into seeing him, and save Murphy and all the other police from the monster MacFinn would become—before they arrested me for trying to do it.

And time was running out.

Chapter 17

Ever wish you had an almanac?

I did, that night. I had no idea what time the moon was supposed to rise, and I hadn't exactly had time to run to the library or a bookstore. I knew that it was supposed to happen an hour or so after sundown, but the way the clouds rolled in had made it uncertain exactly when sundown had happened. Did I have twenty minutes? Ten? An hour?

Or was I already too late?

As I climbed the stairs, I thought about being alone in the building with MacFinn after he had changed. For all my vaunted wizard's knowledge, I had no real idea of his capabilities; although after seeing Kim's body, I had something of an idea of what he could do. Bob had said that loup-garou were fast, strong, virtually immune to magic. What could I do against something like that?

I just had to pray that I would be able to get the circle up around MacFinn before I had to find out. I checked the bucket, to make sure I still had the chalk and the stones I would need to construct the greater circle around MacFinn. You didn't necessarily have to make them out of silver and gold and whatnot. Mostly, you just had to understand how the construct channeled the forces that were being employed. If you knew that, you could figure out how to make it out of less pure materials. The very best wizards don't need much more than chalk, table salt, and a wooden spoon to pull off some remarkable stuff.

My thoughts were rambling now, panic making them scamper around like a frightened chipmunk. That was bad. I needed focus, direction, concentration. I drove my legs a little harder, went up the stairs as fast as I dared, until I came out on the fifth floor. The door to Special Investigations was ten feet away down the hall. The holding cells were down the hall and around the corner, and I started that way at once.

"What do you mean, you can't find him?" Murphy's voice demanded as I walked past the office door.

"Just that. The men on his apartment said that they kept a real good eye on the place, but that he got in and out again without them seeing anything." Carmichael's voice was tired, frustrated.

Murphy snorted. "Christ, Carmichael. Is Dresden going to have to walk right into the office before you can find him?"

I hurried on past the door and down the hall. Tempting as it was to listen to a conversation about myself without the participants knowing, I just didn't have time. I wheeled my wobbling, squeaking bucket down the hall, half jogging in my hurry.

Holding was set up, unsurprisingly, behind bars. There was a swinging barred door that the station guard had to buzz to open, if you didn't have the key. Beyond that was a sort of antechamber with a couple of wooden chairs and not much else besides a counter with a window made of bullet-proof glass. The jailer sat behind the glass at his desk, his expression baggy eyed and bored. Past the jailer's window was another door, made of steel with a tiny little window, which led into the row of cells. The jailer had the controls to that door at his desk as well.

I went to the first barred door, kept my head down, and rapped on the metal slats. I waited for a while, but nothing happened, so I rapped on the bars again. It occurred to me that it would add a nice touch of irony if the same blending potion that got me into the building also kept me from being noticed by the jailer and let inside. I rapped on the bars again, harder this time, with the shaft of my wooden "mop."

It took some determined rapping to get him to look up from his magazine, but he finally did, and peered at me through thick glasses. His colors swirled and gained a bit of tint before settling back toward grey. He frowned at me, glanced back at a calendar on the wall, and then pushed the button.

The barred door buzzed and I shoved it open with my bucket, wheeling inside with my head down. "You're early this week," the jailer said, his eyes back on the magazine.

"Out of town on Friday. Trying to get done sooner," I replied. I kept my voice in a monotone, as grey and boring as I could manage. To my surprise, it came out as I intended it. I'm usually not much of a liar or an actor, so the potion must have been helping me on some subtle and devious level. One thing I'll say for Bob: He's annoying as hell, but he knows his stuff.

"Whatever. Sign here," the jailer said in a bored tone, and shoved a clipboard and a pen at me through a slot at the base of the Plexiglas window. He turned a page in his magazine, showing me a picture of an athletic-looking young woman doing something anatomically improbable with an equally improbable young man.

I hesitated. How in the hell was I supposed to sign in and out? I mean, Bob's potion may have been good, but it wasn't going to change a signature after I'd put it on the paper. I glanced at the inner door, and then at the clock on the wall. To hell with it. I didn't have time to hang around. I went over to the counter and scribbled something unreadable on the admissions sheet.

"Have any trouble tonight?" I asked.

The jailer snorted, turning his magazine to the right by ninety degrees. "Just that rich guy they brought in earlier. He was yelling for a while, but he's shut up now. Probably coming down off of whatever he was on." He collected the clipboard, gave it a perfunctory glance, and hung it back up on its peg beside a bank of black-and-white monitors.

I leaned closer to the monitors, sweeping my eyes over them. Each was apparently receiving a signal from a security camera, because each one of them displayed a scene that was exactly the same except for the actors in it—a small cell, maybe eight feet by eight, with bars serving as one wall, smooth concrete for the other three, a bunk, a toilet, and a single door. Maybe two thirds of the monitors had a strip of masking tape stuck to the lower right-hand corner of the screen, with a name, like HANSON or WASHINGTON, written in black marker. I frantically scanned the bank of monitors until, in the lower corner, I found the one that said MACFINN. I looked at his monitor. The video was blurred, flecked with snow and static, but I could see well enough what had happened.

The cell was empty.

Concrete dust drifted in the air. The wall of bars was missing, apparently torn from the concrete and allowed to fall away. I could see the scraps of MacFinn's denim shorts lying on the floor of the cell.

"Hell's bells," I swore softly. There was a flicker of motion on another monitor, the one next to MacFinn's. The tape at the bottom of the screen read MATSON, and a starved-looking, unshaven man in a sleeveless white undershirt and blue jeans could be seen curled up on the bunk, his back pressed to the rear corner of the cell. His mouth was open and his chest straining, as though he was screaming, but I could hear nothing through the thick security door and the concrete walls. There was a flicker of motion, a huge and furry shape on the camera, out of focus, and Matson threw up his skinny arms to protect himself as something huge and quick shoved its way between the bars, like a big dog going through a rotten picket fence, and engulfed him.

There was a burst of static and violent motion, and then a spattering of black on the grey walls and floor of the cell, as though someone had shaken up a cola and sprayed the walls with it. Then the huge form was gone, and left behind was a ragged, quivering doll of torn flesh and blood-soaked clothing. Matson stared up at the security camera, his dying eyes pleading with mine—and then he jerked once and was gone.

The entire thing had taken perhaps three or four seconds.

My eyes swept over the other security monitors as a sick sort of fascination settled over me. Prisoners were straining to the front of their cells, shouting things out, trying to get enough of a look to see what was going on. I realized that they couldn't see what was happening—they could only hear. They wouldn't be able to look out and see the transformed MacFinn until he was at the bars of their cell.

Fear, sick and horrible and debilitating, swam over me and tangled up my tongue. The creature had gone through the bars of the cell as though they'd been made of cheap plastic, and it had killed without mercy. I stared at Matson's dead eyes, at the ruined mess of what had been his guts, at the detached pieces of meat and bone that had once been his right arm and leg.

Stars above, Harry, I thought to myself. *What the hell are you doing in the same building with that thing?*

On another monitor, there was a replay of what had happened seconds before, and an aging black man named CLEMENT went down beneath the creature, screaming as he died. Seeing what was happening set off some primal, ancient fear, something programmed into my head, a fear of being found in my hiding place, of being trapped in a tiny space from which there was no escape while something with killing teeth and crushing jaws came in to eat me. That same primitive, naked part of me screamed and gibbered and shouted at my rational mind to turn around right now, to turn around and run, fast and far.

But I couldn't let it go on. I had to do something.

"Look," I said and pointed at the monitor. My finger trembled, and my voice came out as a ghost of a whisper. I tried again, jabbing my finger at the monitors and half shouting, "Look!" at the jailer.

He glanced up at me, tilted his head, and frowned. I saw some colors start to bleed into his face, but that didn't matter now. I continued to point at the monitors and tried to step closer to them. "Look, look at the screens, my God, man!" By now my voice was coming out in a high, panicky tone. I pressed as close to the monitors as I could, yelling, excited.

I should have known better, of course. Wizards and technology simply do not mix—especially when the wizard's heart is pounding like the floor of a basketball court and his guts are shaking. The monitors burst into frantic displays of static and snow, flickering images sometimes visible, sometimes not.

The guard gave me a disgusted look and turned around to glance at the monitors. He blinked at them for a second, while a man named MURDOCH died in flickering, poor reception.

"What the hell is wrong with those things now?" the jailer complained, and took off his glasses to clean them. "There's always something going wrong with the damn cameras. I swear, it isn't worth the money they cost to keep on fixing them."

I frantically backed up from the monitors. "They're dying," I said. "God, you've got to let those men out of there before it kills them."

The man nodded. "Uh-huh. Tell me about it. Just goes to show you how smart the city is, right?" I stared at him for a second, and he put his glasses back on to give me a polite, bored smile. His colors had gone back to black and white, and I must have looked like a dull, humdrum old janitor to him once again. The potion had blended my words into something that the guard's brain would accept without comment, and let pass, just boring, everyday conversation like you have with people ninety percent of the time. The potion was fantastic. Way, way too good.

"Look at the monitors," I screamed in frustration and fear. "He's killing them!"

"The monitors won't stop you doing your job," the guard assured me. "I'll just buzz you in." And with that, he pressed a button somewhere behind the Plexiglas window, and the security door that led into the hallway of cells made a humming sound, clicked, and swung three or four inches open.

Screams poured out of the cells, high sounds that you wouldn't think could come from a man's throat, panicked and terrified. There was a horrible, wrenching sound, a screech of protesting metal, and one of the screams peaked at a shivering, violent point—then dissolved into a strangled mishmash of sounds, of tearing and snapping and popping, of gurgling and thudding. And when they were finished, something, something big, with a cavernous, resonating chest, snarled from not ten feet beyond the security door.

I shot a glance to the guard, who had stumbled to his feet and was grabbing for his gun. He headed out of his station, opening a door that led into the antechamber, presumably to investigate.

"No!" I shouted at him, and threw myself at the security door. I sensed, rather than saw, something else, on the other side of the wall, heading for the exit. I could hear its breath, feel its massive motion through the air, and I hurled my shoulder against the door, slamming it forward, just as something huge and strong thrust a paw through the doorway. The edge of the steel security door slammed forward onto the paw, a member that was neither wholly a paw nor a hand, but somewhere in between, tipped with huge black claws, and drenched in wet, dark, blood. I heard the creature on the far side of the door, only three inches of steel away, snarl in a fury and hatred so pure as to be painful to hear.

Then it started shoving at the door.

The first shove was tentative, but though I strained with all my strength, it still slapped me back a foot across the floor, my boots slipping on the tile. That paw-hand turned, and the talons sank into the steel door in a sudden, snapping motion as the thing took hold of it and started wrenching it back and forth in berserk anger.

"Help me!" I shouted at the guard, struggling to force the door closed. The jailer blinked at me for a second, then flooded with color.

"You!" he said. "My God. What is happening?"

"Help me close this door or we're both dead," I snarled, continuing to push forward with every ounce of strength I could summon. On the far side of the door, the loup-garou gathered its weight and hurled itself against the door again just as the guard rushed forward to help me.

The door exploded inward, throwing me back like a doll, past the guard, who stumbled back through the door that led behind the counter where he'd been sitting and fell to the ground. My upper back hit the barred door that led out into the hallway, eliciting an instant flash of hot agony from my wounded shoulder.

There was a snarl, and then the creature that had been Harley MacFinn came through the doorway. The loup-garou was a wolf, in the same way that a velociraptor is a bird—same basic design, vastly different outcome. It must have been five or five and a half feet tall at the tip of its hunched shoulders. It was wider than a wolf, as though a wolf had been squashed down with an extra five or six hundred pounds of muscle. Its pelt was shaggy, jet-black and matte, except where fresh blood was making it glisten. Its ears were ragged, upright, focused forward. It had a muzzle that was too wide to belong to anything natural, a mouthful of teeth, and MacFinn's blazing eyes done in monochrome grey, the whole stained with blood that looked black beneath the influence of the blending potion. Its limbs were disproportionate, though I couldn't say whether they looked too long or too short—just *wrong*. Everything about it was wrong, screamed with malice and hate and anger, and it carried a cloak of supernatural power with it that made my teeth hurt and my hair stand on end.

The loup-garou came through the door, swept its monochrome gaze past me, then turned to its left with unholy grace and flung itself at the jailer.

The man got lucky. He looked up and saw the creature as he was regaining his feet, then convulsed in a spastic reaction to the sight of the fanged horror. The reaction threw him a few inches out of the loup-garou's path. He scrambled back, behind the counter and out of my sight.

The loup-garou turned to pursue the jailer behind the counter, slowed because it had to shoulder its way between the counter and the wall, making the counter buckle outward into the room. The jailer got to his feet, gun in hand, took a creditable shooting stance, and emptied the pistol's clip into the loup-garou's skull in the space of maybe three seconds, filling the little antechamber with the sound of thunder and drowning out the cries of the prisoners in their cells in the hall beyond.

The monster kept coming. The bullets bothered it no more than a fly ramming the forehead of a professional wrestler. It rose up as the guard screamed, "No, no, no, nononononono!" And then it fell upon him, claws and fangs slashing. The jailer tried to turn, to run where there was no place left to go, and the thing turned its head and sank its jaws into the small of the man's back, releasing a spray of blood. The jailer screamed and grabbed frantically at the console, but the loup-garou shook its head violently from left to right, tore him from the console, and hurled him to the floor behind the counter.

I didn't see the guard die. But I saw the way the blood flew up over the hunched, gnarled shoulders of the loup-garou, to decorate the walls and the ceiling. I felt silently grateful when the bent and warping panes of Plexiglas became obscured with scarlet.

It was sometime right around then, as paralyzing agony seared through my shoulder and terrified prisoners screamed and cried out to God or Allah to save them that I noticed that a new noise had been added to the din. The guard had tipped off the alarm when he had scrambled at the console, and it was hooting enthusiastically. Cops were going to come running, and one of the first was going to be Murphy.

The loup-garou was still savaging the jailer's body, and I hoped for his sake that the man wasn't still alive. My best option would have been to slip into the cell block, close the security door behind me, and hope the creature went out into the building at large. Within the cell block, I would have time to put up a warding barrier, something that would keep the monster from coming through the door or the walls to get at me and the prisoners in there. I could fort up there, wait for morning, and live through the night, almost certainly. It was the smart thing to do. It was the survivable thing to do.

Instead, I turned to my staff, at the other side of the little room, and held forth my hand. *"Vento servitas,"* I hissed, forcing out tightly focused will, and a sudden current of air simultaneously threw my staff to me and slammed shut the door to the cells, giving the trapped prisoners what little protection it offered. I caught the staff in my outstretched hand and turned to the barred gate that held me shut in the antechamber with the loup-garou.

I thrust my staff in between the bars and leaned against it as though to pry the bars apart. Had it been only wood and muscle involved, I might have snapped the ancient ash. But a wizard's staff is a tool that helps him to apply forces, to manipulate them and maneuver them to his will. So I leaned my will and my concentration on the staff at the same time I did my body, and worked on multiplying the force I was applying to the steel bars.

"Forzare," I hissed. *"Forzare."* The metal began to strain and buckle.

Behind me, the loup-garou started thrashing around. I heard the shattering of Plexiglas and shot it a look over my shoulder.

The scant protection offered by the potion collapsed, colors flooding my vision. The black of its muzzle warmed to a scarlet-smeared wash of dark brown, stained with wet scarlet. Its fangs were ivory and crimson. Its eyes became a brilliant shade of green. It cut through the blending potion with the ferocity of its stare, and focused on me with an intensity that sent every instinct in my body screaming that death was here, that it was about to jump down my throat and rip me inside out.

"Forzare!" I shouted, shoving against the staff with every ounce of strength I had. The bars bowed out in the middle, parted to an opening perhaps a foot wide and twice as long. The counter exploded outward as the loup-garou came through it, showering me with debris and minor, painful cuts.

I dove through the opening, heedless of my shoulder, conscious only of the beast closing in behind me. My body sailed through with more grace than I could have managed under less panicked circumstances, almost as though the rush of air moving before the charging creature had helped lift me through. And then something closed on my left foot, and I simply lost all sensation in it.

I fell short, to the floor, bumping my chin hard enough to draw blood from the corner of my tongue. I looked over my shoulder to see the loup-garou with one of my boots held in its jaws, its broad head shoved through the opening in the bars and caught there. It was shaking its body back and forth, but its paws were smeared with scarlet blood, and its feet slipped left and right on the tile floor. Incredible strength or no, it couldn't get the leverage it needed to tear the bars apart like tissues.

I heard myself making desperate animal sounds, struggling in a panic, writhing. The alarm was howling all around me now, and I could hear shouts and running footsteps. Dust was falling down around the edges of the bars, and I could see that the loup-garou was slowly tearing them from their mountings in the floor and ceiling, despite its bad footing.

I twisted my foot left and right, horrid images of simply losing it at the ankle flashing in my mind, and then abruptly shot forward several feet along the floor. I glanced down at my leg and saw a bloodstained sock before I scrambled up and started running for my staff.

Behind me, the loup-garou howled in frustration and began to throw itself about. It must have scraped enough of the blood off of its paws, because it then tore through the wall of bars in two seconds flat and rushed after me.

I took up my staff and spun to face the creature, planting my feet on the floor, holding the ash wood before me. *"Tornarius!"* I thundered, thrusting my staff upward, and the thing threw itself at me in a rush of power and mass.

My aim was to reflect the loup-garou's own power and momentum back against it, force equals mass times acceleration, et cetera, but I had underestimated just how much power the thing had. It overloaded my limits and we split the difference. The creature slammed against a solid force in the air that canceled its momentum and flung it to the floor.

Approximately equal force was also applied to me—but I was probably a fifth of the mass of the loup-garou. I was flung back through the air like a piece of popcorn in a sudden wind, all the way to where the hall turned the corner to lead down to Special Investigations. I hit the floor before I hit the wall, thankfully, bounced, rolled, and slapped into the wall at last, grateful to be at a stop and aching all over. I had lost my staff in the tumble. The tile floor was cool against my cheek.

I watched the loup-garou recover itself, focus its burning eyes on me, and hurtle down the hallway. I was in so much pain that I could appreciate the pure beauty of it, the savage, unearthly grace and speed with which it moved. It was a perfect hunter, a perfect killer, fast and strong, relentless and deadly. It was no wonder that I had lost to such a magnificently dangerous being. I hated to go, but at least I hadn't gotten beaten by some scabby troll or whining, angst-ridden vampire. And I wasn't going to turn away from it, either.

I drew in what was to be my last breath, my eyes wide on the onrushing loup-garou.

So I could clearly see as Murphy looked down at me with crystal-blue eyes that saw right through the potion's remaining effects. She gave me a hard glance and placed herself between me and the onrushing monster in a shooter's stance, raising up her gun in a futile gesture of protection.

"Murphy!" I screamed.

And then the thing was on us.

Chapter 18

I tried to make my stunned body respond, to get to my feet, to unleash every ounce of magic at my command to protect Murphy, and to hell with the consequences.

I failed.

The loup-garou hurtled down the hallway, moving faster than I could have believed something so massive *could* move. Its claws gouged into the tile floor like it was soft clay. The walls shook around the beast, as though its very presence was enough to make reality shudder. Bloodstained drool spilled from its foaming jaws, and its green eyes blazed with hellish fury.

Murphy, standing at her full five-feet-and-change tall, was shorter than the loup-garou, its eyes on level with hers. She was wearing jeans again, hiking boots, a flannel shirt rolled up past the elbows, a bandana around her throat. She was without makeup or jewelry, her earlobes curiously naked and vulnerable without earrings. Her punky little haircut fell down around her eyes, and as she raised her gun, she thrust out her lower lip and puffed out a breath, flipping her bangs up out of her vision. She started shooting when the loup-garou was about thirty feet away—useless. The thing had laughed off bullets fired into its skull at point-blank range.

I noticed three things at that point.

First, Murphy's gun was not the usual heavy-caliber Colt semiautomatic she carried. It was smaller, sleeker, with a telescopic sight mounted at its rear.

Second, the gun made a sharp little *bark, bark, bark,* rather than the more customary *wham, wham, wham.*

Third, when the first bullet hit the loup-garou's chest, blood flew, and the creature faltered and buckled, as though surprised. When the second and third shots slammed into its front leg, the limb slipped and went out from under it. The loup-garou snarled and rolled its momentum to the side, put its head down, and simply smashed its way through the wall and into the room beyond.

Murphy and I were left in the dust-clouded hallway, the escape alarm whooping plaintively in the background. Murphy dropped down next to me. "And I told Aunt Edna I'd never get any use out of those earrings," she muttered. "Christ, Dresden, you're covered in blood. How bad is it?" I felt her slip her hand inside an enormous tear in the blue jumpsuit that I hadn't seen before and run her palm over my chest and shoulders, checking the arteries there. "You're under arrest, by the way."

"I'm okay, I'm okay," I panted, when I could breathe. "What the hell happened? How did you do that?"

Murphy rose up, lifted the gun to half raised, and stalked toward the hole the loup-garou had left in the wall. We could hear crashing sounds, heavy thumps, and furious snarling somewhere on the other side. "You have the right to remain silent. What do you think happened, moron? I read your report. I make my own loads for competition shooting, so I ran off a few silver bullets last night. But they're only in twenty-two caliber, so I'm going to have to put one through his eye to take him out. If that will do it."

"Twenty-two?" I complained, still breathless. "Couldn't you have made some thirty-eights, some forty-fours?"

"Bitch and whine," Murphy snarled at me. "You have the right to an attorney. I don't make my loads for work, and I didn't have the materials for it. Be happy with what you have."

I scrambled to my feet and leaned against the wall by the ragged hole. There was the sound of running feet, moving toward us down the hall. "I can't believe you're *arresting* me. What's through that wall?"

"Records, archives," Murphy said, leveling the target pistol at the hole. "A bunch of big old file cabinets and computers. Everyone who works there went home hours ago. How's that thing react to tear gas?"

"Send some in there and I'll tell you," I muttered, and Murphy shot me a dire look.

"Just stay down, Dresden, until I can get you locked up somewhere safe and get a doctor to look at you."

"Murph. Listen to yourself. We're stuck in a building with one of the nastiest creatures around, and you're still trying to *arrest* me. Get some perspective."

"You made your bed, jerk. Now lie in it." Murphy then raised her voice, without turning her head from the hole in the wall. "Carmichael! Down here! I want four on the doors going out of Records, and the rest with me. Rudolph, get down here and get Dresden back to the office, out of the way." She glared at my wrists, where the handcuffs she'd put on me the night before still dangled. "Christ, Dresden," she added in a mutter. "What is it with you and my handcuffs?"

Police, most of them plainclothes guys from Special Investigations, came pouring into the hall. Some of them had pistols, some of them had pump-action riot guns. My vision blurred and swirled between grey tones and Technicolor, and adrenaline made my nerves jangle and jerk. The potion must have been wearing off; most potions only lasted for a couple of minutes, anyway.

I took inventory. The loup-garou's teeth had scored my foot, through the boot. It hurt, and my sock was soaked in blood. I would leave little red footprints on the floor when I started walking. I could taste the blood in my mouth, from where I had bitten into my tongue, and I either had to spit or swallow. I swallowed. No comments, please. My back was mostly numb, and what wasn't numb hurt like hell. My wounded shoulder, naturally, was pounding so hard that I could barely stand.

"Bastard chewed up my good boot," I muttered, and for some reason, the statement struck me as incredibly funny. Maybe I had just seen too much for the evening, but whatever had caused it, I sailed into panting, wheezing gales of laughter.

Carmichael dragged me back. His round face was red with exertion and tension, and his food-stained tie was loose around his throat. He passed me into the custody of a young, good-looking detective, who I didn't recognize. He must have been the rookie at SI. I leaned against the young man and laughed helplessly.

"Take him back to the office, Rudolph," Carmichael said. "Keep him there, out of the way. As soon as this is under control, we'll get him to a doctor."

"Jesus Christ," Rudolph said, his eyes wide, his short, dark hair coated with drifting dust. He had a tense, panicky voice, and in spite of his youth, he was panting twice as heavily as the veteran Carmichael. "You saw it on the security monitors, right? What that thing did to Sergeant Hampton?"

Carmichael grabbed Rudolph by the front of his shirt and shook him. "Listen up, rook," he said, his voice harsh. "It's still there, and it can do it to us just as quick as to Hampy. Shut your hole and do what I told you."

"R-right," Rudolph said. He straightened, and started jerking me back down the hall away from the records office. "Who is this guy, anyway?"

Carmichael glared at me. "He's the guy who knows. If he comes to and says something, listen to him." Then he picked up a riot gun and stomped over to where Murphy was getting set to lead a group through the hole in the wall after the loup-garou. She was going over instructions, that if she went down one of the men was to pick up her gun and try to put out the thing's eyes with it.

The rookie half dragged and half led me around the corner and down the hall to the special investigations office. I stared down at my feet as he did, at the trail of bloody footprints behind me, giggling. Something was nagging at me, somewhere behind the madness of the laughter, where a diffident, rational corner of my mind was waiting patiently for my consciousness to take notice of an important thought it had isolated. Something about blood.

"This isn't happening," Rudolph chanted to himself along the way. "This isn't happening. Sweet Jesus, this is a trick for the new guy. A prank. Got to be." He stank of sour sweat and fear, and he was shaking horribly. I could feel it in my biceps, where he held me.

I think it was his terror that let me see through my own hysteria, fight it down and shove it under control again. He hauled me through the door, into the special investigations office, and I stumbled to the battered, sunken old couch just inside the door. I gasped for air, while the rookie slammed the door and paced back and forth, his eyes bulging, wheezing for air. "This isn't happening," he said. "My God, this isn't happening."

"Hey," I managed, after a minute, struggling to sort out all the input raging through my body—tears, bruises, maybe a sprain or two, a little bit of chill where shock was lurking, and aching sides from the laughter, of all things. The rookie didn't hear me. "Hey, Rudy," I said louder, and the kid snapped his eyes over to me as though shocked that I'd spoken. "Water," I told him. "Need some water."

"Water, right," Rudolph said, and he turned and all but ran to the water fountain. His hands were shaking so hard that he crushed the first two paper cones he took from the dispenser, but he got the third one right. "You're that guy. The fake."

"Wizard," I rasped back to him. "Harry Dresden."

"Dresden, right," the kid said, and came back over to me with the paper cone. I took it and splashed the contents all over my face. It was a cool shock, something else to draw me back from the land of giggles and throbbing nerve endings, and I clawed for all the sane ground I could get. Then I handed the cone back to him. "One more for the inside."

He stared at me as though I was mad (and who's to say, right?) and went to get another cone cup of water. I drank the second one down and started sorting through my thoughts. "Blood, Rudy," I said. "Something about blood."

"God," the rookie panted, the whites of his eyes glaring. "It was all over Hampton. Blood all over the room, splashed on the Plexiglas and the security camera. Blood, goddamn blood everywhere. What the fuck *is* that thing?"

"Just one more tough bad guy. But it bleeds," I said. Then fastened on the idea, my brain churning to a ponderous conclusion. "It bleeds. Murphy shot it and put its blood all over the floor." I gulped down the rest of the water and stood. "It bleeds, and I can nail it." I lifted my fist to shake it defiantly over my head and strode past the stunned Rudolph.

"Hey," he said, feebly. "Maybe you should sit down. You don't look so good. And you're sort of under arrest, still."

"I can't be under arrest right now," I said back to him. "I don't have the time." I limped down the rows of desks and partitions to Murphy's office. It's a little tacked-on office, with cheap walls of wooden paneling and an old wooden door, but it was more than anyone else in the disfavored department had. There was a paper rectangle taped neatly to the door, where a name placard would be on any other office in the building, which read in neat, block letters of black ink: LT. KARRIN MURPHY, SPECIAL INVESTIGATIONS. The powers that be refused to purchase a real name plaque for any director of SI—sort of their way of reminding the person they stuck in the position that they wouldn't be there long enough to matter. Underneath the neat paper square, at an angle, was a red and purple bumper sticker that said: TRESPASSERS WILL BE KILLED AND EATEN.

"I hope she didn't leave her computer on," I mumbled and went into Murphy's office. I took one look around the neatly organized little place and stepped in to pluck my blasting rod, bracelet, amulet, firearm, and other accoutrements I'd had in my possession when I'd been arrested from the table next to the computer. The computer was on. There was a cough from the monitor as my hand passed near it, and a little puff of smoke, then a bright spark from somewhere within the plastic console of the hard drive.

I winced and collected my things, putting on the shield bracelet with fumbling fingers, ducking my head into the loop of my pentacle amulet, stuffing my pistol into the jumpsuit's pocket, and taking my blasting rod firmly in my right hand, the side of the body that projects energy. "You didn't see that, Rudy. Okay?"

The rookie had a stunned look on his face as he stared at me and at the smoking computer and monitor. "What did you do?"

"Nothing, never came close, didn't do anything, that's my story and I'm sticking to it," I muttered. "You got that paper cup? Right, then. All we need is a stuffed animal."

He stared at me. "Wh-what did you say?"

"A stuffed animal, man!" I roared at him. "Don't mess with a wizard when he's wizarding!" I let out a cackle that threatened to bring the wild hysteria that still lurked inside of me back in full force, and banished it with a ferocious scowl. Poor Rudolph bore the brunt of both expressions, got a little more pale than he already was, and took a couple of steps back from me.

"Look. Carmichael still keeps a couple of toys in his desk, right? For when kids have to wait on their parents, that sort of thing?"

"Uh," said the rookie. "I, uh."

I brandished my blasting rod. "Go look!"

Maybe the kid would have taken any excuse at that point, but he seemed willing enough to follow my instructions. He spun and ran out into the main room and started frantically tearing open desks.

I limped out of Murphy's office and glanced back at the bloody footprints I left on the puke-grey carpet behind me with my soaking sock. The room was getting colder as I lost more blood. It wasn't serious, but it was all the way at the bottom of my considerably long body, and if I didn't get the bleeding stopped before too much longer it was bound to cause problems.

I was going to bend over and try to get a better look at my wounded foot, but when I started to, I swayed and wobbled dangerously, and thought it would be a better thing to wait until someone else could do it. I stood up and took a few deep breaths.

Something nagged me about this entire deal, something that was missing, but I'd be damned if I could figure out what it was.

"Rudy," I called. "Get that animal yet?"

The rookie's hand thrust up from one of the partitioned cubicles with a battered stuffed Snoopy doll. "Will this work?"

"Perfect!" I cheered woozily.

And then all hell broke loose.

Chapter 19

From out in the hallway, there came a scream that no human throat could have made, a sound of such fury and insane anger that it made my stomach roil and my guts shake. Gunfire erupted, not in a rattling series of individual detonations, but in a roar of furious thunder. Bullets shot through the wall, somewhere near me, and smashed out a couple of windows in the special investigations office.

I was on my last legs, exhausted, and terrified half crazy. I hurt, all over. There was no way I was going to have the focus, the strength I needed to go up against that monster. Easier to run, to plan something out, to come back when I was stronger. I could win a rematch. It's tough to beat a wizard who knows his enemy, who comes prepared to deal with it. It was the smart thing to do.

But I've never been known for my rational snap judgment. I gripped the blasting rod and started sucking in all the power I could reach, scooping up my recent terror, reaching down into the giggling madness, scraping up all the courage I had left, and pouring it into the kettle with everything else. The power came rushing into me, purity of emotion, complex energies of will, and raw hardheadedness, all combining into a field, an aura of tingling, invisible energy that I could feel enveloping my skin. Shivers ran over me, overriding the pain of my injuries, the ecstasy of power gathering my sensations into its heady embrace. I was pumped. I was charged. I was more than human, and God help anyone who got in my way, because he would need it. I drew in a deep, steadying breath.

And then I simply turned to the wall, pointed my rod at it, and snarled, "*Fuego.*"

Power lanced out through the rod in a flood of scarlet light that charred a six-foot circle of wall into powder and ash and sent it flying. I stepped through it, wishing for my duster, for a second, just for the cool effect it would have.

The hallway was a scene out of hell. Two officers were hauling a third down the hall toward me, while three more with shotguns fired wildly around the corner. I don't think the rescuers had taken the time to note that the body they were dragging away from the combat had no head attached to it.

One of the cops screamed as the riot gun he held ran empty, and something I could not see jerked him forward, around the corner and out of my vision. There was a horrible shriek, a splash of blood, and the two remaining shooters panicked and fled up the hall and toward me.

The loup-garou came around the corner after them, hauling one of the men down and ripping its claws across his spine with a simple, savage motion that left the man quivering on the bloody tiles and hardly made the beast miss a step. It set its eyes on the next man, one of the plainclothes SI detectives, and hamstrung him with a slash of its jaws. The beast left him howling on the tiles and hurtled toward the retreating pair, still frantically dragging their corpse away.

I stepped forward, between the fleeing men and the beast, and lifted the blasting rod. "I don't think so, bub."

The loup-garou crouched down, its massive body moving with unholy grace, its head and forequarters soaked in blood. I saw its eyes widen, and its muscles bunch beneath its dark brown pelt. Power gathered at my fist, red and brilliant, and the length of my blasting rod turned an incandescent white. Energy seethed through me as I prepared to release hell on earth at the monster. My teeth ached and my hair stood on end. I tensed every muscle I had, holding it all back until I could put every scrap of strength I had into the strike.

And then there was the *bark-bark-bark* of Murphy's little target pistol, and the loup-garou's rear flank twitched and threw out little bursts of blood. Its head whipped to one side, back down the short hallway, and its body followed suit, faster than a serpent. There was a surge of enormous muscles, a howl of rage, and then the thing was gone.

I spat a curse and ran down the hall after it. The hamstrung officer lay on the floor screaming, and the other man, the one who'd had his spine ripped out, was choking and twitching, unable to draw in a breath. Red anger flooded me, rage that I realized with some dim part of my mind was as much a part of the beast and its blood-maddened frenzy as it was of me.

I rounded the corner in time to see Murphy, standing in front of a litter of bodies, take a last shot at the loup-garou. And then it snarled and she vanished underneath its bulk.

"No!" I screamed and ran forward.

Carmichael beat me to it. His round belly had been ripped open. There was blood all over his cheap suit, though his food-stained tie had somehow remained untainted. His face was grave pale and set with the sort of intensity that only a dying man can have. He held a bent and twisted riot gun in his hands and he hurled himself onto the loup-garou's back as though he weren't sixty pounds overweight and long past his agile years. He wedged the riot gun between the loup-garou's jaws, but the beast turned and slammed Carmichael into the wall with a sickening crunch of bone and a gout of blood from the man's mouth.

Murphy slithered out from between the beast's paws on her shoulder blades and buttocks, her cute little cheerleader's face set in a berserker's fury. She jammed the end of her little gun beneath the thing's chin. I saw her hands convulse on the trigger. But instead of a flash of light and a dead loup-garou, there was only the whooping of the alarm and a look of shocked surprise on Murphy's face. The gun had run empty.

"Murphy!" I shouted. "Roll!"

She saw me with the blasting rod and her eyes flew wide. The loup-garou shook its shoulders free of Carmichael's corpse and bit completely through the riot gun, thrashing its head left and right. Murphy scuttled sideways across the tiles and through the hole in the wall the beast had made earlier.

It took one snap at her and then whipped its head around to snarl at me. I saw the crimson light reflected in its eyes as I focused every bit of fury in the world on the tip of my rod, and shouted, *"Fuego!"* I saw the reflected image in the beast's eyes brighten to nuclear-white in front of a tall, lean figure of black shadow, saw the flood of energy as big around as my hips rush down the hall like a lance of red lightning and hammer into the beast. Sound rushed along with it, a mountain's roar that made the gunshots and screams of the evening seem like a child's whispers in comparison.

The power lifted the loup-garou, hurtling it over the wounded figures moaning on the floor, down the hall, into holding, through the security door, through the cell door immediately across from it, then through the brick exterior wall of the building and out into the Chicago night. But it wasn't over yet. The lance of power carried the loup-garou across the street, through the windows of the condemned building across from the station, and through a series of walls within, each one shattering with a redbrick roar. Before the red fire died away, I could see the far side of the building across the street, and the lights of the next block over through the hole the loup-garou had made.

I stood in a blood-splattered hallway, filled with the moans of the wounded and the wail of the escape alarm. The sounds of emergency vehicles drifted into the building through the ragged hole in the wall. A slender young black man stood up from the floor of the cell the loup-garou had smashed through and gawked at the hole in the wall, then followed the destruction back down the hallway to where I stood. *"Damn,"* he said, and it had the same hushed tone to it as a holy word.

Murphy struggled out of the hole in the wall to pitch down on the floor of the hallway, gasping. I could see the bulge of bone warping out the skin of her lower arm where it had been snapped, somehow. She lay white faced and gasping, staring at Carmichael's crushed body.

For a moment, I couldn't do anything but stand there gawking. There was another hole in the wall, where the loup-garou must have crashed back into the hall, putting itself between the two groups of policemen, where they couldn't risk shooting at it without hitting one another. Or maybe they had. Some of the men who were down looked as though they had bullet wounds.

And from outside, over the sirens and the moans and the noise of a city night, I heard a long, furious howl.

"You've got to be kidding me," I breathed. My limbs felt like bruised jelly, but I turned to limp back around the corner and found Rudy there, staring, a paper cup in one hand and the Snoopy doll in the other. I took both from him, and stalked back into the hallway, to the second hole the loup-garou had made.

I found what I was looking for at once—blood on the inside of the hole in the wall, where the beast had plowed through it. The loup-garou's blood was thicker, darker than human fluids, and I scooped it into the paper cup before going back into the hallway.

I swept clean a place with my foot, set down my blasting rod, got out my chalk, and drew a circle on the ground. Rudolph approached me, his head jerking back and forth between grisly corpses and splashes of blood. "You. My God. What are you doing?"

I slapped the Snoopy down in the middle of the circle, then smeared the beast's blood over its eyes and mouth, over its ears and nose. "Thaumaturgy," I said.

"Wha—?"

"Magic," I clarified grimly. "Make a symbolic link between a little thing," I nodded at the Snoopy doll, "and a big thing. Make it happen on the smaller scale and it happens on the larger scale, too."

"Magic," Rudolph echoed.

I glanced up at him. "Go downstairs. Send the emergency people up here, Rudy. Go on. Send them up here to help the wounded."

The kid twitched his eyes from the bloody Snoopy back to me and jerked his head in a nod. Then he turned and fled down the hallway.

I turned my attention back to the spell I was working. I had to keep the rage and anger I felt away from the working of my magic. I couldn't afford to flood my spirit with grief, fury, and thoughts of vengeance for the dead men, for their deaths, for the pain that would be visited on their families. But God as my witness, I wanted nothing more than to try to set that thing on fire and hear it burn somewhere outside.

I tried to remind myself that it wasn't MacFinn's fault. He was under a curse, and not to blame. Killing him wouldn't bring back any of the dead men in these bloody hallways. But I could keep any more men from dying tonight.

And I could do that without killing him.

In retrospect, it was just as well that I didn't try to murder MacFinn. Magic like that takes a lot of energy—certainly more than I had. I would probably have killed myself in the effort to finish off the loup-garou. Not to mention that the Council would get their feathers ruffled by the concept—even though technically, MacFinn wasn't a human being at the moment. Killing monsters isn't nearly as much of an issue with the Council. They don't hold with equal-opportunity mercy.

Instead, as my vision started to fade, I began to chant nonsense syllables in a low, musical refrain, focusing the energy I would need inside the circle I had closed around me. It wasn't until later that I would realize that I was babbling a chant of *"Ubriacha, ubrius, ubrium,"* to the Peanuts theme music. I tore off a strip of my own bloodied jumpsuit and bound it across the Snoopy's eyes, its ears. I bound up the ends of its fuzzy, cute little paws. Then its mouth, as though muzzling it.

I felt the spell grow and prepare itself, and when it was ready, I released the power and broke the circle, feeling it flow out into the night, following the blood back to the loup-garou, winding itself about the creature, blinding its eyes, fouling its ears, lashing around its jaws and forcing them shut, crippling its taloned paws. The spell would hamper and confuse the beast, hopefully drive it to ground where no one could disturb it, keep it from venting its rage upon the people of the city. And it would last until dawn. The energy flowed out of me, left me feeling empty, exhausted, dizzy.

And then people were all around me, emergency folk in uniforms, cops and paramedics and firemen, oh my. I stood up from my circle, grabbed my blasting rod, and shambled off blindly.

I walked past Carmichael's corpse, stunned. Murphy was rocking back and forth over it, weeping, shaking, while a man tried to slide a blanket over her shoulders. She didn't notice me. Carmichael looked relaxed in death. I wondered for a minute if he had a family, a wife who would miss him. He'd died saving Murphy from the beast. He'd died a hero.

It seemed so empty to me, at that moment. Meaningless to be a hero. I felt burned on the inside, as though the fire I had hurled at the creature had scoured away all the gentle feelings that had been there and left a fallow ground behind where only red emotions could flourish. I stumbled past Murphy and Carmichael and turned to walk out of the building, dimly realizing that in the confusion I might actually have fair odds of making it back outside where Tera and Susan would be waiting in the car. No one tried to stop me.

The stairs were tough, and for a minute I thought I might just lie down and die on the first landing, but a helpful old fireman lent me a hand down to the first floor, asking me several times if I needed a doctor. I assured him that I was fine and prayed that he didn't notice the handcuffs still dangling from either wrist. He didn't. He was as wide around the eyes as everyone else, stunned.

Outside was chaos. Police were struggling to establish some sort of order. I saw a couple of news vans rolling up the street, while other people crowded around, trying to see. I stood in the door, dismayed, trying to remember how to walk down the steps.

And then someone warm and gentle was at my side, taking some of my weight. I let her have it, and closed my eyes. I smelled Susan's hair when I inhaled, and it made me want to wail and hold on to her, to try to explain what I had seen, to try to clean the stains from inside my head. All that came out was a little choking sound.

I heard Susan speak to someone else, and another person got on the other side of me, helped me down the stairs. Tera, I thought. I dimly remember them guiding me through the hectic area in front of the police station, around ambulances and shouting men, around policemen who were trying to get the bystanders to move away. I heard Susan explain to someone that I was drunk.

Finally there was quiet, and then we were moving among cars in a parking lot, cool light gleaming on cool metal shapes, cool rain coming down on my head, my hair. I tilted my face up to feel the rain, and everything swam crazily.

"I've got you, Harry," Susan murmured against my ear. "Just relax. I've got you. Just relax."

And so I did.

Chapter 20

I awoke in a dark place. It was like the inside of a warehouse, or a big, underground garage, all black, with a smooth, even floor, and a pool of bleak, sterile radiance in the middle of it that came from a source I could not see or identify. I felt like hell, and looked down to see myself covered in scratches, bruises, welts, blood, bandages, and ill-fitting clothing. I wore none of my implements or devices, and there was a curious sense of distance between me and the pain of my injuries—I was more than aware of them, but they seemed to be something that was merely noted in passing, and unimportant to my life as a whole.

I stood just outside the circle of light, and it seemed to me proper that I move forward into it. I did. And as I did, there appeared in the circle opposite me . . . me. Myself. Only better groomed, dressed in a mantled duster of black leather, not the sturdy, if styleless canvas that I wore. My double's pants and boots and shirt were all black as well, and they fit him as though tailor-made, rather than off-the-rack. His eyes were set deep, overshadowed by severe brows, and glittering with dark intelligence. His hair was neatly cut, and the short beard he wore emphasized the long lines of his face, the high cheekbones, the straight slash of his mouth, and the angular strength of his jaw. He stood as tall as I, as long limbed as I, but carried with him infinitely more confidence, raw knowledge, and strength. A faint whiff of cologne drifted over to me, cutting through my own sour sweat and blood smells.

My double tilted his head to one side, looked me up and down for a long minute, and then said, "Harry. You look like hell."

"And you look like *me,*" I said, and limped toward him, peering.

My double rolled his eyes and shook his head. "Hell's bells, you make me sick with how thick skulled you are, sometimes." He took steps toward me, mirroring my own movements. "I don't look like you. I *am* you."

I blinked at him for a few seconds. "You are me. How does that work?"

"You're unconscious, moron," my double said to me. "We can finally talk to one another."

"Oh, I get it," I said. "You're Evil Harry, lurking inside Good Harry. Right? And you only come out at night?"

"Give me a break," my double said. "If you were that simple, you'd be so insufferably boring you'd probably blow your own head off. I'm not Evil Harry. I'm just Subconscious Harry. I'm your inner voice, bub. Your intuition, your instinct, your basic, animal reactions. I make your dreams, and I decide which nightmares to pop in the old psychic VCR at night. I come up with a lot of the good ideas, and pass them along to you when you wake up."

"So you're saying you're wiser than me? Smarter than me?"

"I probably am, in a lot of ways," my double said, "but that's not my job, and it's not why I'm here."

"I see. So what are you doing here, then? You're going to tell me how I'm going to meet three spirits of Harry Past, Present, and Future?" I asked.

My double snorted. "That's good. That really is, the banter thing. I can't do the banter very well. Maybe that's why you're in charge. Of course, if *I* was in charge more often, you'd get laid a lot more—but no, that's not it, either."

"Can we speed this along? I'm too tired to keep on guessing," I complained.

"No joke, jerk. That's why you're asleep. But we don't have long to talk, and there are some issues we need to work through." He said "issues" in the British manner, iss-ewwws.

"Issues to work through?" I said. "What, am I my own therapist, now?" I turned my back on my double and started stalking out of the lighted circle. "I've had some weird dreams, but this has got to be the stupidest one yet."

My double slipped around me and got in my way before I could leave the circle of light. "Hold it. You really don't want to do this."

"I'm tired. I feel like shit. I'm hurt. And what I really don't want is to waste any more time dreaming about you." I narrowed my eyes at my double. "Now get out of my way." I turned to my right and started walking toward the nearest edge of the circle.

My double slipped in front of me again, apparently without needing to cross the intervening space. "It isn't that simple, Harry. No matter where you go, there you are."

"Look, I've had a long night."

"I know," my double said. "Believe me, I know. That's why it's important to get some of this out now, before it settles in. Before you blow a gasket on your sanity, man."

"I've not worried about that," I lied. "I'm as solid as a brick wall."

My double snorted. "If you weren't getting pretty close to crazy, would you be talking to yourself right now?"

I opened my mouth. Closed it again. Shrugged. "Okay. You've got a point."

"I've got more than that," my double said. "Things have been happening to you so quickly that you haven't had time to think. You need to work through some of this, and then you need to do some hard thinking, fast."

I sighed and rubbed at my eyes. "All right, then," I said. "What do you want to hear?"

My double gestured, and there was Murphy as she had appeared in the hallway of the police station, the flesh of her bicep tented out by the broken bone, her face pale, spotted with blood, and streaked with tears and hopeless anguish.

"Murph," I said, quietly, and knelt down by the image. "Stars above. What have I done to you?" The image, the memory, didn't hear me. She just wept silent, bitter tears.

My double knelt on the other side of the apparition. "Nothing, Harry," he said. "What happened at the police station wasn't your fault."

"Like hell it wasn't," I snarled. "If I'd have been faster, gotten there sooner, or if I'd told her the truth from the beginning—"

"But you didn't," my double interjected. "And you had some pretty damned compelling reasons not to. Ease up on yourself, man. You can't change the past."

"Easy for you to say," I snarled.

"No, it isn't," my double said quietly. "Concentrate on what you will do, not what you should have done. You've been trying to protect Murphy all along, instead of making her able to protect herself. She's going to be fighting these kinds of things, Harry, and you won't always be there to baby-sit her. Instead of trying to play shepherd, you need to play coach, and get her into shape to do what she needs to do."

"But that means—"

"Telling her everything," my double said. "The White Council, the Nevernever, all of it."

"The Council won't like it. If I tell her and they hear about it, they might consider her a security risk."

"And if you don't make her able to understand what she's fighting, something's going to eat her face some dark night. Murphy's a big girl. The Council had better be careful if they decide to go messing with her." My double considered Murphy for a moment. "You should ask her out sometime, too."

"I should *what*?" I said.

"You heard me. You're repressing big time, man."

"This is all getting way too Freudian for me," I said, and stood up, intending to walk away again. I was confronted with an image of Susan, as she had appeared on the steps to the police station, tall in her heels and dress suit, elegant and beautiful, her face stretched with worry.

"Think she's going to get a good story out of this?" my double asked.

"Oh, that's below the belt. That's not why she's seeing me."

"Maybe, maybe not. But you're asking yourself that question, aren't you?" My double gestured to himself and to me, demonstratively. "Shouldn't that make you ask a few more questions?"

"Like what?" I asked.

"Like how come you don't trust anyone," my double said. "Not even someone like Susan who has been going out on a limb for you tonight." He lifted a long-fingered hand and stroked at the short beard with his fingertips. "I'm thinking this has to do with Elaine. How about you?"

And then there she was, a girl of elegant height, perhaps eighteen or nineteen years of age—gawky and coltish, all long legs and arms, but with the promise of stunning beauty to add graceful curves to the lean lines of her body. She was dressed in a pair of my blue jeans, cut off at the tops of her muscled thighs, and my own T-shirt, tied off over her abdomen. A pentacle amulet, identical to my own, if less battered, lay over her heart, between the curves of her modest breasts. Her skin was pale, almost luminous, her hair a shade of brown-gold, like ripe wheat, her eyes a startling, storm-cloud grey in contrast. Her smile lit up her face, made her eyes dance with secret fires that still, even after all the years, made me draw in a sharp breath. Elaine. Beautiful, vital, and as poisonous as any snake.

I turned my back on the image, deliberately—before I could see it change into the Elaine that I had last seen—naked, festooned in swirling paints that lent a savage aura to her skin. Her lips had been stained brilliant, wet red, curving around twisting, rolling phrases as she chanted in the midst of her circle, its sigils meant to focus pain and fury into tangible power that had been used to hold a foolish young man helpless while his mentor offered him one last chance to sip from a chalice of fresh, hot blood.

"That's been over for a long time," I said, my voice shaking.

My double answered me quietly, "It isn't over. It isn't over yet, Harry. As long as you hold yourself responsible for Justin's death and Elaine's fall, it still colors everything you think and do."

I didn't answer myself.

"She's still alive," my double said. "You know she is."

"She died in the fire," I said. "She was unconscious. She couldn't have lived through it."

"You'd have known if she died. And they never found a second set of bones."

"She died in the fire!" I screamed. "She's dead."

"Until you stop pretending," my double said, appearing before me, "and try to face reality, you're not going to be able to heal. You're not going to be able to trust anyone. Which reminds me . . ."

My double gestured, and Tera West appeared as I had seen her crouched behind the garbage bin at the rear of the gas station, naked, her body lean, feral, leaves and bits of bracken in her hair, her amber eyes gleaming with cold, alien intelligence. "Why in the *hell* are you trusting *her*?"

"I haven't had much choice," I snapped. "In case you haven't noticed, things have been sort of desperate lately."

"You know she's not human," my double said. "You know she was at the scene of the crime, at Marcone's restaurant, where Spike was torn up. You know she has some kind of hold on a group of young people, the favorite targets of the creatures of the Nevernever. In fact, you can be pretty damn sure that she is a shapeshifter of one kind or another, who isn't telling you the whole truth, but still comes asking for your help."

"Like I can throw stones for not telling the whole truth," I said.

Hngh, my double said in answer. "But you haven't confronted her about what she isn't telling you. Those kids. Who the hell were they, and what were they doing? What is she getting them into?

And why was she keeping it a secret from MacFinn? He didn't recognize the names when you dropped them."

"All right, all right," I said. "I was going to talk to her anyway. As soon as I wake up."

My double chuckled. "If things are that leisurely. These murders are still happening, and they're starting to pile up. Are you serious about doing something about them?"

"You know that I am."

My double nodded firmly. "I'm glad we agree on something. Let's look at some facts. MacFinn couldn't have committed all the murders. Most particularly, he couldn't have committed the most important murder—the industrialist, Marcone's partner. He and his bodyguard were killed the night after the full moon. And Spike was wiped out the night before the full moon. MacFinn doesn't have any control over his shapeshifting. He couldn't have been the one to pull off those murders."

"So who could have?" I asked.

"His fiancée. The men were ripped apart by an animal."

"But the FBI lab said that it wasn't a true wolf that did it."

"Werewolves are slightly different from real wolves," my double said.

"How do you know that?" I demanded.

"I'm the intuition, remember?" my double said. "Think about it. If you were going to change yourself into a wolf, do you think you could hold that image in your head, perfectly exact? Do you think you could make all the millions of subtle, tiny changes in skeletal and muscular structure? Magic doesn't just work—a mind has to direct it, shape it. Your emotions, your feelings toward wolves would color it, too, change the image and the shape. Ask Bob, next chance you get. I'm sure he'll tell you I'm right."

"Okay, okay," I said. "I'll buy that. But the FBI said that there was more than one set of tooth marks and prints, too."

"MacFinn explains some of them. During last month's full moon, he probably killed some people when his circle went kablooey."

"And the group Tera had—they called themselves the Alphas—could explain the rest of them, if they were shapeshifters."

"Now you're catching on," my double said, approval in his tone. "You're smarter than you look."

"Do you think they were behind spoiling MacFinn's containment circle? The fancy one with all the silver and stuff?"

"They had the knowledge to do it, through Tera. Tera could have let them in, providing opportunity," my double said.

"But they didn't have a motive," I said. "Why would they have done it?"

"Because Tera told them to, maybe?"

I frowned and nodded. "She is a creature of the Nevernever. Who knows what's going through her—its head. It doesn't necessarily have to be understandable by human logic."

My double shook his head. "I don't buy that. I saw the way she looked at MacFinn—and how she sacrificed herself to divert the FBI and the police so that he could escape. Your instincts are telling you that she is in love with MacFinn, and that she wouldn't act against him."

"Yeah. You told me that about Elaine, too," I shot back, another pang of memory going through my chest.

"That was a long time ago," my double said defensively. "I've had time to get keener since then. And less easy to distract."

"All right," I sighed. "So where does that leave us?"

"I don't think we've run into the real killers yet. The ones who ruined MacFinn's circle and whacked the mob guys on the non-full-moon nights."

I squinted at my double. "You think so?"

He nodded and stroked his beard again. "Unless the Alphas are doing it without Tera knowing, and they look a little too bright eyed and bushy tailed to be doing that. I think it's someone else entirely. Someone trying to set up MacFinn and take him out of the picture."

"But why?"

"Maybe because they didn't want him putting the Northwest Passage Project through. Or, gee, maybe because he's a freaking werewolf, Harry, and someone caught on to it and wanted him dead. You know that there are organizations who would do that—some of the Venatori Umbrorum, members of the White Council, others who are in the know."

"But you don't think I've seen them, yet?"

"I don't think you've picked them out from the background," my double said. "Keep your eyes open, all right? Which brings us to the next topic of discussion."

"Does it?"

My double nodded. "Threat assessment. You've got all kinds of things staring you right in the face, and you're not noticing them. I don't want you to get killed because you're too distracted."

He glanced to one side, frowned, and said, "We're almost out of time."

"We wouldn't be if you weren't such a wiseass."

"Bite me," my double said. "Don't forget Marcone. You pissed him off by not taking the deal he offered you. He thinks the killers are coming after him next, and he might be right. He's scared, and scared people do stupid things—like trying to off the only man in town who has a chance of stopping what's going on."

"Let me worry about Marcone," I said.

"I *am* you, and I'm worried. Next is the cops. Some of Murphy's people are dead. There is going to be hell to pay once she gets that arm fixed—and someone is going to remember that you were around, and with your luck, they won't remember that you kept even more people from dying. You see Murphy and the police again, you'd better be careful or you're going to get shot to death resisting arrest."

"I'll be careful," I said.

"One more thing," my double said. "You have forgotten about Parker and the Streetwolves entirely. Parker needs you dead if he's going to remain in control of his people."

"Yeah. You'd have thought he'd have been more on the ball than this."

"Exactly," my double said. "You've been hiding and away from your apartment for a while—but you show up in public again, and you can bet that Parker will be on your trail. And *think*. He knew the real deal between you and Marcone, and he's a petty thug in Chicago. There's probably a connection between them, and you've been too dumb to think of it."

"Stars above," I muttered. "It's not as if the situation is very complicated. No pressure, right?"

"At least you're willing to deal with it now, instead of just closing your eyes and pretending that they can't see you. Be careful, Harry. It's a real mess, and you're the only one who can clean it up."

"Who are you, my mother?" I asked.

My double snapped his fingers. "That reminds me, right. Your mother—" He broke off, glancing up and around him, an expression of frustration coming over his face. "Oh, hell."

And then someone was shaking my unwounded shoulder, shaking me roughly awake. I blinked open my eyes in shock, and all the pains of my body came flooding back into me with renewed energy and agony. My brain reeled for a few minutes, trying to shift gears.

I was sitting in the passenger seat of Susan's car. We were rolling down an expressway, somewhere, but rain was clouding the view of the skyline so that I couldn't orient myself to where we were. The glowing numbers of the dashboard clock said that it was only a few minutes after nine. I'd had less than half an hour's sleep. There was an old beach towel wrapped around my wounded foot, and my face felt cool, as though someone had wiped it clean.

"Is he awake?" Susan said, her voice high and panicky. "Is he awake?"

"I'm awake," I said blearily, blinking open my eyes. "Sort of. What? This better be good."

"It is not good," Tera said from the backseat. "If you have any power left, wizard, you should prepare to use it. We are being followed."

Chapter 21

I rubbed at my eyes and mumbled some vague curse at whoever was following us. “Okay, okay. Give me a minute.”

“Harry,” Susan said. “I’m almost on empty. I don’t know if we *have* a minute.”

“It never rains,” I moaned.

Tera frowned at me. “It is raining now.” She turned to Susan. “I do not think he is coherent.”

I snorted and looked around blearily. “It’s a figure of speech. Hell’s bells, you really don’t know *anything* about humans, do you?

“Are you sure there’s someone following us?”

Tera glanced back at the traffic behind us. “Two cars back. And three cars behind that one. Two vehicles are following us.”

“How can you tell?” I asked.

Tera turned those odd amber eyes back to me. “They move like predators. They move well. And I feel them.”

I narrowed my eyes. “Feel them? On an instinctual level?”

Tera shrugged. “I feel them,” she repeated. “They are dangerous.”

The taste of blood was still in my mouth, annoying input, like static on a phone. Of all the people who might be chasing me in cars, I could only think of a few who would trigger the supernatural senses of an inhuman being. I thought that it might be a pretty good idea to listen to what my dapper double had to say. “Susan,” I said, “I want you to get off the expressway.”

Her dark eyes flashed beneath the streetlights as she looked at me, then down at her fuel gauge. “I have to in the next couple of miles anyway. What do you want me to do?”

"Pull off, and get to a gas station."

She flashed me another nervous look, and I had the time to note that she was gorgeous, like some sort of Latin goddess. Of course, I might have been a little less than entirely objective. "Then what?" she said.

I checked my foot and idly took off my remaining boot, so that my hips would be parallel with the floor while I was standing. "Call the police."

"What?" Susan exclaimed and guided her car off the freeway and down an exit ramp.

I felt around in the jumpsuit's tool pouch, until I came out with the little sports bottle with my second potion in it. "Just do it," I said. "Trust me on this one."

"Wizard," Tera said, her voice still utterly calm. "There is no one but you who can help my fiancé."

I shot Tera an annoyed glance. "I'll meet you where you hold your Cub Scout meetings."

"Harry?" Susan said. "What are you talking about?" She pulled the car down the exit ramp, onto a one-way access road.

"I understand what you're doing," Tera said. "I would do the same for my mate."

"Mate?" Susan said indignantly. "Mate? I am most certainly *not* his—"

I didn't get to hear the rest of what Susan said, because I grabbed my blasting rod in one hand, the potion in the other, opened the door to the car, unfastened my seat belt, and rolled out onto the shoulder of the road.

I know, I know. It sounds really stupid in retrospect, even to me. But it made a sort of chivalrous, cockamamie sense at the time. I was pretty sure that Parker and his cronies in the Streetwolves were shadowing us, and I had a precise idea of how dangerous they could be. I had to assume that they were even worse during the full moon. Susan had no idea of the level of danger she was in, and if I stayed near her I would only draw her more deeply into it. And Tera—I still didn't trust Tera. I wasn't sure that I wanted her fighting at my back.

I wanted to deal with my pursuers myself, to deal with my own mistake myself, and not to make an innocent bystander like Susan pay for it.

So I, uh, sort of threw myself out of the passenger seat of a moving car.

Don't look at me like that. I'm telling you, it made sense at the time.

I held out my arms and legs in a circle, as though I were trying to hug a barrel, and then scrape, scrape, rip, bumpity-bumpity-bumpity, whip, whip, whip, and thud. Everything whirled around the whole while. I managed, somehow, to keep my sense of direction, to maintain my momentum largely in a roll, and to angle myself toward the dubious comfort of the thick weeds at the side of the access road. By the time I came to a stop, I was among freshly crushed plants, all damp and cold from the rain, the smell of mud and gas and asphalt and exhaust clogging up my nose.

There was pain, pain everywhere, spreading out from my shoulder and my foot, whirling dizziness, blackness that rode on my eyelids and tried to force them down. I struggled to remember exactly what I had planned on doing when I had thrown open the door to Susan's car.

It came to me in a moment, and I jerked the squeeze top of the sports bottle open with my teeth and then crushed the plastic bottle, forcing the potion inside it out through the narrow nozzle and into my mouth. Eight ounces of cold coffee, I thought, dimly. Yum.

It tasted like stale cardboard and too-old pizza and burned coffee beans. But as it went down my gullet, I could feel the power in the brew spreading out into me, active and alive, as though I had swallowed a huge, hyperkinetic amoeba. My fatigue quite simply vanished, and energy came rushing into me, like it sometimes does at the end of a really good concerto or overture. The pain receded down to levels that I could manage. The soreness lifted out of my muscles, and my cloudy, cloggy thought processes cleared as though someone had flushed my synapses with jalapeno. My heart rate surged, and then held steady, and I came to the abrupt conclusion that things just weren't as bad as I had thought they were.

I pushed myself up using my bad arm, just to spite the injury that Agent Benn had dealt me, and brushed myself off. My jumpsuit was torn and there was fresh blood on it, scrapes from the asphalt and darkening bruises on my arms and legs that I could already see—annoying little bastards. I held them in contempt.

I shook my shield bracelet loose around my left wrist, took my blasting rod in my right hand, and turned toward the access road. I drew in a breath, smelling the odor of the rain on the asphalt, and more distantly the crisp, clean scent of autumn, almost buried by Chicago's stink. I considered how much I loved the autumn, and composed a brief poem about it as I watched traffic force Susan's car along and out of sight. I turned my head to view a pair of cars cut frantically across traffic and cruise down the access road. The lead car was a two-ton pickup, one of the really big ones, and Parker sat behind the wheel, looking around wildly until his eyes lit upon me, standing there in the tall weeds beside the road.

I smiled at him and contemplated his shocked expression to my own satisfaction.

Then I drew in a breath, and my renewed will with it, lifted the rod in my right hand, murmured a phrase in a language I didn't know, and blew the tires off his fucking truck.

They all went at once, in one satisfying THUMP, complete blowouts resulting from a sudden heating of the air inside the tires—a pretty slick spell to pull on the fly, heating up the air inside of the tires of a moving vehicle. The truck slewed left and right, and I could see Parker frantically rolling the steering wheel in an effort to maintain control. Two people sat in the cab with him, faces I didn't recognize from here, and they evidently didn't believe in seat belts. They were tossed about the inside of the truck like toys. The truck careened off the road in a spray of gravel, went past me into the weeds, hit some sort of ditch, and went into a ponderous roll.

There was an enormous crunching sound. Car wrecks, when they happen for real and not on television, are surprisingly noisy. They sound like someone pounding empty trash cans out of shape with a sledgehammer, only louder. Parker's truck tumbled over twice, crunched into the side of a hill, and lay on its passenger side.

"Well then," I said with a certain amount of professional pride. "That should take care of that."

I spoke too soon. There was a brittle, grinding sound, and the windshield of the truck exploded into a hectic spiderweb pattern. The sound repeated itself, and the safety glass shattered outward, followed by a foot wearing a heavy black combat boot. More glass flew outward, and then people started crawling out of the pickup, battered and bloodied. Besides Parker, there was the lantern-jawed lout whose nose I had flattened a few days ago, his nose now swollen and grotesque, and the bloodthirsty woman who had led the group into their berserk fit of lust. They were all dressed in the same variants of denim and leather, and cuts and bruises from the tossing they'd had were much in evidence.

Parker led them out of the truck, looked back at it, stunned—and then he looked at me. I saw fear flicker in his eyes, and it brought out a satisfied surge within my own pounding heart. Served him right, the jerk. I spun my rod around once in my fingers, started whistling a bit from the overture to *Carmen,* and walked toward them through the grass, annoyed that I was limping and that I was dressed in a ridiculous blue jumpsuit that left inches of my arms and legs bare.

Flatnose saw me and grunted out some sort of Neanderthal noise of surprise. He drew a handgun from inside his jacket, and it looked tiny in his hands. Without preamble he started squeezing off shots at me.

I lifted my left hand, forced more of my boundless energy through the shield bracelet, and sang a few phrases in what I supposed could have been taken for Italian to verbally encase the spell. I continued walking forward as bullets bounded off the shield before my hand in cascades of sparks, and I even had enough breath left over to keep on whistling *Carmen.*

Parker snarled and slashed at Flatnose's wrist with the edge of his hand in a martial-arts-style movement. I heard a bone break, very clearly, but Flatnose only jerked his hand back toward his body and flashed Parker a scowl.

"Remember why we're here," the shorter man said. "He's mine."

"Hello there, Mr. Parker," I called cheerfully. I suppose that the image I presented as I walked toward them would have been comic—except for all the blood, and the big smile I felt spreading over my face. It seemed to have a somewhat intimidating effect on the Streetwolves at any rate. The woman snarled at me, and for a second I could feel a wild, savage energy, the same that had surrounded the frenzying lycanthropes at the Full Moon Garage, starting to build in the air around me.

I gave the bitch an annoyed look and slashed my hand at the air, drawling, *"Disperdorus."* I forced out an effort of will I might have found daunting on another night, one when I was feeling a little less all-powerful, and the woman jerked back as though I had slapped her in the mouth. The energy she had been gathering fractured and flew apart as though it had never been. She stared at me, growing tense and nervous, and reached a hand toward a knife in a case at her hip.

"Let's have none of that nonsense. As I was saying," I continued, "hello there, Mr. Parker. I know why you're here. Heard about the ruckus on a police scanner and came down by the station looking for me, right? Hate to disappoint you, but I'm not going to allow you to kill me."

Flatnose scowled and said, "How did you know th—"

Parker shoved the heel of his hand across Flatnose's mouth in a sharp blow, and the big man shut up. "Mr. Dresden," Parker growled. He eyed me up and down. "What exactly makes you think you can stop me from killing you?"

I had to smile at the man. I mean, you have to smile at idiots and children. "Oh, I don't know," I chuckled. "Maybe because the second you step out of line, I'm going to wreck you a whole hell of a lot worse than that truck. And because in just a couple of minutes, the police are going to be arriving to sort you out." There was a momentary flash of dimness, where the streetlight seemed to fade, the rain to grow very cold, and then it was gone again. I blinked a little blood out of my eyes, and renewed my smile. Mustn't let the children see weakness.

Parker snarled his thin lips into a smile. He had bad teeth. "The cops are after your ass too, Dresden," he said. "I don't believe you."

"Once they're here, I'm going to mysteriously disappear," I said. "Just like, well, gosh, magic. But you guys are . . ." I forgot what I had been going to say for a moment. There was something nagging at the back of my mind, a detail I had forgotten.

"I can smell your blood, wizard," Parker said, very quietly. "God, you got no idea what it smells like." Parker didn't move, but the woman let out a little mewling sound and pressed against Flatnose's side. Her eyes were focused intently on me.

"Get a good whiff," I managed to say. "It's the last time you'll smell it." But my smile was gone. A creeping vine of uncertainty was beginning to crack the wall of confidence I had been enjoying. The rain was getting colder, the lights dimmer. My extended left arm began to ache, starting at the wounded shoulder, and my hand shook visibly. Pain started leaking in again, from every part of my battered body.

Sanity returned in a rush. The potion. The potion was giving out on me. I had pushed myself way too hard while the first euphoria was going over me. Dispelling the intimate aura of rage and lust that the woman had begun to gather over them had been a feat I would never have considered in a stable frame of mind.

There were too many unknowns. My heart was laboring along now, and I started panting. I couldn't get enough breath to slow down my rocketing heartbeat.

Parker and his two companions grew tense together, all at once, with no visible signal passing between them. I could feel that wild energy again, coursing down to the lycanthropes from beyond the rain clouds overhead. I swear to you, I could see the cuts on their body, from the crash, closing up before my eyes. Flatnose rolled the wrist that had just been broken, flexed his fingers at me, and gave me a grim smile.

Okay, Harry, I told myself. Keep calm. Do not panic. All you have to do is to hold them here until the cops get here, and then you can bleed to death in peace. Or get to a doctor. Whichever hurts less.

"You know, Parker," I said, and my voice had a fluttering quaver to it, a fast, desperate quality. "I didn't really mean to show up at your garage. Hell, I wouldn't have been there at all if Denton's goon hadn't turned me on to the idea."

"That doesn't matter now," Parker said. His voice had a quiet, certain tone to it, and he had visibly relaxed. He smiled at me, and showed me more of his teeth. "That's all in the past." Then Parker took a step forward, and I panicked.

I jammed the rod at him and snarled, *"Fuego."* I funneled my will through it, and to hell with what the Council thought of me killing someone with magic.

Nothing happened.

I stared in disbelief, first at Parker, and then at the blasting rod. My fingers went numb as I looked at them, and the rune-engraved ash rod fell to the ground, though I tried a clumsy grab to catch it. Instead, my weight came down on my torn foot, and the ripped muscles went into a sudden cramp that sent fresh agony up through my leg. It buckled and pitched me forward into the weeds and the mud. The last wisps of my shield vanished as I fell. My magic had failed me altogether.

Parker laughed, a low and nasty sound. "Nice trick. Got another?"

"One more," I rasped, and fumbled at the jumpsuit's tool pouch. Parker walked slowly toward me, confident, relaxed, and moving like a man thirty years younger than he. My fingers were aching with cold, torn from the asphalt, numb from all the pain and scrapes and bruises. But the handle of my Chief's Special was easy enough to find.

I drew it out, thumbed back the hammer, and pointed it up at Parker. His eyes widened and his weight settled back on his heels—not quite retreating, but not coming any closer, either. From three feet away, even down in the mud, it would be tough to miss him, and he knew it.

"I didn't pick you for the kind to carry a gun," he said. The rain plastered his greasy hair down over his eyes.

"Only on special occasions," I said back. I had to delay him. If I could hold him in place, just for a few minutes, the cops would show up. I had to believe that they would, because if they didn't I was dead meat. Maybe literally. "Stop where you are."

He didn't. He took a step toward me.

So I shot him.

The gun roared, and the bullet smacked into his right kneecap. It exploded in a burst of blood and flying chips of bone, and the leg went out from under him, hurling him to the muddy ground. He blinked once, surprised, but the pain he must have been feeling didn't seem to register. He scooted back a couple of feet and stared at me for a second, reassessing me.

Parker then drew his legs beneath him, and ignoring his ruined knee, hunkered down on his heels and rested his elbows on his thighs as if we were old friends, keeping his hands in plain sight. "You're tougher than you look. We tried to catch you at your apartment, you know," he said, as though I hadn't just shot him. "But the cops were all over it. Police band said you'd gotten arrested, but I guess you got away. We paid the jailer to let us know when they rounded you up." He grinned his snaggletoothed grin and looked almost friendly. "Hell, kid. We were hanging around in a bar two blocks from the station for almost two days, just hoping to be there when they brought you up the steps. Drive-by." He pointed his finger at me in a bang-bang motion, and let his thumb fall forward.

"Sorry to disappoint you," I mumbled. I was working hard not to give in to the shakes, the cold, or the darkness. I knew he was up to something, but there was too much to deal with—too much injury, too much exhaustion, too much blood on my hands. I squinted past him to see Flatnose and the woman still in the same spot, both of them watching me with the intent look of hungry animals.

Parker chuckled. "And instead, everything goes to hell at the station. Gunshots, explosions, sounds like a war inside. Which was fun to watch. And then we see you stumbling out of the middle of it, right there in front of the cop station, with a cute little piece on either side helping you down the stairs. We just rolled out right after your ass."

"I hope you're insured."

Parker shrugged. "Truck wasn't mine." He plucked up a long blade of grass and traced it over the ruin of his knee, painting it red with his blood before crushing it up in his fingers. "Most of my people are out by the lake tonight. They got to let off some steam during the full moon. Damn, but I want to take you out right there in front of all of them. You got a real badass reputation, kid."

"Can't have everything you want," I said. I blinked rain, or blood, from my eyes.

Parker's smile widened. "You know, kid. I think there's something you don't know."

In the distance, I could hear the sound of sirens speeding down the freeway toward me. Hot damn, I thought. I finally did something right. "Oh yeah?" I asked, daring to feel a satisfied thrill of victory.

Parker nodded and looked off to one side. "There were two cars behind you."

And something smashed down on my right hand, making it go numb, and sending the gun to earth. I looked up and had time to see another of the lycanthropes from the garage lift a lead pipe wrapped in electrical tape, and bring it down hard at me. The woman screamed and rushed toward me. She had steel-toed boots. Flatnose lumbered after her, and was content to use the barrel of his pistol as a dumb club.

Parker just sat there, squatting on his heels, and watched them. I could see his eyes. My blood spattered onto his cheek.

I don't like thinking about what they did. They didn't want to kill me. They wanted to hurt me. And they were good at it. I couldn't fight. I couldn't even curl up into a ball. There wasn't that much spirit left in me. I could hear myself making choking sounds, gagging on my own blood, sobbing and retching in pathetic agony. I would have screamed if I could have. You hear stories about men who keep silent through all the torture and agony that anyone inflicts on them, but I'm just not that strong. They broke me.

At some point, the mind says "no more" and it gets the hell away from all that pain. I started going there, to that away-place, and I wasn't sorry to do it at all.

I could dimly hear Parker shoving people off of me, once I

stopped moving. He broke a few more of their bones, and they backed off with snarls of rage. He was walking on the leg again already, though my shot must have torn the joint to pieces. At his orders, they picked me up and carried me to another car, just lugged me along like a sack of broken parts. Duct tape went around my wrists and ankles, knees and elbows and mouth. Then they threw me in the trunk.

Parker reached up to close the lid. I didn't have enough energy to move my eyes. I just stared out, letting them focus wherever they would.

I saw a face behind the wheel of a car going past on the access road—just a sedan, something that would blend in with all the other cars in the city. The face was young, strained, sprinkled with freckles, the hair red, the ears big.

Roger Harris, FBI. Denton's redheaded lackey.

The sedan rolled by without even slowing, and Harris didn't look over at me, didn't break his surveillance. I wasn't the only one, it seemed, who was being followed that night.

Parker slammed shut the trunk, leaving me in darkness. The car started going just as the sirens began to arrive at the access road. My captors' car bounced along and made a casual getaway, leaving me in an agony more thorough, sickening, and acute than any I had felt before.

And, behind the gag, I started laughing. I couldn't help it. I laughed, and it sounded like I was choking on raw sewage.

The pieces had all fallen into place.

Chapter 22

There's a point after which one cannot possibly continue doing complicated things like thinking and keeping one's eyes open. Blackness ensues and everything stops until the body, or the mind, is ready to function again. The blackness came for me and I welcomed it.

When I started to wake up, I smelled motor oil.

That in itself boded ill. I was seated upright, and an upright metal beam pressed into my back. I felt something constricting my wrists and my ankles. Duct tape, still, perhaps. There was cold concrete floor beneath me. I was aching everywhere, and stiff. But there was something soft over me, a blanket, maybe. I wasn't as cold as I might have been.

My first emotion was a vague surprise that I was still alive.

The second was a cold, nasty little shiver. I was a prisoner. And as long as I was, survival was by no means certain. First things first, then. Make it certain. Find out where I was, devise a plan, and get my skinny wizard ass out of there.

After all, it would be a real pity to die when I'd finally put tabs on who had gotten me into this mess—as well as who was responsible for the recent killings that couldn't be attributed to MacFinn, and probably who had set him up as well.

To that end, I opened my eyes and tried to get a look at my surroundings.

I was in the enemy's stronghold, the Full Moon Garage. It was dim inside, and from what I could hear, it was still raining without. There was a dirty, but warm blanket over me, which came as something of a surprise. There was also a little stand with a mostly empty plastic bag of what I took to be blood, dripping down a plastic tube that vanished behind me, out of my sight, and presumably ended at my arm.

I wiggled my feet out from beneath the blanket. My legs had been duct-taped together above and below the knee, and at the ankle. My bitten foot had been wrapped in clean bandages, then covered in my bloodied sock. In fact, I found a number of clean bandages on various cuts and scrapes, and I could smell, faintly, as though my nose had been given a while to get used to it, the sharp, medicine smell of disinfectant. I couldn't feel Murphy's sawed-through handcuffs on my wrists, and found myself vaguely missing them. At least they'd been familiar, if not comfortable.

So, not only was I alive, but I was in considerably better shape, after presumably several hours of sleep and medical attention.

But that didn't explain who had done this to me. Or why.

I looked around the dimness of the garage. My eyes were now adjusted to it, but even so, there were pockets of shadows too deep to see into. An L-shaped ribbon of yellow light showed beneath the door to the manager's office, and the sound of rain on the corrugated roof was a low, soothing roar. I closed my eyes, trying to orient myself, to determine what time it was from the feel of the air and the sound of the rain. Late afternoon? Early evening? I couldn't tell for sure.

I coughed and found my throat dry, but functional. My hands were bound, and I didn't have any way of making a circle. Without a circle, I couldn't use any delicate magic to free myself—all I had access to was the kaboom sort of power, which, while great against nasty loup-garou and other monsters, isn't much good for getting rid of several layers of duct tape resting within half an inch of my own tender skin. Magic was out.

Did I ever tell you about my dad? He was a magician—not a wizard, mind you, but a magician, the kind you see at old-fashioned magic shows. He had a black top hat, a white rabbit, a basket of swords, and everything. He used to travel around the country, performing for the kids and the old folks, barely making enough to scrape by. After Mom died during childbirth, Dad had the job of raising me all by himself, and I guess he did the best he could. He meant well.

I was real young when he died (I refused to believe Chaunzaggoroth's insinuations until I had looked into them further) of a brain aneurism. But I learned a thing or three about what he did before then. He'd named me after three magicians, after all, the first of which was Houdini himself. And one of Houdini's first rules was that the means to escape was always within your grasp. Positive attitude. It's a fact that a human being can escape from just about everything, given enough time.

The only question was, how much time did I have left?

The duct tape was strong, and it was fastened tightly—but it was also cheap, easy to transport, and simple to apply. Even though it was wound about me in multiple layers, it wasn't the best thing for holding people, or else the cops would use duct tape and not handcuffs and manacles. It could be beaten.

So I started looking for ways to beat it.

A little writhing showed me that my hands weren't fastened as tightly as they could have been. I could feel a sharp pain in my forearm, and guessed that was from the IV. They had to loosen the tape on my arms to get the needle into my forearm. I wiggled my shoulders, which set the wounded one to aching fiercely. The tape put pressure on my wrists and tore the hair from my arms with an audible ripping sound, and I clenched my teeth over this particular torment.

It hurt, and it took me the best part of ten minutes, but I got my wrists and hands free. I ditched the IV needle while I was at it, imagining some deadly fluid flowing down the tube into my veins. Then I flexed my arms repeatedly and got them free.

My fingers were numb, stiff, not really responding, but I started fumbling at the tape on my legs as best I could, trying to get tears started so that I could just flex my legs and get the whole thing to go at once. It took more effort than I thought it would, but I finally flexed my legs, thankful that the jumpsuit kept me from losing stripes of hair from my thighs and calves (if not from my ankles). My legs were much stronger than my arms, so snapping the layers of duct tape on them was a lot simpler and quicker.

Just not simple or quick enough.

Before I'd gotten out of the last loop of duct tape, there was a click-clack, and the office door swung open, accompanied by a murmur of low voices and a tinny din of old-time rock-and-roll music.

I panicked. I couldn't run—my ankles were still bound. By the time I got free and struggled to my feet, they'd be on me. So I did the next best thing. I whipped the blanket up and over me, snaked my hands back behind the pole, grabbing up the IV needle as I went and concealing it in my hand, and bent my head far forward as though I were still asleep.

"I still don't get why we can't just put a bullet in him and dump him," said a harsh voice with no nasal tone at all—Flatnose.

"Stupid," Parker growled, his voice like sandpaper. "One, we don't do it without having the others here to see. And two, we don't do it until Marcone's had a chance to see him."

"Marcone," Flatnose said with a sneer in his voice. "What's he want with him?"

Good question, I thought. I kept my head down, my body relaxed, and tried to think sleepy thoughts. Marcone was coming here?

"Who cares?" Parker answered. "I made sure he'd live through the day. Either way, I wanted him here tonight. No skin off my teeth."

Flatnose grunted. "Chicago sees a lot of mobsters. Marcone's just one more. But one call from him, and this wizard character gets a reprieve. Who is this guy, huh? The freaking governor?"

"Always thinking with your balls," Parker said, his voice calm. "Marcone isn't just a mobster. Running Chicago is just his sideline, see. He's got business all over the country, and he owns people from here to the governor's mansion to Washington and back, and he's got more money than God. He can set us up, take us out, have the police on our ass anytime he wants. You don't screw with someone like that lightly."

There was a pause, and then Flatnose said, "Maybe. Or maybe Lana's right. Maybe you're getting soft. Marcone isn't one of us. He doesn't give us orders. The Parker I knew ten years ago wouldn't have thought twice of telling Marcone to fuck off."

Parker's voice became resigned. "Don't do this, man. You were never good enough, even when we were young. The Parker you knew ten years ago would have gotten all of us killed by now. I've kept you in cash, in dope, women, whatever you wanted. So settle down."

"I don't buy it," Flatnose said back. "I think Lana's right. And I say we off this skinny son of a bitch right now." I felt myself tense and prepared to make a run for it, hopeless or not. I'd rather get killed trying to get away than trying to pretend I was asleep.

"Back down," Parker said, and then there was a scuffling noise of boots on old concrete. I heard a couple of grunts and an abrupt yelp, and smelled sour sweat and stale beer as Flatnose was forced to his knees less than a foot away. He kept making small noises of pain, thick with tension, as though Parker was holding him in some kind of lock. I forced myself to relax, not to just stagger up and start running, but I felt a bead of sweat trickle down my face.

Parker snarled over Flatnose's whimpers, "I told you. You were never good enough. Challenge me again, in public or alone, it doesn't matter—and I will rip your heart out." The way he spoke the threat was eerie; not with the hissing, villainous emphasis one would expect, but in a calm, measured, almost bored tone, as though he were mentioning switching out a carburetor or changing a light bulb. There was a rippling sort of sound, and Flatnose let out a howl of pain that dissolved into a string of doglike whimpers. I heard Parker's boots move a few steps away. "Now, get up," he said. "Call Tully's and get the others back here before the moon rises. We'll have blood tonight. And if Marcone isn't polite enough, we'll have a lot more."

I heard Flatnose make his way to his feet and shuffle off in a slow and haphazard fashion. He vanished into the office and closed the door behind him. I waited for a few moments, hoping that Parker would wander off and I could make my escape, but he didn't. Dammit.

I was running out of time. If I waited until the rest of the lycanthropes returned to the garage, I'd never be able to get away. The numbers would be stacked too high. If I was going to make a break for it, logically, the time was now.

Of course, I was still bound. By the time I got my legs free, Parker would be on me. And I had just listened to him disable a man twice his size and threaten to rip his heart out. He'd meant it, too, I could tell. When I had looked inside of him, I had seen a dark and angry place, the source of all that power and force of will. He could tear me to pieces with his bare hands, literally—and what was worse, he would. I had to have a head start if I was going to run.

I could make him mad, maybe. Antagonize him into going to get a baseball bat, or another roll of duct tape for my mouth. Then I could run, make a clean getaway. The one problem with that plan was that he might just rip my heart out on the spot—but nothing ventured, nothing gained. I didn't have time to be picky.

So I lifted up my head enough to squint at him in the semi-darkness and said, "You certainly have a way with people. You must have read a book or something."

My voice startled him, and he spun with the reflexes of a nervous cat. He stared at me for a long minute before starting to relax. "So. You're alive. It's just as well, I suppose."

"Mostly I was just tired. Thanks for the sack time."

He showed me his teeth. "No problem. Checkout is in a couple hours."

That scared me enough to make a rational man pee, but I only shrugged. "No problem. Good thing your people can't hit. They might have made me uncomfortable."

Parker laughed a rough laugh. "You got balls, kid. I'll give you that. At least, until Lana gets her teeth into them, later."

This wasn't going at all well. I had to find some way to piss him off, not make him laugh. "How's the knee?"

Parker narrowed his eyes. "A lot better. It didn't quite heal up before sunrise, but I figure it'll only take an hour or so after the moon comes up."

"I should have aimed higher," I said.

Parker's jaw clenched down a little. "Too late now, kid. Game over."

"Enjoy it while you can. I hear your people are getting a little sick of you. Do you think Lana will be the one to tear *your* balls off when they put you down?"

His boot came out of nowhere and hit me in the side of the head. It threw me hard to my right, and if I hadn't clenched my arms at the last minute, it would have thrown me to the floor and revealed my lack of bonds.

"You just don't know when to keep quiet, do you wizard?"

"What have I got to lose?" I shot back at him. "I mean, hell. It isn't as though all of the people that looked up to me have turned against me, right? It isn't as though I'm getting too old to manage wh—"

"Shut up," Parker snarled, his eyes taking on an eerie, greenish cast in the darkness, a trick of the light, and he kicked me again, this time in the stomach. My breath went out in a whoosh, and I fought to continue speaking.

"Waking up stiffer every morning. Eating less. Maybe not as strong as you used to be, right? Not as fast. Got to beat up on old dogs like Flatnose there, because if you try one of the younger ones, they'll take you down."

The plan was working beautifully. Now all that I needed was for him to stalk out of the room to calm down, or to fetch an instrument of mayhem or some more duct tape, anything. Instead, Parker just spun on his heel, picked up a tire iron, and turned back to me, lifting it high. "Fuck Marcone," he snarled. "And fuck you, wizard."

His muscles bunched beneath his old T-shirt as he raised the iron above his head. His eyes gleamed with the same sort of animalistic fury I had beheld in the other lycanthropes the night before. His mouth was stretched in a feral grin, and I could see the cords in his neck standing out as he wound up to give me the deathblow.

I hate it when a plan falls apart.

Chapter 23

I clenched my teeth and kicked my legs. The duct tape around my ankles gave way, but it was too late to do me any good. I didn't have time to get my weight beneath me, to run, but I made the gesture in any case. Just one of those things you do when you're about to die, I guess.

"Mr. Hendricks," came a very hard, very calm voice. "If Mr. Parker does not put down the tire iron in the next second or two, please shoot him dead."

"Yes sir, Mr. Marcone," Hendricks's rumbling basso answered. I looked over to my right, to see Gentleman Johnny Marcone standing at the door in a grey Italian business suit. Hendricks stood in front of him and a bit to one side, in a much cheaper suit, holding a pump-action shotgun with a short barrel, its stock worked into a pistol grip, in his meaty paws. The gaping black mouth of the barrel was leveled at Parker's head.

Parker's face snapped around to focus on Marcone at the same time as mine did. Parker's jaw clenched and his eyes narrowed to furious slits. His weight shifted from one foot to the other, as though he were preparing to throw the tire iron.

"That's a twelve-gauge riot gun, Mr. Parker," Marcone said. "I'm fully aware of your rather special endurance at this time of the month. Mr. Hendricks's weapon is loaded with solid-slug ammunition, and after several rounds have torn literal pounds of flesh from your body and ruptured the majority of your internal organs, I am reasonably certain that even you would perish." Marcone smiled, very politely, while Hendricks clicked the safety off of the weapon and settled his feet as though he expected firing the gun to knock him down. "Please," Marcone said. "Put down the tire iron."

Parker glanced back at me, and I could see the beast raging in his eyes, wanting to howl out and bathe in blood. It terrified me, made me go cold, right through my gut and down through my loins. There was more fury and rage there than any of the other members of the Streetwolves had demonstrated. Their own berserk losses of control had looked like a child's tantrum next to what I saw in Parker's eyes.

But he controlled it. He lowered his arm, slowly, and took two steps back from me, and I felt my breath whisper out in a sigh of relief. I wasn't dead. Yet. My kick hadn't quite dragged the blanket off of me, and I was still settled with my back against the steel post. They didn't know that I was loose underneath the rough wool. It wasn't much of an advantage, but it was all I had. I needed to find a way to use it, and fast.

"My people are coming," Parker growled. "If you try more of that heavy-handed shit, I'll have you torn apart."

"They are coming," Marcone agreed placidly. "But they are not yet here. Their motorcycles have all suffered flat tires, quite mysteriously. We have time to do business." I heard his shoes cross the concrete floor toward me, and I looked up at him. Marcone met my eyes without fear, a man in his mature prime, his hair immaculately greying at the temples, his custom-made suit displaying a body kept fit in spite of the advancing years. His eyes were the faded green of dollar bills and as opaque as mirrors.

"Hi, John," I said. "You've got good timing."

Marcone smiled. "And you have a way with people, Dresden," he said, glancing at the silent Parker with unveiled amusement. "You must have read a book. I'm already reasonably certain as to your reaction, but I thought I would give you another chance."

"Another chance to what?"

"I received a phone call today," Marcone said. "A Harley MacFinn somehow discovered my personal number. He was quite irate. He said that he knew that it was me who had destroyed his circle and set him up, and that he was going to deal with me tonight."

"I'd say you've had it, then, John. Harley can be fairly destructive."

"I know. I saw the news programs from the station last night. A loup-garou, is he?"

I blinked. "How did you—"

Marcone waved a hand. "The report you gave to Lieutenant

Murphy. Such things have to be paid for, and thus copied and filed and copied and filed. It wasn't hard to obtain a copy for myself."

I shook my head. "Money isn't going to buy off Harley MacFinn."

"Quite," Marcone said. "And my parents, God rest their souls, were in no position to leave me anything, much less articles of silver, or I'd deal with him myself. I have no idea who told him that I had wronged him, or why, but it seems perfectly clear that he believes it. Which brings us to you, Mr. Dresden." He reached into that expensive Italian jacket and drew out a folded sheaf of papers—the contract I'd seen before. "I want to make a deal with you."

I stared at him in silence.

"The same stipulations as before," Marcone continued. "In addition, I will promise you, give you my personal oath, that I will see to it that the pressure is taken off of Lieutenant Murphy. I do have some friends in the mayor's office, and I'm certain something could be worked out."

I started to tell him to go to hell, but bit back the words. I was trapped, at the moment. If I ran, Parker would probably lose it and tear me apart. And if he didn't, Marcone would just point his finger and the hulking Mr. Hendricks would put me down with a twelve-gauge slug.

And Murphy, in spite of recent misunderstandings, was my friend. Or maybe it was more accurate to say that in spite of what had gone on lately, I was still Murphy's friend. Saving her job, getting the pressure from the politicians off of her—isn't that why I had gotten involved in this to begin with? Wouldn't Murphy thank me for helping her?

No, I thought. Not like that. She wouldn't want that kind of help. Magic, she could accept. Help from money generated by human suffering, graft, and deception was a different story. Marcone looked good in his grey suit and his perfect hair and his manicured hands, but he wasn't.

My own hands weren't clean—but they were free. Things were desperate, and getting worse the longer I waited. Maybe I could pull off enough magic to get myself out of this.

I drew in a breath, and focused on a pile of loose tools and metal parts on a workbench twenty feet away. I gathered together threads of will, feeling the pressure build with a sort of skewed intangibility to it, something I hadn't ever felt before. I focused on my goal, on the rush of air that would lift the tools and parts and hurl them at Marcone, Parker, and Hendricks like so many bullets, and I prayed that I wouldn't catch myself in the edges of it by accident and get myself killed. I'd be breaking the First Law of Magic if one of them died, and I might have to deal with the White Council later; but hell's bells, I did not want to die on that concrete floor.

My head pounded, but I pushed the pain aside, focused, and breathed out, *"Vento servitas."*

The energy I had gathered whispered out of me. The tools jumped and rattled in place—and then fell still again.

Fire erupted behind my eyes. The pain was blinding, and I sucked in a breath and bowed my head forward, struggling not to fall to one side and reveal my lack of duct-tapedness. Oh, stars, it hurt like hell, and I clenched my teeth to keep from crying out. My chest heaved and strained to give me enough breath.

I blinked tears out of my eyes and straightened again, facing Marcone. I didn't want him to see the weakness. I didn't want him to know that my magic had failed.

"Interesting," Marcone said, glancing at the workbench, and then back at me. "Perhaps you've been working too hard," he suggested. "But I'm still willing to make the offer, Mr. Dresden. Otherwise, you understand, I have no interest in your well-being, and I will be forced to leave you here with Mr. Parker and his associates. If you do not come to work for me, you'll die."

I glared up at Marcone and gathered in a breath to spit out a curse at him. To hell with him and his whole stinking breed of parasites. Polite and smiling bastards who didn't care about the lives they ruined, the people they destroyed, so long as business continued as usual. If I was going to die here, I was going to lay out a curse on Marcone that would make the grimmest old fairy tales you ever heard sound like pleasant daydreams.

And then I glanced at Parker, who was glaring suspiciously at Marcone, and stifled the curse as well. I lowered my head, to hide my expression from Marcone. I had an idea.

"He dies anyway," Parker growled. "He's mine. You never said anything about him leaving with you."

Marcone stood, his mouth settled in a tight smile. "Don't start with me, Parker," Marcone said. "I'll take what I want to take. Last chance, Mr. Dresden."

"This wasn't part of the deal," Parker said. "I need him. I'll kill you before I let you take him." Parker put one hand behind his back, as though scratching at an itch. I glanced over, toward the office door behind him, and saw Flatnose crouched there in the doorway, mostly shielded by the door and unnoticed. Perfect.

"You needn't worry, Parker," Marcone said, his tone satisfied. "He won't accept my offer. He'd rather die."

I lifted up my head, and kept my expression as blank as I could. "Give me a pen," I said.

Marcone's mouth dropped open, and it was an intense pleasurc to see the surprise on his face. "What?" he said.

I enunciated each word carefully. "Give me a pen. I'll sign your contract." I glanced aside, at Parker, and said more loudly, "Anything to get away from these animals."

Marcone stared at me for a moment and then reached toward his pocket. I could see his eyes, see him searching my expression. The gears were spinning in his head as he tried to work out what I was doing.

Parker let out a sudden scream of rage and hurled the tire iron at Hendricks, who dodged to one side, too quickly for a man his size, and lifted his weapon. The office door exploded open, and Flatnose threw himself onto the big man. They both went down to the concrete, struggling for possession of the shotgun.

"The wizard's mine!" Parker howled, and threw himself at Marcone. Marcone moved like a snake in his zillion-dollar business suit and made a curved knife appear in his hands. He swept it in an arc that was followed by a spray of blood from Parker's wrist, and the lycanthrope howled.

I got up and ran like hell toward the door. My legs were shaky, and my balance wasn't great, but I was moving again, and I thought I had a fair chance of getting away. Over to my left, there was the roar of the shotgun going off, and a wet, red spray that went all over one wall and the ceiling. I didn't stop to see who had been killed, just jerked open the door.

Agent Phillip Denton stood five feet away from me, in the cold mist of autumn rain. The veins in his forehead were throbbing, and his short hair was frosted by the mist. He was flanked by the potbellied Agent Wilson, in his rumpled suit, his mostly bald head shining, and by the lean, savage-looking woman, Benn, her dark skin even darker in the evening's gloom and the glow of streetlights, her sensuous mouth peeling back into a startled snarl.

Denton blinked in surprise, and then narrowed his intensely grey eyes. "The wizard mustn't escape," he said, his voice calm and precise. "Kill him."

Benn's eyes gleamed, and she hissed something under her

breath while reaching a hand into her jacket. Wilson did the same. I brought my forward momentum to a sudden halt, fell, and started scrambling back into the building.

But instead of drawing guns out of their jackets, they changed. It happened fast, nothing like you see in the movies. One moment, there were two human beings standing there, and the next there was a flicker of shadow and a pair of enormous, gaunt wolves, one the grey of Benn's mane, one the same brown as Wilson's receding hairline.

They were huge, six feet long not including the tail, and as high as my belly at their shoulders. Their entirely human eyes shone, as did their bared fangs. Denton stood between them, his eyes gleaming with some dark breed of joy, and then he hissed, throwing his hands toward me. As though thrown by the motion, both wolves hurtled forward.

I flung myself back through the door and slammed it closed. There were heavy thuds as the wolves hit the door behind me. I saw a motion to my right and threw myself down just before Hendricks pulled the trigger. The riot gun belched forth flame and huge sound and blew a hole the size of my face in the door behind me. I could still hear Parker's furious snarling somewhere in the dark, and I scrambled forward, behind the bulk of a car, and then ran toward the back of the cavernous garage, staying low.

Outside, there was the sudden thunder of a dozen engines, and the sharp, heavy sounds of gunfire. Evidently, the Streetwolves had returned.

I stumbled through the darkness and tried not to make enough sound to give someone a chance to shoot me. The door flew open at the front of the garage, letting in a flood of dim light that didn't help me much. I heard people screaming.

I reached the back corner and sank down into it, then grabbed at something that turned out to be a toolbox. I came out with a heavy wrench and gripped it tightly. I was alone. I'd hurt myself using too much of my magic while on the go-go potion, and I didn't have anything left to throw now. Except for the wrench in my hands, I was unarmed. All around me, in the garage, there were the sounds of gunshots and screams and thuds of flesh as the animals fought for control of the jungle, and it was only a matter of time before one of them stumbled across a weakened and exhausted wizard named Harry Dresden.

Talk about frying pans and fires.

Chapter 24

It couldn't possibly get any worse than this, I thought. I cowered in the corner, clutching my captured wrench like a child's teddy bear, with no way out, and full of the knowledge that my magic had failed me.

Oddly, that thought troubled me more than probable death. A lot more. Death was something that happened to everyone—only the timing is different, for each of us. I knew that I would, eventually, die. Hell, I even knew that I might die horribly. But I had never thought that the magic would fail me. More accurately, I had never guessed that I might fail *it*. I had pushed too hard and my body wouldn't conduct the power I needed to utilize the forces I was accustomed to commanding. Granted, maybe I should have started with something smaller than a large and violent telekinesis, but the indication was there that I had burned out some internal circuitry. It might not ever come back.

It was a loss of identity. I was a wizard. It was more than just a job, more than just a title. Wizardry was at the core of my being. It was my relationship with my magic, the way I used it, the things it let me do that defined me, shaped me, gave me purpose.

I dwelled on these things while death danced over the concrete floor, clutching them like a sailor clinging to the wreckage of his ship, trying to ignore the storm that blasted it to pieces. I noted peripheral details from my pathetic hiding place. Marcone made a break for one of the garage doors, only to be pinned down behind a rusted truck by gunfire from some of the Streetwolves. Hendricks joined him, and a moment later, the truck roared to life and crashed out through the garage door and into the gravel parking lot. Hendricks, in the rear of the truck, fired several blasts from the big shotgun back into the building, while the Streetwolves sent rounds skewing off after the truck.

The real battle, though, took place between the Streetwolves and the FBI.

It was largely a gunfight. Denton was armed with his FBI-issue automatic and what looked like an Uzi submachine gun. He cut down three of the lycanthropes with a swath of fire from the automatic weapon as he came in through the door, and the two great wolves with him hurtled into the darkness. Screams and savage snarling erupted from the shadows, and I could hear more of the lycanthropes dying, being torn apart by the enormous wolves that had once been Agents Benn and Wilson. Parker screamed orders somewhere in the dark, half incoherent with rage. Denton reached into his jacket for a fresh clip for the Uzi, and I saw something across his belly that I noted for future reference, should I have any future.

I watched the killing, and I hid, and I prayed that there would be an opportunity to flee toward the open doors of the garage before Denton or Parker noticed me. It went on forever. Oh, I knew, in some rational part of my brain, that only seconds were going by, but it felt like days. I was terrified, and my head and my body hurt, and I couldn't use magic to protect myself.

There was a sound near my ankle, and my heart leapt up out of my throat. I flinched violently away from it. The sound repeated itself in a continuous scrabble of noise. The floor, I noticed, was rough dirt and broken concrete in this corner, where the foundation platform was flawed. The scrabbling noise came from the very base of the wall, where the dirt was stirring and moving.

Something was trying to dig its way beneath the wall and into the garage, practically right underneath my butt. I felt a chill of fear, followed swiftly by anger at the thing that had added to an already overabundant flow of adrenaline. I clutched my makeshift weapon in hand and moved to crouch over the source of the disturbance, lifting it in preparation to strike at whatever came through.

I saw it in the dimness, and there was no mistaking the shape. A paw, a huge canine paw, scrabbled at the earth, digging out a shallow hole beneath the wall, frustrated by bits of concrete that got in the way. Between shots, I could hear animal sounds outside, panting whimpers of eagerness, it seemed. Whatever was out there wanted to dig its way inside, and wanted it bad.

"Dig this," I muttered, and swung the wrench down on the paw, hard.

There was an instant yelp of pain, and the paw jerked its way back out from beneath the corrugated-metal wall. It was followed by a snarl, and the paw appeared again, whereupon I slammed the wrench down on it once more, with similar results. I heard a furious snarling sound from the other side, and I released a small surge of vindictive satisfaction by leaning down close enough to the hole to say, "Hah. Bring another one in here and I'll give you the same."

I heard sounds outside for a moment, then a crunch of gravel, and Tera West's smooth, unmistakable voice. "Wizard," she hissed. "Stop that."

I blinked, startled, and leaned down close to the hole. "Tera? Is that you? How did you know it was me?"

"You are the only man I ever met," Tera growled, "who would smash the paws that are trying to free you from certain death." I flinched at another burst of gunfire from the far side of the garage. "I am going to tell them to dig again. Do not strike at their paws."

"Them?" I demanded. "Them who?"

But she didn't answer me. Instead, the scrabbling sounds began again. I looked over my shoulder at the rest of the room. I saw Streetwolves moving swiftly out through the door and the gaping hole Marcone had left in the garage door when he escaped. In a flash of automatic muzzle-flare, I saw Denton standing over the form of a lanky woman and firing down into it, apparently making absolutely certain that she would never rise again. I had enough time to recognize Lana's face, now screwed up with pain rather than blood lust. Her body jerked and twitched as Denton emptied the remainder of the clip into her. And then everything went dark again.

By my feet, the scrabbling sounds continued—and then broke off in a yelp. I heard a series of vicious snarls and yelps from the half-dug hole beneath the wall, and I cursed.

"Tera," I whispered, as loudly as I dared. "What's going on?"

There was only more growling for answer, and a sharp yelp that carried to the far side of the garage.

I threw myself flat behind the toolbox and a pile of junk, just before a flashlight beam swept over the corner where I had been hiding. "It's that bitch," Denton snarled. "Roger's got her outside."

There was a whispering sound, and a tingling feeling along

my spine. Then a throaty, sensual female voice purred, "Parker's still in here. So is that wizard. I can smell them."

"Dammit," Denton growled. "The wizard knows too much. Wilson, go help Roger."

"What about me, lover?" the female voice said, a husky laugh added to the end. Agent Benn sounded like she'd just had too much sex, drugs, and rock and roll, and was hungry for more.

"You and I stay in here. I'll cover the doors. Flush them toward me."

There was a mewling sound of pleasure from the woman. "Come with me," she urged. "Change. You know you love it so much. You know how good it feels."

I could visualize Denton's veins throbbing. "Smarter for one of us to cover the door with a gun." But there was a sort of heavy reluctance to his tone.

"Fuck smart," Benn purred. "Come with me. Change."

"It's not why we did this. Not why we made the bargain."

Benn made another sound, utterly sexual in nature. "It doesn't matter now. Taste it," she urged him. "Taste the blood." The light wavered and dropped from the corner where I hid.

I chanced a look up. Agent Benn, spattered in gore, stood before Denton in the wash of his flashlight from the floor. She had three of her fingers pressed together, and was sliding them between his lips. Denton was shaking, and his eyes were squeezed tightly closed. He suckled at her fingers, something frighteningly erotic in the motion. One of the huge, gaunt beasts from earlier, Wilson I supposed, stood nearby, watching the pair of them with gleaming eyes.

Denton made a growling sound and grasped Benn by her mane of greying hair, jerking her chin up so that he could nuzzle and lick at the blood smeared over her throat. She laughed and arched into him, her hips undulating against him in urgent motions. "Change," she moaned. "Change. Do it."

There was a howl of rage, and flash of motion, and Parker staggered from the darkness, one arm dangling uselessly, a heavy knife in his other hand, and defiance and insane anger in his glazed eyes. Denton and Benn looked up, and then they reached to their waists, flickered, and changed into a pair of the nightmare-sized wolves, their eyes glowing in the ambient light, jaws dropping open to reveal lolling tongues and vicious fangs. Parker lurched forward, greasy hair flying, and the three wolves leapt on him.

I stared in a sort of sickened fascination. The wolves buried him under a mound of fangs and fur and blood and absolute fury. He screamed, the knife flailing, and then it was cast aside, out of his hands, to land spinning on the floor not far from me. Parker tried to fight, tried to struggle up and kick, but it was hopeless. There were flashes of blood, and he screamed again and went still.

And then the wolves started to eat him. They bit off chunks of muscle and gulped them down, ripping aside clothing to get to more meat. They snarled and snapped at one another, and one of the males mounted the female, even as she continued to tear at the body, burrowing her muzzle down through the layers of stomach muscle to get at the vitals. My gorge rose, and if I'd had anything in my stomach, I would have emptied it onto the concrete floor.

Instead, I turned back to the half-finished hole in the floor and started digging at it with my wrench, frantic. I didn't want to be the next thing on the menu.

There were more yelps from outside, more growls, and I opened the hole up enough that I thought I might be able to get out. I flattened myself down and wormed my way into the dirt, the corrugated metal scraping at my back, my wounded shoulder paining me again.

I jerked my way out into the open air, to find myself in an alley behind the garage, dimly lit by a distant streetlight.

There were wolves everywhere.

Three wolves, smaller than the ones I had seen before, were spread in a loose ring about a great russet-furred beast with bat-like ears. The great wolf's coat was spattered with blood, and two of the smaller wolves lay nearby, yelping in pain, stirring weakly, blood matting their coats. Tera was a part of the ring around the great beast as well, naked and lean, a length of pipe held in either hand. When the great wolf turned toward one of the others, the rest would begin to close in around him, and he would spin, jaws flashing, trying to pin down one of those who encircled him.

"You took your time, wizard," Tera snarled, without looking back at me.

I got to my feet, wrench in hand, and shook my head to clear it of cold sweat. "Tera," I said. "We've got to get out of here. Denton and the others will be coming."

"Go," she responded. "Help MacFinn. We will hold them." The great russet wolf lunged at her, and she skittered back, cooly staying a hair's breadth from his fangs. She fetched him a sharp blow across the nose with more speed than I could have believed and a contemptuous snort. The three smaller wolves rushed the great beast, and he spun to drive them back and away from him, drawing a yelp from one that wasn't swift enough to entirely evade his jaws.

"You can't stop them all," I said. "There's three more like this one."

"There are pack on the ground," she snarled, and jerked her head toward the wounded wolves. "We do not abandon our own."

I let out an acid curse. I needed Tera. She could confirm everything, help me sort out all my facts, make sure that I understood what was going on. She was offering to give her life for me, to stay and occupy Denton and the others for as long as she and her compatriots could, but I had seen enough people dying already tonight. I wasn't going to accept another loss on my behalf.

And I was abruptly more furious than afraid. I'd been run around and treated like a piece of baggage or a choice item on the menu for long enough. I'd flailed around in the dark and been helpless and ineffective for way too long. Too many people had been hurt, too much suffering caused by creatures of magic and the night, things that I should have been handling. It didn't matter to me, at that moment, that I couldn't work any of my spells against them. I might not have any magic available to me, but that didn't make me any less of a wizard, one of the magi, the wise. That's the true power of a wizard.

I know things.

Knowledge is power.

With power comes responsibility.

That made the entire thing pretty simple. I clutched the wrench in my hand, took a deep breath, and threw myself forward, at the great wolf's back. The huge wolf sensed me coming, spun with abrupt speed, and met me in the air. It slammed me down to the concrete and bent its jaws toward my throat. I heard Tera cry out, and she and the other wolves moved forward—but they would never have been able to get to the thing before it killed me. That wasn't the point.

I jammed the wrench into the wolf's jaws, feeling some teeth tear at one of my fingers as I did. The wolf snarled and jerked the wrench out of my hands. It spun end over end away from me, and the great beast turned back toward me, its eyes glowing.

I had time to watch it all in great detail. The wolf's power, its speed, simply shocked me. It was huge, quick, and I didn't have a prayer against it. The distant streetlight gleamed off of its reddened fangs as its muzzle sped toward my throat.

Chapter 25

The wolf's fur was speckled with drops of blood that had beaded on it like rain. The gravel in the alley shone in the half-light from the distant street lamps. The wolf's muzzle, a little shorter and broader than I had seen on *Wild Kingdom,* was drawn back, black lips from fangs striped white and red like peppermints. Its eyes were blue, rather than any proper lupine shade, and gleamed with a sort of demented awareness.

I had time to see all those details because I didn't need my eyes for what I wanted to do. I thrust my hands into the beast's pelt as he went for my throat, and wormed my way down between his forelegs with my buttocks, fingers digging, until I felt what I was looking for—the sharp metal edges of a belt buckle, down against the skin, almost flush to the surface. As the wolf's jaws came toward my throat, I furiously worked the buckle, feeling skin rip and tear from the wolf's hide as I jerked it open, and then threw my arm to one side, clutching hard at the trailing strap.

And abruptly, a wolf-pelt belt was sliding out from beneath the grey suit jacket of Roger Harris, the forensic specialist for the local FBI office, the kid with the red hair and the big ears. He crouched over me for a second, blinking in stunned amazement at me, blood on his mouth and lips.

"*Hexenwulf* jerk-off," I snarled and slammed my knee up into his groin. It hit home hard.

Harris gasped and rolled off me, reaching into his jacket, but I didn't let him get his gun. I stayed with him, keeping too close to him to let him move his arms freely, grabbed him by those big ears, and started slamming his head repeatedly against the gravel.

He struggled against me for a few seconds, but I'd taken him by surprise. His skull banged against the rocks over and over, and after a half-dozen solid blows, he stopped struggling.

I released his ears with a little jerk and looked up at Tera and the wolves. They were closing in around him like a pack of sharks around a wounded dolphin, and I could read the blood in their eyes, in the bared fangs, and in the white-knuckled grip of Tera's hands on her lead pipes. I felt a sudden surge of frustration. Bad enough to have bloodthirsty animals roaming all over the city—I didn't need more of them on my team.

"Everyone back off," I snarled.

"He's ours," Tera answered me in kind. "He hurt those of the pack."

"Then why don't you get them some help instead of wasting your time on this guy?" I said.

"His blood is ours," Tera said, and the wolves confirmed this with a chorus of angry growls.

"He can't hurt you now. Killing him won't make your friends any better. And the lost time might finish them."

"You do not understand, wizard," Tera snarled, and the wolves echoed her in a chorus, white fangs showing. "It is our way."

I stood up slowly, to my full height. "I understand," I said in a very low and even voice, "that you do not want to make me any more angry than I already am." I met Tera's eyes and stared, hard. My jaws ached from clenching. "There's been enough killing. Take him out now, and you're no different than he is."

"Wrong," Tera said. "I would be alive, and he dead."

"Not if you cross me, you won't be."

We held the tension for a moment, glaring at one another.

I saw uncertainty waver across her face. She didn't know that I was out of gas, magically speaking, and she had seen me do too many impressive things with my powers to want to defy me lightly. She blinked first and looked away from me with a sullen sound in the back of her throat. "As you wish, wizard," she said. "We don't have the time to waste fighting one another. The rest of his pack is coming. And we have wounded to tend to."

I nodded and swept my gaze around at the three wolves around me. "Anybody else?" I challenged. They all backed away from me, and didn't meet my eyes. "All right, then," I said, and stooped to recover Harris's gun and the wolf-pelt belt. "Do you have transportation out of here?"

"Yes," Tera said. "Georgia."

One of the wolves, a leggy, lanky, pale-brown beast shuddered and paced in a circle, making small, whimpering sounds. A moment later, there was a whisper of power. The she-wolf shivered, and went still, her head bowed. And then she shook herself, and all that pale-brown hair faded from paler skin, leaving me staring at the lanky, dark-blonde girl I had seen in the department store a few days ago, sans all the black leather. Georgia rose to her feet and said, “I’ll have her bring the van around on the next street. Can you get them to it?” Her expression was tense, her eyes a little wide.

“Yes,” Tera said. “Everyone, come back to yourselves.” The other two ambulant wolves began to pace in a slow circle, gathered their own power, and their own transformations commenced, until they stood before me as a pair of naked young men—one of them the short, stout boy who had been arguing against Georgia—Billy—and the other a face I recognized but couldn’t name.

Tera took charge of the situation while I held Harris’s gun and kept watch down the alley. She and the two young men made a litter for one of the wolves out of Harris’s jacket, and the other Tera simply picked up with a flexion of wire-tight muscle and carried, though it must have weighed a hundred and fifty pounds. The wounded wolves yelped piteously, and Tera and the two young men cast dark glances at the downed Harris while they headed down the alley, and over toward the beach, leaving me alone with the kid.

I hunkered down beside him and slapped his face until his eyes rolled open. He blinked once and then jerked, as though he was about to sit up. I stuck the barrel of the semiautomatic in the hollow of his throat and said, in a calm voice, “Hold still.”

He froze, staring up at me with wide eyes.

“I’m going to ask some questions, kid. I think I’ve got the answers already, but you’re going to talk to me, quietly and honestly. Or I demonstrate point-blank bullet impact for you right here and now. Got it?”

Harris’s mouth twitched a few times before he managed to speak. “If you kill me,” he said, “Denton won’t stop until you’re dead.”

“Give me a break, Roger,” I said back in a reasonable tone. “Denton wants me dead anyway. I could kill you now and it wouldn’t make any difference in what he has to do.”

Roger licked his lips and rolled his eyes about without moving his head, as though hoping for rescue. "How did you know? About the belt."

"I saw Denton's inside. And I saw that before you all changed, you had to reach inside your jackets for something. I figure that first night, Agent Benn was reaching into her jacket to touch the belt and tear Murphy's head off, when she got mad. But she managed to remember not to do it in time and drew her gun instead. Right?"

Harris's head twitched in a slight nod.

"The bargain," I said. "You're *Hexenwulfen,* so you've made a bargain with someone to get the power to change, to get the belts. Who is it?"

"I don't know," Harris said, and his eyes widened. "God, I don't know. Denton handled all of it."

I narrowed my eyes at him and drew back the hammer on the gun.

"Please," he squealed, breathless. "I don't know. I swear to God, Denton handled all of that. He just came to us, asked us if we wanted to back him, if we wanted to nail some of the scum that kept getting away from the law, and I told him I did. Jesus, I didn't know it was going to lead to this."

"Lead to what, Roger?" I asked, my tone frosty. "Start from the beginning, and make it quick."

"Marcone," he said, eyes on the gun. "It was all about Marcone. Denton wanted to take him down."

"You mean kill him."

His eyes flickered up to me. "He told us there was no other way to get to him. That he was doing more to poison this city than anyone alive. And he was right. Marcone's bought enough influence in this town to stay clear of city police forever, and he carries weight on the national level, too. The bureau has had more than one investigation on him called off. He's untouchable."

"So you planned to use the belts to kill him."

He nodded. "But there would be evidence. No one would believe he'd just been mauled by wild dogs. There would be a full investigation, forensics, the works."

I understood and nodded. "So you needed someone to make it a neat package. Let me guess: the Streetwolves."

Harris showed his teeth. "A gang of felons and troublemakers with a wolf motif. Murder of a criminal figure by persons with a wolf motif. No one would bother to check the figures on that one. It's obvious. And we get one more dangerous group off the street."

"Yeah, Roger, except that they'd be innocent of that particular crime. Did you think of that? Innocent like those other people who died the nights around the full moon last month. You killed them. You and the rest of Denton's team."

He closed his eyes, his face going pale, and he shuddered. "The change. When . . . when you're changed, when you're a beast, it's so incredible. So much speed, power. Your body just sings with it. I tried coke once, in college, and it was nothing compared to this. The blood . . ." His tongue flicked out again over his bloodstained lips, a thirsty motion this time, rather than a nervous one.

"I think I'm starting to see. Denton didn't tell you about that part. About how your thoughts are influenced. He probably didn't know himself. And when you've done it once . . ."

Harris nodded emphatically. "You just can't stop, man. It gets to where you're pacing the room at night. And it's better than sleep, when you get finished hunting, you feel so *alive*." He opened his eyes again, staring up at me, pleading. "I didn't mean to kill those people. We started off with criminals. Some gangsters dealing drugs. We were just going to scare them, but it was too much. They screamed and ran and we were after them, and . . . We killed them. And my God, Dresden, it was beautiful."

"And it happened again," I said. "A couple of times. Innocent people. Just poor schmucks in the wrong place at the wrong time."

Harris turned his head away from me and nodded. "Denton said that we could salvage it. He said that we could pin those killings on the Streetwolves as well. Make everyone think they had done it. And we just went along with him."

I shook my head. "That doesn't explain why you dragged MacFinn into this."

"Denton," the kid said. "It was all him. He said there was someone else we could also set up to take the blame, to be certain we'd be in the clear. That he had the man for it. We broke into MacFinn's house, and there was all this occult stuff. We messed up some of it and left. And . . . the next night, more people were dead. And more, the next night. That's when we went after that slime Marcone's business partner, and wasted the bastard and his goon."

"And then you laid low for a month."

Harris swallowed and nodded. "Denton took the belts. He hid them from us. He'd held out better than anyone. And my God, poor Benn was so far gone, it was like she wasn't even human anymore. Wilson wasn't much better. But we lasted out the month."

"And then you killed Marcone's bodyguard at the Varsity."

Harris's eyes flared. "Yes. You should see his record. The things we know he did, but that we can't get through a court. My God, Dresden, he had it coming."

"Maybe. Maybe not. Who are we to judge?"

"Who are we *not* to?" Harris demanded. "The power was in our hands. We had a responsibility to use it for the good. To do our jobs. Hell, Dresden. If you're such a do-gooder, you should be helping us, not getting in the way. These men are untouchable and you know it."

I shifted my weight uncomfortably. "I don't agree with your methods. With setting people up to take the blame for your killings."

Harris sneered. "Like MacFinn has never killed anyone. Hell, he's a murderer now, isn't he? After that scene at the police station, anyone would be convinced he was a killer."

"Except me," I said. "MacFinn would never have been there if you hadn't messed up the circle that held him."

"Yeah," Harris said, a spiteful, frustrated edge to his tone. "Except you. You got to poking around in our business. Christ, that crazy report to Murphy even talked about the belts. That was when Denton started taking you seriously. If you had any brains at all, you'd pull that trigger and get the hell out now, before Denton and the others come out of the haze and come after you. Because you know way too much."

"Why the Streetwolves?" I said, instead of shooting him. "Why send me off to check them out?"

"Denton figured they'd kill you," Harris spat. "And get you out of our hair."

I nodded. It figured, that someone else had been trying to kill me the whole while, and I hadn't really noticed. "And he knew that they were after me, after I got away from them the first time."

"Yeah. And had me tailing them, so we could find you and make sure you were dead. When I saw you in the back of that car, I figured you were. So we planned the hit on the Streetwolves to go down tonight, before MacFinn went after Marcone."

"How'd you know about that?" I asked.

Harris snorted. "Marcone told us. The snake called asking for police protection."

I almost smiled. "Did he get it?"

"Hell, no," Harris answered me. He lifted his chin, and balled his hands into fists, and I felt him tighten up beneath me. "I'm done talking," he said. "If you aren't going to sign on with us, then get the hell out of here. Or pull the trigger. But quit wasting my time."

"I'm not done talking," I said, and I jammed the gun crosswise over the kid's throat, strangling him. "You're going to give Denton a message for me. I'm sick of dancing around. Tell him that he'll get his shot at me at moonrise, at Marcone's place."

Harris squirmed beneath me, making rasping, gagging sounds. His eyes widened at my words. "It doesn't take a genius to figure out that he'll try to be there when MacFinn shows up," I said. "That he'll want to make sure everyone there is dead so that he's the only one who can report what happened. You tell him that I'll be there. And tell him that he's not going to get away with it. Do you understand me, kid?"

I let up on the pressure, and Harris croaked out a vague affirmative. I rose away from him, keeping the gun in one hand and the belt in the other. I saw his eyes flicker to the belt, tracking its movement with a tense, strained sort of hunger.

"Why tell me?" the kid asked. "Why warn us?"

I stared down at him for long seconds before I answered him in a quiet voice. "Because I don't like what you're doing. What you are. You aren't using the power you've been given. It's using you. You're turning into animals. You're using savagery and fear to try to uphold the peace. Now it's your turn to see what it's like to be afraid."

Harris rose to his feet, his red hair askew, blood drying on his mouth, and backed several paces from me, his eyes darting around. "My belt," he said. "I want my belt."

"Forget it, kid," I told him. "The smartest thing you can do is go lock yourself in your room, and stay there until all of this is over. Because one way or another, you aren't using this belt again."

His face whitened, and he took a step toward me. I pointed the gun at him, and he froze, his hands balling into fists. "You won't get away with this," he said, his voice thick with tension.

"Moonrise," I told him, then turned on my heel and walked quickly from the alley, although my sock feet on the gravel, combined with my limp, probably spoiled the badass image.

Thirty feet down the alley, Tera appeared from the shadows and fell into step beside me, close enough to support me if I should fall. "You were wrong, wizard," she said.

I looked down at her, and she met my gaze with her soulless amber eyes. "How so?"

"They have not become animals." She looked over her shoulder, her eyes narrowed. "Animals do not do what they have done. Animals kill to eat, to defend themselves or their own, and to protect their territory. Not for the joy of it. Not for the lust of it." She looked back up at me. "Only humans do that, wizard."

I grimaced, but couldn't really refute her. "I guess you're right."

"Of course," Tera said. We walked in silence for a moment. "You will try to help my fiancé?"

"I'll try," I said. "But I can't let his curse claim any more lives."

She nodded, her eyes dark. "He would want it that way. He thinks of others before himself."

"He sounds like a good man."

She shrugged, but there was a sudden, worried weight in her shoulders. "And these others. The FBI. They will try to stop you."

"Yes."

"And when they do?"

"I can't let them go on like they have. They're out of control. I don't think they can stop themselves from killing, now." I didn't look down at Tera, just focused on taking steps, one at a time. "When they do . . ." I said. "When they do . . . I guess I'm going to need to get very human."

Chapter 26

Tera and I walked toward the shores of Lake Michigan. There, along Forty-ninth Street, idled a big old van, its engine rattling. Its headlights came on as we approached, and the driver got out to roll open the side door for us.

"Harry?" she said. "Oh, God. What did they do to you?" She hurried over to me, and then I felt Susan's warmth against me as she slid one of my arms over her shoulder and pressed up against my side. She was wearing jeans that showed off her long legs, and a dark red jacket that complemented her dark skin. Her hair was tied back into a ponytail, and it made her neck look slender and vulnerable. Susan felt soft and warm beyond belief, and smelled clean and delightfully feminine, and I found myself leaning against her. All the aches and pains that had faded into the background came throbbing back to the forefront of my awareness, in comparison to her soft warmth and gentle support. I liked the way Susan felt better than the way I did.

"They beat him," Tera explained. "But they kept him alive, as I told you they might."

"Your face looks like a sack of purple potatoes," Susan said, her dark eyes studying me, the lines in her face deepening.

"You say the sweetest things," I mumbled.

They loaded me into the van, where Georgia, Billy, and the other Alphas were crouched. Two of the young people, a boy with blinking, watery blue eyes, and a girl with mousy brown hair, lay on their backs, gasping quietly. Clean white bandages had been wrapped around their wounds. Georgia had, evidently, been the attending medic. All of the Alphas were dressed in plain, dark bathrobes, rather than in their birthday suits, and I felt an oddly grateful feeling toward them for it. Things were weird enough without needing to ride around in a van with a bunch of naked, somewhat geeky college students.

I put my seat belt on and noted the bruises on my hands and forearms—ugly, dark purple-and-brown splotches, so thickly scattered over my skin that in places I couldn't tell where one stopped and the next began. I sat down and leaned against the window, pillowing my head on my right hand.

"What are you doing here with these people?" I asked Susan when she got into the driver's seat.

"Driving," she said. "I was the only one old enough to rent the van."

I winced. "Ouch."

"Tell me about it," she said and started the engine. "After you jumped out of the car, and I finished with my heart attack, we called the police, just like you said. Tera went to look for you and told me that the police had shown up too late, and that the Streetwolves had taken you. How did that truck crash like that?"

"Bad luck. Someone made all their tires explode at the same time."

Susan gave me an arch look and started up the van. "Those bastards. Just lie still, Harry. You look like a train wreck. We'll get you to someplace quiet."

"Food," I said. "I'm starving. Tera, can you keep track of moonrise?"

"I will," she said. "The clouds are moving away. I can see the stars."

"Fantastic," I mumbled. And then I went to sleep, ignoring the jostling of the van. I didn't wake up until the smell of fried grease and charred meat made me look up at the drive-thru window of a fast-food burger joint. Susan paid for everything in cash, passing paper sacks to everyone. I snagged a golden paper crown from one of the bags and idly joined it into a circle and put it on my head. Susan blinked at me, then let out a brief laugh.

"I am," I intoned, with an imperious narrowing of my eyes, "the burger king." Susan laughed again, shaking her head, and Tera gave me a serious, level gaze. I checked the status of the young people in the back of the van, and found them, even the wounded ones, hungrily wolfing (no pun intended) down the food.

Tera caught the direction of my glance and leaned toward me. "Puppies," she said, as though the word should explain more than it did. "They were not hurt so badly as they thought. They will hardly have scars to show for it."

"That's good to know," I said and sipped at my cola and chomped down steaming-hot french fries. "But what I'm really interested in," I said, "is in knowing why your blood was in Marcone's restaurant the night before the full moon."

Tera took the hamburger patty off of the bun and started nibbling on it, holding it in her fingers. "Ask another time."

"No offense," I said, "but I'm not so sure there's going to be another time. So tell me."

Tera took another bite of meat, and then shrugged. "I knew that the pack that had harassed my fiancé was about. I deduced where they might strike, and went there to attempt to stop them."

"All by yourself?"

Tera sniffed. "Most of those who turn themselves into wolves know little about *being* wolf, wizard. But these had taken too much of the beast inside. I ran through the window glass and fought, but they outnumbered me. I left before I could be killed."

"And what about these kids?" I said, nodding toward the back of the van.

She glanced back at them, and for a moment, I saw warmth and pride gleaming in her eyes, subverting the remote, alien lines of her face. "Children. But with strong hearts. They wished to learn, and I taught. Let them tell you their tale."

"Maybe later," I said and finished off the french fries. "Where are we going?"

"To a safe place, to arm and prepare ourselves."

"Myself," I contradicted her. "To prepare myself. I'm not taking you with me."

"You are incorrect," Tera said. "I am going with you."

"No."

She fastened her amber eyes on mine. "You are strong, wizard. But you have not yet seen my beast. The men you will oppose would take my fiancé from me. I will not allow that. I will be with you, or you will kill me to stop me."

This time, it was I who looked away first. I sipped at my drink, scowling, while Tera placidly ate more of the hamburger patty. "Who are you?" I asked her finally.

"One who has lost too many of her family already," she said. And then she settled back on the seat and withdrew from the conversation, falling silent.

"One who has lost too many . . ." I grumbled, frustrated,

mocking her beneath my breath. I turned back to the front of the van and hunched my shoulders over my burger. "Put some clothes on, you weird, yellow-eyed, table-dancing, werewolf-training, cryptic, stare-me-right-in-the-eyes-and-don't-even-blink wench."

There was a hissing sound from the back seat, and I flicked a scowl back over my shoulder. Tera was chewing on her meat. Her eyes were shining, her mouth was curved at the corners, and her breath was puffing out her nostrils in near-silent laughter.

The safe place we were going to turned out to be a big house up near the Gold Coast, not far from Marcone's own minipalace. The house wasn't large, by the neighborhood's standards, but that was like saying that a bale of hay isn't much to eat, by elephant standards. Susan drove the van up through a break in a high hedge, up a long driveway of white concrete, and into a six-car garage whose doors rolled majestically up before us.

I got out of the van, in the garage, and stared at the Mercedes and the Suburban also parked in it. "Where are we?" I said.

Tera opened the side door of the van, and Georgia, Billy, and the other young man emerged, assisting the two wounded werewolves. Georgia stretched, which did interesting things to the dark bathrobe, and drew her mane of tawny hair back from her lean face with one hand. "It's my parents' place. They're in Italy for another week."

I rubbed a hand over my face. "They aren't going to mind you having a party, are they?"

She flashed me an annoyed look and said, "Not as long as we clean up all the blood. Come on, Billy. Let's get these two inside and into bed."

"You go on," he said, fastening his eyes on me. "I'll be along in a minute."

Georgia looked like she wanted to give him an argument, but shook her head instead, and with the help of the other young man, took the two invalids inside. Tera, still naked and supremely unconcerned about it, followed them, glancing back over her shoulder at me before she disappeared. Susan promptly stepped in front of me, somewhat obstructing the view, and said, "Five minutes, Dresden. Come find me then."

"Uh," was my rapier reply, and then Susan went into the house, too.

I stood in the dark with Billy, the stout, short kid in thick glasses. He had his hands stuffed into his bathrobe pockets, and he was peering at me.

"Do all wizards," he said, "get the kiddie crowns and wear them around? Or is that only for special occasions?"

"Do all werewolves," I shot back, snatching the crown from my head, "wear glasses and too much Old Spice? Or is that only for full moons?"

He grinned at me, rather than taking umbrage. "You're quick," he said. "I always wanted to be that way." He stuck out his hand toward me. "Billy Borden."

I traded grips with him wearily, and he tried to crush my hand in his. "Harry Dresden," I told him.

"You look pretty beat up, Mr. Dresden," he said. "Are you sure you can handle going out again tonight?"

"No," I answered, in a spurt of brutal honesty.

Billy nodded, and pushed his glasses up higher onto his nose. "Then you need our help."

Oh, good grief. The Mickey Mouse Club of werewolves wanted to throw in on my side. Werewolfkateer role call: Billy. Georgia. Tommy. Cindy. Sheesh.

"No way," I said. "Absolutely not."

"Why not?" he said.

"Look, kid. You don't know what these *Hexenwulfen* can be like. You don't know what Marcone can be like, and you sure as hell have never seen anything like MacFinn outside of a movie theater. And even if you had the skills to deal with it, what makes you think you have a right to be going along?"

Billy considered the question seriously. "The same thing that makes you think that you do, Mr. Dresden," he said.

I opened my mouth. And closed it again.

"I know I don't know a lot, compared to you," Billy said. "But I'm not stupid. I've got eyes. I see some things everyone else tries to pretend aren't there. This vampire craze sweeping the nation. Why the hell shouldn't there be some genuine vampires in it? Did you know that violent crimes have increased nearly forty percent in the last three years, Mr. Dresden? Murder alone has almost doubled, particularly in heavy urban areas and isolated rural areas. Abductions and disappearances have gone up nearly three hundred percent."

I blinked at the kid. I hadn't really read the numbers. I knew that Murphy and some of the other cops said that the streets were getting worse. And I knew myself, on some deep level, that the world was getting darker. Hell, it was one of the reasons I did idiotic things like I was doing tonight. My own effort to lift up a torch.

"I'm sort of a pessimist, Mr. Dresden. I think that people are almost too incompetent to hurt themselves so badly. I mean, if criminals were *trying,* they couldn't increase their production by three hundred percent. And I hear stories, read the tabloids sometimes. So what if the supernatural world is making a comeback? What if that accounts for some of what is going on?"

"What if it does?" I asked him.

Billy regarded me steadily, without looking me in the eyes. "Someone has to do something. I can. So I should. That's why we're here, the Alphas. Tera offered us the chance to do something, when she met us through the Northwest Passage Project, and we took it."

I stared at the kid. I could have argued with him, but there wouldn't be much point to it. I knew his argument, backward and forward. I'd worked it out myself. If I was ten years younger, a foot shorter, and a couple of pounds heavier, that could have been me talking. And I had to admit, the kid did have power. I mean, turning yourself into a wolf is no cheap parlor trick. But I did have one angle to play, and I took it. I didn't want this kid's blood on my hands.

"I don't think you're ready for the big leagues yet, Billy."

"Could be," he said. "But there's no one else in the bull pen."

I had to give the kid credit. He had resolve. "Maybe you should sit this one out, and live to fight another day. It could all go bad, and if it does, those *Hexenwulfen* we took on down by the beach are going to be coming for you. Someone will need to stay with your wounded people, to protect them."

"More likely, if they go through you, they're going to go through us, too. It would be smarter to pile on everything we've got in one place. With you."

I chuckled. "All your eggs in one basket?"

He shook his head. "All the money on the most likely winner."

I studied him in silence for a long minute. I was confident of his sincerity. It just oozed out of him, in a way that only the really inexperienced and idealistic can manage. It was comforting, and at the same time it was the most frightening thing about him. His ignorance. No, not ignorance, really. Innocence. He didn't know what he would be going out to face. If I let him go along, I'd be dragging him down with me. Despite what he'd seen tonight,

I'd be exposing him to a whole new, violent, bloody, and dangerous world. One way or another, if I let Billy Borden and his buddies go with me, these innocent children wouldn't live to see the sunrise.

But, God help me. He was right about one thing. I needed the help.

"Everyone who's going takes orders from me," I said, and he drew in a sharp breath, his eyes gleaming. "Not Tera. You do what I say, and you do it when I say it. And if I tell you to leave, you go. No questions. You got it?"

"I got it," Billy said, and gave me a cocky grin that simply did not belong on the face of a geeky little college nerd in a black bathrobe. "You're a smart man, Mr. Dresden."

I snorted at him, and just then the automatic light on the garage door opener went out, leaving us in darkness. There was a disgusted sound from the doorway, and then the lights came on again. Georgia, in all her willowy, annoyed glory, was standing in the doorway to the garage.

"Billy Borden," she said. "Don't you have any better sense than to stay here in the dark?" She stalked out toward him, scowling.

He looked up at her calmly and said, "Tell everyone we're going along. Dresden's in charge. If they can handle that, they're in, and if not, they're staying here to guard Cindy and Alex."

Georgia's eyes widened and she gave a little whoop of excitement. She turned to me and threw her arms around me for a moment, making my shoulder scream in pain, and then whirled to Billy and bent down to do the same thing. He winced when she did, and she stood up and jerked back his black bathrobe, clearing it off of one side of his pale chest. To give the kid credit, his stoutness was the result of what looked like quite a bit of solid muscle, and along the line of his chest there was a thickly clotted wound, still trickling blood in a few places.

"What's this?" Georgia said. "You idiot. You didn't tell me you'd gotten hurt."

Billy shrugged, and pulled his robe straight again. "It closed. And you can't bandage it and keep it on me when I change, anyway."

Georgia clucked her teeth, annoyed. "You shouldn't have gone for the hamstring on that wolf. He was too fast."

Billy flashed her a grin. "I almost got him, though."

"You almost got yourself killed," she said, but her voice had softened a few shades. I noticed that she hadn't moved her hand from the other side of Billy's chest, and he was looking up at her with an expectant expression. She fell silent, and they stared at one another for a minute. I saw her swallow.

Please, help me. Young werewolves in love. I turned to walk into the house, moving carefully.

I had never much believed in God. Well, that's not quite true. I believed that there was a God, or something close enough to it to warrant the name—if there were demons, there had to be angels, right? If there was a Devil, somewhere, there had to be a God. But He and I had never really seen things in quite the same terms.

All the same. I flashed a look up at the ceiling. I didn't say or think any words, but if God was listening, I hoped he got the message nonetheless. I didn't want any of these children getting themselves killed.

Chapter 27

Susan's perfume led me to her. She was waiting for me in a bedroom on the first floor. She stood in the simply furnished room, in her jeans and a white T-shirt blazoned with the words, EAT IT? I WOULDN'T SIT ON IT! It was one of mine. She lifted her chin up high when she saw me, as though trying to keep the tears in her eyes from falling.

Our gazes met, and held. We had looked into one another before, more than a year ago. She'd fainted when she saw what was inside of me through the soulgaze. I don't know what it was she saw. I don't look too hard into mirrors.

Inside of her, though, I'd seen passion, like I'd rarely known in people other than myself. The motivation to go, to do, to act. It was what drove her forward, digging up stories of the supernatural for a half-comic rag like the *Arcane*. She had a gift for it, for digging down into the muck that people tried to ignore, and coming up with facts that weren't always easily explained. She made people think. It was something personal for her—I knew that much, but not why. Susan was determined to make people see the truth.

I shut the door behind me and limped toward her.

"They'll kill you," she said. "Don't go." As I reached her, she put her hands against my chest, then her cheek.

"I've got to. Denton can't afford to let me live now. I need to finish this business, before it gets any more out of hand. Before more people die. If I don't go tonight, Denton will be able to kill Marcone and MacFinn and set MacFinn up for all the killings.

He'll get away clean, and then he'll be able to focus on me. And maybe on you, too."

"We could go somewhere," she said quietly. "We could hide."

I blinked my eyes closed. She'd said "we." She hadn't really done that much, before. I hadn't really thought in those terms, either. I hadn't much thought in those terms for a lot of years. Not since the last time.

I should have said something about it. Acknowledged the implication. I knew it was there, and she knew that I had noticed it. She held still, waiting.

Instead, I said, "I'm not much good at hiding. Neither are you."

Her breath went out in a little whisper, and I felt her tighten a little against me. There would be tears on my shirt, I knew, but I didn't look down at her.

"You're right," she said a moment later. Her voice was shaking. "And I know you are. But I'm afraid, Harry. I mean, I know we haven't been really close. Friends, and lovers, but . . ."

"Work," I said. I closed my eyes.

She nodded. "Work." Her fingers tightened on my shirt, and she looked up at me, dark eyes swimming with tears, still more on the smooth lines of her cheek. "I don't want to lose you now. I don't want the work to be all that's left."

I tried to think of something smart to say. Something that would reassure her, calm her, help her to feel better, to understand what I felt for her. But I wasn't even sure what it was that I felt.

I found myself kissing her, the rough growth on my mouth and chin brushing her soft skin. She tensed at first, and then melted against me with a deliciously feminine sort of willingness, a soft abandoning of distance that left her body, in all its dark beauty, pressed against mine. The kiss deepened, slowed, became something intense and erotic and self-contained. The motion of our lips, the warmth of our bodies pressed together. The touch of my fingertips on her face, featherlight. The scratch of her nails as her fingers kneaded at my shirt. My heart was pounding, and I could feel hers, too, racing.

She broke the kiss first, and I swayed on my feet, my breath gone. Without speaking, she guided me down to the edge of the bed, and sat me there. Then she vanished into the bathroom, reappearing with a basin of warm water, some soap, and a washcloth.

She undressed me. Slowly. Delicately. She changed the bandages, murmuring softly to me when it hurt, kissing my eyes and forehead to soothe me. She bathed me with the water, its warmth washing away the dried sweat, the blood, and some of the pain. Patiently, more gentle than rain, she made me clean, while I drifted, my eyes closed. I could hear myself make a soft sound, now and then, in response to her touches.

I felt her come to me. Felt her bare skin against mine, hot and smooth. I opened my eyes and saw the silver haze of the moon on the far horizon, across the lake. I saw Susan outlined in it, all sweetly feminine curves and lines, a beautiful shadow. She kissed me again, and I returned it in kind, and it was a liquid, smooth thing, as restrained and desperate as the near-still surface of a rushing river. Her lips passed from my mouth and roamed over the skin she had just cleaned, and when I tried to touch her, she gently pressed my hands back down, telling me without words to be still.

It went on like that, all skin and light touches, soft sighs, pounding hearts, until she settled atop me, keeping her weight off me with her legs, her hands, afraid to cause any pain. We moved together, feeling the power of our need, our hunger for one another, a pure blend of desire and warmth and affection and incredible intimacy that shook us to the core. It ended in silence, the sensation all the more piercing for that, our mouths together, our breath mingling.

She lay down beside me until our pounding hearts slowed down. Then she rose, and said, "I don't know if I want to fall in love with you, Harry. I don't know if I could stand it."

I opened my eyes, and answered softly, "I've never wanted to hurt you. I don't know what's right."

"I know what feels right," she said, and kissed me again, then started touching my forehead, lifting her head up to study me with gentle, compassionate eyes. "You see so much pain. I just wanted to remind you that there was something else in the world."

I'm a pretty tough guy. I mean, look at me. I can handle some rough stuff. But some things I'm not so tough about. I started crying, hard, and Susan held me, rocked me gently, until the tears had gone away.

I wanted to stay there, where it was warm, and where I was clean, and where there wasn't anyone dying. There wasn't any blood or snarling animals, and no one was trying to kill me. I liked the idea of being there, with Susan, in her arms, a whole lot more than I liked the idea of going out into the silver light of the full moon, which was growing greater underneath the horizon, coming up in a hazy nimbus.

Instead, I drew away from her a little and sat up.

It was a fool's moon.

She rose from the bed and returned with an overnight bag and drew out a pair of my black jeans, my black sneakers, socks, a heavy, dark grey shirt, dark undies to complete the color theme, and bless her heart, ibuprofen. I rose to dress, but she pressed a hand on my shoulder and made me sit down—then dressed me herself, slowly and carefully, her attention focused on the task. Neither of us spoke.

Ever had a beautiful, naked woman dress you? Talk about girding your loins for battle. There was something indescribably soothing and at the same time, exciting, about it. I could feel my body becoming more relaxed and aware, my senses more in tune with what was around me.

I heard footsteps in the hall, and a knock at the door. Tera's voice called, "Wizard. It is time."

I stood up, but Susan grabbed my wrist. "Harry," she said. "Wait a minute." She knelt down by the bag and drew out a heavy box, flat and broad. "I was going to give it to you for your birthday. But I thought you could use it."

I tilted my head and took the box in hand. It was heavy. "What is it?" I asked her.

"Just open it, dummy," she answered, smiling up at me. I did, and inside was the smell of soft, worked leather, sensuous and thick, wrapped up in translucent paper. I tossed the lid aside, took the paper off, and found dark leather, new and matte black, hardly casting back the light. I took it out of the box, and it unfolded into a heavy, long coat, like my own duster in design, even to the mantle around the shoulders and arms, but all made of the finer material.

I blinked at the coat. "It must have cost you a fortune."

She laughed wickedly. "Yeah. But I got to wear it around naked, just to feel it on my skin." Her face sobered. "I want you to have it, Harry. Something from me. For luck." She glided to my side and helped me into the coat.

The coat settled around me with a comforting heaviness and a peculiar sort of familiarity. It just felt right. I plucked my mother's pentacle on its chain from beneath my shirt and wore it openly. And then I got Harris's confiscated side arm from my coveralls' tool pouch, and put it in the coat's pocket. I didn't have any other magical tools. And maybe not even any more magic. The gun, all things considered, seemed an uncertain weapon at best.

But I was as ready as I was going to be.

I turned to say good-bye to Susan, to find her hurriedly stepping into her clothes. "What are you doing?" I asked.

"Getting dressed," she said.

"Why?"

"Someone's got to drive the van, Dresden." She tugged on her T-shirt, slung her jacket over her shoulder, and walked past me, pausing to give me a narrow glance. "Besides. This could be the biggest paranormal event I've ever had the chance to cover. Did you expect me to stay behind?" She pushed the door open and gave me an expectant look.

Damn, I thought. *And double damn.* One more person to worry about. One more person to protect. Susan wasn't a werewolf. She wasn't a wizard. She didn't even have a gun. It was crazy to let her even think about going along. But I found myself wanting to make sure she was somewhere close.

"All right," I said. "But the same rules I gave the kids. I'm in charge. You do what I say, when I say, or you stay here."

Susan pursed her lips and narrowed her eyes. "I kind of like the sound of that," she said, teasing me. "I like that look on you, too. Have you ever thought about growing a beard?" Then she smiled, and vanished out into the hallway.

I scowled after her. She'd stay away from the worst of it. I'd make sure of that, if I had to tie her to the van myself. I muttered something grouchy, bent my head to one side, and inhaled, smelling the smell of new leather, of fresh clothes and soap, and of *eau de Susan* still lingering on my skin. I liked it. The jacket creaked as I started forward, and I caught sight of myself in the dresser mirror.

My double, the one from the dream, stared back out at me. Only the roughness of the three-day growth of dark whiskers, and the bruises, were at contrast with the subconscious-me's neatly trimmed beard. Everything else was precisely the same.

I turned my face away rather quickly and paced from the room, out to the van, where the others were waiting.

Show time.

Chapter 28

The moon rose in silver splendor into an October sky strewn with pale clouds and brilliant stars. The clouds churned, a white-foam sea, and the moon was a vast, graceful clipper ship, its sails full of spectral light as it ran before the strength of the cold autumn winds. Pale light bleached each of the uncut stones on the nine-foot wall around Gentleman Johnny Marcone's estate, making edges sharper, shadows blacker, until it looked like a barrier made of gaping white skulls. Trees grew up thick on the other side of the wall, blocking the view of the interior, though no branches extended far enough to provide a way to climb over it.

"We've got to get over the wall," I said to the enormous, dark wolf beside me, keeping my voice low as we all crouched in the shadows of the bushes across the street from Marcone's estate. "There will be security on it. Maybe cameras, maybe infrared beams, maybe something else. I want you to find us a way past it." The wolf flickered her amber eyes toward me and made a soft, assenting growl. Then she simply turned and faded into the darkness, leaving five more furry, crouching shapes grouped around me.

The Alphas didn't exactly inspire confidence, but they had all managed to master enough rudimentary magic to transform themselves into very, very close approximations of wolves, at least. It was something.

Susan had parked the van on a hill leading up to Marcone's estate, and remained with it, in case we needed a quick getaway. When we'd arrived, a nude Tera West and five young people, three female and two male, had leapt out of the van, the Alphas hurriedly tumbling out of their robes.

"Hell's bells," I'd complained, "we're on a public street. Can you be something besides naked, here, people?"

Tera had smirked and, in a liquid shimmer, become a gaunt, dark wolf, a beast fully as large as Denton and his cronies had been, but with a narrower muzzle and cleaner proportions. Like Denton and his crew of *Hexenwulfen,* she kept the exact same shade and color of her eyes, even in wolfish form.

"Well?" I'd demanded of the others. "Let's hurry it up."

Georgia had slipped her lean body from her dark robe and melted in a few seconds into her wolf shape, then had quickly slipped past me to go to Tera. Billy had growled something under his breath as he shrugged out of his robe, catching one sleeve on his arm as he'd begun to change.

Billy-wolf had stumbled over the robe still hanging on to his forepaw, tripped, and tumbled onto the street with a whuff of expelled breath and a little whimper.

I'd rolled my eyes. Billy-the-wolf had snarled and struggled out of his robe, picked it up carefully in his teeth, like a large and particularly grumpy-looking Benji, and put it back in the van.

"Um," one of the other girls had said, a redheaded lass who filled out her robe a little too generously. "We're still a little new at this." She'd covered herself with her arms awkwardly, letting her robe fall from her shoulders as she whispered a little chant, and had become a rather round, hefty-looking she-wolf with dark auburn fur. She'd moved daintily to the edge of the cargo van and had minced, despite her weight, down to the street. The other two young people, a lanky, dark-haired boy and a scrawny girl with mouse-brown hair, had made the change and loped up the hill after Tera, and then we all had moved as quietly as we could to the rear of Marcone's estate.

Surrounded by a high stone wall, the property occupied an entire block, bounded on all four sides by individual streets. None of us had known the layout to Marcone's place, so we'd chosen to approach from the rear, on general principles of sneakiness. I hadn't thought it would be wise to walk in the front door, so I had dispatched Tera to find us a way in, while I'd remained behind with the Alphas.

I found myself tapping my fingers on my thighs as I crouched, restless. I soon realized that if I was tense, the would-be werewolves were twice as keyed up. The darkest-furred one, Billy, I thought, rose to his paws and started away, in the opposite direction from which Tera had gone. Georgia growled at him, Billy growled back, and the other male rose to follow him.

Great, I thought. I couldn't afford to let the Alphas wander off now, no matter how restless they were.

"Hey," I said quietly. "You can't go haring off now. If there's a way inside, Tera will find it."

The wolves all turned their heads, and their very human eyes, toward me.

Billy planted his paws stubbornly and growled.

"Oh, don't give me that," I snapped, glaring at him without meeting his eyes. "You promised you'd play this my way, Billy. This isn't a time to be messing around."

Billy's stance became less certain, and I beckoned all of them toward me. If I could keep them listening until Tera got back, I could at least be sure that they'd be around when I needed them. "Huddle up, everyone," I said. "I want to go over some things before we go in."

There was a brief silence, and then a crowding of furry, heavy bodies, and a snuffling of wet noses. Ten ears pricked up and rotated toward me, and ten bright, human eyes fastened upon me from lupine faces. I suppressed a sudden urge to say, "Good evening, class. I'm your teacher, Mr. Dresden," and instead put on my most serious expression.

"You all know what's at stake tonight," I said. "And that we could all get killed. We're going to be confronting a bunch of law-enforcement people who have gotten hold of some magic that's as black as anything I've ever seen, and are using it to turn themselves into wolves. They've lost control of the power they've grabbed. They're killing people, and if we don't stop them they're going kill a lot more. Especially me, because I know too much. I'm a danger to them.

"But I don't want that. I don't want anyone to get killed. Not us, and not them. Maybe they deserve it. Maybe not. The power they grabbed has turned into a drug for them, and they're not really in control of themselves anymore. I just don't think we'd be much different than them if we went in there planning to wipe them out. It isn't enough to stand up and fight darkness. You've got to stand apart from it, too. You've got to be different from it."

I cleared my throat. "Hell. I'm not good at this. Go for their belts, if you can, just like I did in the alley. Once their belts are off, they're not going to be as crazy, and maybe we'll be able to talk to them." I glanced up at the wall and back down. "Just don't get killed, guys. Do what you have to do to stay alive. That's your first priority. And if you've got to kill them to do it, then don't hesitate."

There was a chorus of growls from around me, led by the wolf Billy, but that was the great thing about being the only human being there—I was the only one who could talk. There wouldn't have been any arguments, even had they disagreed. Their enthusiasm was a little intimidating.

"If you are any louder, wizard," Tera's soft voice came from behind me, "we might as well walk through the front gate." I jumped and looked up to see Tera, naked and human, crouched down a few feet away.

"I wish you wouldn't *do* that," I hissed at her. "Did you find a way in?"

"Yes," she said. "A place where the wall has crumbled. But it is far for you to walk, around along the eastern wall, toward the front of the property. We must run if we are to get inside in time."

I grimaced. "I'm not in any shape to run anywhere."

"It would seem you have little choice. I also saw many streaks of light across the front gate. And there are black boxes with glass eyes every seventy or eighty paces. They do not see the crumbled place. It is a fortunate position."

"Cameras," I muttered. "Hell."

"Come, wizard," Tera said, crouching down on all fours. "We have no time to waste if you are to join us. The pack can cover the distance in moments, but you must hurry."

"Tera. I've had a rough couple of days. I'd fall over in about two minutes if I tried to run somewhere."

The woman blinked passionless amber eyes up at me. "Your point?"

"I'm going over the wall right here," I said.

Tera looked at the wall and shook her head. "I cannot bring the pack over that wall. They are not strong enough to keep changing back and forth, and they have no hands in their wolf form."

"Just me then. I guess you all can find me?"

Tera snorted. "Of course. But it is foolish for you to go over the wall alone. And what if the cameras see you?"

"Let me worry about the cameras," I said. "Help me up to the top. Then you and the Alphas circle around and rendezvous with me."

Tera scowled, the expression dark. "I think this foolish, wizard. If you are too wounded to run, then you are too wounded to go in alone."

"We don't have time," I said with a glance up at the moon, "to argue about this. Do you want my help or don't you?"

Tera let out a sound somewhere between a snort and a snarl, and for a moment tension in her muscles made them stand out hard against her skin. One of the Alphas let out a little whimper, and stepped away from us.

"Very well, wizard," Tera said. "I will show you the nearest camera and help you over the wall. Do not move from where you land. We do not know who is on the other side of the wall, or where."

"Don't worry about me," I said. "Worry about yourself. If there's a good way through the wall, Denton might show up there, too, to go in. Or MacFinn might."

"MacFinn," Tera said, traces of pride in her voice and fear in her eyes, "will not even notice that the wall got in his way."

I grimaced. "Just show me the camera."

Tera led me forward through the dark, silent and naked and looking as though she didn't mind the cold evening at all. The grass was damp, plush, and deep. Tera pointed out the small, silent square of the video camera settled onto the wall across the street, and almost entirely hidden by the shadows of the trees.

I licked my lips and leaned toward the camera, keeping my own form obscured by the bushes. I squinted my eyes and drew in my will, trying to focus. My head started to pound at once, and I felt sweat break out beneath my arms and across my forehead. Hexing up anything mechanical is usually fairly simple. The field of magic that surrounds practitioners of the Art plays havoc with the implements of technology. A passing thought, on the right kind of day, can blow out a cellular telephone or kill a photocopier.

This was the wrong kind of day. That field of energy around me was severely depleted from its usual levels, and the metaphysical "muscles" I would normally use to manipulate that energy were in screaming agony, reflected in pains throughout my body.

But I needed to get inside, and I really did think that I wouldn't be able to make it all the way around the property. I was running on empty already, and too much more would leave me gasping like a fish out of water and wishing I was at home in bed.

I forced calm on my thoughts and focused all the energy I had, and it hurt me, starting in my head and spreading into weary aches in my knees and elbows. But the energy built, and built, and with it the pain, until I could hold it together no longer.

"Malivaso," I whispered, and pushed my hand out at the square shape, like a grade-school girl throwing a baseball wrong handed. The power I'd gathered, though it felt like it was about to split me at the seams, rushed out in an almost impotent little hiccup of magic and swirled drunkenly toward the security camera.

For a long minute, nothing happened. And then there was a flash of light, and a tiny shower of sparks from the rear of the box. Smoke drizzled up from the camera in a quavering plume, and I felt a small surge of triumph. At least I had *something* left in me, even if it was aneurism-causing labor to perform the mildest of tasks.

"All right then," I said a second later, my voice somewhat thready. "Let's go."

We looked around and made sure no cars were about, and then Tera, the Alphas, and I rushed across the road, through some decorative, leafy bushes, to the high stone wall. Tera laced her fingers together to form a stirrup. I put my good foot into it, and pushed up hard. She heaved me up, and half threw me over the wall. I caught myself at the top, saw a car's headlights coming, and swiftly rolled down the other side, falling heavily to damp, muddy earth.

It was dark. It was really dark. I was crouched at the base of the wall, underneath a spreading canopy of bare tree branches and stubborn sycamore leaves. Moonlight filtered through in random places, but it only served to make the dark spots all the more gloomy. My own black leather duster was utterly invisible, and I remembered reading somewhere that the gleam of my eyes and teeth would be the most likely to give me away—but since I didn't feel like sitting in the dark with my eyes closed, I didn't. Instead, I crouched and got my confiscated gun ready in one pocket, and took my ace in the hole out of the other, getting that ready as well.

I shivered, and worked hard to remind myself not to be afraid. Then I waited in the darkness for my allies. And waited. And waited. Time passed, and I knew that a minute would feel like an hour, so I began counting, one number for every deliberate breath.

The wind blew through the trees, brisk and cool. Leaves rustled, and droplets of rainwater fell from the trees around me, making little pattering sounds as they struck my new coat. They clung to the leather in tight beads and caught pieces of moonlight in them, brilliant against the black. The smell of rich earth and damp stone rose up with the wind, and for a moment it did almost feel as though I was in a forest rather than on a crime lord's private estate in the north end of Chicago. I took deep breaths, a little comforted by the illusion, and kept on counting.

And waited.

Nothing happened. No wolves, no sounds.

Nothing.

It wasn't until I got to one hundred that I started to get really nervous, my stomach beginning a slow twist that made weak sensations lace out through my arms and legs like slivers of ice. Where was Tera? Where were the Alphas? It shouldn't have taken them nearly so long to get inside the wall and then to cover the distance back to me. Though the estate was huge, the distance surely meant little to the flashing speed of a wolf.

The evening had obviously been moving along entirely too smoothly, I thought.

Something had gone wrong. I was alone.

Chapter 29

Alone.

It's one of those small words that means entirely too much. Like fear. Or trust. I'm used to working alone. It goes with the territory. Wizards of my level of skill and strength (well, my usual levels) are few and far between—maybe no more than two dozen in the United States, with a slightly higher concentration of them in Europe, Africa, and Asia. But there is a difference between working alone and finding yourself facing a hatful of foes, on a cold night, while wounded, and in the dark, and practically helpless. It took me about ten seconds to become acutely aware of that difference.

Fear settled in comfortably. Fear was something I was used to. I was able to think past it, to focus on my predicament. Yay for me. My body reacted the same old way, keying up for fight or flight, while I forced my breathing to stay even.

The smart thing to do would be to run, to turn around and go back to the van and to have Susan drive me the hell away. Granted, I probably couldn't even climb the wall on my own, but I could have tried.

But I was already committed. I was here to do battle with the forces of evil, such as they were. I had dropped the challenge to them, not the other way around. Besides, if Tera and the kids were in trouble, I was the only one who could help them.

I climbed to my feet, getting out the gun, and moved forward through the woods, in a direction that seemed perpendicular to the line of the stone wall behind me. The woods were thick, sycamores and poplars giving way to evergreens with scratchy, low branches. I slipped through them as best I could, moving as quietly as I could manage. I didn't think I made more noise than the wind did, as it rattled the branches and the fallen leaves, and stirred more droplets of water to fall. In time, maybe three or four minutes, I came to the edge of the woods, and looked out on to Gentleman Johnny Marcone's estate.

It was magnificent, something out of a home-and-garden magazine. You could have put a small golf course in Marcone's backyard. A long ways off, at the front of the property, Marcone's huge white house stood serene and flawless, artistically illuminated by dozens of lights, with a veranda or patio larger than a dance floor plotted out at its rear. Behind it, three enormous square plots, side-by-side, contained lit and lovely gardens, terraced down a gently sloping hill toward me. At the hill's base was a pretty little vale, and there lay a small pond, which I realized after a moment was an enormous, concrete-lined swimming pool, lit from beneath the surface. The pool was irregularly shaped, and one corner of the pool stirred, near the surface. Steam lay thick over the water.

Standing stately sentinel toward the center of the vale was a ring of evergreens, thick and stocky trees that concealed whatever was at their center. Two rounded hillocks decorated the left side of the vale's landscape, one of them surmounted by what looked like a replica of a small, ruined shrine or temple, all cracked marble and fallen columns.

The whole place was well lit, both by silver moonlight and by lighting placed at strategic intervals. The lawn was immaculate, and trees dotted the grounds in the sort of careless perfection that only an army of expensive gardeners could have maintained.

And they say that crime doesn't pay.

I took a position behind a screen of trees and brush and looked around the grounds with careful, stealthy caution. I didn't have long to wait.

There was a rush of motion from beneath one of the trees on the far side of the estate, and a swift form, a dark-furred wolf, Billy, I thought, flew from beneath one tree and toward a patch of dark shadow on the grass, not twenty feet from me. I tensed, and started to rise from my hiding place in the brush, to call out to the wolf as he ran.

A bright red dot of light appeared against the wolf's fur. There was a hollow sound, something I could barely hear, like a politely covered cough. I saw the wolf jerk as a flash of blue feathered against its fur, and then the beast tumbled into a roll and fell to the ground. It struggled for a moment, back to its feet, and reached for the dart in its flanks with its jaws. Its balance wavered, and the wolf staggered to one side and fell. I could see its chest heaving, and one of its rear legs twitched spasmodically. I thought I saw the beast's eyes, Billy's eyes, focus on me for a moment, and then they glazed over and went vacant.

"Nice shot," called a deep, tense voice. In the ring of evergreens, there was motion, and then Denton appeared, walking out across the grass toward the fallen wolf. His dark, short hair was still immaculately rigid. I couldn't see the veins in his forehead, despite the bright light. It was a subtle change in him, one of several. His tie was loose. His jacket was unbuttoned. He moved with less steel in his backbone, more fire in his belly. There was an animal quality to him, a surety and savagery of purpose that had been uncertain before, and what it meant was a lot more significant than the changes that showed on his exterior.

His restraint was gone. Whatever last remnants of doubt or regret that had enabled him to maintain his own self-control, and some measure of control over the other *Hexenwulfen,* had vanished with the blood frenzy in the Full Moon Garage. It was in every line of him now, in each step and every flicker of his eyes.

The man had become a predator.

From the evergreens behind him appeared the rest of the *Hexenwulfen:* Benn, now dressed only in a white dress shirt and a grey business skirt, her legs dark and rippling with muscle in the moonlight; Harris, his ears still sticking out, his freckles dark spots against pale skin, his manner restless and hungry; and Wilson, still in his wrinkled suit, but with the shirt unbuttoned, his potbelly overlapping the belt of dark fur around his waist. He stroked and patted it with his fat fingers. His mouth was set in an odd, dangerous grin.

Denton moved across the grass to the fallen wolf, and nudged it with his toe. "Six," he said. "Did you count six?"

"Six," Benn confirmed, her voice throaty. "Can we have them now?" She reached Denton's side and pressed up against him, lifting one leg to rub against his, baring it to the top of her thigh as she did.

"Not yet," Denton said. He looked around him thoughtfully, and my gaze followed his. Scattered around a circle of perhaps fifty-yards diameter were several dark lumps I had taken to be indentations in the ground, shadows cast by the moon and the grounds lighting. I looked again and saw, with a surge of fearful understanding, that they weren't indentations. They were the wolves, my allies. The dark patch Billy had been running for gave a little whimper, and I thought I saw the moon glint off of Georgia's tawny coat. I looked around and counted the fallen.

Six. I couldn't tell them apart very well, couldn't tell which of them, if any, was Tera, but I counted six fallen wolves upon the ground. All of them, I thought, with a panicked rush of fear. All of them had been taken.

"Come *on,*" Harris said, his voice tight, strained. "Fuck MacFinn, he isn't showing up. Let's take them out, all of them, and go find Dresden."

"We'll get to your belt soon enough, kid," Wilson snorted, his fingers stroking at the fur belt over his belly. "If you hadn't been so stupid as to lose it—"

Harris snarled, and Denton shook Benn from his side to get between the other two men. "Shut up. Now. We don't have time for this. Harris, we'll go after the wizard as soon as we can. Wilson, keep your fat mouth shut, if you like your tongue where it is. And both of you back off." The men made low, growling noises, but they took steps away from one another.

I licked my lips. I was shaking. The gun felt heavy in my hand. There were only the four of them, I thought. They weren't more than thirty feet away. I could start shooting right now. If I got lucky, I could down them all. They were werewolves, but they weren't invincible.

I slipped the safety off of the pistol, and drew in a steadying breath. It was a damn fool thing to do, and I knew it. Life is not the movies. It wasn't likely that I would be able to shoot them all before they could draw and shoot back. But I didn't have much choice.

Denton turned toward the first hillock, with its artfully ruined temple, and waved. "All right," he called. "That's all of them."

A pair of shapes appeared in the lights that shone on the temple, and then came down the hill toward Denton and the *Hexenwulfen*. Marcone was dressed in a flannel shirt, jeans, and a hunter's vest, and he bore a gleaming rifle, an enormous scope mounted on it, in one hand. Hendricks, hulking beside him in muscle-bound silence, was dressed in what looked like black military fatigues, bearing the gun I'd seen earlier, a knife, and various other gear. Hendricks's eyes flickered over Denton and his associates warily.

I stared at Marcone in shock. It took me a moment to pick my jaw up off the ground and to piece together what was going on. Marcone didn't know. He didn't know that Denton and company were out to get him. They must have blamed the other killings on MacFinn and the Alphas.

So now Denton had Marcone and the Alphas there. Once MacFinn arrived, he would be able to kill everyone he wanted dead, everyone who knew what was going on, and be able to make up any story he damned well pleased. Everyone but me, that is. He did not, as yet, have his hands on me.

"These are all we saw on the monitors," Marcone corrected. "There was a malfunction in camera six, at the rear line of the property. Mr. Dresden and such malfunctions tend to go hand in hand."

Dammit.

"Are you sure the wizard isn't one of them?" Denton demanded. "One of these wolves?"

"I think not," Marcone answered. "But I suppose anything is possible."

Denton scowled. "Then he's not here."

"If he truly offered you a challenge, he's here," Marcone said, his tone completely confident. "I'm certain of it."

"And he just watched his werewolf friends get shot down?" Denton asked.

"Wolves run faster than men," Marcone pointed out. "Possibly, he hasn't caught up to them yet. He could even be watching us now."

"You're giving him too much credit," Denton said. But I saw his eyes shift instinctively toward the blackness of the growth of woods. If I stood up, he would be looking right at me. I froze, holding my breath.

"Am I?" Marcone smiled, and leaned down to pluck the feathered dart from Billy's furry flank. "The tranquilizers likely won't hold these beasts for very long. Decisions need to be made, gentlemen. And if you are to hold to your end of the bargain, you had best get to work producing."

I don't know if Marcone noticed Benn's sudden tension, the way she slid her hands over her stomach, but I did. "Kill these dogs now," she said in a low, heated voice. "It prevents complications later in the evening."

Marcone tsked. "Shortsighted. Let MacFinn tear them to pieces when he arrives, and any medical examiner won't bother to look for the tranquilizers. If one of you does it, it will create awkward questions once forensics takes a look at things. And I thought that was the point of you coming to me with this offer. Reducing questions."

Benn lifted her lips away from her teeth, and I saw the tips of her breasts stiffen beneath her white shirt. "I hate slimy scum like you, Marcone," she purred, sliding her hand from her thigh up over her hip and beneath the buttons of her shirt. Marcone's eyes narrowed on her, and as though connected to the crime lord by a telepathic leash, Hendricks made one simple motion, a shift of his forward arm, that chambered a round on the gun with a cold little *click-clack*.

Denton gave Marcone a sharp look and took hold of Benn's wrist with his hand. The woman tensed for a second, resisting him, but then she allowed Denton to draw her hand away from the belt that was surely beneath her shirt. Denton released her, and Benn lowered her hands, visibly relaxing. Marcone and Hendricks never so much as blinked, or broke a sweat. Fragile situations like this one were evidently second nature to them.

I let out the breath I'd been holding for a long time. Six to one and ready for a fight. If I attacked them now, I didn't have a prayer. If I tried to move, to fade back into the trees, they would be likely to notice me. Damn.

Denton glanced at the trees once more, and I held my breath again. "Don't worry, Marcone," he said. "We'll turn the wizard over to you, once we find him. No questions asked."

"That being the case," Marcone said, "I suggest you start looking, while I make preparations for Mr. MacFinn. Please remember that I want Dresden alive, if possible."

My throat constricted, and if I hadn't been holding my breath, I think I would have let out a squeak. What in the world could John Marcone want with me, after the incident in the parking garage? Nothing good, certainly. Nothing I wanted to think about. Damn, damn. This night was getting spookier all the time.

"Of course, Mr. Marcone," Denton said, his tone a little too polite. "Do you have any suggestions of where we should start looking?"

Marcone ignored the sarcasm, flicked a switch on the sight on his rifle, and pointed it negligently at the tree line. "Over there ought to do."

The red dot of the laser sight settled onto a leaf six inches to the left of my head, and the thready pulse of fear in my chest turned into an icy white streak of terror.

Damn, damn, damn.

Chapter 30

If I ran, I would be seen and pursued, and likely torn apart. If I remained where I was hidden, I would be found and *then* torn apart, or shot, or tranquillized and given to Johnny Marcone. A poor set of choices, but I wasn't going to get any better ones by sitting on my ass. So I got my feet underneath me and started easing back into the woods, the confiscated semiautomatic still in my hand.

"Hold it," Denton said. "Did you hear that?"

"What?" Benn asked. I could hear the sudden, eager tension in her voice, and I struggled not to make any more noise as I hurried my pace back into the shelter of the deeper trees.

"Quiet," Denton snarled, and I froze in place. Wind and rain were the only sounds for a few moments, in the chilly autumn night. "Over there," Denton said after a moment. "I think I heard it over that way."

"Could be a raccoon. Squirrel. Or a cat," Wilson suggested.

"Don't be naive," came Marcone's voice, laced with scorn. "It's *him*."

There was the immediate sound of a slide being worked on a handgun, a round being chambered into place. "Move forward," said Denton. "That way. Fan out and we'll take him. Watch yourself. We don't know all of what he can do. Don't take any chances." His voice came closer as he spoke, and I nearly bolted. There was a chorus of assenting sounds, and another couple of weapons being readied. Footsteps came toward me through the grass.

After that, I did bolt, just stood up and ran bent over as low as

I could. There was a shout from behind me and a bark of a gun being fired. I pointed the semiautomatic above me, afraid to fire back at them for fear of hitting Tera or one of the Alphas by mistake, and pulled the trigger twice. The gunshots must have surprised them, because Denton and the others scattered for cover behind the nearest trees.

I ran deeper into the woods, marshaling my thoughts. I had gained a little time, but time to do what? Running would only put me up against a stone wall. I doubted I'd be able to climb it, with a bum foot and a wounded shoulder. And I could only play the rabbit in the woods for so long before I was found.

Dammit, I thought. *I'm no rabbit.*

It was about time the hunters became the hunted around here. I moved ahead, silent and intent now, and scanned around me, searching for the sort of place I would need. I found it almost at once, an inward-curving hollow at the base of a large tree, and slid into it, nestling into the wood's embrace. I put my head down, hiding the paleness of my face and the gleam of the whites of my eyes. And Listened.

They came forward quietly, and without any lights flickering around at the edges of my vision. Maybe Denton and his cronies were getting used to the darkness. They were moving forward in a ragged line, twenty or thirty paces apart, and somehow keeping mostly parallel. They were all still on two feet, by the sound of the steps, thank my lucky stars. If they'd gone to wolf form they might have had me—of course, on two legs, they still had hands free to hold guns of their own. There are pros and cons to everything, I suppose.

I held my breath when footsteps approached me. They came within ten feet. Then five. I felt the brush stir when someone walked past no more than a foot away, making leaves brush up against me. They stopped, right there, and I heard a little, whuffling sound. Sniffing. I thought of the aroma of my brand-new leather jacket, and clenched my jaws down slightly, tension thrumming through me and making my legs shake.

About ten billion years went by. And then whoever it was began walking again, forward and past me. I would have let out a sigh of relief, if the most dangerous part of my plan wasn't still to come.

I got up from my hiding place, stepped forward and jammed the barrel of the semiautomatic against the back of the neck of the person before me. It was Denton. His back arched and he sucked in a stunned breath.

"Quiet," I whispered. "Don't move."

Denton hissed, but froze in place. "Dresden. I should kill you right now."

"Try it," I said, and thumbed back the hammer of the gun. "But after the loud noise, remember to keep going down the tunnel and toward the light."

Denton's shoulders shifted a fraction and I said, "Don't move your arms, at all. Reach for that belt and I'll kill you before you're halfway to furry, Denton. Drop the gun."

Denton moved his fingers enough to close the safety on his gun and let it fall. "Not bad, Dresden," he said. "But this isn't going to do you any good. Put the gun down, and we can talk about this."

"Smooth, polite, nice delivery," I said. "They teach you that at the FBI?"

"Don't make this any harder on yourself than it has to be, Dresden," Denton said, his voice toneless. "You can't get out of this."

"They always say that," I said and used my free hand, though it made my shoulder twitch, to take him by the collar and hold him steady. "My arm's feeling a little weak," I said. "Don't do anything to make me slip."

I felt his body tense at my words. "What are you doing, Dresden?"

"You and me, we're going to turn around," I said with a little shove of the gun against his neck to emphasize the point. "And then you're going to order all of your people out of the trees and back into the light. They'll each call to you from there, so that I know they're in front of me, and then we're going to go see them."

"What do you hope to accomplish here, Dresden?" Denton said.

I let go of his neck, pressed close, and reached around him to remove the wolf-pelt belt from around his middle. I saw his jawline shift as I took the belt away, but he remained still and quiet, his hands in the air. "I was just going to ask you the same thing, Denton," I said. "Now, call your buddies out of the trees."

Denton might have been a cool customer, maybe a treacherous sneak, maybe a murderer, but one thing he wasn't was a fool. He called out to the other three agents, and told them to get out of the trees.

"Dent?" Wilson called. "Are you okay?"

"Just do it," Denton answered. "It will all be clear in a minute."

They did it. I heard them move out of the woods and call to him from the cut, level grass of Marcone's estate. "Now," I said. "Walk. Don't trip, because I swear to God I would rather blow your head off over a misunderstanding than get suckered by a trick and killed."

"Maybe you should put the safety on," Denton said. "Because if you kill me, you'll never get out of here alive."

I hate it when the bad guys have a point, but I chose to err on the side of Denton getting blown apart, and left the safety where it was. I slung the wolf belt over my shoulder, took Denton's collar again, and said, "Walk." He did. We walked out of the deep darkness of the woods and into the light.

I kept at the edge of the darkness and put a tree's trunk to my back, keeping Denton between me and the bad guys. They were spread out, the three of them, in a half circle about thirty feet away, and they all had guns. It would have been one hell of a marksman who could get at me with Denton's broad, solid form in front of me, and the shadows veiling me, but I didn't take chances. I crouched down behind him some, leaving nothing but the corner of my head and one eye showing. At least that way, I thought, if they shot me, I'd never feel it.

"Uh. Hi guys," I said a bit lamely. "I've got your boss. Put the guns down, take your belts off, and walk away from them nice and slow, or I kill him." A part of me, probably the smarter part, groaned at my course of action and started cataloguing the number of federal and state criminal codes I was breaking into tiny pieces by taking a member of the Federal Bureau of Investigation hostage and threatening to kill him and attempting to take hostage three more. I stopped counting broken laws at ten, and waited to see the *Hexenwulfen's* response.

"To hell with you," Benn snarled. The silver-haired young woman dropped her gun, and ripped off her shirt, revealing a torso that was impressive in a number of senses—and another wolf-hide belt. "I'll tear your fucking throat out myself."

"Deborah," Denton said, his voice strained. "Don't. Please."

"Go ahead, bitch," growled Harris. His big ears created little half-moon shadows of blackness on the sides of his head. "Denton buys it and we all get promoted. Hell, the wizard will probably shoot you, while he's at it." Benn whirled toward Harris, lifting her hands as though she would strangle him, fingers clenching like talons.

"Shut up," I said. "Both of you. Put your guns down. Now."

Harris sneered at me. "You won't, Dresden. You don't have the guts."

"Roger," Denton said very quietly. "You're an idiot. The man's in a corner. Now. Put *down* your gun."

I blinked, surprised at the unexpected support. It made me instantly suspicious. That Marcone was out of sight did not mean that he was out of mind, either. Where was he? Crouched somewhere, aiming that rifle at me? I kept an eye out for bright red dots.

"That's right," I appended to Denton's statement. "You *are* an idiot. Drop the gun. You too, Wilson," I added, glancing at the overweight agent. "And you and Benn, take the belts off, too. Leave them on the ground."

"Do it," Denton confirmed, and I got a little more nervous. The man was relaxed now, not resisting me. His voice was solid, confident, unimpressed. That was bad. Denton's pack obeyed him, if reluctantly. Benn dropped the belt to the ground in the same way Scrooge might have let fall a string of diamonds, a visible ache in the motion. Wilson grunted as his belt came unfastened, and his belly flopped out a little as the catch released. He left it on the ground by his gun. Harris glared at me, but he lowered his gun, too.

"Now, step back. All of you."

"Yes," Denton said. "Harris, Wilson. Step back to the trees and bring out what we left there."

"Hey," I said. "What the hell are you talking about? Don't move, any of you." Harris and Wilson smirked at me, and began walking toward the trees. "Get your asses back here."

"Shoot at them, Mr. Dresden," Denton said, "and you will have to take your gun off me. I think I can reach it, if you do that, and turn this into a fight. You are resourceful, and intelligent, but you are also wounded. I don't think you could overcome me in hand to hand."

I glanced between the two men and Denton. "Dammit," I said. "What are you up to, Denton? You try anything funny, anything at all, and you're not going to live to regret it."

"I'm with the FBI. I don't do anything that could be construed as funny, Mr. Dresden."

I swore quietly, and could all but feel Denton's mouth stretch into a smile. "Why?" I asked him. "Why did you get involved with these belts? Why are you doing this?"

Denton began to shrug, but evidently thought better of it. "Too many years of seeing men like Marcone laugh at the law. Of seeing people hurt by him, death, misery brought on by him and people like him. I was tired of just watching. I decided to stop him. And men like him."

"By killing them," I said.

"I was given the power. I used it."

"What gives you the right to mandate their deaths?"

"What gives them the right," Denton asked, "to kill? Should I stand by and let them slaughter, Dresden, if I can stop it? I have the power, and the responsibility to use it."

I felt a little shiver run through me, as the words struck close to home. "And the other people? The innocents who have died?"

Denton hesitated. His reply was quiet. "It was unfortunate. An accident. It was never my intention."

"The belts do more than make you fuzzy, Denton. They change the way you think. The way you act."

"I can control my people," Denton began.

"Like you did last month?" I asked.

He swallowed, and said nothing.

"And you knew, didn't you? You knew that I'd find out. That's why you sent me to the Full Moon Garage."

The vein on his forehead pulsed. "After the deaths, I was warned about a governing body. A sort of magic police. The White Council. That you worked for them."

I almost laughed. "Yeah, well someone told you part of the story, anyway, Denton. That's why you messed up MacFinn's circle, isn't it? You needed a patsy and you turned MacFinn loose knowing that the Council would suspect him. The Streetwolves for the cops, and MacFinn for the Council."

Denton snarled. "Necessary sacrifices. There was work to be done, Dresden."

"Oh yeah? As one of the aforementioned sacrifices, I don't find myself agreeing with you," I said. "To hell with the law, right? That's what you're saying—that you're above the law. Like Marcone."

Denton grew tense again and turned his head a bit toward me. Like he might have been listening.

I pressed him, hard, desperate to reach him. If I could, I might get out of this situation after all. "These belts, man, the power they've given you. It's *bad*. You can't handle it. It's gotten into your head and you aren't thinking straight. Give them up. You can still walk away from all of this, do the right thing. Come on, Denton. Don't throw away everything you fought for all those years. There's a better way than this."

Denton was silent for a long time. Harris and Wilson disappeared into the thick ring of pine trees. Benn watched us, her eyes bright, her body muscled and firm in the moonlight, her breasts rather pretty and distracting as she breathed. She looked from the pair of us to the fur belt on the ground, alternately, and her breaths became ragged. "Look at her," I said. "Those belts are like a drug. Is this the kind of person she was? Is this the kind of person you want to be? Wilson, Harris, were they always like they are now? You're turning into monsters, man. You've got to get out of this. Before you're all the way gone."

Denton closed his eyes. Then shook his head once. "You're a decent man, Mr. Dresden. But you've got no idea of how the world works. I'm sorry you've gotten in the way." He opened his eyes again. "Necessary sacrifices."

"Dammit," I said. "Don't you see that this won't do you any good? Even if you do get away with wiping out everyone here tonight, Murphy is going to piece together what happened."

Denton glanced at me and said, like a mantra, "Necessary sacrifices."

I swallowed, suddenly more cold than I had been. It was eerie, the way Denton said the words—so matter-of-fact, calm, rational. There was no doubt in him, when he should have been afraid. Only fools and madmen know that kind of certainty. And I had already noted that Denton was no fool.

Harris and Wilson emerged from the trees, carrying something between them. Someone, hooded, arms and legs bound. Harris had a knife in one hand, and it was against the base of the hood, which looked to be a pillowcase. His big ears and freckles were at sharp odds with the arrogant competence with which he held the knife.

"Damn you," I said quietly. Denton said nothing. Benn's eyes glittered in the moonlight, bright and vacant of anything but lust and hunger.

The two agents brought the prisoner over, and Wilson dropped the legs. Harris kept the knife steady, while the overweight man went to remove the hood, but I had already seen the cast on the prisoner's arm.

Murphy's face was pale, her golden hair bleached to silver by the moonlight, and falling down around her eyes. Her mouth was covered in cloth or duct tape, one of the two, and there was blood clotted at the base of one nostril, a bruise purpling over one eye. She blinked for a moment, and then kicked at Wilson. With her legs bound, it was ineffective, and when Harris snarled and pressed the knife against her throat, she stopped struggling. Her blue eyes glared in fury at Harris and then Wilson. And then they settled on me and widened.

"Kill me, Mr. Dresden," Denton said quietly, "and Harris will cut the Lieutenant's throat. Benn will go for her gun, as will Wilson. Likely, they will kill you. And then they will kill these wolves you brought with you, your allies. But even if you get all of us first, Murphy will be dead, and you will be holding the weapon that killed four agents of the FBI."

"You bastard," I said. "You cold-blooded bastard."

"Necessary sacrifices, Mr. Dresden," Denton said, but it wasn't a calm phrase anymore. It was eager, somehow, warmth curving around and through the words like a lover's hands. "Drop your gun."

"No," I said. "I won't." He wouldn't kill another cop. Would he?

"Then Murphy dies," Denton said. "Harris."

The redhead's shoulders bunched, and Murphy tried to scream, through the gag. I cried out and swung the barrel of the gun toward Harris.

Denton's elbow came back into my gut and then his fist snapped up into my nose, casting a field of stars across my vision. The gun went off, pointed somewhere, but then Denton slapped it from my hand and drove another blow into my throat that sent me sprawling to the ground, unable to breathe or to move.

Denton stooped to recover the gun and said, "You should have shot me while you had the chance, Mr. Dresden, instead of moralizing." He pointed it at me, and I watched his lips curve into a slow, hungry smile. "Beautiful moon tonight," he said. "Sort of reminds me of a story. How did it go . . . ?"

I tried to tell him where he could stick the moon and his story, but it came out a strangled gasp. I still couldn't move. It hurt too much.

Denton thumbed back the trigger, sighted down the barrel at my left eye, and said, "Ah, yes. 'And I'll huff. And I'll puff. And I'll blow your house down.' Good-bye, wizard."

Death by nursery tale. Hell's bells.

Chapter 31

The barrel of Denton's gun looked bigger and deeper than the national debt as it swung to bear on my face. His grey eyes glittered down the sights at me, and I saw the decision to pull the trigger flash across them. Before he could, I met his eyes hard, shoved myself out toward him with a sudden screaming pain in my temples, and locked him into a soulgaze.

There was a rushing sensation, as there usually was, a feeling of movement forward and then down, like being sucked into a whirlpool. I rode the sensation into Denton's head, a brief doubt crossing my mind. Maybe getting shot would have been better than wading heart deep into Denton's soul.

I can't describe what I found there very well. Try to imagine a place, a beautifully ordered structure, like the Parthenon or Monticello. Imagine that everything is balanced, everything is in proportion, everything is smooth and secure. Stick in blue skies overhead, green grass all around, puffy white clouds, flowers, and children running and playing.

Now, add a couple hundred years of wear and tear to it. Dull the edges. Round the corners a little. Imagine water stains, and worn spots where the wind has gotten to it. Turn the skies dirty brown with smog. Kill the grass, and replace it with tall, ugly ragweed. Ditch the flowers, and leave in their places only dried up, skeletal rose vines. Age the male children into adult winos, faces haggard with despair and self-loathing and flushed with drink, and the girls into tired, jaded strumpets, faces hard, eyes cold and calculating. Give the place of beauty an aura of rage and feral abandon, where the people who walk about watch the shadows like hungry cats, waiting to pounce.

And then, after all of that, after all the cares and trials and difficulties of the world a cop inhabits have been fairly represented, coat everything in a thick, sticky black sludge that smells like swamps and things that attract dun-colored flies. Paint it on, make it a coating that emphasizes the filth, the decay, the despair all around, that brings out that painful decline to the utmost degree. The sludge makes things stronger, and more bitter, more rotten, more putrid all at the same time.

That was Denton, inside. A good man, jaded by years and poisoned by the power that had taken control of him, until that good man had been buried and only the filth and decay remained. Until the existence of the man who had once been was only a bitter reminder that made the man who was now seem all the more downfallen by comparison.

I understood Denton's pain and his rage, and I understood how the dark power he'd taken had pushed him over the edge. There was an image of him kneeling at someone's feet as a wolf-fur belt was passed into his hands, and then it was gone. Knowing the man he had once been made clear to me the beast he had become, all violence and hunger and craving.

I felt tears on my cheeks, and violent shudders shaking down my spine. I could pity Denton, and the others with him, but now, more than ever, they scared the crap out of me. I had bought myself a few seconds, at least, with the soulgaze—but would it be enough to keep Denton from blowing my head off?

Denton stared at me as the soulgaze broke and we were released. He wasn't reacting well to whatever it was he had seen inside of me. His face had gone white, and his hand was trembling, the barrel of the gun wavering every which way. He lifted his other hand to mop beads of cold sweat away from his face.

"No," Denton said, white showing all around the grey irises of his eyes. "No, wizard." He raised his gun. "I don't believe in hell. I won't let you." He screamed then, at the top of his lungs. "I won't let you!" I tensed up, preparing for a futile attempt to throw myself out of the way of a speeding bullet.

"Yes," said a calm voice. "You will." A bright red dot appeared right on the middle of Denton's chest, cheerful as a Christmas light. I twisted my head around to see Marcone walking over the turf, his weapon pointed steadily at Denton, Hendricks looming to one side. Denton's lackeys were watching Marcone with bright, steady eyes. Murphy lay on the grass, her feet toward me, her head away. I couldn't see what condition she was in, and both fear and frustration leapt up into me, for her sake.

"Marcone," Denton said. His back straightened and his eyes narrowed. "You treacherous scum."

Marcone clucked with his teeth. "Our bargain was that you would bring him to me alive. Not execute him. Additionally, you may want to rethink the wisdom of using your own weapons. Let MacFinn kill him when he arrives."

"If he arrives," Denton snarled.

"My spotters," Marcone said, "tell me that the animals I sent out with them went mad with fear about two minutes ago, three miles west of here. I think it will not take him much longer to show up, Mr. Denton." His smile widened, but his money-colored eyes grew harder. "Now. Shall we cease antagonizing one another and finish our business?" Marcone lowered the rifle and flicked the laser sight off.

Denton looked from me to Marcone, and I saw the blackness rise up in his eyes, gather behind them, and get ready to come rolling out. "Marcone," I said. "Just shoot him now."

"I think we've both had enough of your attempts to divide and conquer, Mr. Dresden," Marcone said, his voice bored. "You're beaten. Acknowledge it with grace."

I watched a slow smile spread over Denton's face as he kept the gun pointed at my head. My voice rose by a couple notes of alarm. "I mean it, John. I really do, I shit you not. This entire thing is about them killing you."

"What a vulgar reassurance," Marcone said. "Agent Denton, we have a few details to attend to. Lower your gun and let us be about them."

"I don't think so," Denton said. And he pointed the gun at Hendricks and started pulling the trigger. The gun roared so many times, so quickly, that I couldn't tell how often Denton fired.

Hendricks snapped back onto his heels and was driven flat onto his back by the force of the bullets slamming into him. He didn't have time to twitch, much less scream, and he dropped like a felled tree. I felt it in the earth when his massive body hit the ground.

Marcone started to raise his gun, but Wilson and Harris hurtled at his back and dragged him to the ground, pounding on him with their fists. Marcone writhed like an eel and slipped away from them, but Denton stepped into his path and thrust the gun into Marcone's face.

"That's enough," he said, his voice gone hoarse. "Get them all and take them to the pit. MacFinn will be here any moment."

I took the moment to roll to my hands and knees and attempt to slip away unnoticed, but was brought up short by a pair of bare, muscular, feminine legs. My gaze followed the legs up, past the skirt, to a magnificently bare-breasted torso encircled by a wolf-pelt belt, and then to a face dominated by eyes made eerie by the lack of anything recognizably sentient in them. Benn smiled at me, set her foot against my wounded shoulder, and with a sadistic twist of her ankle and a shove of her muscled leg, sent searing pain screaming through my body, making me crumple to the ground in agony.

I remember them dragging me across the grounds. We passed into the ring of evergreens, and I remember thinking that any sounds originating in that circle of pines would be heavily muffled by their branches and needles, further muffled by the trees surrounding the property, as well as the high stone wall. Gunshots, for example, might not even be heard at all, off the property. It was the clearest thought I had while my shoulder exploded.

The next thing I remember was being shoved roughly forward. I fell, straight and hard in the dispassionate grip of gravity, and after long enough for me to start to suck in a breath, I hit water. It was only about six or eight inches deep, and beneath it was swirling, soft mud. I had a brief pang for my leather duster and then I sank down into the water, my hands slipping into the mud and getting stuck there. Cold water burbled around my face, and felt nice, for a moment, on my aching shoulder.

Someone grabbed me by the collar and hauled me out of the water, to sit on my butt. Hands steadied me, and I sat with my shoulder aching and my head whirling until I could squint up at who was there.

Murphy dropped to one knee in the water beside me and smoothed back my damp hair. "Dresden," she said. "You okay?"

I took a look around me. I was at the bottom of an enormous pit, a square maybe twenty feet deep and twice that across. Muddy water, maybe from the rain, covered the bottom of the pit, and the moon tinted its surface silvery brown. Directly above the pit's center, maybe forty feet above me, was a square made of wooden planks, maybe five by five. It was a hunter's platform, suspended by ropes leading from the circle of evergreens that surrounded the pit. I could see the tops of the trees against the moon and the clouds.

"Dresden," Murphy said again. "Are you all right?"

"I'm alive," I said. I blinked at her for a second and then said, "I thought they killed you."

Her blue eyes sparkled briefly. Her hair was a mess, and her jeans and flannel shirt were rumpled and soaked with muddy water. She was shivering from the cold. "I thought they had, too. But they stopped as soon as Denton took you out, and tossed me down here. I can't figure why they didn't do the deed themselves, instead of leaving it to MacFinn."

I grimaced. "Trying to cover their tracks from the White Council," I said. "Denton wants MacFinn to take the fall for all the deaths. I think he's lost it."

"I always wind up in the nicest places when I hang with you, Dresden."

"You were tied up," I said. "How'd you get loose?"

"She had help," someone said in a slurred, heavy voice. "For all the good it will do her." I turned my head to see a naked and dirty Tera West, sitting with her back against another wall of mud. There were five soggy, motionless forms lying around her, the Alphas in their wolf-shapes. Tera held their heads upon her lap, up out of the water. She looked bedraggled and anguished, touching each of them in turn, very gently. Her amber eyes were dull.

"I don't get it," I said. "Why did they stick us down here? Marcone just keeps a pit trap dug in his yard?"

"He was planning on trapping MacFinn down here until morning." Tera said. "When he would be vulnerable."

"Whoa, whoa," Murphy said, face pensive. "You're saying Denton was responsible for the deaths? All of them?"

"One way or another. Yeah." I gave Murphy the rundown on Denton. The way he'd gotten the belts for him and his people, lost control of the power they'd given him, and set up the Streetwolves and then MacFinn to take the blame.

Murphy broke out into acidic swearing. "That was the angle I was missing. Dammit. No wonder Denton was so hot to keep you off of the case and out of the way, and why he wanted to find you so bad after the scene at MacFinn's place. That's how he kept showing up everywhere so fast, too—he already knew that someone was dead."

There were shouts from above, and we looked up to see

Marcone swing out from the edge of the pit. He hung limply from a rope. His eyes were closed. I watched as he was drawn up in a series of short jerks until his bowed head bumped the bottom of the hunter's platform above and then was left there.

"What the hell?" Murphy said, her voice soft.

"Bait," I replied. I closed my eyes for a moment. "Denton's stringing him up as bait for MacFinn. The loup-garou comes in, jumps up to get Marcone, then Denton cuts the rope and drops MacFinn down in here."

"With us," Murphy said quietly. I felt her shivers grow a little more severe. "They're going to drop that thing into this pit with us. Oh, God, Harry."

"Denton or one of his people must have gotten some silver bullets made," I said. "They'll just let MacFinn slaughter us, then shoot him from up there." I squinted up at the edge of the pit. "Pretty good plan."

"What can we do?" Murphy asked. She hugged herself, hard.

I shook my head. "I don't know."

"Nothing," Tera said quietly. Murphy and I turned to look at her. One of the Alphas was stirring, Billy maybe, and wobbled and fell when he tried to sit up. But at least he could hold his head up out of the water. "Nothing," she repeated. "We are beaten."

I closed my eyes and tried to order my thoughts, to push the pain and fatigue back down and put together some sort of plan. Murphy settled beside me, a shivering spot against my side. The cast on her arm pressed against my ribs. I opened my coat, more a polite gesture than anything else, given that it, too, was soaked, and slipped the edge of it around her shoulders with my arm. Her back stiffened and she flashed me a look of indignation, but after a second just pressed as far under the coat as she could.

After a moment, she spoke. Her voice came out quiet, uncertain—a far cry from her normal, brisk tones. "I've done some thinking, Dresden. I've decided that there's a reasonable chance you aren't involved with the killings."

I smiled a little. "That's real big of you, Murph. Doesn't what Denton did to you sort of prove I'm not involved?"

She half smiled and shook her head. "No, Harry. It just means that he wants to kill you and me both. It doesn't mean that I trust everything you're saying."

"He wants me dead, Murph. That should mean something in my favor, shouldn't it?"

"Not really," she said, and squinted up at the top of the pit. "From what I can tell, Denton wants pretty much everybody dead. And you could still be lying to me."

"I'm not, Murph," I said, my voice soft. "Cross my heart."

"I can't just take your word on it, Harry," she whispered. "There are too many people dead. My men. My people. Civilians, the ones I'm supposed to protect. The only way to be sure is to take you all, everyone involved, and sort things out with you behind bars."

"No," I said. "There's more to it than what you can prove, Murph, more than what's going to stand up in court. Come on. You and me, we've known each other for years. You should be able to trust me by now, right?"

"I should be able to," Murphy agreed. "But after what I've seen, all the blood and death . . ." She shook her head. "No, Harry. I can't trust anyone anymore." She half smiled and said, "I still like you, Dresden. But I can't trust you."

I tried to match her smile, but my feelings were in too much turmoil. Pain, mostly. Physical pain, and a deeper heart hurt, both for Murphy's sake and for the sake of our friendship. She was so alone. I wanted to go to the rescue, somehow, to make her hurting go away.

She'd have spit in my face if I'd tried. Murphy wasn't the sort of person who wanted to be rescued, from anything. That she accepted as much comfort as my wet coat offered her came as a surprise to me.

I looked around the pit again intently. The other Alphas were recovering, enough to sit up, but apparently not enough to move. Tera just sat with her back against the wall, defeated and exhausted. Marcone swung from the platform high above me, not moving, though I thought I might have heard a moan from him at one point. I felt a pang of sympathy for him. However much of a heartless bastard he might be, no one deserved to dangle like bait from a hook.

The Alphas, Tera, Marcone, Murphy. They were all where they were because of me. It was my fault we were there, my doing that we were all about to die. Carmichael, the poor jerk, was dead, also because of me. So were other good cops. So was Hendricks.

I had to do something about it.

"I need to get out of here," I told Murphy. "Get me out of here, and maybe I can do something."

Murphy turned her head toward me. "You mean . . . ?" She waved the fingers of her unbroken arm in a vaguely mystic gesture.

I nodded. I still had my ace in the hole. "Something like that."

"Right. So how do we get you out of here?"

"You going to trust me, Murph?"

Her jaw clenched. "It doesn't look as though I have much choice, does it?"

I smiled back at her, and rose to my feet, sloshing around in the water. "Maybe we could dig into the walls a bit. Make climbing holes."

"You'll probably get shot once you get to the top," Murphy said.

"No," I said, "I don't think they'll want to hang around the pit with MacFinn coming. They're bloodthirsty, but not stupid."

"So," Murphy said. "All we need to do is get you up to the top of the pit, and then you're going to go one-on-four with a bunch of armed FBI agents-cum-werewolves and beat them in time to go up against the loup-garou that we couldn't stop before with all of your magical gizmos and a building full of police officers."

"Essentially," I answered.

Murphy looked up at me and then shrugged and let out a short, defiant laugh. She stood up too, flicked her hair back from her eyes with a toss of her head, and said, "I guess it could be worse."

There was a soft sound from above and behind me. Murphy froze, staring upward, her eyes becoming almost impossibly wide.

I turned my head very slowly.

The loup-garou crouched up at the lip of the pit, huge and gnarled and muscled and deadly. Its foaming jaws were open, showing the rows of killing teeth. Its eyes gleamed with scarlet flames in the moonlight, and they were fastened on the dangling figure of Gentleman Johnny Marcone. I quivered, and the motion made a slight sound against the water. The beast turned its head down, and when it saw me its eyes narrowed to glowing slits, and it let out a harsh, low growl. Its claws dug into the earth at the edges of the pit, tearing through it like sand.

It remembered me.

My heart started ripping a staccato rhythm in my chest. That same raw, sharp, primitive fear I'd felt before, the fear of simply being jumped on and *eaten,* returned in full force and for a moment swept away all thoughts and plans.

"You had to say that," I said to Murphy, my voice wan and pale. "Happy? It's worse."

Chapter 32

"Okay," I said, fear making my voice weak. "This is bad. This is very, very bad."

"Wish I had my pistol," Murphy said, her tone resolute. "I wish we'd had some more time to talk things out, Harry."

I glanced over at Tera. One of the Alphas, the mouse-haired girl in her wolf-shape, was leaning against her and whimpering. "Close your eyes," Tera said softly and covered the little wolf's eyes with her hand. Her amber eyes met mine, without hope, without any sparkle of life.

They were going to die because of me. Dammit all, it wasn't fair. I hadn't done anything grossly stupid. It wasn't fair to have come so far, sacrificed so much, and to buy it down here in the mud, like some kind of burrowing bug. I searched the pit again desperately, but it was a fiendishly simple and complete trap. There were no options down here.

My eyes went up. Straight up.

"Marcone!" I shouted. "John Marcone! Can you hear me?"

The limp figure suspended above me stirred weakly. "What do you want, Mr. Dresden?"

"Can you move?" I asked. The loup-garou growled, low, and started pacing a circuit of the pit, glowing eyes flashing between us down at the bottom and Marcone, trying to decide who to rip apart first.

"An arm," Marcone confirmed a few seconds later.

"Do you still keep that knife on you? The one I saw at the garage?"

"Denton and his associates searched me and found it, I am afraid," came Marcone's voice.

"Dammit all. You're a miserable, stupid bastard for making a deal with Denton, Marcone. Now do you believe he wanted to kill you all along?"

The figure above me wiggled and writhed, swinging from the ropes that held him trussed up there. "Yes, do tell me that you told me so with your last breath, Mr. Dresden. I was already rather acutely aware of that," Marcone said, his voice dry. "But perhaps I'll yet have a chance to make amends."

"What are you doing?" I asked. I kept my eyes on the loup-garou, as it circled the pit, and kept myself opposite the creature, where I could see it.

"Reaching for the knife they *didn't* find," Marcone replied. He grunted, and then I saw a flicker of light on something shiny up above me.

"Forget it," Murphy said quietly, stepping close to my side as she watched Marcone. "He's just going to cut himself loose and leave us to rot here."

"We won't get the chance to rot," I pointed out. But I thought she was right.

Marcone started to spin slowly on his rope, wriggling around until his whole body was rotating on the end of it. He began to speak, his voice calm. "Ironic, isn't it? I'd planned to wait for the creature on the platform and tempt it into the pit. There are some nets ready to drop on it, after that. I would have held it until morning."

"You do know that it's right beneath you now, don't you, John?" I asked.

"Mr. Dresden," Marcone said crossly. "I've asked you not to call me that."

"Whatever," I said, but I had to admire the raw courage of the man to banter while dangling up there like a ripe peach.

"I use this place to conduct noisy business," Marcone said. "The trees muffle the sound, you see. You can barely hear even shotgun blasts on the other side of the wall." He continued to spin on the rope, slow and lazy, a shadow against the moon and the stars.

"Well. That's nice," I said, "and despicable." The loup-garou looked down at me and snarled, and I took an involuntary step back from it. The mud wall of the pit stopped me.

"Oh, quite," Marcone agreed. "But necessary."

"Is there *anything* you're not shameless about, Marcone?" I asked.

"Of course. But you don't think I'm going to tell you, do you? Now, be quiet if you please. I don't need the distraction." And then I saw Marcone's arm curl in and straighten outward. There was a flutter of metallic motion in the air, and a snapping sound from the base of one of the ropes that held the platform suspended, at its far end where it was secured to one of the pine trees.

The rope abruptly sagged, and the platform—and Marcone with it—swayed drunkenly. Marcone grunted, and bounced against his ropes a few times, making the whole affair of ropes lurch about—and then the damaged line snapped and came entirely free. It whipped out toward Marcone, lost momentum, and then fell through the evening air.

Straight down into the pit in front of me. One end was still attached to the platform above, now off center from the pit and listing to one side.

I blinked at it for a moment, and Murphy said, "Holy shit. He did it."

"I don't recommend waiting about, Mr. Dresden," Marcone said. I saw him twist his head to look at the loup-garou, and tense up as the beast trotted around the edge of the pit to the side closest to him. If it had noticed the rope that had fallen down from above, it gave no sign.

Hope lurched in my chest like sudden thunder. I grabbed on to the rope with both hands and started shinnying up it like a monkey, pushing with my legs and using mostly my good arm to hang on with while I lifted my legs up higher for another grip.

I got up to even with the lip of the pit and started rocking the rope back and forth, getting a swinging momentum going so that I could leap off the rope and to the ground outside the pit. The ropes above creaked dangerously as I did, and Marcone swayed back and forth, still spinning about gently.

"Dresden," he shouted. "Look out!"

I had been intent on my escape, and given the loup-garou no thought. I turned my head around to see it flying through the air toward me. I could see its gleaming eyes and felt sure that I could have counted its teeth if I had waited around for it. I didn't. I let out a yelp and let go of the rope, dropping several feet straight down before clamping on to it again. The loup-garou sailed past me overhead like some huge, obscenely graceful bat, and landed on the far side of the pit with barely a sound.

My fingers felt weak, I was so shocked and terrified, but I started hauling my way up again, swinging desperately as I went. The loup-garou turned and focused its eyes on me again, but Marcone let out a sharp whistle, and the thing turned toward him, pricking its misshapen ears forward in a weirdly doggy mannerism, before it snarled and leapt upward. I bounced on the rope, and Marcone bobbed down and then back up again. The loup-garou missed him by bare inches, I think, but I didn't hang around to watch. I let out a yell and threw myself at the edge of the pit as the rope reached the apex of its swing.

I missed, my belly hitting the lip of the pit, but I started clawing at the earth and kept myself from falling. I strained and kicked, thrashing and whimpering in desperation, and managed to gain a few inches, slowly worming my way up onto the ground, until I got my feet underneath me. The loup-garou, on the far side of the pit, turned toward me and let out a sound that can best be described as a furious roar. Shouts erupted from elsewhere in the estate—Denton and his lackeys must have been watching the pit, I thought, but they were the second scariest bad guys on the field at the moment. I had bigger things on my mind.

Said thing threw itself at me, and I had a few seconds to start running, trying to arrange things so that the pit would be between me and it when it landed. I was only partly successful. The loup-garou tore up the earth where I had been standing when it came down, and turned toward me again, facing me across a scant ten feet of space, from one side of the square pit to the side adjacent to it.

The rope started bobbing again, and then with a motion full of grace and power, Tera swung up out of the pit and landed in a crouch on the ground beside me.

"Go, wizard," she snarled. "Denton and the others will kill us all if they are not stopped. I will handle MacFinn."

"No way," I said. "You can't possibly take him on."

"I know him," she responded. And then there was, in her place, the huge she-wolf, dark fur peppered with grey. She snarled and bounded at the loup-garou and it reared up like a cat about to take a mouse, plunging toward her with abrupt speed.

And that's when I saw the difference between Tera and the Alphas, Tera and Denton's *Hexenwulfen,* even Tera and the loup-garou. Where they were fast, Tera was fast *and* graceful. Where they were quick, Tera was quick *and* elegant. She made them look like amateurs. She was something more primal, more in tune with the wild than they would ever be.

As the loup-garou threw itself at her, she slipped to one side like wind, threw her shoulder beneath the beast's planted forepaw, and shouldered it off-balance, making it stumble. It recovered and spun toward her, but she was already gone, farther away from the pit, growling defiance at the supernatural creature. It followed, impervious and snarling with rage.

I heard a gunshot, and a bullet smacked into one of the trees behind me. Benn's voice repeated a low, frantic chant, and then I heard her words turn into an animal's snarls. Denton and the others were coming. It was time to play the last option I had, the one I hadn't wanted to be forced to use. I wasn't sure what would happen if I did, but there wasn't much choice.

I slipped my hand beneath my shirt and touched the wolf belt I'd taken from Agent Harris in the alley behind the Full Moon Garage.

It was vibrating beneath my fingers, warm to the touch, alive in its own fashion, and full of the power and strength that had been channeled into it. I closed my eyes and let that dark, wild power spill into me, mingle with all the fear and pain and weariness inside of me. It was easy. It was easier than any magic I'd ever done, leaping into me with a sort of hungry eagerness, seeping into me, making pain and fatigue and fear vanish and replacing it with nothing but strength, ferocity.

Power.

"Lupus," I whispered. *"Lupus, lupara, luperoso."*

It took no more of a chant than that for the change to take me. It wasn't something that I noticed, really. But when I opened my eyes again, things were simply as they should be, *right* in a way so fundamentally profound that I wondered why I had never noticed its lack before.

My vision was sharp and clear enough to count the hairs on the head of the she-wolf orienting on me a few feet away. I could hear the pounding of her heart, the restless motion of the wind, the heavy breaths of the other agents in the trees, moving toward me like great, clumsy cows. If the sun had suddenly risen into the sky, I could not have seen any more clearly than I did, all in glorious shades of blue and green and maroon and purple, as though God had dipped his brush into a late summer twilight and replaced all the darkness with those colors.

I dropped open my mouth in a silent laugh and felt my tongue glide over the gleaming, sharp tips of my fangs. What a beautiful night. I could smell blood on the air, hear the eagerness of my enemies to kill, and I felt that same hunger rising from my own heart and surging through me. It was perfect.

Benn came through the trees first, fast and powerful, but clumsy and impatient and stupid. I could smell her excitement, pitched to an almost sexual level. She was expecting an easy kill, a sudden rush over one of the slow, graceless two-legs and then the hot, spurting blood, the frenzied writhing. I did not oblige her. As she came through the trees, I leapt forward and was at her throat before she even realized I was there. A quick rip, hot blood, and she yelped in agony and fear, throwing herself to one side.

Stupid bitch. I'd missed the heart's blood, but she was badly hurt. Two snaps severed her hamstrings as she tried to flee and left her writhing on the ground, helpless and terrified. I felt my body thrill with abrupt and vicious excitement. The bitch was mine now. She would live or die as I wished.

The surge of power and elation that flew through me at that realization could have carried me off the earth and to the silver glory of the moon and stars themselves. To the victor go the spoils. Her blood, her life, was mine to take and that was exactly how it *should* be. I stalked forward to finish her, as was only proper.

There was a puff of breath, and then Wilson, in his wolf-form, came hurtling from the woods. I slipped aside easily as he rushed by. The wounded Benn snarled and snapped blindly at him. Wilson turned on her, his fury out of control, and latched his jaws onto her throat. Blood was a black, rich, heady smell in the moonlight, and I swayed, drunk on the aroma of it. My mouth watered, jaws growing damp with saliva, as I smelled the bitch's blood, and I wanted to fling myself at her, tear her apart myself as she went screaming to her death.

"Those wolves!" screamed Harris. "They got out! They got Benn!" He came plunging out of the trees, gun at the ready, his nearly useless eyes wide and staring and panicked. He started shooting at Wilson, who released the dead Benn's throat. The first bullet smashed his left front paw to pulp. The second and third slugs hammered into his chest, and Wilson-wolf staggered to one side, yelping in sudden agony. He twisted and strained as he went down, paws scrabbling at his own stomach, until there was abruptly a balding, overweight man lying on the earth beside the dead wolf, his jacket open, his shirt unbuttoned to show the unfastened wolf belt. There was blood all over Wilson, bubbling out of his mouth.

"Holy . . ." Harris breathed, pacing closer, his gun held up, until he could see what he had done. "George? Oh, God. Oh, God, I thought you were one of them. What the hell . . ."

Agent Wilson didn't answer the redheaded kid. He simply drew his gun from his jacket and started shooting.

In their human forms, they couldn't see each other very well in the dark, I thought. They both started shooting at the muzzle flashes. More blood flooded the air, along with the sharp, acrid smell of burning gunpowder. Both men went down, bleeding out onto the earth, and I felt my jaws open in another smile, on another sense of warm satisfaction. Idiots. Who did they think they were dealing with here? They'd been making my life miserable, and the lives of others, and now they had gotten their just desserts. It would have been better had I torn out their throats myself, admittedly.

But then, I thought, there was still Denton to deal with.

That thought cheering me, I turned and made my way into the woods, hunting the last of them. My heart was pounding hard, and relaxed and steady with excitement as I melded in with the night and searched for prey.

Denton and I met as I emerged from the circle of trees. He stood in the moonlight, in the right shape, the only real shape, the moon streaking his brown coat shades paler and making his eyes glow. He was powerfully built, as in his two-leg shape, and looked quick and strong. His eyes burned with the lust of the moon, the night, with blood need and raging, wild strength, just as mine did. We faced one another and there was a mad sort of joy in it. I would have giggled if I could have.

A snarl bubbled up out of my chest like music, and I launched myself at him. We met in a tangle of scratching claws, snapping teeth, dark fur. He was the stronger, I the quicker. The fight was silent, with no breath wasted. It was a duel between us; our fangs were our swords, thick fur ruffs used as shield and armor.

I tasted his blood in my mouth from a slash to an ear and it hit me like a drug, sent a fury and power coursing through me like I had never known. I threw myself at him again, and an instant later was rewarded for my overeagerness with a hot pain on my foreleg. Scarlet-black blood stained Denton's fangs in the moonlight.

We separated and stalked one another in a slow circle, looking for weakness, our eyes never leaving one another. I laughed at him silently, and he answered me in much the same way. I understood him, then, and rejoiced with him in the power he had found. In that moment, I loved the man, felt him a brother, and longed to hold his throat in my jaws as the last of his blood flowed out of him. It was the most ancient of struggles, the deepest of conflicts: survival of the fittest. One of us would live to run again, to hunt, to kill, to taste the hot blood. And the other would be dead and cold on the grass.

It was *good*.

We came together again like partners in a dance, moving over the grass together. Dimly, of course, I was aware of Tera dancing with the loup-garou, but that didn't matter to me, really. They were far away, dozens of yards, and I took no notice of them. My joy was *here*.

We danced under the moon—and he made the first misstep. I threw myself into the opening he'd left me, knocked him to the ground with my shoulder, and as he rolled and twisted away, I took his back leg, right across the big tendon. He screamed his fury, but I heard the fear in it, too. He scrambled to his three good paws again and turned to face me, but there was terrible knowledge in his eyes, just as there was in mine. We both knew that it was all over but the bleeding.

I shuddered. Yes. The bleeding.

He could still face me, could still hurt me if I were foolish—but I wasn't. I began to wear him down, pressing him with short rushes and quick withdrawals that forced him to shift his weight awkwardly, stumble on his three working limbs, to wear him out. As his reactions became slower, I tested him with a few flashing passes of fangs. Once more, I tasted his blood.

I gave him a dozen small wounds and each taste of him made my frenzy all the more satisfying. The night, the dance, the violence, the blood—all of it was overwhelming, more than any power I had ever felt, any medicine I'd ever tasted, even in my dreams or in the wild realms of the Nevernever. It was pure beauty, pure pleasure, pure power. Victory was mine.

I grew contemptuous of him as he began to whimper, to seek escape. The fool. He should never have tested himself against me. Should never have tried his strength against mine. Had he yielded to me at once, I would have been content to lead him, to accept him as a follower, and taken him with me on the hunts. It was sad, in a way. But then, I could always find others. It would not be difficult to make the belts, I thought. To give them to a few people to try. Once they had, they'd never take them off again.

I stalked Denton as he faltered, and I thought of running with

Susan, of filling our mouths with hot, sweet blood, of taking her in the ecstasy of the night and the kill and it made me shake with anticipation. I threw myself at Denton, knocked him over, and went for his throat. The fool scrambled and took his belt off, melting into the ugly two-leg form, his suit covered in blood.

"Please," he croaked. "Oh, God. Please. Don't kill me. Don't *kill* me."

I snarled in answer, and let my fangs tighten on his neck. I could feel his pulse against my tongue. Don't kill him. That he would beg at all was contemptuous. He should have known the law of the jungle before he started trying to rule it. Who did he think he was dealing with? Someone who would give him mercy, let him survive, crippled and pathetic, and feed him when he whined again? I wanted to laugh.

My jaws tightened on his throat. I wanted to feel him *die*. Something told me that everything else I'd experienced since I discovered my true self was child's candy next to the passing of a life beneath me. I shook with eagerness. Denton continued to beg, and it made me hesitate. I snarled, annoyed. No. No weakness. No mercy. I wanted his blood. I wanted his life. He had tried me and failed. Kill him. Kill him and take my rightful place.

Who did he think I was?

"Harry?" whispered a terrified voice.

Without releasing his throat, I looked up. Susan stood there in the moonlight, slender and graceful for a two-legs. Her camera was in one hand, dangling forgotten at her side. Her eyes were wide with desire, and she smelled of perfume and our mating and of fear. Something pressed at my awareness, and though part of me wanted to ignore her, to rip and rend, I focused on Susan, on her expression.

On her eyes. They weren't wide with desire.

They were terrified.

She was terrified of me.

"My God," Susan said. "Harry." She fell to her knees, staring at me. At my eyes.

I felt Denton's pulse beneath my tongue. Felt his whimpers vibrate into my mouth. So easy. One simple motion, and I would never have doubts, fears, questions. Never again.

And, something inside of me said in a calm tone, *you'll never be Harry Dresden again.*

Power. I could feel the belt's power in me, its magic, its strength. I recognized it now. That dark surety, that heady and careless delight. I recognized why there were parts of me that loved it so much.

I released Denton's throat and backed away from him. I scrambled with my paws, my stomach twisting in sudden nausea, rebelling at the very idea of what I had been about to do. I sobbed and tore the belt from my waist, ripping my shirt in the process, feeling my body grow awkward and heavy and clumsy and pained again. Injuries that had been nothing to my tru—to the *wolf* form returned in vengeance to my human frailty. I threw the belt away from me, as far as it would go. I felt hot tears on my face, at the loss of that joy, that energy, that impervious strength.

"You bastard," I said to Denton. "Damn you. You poor bastard." He lay on his side now, whimpering from his injuries, bleeding from many wounds, one leg curled limp and useless beneath him. I crawled to him and took his belt away. Threw it after the other.

Susan rushed over to me, but I caught her before she could embrace me. "Don't touch me," I told her, and I meant it with every cell in me. "Don't touch me now."

Susan flinched away from me as though the words had burned her. "Harry," she whispered. "Oh, God, Harry. We've got to get you away from all of this."

From the far side of the ring of trees, there was another furious bellow. There was motion in the trees, and then Murphy, leading a stumbling, clumsy string of naked Alphas, came out of the woods toward me, staying low. She had a gun, probably taken from one of the bodies, in her good hand.

"All right," I said, as they approached, and turned a shoulder to Susan, pressing her away. I couldn't even look at her. "Murphy, you and Susan get these kids out of here, *now*."

"No," Murphy said. "I'm staying." Her eyes flickered to Denton, narrowed in a flash of anger, and then dismissed him again as quickly. She made no move to examine his injuries. Maybe she didn't care if he bled to death, either.

"You can't hurt MacFinn," I said.

"And you can?" she asked. She leaned closer and peered at me. "Christ, Dresden. You've got blood all over your mouth."

I snarled. "Take the kids and go, Karrin. I'm handling things here."

Murphy, for answer, slipped the safety off of the gun. "I'm the cop here," she said. "Not you. This is a bust in progress. I'm staying until the end." She smiled, tight. "When I can sort out who is a good guy and who isn't."

I spat out another curse. "I don't have time to argue this with you. Susan, get the kids back to the van."

"But Harry . . ." she began.

Fury rose to the top of the rampant emotions coursing through me. "I've got enough blood on my hands," I screamed. "Get these kids out of here, damn you."

Susan's dark-toned face went pale, and she turned to the nearest of the naked, wet, shivering Alphas, Georgia as it happened. She took the young woman's hand, had the others line up in drug-hazed confusion and join hands, and then led them away. I watched them go and felt the seething anger and sorrow and fear in me twist around in confusion.

From the far side of the woods, there was another bellow of rage, a shaking of one of the evergreens, and then a sharp, sudden yelp of purest anguish. Tera. The sound of the she-wolf's pain rose to a frantic gargling sound, and then went silent. Murphy and I stared at the trees. I thought I saw a flicker of red eyes somewhere behind them, and then it was gone.

"It's coming around," Murphy said. "It will circle around to get to us."

"Yeah," I said. The loup-garou's blood was up, after the infuriating chase after Tera. It would go after whatever it saw next. My mouth twisted bitterly. I had a unique insight to its point of view now.

"What do we do?" Murphy said. Her knuckles whitened on the gun.

"We go after it and try to hold it long enough for Susan and the kids to get away," I said. "What about Marcone?"

"What about him?"

"He saved our lives," I said. Murphy's expression said she wasn't happy with that idea. "We owe him."

"You want to get him out of there?"

"I don't want to leave anyone else to that thing," I said. "How about you?"

She closed her eyes and let out a breath. "All right," she said. "But God, this smells like you're trying to set me up, Dresden. If you get me killed, there's no one left who saw what happened here, is there?"

"If you want to be safe, go after Susan," I said bluntly. "We split up. One of us attracts its attention, maybe the other one will get through."

"Fine," Murphy snarled. "Fuck you, Harry Dresden."

Famous last words, I thought, but I didn't waste any breath on voicing it.

It was time to face the loup-garou.

Chapter 33

I circled into the trees and stepped over Harris's corpse. The kid's face had been smashed in by two bullets, though the semiautomatic was still in his dead hand. Murphy must have had Wilson's gun. Wilson lay not far from Harris, also dead. Wounds to the chest, massive bleeding. Benn lay next to him, naked but for a business skirt soaked in blood. There was a line of greenish goo around her waist, probably the remains of the wolf belt. Its magic must have died when she did. I tried not to look at the mangled meat on the back of her thighs, or the tears near her jugular. I tried not to smell her blood, or to notice the dark surge of contemptuous pride that went through me, leftovers from my experience with my own wolf belt.

I shuddered and went past the bodies. The night was silent, but for wind, and the creaking of the ropes that supported the platform in the middle of the encircling evergreens. I could still see Marcone hog-tied up there. The position must have been excruciating—it isn't every day that you get crucified and hung up as dinner for a monster, and you can't really train your muscles for it. I couldn't see Marcone's expression, but I could almost feel his agony.

I waved a hand as he spun gently toward me, and he nodded his head, silent. I pointed at my eyes, and then around at the shadowed trees, trying to ask him if he knew where the loup-garou was, but he shook his head. Either he didn't understand me or he couldn't see it, and either way it didn't do me any good.

I grimaced and moved forward through the trees, skirting the edge of the pit. I looked for the rope that had been used to haul

Marcone up to his current position. It had to have been tied off somewhere low. I peered through the near dark, followed the strand of rope back down to the tree it was tied to, and headed over toward it.

Maybe I could get out of this. Maybe Murphy and I could escape with Marcone, join Susan and the others, and get out of here.

No. That was a happy fantasy. Even if I did get everyone out, I knew I couldn't live with myself if I let the loup-garou go loose tonight, on another killing spree. I had to try to stop it.

I was already going to have a hard enough time living with myself.

The rope supporting Marcone had been secured with a hasty knot, easily undone. I started working it, rubbernecking all around, listening, trying to locate the loup-garou. It wouldn't have just run off and left us here alive. Would it?

I took a turn around the tree with the rope to give me a little leverage, and then, very carefully because of my bum arm, started lowering Marcone. If I could get him low enough, I could have him swing over to me from the pit's center, catch him, balance him, and then go back and release the rope. It would have been easier if Murphy was there, but I hadn't seen her.

A nasty thought hit me. What if Murphy had run across the loup-garou and it had killed her silently? What if it was, even now, trying to get to me?

I secured the rope and moved back over to the pit. Marcone, no dummy, was already swinging back and forth as best he could, trying to get himself over to me. I went to the edge of the pit and crouched down, keeping my weight well away from the crumbling earth at the pit's lip.

Marcone let out a sudden startled hiss and said, "Dresden! The pit!"

I looked down and saw the loup-garou's eyes glowing, down in the darkness of the pit, only a heartbeat before they surged toward me with a howl of rage. It was coming *up* the wall of the pit, simply gouging its claws into the mud and hauling itself upward, toward me. I reeled back from the thing, threw out a hand and screamed, *"Fuego!"*

Nothing happened, except a little puff of steam, like a breath exhaled on a cold night, and sudden, blinding pain in my head. The loup-garou hurtled toward me, and I threw myself down to the earth, rolling away from its claws as it came up over the edge of the pit. It raked at me, caught the edge of my leather duster, and pinned it to the earth.

I liked the coat, but I didn't like it *that* much. I slipped out of it, as the loup-garou clawed with its rear legs, much as I had only moments before, and inched up out of the pit. I was already running by the time it got out, and I heard it snarl, get its bearings, and then come after me.

I was dead. I was so dead. I had gotten the kids out, and Susan, and I had stopped Denton and his cronies, but I was about to pay the price. I slipped through the trees and out onto the grass again, panting, cold now that my jacket was off. My shoulder ached from the running, from all the motion, and my foot hurt abominably as well. I couldn't run any longer—physically *couldn't*. My steps slowed, despite the commands of my brain, and I wept with frustration, weaving around just to keep on my feet.

I was at the end of my rope. It was over. I turned to face the trees, to watch the loup-garou coming. I wanted to see it coming, at least. If I was going to be killed, I wanted to face it on my feet, head on. Go down with a little dignity.

I saw its red eyes back among the trees. It came forward, slow, low to the ground, wary of some trick. I had stung it before, if not actually hurt it. It didn't want to fall victim to another such attack, I thought. It wanted to make absolutely sure that I was dead.

I drew in a breath and straightened my back. I lifted my chin, trying to prepare myself. If I was going to go down, I'd go down as a wizard should—proud and ready to face what was beyond. I could spill out my death curse, a potent working of magic, if I had time to speak it. Maybe I could counter MacFinn's curse with it, take the horrid transformation off of him that Saint Patrick had allegedly laid on him. Or maybe I could bring down Marcone's criminal empire with it.

I debated these things, as I drew out the silver pentacle amulet I had inherited from my mother, so that it would lie bright on my chest.

My mother's amulet.

Silver.

Amulet.

Inherited from my mother.

Inherited silver.

My eyes widened and my hands started to shake. A drowning man will reach for anything that floats. The idea floated—if only

I could pull it off. If only my brainlessness hadn't kept me from realizing what I had until it was too late.

I took the silver pentacle off of my neck, breaking the chain in my haste. I caught the broken ends in my fist as I fastened my eyes on the loup-garou, and started to whirl the amulet in a circle above my head with my good arm. The amulet described a circle in the night air as I spun it, and I invested that circle with a tiny spark of will, a tiny bit of power. My head pounded. I felt the circle close around me, containing magical energies, focusing them.

I hurt. I was weary. I felt as though I had betrayed myself, given myself over to the darkness I'd tried so hard to resist by donning the evilly enchanted wolf belt—because let there be no mistaking, that *is* evil. Anything with that much power and that little control, that utter lack of concern for anything but self is evil in the most effective sense of the word. There was nothing left inside of me.

But I had to find it. I had to find enough magic to stop this bloodletting, once and forever.

I searched inside of me, where everything was numb and empty and tired. Magic comes from the heart, from your feelings, your deepest expressions of desire. That's why black magic is so easy—it comes from lust, from fear and anger, from things that are easy to feed and make grow. The sort I do is harder. It comes from something deeper than that, a truer and purer source—harder to tap, harder to keep, but ultimately more elegant, more powerful.

My magic. That was at the heart of me. It was a manifestation of what I believed, what I lived. It came from my desire to see to it that someone stood between the darkness and the people it would devour. It came from my love of a good steak, from the way I would sometimes cry at a good movie or a moving symphony. From my life. From the hope that I could make things better for someone else, if not always for me.

Somewhere, in all of that, I touched on something that wasn't tapped out, in spite of how horrible the past days had been, something that hadn't gone cold and numb inside of me. I grasped it, held it in my hand like a firefly, and willed its energy out, into the circle I had created with the spinning amulet on the end of its chain.

It began to glow, azure-blue like a candle flame. The light spread down the chain and to the amulet, and when it reached it the light became incandescent, the pentacle a brilliant light at the end of the chain, spinning a circle of light around me, trailing motes of dust that fell like starlight to the grass around me.

"*Vento,*" I whispered, and then called, more loudly, "*Vento servitas. Ventas, vento servitas!*" In the bushes, the loup-garou snarled quietly, and its eyes brightened, burned with scarlet fury. It started moving toward me.

Without warning, Murphy stepped between me and the loup-garou, her gun held in both hands in a shooter's stance, though the cast made that awkward. She held her gun pointed directly at me. "Harry," she said in a very calm tone. "Get down on the ground. Right now."

My eyes widened. I could see over Murphy. I could see the loup-garou, moving rapidly toward her through the trees. I saw it focus on her, felt its malice and hunger spread toward her and envelop her.

I couldn't speak. I couldn't break the chant, or stop whirling the amulet. To do so would have released the energy I'd gathered, the very last strength I had in me. My head hammered with pain that would have had me screaming on any other night. I kept the amulet whirling, spraying motes of light, the brilliant white pentacle at the end of a leash of blue light.

"I mean it, Harry," Murphy said. "I don't know what you're doing, but *get down*." Her eyes were intense, and she lifted the gun, thumbing back the hammer.

Trust. Whatever trust she'd had in me was gone. She'd seen or thought of something that made her think I was trying to betray her. The loup-garou rushed closer, and I thought, with a sick feeling in my stomach, that Susan and the Alphas hadn't even had time to make it off the estate yet, much less all the way back to the van. If the loup-garou got through me, it would kill them, one by one, follow their trail like a hound and tear them apart.

"Harry," Murphy said, her voice pleading. Her hand was shaking. "Please, Harry. Get down."

The loup-garou came through the woods in a sudden rush, and Murphy drew in a breath, ready to fire. I kept the amulet whirling and felt the power grow, my head splitting with agony. And made my choice. I just hoped that I could finish the job before Murphy gunned me down. Everything of the past few days came down to that single instant.

It all slowed down, giving me time to view it in agonizing detail.

The loup-garou rose up behind Murphy, leaping toward her through the air. It was still huge, still powerful, and more terrifying than ever. Its jaws were open wide, aimed for her blonde head, and could crush it with a single snap.

Murphy narrowed her eyes, peering down the shaking barrel of her gun. Flame blossomed from the barrel, reaching out toward me. She wasn't twenty feet away from me. I didn't think there was any way she could miss, and I thought, with a pang of sadness, that I wanted a chance to apologize to her before the end. For everything.

"Vento servitas!" I shouted and released the spell, the circle, and the amulet, as the sound of the shot hit me like a slap in the face. Power rushed out of me, everything I had left in me, focused and magnified by the circle and the time I had taken to refine it, flying forward at the leaping loup-garou. Something hot and painful hammered into my torso—almost like it had hit my back. I toppled forward, too weak and tired to care anymore. But I watched what happened to the amulet.

The pentacle flew toward the loup-garou like a comet, incandescent white, and struck the creature's breast like lightning hammering into an ancient tree. There was a flash of light, too much power unleashed in a flaring of energy as the mystic substance shattered the loup-garou's invulnerability, carved into it, coursed through it in a blinding blue-white shower of sparks. Blue fire erupted from its chest, its black heart's blood ignited into blinding flame, and the creature screamed, arching backward in agony. There was the sound of thunder, flashes of more light, someone screaming. Maybe it was me.

The loup-garou fell to earth. And changed. Muzzle melted back into human face. Fangs and claws faded. Warped muscles slithered away into globs of clear, preternatural ooze that would quickly vanish. Fur disappeared. Knotted limbs straightened into clean arms and legs—until Harley MacFinn lay before me, partly upon his side, one hand pressed to his heart.

The silver of my amulet's chain spilled out between his fingers and dangled down his chest. He stared down at the wound for a moment, and then I saw him relax. MacFinn looked up, and in his face I saw all the grief and agony and impotent rage, everything he'd felt during all those years of being unable to control himself, cursed to cause death and destruction when all he wanted was to open a park for the wildlife. And then it all flooded out of him. His eyes cleared and warmed as he looked at me, and he gave me a small, quiet smile. It was an expression of forgiveness. Something to let me know that he understood.

Then he laid down his head, and was gone.

My own blackness followed soon after.

Chapter 34

I woke up.

That surprised me, in itself.

I woke up to see the moon still high overhead, and to feel Murphy's hand on my forehead. "Come on, Harry," she whispered. "Don't do this to me."

I blinked my eyes a few times and whispered, "You *shot* me, Murph. I can't believe you shot me."

She blinked her eyes at me, to hold back tears. "You stupid jerk," she said, her voice gentle. "You should have got down when I told you to."

"I was busy."

She glanced over her shoulder, at MacFinn's silent, still form. "Yeah. I saw, after." She turned back to me, looking a little past me, focused elsewhere.

"It's all right," I said. "I forgive you." I thought it very generous of me, appropriate to the last moments of a man's life.

Murphy blinked at me. And then stiffened. "You what?"

"Forgive you, Murph. For shooting me. Your job and all, I understand."

Murphy's eyes narrowed dangerously. "You think . . ." she said. Her face twisted with disgust and she sputtered for a moment, and then spat to one side. She began again. "You think that I thought you were one of the bad guys, still, and I shot you because you wouldn't surrender?"

I felt too weak and dizzy to argue. "Hey. It's understandable. Don't worry about it." I shivered. "I'm so cold."

"We're *all* cold, moron," Murphy snapped. "A front came

through about the same time they threw us in that freaking pit. It must be below forty, already, and we're wet besides. Sit up, El Cid."

I blinked at her. "I . . . Uh. What?"

"Sit up, dummy," Murphy said. "Look behind you."

I did sit up, and it didn't hurt much worse than it had earlier this evening, surprising me again. I looked behind me.

Denton was there. He held a fallen branch in one hand, like a club. His eyes were wide and staring and savage, his face pale with loss of blood. There was a neat hole in his forehead, right in the middle. I blinked at the body for a moment.

"But . . . How did he . . . ?"

"I shot *him,* you jerk. He came running up behind you, just as I came back from giving first aid to that naked woman. Tera West. I was shaking too hard to have a safe shot with you standing, and I didn't know the loup-garou was coming up behind *me*." Murphy stood up. "I can't believe this," she said and turned to walk away. "You thought I shot you."

"Murph," I protested. "Murph, give me a break. I mean, I thought . . ."

She snorted at me over her shoulder. She snorts well for someone with a cute little button of a nose. "You *didn't* think, Dresden," she said, flipping her hair back from her eyes. "Dramatic death scene. Noble sacrifice, right? Tragically misunderstood? Hah! I understand you, buddy. You're such a pompous, arrogant, pretentious, chauvinistic, hopelessly old-fashioned, stupidly pigheaded . . ." Murphy went on in graphic detail and at great length about me as she walked away to call the police, and an ambulance, and it was music to my ears.

I lay back on the grass, tired but smiling. Things were all right between us.

The police had one hell of a time sorting out the mess at Marcone's place. I made sure to collect all the wolf belts. Murphy helped me. We burned them, right there, in a stinking fire made of tree branches. It was too hard for me to throw them in. Murph did it for me. She understands things, sometimes, that I couldn't ever explain to her. Later, I went with Murph to Carmichael's funeral. She went with me to Kim Delaney's. Those are the kind of things friends do for each other.

Mr. Hendricks, as it turns out, had worn his Kevlar under the black fatigues. They put me next to him in the ambulance that night when I finally left the scene. They'd bared his chest, and it was a solid mass of purple bruises, so that we were a matched set. He glowered at me in silence, but he breathed steadily through the oxygen mask on his face. I felt absurdly cheered when I saw him alive. All things considered, can you blame me?

Marcone got arrested on general principles, but nothing stuck. Though everything had happened on his property, injuries on the FBI agents indicated that they had all done one another in, or been killed by an animal—except for Denton, of course. None of the peace officers there had possessed a warrant, et cetera, et cetera. I hear his lawyers had him out in less than three hours.

Marcone called me a few days later and said, "You owe me your life, Mr. Dresden. Are you sure we can't talk business?"

"The way I see it, John," I told him, "you owe me *your* life. After all, even if you'd cut yourself free, you'd have just fallen down into the pit and got eaten up with the rest of us. I figure you thought your highest chances of survival were in freeing me, the wizard who deals with this kind of thing, to handle it."

"Of course," Marcone said, with a note of disappointment in his voice. "I'd just hoped you hadn't realized it. Nonetheless, Harry—"

"Don't call me Harry," I said, and hung up on him.

Susan filmed the death of the loup-garou from less than fifty yards away with a pretty good zoom lens and special light-sensitive film. The light from my amulet illuminated the scene rather dramatically without really showing many details. You can only see my back, and it looks like I'm swinging a glow stick around, and then throwing it at the monster, which can be seen only in shadowy detail as something large and furry. At the point where I released the spell, there's a burst of static about a second long, where the magic messed up Susan's camera, even from that far away.

In the film, the static clears and you can see Murphy shoot Denton off of my back, just before he brains me with his club. Then she spins around like Rambo, jumps out of the way of the leaping furry something-or-other, and empties the rest of her clip into the thing out of reflex.

Murph and I both know the bullets didn't hurt it at all, that it was just a reflexive gesture on her part, but I don't need the attention. She was quite the hero according to the camera, and that was fine with me.

Susan's film went on the morning news and was shown for about two days afterward, exclusively on WGN Channel Nine, and it impressed Chicago a lot. The film made Murphy popular enough, with voters, that a bunch of city councilmen went to bat for her, and the internal affairs investigation got called off. She carries a little bit more clout now than she did before. The politicians down at City Hall paid for a real name tag for her office door.

The weird thing was that the film just vanished after two days. No one knew what happened to it, but the film technician in the room with the exclusive WGN Channel Nine videotape disappeared, too, leaving only a few scattered and low-quality copies. A couple of days later, some experts spoke up claiming that the tape had to be fake, and decrying it as a simple hoax perpetrated by a tabloid.

Some people just can't deal with the thought of the supernatural being real. Federal government is like that, a lot. But I'm thinking that if anyone in the government *did* believe, they would just as soon not have had proof of the existence of werewolves and the instability of a local FBI agent showing at five, six, and ten.

The film's disappearance didn't stop Susan from getting a promotion at the *Arcane,* a big raise, and a guest slot on the Larry King show, plus a few other places. She looked good doing it, too, and made people think. She's getting her column syndicated. Maybe, in a few hundred years, people might actually be willing to consider what was real in the world with an open mind.

But I doubted it.

I didn't call Susan for a while, after she had seen me so far gone into being a monster that I might as well have been one. She didn't pressure me, but kept her presence known. She'd send me flowers, sometimes, or have a pizza delivered to my office when I was working late. Hell of a girl.

Tera was badly injured, but recovered thanks to her own reversion to human form, and Murphy's quick first aid. She asked me to meet her at Wolf Lake Park a few weeks later, and when I showed up, she was there, wearing just a long black cloak.

"I wished to tell you that what you did was necessary. And I wished to tell you good-bye," she said. And slipped the cloak off. She was naked, with a few new, wrinkled scars. "Good-bye."

"Where will you go?" I asked.

She tilted those odd amber eyes at me. "I have family," she said. "I have not seen them in a long time. I will return to them now."

"Maybe you'll call, sometime?"

Her eyes sparkled, and she smiled at me, a little sadly. "No, Harry Dresden. That is not the way of my kind. Come to the great mountains in the Northwest one winter. Perhaps I will be there." And then she shimmered into the shape of a great timber wolf, and vanished into the sunset.

All those people shapeshifting into wolves, and I had never once considered the possibility of a wolf shapeshifting into a person. I picked up Tera's cloak, musing, and took it home with me, as a reminder to keep my mind even more open to the realms of possibility.

The Alphas decided that I'm about the greatest thing since sliced bread. Which isn't exactly the most thrilling thing in the world for me. They asked me to a camp out with them, which I reluctantly attended, where all dozen-odd young people swore friendship and loyalty to me, and where I spent a lot of time blinking and trying to say nothing. They're just itching for me to lead them in some meaningful crusade against evil. Hell, I have trouble just paying the bills.

When I took some time to think about all that had happened, I couldn't help but think that the last several months had been a little too crazy for coincidence. First, a power-drunk warlock had appeared out of nowhere, and I had to duke it out with him in his own stronghold before he murdered me outright. And then, Denton and his people showed up with enchanted wolf belts and raised hell.

I never had found out who exactly was behind the warlock who showed up the previous spring. Black wizards don't just grow up like toadstools, you know. Someone has to teach them complicated things like summoning demons, ritual magic, and clichéd villain dialogue. Who had been his teacher?

And Denton and company had shown up six months later. Someone had provided them with those belts. Someone had warned Denton that I was dangerous, that I or someone like me from the Council would go after him. And by telling him that, they had pointed him at me like a gun, determined to kill me.

I'm not much of a believer in coincidence. Could it have been one of my enemies on the White Council? One of the beings of the Nevernever who had come to hate me? I was on the list of a number of nasty things, for one reason or another.

"You know what?" I told Mister one night in front of the fire. "Maybe I've finally gone around the bend, but I think someone might be trying to kill me."

Mister looked up at me, his feline features filled with a supreme lack of concern, and rolled over so that I could rub his tummy. I did, pensive and comfortable before the fire, and thought about who it might be. And then thought that I might be getting a little stir-crazy. I hadn't gone anywhere but to work and back home for a couple of weeks. Too much work and no play makes Harry a paranoid boy.

I reached for the phone and started spinning the dial to Susan's number. Mister batted at my hand approvingly.

"Or maybe I'm just too stupid to get out of trouble's way, eh?"

Mister rumbled a deep, affirmative purr in his chest. I settled back to ask Susan over, and enjoyed the warmth of the fire.

GRAVE PERIL

Chapter 1

There are reasons I hate to drive fast. For one, the *Blue Beetle*, the mismatched Volkswagen bug that I putter around in, rattles and groans dangerously at anything above sixty miles an hour. For another, I don't get along so well with technology. Anything manufactured after about World War II seems to be susceptible to abrupt malfunction when I get close to it. As a rule, when I drive, I drive very carefully and sensibly.

Tonight was an exception to the rule.

The *Beetle's* tires screeched in protest as we rounded a corner, clearly against the NO LEFT TURN sign posted there. The old car growled gamely, as though it sensed what was at stake, and continued its valiant puttering, moaning, and rattling as we zoomed down the street.

"Can we go any faster?" Michael drawled. It wasn't a complaint. It was just a question, calmly voiced.

"Only if the wind gets behind us or we start going down a hill," I said. "How far to the hospital?"

The big man shrugged his shoulders and shook his head. He had that kind of salt-and-pepper hair, dark against silver, that some men seem lucky enough to inherit, though his beard was still a solid color of dark brown, almost black. There were worry and laugh lines at the corners of his leathery face. His broad, lined hands rested on his knees, which were scrunched up due to the dashboard. "I don't know for certain," he answered me. "Two miles?"

I squinted out the *Beetle's* window at the fading light. "The sun is almost down. I hope we're not too late."

"We're doing all we can," Michael assured me. "If God wills it, we'll be there in time. Are you sure of your . . ." his mouth twisted with distaste, "source?"

"Bob is annoying, but rarely wrong," I answered, jamming on the brakes and dodging around a garbage truck. "If he said the ghost would be there, it will be there."

"Lord be with us," Michael said, and crossed himself. I felt a stirring of something; powerful, placid energy around him—the power of faith. "Harry, there's something I've been meaning to talk to you about."

"Don't ask me to Mass again," I told him, uncomfortable. "You know I'm just going to say no." Someone in a red Taurus cut me off, and I had to swerve around him, into the turn lane, and then ahead of him again. A couple of the *Beetle's* wheels lifted off the ground. "Jerk!" I howled out the driver's window.

"That doesn't preclude asking," Michael asked. "But no. I wanted to know when you were going to marry Miss Rodriguez."

"Hell's Bells, Michael," I scowled. "You and I have been chasing all over town for the past two weeks, going up against every ghost and spirit that has all of a sudden reared its ugly head. We still don't know what's causing the spirit world to go postal."

"I know that, Harry, but—"

"At the moment," I interrupted, "we're going after a nasty old biddy at Cook County, who could kill us if we aren't focused. And you're asking me about my love life."

Michael frowned at me. "You're sleeping with her, aren't you," he said.

"Not often enough," I growled, and shifted lanes, swerving around a passenger bus.

The knight sighed. "Do you love her?" he asked.

"Michael," I said. "Give me a break. Where do you get off asking questions like that?"

"Do you love her?" he pressed.

"I'm trying to drive, here."

"Harry," he asked, smiling. "Do you love the girl or don't you? It isn't a difficult question."

"Speaks the expert," I grumbled. I went past a blue-and-white at about twenty miles an hour over the speed limit, and saw the police officer behind the wheel blink and spill his coffee as he saw me go past. I checked my rearview mirror, and saw the blue bulbs on the police car whirl to life. "Dammit, that tears it. The cops are going to be coming in right after us."

"Don't worry about them," Michael assured me. "Just answer the question."

I flashed Michael a glance. He watched me, his face broad and honest, his jaw strong, and his grey eyes flashing. His hair was cropped close, Marine-length, on top, but he sported a short, warrior's beard, which he kept clipped close to his face. "I suppose so," I said, after a second. "Yeah."

"Then you don't mind saying it?"

"Saying what?" I stalled.

"Harry," Michael scolded, holding on as we bounced through a dip in the street. "Don't be a child about this. If you love the woman, say so."

"Why?" I demanded.

"You haven't told her, have you. You've never said it."

I glared at him. "So what if I haven't? She knows. What's the big deal?"

"Harry Dresden," he said. "You, of all people, should know the power of words."

"Look, she knows," I said, tapping the brakes and then flattening the accelerator again. "I got her a card."

"A card?" Michael asked.

"A Hallmark."

He sighed. "Let me hear you say the words."

"What?"

"Say the words," he demanded. "If you love the woman, why can't you say so?"

"I don't just go around *saying* that to people, Michael. Stars and sky, that's . . . I just couldn't, all right?"

"You don't love her," Michael said. "I see."

"You know that's not—"

"*Say* it, Harry."

"If it will get you off my back," I said, and gave the *Beetle* every ounce of gas that I could. I could see the police in traffic somewhere behind me. "All right." I flashed Michael a ferocious, wizardly scowl and snarled, "I love her. There, how's that?"

Michael beamed. "You see? That's the only thing that stands between you two. You're not the kind of person who says what they feel. Or who is very introspective, Harry. Sometimes, you just need to look into the mirror and see what's there."

"I don't like mirrors," I grumbled.

"Regardless, you needed to realize that you *do* love the woman. After Elaine, I thought you might isolate yourself too much and never—"

I felt a sudden flash of anger and vehemence. "I don't *talk* about Elaine, Michael. Ever. If you can't live with that, get the hell out of my car and let me work on my own."

Michael frowned at me, probably more for my choice of words than anything else. "I'm talking about Susan, Harry. If you love her, you should marry her."

"I'm a wizard. I don't have *time* to be married."

"I'm a knight," Michael responded. "And I have the time. It's worth it. You're alone too much. It's starting to show."

I scowled at him again. "What does that mean?"

"You're tense. Grumpy. And you're isolating yourself more all the time. You need to keep up human contact, Harry. It would be so easy for you to start down a darker path."

"Michael," I snapped, "I don't need a lecture. I don't need the conversion speech again. I don't need the 'cast aside your evil powers before they consume you' speech. *Again.* What I need is for you to back me up while I go take care of this thing."

Cook County Hospital loomed into sight and I made an illegal U-turn to get the *Blue Beetle* up into the Emergency entrance lane.

Michael unbuckled his seat belt, even before the car had come to a stop, and reached into the back seat to draw an enormous sword, fully five feet long in its black scabbard, from the backseat. He exited the car and buckled on the sword. Then he reached back in for a white cloak with a red cross upon the left breast, which he tossed over his shoulders in a practiced motion. He clasped it with another cross, this one of silver, at his throat. It clashed with his flannel workman's shirt, blue jeans, and steel-toed work boots.

"Can't you leave the cloak off, at least?" I complained. I opened the door and unfolded myself from the *Beetle's* driver's seat, stretching my long legs, and reached into the backseat to recover my own equipment—my new wizard's staff and blasting rod, each of them freshly carved and still a little green around the edges.

Michael looked up at me, wounded. "The cloak is as much a part of what I do as the sword, Harry. Besides, it's no more ridiculous than that coat you wear."

I looked down at my black leather duster, the one with the large mantle that fell around my shoulders and spread out as it billowed in a most heavy and satisfactory fashion around my legs. My own black jeans and dark Western shirt were a ton and a half more stylish than Michael's costume. "What's wrong with it?"

"It belongs on the set of *El Dorado*," Michael said. "Are you ready?"

I shot him a withering glance, to which he turned the other cheek with a smile, and we headed toward the door. I could hear police sirens closing in behind us, maybe a block or two away. "This is going to be close."

"Then we best hurry." He cast the white cloak back from his right arm, and put his hand on the hilt of the great broadsword. Then he bowed his head, crossed himself, and murmured, "Merciful Father, guide us and protect us as we go to do battle with the darkness." Once more, there was that thrum of energy around him, like the vibrations of music heard through a thick wall.

I shook my head, and fetched a leather sack, about the size of my palm, from the pocket of my duster. I had to juggle staff, blasting rod, and sack for a moment, and wound up with the staff in my left hand, as was proper, the rod in my right, and the sack dangling from my teeth. "The sun is down," I grated out. "Let's move it."

And we broke into a run, knight and wizard, through the emergency entrance of Cook County Hospital. We drew no small amount of stares as we entered, my duster billowing out in a black cloud behind me, Michael's white cloak spreading like the wings of the avenging angel whose namesake he was. We pelted inside, and slid to a halt at the first intersection of cool, sterile, bustling hallways.

I grabbed the arm of the first orderly I saw. He blinked, and then gawked at me, from the tips of my Western boots to the dark hair atop my head. He glanced at my staff and rod rather nervously, and at the silver pentacle amulet dangling at my breast, and gulped. Then he looked at Michael, tall and broad, his expression utterly serene, at odds with the white cloak and the broadsword at his hip. He took a nervous step back. "M-m-may I help you?"

I speared him into place with my most ferocious, dark-eyed smile and said, between teeth clenched on the leather sack, "Hi. Could you tell us where the nursery is?"

Chapter 2

We took the fire stairs. Michael knows how technology reacts to me, and the last thing either of us wanted was to be trapped in a broken elevator while innocent lives were snuffed out. Michael led the way, one hand on the rail, one on the hilt of his sword, his legs churning steadily.

I followed him, huffing and puffing. Michael paused by the door and looked back at me, white cloak swirling around his calves. It took me a couple of seconds to come gasping up behind him. "Ready?" he asked me.

"Hrkghngh," I answered, and nodded, still clenching my leather sack in my teeth, and fumbled a white candle from my duster pocket, along with a box of matches. I had to set my rod and staff aside to light the candle.

Michael wrinkled his nose at the smell of smoke, and pushed open the door. Candle in one hand, rod and staff in the other, I followed, my eyes flicking from my surroundings to the candle's flame and back.

All I could see was more hospital. Clean walls, clean halls, lots of tile and fluorescent lights. The long, luminescent tubes flickered feebly, as though they had all gone stale at once, and the hall was only dimly lit. Long shadows stretched out from a wheelchair parked to the side of one door and gathered beneath a row of uncomfortable-looking plastic chairs at an intersection of hallways.

The fourth floor was a graveyard, bottom-of-the-well silent. There wasn't a flicker of sound from a television or radio. No intercoms buzzed. No air conditioning whirred. Nothing.

We walked down a long hall, our steps sounding out clearly despite an effort to remain quiet. A sign on the wall, decorated with a brightly colored plastic clown, read: NURSERY/MATERNITY, and pointed down another hall.

I stepped past Michael and looked down that hallway. It ended at a pair of swinging doors. This hallway, too, was quiet. The nurse's station stood empty.

The lights weren't just flickering here—they were altogether gone. It was entirely dark. Shadows and uncertain shapes loomed everywhere. I took a step forward, past Michael, and as I did the flame of my candle burned down to a cold, clear pinpoint of blue light.

I spat the sack out of my mouth and fumbled it into my pocket. "Michael," I said, my voice strangled to hushed urgency. "It's here." I turned my body, so that he could see the light.

His eyes flicked down to the candle and then back up, to the darkness beyond. "Faith, Harry." Then he reached to his side with his broad right hand, and slowly, silently, drew *Amoracchius* from its sheath. I found it a tad more encouraging than his words. The great blade's polished steel gave off a lambent glow as Michael stepped forward to stand beside me in the darkness, and the air fairly thrummed with its power—Michael's own faith, amplified a thousandfold.

"Where are the nurses?" he asked me in a hoarse whisper.

"Spooked off, maybe," I answered, as quietly. "Or maybe some sort of glamour. At least they're out of the way."

I glanced at the sword, and at the long, slender spike of metal set into its cross guard. Perhaps it was only my imagination, but I thought I could see flecks of red still upon it. Probably rust, I reasoned. Sure, rust.

I set the candle down upon the floor, where it continued to burn pinpoint-clear, indicating a spiritual presence. A big one. Bob hadn't been lying when he'd said that the ghost of Agatha Hagglethorn was no two-bit shade.

"Stay back," I told Michael. "Give me a minute."

"If what the spirit told you is correct, this creature is dangerous," Michael replied. "Let me go first. It will be safer."

I nodded toward the glowing blade. "Trust me, a ghost would feel the sword coming before you even got to the door. Let me see what I can do first. If I can dust the spook, this whole contest is over before it begins."

I didn't wait for Michael to answer me. Instead, I took my

blasting rod and staff in my left hand, and in my right I grasped the pouch. I untied the simple knot that held the sack closed, and slipped forward, into the dark.

When I reached the swinging doors, I pressed one of them slowly opened. I remained still for a long moment, listening.

I heard singing. A woman's voice. Gentle. Lovely.

Hush little baby, don't say a word. Mama's gonna buy you a mockingbird.

I glanced back at Michael, and then slipped inside the door, into total darkness. I couldn't see—but I'm not a wizard for nothing. I thought of the pentacle upon my breast, over my heart, the silver amulet that I had inherited from my mother. It was a battered piece of jewelry, scarred and dented from uses for which it was never intended, but I wore it still. The five-sided star within the circle was the symbol of my magic, of what I believed in, embodying the five forces of the universe working in harmony, contained inside of human control.

I focused on it, and slid a little of my will into it, and the amulet began to glow with a gentle, blue-silver light, which spread out before me in a subtle wave, showing me the shapes of a fallen chair, and a pair of nurses at a desk behind a counter, slumped forward over their stations, breathing deeply.

The soothing, quiet lullaby continued as I studied the nurses. Enchanted sleep. It was nothing new. They were out, they weren't going anywhere, and there was little sense in wasting time or energy in trying to break the spell's hold on them. The gentle singing droned on, and I found myself reaching for the fallen chair, with the intention of setting it upright so that I would have a comfortable place to sit down for a little rest.

I froze, and had to remind myself that I would be an idiot to sit down beneath the influence of the unearthly song, even for a few moments. Subtle magic, and strong. Even knowing what to expect, I had barely sensed its touch in time.

I skirted the chair and moved forward, into a room filled with dressing hooks and little pastel hospital gowns hung upon them in rows. The singing was louder, here, though it still drifted around the room with a ghostly lack of origin. One wall was little more than a sheet of Plexiglas, and behind it was a room that attempted to look sterile and warm at the same time.

Row upon row of little glass cribs on wheeled stands stood in the room. Tiny occupants, with toy-sized hospital mittens over their brand-new fingernails, and tiny hospital stocking caps over their bald heads, were sleeping and dreaming infant dreams.

Walking among them, visible in the glow of my wizard's light, was the source of the singing.

Agatha Hagglethorn had not been old when she died. She wore a proper, high-necked shirt, as was appropriate to a lady of her station in nineteenth-century Chicago, and a long, dark, no-nonsense skirt. I could see through her, to the little crib behind her, but other than that she seemed solid, real. Her face was pretty, in a strained, bony sort of way, and she had her right hand folded over the stump at the end of her left wrist.

If that mockingbird don't sing, mama's going to buy you . . .

She had a captivating singing voice. Literally. She lilted out her song, spun energy into the air that lulled listeners into deeper and deeper sleep. If she was allowed to continue, she could draw both infants and nurses into a sleep from which they would never awaken, and the authorities would blame it on carbon monoxide, or something a little more comfortably normal than a hostile ghost.

I crept closer. I had enough ghost dust to pin down Agatha and a dozen spooks like her, and allow Michael to dispatch her swiftly, with a minimum of mess and fuss—just as long as I didn't miss.

I hunkered down, kept the little sack of dust gripped loosely in my right hand, and slipped over to the door that led into the roomful of sleeping babies. The ghost did not appear to have noticed me—ghosts aren't terribly observant. I guess being dead gives you a whole different perspective on life.

I entered the room, and Agatha Hagglethorn's voice rolled over me like a drug, making me blink and shudder. I had to keep focused, my thoughts on the cool power of my magic flowing through my pentacle and coming out in its spectral light.

If that diamond ring don't shine . . .

I licked my lips and watched the ghost as it stooped over one of the rolling cradles. She smiled, loving-kindness in her eyes, and breathed out her song over the baby.

The infant shuddered out a tiny breath, eyes closed in sleep, and did not inhale.

Hush little baby . . .

Time had run out. In a perfect world, I would have simply dumped the dust onto the ghost. But it's not a perfect world:

Ghosts don't have to play by the rules of reality, and until they acknowledge that you're there, it's tough, very, very tough, to affect them at all. Confrontation is the only way, and even then, knowing the shade's identity and speaking its name aloud is the only sure way to make it face you. And, better and better, most spirits can't hear just anyone—it takes magic to make a direct call to the hereafter.

I rose fully to my feet, bag gripped in my hand and shouted, forcing my will into my voice, "Agatha Hagglethorn!"

The spirit started, as though a distant voice had come to her, and turned toward me. Her eyes widened. The song abruptly fell silent.

"Who are you?" she said. "What are you doing in my nursery?"

I struggled to keep the details Bob had told me about the ghost straight. "This isn't your nursery, Agatha Hagglethorn. It's more than a hundred years since you died. You aren't real. You are a ghost, and you are dead."

The spirit drew itself up with a sort of cold, high-society haughtiness. "I might have known. Benson sent you, didn't he? Benson is always doing something cruel and petty like this, then calling me a madwoman. A madwoman! He wants to take my child away."

"Benson Hagglethorn is long dead, Agatha Hagglethorn," I responded, and gathered back my right hand to throw. "As is your child. As are you. These little ones are not yours to sing to or bear away." I steeled myself to throw, began to bring my arm forward.

The spirit looked at me with an expression of lost, lonely confusion. This was the hard part about dealing with really substantial, dangerous ghosts. They were almost human. They appeared to be able to feel emotion, to have some degree of self-awareness. Ghosts aren't alive, not really—they're a footprint in stone, a fossilized skeleton. They are shaped like the original, but they aren't it.

But I'm a sucker for a lady in distress. I always have been. It's a weak point in my character, a streak of chivalry a mile wide and twice as deep. I saw the hurt and the loneliness on the ghost-Agatha's face, and felt it strike a sympathetic chord in me. I let my arm go still gain. Perhaps, if I was lucky, I could talk her away. Ghosts are like that. Confront them with the reality of their situation, and they dissolve.

"I'm sorry, Agatha," I said. "But you aren't who you think you are. You're a ghost. A reflection. The true Agatha Hagglethorn died more than a century ago."

"N-no," she said, her voice shaking. "That's not true."

"It *is* true," I said. "She died on the same night as her husband and child."

"No," the spirit moaned, her eyes closing. "No, no, no, no. I don't want to hear this." She started singing to herself again, low and desperate—no enchantment to it this time, no unconscious act of destruction. But the infant girl still hadn't inhaled, and her lips were turning blue.

"Listen to me, Agatha," I said, forcing more of my will into my voice, lacing it with magic so that the ghost could hear me. "I know about you. You died. You remember. Your husband beat you. You were terrified that he would beat your daughter. And when she started crying, you covered her mouth with your hand." I felt like such a bastard to be going over the woman's past so coldly. Ghost or not, the pain on her face was real.

"I didn't," Agatha wailed. "I didn't hurt her."

"You didn't mean to hurt her," I said, drawing on the information Bob had provided. "But he was drunk and you were terrified, and when you looked down she was gone. Isn't that right?" I licked my lips, and looked at the infant girl again. If I didn't get this done quickly, she'd die. It was eerie, how still she was, like a little rubber doll.

Something, some spark of memory caught a flame in the ghost's eyes. "I remember," she hissed. "The axe. The axe, the axe, the axe." The proportions of the ghost's face changed, stretched, became more bony, more slender. "I took my axe, my axe, my axe and gave my Benson twenty whacks." The spirit grew, expanding, and a ghostly wind rustled through the room, emanating from the ghost, and rife with the smell of iron and blood.

"Oh, crap," I muttered, and gathered myself to make a dash for the girl.

"My angel gone," screamed the ghost. "Benson gone. And then the hand, the hand that killed them both." She lifted the stump of her arm into the air. "Gone, gone, gone!" She threw back her head and screamed, and it came out as a deafening, bestial roar that rattled the nursery walls.

I threw myself forward, toward the breathless child, and as I did the rest of the infants burst into terrified wails. I reached the child and smacked her little upturned baby butt. She blinked her eyes open in sudden shock, drew in a breath, and joined the rest of her nursery mates in crying.

"No," Agatha screamed, "no, no, no! He'll hear you! He'll hear you!" The stump of her left arm flashed out toward me, and I felt the impact both against my body and against my soul, as though she had driven a chip of ice deep into my chest. The power of the blow flung me back against a wall like a toy, hard enough to send my staff and rod clattering to the floor. By some miracle or other, I kept hold of my sack of ghost dust, but my head vibrated like a hammer-struck bell, and cold shivers wracked my body in rapid succession.

"Michael," I wheezed, as loudly as I could, but already I could hear doors being thrown open, heavy work boots pounding toward me. I struggled to my feet and shook my head to clear it. The wind rose to gale force, sending cribs skittering around the room on their little wheels, tearing at my eyes so that I had to shield them with one hand. Dammit. The dust would be useless in such a gale.

"Hush little baby, hush little baby, hush little baby." Agatha's ghost bowed over the infant girl's cradle again, and thrust the stump of her left arm down and *into* the mouth of the child, her translucent flesh passing seamlessly into the infant's skin. The child jerked and stopped breathing, though she still attempted to cry.

I shouted a wordless challenge and charged the spirit. If I could not cast the dust upon her from across the room, I could thrust the leather bag into her ghostly flesh and pin her into place from within—agonizing, but undoubtedly effective.

Agatha's head whipped toward me as I came, and she jerked away from the child with a snarl. Her hair had come free in the gale and spread about her face in a ferocious mane well suited to the feral features that had replaced her gentle expression. She drew back her left hand, and there suddenly appeared, floating just above the stump, a short, heavy-headed hatchet. She shrieked and brought the hatched down at me.

Ghostly steel chimed on true iron, and *Amoracchius's* light flared bright-white. Michael slid his feet into position on the floor, gritting his teeth with effort, and kept the spirit-weapon from touching my flesh.

"Dresden," he called. "The dust!"

I fought my way forward, through the wind, shoved my fist into Agatha's weapon-arm, and shook loose some of the ghost dust from the leather sack.

Upon contact with her immaterial flesh, the ghost dust flared into blazing motes of scarlet light. Agatha screamed and jerked back, but her arm remained in place as firmly as if it had been set in concrete.

"Benson!" Agatha shrieked. "Benson! Hush little baby!" And then she simply tore herself away from her arm at the shoulder, leaving her spirit flesh behind, and vanished. The arm and hatchet collapsed to the floor in a sudden spatter of clear, semi-fluid gelatin, the remnants of spirit-flesh when the spirit was gone, ectoplasm that would swiftly evaporate.

The gale died, though the lights continued to flicker. My blue-white wizard light, and the lambent glow of Michael's sword were the only reliable sources of illumination in the room. My ears shrieked with the sudden lack of sound, though the dozen or so babies, in their cribs, continued a chorus of steady, terrified little wails.

"Are the children all right?" Michael asked. "Where did it go?"

"I think so. The ghost must have crossed over," I guessed. "She knew she'd had it."

Michael turned in a slow circle, sword still held at the ready. "It's gone, then?"

I shook my head, scanning the room. "I don't think so," I responded, and bent over the crib of the infant girl who had nearly been smothered. The name on her wrist bracelet read Alison Ann Summers. I stroked her little cheek, and she turned her mouth toward my finger, baby lips fastening on my fingertip, cries dying.

"Take your finger out of her mouth," Michael chided. "It's dirty. What happens now?"

"I'll ward the room," I said. "And then we'll get out of here before the police show up and arres—"

Alison Ann jerked and stopped breathing. Her tiny arms and legs stiffened. I felt something cold pass over her, heard the distant drone of mad lullaby.

Hush little baby . . .

"Michael," I cried. "She's still here. The ghost, she's reaching here from the Nevernever."

"Christ preserve," Michael swore. "Harry, we have to step over."

My heart skipped a beat at the very thought. "No," I said. "No way. This is a big spook, Michael. I'm not going to go onto her home ground naked and offer to go two out of three."

"We don't have a choice," Michael snapped. "Look."

I looked. The infants were falling silent, one by one, little cries abruptly smothered in mid-breath.

Hush little baby . . .

"Michael, she'll tear us apart. And even if she doesn't, my godmother *will*."

Michael shook his head, scowling. "No, by God. I won't let that happen." He turned his gaze on me, piercing. "And neither will you, Harry Dresden. There is too much good in your heart to let these children die."

I returned his stare, uncertain. Michael had insisted that I look him in the eyes on our first meeting. When a wizard looks you in the eyes, it's serious. He can see inside of you, all of your dark secrets and hidden fears of your soul—and you see his in return. Michael's soul had made me weep. I wished that my soul would look liked his had to me. But I was pretty damned sure that it didn't.

Silence fell. All the little babies hushed.

I closed the sack of ghost dust and put it away in my pocket. It wouldn't do me any good in the Nevernever.

I turned toward my fallen rod and staff, thrust out my hand, and spat, *"Ventas servitas."* The air stirred, and then flung staff and rod into my open hands before dying away again. "All right," I said. "I'm tearing open a window that will give us five minutes. Hopefully, my godmother won't have time to find me. Anything beyond that and we're going to be dead already or back here, in my case."

"You have a good heart, Harry Dresden," Michael said, a fierce grin stretching his mouth. He stepped closer to my side. "God will smile on this choice."

"Yeah. Ask Him not to Sodom and Gomorrah my apartment, and we'll be even."

Michael gave me a disappointed glance. I shot him a testy glare. He clamped a hand onto my shoulder and held on.

Then I reached out, caught hold of reality in my fingertips, and with an effort of will and a whispered, *"Aparturum,"* tore a hole between this world and the next.

Chapter 3

Even days that culminate in a grand battle against an insane ghost and a trip across the border between this world and the spirit realm usually start out pretty normally. This one, for example, started off with breakfast and then work at the office.

My office is in a building in midtown Chicago. It's an older building, and not in the best of shape, especially since there was that problem with the elevator last year. I don't care what anyone says, that wasn't my fault. When a giant scorpion the size of an Irish wolfhound is tearing its way through the roof of your elevator car, you get real willing to take desperate measures.

Anyway, my office is small—one room, but on the corner, with a couple of windows. The sign on the door reads, simply, HARRY DRESDEN, WIZARD. Just inside the door is a table, covered with pamphlets with titles like: *Magic and You*, and *Why Witches Don't Sink Any Faster Than Anyone Else—a Wizard's Perspective*. I wrote most of them. I think it's important for we practitioners of the Art to keep up a good public image. Anything to avoid another Inquisition.

Behind the table is a sink, counter, and an old coffee machine. My desk faces the door, and a couple of comfortable chairs sit across from it. The air conditioning rattles, the ceiling fan squeaks on every revolution, and the scent of coffee is soaked into the carpet and the walls.

I shambled in, put coffee on, and sorted through the mail while the coffee percolated. A thank you letter from the Campbells, for chasing a spook out of their house. Junk mail. And, thank goodness, a check from the city for my last batch of work for the Chicago P.D. That had been a nasty case, all in all. Demon summoning, human sacrifice, black magic—the works.

I got my coffee and resolved to call Michael to offer to split my earnings with him—even though the legwork had been all mine, he and *Amoracchius* had come in on the finale. I'd handled the sorcerer, he'd dealt with the demon, and the good guys won the day. I'd turned in my logs and at fifty bucks an hour had netted myself a neat two grand. Michael would refuse the money (he always did) but it seemed polite to make the offer; especially given how much time we'd been spending together recently, in an attempt to track down the source of all the ghostly happenings in the city.

The phone rang before I could pick it up to call Michael. "Harry Dresden," I answered.

"Hello there, Mr. Dresden," said a warm, feminine voice. "I was wondering if I could have a moment of your time."

I kicked back in my chair, and felt a smile spreading over my face. "Why, Miss Rodriguez, isn't it? Aren't you that nosy reporter from the *Arcane*? That useless rag that publishes stories about witches and ghosts and Bigfoot?"

"Plus Elvis," she assured me. "Don't forget the King. And I'm syndicated now. Publications of questionable reputation all over the world carry my column."

I laughed. "How are you today?"

Susan's voice turned wry. "Well, my boyfriend stood me up last night, but other than that . . ."

I winced a little. "Yeah, I know. Sorry about that. Look, Bob found a tip for me that just couldn't wait."

"Ahem," she said, in her polite, professional voice. "I'm not calling you to talk about my *personal* life, Mr. Dresden. This is a business call."

I felt my smile returning. Susan was absolutely one in a million, to put up with me. "Oh, beg pardon, Miss Rodriguez. Pray continue."

"Well. I was thinking that there were rumors of some more ghostly activity in the old town last night. I thought you might be willing to share a few details with the *Arcane*."

"Mmmm. That might not be wholly professional of me. I keep my business confidential."

"Mr. Dresden," she said. "I would as soon not resort to desperate measures."

"Why, Miss Rodriguez." I grinned. "Are you a desperate woman?"

I could almost see the way she arched one eyebrow. "Mr. Dresden. I don't want to threaten you. But you must understand that I am well acquainted with a certain young lady of your company—and that I could see to it that things became *very* awkward between you."

"I see. But if I shared the story with you—"

"Gave me an exclusive, Mr. Dresden."

"An exclusive," I amended, "then you might see your way clear to avoiding causing problems for me?"

"I'd even put in a good word with her," Susan said, her voice cheerful, then dropping into a lower, smokier register. "Who knows. You might get lucky."

I thought about it for a minute. The ghost Michael and I had nailed last night had been a big, bestial thing lurking in the basement of the University of Chicago library. I didn't have to mention the names of any people involved, and while the university wouldn't like it, I doubted it would be seriously hurt by appearing in a magazine that most people bought along with every other tabloid in the supermarket checkout lines. Besides which, just the thought of Susan's caramel skin and soft, dark hair under my hands . . . Yum. "That's an offer I can hardly refuse," I told her. "Do you have a pen?"

She did, and I spent the next ten minutes telling her the details. She took them down with a number of sharp, concise questions, and had the whole story out of me in less time than I would have believed. She really was a good reporter, I thought. It was almost a shame that she was spending her time reporting the supernatural, which people had been refusing to believe in for centuries.

"Thank you very much, Mr. Dresden," she said, after she squeezed the last drips of information out of me. "I hope things go well between you and the young lady tonight. At your place. At nine."

"Maybe the young lady would like to discuss the possibilities with me," I drawled.

She let out a throaty laugh. "Maybe she would," Susan agreed. "But this is a business call."

I laughed. "You're terrible, Susan. You never give up, do you?"

"Never, ever," she said.

"Would you really have been mad at me if I hadn't told you?"

"Harry," she said. "You stood me up last night without a word. I don't usually stand for that kind of treatment from any man. If you hadn't had a good story for me, I was going to think that you were out horsing around with your friends."

"Yeah, that Michael." I chuckled. "He's a real party animal."

"You're going to have to give me the story on him sometime. Have you come any closer to working out what's going on with the ghosts? Did you look into the seasonal angle?"

I sighed, closing my eyes. "No, and yes. I still can't figure why the ghosts seem to be freaking out all at once—and we haven't been able to get any of them to hold still long enough for me to get a good look at them. I've got a new recipe to try out tonight—maybe that will do it. But Bob is sure it isn't a Halloweeny kind of problem. I mean, we didn't have any ghosts last year."

"No. We had werewolves."

"Different situation entirely," I said. "I've got Bob working overtime to keep an eye on the spirit world for any more activity. If anything else is about to jump, we'll know it."

"All right," she said. She hesitated for a moment and then said, "Harry. I—"

I waited, but when she stalled I asked, "What?"

"I, uh . . . I just want to be sure that you're all right."

I had the distinct impression that she had been going to say something else, but I didn't push. "Tired," I said. "A couple of bruises from slipping on some ectoplasm and falling into a card catalog. But I'm fine."

She laughed. "That creates a certain image. Tonight then?"

"I'm looking forward to it."

She made a pleased little sound with more than a hint of sexuality in it, and let that be her goodbye.

The day went fairly quickly, with a bunch of the usual business. I whipped up a spell to find a lost wedding ring, and turned down a customer who wanted me to put a love spell on his mistress. (My ad in the Yellow Pages specifically reads "No love potions," but for some reason people always think that their case is special.) I went to the bank, referred a caller to a private detective I knew, and met with a fledgling pyromancer in an attempt to teach him to stop igniting his cat accidentally.

I was just closing down the office when I heard someone come out of the elevator and start walking down the hallway toward me. The steps were heavy, as though from boots, and rushed.

"Mr. Dresden?" asked a young woman's voice. "Are you Harry Dresden?"

"Yes," I said, locking the office door. "But I'm just leaving. Maybe we can set up an appointment for tomorrow."

The footsteps stopped a few feet away from me. "Please, Mr. Dresden. I've got to talk to you. Only you can help me."

I sighed, without looking at her. She'd said the exact words she needed to in order to kick off my protective streak. But I could still walk away. Lots of people got to thinking that magic could dig them out of their troubles, once they realized they couldn't escape. "I'll be glad to, Ma'am. First thing in the morning." I locked the door and started to turn away.

"Wait," she said. I felt her step closer to me, and she grabbed by hand.

A tingling, writhing sensation shot up my wrist and over my elbow. My reaction was immediate and instinctive. I threw up a mental shield against the sensation, jerked my hand clear of her fingers, and took several steps back and away from the young woman.

My hand and arm still tingled from brushing against the energy of her aura. She was a slight girl in a black knit dress, black combat boots, and hair dyed to a flat, black matte. The lines of her face were soft and sweet, and her skin was pale as chalk around eyes that were sunken, shadowed, and glittering with alley-cat wariness.

I flexed my fingers and avoiding meeting the girl's eyes for more than a fraction of a second. "You're a practitioner," I said, quietly.

She bit her lip and looked away, nodding. "And I need your help. They said that you would help me."

"I give lessons to people who want to avoid hurting themselves with uncontrolled talent," I said. "Is that what you're after?"

"No, Mr. Dresden," the girl said. "Not exactly."

"Why me, then? What do you want?"

"I want your protection." She lifted a shaking hand, fidgeting with her dark hair. "And if I don't have it . . . I'm not sure I'll live through the night."

Chapter 4

I let us both back into the office, and flicked on the lights. The bulb blew out. It does that a lot. I sighed, and shut the door behind us, leaving stripes of golden autumn light pouring through the blinds, interweaving with shadows on the floor and walls.

I drew out a seat in front of my desk for the young woman. She blinked at me in confusion for a second before she said, "Oh," and sat. I walked around the desk, leaving my duster on, and sat down.

"All right," I said. "If you want my protection, I want a few things from you first."

She pushed back her asphalt-colored hair with one hand and gave me a look of pure calculation. Then she simply crossed her legs, so that the cut of her dress left one pale leg bare to mid-thigh. A subtle motion of her back thrust out her young, firm breasts, so that their tips pressed visibly against the fabric. "Of course, Mr. Dresden. I'm sure we can do business." The look she gave me was direct, sensual, and willing.

Nipple erection on command—now that's method acting. Oh, she was pretty enough, I suppose. Any adolescent male would have been drooling and hurling himself at her, but I'd seen acts a lot better. I rolled my eyes. "That's not what I meant."

Her sex-kitten look faltered. "It . . . it isn't?" She frowned at me, eyes scanning me again, reassessing me. "Is it . . . are you . . . ?"

"No," I said. "I'm not gay. But I'm not buying what you're selling. You haven't even told me your name, but you're willing to spread your legs for me? No thanks. Hell's Bells, haven't you ever heard of AIDS? Herpes?"

Her face went white, and she pressed her lips together until they were white, too. "All right, then," she said. "What do you want from me?"

"Answers," I told her, jabbing a finger at her. "And don't try lying to me. It won't do you any good." Which was only a marginal lie, in itself. Being a wizard doesn't make you a walking lie detector, and I wasn't going to try a soulgaze on her to find out if she was sincere—it wasn't worth it. But another great thing about being a wizard is that people attribute just about anything you do to your vast and unknowable powers. Granted, it only works with those who know enough to believe in wizards, but not enough to understand our limits—the rest of the world, the regular people who think magic is just a joke, just look at you like someone is going to stuff you into a little white coat any second now.

She licked her lips, a nervous gesture, not a sexy one. "All right," she said. "What do you want to know?"

"Your name, for starters."

She let out a harsh laugh. "You think I'm going to give you that, wizard?"

Point. Serious spell-slingers like me could do an awful lot with a person's name, given by their own lips. "All right, then. What do I call you?"

She didn't bother to cover her leg again. A rather pretty leg, actually, with a tattoo of some kind encircling her ankle. I tried not to notice. "Lydia," she said. "Call me Lydia."

"Okay, Lydia. You're a practitioner of the Art. Tell me about that."

"It doesn't have anything to do with what I want from you, Mr. Dresden," she said. She swallowed, her anger fading. "Please. I need your help."

"All right, all right," I said. "What kind of help do you need? If you're into some kind of gang-related trouble, I'm going to recommend that you head for the police. I'm not a bodyguard."

She shivered, and hugged herself with her arms. "No, nothing like that. It's not my body I'm worried about."

That made me frown.

She closed her eyes and drew in a breath. "I need a talisman," she said. "Something to protect me from a hostile spirit."

That made me sit up and take notice, metaphorically speaking.

With the city flying into spiritual chaos as it was, I had no trouble believing that a girl gifted with magical talent might be experiencing some bad phenomena. Ghosts and spooks are drawn to the magically gifted. "What kind of spirit?"

Her eyes shifted left and right, never looking at me. "I can't really say, Mr. Dresden. It's powerful and it wants to hurt me. They . . . they told me you could make something that would keep me safe."

True, in point of fact. Around my left wrist at that very moment was a talisman made from a dead man's shroud, blessed silver, and a number of other, more difficult to come by ingredients. "Maybe," I told her. "That depends on why you're in danger, and why you feel you need protection."

"I c-can't tell you that," she said. Her pale face pinched into an expression of worry—real worry, the kind that makes you look older, uglier. The way she hugged herself made her look smaller, more frail. "Please, I just need your help."

I sighed, and rubbed at one eyebrow with my thumb. My first rampant instincts were to give her a cup of hot chocolate, put a blanket around her shoulders, tell her everything would be all right and strap my talisman onto her wrist. I tried to rein those in, though. Down, Quixote. I still knew nothing about her situation, or what she needed protection from—for all I knew, she was trying to stave off an avenging angel coming after her in retribution for some act so vile that it stirred the Powers that be to take immediate action. Even vanilla ghosts sometimes come back to haunt someone for a darned good reason.

"Look, Lydia. I don't like to get involved in anything without knowing something about what's going on." *Which hadn't slowed me down before,* I noted. "Unless you can tell me a little bit about your situation, convince me that you are in legitimate need of protection, I won't be able to help you."

She bowed her head, her asphalt hair falling across her face for a long minute. Then she drew in a breath and asked, "Do you know what Cassandra's Tears is, Mr. Dresden?"

"Prophetic condition," I said. "The person in question has random seizures—visions of the future, but they're always couched in terms of conditions that make explanation of the dreams seem unbelievable. Doctors mistake it for epilepsy in children, sometimes, and prescribe a bunch of different drugs for it. Pretty accurate prophecy, as it goes, but no one ever buys into it. Some people call it a gift."

"I'm not one of them," she whispered. "You don't know how horrible it is. To see something about to happen and to try to change it, only to have no one believe you."

I studied her for a minute in silence, listening to the clock on my wall count down the seconds. "All right," I said. "You say that you have this gift. I guess you want me to believe that one of your visions warned you about an evil spirit coming after you?"

"Not one," she said. "Three. *Three*, Mr. Dresden. I only got one vision when they tried to kill the President. I got two for that disaster at NASA, and for the earthquake in Laos. I've never had three before. Never had something appear so clearly . . ."

I closed my eyes to think about this. Again, my instincts told me to help the girl, smash the bad ghost or whatever, and walk off into the sunset. If she was indeed afflicted with Cassandra's Tears, my actions could do more than save her life. My faith could change it for the better.

On the other hand, I'd been played for a sucker before. The girl was obviously a competent actress. She had shifted smoothly to the role of willing seductress, when she thought I had been asking for sex in payment. That she would immediately make that conclusion based on my own fairly neutral statement said something about her, all by itself. This wasn't a girl who was used to playing things fair and square. Unless I was grossly misreading her, she had bartered sex for goods and services before—and she was awfully young to be so jaded about the entire matter.

The entire Cassandra's Tears angle was a perfect scam, and people had used it before, among the circles of the magically endowed. The story required no proof, no performance on the part of the person running the scam. All she would need would be a smidgen of talent to give her the right aura, maybe enough kinetomancy to tilt the dice a little on their way down. Then she could make up whatever story she wanted about her supposed prophetic gifts, put on a little-girl-lost act, and head straight for the local dummy, Harry Blackstone Copperfield Dresden.

I opened my eyes to find her watching me. "Of course," she said. "I could be lying. Cassandra's Tears can't be analyzed or observed. I could be using it as an excuse to provide a reasonable explanation why you should help a lady in distress."

"That's pretty much what's going through my mind, Lydia, yeah. You could just be a small-time witch who stirred up the wrong demon and is looking for a way out."

She spread her hands. "All I can tell you is that I'm not. I know that something's coming. I don't know what, and I don't know why or how. I just know what I see."

"Which is?"

"Fire," she whispered. "Wind. I see dark things and a dark war. I see my death coming for me, out of the spirit world. And I see you at the middle of it all. You're the beginning, the end of it. You're the one who can make the path go different ways."

"*That's* your vision? Iowa has less corn."

She turned her face away. "I see what I see."

Standard carny procedure. Flatter the ego of the mark, draw him in, get him good and hooked, and fleece him for everything he's got. Sheesh, I thought, someone else trying to get something out of me. My reputation must be growing.

Still, there was no sense in being rude. "Look, Lydia. I think maybe you're just overreacting, here. Why don't we meet again in a couple of days, and we'll see if you still think you need my help."

She didn't answer me. Her shoulders just slumped forward and her face went slack with defeat. She closed her eyes, and I felt a nagging sensation of doubt tug at me. I had the uncomfortable impression that she wasn't acting.

"All right," she said, softly. "I'm sorry to have kept you late." She got up and started walking toward the door of my office.

My better judgement propelled me up out of my chair and across the room. We reached the door at the same time.

"Wait a minute," I said. I unbound the talisman from my arm, feeling the silent *pop* of energy as the knot came undone. Then I took her left wrist and turned her hand over to tie the talisman onto her. There were pale scars on her arm—the vertical kind that run along the big veins. The ones you get when you're really serious about killing yourself. They were old and faded. She must have gotten them when she was . . . what? Ten years old? Younger?

I shuddered and secured the little braid of musty cloth and silver chain about her wrist, willing enough energy into it to close the circle once the knot was tied. When I finished, I touched her forearm lightly. I could just feel the talisman's power, a tingling sensation that hovered a half-inch off of her skin.

"Faith magic works best against spirits," I said quietly. "If you're worried, get to a church. Spirits are strongest just after the sun goes down, around the witching hour, and again just before the sun comes up. Go to Saint Mary of the Angels. It's a church at the corner of Bloomingdale and Wood, down by Wicker Park. It's huge, you can't miss it. Go around to the delivery door and ring the bell. Talk to Father Forthill. Tell him that Michael's friend said that you need a safe place to stay for a while."

She only stared at me, her mouth open. Tears formed in her eyes. "You believe me," she said. "You believe me."

I shrugged, uncomfortable. "Maybe. Maybe not. But things have been bad, the past few weeks, and I would rather not have you on my conscience. You'd better hurry. It's going to be sundown soon." I pressed some bills into her hand and said, "Take a cab. Saint Mary of the Angels. Father Forthill. Michael's friend sent you."

"Thank you," she said. "Oh, God. Thank you, Mr. Dresden." She seized my hand in both of hers and pressed a tearstained kiss to my knuckles. Her fingers were cold and her lips too hot. Then she vanished out the door.

I shut it behind her and shook my head. "Harry, you idiot. Your one decent talisman that would protect you against ghosts and you just gave it away. She's probably a plant. They probably sent her to you just to get the talisman off you, so that they can eat you up the next time you go spoil their fun." I glared down at my hand, where the warmth of Lydia's kiss and the dampness of her tears still lingered. Then I sighed, and walked to the cabinet where I kept fifty or sixty spare light-bulbs on hand, and replaced the one that had burned out.

The phone rang. I got down off my chair and answered it sourly. "Dresden."

There was silence and scratchy static on the other end of the line.

"Dresden," I repeated.

The silence stretched on, and something about it made the hairs on the back of my neck stand up. There was a quality to it that is difficult to describe. Like something waiting. Gloating. The static crackled louder, and I thought I could hear voices underneath it, voices speaking in low, cruel tones. I glanced at the door, after the departed Lydia. "Who is this?"

"Soon," whispered a voice. "Soon, Dresden. We will see one another again."

"Who is this?" I repeated, feeling a little silly.

The line went dead.

I stared at the phone before hanging it up, then ran my hand back through my hair. A chill crawled neatly down my spine and took up residence somewhere a little lower than my stomach. "All right, then," I said, my own voice a little too loud in the office. "Thank God that wasn't too creepy or anything."

The antique radio on the shelf beside the coffee machine hissed and squalled to life and I almost jumped out of my shoes. I whirled to face it in a fury, hands clenched.

"Harry?" said a voice on the radio. "Hey, Harry, is this thing working?"

I tried to calm my pounding heart, and focused enough will on the radio to let my voice carry through. "Yeah, Bob. It's me."

"Thank the stars," Bob said. "You said you wanted to know if I found out anything else ghostly going on."

"Yeah, yeah, go ahead."

The radio hissed and crackled with static—spiritual interference, not physical. The radio wasn't set up to receive AM/FM any more. Bob's voice was garbled, but I could understand it. "My contact came through. Cook County Hospital, tonight. Someone's stirred up Agatha Hagglethorn. This is a bad one, Harry. She is one mean old biddy."

Bob gave me the rundown on Agatha Hagglethorn's grisly and tragic death, and her most likely target at the hospital. I glanced down at my bare left wrist, and abruptly felt naked. "All right," I said. "I'm on it. Thanks, Bob."

The radio squalled and went silent, and I dashed out the door. Sundown would come in less than twenty minutes, rush hour had been going for a while now, and if I wasn't at Cook County by the time it got dark, all kinds of bad things could happen.

I flew out the front door, the sack of ghost dust heavy in my pocket, and all but slammed into Michael, tall and broad, toting a huge athletic bag over his shoulder, which I knew would contain nothing but *Amoracchius* and his white cloak.

"Michael!" I burst out. "How did you get here?"

His honest face split into a wide smile. "When there is a need, He sees to it that I am there."

"Wow," I said. "You're kidding."

"No," he said, his voice earnest. Then he paused. "Of course, you've gotten in touch with me every night for the past two weeks. Tonight, I just thought I'd save Him the trouble of arranging coincidence, so I came on over as soon as I got off work." He fell into step beside me and we both got into the *Blue Beetle*—he got in the red door, I got in the white one, and we peered out over the grey hood as I pulled the old VW into traffic.

And that was how we ended up doing battle in the nursery at Cook County.

Anyway, you see what I mean about a day being fairly normal before it falls all to pieces. Or, well. Maybe it hadn't been all that normal. As we took off into traffic and I gave the *Beetle* all the gas it could take, I got that sinking feeling that my life was about to get hectic again.

Chapter 5

Michael and I plunged through the hole I'd torn in reality and into the Nevernever. It felt like moving from a sauna into an air-conditioned office, except that I didn't feel the change on my skin. I felt it in my thoughts and my feelings, and in the primitive, skin-crawling part of me at the base of my brain. I stood in a different world than our own.

The little leather sack of ghost dust in my duster pocket abruptly increased its weight, dragging me off balance and to the ground. I let out a curse. The whole point of the ghost dust was that it was something extra-real, that it was heavy and inert and locked spiritual matter into place when it touched it. Even inside its bag, it had become a sudden stress on the Nevernever. If I opened the bag here, in the world of spirit, it might tear a hole in the floor. I'd have to be careful. I grunted with effort and pulled the little pouch out of my pocket. It felt like it weighed thirty or forty pounds.

Michael frowned down at my hands. "You know. I never really thought to ask before—but what *is* that dust made of?"

"Depleted uranium," I told him. "At least, that's the base ingredient. I had to add in a lot of other things. Cold iron, basil, dung from a—"

"Never mind," he said. "I don't want to know." He turned away from me, his arms steadily holding the massive sword before him. I recovered staff and rod, and stood beside him, studying the lay of the as-it-were land.

This part of the Nevernever looked like Chicago, at the end of the nineteenth century—no, strike that. This was the ghost's demesne. It looked like a mishmash of Agatha Hagglethorn's memories of Chicago at the end of her life. Edison's bulbs were mounted in some of the streetlights, while others burned with flickering gas flames. All of them cast hazy spheres of light, doing little to actually illuminate their surroundings. The buildings stood at slightly odd angles to one another, with parts of them seamlessly missing. Everything—streets, sidewalks, buildings—was made of wood.

"Hell's bell," I muttered. "No wonder the real Chicago kept burning down. This place is a tinderbox."

Rats moved in the shadows, but the street was otherwise empty and still. The rift that led back to our world wavered and shifted, fluorescent light and sterile hospital air pouring onto the old Chicago streets. Around us pulsed maybe a dozen shimmering disturbances in the air—the rich life forces of the infants back in the infirmary, showing through into the Nevernever.

"Where is she?" Michael asked, his voice quiet. "Where's the ghost?"

I turned in a slow circle, peering at the shadows, and shook my head. "I don't know. But we'd better find her, fast. And we need to get a look at this one if we can."

"To try to find out what's gotten it stirred up," Michael said.

"Exactly. I don't know about you, but I'm getting a little tired of chasing all over town every night."

"Didn't you already get a look at her?"

"Not the right kind of look," I said with a grimace. "There could be spells laid on her, some kind of magic around her to clue me in on what's going on. I need to be not in mortal peril for a couple of minutes to examine her."

"Provided she doesn't kill us first, all right," Michael assented. "But time is short, and I don't see her anywhere. What should we do?"

"I hate to say it," I said, "but I think we should—"

I was going to say "split up," but I didn't get the chance. The heavy wooden timbers of the roadway beneath us exploded up and out in a deadly cloud of splinters. I threw one leather-clad arm across my eyes and went tumbling one way. Michael went the other.

"My little angels! Mine, mine, MINE!" screamed a voice that roared against my face and chest and made my duster flap around as though made of gauze.

I looked up, to see the ghost, quite real and solid now, clawing its one-armed way up from the sub-street. Agatha's face was lean and bony, twisted in rage, and her hair hung about her in a shaggy mane, sharply at odds with her crisp white shirt. Her arm was missing from its shoulder, and dark fluid stained the cloth beneath it.

Michael rose to his feet with a shout, one of his cheeks cut and bleeding, and went after her with *Amoracchius*. The spirit back-handed him away with her remaining arm as though he weighed no more than a doll. Michael grunted and went flying, rolling along the wooden street.

And then, snarling and drooling, her eyes wide with frenzied madness, the ghost turned toward me.

I scrambled to my feet and held out my staff across my body, a slender barrier between me and the ghost on its home turf. "I guess it's too late to have a reasonable discussion, Agatha."

"My babies!" the spirit screamed. "Mine! Mine! Mine!"

"Yeah, that's what I thought," I breathed. I gathered my forces and started channeling them through the staff. The pale wood began glowing with a gold-and-orange light, spreading out before me in a quarter-dome shape.

The ghost screamed again and hurtled toward me. I stood fast and shouted, "*Reflettum!*" at the top of my lungs. The spirit impacted against my shield with all the momentum of a bull rhinoceros on steroids. I've stopped bullets and worse with that shield before, but that was on my home turf, in the real world. Here, the Nevernever, Agatha's ghost overloaded my shield, which detonated with a thunderous roar and sent me sprawling to the ground. Again.

I jammed my scorched staff into the ground and groaned to my feet. Blood stained my tingling fingers, the skin swelling with dark bruises and burst blood vessels.

Agatha stood several paces away, shaking with rage, or if I was lucky, with confusion. Bits of my shield-fire played over her shape and slowly winked out. I fumbled for my blasting rod, but my fingers had gone numb and I dropped it. I bent over to pick it up, swayed, and stood up again, red mist and sparkling dots swimming through my vision.

Michael circled the stunned spirit and arrived at my side. His expression was concerned, rather than frightened. "Easy, Harry, easy. Good Lord, man, are you all right?"

"I'll make it," I croaked. "There's good news and bad news."

The knight brought his sword to guard again. "I've always been partial to the good news."

"I don't think she's interested in those babies anymore."

Michael flashed me a swift smile. "That *is* good news."

I wiped some sweat from my eyes. My hand came away scarlet. I must have gotten a cut, somewhere along the way. "The bad news is that she's going to come over here and tear us apart in a couple more seconds."

"Not to be negative, but I'm afraid the news gets worse," Michael said. "Listen."

I glanced at him, and cocked my head to one side. Distantly, but quickly growing nearer, I could hear haunting, musical baying, ghostly in the midnight air. "Holy shit," I breathed. "Hellbounds."

"Harry," Michael said sternly. "You know I hate it when you swear."

"You're right. Sorry. Holy shit," I breathed, "heckhounds. Godmother's out hunting. How the hell did she find us so damned fast?"

Michael grimaced at me. "She must have been close already. How long before she gets here?"

"Not long. My shield made a lot of noise when it buckled. She'll home in on it."

"If you want to go, Harry," Michael said, "go on and leave. I'll hold the ghost until you can get back through the rift."

I was tempted. There aren't a lot of things that scare me more than the Nevernever and my godmother in tandem. But I was also angry. I hate it when I get shown up. Besides, Michael was a friend, and I'm not in the habit of leaving friends to clean up my messes for me. "No," I said. "Let's just hurry."

Michael grinned at me, and started forward, just as Agatha's ghost extinguished the last residual bits of my magic that had been plaguing it. Michael send *Amoracchius* whistling at the ghost, but she was unthinkably swift, and dodged each blow with a circling, swooping sort of grace. I lifted my blasting rod and narrowed my focus. I tuned out the baying of the hellhounds, now a lot nearer, and the sound of galloping hoofbeats that sent my pulse racing. I methodically blanked out everything but the ghost, Michael, and the power funneling into the blasting rod.

The ghost must have sensed the strike gathering, because she turned and flew at me like a bullet. Her mouth opened in a scream, and I could see jagged, pointed teeth lining her jaws, the empty white fire of her eyes.

"Fuego!" I shouted, and then the spirit hit me, full force. A beam of white fire spewed out from my blasting rod and across the wooden storefronts. They burst into flame as though soaked in gasoline. I went down, rolling, the spirit going after my throat with her teeth. I jammed the end of the blasting rod into her mouth and prepared to fire again, but she tore it from my hands with a ferocious dog-like worrying motion and it tumbled away. I swiped the staff at her awkwardly, to no avail. She went for my throat again.

I shoved a leather-clad forearm into her mouth and shouted, "Michael!" The ghost ripped at me with her nails and clamped down on my forearm. I dropped the ghost dust and scrabbled furiously at her with my free hand, trying to lever her off of me, but didn't do much more than muss up her clothing.

She got her hand on my throat and I felt my breath cut off. I writhed and struggled to escape, but the snarling ghost was a lot stronger and faster than me. Stars swam in front of my eyes.

Michael shouted, and swept *Amoracchius* at the spirit. The great blade bit into her back with a wooden-sounding thunk and made her arch up, screaming in pain. It was a deathblow. The white light of the blade touched her spirit-flesh and set it alight, sizzling away from the edges of the wound. She twisted, screaming in fury, and the motion jerked the blade from Michael's hands. Agatha Hagglethorn's blazing ghost prepared to fly at his throat.

I sat up, seized the sack of ghost dust, and with a grunt of effort swept it at the back of her head. There was a sharp sound when the improvised cosh struck her, the superheavy matter I'd enchanted hitting like a sledgehammer on china. The ghost froze in place for a moment, her feral mouth wide—and then toppled slowly to one side.

I looked up at Michael, who stood gasping for breath, staring at me. "Harry," he said. "Do you see?"

I lifted a hand to my aching throat and looked around me. The sounds of baying hounds and thundering hooves had gone. "See what?" I asked.

"Look." He pointed at the smoldering ghost-corpse.

I looked. In my struggles with Agatha's ghost, I had torn aside the prim white shirt, and she must have ripped up the dress when she'd been crashing through sidewalks and strangling wizards and so on. I crawled a bit closer to the corpse. It was burning—not blazing, but steadily being eaten away by *Amoracchius's* white fire, like newsprint slowly curling into flame. The fire didn't hide what Michael was talking about, though.

Wire. Strands of barbed wire ran about the ghost's flesh, beneath her torn clothing. The barbs had dug cruelly into her flesh every two inches or so, and her body was covered with small, agonizing wounds. I grimaced, picking away at the burning cloth in tentative jerks. The wire was a single strand that began at her throat and wrapped about her torso, beneath the arms, winding all the way down one leg to her ankle. At either end, the wire simply vanished into her flesh.

"Sun and stars," I breathed. "No wonder she went mad."

"The wire," Michael asked, crouching down next to me. "It was hurting the ghost?"

I nodded. "Looks like. Torturing it."

"Why didn't we see this in the hospital?"

I shook my head. "Whatever this is . . . I'm not sure it would be visible in the real world. I don't think we would have seen it if we hadn't come here."

"God smiled on us," Michael said.

I eyed my own injuries, then glowered at the bruises already spreading over Michael's arm and throat. "Yeah, whatever. Look, Michael—this kind of thing doesn't just happen. Someone had to do it to this ghost."

"Which implies," Michael said, "that they had a reason to want this ghost to hurt those children." His face darkened into a scowl.

"Whether or not that was their goal, what it implies is that some*one* is behind all the recent activity—not some thing or condition. Someone is purposefully doing this to the ghosts in the area." I stood up and brushed myself off, as the corpse continued to burn, like the buildings around us. Fire raged up the sides of anything vertical, and began to chew its way across the streets and sidewalks as well. A haze of smoke filled the air, as the spirit's demesne in the Nevernever crumbled along with its remains.

"Ow," I complained. I keep my complaints succinct.

Michael took the handle of his sword and drew it out of the flames, shaking his head. "The city is burning."

"Thank you, Sir Obvious."

He smiled. "Can the flames hurt us?"

"Yes," I said, emphatic. "Time to go."

Together, we headed back to the rift at a quick trot. At one point, Michael shouldered me out of the way of a tumbling chimney, and we had to skirt around the pile of shattered bricks and blazing timbers.

"Wait," I said suddenly. "Wait. Do you hear that?"

Michael kept me hustling over the ground, toward the rift. "Hear what? I don't hear anything."

"Yeah." I coughed. "No more hounds howling."

A very tall, slender, inhumanly beautiful woman stepped out of the smoke. Reddish hair curled down past her hips in a riotous cascade, complementing her flawless skin, high cheekbones, and lush, full, bloodred lips. Her face was ageless, and her golden eyes had vertical slits instead of pupils, like a cat. Her gown was a flowing affair of deep green.

"Hello, my son," Lea purred, evidently unaffected by the smoke and unconcerned about the fire. Three great shapes, like mastiffs built from shadows and soot, crouched about her feet, watching us with flat, black eyes. They stood between us and the rift that led back home.

I swallowed and forced down a sudden feeling of childlike panic that started gibbering down in my belly and threatened to come dancing up out of my throat. I stepped forward, between the faerie and Michael and said, in a rough voice, "Hello, Godmother."

Chapter 6

My godmother looked around at the inferno and smiled. "It reminds me of times gone by. Doesn't it remind you, my sweet?" She idly reached down and stroked the head of one of the hounds at her side.

"However did you find me so quickly, Godmother?" I asked.

She gave the hellhound a benign smile. "Mmmm. I have my little secrets, sweet. I only wanted to greet my long-estranged godson."

"All right. Hi, good to see you, have to do it again sometime," I said. Smoke curled up into my mouth and I started coughing. "We're kind of in a hurry here, so—"

Lea laughed, a sound like bells just a shade out of tune. "Always in such a rush, you mortals. But we haven't seen each other in ages, Harry." She walked closer, her body moving with a lithe, sensuous grace that might have been mesmerizing in other circumstances. The hounds spread out silently behind her. "We should spend some time together."

Michael lifted his sword again, and said, calmly, "Madame, step from our path, if you please."

"It does *not* please me," she spat, sudden and vicious. Those rich lips peeled back from dainty, sharp canines, and at the same time the three shadowy hounds let out bubbling growls. Her golden eyes swept past Michael and back to me. "He is mine, sir Knight, by blood right, by Law, and by his own broken word. He has made a compact with me. You have no power over that."

"Harry?" Michael shot me a quick look. "Is what she says true?"

I licked my lips, and gripped my staff. "I was a lot younger, then. And a lot more stupid."

"Harry, if you have made a covenant with her of your own free will then she is right—there is little I can do to stop her."

Another building fell with a roar. The fires gathered around us, and it got hot. Really, really hot. The rift wavered, growing smaller. We didn't have much time left.

"Come, Harry," Lea purred, her voice gone, pardon the pun, smoky again. "Let the good Knight of the White God pass on his way. And let me take you to waters that will soothe your hurts and balm your ills."

It sounded like a good idea. It sounded *really* good. Her own magic saw to that. I felt my feet moving toward her in a slow, leaden shuffling.

"Dresden," Michael said, sharply. "Good Lord, man! What are you doing?"

"Go home, Michael," I said. My voice came out thick, dull, as though I'd been drinking. I saw Lea's mouth, her soft, lovely mouth, curl upward in a triumphant smirk. I didn't try to fight the pull of the magic. I wouldn't have been able to stop my legs in any case. Lea'd had my number for years, and as far as I could tell she always would. I hadn't a prayer of taking control back for more than a few seconds. The air grew cooler as I got closer to her, and I could smell her—her body, her hair, like wildflowers and musky earth, intoxicating. "There isn't much time before the rift closes. Go home."

"Harry!" Michael shouted.

Lea placed one long-fingered, slender hand upon my cheek. A wash of tingling pleasure went through me. My body reacted to her, helpless and demanding at the same time, and I had to fight to keep thoughts of her beauty from preoccupying me altogether.

"Yes, my sweet man," Lea whispered, golden eyes bright with glee. "Sweet, sweet, sweet. Now, lay aside your rod and staff."

I watched dully, as my fingers released both. They clattered to the ground. The flames grew closer, but I didn't feel them. The rift glowed and shrank, almost closed. I narrowed my eyes, gathering my will.

"Will you complete your bargain now, sweet mortal child?" Lea murmured, sliding her hands over my chest and then over my shoulders.

"I will go with you," I answered, letting my voice come out thick, slow. Her eyes lit with malicious glee, and she threw her head back and laughed, revealing creamy, delicious expanses of throat and bosom.

"When Hell freezes over," I added, and drew out the little sack of ghost dust for the last time. I dumped it all over and down the previously mentioned bosom. There isn't much lore about faeries and depleted uranium, yet, but there's a ton about faeries and cold iron. They don't like it, and the iron content of the dust's formula was pretty high.

Lea's flawless complexion immediately split into fiery scarlet welts, the skin drying and cracking before my eyes. Lea's triumphant laugh turned into an agonized scream, and she released me, tearing her silken gown away from her chest in a panic, revealing more gorgeous flesh being riven by the cold iron.

"Michael," I shouted, "now!" I gave my godmother a stiff shove, scooped up my staff and rod, and dove for the rift. I heard a snarl, and something fastened around one of my boots, dragging me to the ground. I thrust my staff down at one of the hellhounds, and the wood struck it in one of its eyes. It roared in rage, and its two pack mates came rushing toward me.

Michael stepped in the way and swept his sword at one of them. The true iron struck the faerie beast, and blood and white fire erupted from the wound. The second one leapt upon Michael and fastened its fangs onto his thigh, ripping and jerking.

I brought my staff down hard on the beast's skull, driving it off Michael's leg, and started dragging my friend back toward the swiftly vanishing line of the rift. More hellhounds appeared, rushing from the burning ruins around us. "Come on!" I shouted. "There's no time!"

"Treacher!" spat my godmother. She rose up from the ground, blackened and burned, her fine dress in tatters about her waist, her body and limbs stretched, knobby, and inhuman. She clenched her hands into fists at her sides, and the fire from the building around us seemed to rush down, gathering in her grasp in a pair of blazing points of violet and emerald light. "Treasonous, poisonous child! You are mine as your mother swore unto me! As you swore!"

"You shouldn't make contracts with a minor!" I shouted back, and shoved Michael forward, into the rift. He wavered for a moment on the narrow opening, and then fell through and vanished back into the real world.

"If you will not give me your life, serpent child, then I will have your *blood*!" Lea took two huge strides toward me and hurled both hands forward. A thunderbolt of braided emerald and violet power rushed at my face.

I hurled myself backwards, at the rift, and prayed that it was still open enough to let me fall through. I extended my staff toward my godmother and threw up whatever weak shield I could. The faerie fire hammered into the shield, hurling me back into the rift like a straw before a tornado. I felt my staff smolder and burst into flames in my hand as I went sailing through.

I landed on the floor of the nursery back in Cook County Hospital, my leather duster trailing with it a shroud of smoke that swiftly converted itself to a thin, disgusting coating of residual ectoplasm, while my staff burned with weird green and purple fire. Babies, in their little glass cribs, screamed lustily all around me. Confused voices babbled from the next room.

Then the rift closed, and we were left back in the real world, surrounded by crying babies. The fluorescent lights all came back up, and we could hear more worried words from the nurses back at the duty station. I beat out the fires on my staff, and then sat there, panting and hurting. None of the matter of the Nevernever may have come back to the real world—but the injuries gained there were very real.

Michael got up, and looked around at the babies, making sure that they were all in satisfactory condition. Then he sat down next to me, wiped the patina of ectoplasm from his brow, and started pressing the material of his cloak against the oozing gashes in his leg, where the hellhound's fangs had sunk through his jeans. He gave me a pensive, frowning stare.

"What?" I asked him.

"Your godmother. You got away from her," he said.

I laughed, weakly. "This time, yeah. So what's bothering you?"

"You lied to her to do it."

"I tricked her," I countered. "Classic tactics with faeries."

He blinked, and then used another section of his cloak to clean the ecto-gook off of *Amoracchius*. "I just thought you were an honest man, Harry," he said, his expression injured. "I can't believe you lied to her."

I started to laugh, weakly, too exhausted to move. "You can't believe I lied to her."

"Well, no," he said, his voice defensive. "That's not the way we're supposed to win. We're the good guys, Harry."

I laughed some more, and wiped a trickle of blood off of my face.

"Well, we are!"

Some kind of alarm started going off. One of the nurses stepped into the observation room, took one look at the pair of us, and ran out screaming.

"You know what bothers me?" I asked.

"What's that?"

I set my scorched staff and rod aside. "I'm wondering how in the world my godmother happened to be right at hand, when I stepped through into Nevernever. It isn't like the place is a small neighborhood. I wasn't there five minutes before she showed up."

Michael sheathed his sword and set it carefully aside, out of easy arm's reach. Then unfastened his cloak, wincing. "Yes. It seems an unlikely coincidence."

We both put our hands up on top of our heads, as a Chicago P.D. patrolman, his jacket and pants stained with spilled coffee, burst into the nursery, gun drawn. We both sat there with our hands on our head, and did our best to look friendly and non-threatening.

"Don't worry," Michael said, quietly. "Just let me do the talking."

Chapter 7

Michael rested his chin in his hands and sighed. "I can't believe we're in jail."

"Disturbing the peace," I snorted, pacing the confines of the holding cell. "Trespass. Hah. They'd have seen disturbed peace if we hadn't shown up." I jerked a fistful of citations out of my pants pocket. "Look at this. Speeding, failure to obey traffic signs, dangerous and reckless operation of a motor vehicle. And here's the best one. Illegal *parking*. I'm going to lose my license!"

"You can't blame them, Harry. It isn't as though we could explain what happened in terms that they would understand."

I kicked at the bars in frustration. Pain lanced up my leg and I immediately regretted it—they'd taken away my boots when I'd been put through processing. Added to my aching ribs, the wounds on my head, and my stiffening fingers, it was too much. I sat down on the bench next to Michael with a *whuff* of expelled breath. "I get so sick of that," I said. "People like you and me stand up to things that these jokers"—I made an all-encompassing gesture—"would never even dream existed. We don't get paid for it, we hardly even get thanked for it."

Michael's tone was unruffled, philosophical. "It's the nature of the beast, Harry."

"I don't mind it so much. I just hate it when something like this happens." I stood up, frustrated again, and started pacing the interior of the cell. "What really galls me is that we still don't know why the spirit world's been so jumpy. This is big, Michael. If we don't pin down what's causing it—"

"Who's causing it."

"Right, who's causing it—who knows what could happen."

Michael half-smiled. "The Lord will never give you a burden bigger than your shoulders can bear, Harry. All we can do is face what comes and have faith."

I gave him a sour glance. "I need to get myself some bigger shoulders, then. Someone in accounting must have made a mistake."

Michael let out a rough, warm laugh, and shook his head, then lay back on the bench, crossing his arms beneath his head. "We did what was right. Isn't that enough?"

I thought of all those babies, snuffling and making cute, piteous little sounds as the nurses had rushed about, gathering them up and making sure that they were all right, carrying them off to their mommies. One, a fat little Gerber candidate, had simply let out an enormous burp and promptly fallen asleep on the nurse's shoulder. About a dozen little lives, all told, with an open future laid out before them—a future that would have abruptly ended if I hadn't acted.

I felt a stupid little smile playing at the corners of my mouth, and a very small, very concrete sense of satisfaction that my indignation hadn't managed to erase. I turned away from Michael, so that he wouldn't see the smile, and forced myself to sound resigned. "Is it enough? I guess it's going to have to be."

Michael laughed again. I flashed him a scowl, and it only drew more merry laughter, so I gave up trying, and just leaned against the bars. "How long before we get out of here, do you think?"

"I've never been bailed out of jail before," Michael said. "You'd be a better judge."

"Hey," I protested, "what's that supposed to mean?"

Michael's smile faded. "Charity," he predicted, "is not going to be very happy."

I winced. Michael's wife. "Yeah, well. All we can do is face what comes and have faith, right?"

Michael grunted, somehow making it wry. "I'll say a prayer to Saint Jude."

I leaned my head against the bars and closed my eyes. I ached in places I didn't know could ache. I could have dozed off right there. "All I want," I said, "is to get home, get clean, and go to sleep."

An hour or so later, a uniformed officer appeared and opened the door, informing us that we'd made bail. I got a sickly little feeling in my stomach. Michael and I shuffled out of the holding area into the adjacent waiting room.

A woman in a roomy dress and a heavy cardigan stood waiting for us, her arms folded over her seventh or eighth month of pregnancy. She was tall, with gorgeous, silken blonde hair that fell to her waist in a shining curtain, timelessly lovely features, and dark eyes smoldering with contained anger. "Michael Joseph Patrick Carpenter," she snapped, and stalked toward us. Well, actually she waddled, but the set of her shoulders and her determined expression made it seem like a stalk. "You're a mess. This is what comes of taking up with bad company."

"Hello, angel," Michael rumbled, and leaned over to give the woman a kiss on the cheek.

She accepted it with all the loving tolerance of a Komodo dragon. "Don't you hello angel me. Do you know what I had to go through to find a baby-sitter, get all the way out here, get the money together and then get the sword back for you?"

"Hi Charity," I said brightly. "Gee, it's good to see you, too. It's been, what, three or four years since we've talked?"

"Five years, Mr. Dresden," the woman said, shooting me a glare. "And the Good Lord willing it will be five more before I have to put up with your idiocy again."

"But I—"

She thrusted her swollen stomach at me like the ram on a Greek warship. "Every time you come nosing around, you get Michael into some sort of trouble. And now into jail! What will the children think?"

"Look, Charity, it was really imp—"

"*Missus* Carpenter," she snarled. "It's *always* really important, Mr. Dresden. Well, my husband has engaged in many important activities without what I dubiously term your 'help.' But it's only when you're around that he seems to come back to me covered in blood."

"Hey," I protested. "I got hurt too!"

"Good," she said. "Maybe it will make you more cautious in the future."

I scowled down at the woman. "I'll have you know—"

She grabbed the front of my shirt and dragged my face down to hers. She was surprisingly strong, and she could glare right at me without looking me square in the eyes. "I'll have *you* know," she said, voice steely, "that if you *ever* get my Michael into trouble so deep that he can't come home to his family I will make you sorry for it." Tears that had nothing to do with weakness made her eyes bright for a moment, and she shook with emotion. I have to admit, at that particular moment, her threat scared me, waddling pregnancy and all.

She finally released me and turned back to her husband, gently touching a dark scab on his face. Michael put his arms around her, and with a little cry she hugged him back, burying her face against his chest and weeping without making any sound. Michael held her very carefully, as if he were afraid of breaking her, and stroked her hair.

I stood there for a second like a floundering goob. Michael looked up at me and met my gaze for a moment. He then turned, keeping his wife under one arm, and started walking away.

I watched the two of them for a moment, walking in step beside one another, while I stood there alone. Then I stuck my hands into my pockets, and turned away. I hadn't ever noticed, before, how well the two of them matched one another—Michael with his quiet strength and unfailing reliability, and Charity with her blazing passion and unshakeable loyalty to her husband.

The married thing. Sometimes I look at it and feel like someone from a Dickens novel, standing outside in the cold and staring in at Christmas dinner. Relationships hadn't ever really worked for me. I think it's had something to do with all the demons, ghosts, and human sacrifice.

As I stood there, brooding, I sensed her presence before I smelled her perfume, a warmth and energy about her that I'd grown to know over the time we'd been together. Susan paused at the door of the waiting room, looking back over her shoulder. I studied her. I never got tired of that. Susan had dark skin, tanned even darker from our previous weekend at the beach, and raven-black hair cut off neatly at her shoulders. She was slender, but curved enough to draw an admiring look from the officer behind the counter as she stood there in a flirty little skirt and half-top which left her midriff bare. My phone call caught her just as she'd been leaving for our rendezvous.

She turned to me and smiled, her chocolate-colored eyes worried but warm. She tilted her head back toward the hallway behind her, where Michael and Charity had gone. "They're a beautiful couple, aren't they?"

I tried to smile back, but didn't do so well. "They got off to a good start."

Susan's eyes studied my face, the cuts there, and the worry in her eyes deepened. "Oh? How's that?"

"He rescued her from a fire-breathing dragon." I walked toward her.

"Sounds nice," she said, and met me halfway, giving me a long and gentle hug that made my bruised ribs ache. "You okay?"

"I'll be okay."

"More ghostbusting with Michael. What's his story?"

"Off the record. Publicity could hurt him. He's got kids."

Susan frowned, but nodded. "All right," she said, and added a flair of melodrama to her words. "So what is he? Some kind of eternal soldier? Maybe a sleeping Arthurian knight woken in this desperate age to battle the forces of evil?"

"As far as I know he's a carpenter."

Susan arched a brow at me. "Who fights ghosts. What, has he got a magic nailgun or something?"

I tried not to smile. The muscles at the corners of my mouth ached. "Not quite. He's a righteous man."

"He seemed nice enough to me."

"No, not self-righteous. Righteous. The real deal. He's honest, loyal, faithful. He lives his ideals. It gives him power."

Susan frowned. "He looked average enough. I'd have expected . . . I'm not sure. Something. A different attitude."

"That's because he's humble too," I said. "If you asked him if he was righteous, he'd laugh at the idea. I guess that's part of it. I've never met anyone like him. He's a good man."

She pursed her lips. "And the sword?"

"Amoracchius," I supplied.

"He named his sword. How very Freudian of him. But his wife just about reached down that clerk's throat to get it back."

"It's important to him," I said. "He believes that it is one of three weapons given by God to mankind. Three swords. Each of them has a nail that is supposed to be from the Cross worked into its design. Only one of the righteous can wield them. The ones who do call themselves the Knights of the Cross. Others call them the Knights of the Sword."

Susan frowned. "*The* Cross?" she said. "As in *the* Crucifixion, capital *C*?"

I shrugged, uncomfortably. "How should I know? Michael believes it. That kind of belief is a power of its own. Maybe that's enough." I took a breath and changed the subject. "Anyway, my car got impounded. I had to drive fast and C.P.D. didn't like it."

Her dark eyes sparkled. "Anything worth a story?"

I laughed tiredly. "Don't you ever give up?"

"A girl's got to earn a living," she said, and fell into step beside me on the way out, slipping her arm through mine.

"Maybe tomorrow? I just want to get back home and get some sleep."

"No date, I guess." She smiled up at me, but I could see the expression was strained around the edges.

"Sorry. I—"

"I know." She sighed. I shortened my steps a little and she lengthened hers, though neither of us moved quickly. "I know what you're doing is important, Harry. I just wish, sometimes, that—" She broke off, frowning.

"That what?"

"Nothing. Really. It's selfish."

"That what?" I repeated. I found her hand with my bruised fingers and squeezed gently.

She signed, and stopped in the hall, turning to face me. She took both of my hands, and didn't look up when she said, "I just wish that I could be that important to you, too."

An uncomfortable pang hit me in the middle of my sternum. Ow. It hurt to hear that, literally. "Susan," I stammered. "Hey. Don't ever think that you're not important to me."

"Oh," she said, still not looking up, "it's not that. Like I said, just selfish. I'll get over it."

"I just don't want you to feel like . . ." I frowned and took a breath. "I don't want you to think that I don't . . . What I mean to say is that I . . ." *Love you.* That should have been simple enough to say. But the words stuck hard in my throat. I'd never said them to anyone I didn't lose, and every time I told my mouth to make the sounds, something shut down somewhere along the way.

Susan looked up at me, her eyes flickering over my face. She reached up a hand and touched the bandage on my forehead, her fingers light, gentle, warm. Silence fell heavy on the hallway. I stood there staring stupidly at her.

Finally, I leaned down and kissed her, hard, like I was trying to push the words out of my useless mouth and into her. I don't know if she understood, but she melted to me, all warm, soft tension, smelling of cinnamon, the sweetness of her lips soft and pliant beneath mine. One of my hands drifted to the small of her back, to the smooth, rounded ridges of muscle on either side of her spine, and drew her against me a little harder.

Footsteps coming from the other direction made us both smile and break away from the kiss. A female officer walked by, her lips twisted into a knowing little smirk, and I felt my cheeks flush.

Susan took my hand from her back, bending her mouth to put a gentle kiss on my bruised fingers. "Don't think you're getting off that easy, Harry Dresden," she said. "I'm going to get you to start talking if it kills you." But she didn't press the issue, and together we reclaimed my stuff and left.

I fell asleep on the drive back to my apartment, but I woke up when the car crunched into the gravel parking lot beside the stone stairs leading down to my lair, in the basement of an old boardinghouse. We got out of the car, and I stretched, looking around the summer night with a scowl.

"What's wrong?" Susan asked.

"Mister," I said. "He's usually running right up to me when I come home. I let him out early this morning."

"He's a cat, Harry," Susan said, flashing me a smile. "Maybe he's got a date."

"What if he got hit by a car? What if a dog got him?"

Susan let out a laugh and walked over to me. My libido noted the sway of her hips in the little skirt with an interest that made my aching muscles cringe. "He's as big as a horse, Harry. I pity the dog that tries something."

I reached back into the car for my staff and rod, then slipped an arm around her. Susan's warmth beside me, the scent of cinnamon drifting up to me from her hair, felt incredibly nice at the end of a long day. But it just didn't feel right, to not have Mister run up to me and bowl into my shins in greeting.

That should have been enough to tip me off. I'll plead weariness, achiness, and sexual distraction. It came as a total shock to me to feel a wave of cold energy writhe into my face, in tandem with a shadowy form rising up from the steps leading down to my apartment. I froze and took a step back, only to see another silent shape step around the edge of the boardinghouse and start walking toward us. Gooseflesh erupted up and down my arms.

Susan caught on a second or two after my wizard's senses had given me warning. "Harry," she breathed. "What is it? Who are they?"

"Take it easy, and get out your car keys," I said, as the two shapes approached us, the waves of cool energy increasing as they did. Light from the distant street lamp reflected in the nearest figure's eyes, gleaming huge and black. "We're getting out of here. They're vampires."

Chapter 8

One of the vampires let out a velvet laugh, and stepped out into the dim light. He wasn't particularly tall, and he moved with a casual and dangerous grace that belied his crystal-blue eyes, styled blond hair, and the tennis whites he wore. "Bianca told us you'd be nervous," he purred.

The second of the pair kept coming toward us from the corner of the boardinghouse. She, too, was of innocuous height and build, and possessed the same blue eyes and flawless golden hair as the man. She too was dressed in tennis whites. "But," she breathed, and licked her lips with a cat-quick tongue, "she didn't tell us you would smell so delicious."

Susan fumbled with her keys, and pressed up against me, tight with tension and fear. "Harry?"

"Don't look them in the eyes," I said. "And don't let them lick you."

Susan shot me a sharp look from beneath raven brows. "Lick?"

"Yeah. Their saliva's some kind of addictive narcotic." We reached her car. "Get in."

The male vampire opened his mouth, showing his fangs, and laughed. "Peace, wizard. We're not here for your blood."

"Speak for yourself," the girl said. She licked her lips again, and this time I could see the black spots on her long, pink tongue. Ewg.

The male smiled and put a hand on her shoulder, a gesture that was half affection, half physical restraint. "My sister hasn't eaten tonight," he explained. "She's on a diet."

"Vampires on a diet?" Susan murmured beneath her breath.

"Yeah," I said back, sotto voce. "Make hers a Blood Lite."

Susan made a choking sound.

I eyed the male and raised my voice. "Who are you, then? And why are you at my house?"

He inclined his head politely. "My name is Kyle Hamilton. This is my sister, Kelly. We are associates of Madame Bianca's, and we are here to give you a message. An invitation, actually."

"It only takes one of you to deliver a message."

Kyle glanced at his sister. "We were just on the way to our game of doubles."

I snorted. "Yeah, right," I told him. "Whatever it is you're selling, I don't want any. You can go now."

Kyle frowned. "I urge you to reconsider, Mr. Dresden. You, of all people, should know Madame Bianca is the most influential vampire in the city of Chicago. Denying her invitation could have grave consequences."

"I don't like threats," I shot back. I hefted my blasting rod and leveled it at Kyle's baby blues. "Keep it up and there's going to be a greasy spot right about where you're standing."

The pair of them smiled at me—innocent angels with pointed teeth. "Please, Mr. Dresden," Kyle said. "Understand that I am only pointing out the potential hazards of a diplomatic incident between the Vampire Court and the White Council."

Whoops. That changed things. I hesitated, and then lowered the blasting rod. "This is court business? Official business?"

"The Vampire Court," Kyle said, a measured cadence to his words, "extends a formal invitation to Harry Dresden, Wizard, as the local representative of the White Council of Wizards, to attend the reception celebrating the elevation of Bianca St. Claire to the rank of Margravine of the Vampire Court, three nights hence, reception to begin at midnight." Kyle paused to produce an expensive-looking white envelope and to refresh his smile. "The safety of all invited guests is assured, by word of the assembled court, of course."

"Harry," Susan breathed. "What's going on?"

"Tell you in a minute," I said. I stepped away from Susan. "You are acting as an ordained herald of the court, then?"

"I am," Kyle said.

I nodded. "Bring me the invitation."

The pair of them started toward me. I lifted my blasting rod and muttered a word. Power flooded through the rod, and the far tip began to glow with an incandescent light. "Not her," I said, nodding to the herald's sister. "Just you."

Kyle kept his smile, but his eyes had changed from blue to a shade of angry black that was rapidly expanding to cover the whites. "Well," he said, his voice tense, "aren't we the little lawyer, Mr. Dresden."

I smiled back at him. "Look, Sparky, you're the herald. You should know the accords as well as I do. You've license to deliver and receive messages and to have safe passage granted you so long as you don't start any trouble." I waved the tip of the rod toward the girl beside him. "She doesn't. And she's not obliged to keep the peace, either. Let's just say I'd rather we all walked away from this."

They both made a hissing sound that no human could quite have duplicated. Kyle pushed Kelly roughly back behind him, where she remained, her soft-looking hands pressed to her stomach, her eyes flooded entirely black and empty of humanity. Kyle stalked toward me and thrust the envelope at me. I swallowed my fear, lowered my blasting rod, and took it.

"Your business here is complete," I told him. "Blow."

"You'd better be there, Dresden," Kyle snarled, pacing back to his sister's side. "My lady will be most upset if you are not."

"I told you to blow, Kyle." I lifted my hand, gathered my anger and my fear as handy sources of fuel, and said, quietly, "*Ventas servitas.*"

Energy flowed out of me. Wind roared up in response to my command, and whipped out toward the pair of vampires, carrying a cloud of dust and dirt and debris with it. They both staggered, lifting a hand to shield their eyes against flying particles.

As the wind faded I sagged, wearied by the effort of moving that much air, and watched the vampires gather their wits and blink their eyes clear. Their perfect tennis whites were stained, their beautiful complexions were mussed, and best of all, their flawless hair was standing up every which way.

They hissed at me and crouched, bodies oddly balanced and held with an inhuman lightness. Then there was a blur of tennis whites, and they were gone.

I didn't assume that they had left until I let my senses drift out from me, tasting the air for the cold energy that had surrounded them. It had faded, as well. Only then, when I was absolutely sure they were gone, did I relax. Well, it felt like simple relaxing—but generally when I relax, I don't stagger and need to plant my staff firmly on the ground to keep from falling over. I stood there like that for a second, my head swimming.

"Wow." Susan came toward me, her face concerned. "Harry, you sure know how to make friends."

I wobbled a little, hardly able to stand. "I don't need friends like that."

She got close enough for me to lean on, and spared my ego by slipping underneath my arm as though for my protection. "Are you all right?"

"Tired. I've been working too hard tonight. Must have gotten out of shape."

"Can you walk?"

I gave her a smile that probably looked strained, and started walking toward the stairs leading down to my apartment. Mister, my grey cat, came flying over the ground from the darkness somewhere and threw himself fondly against my legs. Thirty pounds of cat is a lot of fondness, and I had to have Susan's help to keep from falling over. "Eating small children again, Mister?"

My cat meowed, then padded down the stairs and pawed at the door.

"So," Susan said. "The vampires are throwing a party."

I fished my keys out of my duster's pocket. I unlocked the door to the old place, and Mister bolted inside. I shut the door behind us, and stared wearily at my living room. The fire had died down to glowing embers, but still shed red-golden light over everything. I decorated my apartment in textures, not colors, in any case. I like the smooth grain of old woods, the heavy tapestries on the bare stone walls. The chairs are all thickly padded and comfortable looking, and rugs are strewn over the bare stone floor in a variety of materials, patterns, and weaves, from Arabian to Navajo.

Susan helped me hobble in until I could collapse on my plushly cushioned couch. She took my staff and blasting rod from me, wrinkling her nose at the charred smell, and set them in the corner next to my cane sword. Then she came back over to me and knelt down, flashing a lot of bare, pretty leg. She took my boots off, and I groaned as my feet came free.

"Thanks," I said.

She plucked the envelope from my hand. "Could you get the candles?"

I groaned, for an answer, and she sniffed. "Big baby. You just want to see me walk around in this skirt."

"Guilty," I said. She quirked a smile at me, and went to the fireplace. She added a few logs to it from the old tin hod, and then stirred the embers with a poker until licks of flame came up. I don't have any electric lights in my apartment. Gadgets go out so often that there's no point in constantly replacing them. My refrigerator is an old-style icebox. The kind with ice. I shuddered to think of what I could do to gas lines.

So, I lived without heat, except for my fireplace, and without hot water, without electricity. The curse of a wizard. It saves on the utilities bills, I have to admit, but it can be damned inconvenient.

Susan had to bend down far over the fire to thrust a long candlestick's tip down into the small flames. The orange light curved around the lean muscles of her legs in a fashion I found positively fascinating, even as wearied as I was.

Susan rose with the lighted candle in her hand and cast a smirk at me. "You're staring, Harry."

"Guilty," I said again.

She lit several candles on the mantel from the first, and then opened the white envelope, frowning. "Wow," she said, and held the invitation inside up to the light. I couldn't make out the words, but they had that white-yellow glint that you only get from true gold. "The bearer, Wizard Harry Dresden, and an escort of his choosing are hereby courteously invited to a reception . . . I didn't think they used invitations like this anymore."

"Vampires. They can be a couple hundred years out of style and not notice."

"Harry," Susan said. She flicked the invitation against the heel of her hand a couple of times. "You know, something occurs to me."

My brain tried to stir from its congealment. Some instinct twitched, warning me that Susan was up to something. "Um," I said, blinking my eyes in an effort to clear my thoughts. "I hope you're not thinking what a great opportunity it would be for you to go to the ball."

Her eyes glinted with something very much like lust. "Think of it, Harry. There could be beings there hundreds of years old. I could get enough stories from a half hour of chat to last me—"

"Hang on, Cinderella," I said. "In the first place, I'm not going to the ball. In the second, even if I was I wouldn't take you with me."

Her back straightened and she put one fist on her hip. "And just what is that supposed to mean?"

I winced. "Look, Susan. They're *vampires*. They eat people. You've got no idea how dangerous it would be for me there—or for you, for that matter."

"What about what Kyle said? The guarantee of your safety?"

"Talk is cheap," I said. "Look, everyone in the old circles is big on the old laws of courtesy and hospitality. But you can only trust them to adhere to the letter of the law. If I happened to get served a bad batch of mushrooms, or someone drove by and filled the whole place with bullets and I was the only mortal there, they'd just say, 'Oh my, what a terrible shame. So sorry, really, it won't happen again.' "

"So you're saying they'd kill you," Susan said.

"Bianca has a grudge against me," I said. "She couldn't just sneak up on me and tear my throat out, but she could arrange for something to happen to me more indirectly. It's probably what she has in mind."

Susan frowned. "I've seen you handle things a lot worse than those two out there."

I let out a breath in exasperation. "Maybe, sure. But what's the point in taking chances?"

"Can't you see what this might mean to me?" she said. "Harry, that footage I shot of the werewolf—"

"Loup-garou," I interrupted.

"Whatever. It was ten seconds of footage that was only aired for three days before it vanished—and it put me further ahead than five *years* of legwork. If I could publish actual interviews with vampires—"

"Sheesh, Susan. You're reading too much off the bestseller list. In the real world, the vampire eats you before you get to hit the record button."

"I've taken chances before—so have you."

"I don't go *looking* for trouble," I said.

Her eyes flashed. "Dammit, Harry. How long have I been putting aside the things that happen to you? Like tonight, when I was supposed to be spending the evening with my boyfriend and instead I'm bailing him out of jail."

Ouch. I glanced down. "Susan, believe me. If I could have done anything else—"

"This could be a fantastic opportunity for me."

She was right. And she had bailed me out of trouble often

enough before that maybe I owed her that opportunity, dangerous as it might be. She was a big girl and could make her own choices. But dammit, I couldn't just nod my head and smile and let her walk into that kind of danger. Better to try to sidetrack her. "No," I said. "I've got enough problems without pissing off the White Council again."

Her eyes narrowed. "What's this White Council? Kyle talked to you as though it were some kind of ruling body. Is it like the Vampire Court, only for wizards?"

Exactly like that, I thought. Susan hadn't gotten as far as she had by being stupid. "Not really," I told her.

"You're a horrible liar, Harry."

"The White Council is a group of the most powerful men and women in the world, Susan. Wizards. Their big currency is in secrets, and they don't like people knowing about them."

Her eyes gleamed, like a hound on a fresh scent. "And you're . . . some kind of ambassador for them?"

I had to laugh at the notion. "Oh, God, no. But I'm a member. It's sort of like having a black belt. It's a mark of status, of respect. With the council, it means that I get to vote, when issues come up, and that I have to abide by their rules."

"Are you entitled to represent them at a function like this?"

I didn't like the direction this conversation was headed. "Um. Obligated to, really, in this case."

"So if you *don't* show up, you'll be in trouble."

I scowled. "Not as much trouble as I'll be in if I go. The worst the council'd be able to accuse me of is being impolite. I can live with that."

"And if you do show up? Come on, Harry. What's the worse that could happen?"

I threw up my hands. "I could get myself killed! Or worse. Susan, you really don't understand what you're asking of me." I pushed myself up off the couch, to go to her. Bad idea. My head swam and my vision blurred.

I would have fallen, but Susan dropped the invitation and caught me. She eased me back down to the couch, and I kept my arm around her, drawing her down with me. She felt soft and warm.

We lay there for a minute, and she rubbed her cheek against the duster. Leather creaked. I heard her sigh. "I'm sorry, Harry. I shouldn't hit you with this right now."

"It's all right," I said.

"I just think that it's something big. If we—"

I turned a little, tangled my fingers in the dark softness of her hair, and kissed her.

Her eyelids opened wide for a second, and then lowered. Her words broke off into a low, growling sound, and her mouth softened beneath mine, warm and getting warmer. In spite of my aches and bruises, the kiss felt good. It felt really good. Her mouth tasted nice, the softness of her lips mobile and eager beneath mine. I felt her slide a few fingers in between the buttons of my shirt, caressing the skin there, and electric sensation thrilled through me.

Our tongues met, and I dragged her closer. She moaned again, then abruptly pushed me back enough to straddle my hips with those long and lovely legs and begin to kiss me as though she meant to inhale me. I ran my hands over her hips, lingering on the small of her back, and she moved them, grinding against me. I moved my hands to the taut tension of her thighs and slid them up over the bare, smooth skin, lifting the skirt up, baring her legs, her hips.

I faltered in surprise for a half-second when I realized she wasn't wearing anything underneath—but then, we'd been planning on an evening in. A spasm of need and hunger pounded through all the exhaustion, and I clutched her, felt her gasp again, willing and as hungry as me, her body tensing against me, beneath my hands.

She started jerking at my belt, gasping, her breath hot in my face. "Harry. You jerk. Don't you think this is going to distract me forever."

Shortly after that, we made sure that neither of us could think of anything at all, and fell asleep a goodly while after that, tangled together in a sprawl of exhausted limbs, dark hair, and soft blankets in front of the fire.

All right, so. The *entire* day wasn't a living hell.

But, as it turned out, hell got up awfully early in the morning.

Chapter 9

I dreamed.

The nightmare felt familiar, almost comfortable, though it had been years since I'd gone through it. It began in a cave, its walls made of translucent crystal, all but glowing in the dim light of the fire beneath the cauldron. The silver manacles were tight on my wrists, and I was too dizzy to keep my own balance. I looked to the left and right and watched my blood glide down over the manacles from where they pierced my wrists like thorns, then fall into a pair of earthen bowls set out beneath them.

My godmother came to me, pale and breathtaking in the firelight, her hair spilling down around her like a cloud of silk. The sidhe lady was beautiful beyond the pale of mortals, her eyes bewitching, her mouth more tempting than the most luscious fruit. She kissed my bare chest. Shudders of cold pleasure ran through me.

"Soon," she whispered, between kisses. "Only a few more nights of the dark moon, my sweetling, and you will be strong enough."

She kept kissing me, and I began to lose my vision. Cold pleasure, faerie magic, coursed through her lips like a drug, so sweet that it was almost an agony of its own, and made the torment of the bonds, the blood loss, almost worthwhile. Almost. I felt myself gasping for breath, and stared at the fire, focusing on it, trying to keep from falling into the darkness.

The dream changed. I dreamt of fire. Someone I had once loved like a father stood in the middle of it, screaming in agony. They were black screams, horrible screams, high-pitched and utterly without pride or dignity or humanity. In the dream, as in life, I forced myself to watch flesh blacken and flake away from sizzling muscle and baking bone, watched muscles contract in tortured spasms while I stood over the fire and, metaphorically speaking, blew on the coals.

"Justin," I whispered. In the end, I couldn't watch any longer. I closed my eyes and bowed my head, listening to the thunder of my own heart pounding in my ears. Pounding. My heart pounding.

I came out of the dream, blinked opened my eyes. My door rattled on its frame under a series of hammering blows. Susan woke up at the same time, sitting up, the blanket we'd been curled under gliding down over the curves of her breasts. It was still dark outside. The longest candle hadn't yet burned away, but the fire was down to embers again.

My body ached all over, the day-after ache of tired joints and muscles demanding time to recuperate. I rose as the pounding went on, and went to the kitchen drawer. My .38 had been lost in the battle with the gang of half-mad lycanthropes the year before, and I'd replaced it with a medium-barreled .357. I must have been feeling insecure that day, or something.

The gun weighed about two thousand pounds in my hand. I made sure that it was loaded and turned to face the door. Susan pushed her hair out of her eyes, blinked at my gun, and backed away, making damn sure she was out of my line of fire. Smart girl, Susan.

"You're not going to have much luck breaking down that door," I called out. I didn't point the gun at the door, yet. Never point a gun at anything you aren't sure you want dead. "I replaced the original one with a steel door and a steel frame. Demons, you know."

The pounding ceased. "Dresden," Michael called from the other side of the door. "I tried to reach you on the phone, but it must be off the hook. We've got to talk."

I frowned, and put the gun back in the drawer. "Okay, okay. Sheesh, Michael. Do you know what time it is?"

"Time to work," he answered. "The sun will be up shortly."

"Lunatic," I mumbled.

Susan looked around at the remains of our clothing, scattered pretty much everywhere, the sprawl of blankets and pillows and cushions all over the floor. "I think maybe I'll just wait in your room," she said.

"Right, okay." I opened the kitchen closet and got my heavy

robe out, the one I usually save for working in the lab, and slipped into it. "Stay covered up, all right? I don't want you to get sick."

She gave me a sleepy half-smile and rose, all long limbs and grace and interesting tan lines, then vanished into my little bedroom and shut the door. I walked across the room, and opened the door for Michael.

He stood there in blue jeans, a flannel shirt, and a fleece-lined denim jacket. He had his big gym bag slung over his shoulder, and *Amoracchius* was a silent tension I could just barely feel within it. I looked from the bag to his face and asked, "Trouble?"

"Could be. Did you send someone to Father Forthill last night?"

I rubbed at my eyes, trying to get the sleep out of them. Coffee. I needed coffee. Or a Coke. Just as long as there was caffeine somewhere. "Yes. A girl named Lydia. She was worried that a ghost was after her."

"He called me this morning. Something spent the night trying to get into the church."

I blinked at him. "What? Did it get inside?"

He shook his head. "He didn't have time to tell me much. Can you come down there with me and take a look around?"

I nodded, and stepped back from the door. "Give me a couple of minutes." I headed for the icebox and got out a can of Coke. My fingers worked enough to open it, at least, though they still felt stiff. My stomach reminded me that I'd been ignoring it, and I got out the plate of cold cuts while I was there.

I swigged Coke and made myself a big sandwich. I looked up a minute later to see Michael eyeing the destruction that had been the living room. He nudged one of Susan's shoes with his foot, and glanced up at me apologetically. "I'm sorry. I didn't know anyone was here."

"It's okay."

Michael smiled briefly, then nodded. "Well. Do I need to lecture you on sexual involvement before marriage?"

I growled something about early morning and inconvenient visitors and toads. Michael only shook his head, smiling, while I wolfed down food. "Did you tell her?"

"Tell her what?"

He lifted an eyebrow at me.

I rolled my eyes. "Almost."

"You almost told her."

"Sure. Got distracted."

Michael nudged Susan's other shoe with his foot and let out a delicate cough. "So I see."

I finished the sandwich and part of the Coke, then walked across the room and slipped into the bedroom. The room was freezing, and I could see Susan curled into a ball beneath the heavy blankets on my bed. Mister had lain down with his back against hers, and watched me with sleepy, self-satisfied eyes as I came in.

"Rub it in, fuzzball," I growled at him, and dressed quickly. Socks, jeans, T-shirt, heavy flannel work shirt over that. Mom's amulet, around my neck, and a little silver charm bracelet with a half-dozen shields dangling off it, fixed to my left wrist in place of the charm I'd given to Lydia. A plain silver ring, its interior surface inscribed with a number of runes, went onto my right hand. Both pieces of jewelry tingled with the enchantments I'd laid on them, still fairly fresh.

I leaned over the bed and kissed Susan's cheek. She made a sleepy, murmuring sound, and snuggled a little deeper beneath the covers. I thought about getting under there with her and making sure she was nice and warm before leaving—but instead went out, shutting the door carefully behind me.

Michael and I left, piling into his truck, a white (of course) Ford pick-up with extra wheels and enough hauling power to move mountains, and headed for Saint Mary of the Angels.

Saint Mary of the Angels is a big church. I mean, a *big* church. It's been looming over the Wicker Park area for more than eighty years, and has seen the neighborhood grow up from a collection of cheap homes for immigrants mixed in with rich folks' mansions to Little Bohemia today, packed with yuppies and artsies, success stories, and wannabes. The church, I'm told, is modeled after St. Peter's Basilica in Rome—which is to say, enormous and elegant and maybe a bit overdone. It takes up an entire city block. I mean, sheesh.

The sun came up as we entered the parking lot. I felt the golden rays slice across the morning skies, the sudden, subtle shift of forces playing about the world. Dawn is significant, magically speaking. It is a time of new beginnings. Magic isn't as simple as good and evil, light and dark, but there's a lot of correlations between the powers particular to night and the use of black magic.

We drove around to the rear parking lot of the church and got out of the truck. Michael walked in front of me, carrying his bag. I stuffed my hands down in the pockets of my duster as I followed him. I felt uncomfortable, approaching the church—not for any weirdo quasi-mystical reason. Just because I'd never felt comfortable with churches in general. The Church had killed a lot of wizards in its day, believing them in league with Satan. It felt strange to just be strolling up on business. Hi, God, it's me, Harry. Please don't turn me into a pillar of salt.

"Harry," Michael said, bringing me out of my reverie. "Look."

He had stopped beside a pair of worn old cars parked in the back lot. Someone had done one hell of a job on them. The windows had all been smashed, their safety glass fractured and dented. The hoods were dented as well. The headlights lay mostly on the ground in front of the cars, and all the tires were flat.

I walked around to the back of the cars, frowning. The taillights lay shattered on the ground. The antenna had been torn off each car, and were not in sight. Long scratches, in three parallel rows ran down the sides of both cars.

"Well?" Michael asked me.

I looked up at him and shrugged. "Probably something got frustrated when it couldn't get inside the church."

He snorted. "Do you think?" He adjusted the gym bag until *Amoracchius's* handle lay jutting outside the zipper. "Any chances that it's still around?"

I shook my head. "I doubt it. Come daylight, ghosts usually head back to the Nevernever."

"Usually?"

"Usually. Almost without exception."

Michael eyed me and kept one hand on the hilt of the sword. We walked on up to the delivery door. Compared to the grandeur of the church's front, it looked stunningly modest. On either side of the double doors, someone had gone to a lot of trouble to plant and care for a half-dozen rosebushes. Someone else had gone to a lot of trouble to tear them to shreds. Each plant had been uprooted. Thorny branches lay strewn across several dozen square yards around the door.

I crouched down beside several fallen branches, picking them up one at a time, squinting at them in the dawn dimness.

"What are you looking for?" Michael asked me.

"Blood on the thorns," I said. "Rose thorns can poke little holes in just about anything—and something that tore them up this hard would have been scratching itself on them."

"Any blood?"

"No. No footprints in the earth, either."

Michael nodded. "A ghost, then."

I squinted up at Michael. "I hope not."

He tilted his head and frowned at me.

I dropped a branch and spread my hands. "A ghost can usually only manage to move things, physically, in bursts. Throwing pots and pans. Maybe really stretch things and stack up a bunch of books or something." I gestured at the torn plants, and then back toward the wrecked cars. "Not only that, but it's limited to a certain place, time, or event. The ghost, if it is one, followed Lydia here and rampaged around on blessed ground tearing things apart. I mean, wow. This thing is way stronger than any ghost I've ever heard about."

Michael's frown deepened. "What are you saying, Harry?"

"I'm saying we might be getting out of our depth, here. Look, Michael, I know a lot about spooks and nasties. But they aren't my specialty or anything."

He frowned at me. "We might need to know more."

I stood up, brushing myself off. "That," I said, "is my specialty. Let's talk to Father Forthill."

Michael knocked on the door. It opened at once. Father Forthill, a greying man of slight build and only medium stature, blinked anxiously up at us through a pair of wire-rimmed spectacles. His eyes were normally a shade of blue so bright as to rival robin's eggs, but today they were heavily underlined, shadowed. "Oh," he said. "Oh, Michael. Thank the Lord." He opened the door wider, and Michael stepped over the threshold. The two embraced. Forthill kissed Michael on either cheek and stepped back to peer at me. "And Harry Dresden, professional wizard. I've never had anyone ask me to bless a five-gallon drum into holy water before, Mr. Dresden."

Michael peered at me, evidently surprised that the priest and I knew each other. I shrugged, a little embarrassed, and said, "You told me I could count on him in a pinch."

"And so you can," Forthill said, his blue eyes sparkling for a moment behind the spectacles. "I trust you have no complaints about the blessed water?"

"None at all," I said. "Talk about your surprised ghouls."

"Harry," Michael chided. "You've been keeping secrets again."

"Contrary to what Charity thinks, Michael, I don't go running to the phone to call you every time I have a little problem." I clapped Michael on the shoulder in passing and offered my hand to Father Forthill, who shook it gravely. No hug and kiss on each cheek for me.

Forthill smiled up at me. "I look forward to the day when you give your life to God, Mr. Dresden. He can use men with your courage."

I tried to smile, but it probably looked a little sickly. "Look, Father. I'd love to talk about it with you sometime, but we're here for a reason."

"Indeed," Forthill said. The sparkle in his eyes faded, and his manner became absolutely serious. He began to walk down a clean hallway with dark, heavy beams of old wood overhanging it and paintings of the Saints on the walls. We kept pace with him. "The young woman arrived yesterday, just before sunset."

"Was she all right?" I asked.

He lifted both eyebrows. "All right? I should say not. All the signs of an abused personality. Borderline malnutrition. She had a low-grade fever as well, and hadn't bathed recently. She looked as though she might be going through withdrawal from something."

I frowned. "Yeah. She looked like she was in pretty bad shape." I briefly recounted my conversation with Lydia and my decision to help her.

Father Forthill shook his head. "I provided fresh clothes and a meal for her and was getting set to put her to bed on a spare cot at the back of the rectory. That's when it happened."

"What happened?"

"She began to shake," Forthill said. "Her eyes rolled back into her head. She was still sitting at the dinner table, and spilled her soup onto the floor. I thought she was having a seizure of some sort, and tried to hold her down and to get something into her mouth to keep her from biting her tongue." He sighed, clasping his hands behind his back as he walked. "I'm afraid that I was of little help to the poor child. The fit seemed to pass in a few moments, but she still trembled and had gone absolutely pale."

"Cassandra's Tears," I said.

"Or narcotic withdrawal," Forthill said. "Either way, she needed help. I moved her to the cot. She begged me not to leave her, so I sat down and began to read part of St. Matthew's gospel to her. She seemed to calm somewhat, but she had such a look in her eyes . . ." The old priest sighed. "That resolved look that they get when they're sure that they're lost. Despair, and in one so young."

"When did the attack begin?" I asked.

"About ten minutes later," the priest said. "It started with the most terrible howling of wind. Lord preserve me, but I was sure the windows would rattle out of their frames. Then we started to hear sounds, outside." He swallowed. "Terrible sounds. Something walking back and forth. Heavy footsteps. And then it started calling her name." The priest folded his arms and rubbed his palms against either arm.

"I rose and addressed the being, and asked its name, but it only laughed at me. I began to compel it by the Holy Word, and it went quite mad. We could hear it crushing things outside. I don't mind telling you that it was quite the most terrifying experience I have ever had in my life.

"The girl tried to leave. To go out to it. She said that she didn't want me harming myself, that it would only find her in any case. Well, I forbade her, of course, and refused to let her past me. It kept on, outside, and I kept on reading the Word aloud to the girl. It waited outside. I could . . . feel it, but could see nothing outside the windows. Such a darkness. And every so often it would destroy something else, and we'd hear the sound of it.

"After several hours, it seemed to grow quiet. The girl went to sleep. I walked the halls to make sure all the doors and windows were still closed, and when I came back she was gone."

"Gone?" I asked. "Gone as in left or as in just gone?"

Forthill gave me a smile that looked a bit shaky. "The back door was unlocked, though she'd shut it after herself." The older man shook his head. "I called Michael at once, of course."

"We've got to find that girl," I said.

Forthill shook his head, his expression grave. "Mr. Dresden, I am certain that only the power of the Almighty kept us safe within these walls last night."

"I won't argue with you, Father."

"But if you could have sensed this creature's anger, its . . . rage. Mr. Dresden, I would not wish to encounter this being outside of a church without seeking God's help in the matter."

I jerked a thumb at Michael. "I *did* seek God's help. Heck, is one Knight of the Cross not enough? I could always put out the Bat-signal for the other two."

Forthill smiled. "That's not what I meant, and you know it. But as you wish. You must come to your own decision." He turned to Michael and me both and said, "I hope, gentlemen, that I can trust your discretion on this matter? The police report will doubtless reflect that persons unknown perpetuated the vandalism."

I snorted. "A little white lie, Father?" I felt bad the minute I'd said it, but heck. I get tired of the conversion efforts every time I show up.

"Evil gains power from fear, Mr. Dresden," Forthill replied. "Within the Church, we have agencies for dealing with these matters." He put a hand on Michael's shoulder, briefly. "But spreading word of it to everyone, even to all of the brethren would accomplish nothing but to frighten many people and to make the enemy that much more able to do harm."

I nodded at the priest. "I like that attitude, Father. You almost sound like a wizard."

His eyebrows shot up, but then he broke into a quiet, weary laugh. "Be careful, both of you, and may God go with you." He made the sign of the cross over both of us, and I felt the quiet stirring of power, just as I sometimes did around Michael. Faith. Michael and Forthill exchanged a few quiet words about Michael's family while I lurked in the background. Forthill arranged to christen the new baby, whenever Charity delivered. They exchanged hugs again; Forthill shook my hand, businesslike and friendly, and we left.

Outside, Michael watched me as we walked back to his truck. "Well?" he asked. "What's next?"

I frowned, and stuffed my hands into my pockets. The sun was higher now, painting the sky blue, the clouds white. "I know someone who's pretty close to the spooks around here. That psychic in Oldtown."

Michael scowled and spat. "The necromancer."

I snorted. "He's no necromancer. He can barely call up a ghost and talk to it. He's got to fake it most of the time." Besides. Had he been a real necromancer, the White Council would already have hounded him down and beheaded him. Doubtless, the man I was thinking of had already been visited by at least one Warden and warned of the consequences of dabbling too much into the dark arts.

"If he's so inept, why speak to him at all?"

"He's probably closer to the spirit world than anyone else in town. Other than me, I mean. I'll send out Bob, too, and see what kind of information he can run down. We're bound to have different contacts."

Michael frowned at me. "I don't trust this business of communing with spirits, Harry. If Father Forthill and the others knew about this familiar of yours—"

"Bob isn't a familiar," I shot back.

"He performs the same function, doesn't he?"

I snorted. "Familiars work for free. I've got to pay Bob."

"Pay him?" he asked, his tone suspicious. "Pay what?"

"Mostly romance novels. Sometimes I splurge on a—"

Michael looked pained. "Harry, I really don't want to know. Isn't there some way that you could work some kind of spell here, instead of relying upon these unholy beings?"

I sighed, and shook my head. "Sorry, Michael. If it was a demon, it would have left footprints, and maybe some kind of psychic trail I could follow. But I'm pretty sure this was pure spirit. And a goddamned strong one."

"Harry," Michael said, voice stern.

"Sorry, I forgot. Ghosts don't usually inhabit a construct—a magical body. They're just energy. They don't leave any physical traces behind—at least none that last for hours at a time. If it was *here,* I could tell you all kinds of things about it, probably, and work magic on it directly. But it's not here, so—"

Michael sighed. "Very well. I will put out the word to those I know to be on the lookout for the girl. Lydia, you said her name was?"

"Yeah." I described her to Michael. "And she had a charm on her wrist. The one I'd been wearing the past few nights."

"Would it protect her?" Michael asked.

I shrugged. "From something as mean as this thing sounded . . . I don't know. We've got to find out who this ghost was when it was alive and shut it down."

"Which still will not tell us who or what is stirring up the spirits of the city." Michael unlocked his truck, and we got inside.

"That's what I like about you, Michael. You're always thinking so positively."

He grinned at me. "Faith, Harry. God has a way of seeing to it that things fall into place."

He started driving, and I leaned back in my seat and closed my eyes. First off to see the psychic. Then to send Bob out to find out more about what looked to be the most dangerous ghost I'd seen in a long time. And *then* to keep on looking for whoever it was behind all the spooky goings-on and to rap them politely on the head until they stopped. Easy as one, two, three. Sure.

I whimpered, sunk down in my seat a little more, and wished that I had kept my aching, sore self in bed.

Chapter 10

Mortimer Lindquist had tried to give his house that gothic feel. Greyish gargoyles stood at the corners of his roof. Black iron gates glowered at the front of his house and statuary lined the walk to his front door. Long grass had overgrown his yard. If his house hadn't been a red-roofed, white-walled stucco transplant from somewhere in southern California, it might have worked.

The results looked more like the Haunted Mansion at Disneyland than an ominous abode of a speaker to the dead. The black iron gates stood surrounded by plain chain-link fence. The gargoyles, on closer inspection, proved to be plastic reproductions. The statuary, too, had the rough outlines of plaster, rather than the clean, sweeping profile of marble. You could have plopped a pink flamingo down right in the middle of the unmowed weeds, and it would have somehow matched the decor. But, I supposed, at night, with the right lighting and the right attitude, some people might have believed it.

I shook my head and lifted my hand to rap on the door..

It opened before my knuckles touched it, and a well-rounded set of shoulders below a shining, balding head backed through the doorway, grunting. I stepped to one side. The little man tugged an enormous suitcase out onto the porch, never taking notice of me, his florid face streaked with perspiration.

I sidled into the doorway as he turned to lug the bag out to the gate, muttering to himself under his breath. I shook my head and went on into the house. The door was a business entrance—there was no tingling sensation of crossing the threshold of a dwelling uninvited. The front room reminded me of the house's exterior.

Lots of black curtains draped down over the walls and doorways. Red and black candles squatted all over the place. A grinning human skull leered from a bookshelf straining to contain copies of the *Encyclopedia Britannica* with the lettering scraped off their spines. The skull was plastic, too.

Morty had a table set up in the room, several chairs around it with a high-backed chair at the rear, wood that had actually been carved with a number of monstrous beings. I took a seat in the chair, folded my hands on the table in front of me, and waited.

The little man came back in, wiping at his face with a bandana handkerchief, sweating and panting.

"Shut the door," I said. "We need to talk, Morty."

He squealed and whirled around.

"Y-you," he stammered. "Dresden. What are you doing here?"

I stared at him. "Come in, Morty."

He came closer, but left the door open. In spite of his pudginess, he moved with the nervous energy of a spooked cat. His white business shirt showed stains beneath his arms reaching halfway to his belt. "Look, Dresden. I told you guys before—I get the rules, right? I haven been doing *anything* you guys talked about."

Aha. The White Council *had* sent someone to see him. Morty was a professional con. I hadn't planned on getting any honest answers out of him without a lot of effort. Maybe I could play this angle and save myself a lot of work.

"Let me tell you something, Morty. When I come into a place and don't say a thing except, 'Let's talk,' and the first thing I hear is 'I didn't do it,' it makes me think that the person I'm talking to must have done something. You know what I'm saying?"

His florid face lost several shades of red. "No way, man. Look, I've got nothing to do with what's been going on. Not my fault, none of my business, man."

"With what's been going on," I said. I looked down at my folded hands for a moment, and then back up at him. "What's the suitcase for, Morty? You do something that means you need to leave town for a while?"

He swallowed, thick neck working. "Look, Dresden. Mister Dresden. My sister got sick, see. I'm just going to help her out."

"Sure you are," I said. "That's what you're doing. Going out of town to help your sick sister."

"I swear to God," Morty said, lifting a hand, his face earnest.

I pointed at the chair across from me. "Sit down, Morty."

"I'd like to, but I got a cab coming." He turned toward the door.

"Ventas servitas," I hissed, nice and dramatic, and threw some will at the door. Sudden wind slammed it shut right in front of his eyes. He squeaked, and backed up several paces, staring at the door, then whirling to face me.

I used the remnants of the same spell to push out a chair opposite me. "Sit down, Morty. I've got a few questions. Now, if you cut the crap, you'll make your cab. And, if not . . ." I left the words hanging. One thing about intimidation is that people can always think up something worse that you could do to them than you can, if you leave their imagination some room to play.

He stared at me, and swallowed again, his jowls jiggling. Then he moved to the chair as though he expected chains to fly out of it and tie him down the moment he sat. He balanced his weight on the very edge of the chair, licked his lips, and watched me, probably trying to figure out the best lies for the questions he expected.

"You know," I said. "I've read your books, Morty. *Ghosts of Chicago. The Spook Factor*. Two or three others. You did good work, there."

His expression changed, eyes narrowing in suspicion. "Thank you."

"I mean, twenty years ago, you were a pretty damn good investigator. Sensitivity to spiritual energies and apparitions—ghosts. What we call an ectomancer in the business."

"Yeah," he said. His eyes softened a little, if not his voice. He avoided looking directly in my face. Most people do. "That was a long time ago."

I kept my voice in the same tone, the same expression. "And now what? You run séances for people. How many times do you actually get to contact a spirit? One time in ten? One in twenty? Must be a real letdown from the actual stuff. Playacting, I mean."

He was good at covering his expressions, I'll give him that. But I'm used to watching people. I saw anger in the way he held his neck and shoulders. "I provide a legitimate service to people in need."

"No. You play on their grief to take them for all you can. You don't believe that you're doing right, Morty, deep down. You can justify it any way you want, but you don't *like* what you're doing. If you did, your powers wouldn't have faded like they have."

His jaw set in a hard line, and he didn't try to hide the anger anymore—the first honest reaction I'd seen out of him since he'd cried out in surprise. "If you've got a point, Dresden, get to it. I've got a plane to catch."

I spread my fingers over the tabletop. "In the past two weeks," I said, "the spooks have been going mad. You should see the trouble they've caused. That poltergeist in the Campbell house. The Basement Beast at U. of C. Agatha Hagglethorn, down at Cook County."

Morty grimaced and wiped at his face again. "Yeah. I hear things. You and the Knight of the Sword have been covering the worst of it."

"What else has been happening, Morty? I'm getting a little cranky losing sleep, so keep it short and simple."

"I don't know," he said, sullen. "I've lost my powers, remember."

I narrowed my eyes. "But you hear things, Morty. You've still got some sources in the Nevernever. Why are you leaving town?"

He laughed, and it had a shaky edge to it. "You said you read all of my books? Did you read *They Shall Rise*?"

"I glanced over it. End-of-the-world-type stuff. I figured you had been talking to the wrong kind of spirits too much. They love trying to sell people on Armageddon. A lot of them are cons like you."

He ignored me. "Then you read my theory on the barrier between our world and the Nevernever. That it's slowly being torn away."

"And you think it's falling to pieces, now? Morty, that wall has been there since the dawn of time. I don't think it's going to collapse right now."

"*Wall.*" He said the word with a sneer. "More like Saran Wrap, wizard. Like Jell-O. It bends and wiggles and stirs." He rubbed his palms on his thighs, shivering.

"And it's falling now?"

"Look around you!" he shouted. "Good God, wizard. The past two weeks, the border's been waggling back and forth like a hooker at a dockworker's convention. Why the hell do you think all of these ghosts have been rising?"

I didn't let the sudden volume of his tone make me blink. "You're saying that this instability has been making it easier for ghosts to cross over from the Nevernever?"

"And easier to form bigger, stronger ghosts when people die," he said. "You think you've got some pissed-off ghosts now? Wait until some honor student on her way out of the south side with a college scholarship gets popped by accident in a gang shootout. Wait until some poor sap who got AIDS from a blood transfusion breathes his last."

"Bigger, badder ghosts," I said. "Superghosts. That's what you're talking about."

He laughed, a nasty little laugh. "New generation of viruses is coming, too. Things are going to hell all over. Eventually, that border's going to get thin enough to spit through, and you'll have more problems with demon attacks than gang violence."

I shook my head. "All right," I said. "Let's say that I buy that the barrier is fluid rather than concrete. There's turbulence in it, and it's making crossing over easier, both ways. Could something be causing the turbulence?"

"How the hell should I know?" he snarled. "You don't know what it's like, Dresden. To speak to things that exist in the past and in the future as well as in the now. To have them walk up to you at the salad bar and start telling you how they murdered their wife in her sleep.

"I mean, you think you've got a hold on things, that you understand, but in the end it all falls to pieces. A con is simpler, Dresden. You *make* order. People don't give a flying fuck if Uncle Jeffrey really forgives them for missing his last birthday party. They want to know that the world is a place where Uncle Jeffrey *can* and *should* forgive them." He swallowed, and looked around the room, at the fake tomes and the fake skull. "That's what I sell them. Closure. Like on television. They want to know that it's all going to work out in the end, and they're happy to pay for it."

A car honked outside. Morty glared at me. "We're through."

I nodded.

He jerked to his feet, splotches of color in his cheeks. "God, I need a drink. Get out of town, Dresden. Something came across last night like nothing I've ever felt."

I thought of ruined cars and rosebushes planted in consecrated ground. "Do you know what it is?"

"It's big," Morty said. "And it's pissed off. It's going to start killing, Dresden. And I don't think you or anyone else is going to be able to stop it."

"But it's a ghost?"

He gave me a smile that showed me his canines. It was creepy on that florid, eyes-too-wide face. "It's a nightmare." He started to turn away. I wanted to let him go, but I couldn't. The man had become a liar, a sniveling con, but he hadn't always been.

I rose and beat him to the door, taking his arm in one hand. He spun to face me, jerking his arm away, glaring defiantly at my eyes. I avoided locking gazes. I didn't want to take a look at Mortimer Lindquist's soul.

"Morty," I said, quietly. "Get away from your séances for a while. Go somewhere quiet. Read. Relax. You're older now, stronger. If you give yourself a chance, the power will come back"

He laughed again, tired and jaded. "Sure, Dresden. Just like that."

"Morty—"

He turned away from me and stalked out the door. He didn't bother to lock the place up behind him. I watched him head out to the cab, which waited by the curb. He lugged his bag into the backseat, and then followed it.

Before the cab pulled out, he rolled down the window. "Dresden," he called. "Under my chair there's a drawer. My notes. If you want to kill yourself trying to stand up to this thing, you might as well know what you're getting into."

He rolled the window back up as the cab pulled away. I watched it go, then went back inside. I found the drawer hidden in the base of the carved wooden chair, and inside I found a trio of old leather-bound journals, vellum pages covered in script that started out neat in the oldest one and became a jerky scrawl in the most recent entries. I held the books up to my mouth and inhaled the smell of leather, ink, paper; musty and genuine and real.

Morty hadn't had to give me the notes. Maybe there was some root of the person he had been, deep down somewhere, that wasn't dead yet. Maybe I'd done him a little good with that advice. I'd like to think that.

I blew out a breath, found a phone and called a cab of my own. I needed to get the *Beetle* out of impound if I could. Maybe Murphy could fix it for me.

I gathered the journals and went to the porch to wait for the cab, shutting the door behind me. Something big was coming through town, Morty had said.

"A nightmare," I said, out loud.

Could Mort be right? Could the barrier between the spirit world and our own be falling apart? The thought made me shudder. Something had been formed, something big and mean. And my gut instinct told me that it had a purpose. All power, no matter how terrible or benign, whether its wielder is aware of it or not, has a purpose.

So this Nightmare was here for something. I wondered what it wanted. Wondered what it would do.

And worried that, all too soon, I would find out.

Chapter 11

An unmarked car sat in my driveway with two nondescript men inside.

I got out of the taxi, paid off the cabby, and nodded at the driver of the car, Detective Rudolph. Rudy's clean-cut good looks hadn't faded in the year since he'd started with Special Investigations, Chicago's unspoken answer to the officially unacknowledged world of the supernatural. But the time had hardened him a bit, made him a little less white around the eyes.

Rudolph nodded back, not even trying to hide his glower. He didn't like me. Maybe it had something to do with the bust several months back. Rudy had cut and run, rather than stick it out next to me. Before that, I'd escaped police custody while he was supposed to be watching me. I'd had a darn good reason to escape, and it wasn't really fair of him to hold that against me, but hey. Whatever got him through the day.

"Heya, Detective," I said. "What's up?"

"Get in the car," Rudolph said.

I planted my feet and shoved my hands in my pockets with a certain nonchalance. "Am I under arrest?"

Rudolph narrowed his eyes and started to speak again, but the man in the passenger seat cut him off. "Heya, Harry," Detective Sergeant John Stallings said, nodding at me.

"How you doing, John? What brings you out today?"

"Murph wanted us to ask you down to a scene." He reached up and scratched at several days' worth of unshaven beard beneath a bad haircut and intelligent dark eyes. "Hope you got the time. We tried at your office, but you haven't been in, so she sent us down here to wait for you."

I shifted Mort Lindquist's books in my arms. "I'm busy today. Can it wait?"

Rudolph spat, "The lieutenant says she wants you down there now, you get your ass down there. Now."

Stallings gave Rudolph a look, and then rolled his eyes for my benefit. "Look, Harry. Murphy told me to tell you that this one was personal."

I frowned. "Personal, eh?"

He spread his hands. "It's what she said." He frowned and then added, "It's Micky Malone."

I got a sickly little feeling in my stomach. "Dead?"

Stallings's jaw twitched. "You'd better come see for yourself."

I closed my eyes and tried not to get frustrated. I didn't have time for detours. It would take me hours to grind through Mort's notes, and sundown, when the spirits would be able to cross over from the Nevernever, would come swiftly.

But Murphy did plenty for me. I owed her. She'd saved my life a couple of times, and vice versa. She was my main source of income, too. Karrin Murphy headed up Special Investigations, a post that had traditionally resulted in a couple of months of bumbling and then a speedy exit from the police force. Murphy hadn't bumbled—instead, she'd hired the services of Chicago's only professional wizard as a consultant. She was getting to where she had a pretty good grasp on the local preternatural predators, at least the most common of them, but when things got hairy she still called me in. Technically, I show up on the paperwork as an investigative consultant. I guess the computer records system doesn't have numerical codes for demon banishment, divination spells, or exorcisms.

S.I. had gone toe to toe with one of the worst things anyone but a wizard like me was ever likely to see, only the year before—a half-ton of indestructible loup-garou. They'd taken some serious casualties. Six dead, including Murphy's partner. Micky Malone had gotten hamstrung. He'd gone through therapy, and had come along for one last job when Michael and I took down that demon-summoning sorcerer. After that, though, he'd decided that his limp was going to keep him from being a good cop, and retired on disability.

I felt guilty for that—maybe irrational, true, but if I'd been a little smarter or a little faster, maybe I could have saved those people's lives. And maybe I could have saved Micky's health. No one else saw it that way, but I did.

"All right," I said. "Give me a second to put these away."

The ride was quiet, except for a little meaningless chatter from Stallings. Rudolph ignored me. I closed my eyes and ached along the way. Rudolph's radio squawked and then fell abruptly silent. I could smell burnt rubber or something, and knew that it was likely my fault.

I opened one eye and saw Rudolph scowling back at me in the mirror. I half-smiled, and closed my eyes again. Jerk.

The car stopped in a residential neighborhood near West Armitage, down in Bucktown. The district had gotten its name from the number of immigrant homes once there, and the goats kept in people's front yards. The homes had been tiny affairs, stuffed with too-large families and children.

Bucktown had been lived in for a century and it was all grown up. Literally. The houses on their tiny lots hadn't had much room to expand out, so they'd grown up instead, giving the neighborhood a stretched, elongated look. The trees were ancient oaks and sycamores, and decorated the tiny yards in stately majesty, except where they'd been roughly hacked back from power lines and rooftops. Shadows fell in sharp slants from all the tall trees and tall houses, turning the streets and sidewalks into candy canes of light and darkness.

One of the houses, a two-story white-on-white number, had its small driveway full and another half-dozen cars parked out on the street, plus Murphy's motorcycle leaning on its kickstand in the front yard. Rudolph pulled the car up alongside the curb across the street from that house and killed the engine. It went on rattling and coughing for a moment before it died.

I got out of the car and felt something *wrong*. An uneasy feeling ran over me, prickles of sensation along the nape of my neck and against my spine.

I stood there for a minute, frowning, while Rudolph and Stallings got out of the car. I looked around the neighborhood, trying to pin down the source of the odd sensations. The leaves in the trees, all in their autumn motley, rustled and sighed in the wind, occasionally falling. Dried leaves rattled and scraped over the streets. Cars drove by in the distance. A jet rumbled overhead, a deep and distant sound.

"Dresden," Rudolph snapped. "Let's go."

I lifted a hand, extending my senses out, pushing my perception out along with my will. "Hang on a second," I said. "I need to . . ." I quit trying to speak, and searched for the source of the sensation. What the hell was it?

"Fucking showboat," Rudolph growled. I heard him start toward me.

"Hang on, kid," Stallings said. "Let the man work. We've both seen what he can do."

"I haven't seen shit that can't be explained," Rudolph growled. But he stayed put.

I drifted across the street, to the yard of the house in question, and found the first body in the fallen leaves, five feet to my left. A small, yellow-and-white furred cat lay there, twisted so that its forelegs faced one way, its hindquarters the opposite. Something had broken its neck.

I felt a pang of nausea. Death isn't ever pretty, really. It's worst with people, but with the animals that are close to mankind, it seems to be a little nastier than it might be elsewhere in the wild kingdom. The cat couldn't have reached its full growth, yet—maybe a kitten from early in the spring, roaming the neighborhood. There was no collar on its neck.

I could feel a little cloud of disturbance around it, a kind of psychic energy left by traumatic, agonizing, and torturous events. But this one little thing, one animal's death, shouldn't have been enough to make me aware of it all the way over from my seat in the police car.

Five feet farther on, I found a dead bird. I found its wings in two more places. Then two more birds, without heads. Then something that had been small and furry, and was now small and furry and squishy—maybe a vole or a ground squirrel. And there were more. A lot more—all in all, maybe a dozen dead animals in the front yard, a dozen little patches of violent energies still lingering. No single one of them would have been enough to disturb my wizard's sense, but all of them together had.

So what the hell had been killing these animals?

I rubbed my palms over my arms, a sickly little feeling of dread rolling through me. I looked up to see Rudolph and Stallings following me around. Their faces looked kind of greenish.

"Jesus," Stallings said. He prodded the body of the cat with one toe. "What did this?"

I shook my head and rolled my shoulders in a shrug. "It might take me a while to find out. Where's Micky?"

"Inside."

"Well then," I said, and stood up, brushing off my hands. "Let's go."

Chapter 12

I stopped outside the doorway. Micky Malone owned a nice house. His wife taught elementary school. They wouldn't have been able to afford the place on his salary alone, but together they managed. The hardwood floors gleamed with polish. I saw an original painting, a seascape, hanging on one of the walls of the living room, adjacent to the entryway. There were a lot of plants, a lot of greenery that, along with the wood grain of the floors, gave the place a rich, organic glow. It was one of those places that wasn't just a house. It was a home.

"Come on, Dresden," Rudolph snapped. "The lieutenant is waiting."

"Is Mrs. Malone here?" I asked.

"Yes."

"Go get her. I need her to invite me in."

"What?" Rudolph said. "Give me a break. Who are you, Count Dracula?"

"Drakul is still in eastern Europe, last time we checked," I replied. "But I need her or Micky to ask me in, if you want me to do anything for you."

"What the hell are you talking about?"

I sighed. "Look. Homes, places that people live in and love and have built a life in have a kind of power of their own. If a bunch of strangers had been trouping in and out all day, I wouldn't have any trouble with the threshold, but you're not. You guys are friends." Like Murphy had said—this one was personal.

Stallings frowned. "So you can't come in?"

"Oh, I could come in," I said. "But I'd be leaving most of what

I can do at the door. The threshold would mess with me being able to work any forces in the house."

"What shit," Rudolph snorted. "Count Dracula."

"Harry," Stallings said. "Can't we invite you in?"

"No. Has to be someone who lives there. Besides, it's polite," I said. "I don't like to go places where I'm not welcome. I'd feel a lot better if I knew it was all right with Mrs. Malone for me to be here."

Rudolph opened his mouth to spit venom on me again, but Stallings cut him off. "Just do it, Rudy. Go get Sonia and bring her back here."

Rudolph glowered but did what he was told, going into the house.

Stallings tapped out a cigarette and lit up. He puffed for a second, thoughtfully. "So you can't do magic inside a house unless someone asks you in?"

"Not a house," I said. "A home. There's a difference."

"So what about Victor Sells's place? I hear you took him on, right?"

I shook my head. "He'd screwed up his threshold. He was running his business out of it, using the place for dark ceremonies. It wasn't a home anymore."

"So you can't mess with anything on its own turf?"

"Can't mess with mortals, no. Monsters don't get a threshold."

"Why not?"

"How the hell should I know," I said. "They just don't. I can't know everything, right?"

"Guess so," Stallings said, and after a minute he nodded. "Sure, I see what you mean. So it shuts you down?"

"Not completely, but it makes it a lot harder to do anything. Like wearing a lead suit. That's why vampires have to keep out. Other nasties like that. If you give them that much of a handicap, they have trouble just staying alive, much less using any freaky powers."

Stallings shook his head. "This magic crap. I never would have believed it before I came here. I still have trouble with it."

"Yeah? That's good. Means you aren't running into it too much."

He blew out twin columns of smoke from his nostrils. "Could be changing. Last couple of days, we've had some people go missing. Bums, street people, folks some of the cops and detectives know."

I frowned. "Yeah?"

"Yeah. It's all rumors so far. And people like that, they can just be gone the next day. But since I started working S.I., stuff like that makes me nervous."

I frowned, and debated telling Stallings what I knew about Bianca's party. Doubtless, there would be a whole flock of vampires in from out of town for the event. Maybe she and her flunkies were rounding up hors d'oeuvres. But I had no proof of that—for all I knew, the disappearances, if they *were* disappearances, could be related to the turbulence in the Nevernever. If so, the cops couldn't do anything about it. And if it was something else, I could be starting a very nasty exchange with Bianca. I didn't want to sic the cops on her for no reason. I'm pretty sure Bianca had the resources to send them back at me—and she could probably make it look like I'd done something to deserve it, too.

Besides that, in the circles of the supernatural community, an Old World code of conduct still ruled. When you have a problem, you settle it face to face, within the circle. You don't bring in the cops and the other mortals as weapons. They're the nuclear missiles of the supernatural world. If you show people a supernatural brawl going on, it's going to scare the snot out of them and the next thing you know, they're burning everything and everyone in sight. Most people wouldn't care that one scary guy might have been right and the other was wrong. Both guys are scary, so you ace both of them and sleep better at night.

It had been that way since the dawn of the Age of Reason and the rising power of mortal kind. And more power to the people, I say. I hated all these bullies, vampires, demons, and bloodthirsty old deities rampaging around like they ruled the world. Never mind that, until a few centuries ago, they really had.

In any case, I decided to keep my mouth shut about Bianca's gathering until I knew enough to be certain, either way.

Stallings and I made small talk until Sonia Malone appeared at the door. She was a woman of medium height, comfortably overweight and solid-looking. Her face would have been gorgeous when she was a young woman, and it still carried that beauty, refined by years of self-confidence and steady reliability. Her eyes were reddened, and she wore no makeup, but her features seemed composed. She wore a simple dress in a floral print, her only jewelry the wedding band on her finger.

"Mr. Dresden," she said, politely. "Micky told me that you saved his life, last year."

I coughed and looked down. Though I guess that was true, technically, I still didn't see it that way. "We all did everything we could, ma'am. Your husband was very brave."

"Detective Rudolph said that I needed to invite you in."

"I don't want to go where I'm not welcome, ma'am," I replied.

Sonia wrinkled up her nose and eyed Stallings. "Put that out, Sergeant."

Stallings dropped the cigarette and mushed it out with his foot.

"All right, Mr. Dresden," she said. For a moment, her composure faltered and her lips began to tremble. She closed her eyes and took a deep breath, smoothing over her features, then opened her eyes again. "If you can help my Micky, please come in. I invite you."

"Thank you," I said. I stepped forward, through the door, and felt the silent tension of the threshold parting around me like a beaded curtain rimed with frost.

We went through a living room where several cops, people I knew from S.I., sat around talking quietly. It reminded me of a funeral. They looked up at me as I went by, and talk ceased. I nodded to them, and we went on past, to a staircase leading up to the second floor.

"He was up late last night," she told me, her voice quiet. "Sometimes he can't sleep, and he didn't come to bed until late. I got up early, but I didn't want to wake him, so I let him sleep in." Mrs. Malone stopped at the top of the stairs, and pointed down the hall at a closed door. "Th-there," she said. "I'm sorry. I c-can't . . ." She took another deep breath. "I need to see about lunch. Are you hungry?"

"Oh. Yes, sure."

"All right," she said, and retreated back down the stairs.

I swallowed and looked at the door at the end of the hall, then headed toward it. My steps sounded loud in my own ears. I knocked gently on the door.

Karrin Murphy opened it. She wasn't anyone's idea of a leader of a group of cops charged with solving every bizarre crime that fell between the lines of the law enforcement system. She didn't look like someone who would stand, with her feet planted, putting tiny silver bullets into an oncoming freight train of a loup-garou, either—but she was.

Karrin looked up at me from her five-foot-nothing in height. Her blue eyes, normally clear and bright, looked sunken. She'd shoved her golden hair under a baseball cap, and wore jeans and a white T-shirt. Her shoulder harness wrinkled the cotton around the shoulder where her side arm hung. Lines stood out like cracks in a sunbaked field, around her mouth, her eyes. "Hi, Harry," she said. Her voice too was quiet, gruff.

"Hiya, Murph. You don't look so good."

She tried to smile. It looked ghastly. "I . . . I didn't know who else to call."

I frowned, troubled. On any other day, Murphy would have returned my mildly insulting comment with compounded interest. She opened the door farther, and let me in.

I remembered Micky Malone as an energetic man of medium height, balding, with a broad smile and a nose that peeled in the sun if he walked outside to get his morning paper. The cane and limp were additions too recent for me to have firmly stuck in my memory. Micky wore old, quality suits, and was careful never to get the jackets messy or his wife would never let him hear the end of it.

I didn't remember Micky with a fixed, tooth-baring grin and eyes spread out in that Helter-Skelter gleam of madness. I didn't remember him covered in small scratches, or his fingernails crusted with his own blood, or his wrists and ankles cuffed to the iron-framed bed. He panted, grinning around the neatly decorated little room. I could smell sweat and urine. There were no lights on in the room, and the curtains had been drawn over the windows, leaving it in a brownish haze.

He turned his head toward me and his eyes widened. He sucked in a breath and threw back his head in a long, falsetto-pitched scream like a coyote's. Then he started laughing and rocking back and forth, jerking on the steel restraints, making the bed shake in a steady, squeaking rhythm.

"Sonia called us this morning," Murphy said, toneless. "She'd locked herself into her closet and had a cellular. We got here right before Micky finished breaking down the closet door."

"She called the cops?"

"No. She called me. Said she didn't want them to see Micky like this. That it would ruin him."

I shook my head. "Damn. Brave lady. And he's been like this ever since?"

"Yeah. He was just . . . crazy mean. Screaming and spitting and biting."

"Has he said anything?" I asked.

"Not a word," Murphy said. "Animal noises." She crossed her

arms and looked up at me, at my eyes for a second, before looking away. "What happened to him, Harry?"

Micky giggled and started bouncing his hips up and down on the bed as he rocked, making it sound as though a couple of hyperkinetic teenagers were coupling there. My stomach turned. No wonder Mrs. Malone hadn't been willing to come back into this room.

"You better give me a minute to find out," I said.

"Could he be . . . you know. Possessed? Like in the movies?"

"I don't know yet, Murph."

"Could it be some kind of spell?"

"Murphy, I don't know."

"Dammit, Harry," she snapped. "You'd damned well better find out." She clenched her fists and shook with suppressed fury.

I put my hand on her shoulder. "I will. Give me some time with him."

"Harry, I swear, if you can't help him—" Her voice caught in her throat, and tears sparkled in her eyes. "He's one of *mine*, dammit."

"Easy, Murph," I told her, making my voice as gentle as I knew how. I opened the door for her. "Go get some coffee, all right? I'll see what I can do."

She glanced up at me and then back at Malone. "It's okay, Micky," she said. "We're all here for you. You won't be alone."

Micky Malone gave her that fixed grin and then licked his lips before bursting out into another chorus of giggles. Murphy shivered and then walked out of the room, her head bowed.

And left me alone with the madman.

Chapter 13

I drew up a chair beside the bed and sat down. Micky stared at me with white-rimmed eyes. I rummaged around in the inside pocket of my duster. I had some chalk there, in case I needed to draw a circle. A candle and some matches. A couple of old receipts. Not much, magically speaking, to work with.

"Hi, there, Micky," I said. "Can you hear me in there?"

Micky broke out in another fit of giggles. I made sure to keep my eyes away from his. Hells bells, I did *not* want to get drawn into a soulgaze with Micky Malone at the moment.

"All right, Micky," I said, keeping my voice calm, low, like you do with animals. "I'm going to touch you—okay? I think I'll be able to tell if there's anything inside of you if I do. I'm not going to hurt you, so don't freak out." As I spoke, I reached out a hand toward his bare arm and laid it lightly upon Micky's skin.

He was fever-hot to the touch. I could sense some kind of force at work on him—not the tingling energy of a practitioner's aura, or the ocean-deep power of Michael's faith, but it was there, nonetheless. Some kind of cold, crawling energy oozed over him.

What the hell?

It didn't feel like any kind of spell I'd ever experienced. And it wasn't a possession, I was sure of that. I would have been able to sense any kind of spirit-being in him, through a physical touch.

Micky stared at me for a second and then thrust his head at my hand, his teeth making snapping motions. I jerked back even though he couldn't have reached me. Someone trying to bite you makes you react, more than if they take a punch at you. Biting is just more primal. Spooky.

Micky started giggling again, rocking the bed back and forth.

"All right," I breathed. "I'm going to have to get a little desperate, here. If you weren't a friend, Micky . . ." I closed my eyes for a moment, steeling myself, then focused my will into a spot right between my eyebrows, only a little higher. I felt the tension gather there, the pressure, and when I opened my eyes again, I'd opened my wizard's Sight, too.

The Sight is a blessing and a curse. It lets you see things, things you couldn't normally see. With my Sight, I can see even the most ethereal of spirits. I can see the energies of life stirring and moving, running like blood through the world, between the earth and the sky, between water and fire. Enchantments stand out like cords braided from fiber-optic cables, or maybe Las Vegas-quality neon, depending on how complicated or powerful they are. You can sometimes see the demons that walk among mankind in human form, this way. Or the angels. You see things the way they really are, in spirit and in soul, as well as in body.

The problem is that anything you see stays with you. No matter how horrible, no matter how revolting, no matter how madness-inducing or terrifying—it stays with you. Forever. Always right there in your mind in full technicolor, never fading or becoming easier to bear. Sometimes you see things that are so beautiful you want to keep them with you, always.

But more often, in my line of work, you see things like Micky Malone.

He was dressed in boxers and a white undershirt, stained with bits of blood and sweat and worse. But when I turned my Sight on him, I saw something different.

He had been ravaged. Torn apart. He was missing flesh, everywhere. Something had attacked him and taken out sections of him in huge bites. I'd seen pictures of people who'd been attacked by sharks, had hunks of meat just taken, gone. That's what Micky looked like. It wasn't visible to the flesh, but something had torn his mind, and maybe his soul, to bloody shreds. He bled and bled, endlessly, never staining the sheets.

And wound around him, starting at his throat and running down to one ankle was a strand of black wire, oversized barbs gouging into his flesh, the ends disappearing seamlessly into his skin.

Just like Agatha Hagglethorn.

I stared at him, horrified, my stomach writhing and heaving. I had to fight to keep from throwing up. Micky looked up at me and seemed to sense something was different, because he went abruptly still. His smile didn't look mad to me anymore. It looked agonized, like a grimace of pain twisted and cranked until the muscles of his face were at the snapping point.

His lips moved. Shook, his whole face writhing with the expression. "Uh, uh, uh," he moaned.

"It's all right, Micky," I said. I clasped my hands together to keep them from shaking. "I'm here."

"Hurts," he breathed at last, barely a whisper. "It hurts, it hurts, it hurts, it hurts, it hurts, it hurts . . ." He went on and on repeating it until he ran out of breath. Then he squeezed his eyes shut. Tears welled out and he broke into another helpless, maddened giggle.

What the hell could I do for *that*? The barbed wire had to be a spell of some kind, but it didn't look like anything I had ever seen before. Most magic throbbed and pulsed with light, life, even if it was being used for malevolent purposes. Magic comes from life, from the energy of our world and from people, from their emotions and their will. That's what I had always been taught.

But that barbed wire was dull, flat, matte-black. I reached out to touch it, and it almost seared my fingers with how cold it was. Micky, God. I couldn't imagine what he must have been going through.

The smart thing to do would have been to fall back. I could get Bob and work on this, research it, figure out how to get the wire from around Micky without hurting him. But he had already been suffering through this for hours. He might not make it through many more—his sanity was going to be hard-pressed to survive the spiritual mauling he had taken. Adding another day of this torture onto it all might send him someplace from where he'd never come back.

I closed my eyes and took a breath. "I hope I'm right, Micky," I told him. "I'm going to try to make it stop hurting."

He let out a whimpering little giggle, staring up at me.

I decided to start at his ankle. I swallowed, steeling myself again, and reached down, getting my fingers between the burning cold barbed wire and his skin. I clenched my teeth, forcing will, power, into the touch, enough to be able to touch the material of the spell around him. Then I started pulling. Slowly, at first, and then harder.

The metal strands burned into me. My fingers never went numb—they just began to ache more and more violently. The barbed wire resisted, barbs clinging at Micky's flesh. The poor man screamed aloud, agonized, though there was that horrible, tortured laughter added to it as well.

I felt tears burn into my eyes, from the pain, from Micky's scream, but I kept pulling. The end of the wire tore free of his flesh. I kept pulling. Barb by barb, inch by inch, I tore the wire-spell free, drawing it up *through* his flesh at times, pulling that dead, cold energy away from Micky. He screamed until he ran out of breath and I heard whimpers coming from somewhere else in the room. I guess it was me. I started using both hands, struggling against the cold magic.

Finally, the other end slithered free from Micky's neck. His eyes flew open wide and then he sagged down, letting out a low, exhausted moan. I gasped and stumbled back from the bed, keeping the wire in my hands.

It suddenly twisted and spun like a serpent, and one end plunged into my throat.

Ice. Cold. Endless, bitter, aching cold coursed through me, and I screamed. I heard footsteps running down the hall outside, a voice calling out. The wire whipped and thrashed around, the other end darting toward the floor, and I seized it in both hands, twisted it up and away from attaching itself at the other end. The loose strands near my neck started rippling, cold barbs digging into me through my clothes, my skin, as the dark energy tried to attach itself to *me*.

The door burst open. Murphy came through it, her eyes living flames of azure blue, her hair a golden coronet around her. She held a blazing sword in her hand and she shone so bright and beautiful and terrifying in her anger that it was hard to see. The Sight, I realized, dimly. I was seeing her for who she was.

"Harry! What the hell?"

I struggled against the wire, knowing that she couldn't see it or feel it, gasping. "The window. Murph, open the window!"

She didn't hesitate for a second, but crossed the floor and threw open the window. I staggered after her, winding the frozen wire around one hand, my mind screaming with the agony of it. I fought it down, dragged it into a coil, my face twisted into a snarl as I did it. Anger surged up, hot and bright, and I reached for that power as I jerked the wire from my throat and threw it out the window as hard as I could, sending it sailing into the air.

I snarled, jabbed a finger at it, took all that anger and fear and sent it coursing out of me, toward that dark spell. *"Fuego!"*

Fire came to my call, roared forth from my fingertips and engulfed the wire. It writhed and then vanished in a detonation that rattled the house around me and sent me tumbling back to the floor.

I lay there for a minute, stunned, trying to get a handle on what was happening. Damn the Sight. It starts blurring the lines between what's real and what isn't. A guy would go crazy that way. Fast. Just keep it open all the time and let everything pour in and really *know* what everything is like. That sounded like a good idea, really. Just bask in all the beauty and horror for a while, just drink it all in and let it erase everything else, all that bother and worry about people being hurt or not being hurt—

I found myself sitting on the floor, aching from cold that had no basis in physical reality, giggling to myself in a high-pitched stream, rocking back and forth. I had to struggle to close my Sight again, and the second I did, everything seemed to settle, to become clearer. I looked up, blinking tears out of my eyes, panting. Outside, dogs were barking all over the place, and I could hear several car alarms whooping, touched off by the force of the blast.

Murphy stood over me, her eyes wide, her gun held in one hand and pointed at the door. "Jesus," she said, softly. "Harry. What happened?"

My lips felt numb and I was freezing, all over, shaking. "Spell. S-something attacked him. L-laid a spell on him after. H-had to burn it. Fire even burns in the s-spirit world. S-sorry."

She put the gun away, staring at me. "Are you all right?"

I shook some more. "H-how's Micky?"

Murphy crossed the room to lay a hand on Micky's brow. "His fever's gone," she breathed. "Mick?" she called gently. "Hey, Malone. It's Murph. Can you hear me?"

Micky stirred, and blinked open his eyes. "Murph?" he asked quietly. "What's going on?" His eyes fell closed again, exhausted. "Where's Sonia? I need her."

"I'll get her," Murphy breathed. "You wait here. Rest."

"My wrists hurt," Micky mumbled.

Murphy looked back at me, and I nodded to her. "He should be all right, now." She unfastened the cuffs from him, but it looked as though he had already fallen into a deep, exhausted sleep.

Murphy drew the covers up over him, and smoothed his hair back from his forehead. Then she knelt down on the floor beside me. "Harry," she said. "You look like . . ."

"Hell," I said. "Yeah, I know. He's going to need rest, Murph. Peace. Something tore him up inside, real bad."

"What do you mean?"

I frowned. "It's like . . . when someone close to you dies. Or when you break off a relationship with someone. It tears you up inside. Emotional pain. That's kind of what happened to Micky. Something tore him up."

"What did it?" Murphy asked. Her voice was quiet, steel-hard.

"I don't know yet," I said. I closed my eyes, shaking, and leaned my head back against a wall. "I've been calling it the Nightmare."

"How do we kill it?"

I shook my head. "I'm working on it. It's staying a couple steps ahead of me, so far."

"Damn," Murphy said. "I get sick of playing catch-up, sometimes."

"Yeah. So do I."

More footsteps came pounding down the hall, and Sonia Malone burst into the room. She saw Micky, laying quietly, and went to him as if she feared to stir the air too much, each movement fragile. She touched his face, his thinning hair, and he awoke enough to reach for her hand. She held onto it tightly, kissed his fingers, and bowed her head to rest her cheek against his. I heard her crying, letting it out.

Murphy and I traded a look, and rose by mutual consent to leave Sonia in peace. Murphy had to help me up. I ached, everywhere, felt as though my bones had been frozen solid. Walking was hard, but Murphy helped me.

I took a last look at Sonia and Micky, and then quietly closed the door.

"Thank you, Harry," Murphy said.

"Any time. You're my friend, Murph. And I'm always up to helping a lady in distress."

She glanced up at me, a sparkle in her eyes underneath the brim of the baseball cap. "You are such a chauvinist pig, Dresden."

"A hungry chauvinist pig," I said. "I'm starving."

"You should eat more often, beanpole." Murphy sat me down on the top step and said, "Stay here. I'll get you something."

"Don't take too long, Murph. I've got work to do. The thing that did this comes out to play at sundown."

I leaned against the wall and closed my eyes. I thought of dead animals and smashed cars and frozen agonies wrapped around Micky Malone's tortured soul. "I don't know what the hell this Nightmare is. But I'm going to find it. And I'm going to kill it."

"That sounds about right," Murphy said. "If I can help, you've got it."

"Thanks, Murph."

"Don't mention it. Um, Harry?"

I opened my eyes. She was watching me, her expression uncertain. "For a minute there, when I came in. You stared at me. You stared at me with the strangest damned expression on your face. What did you see?" she asked.

"You'd laugh in my face if I told you," I said. "Go get me something to eat."

She snorted and turned to go down the stairs and sort things out with the excited S.I. officers roaming around on the first floor. I smiled, remembering the vision, sharp and brilliant in my mind's eye. Murphy, the guardian angel, coming through the door in a blaze of wrath. It was a picture I wouldn't mind keeping with me. Sometimes you get lucky.

And then I thought of that barbed wire, the hideous torment I'd seen and briefly felt. The ghosts rising of late had been suffering from the same thing. But who could be doing it to them? And how? The forces used in that torture-spell weren't like anything I had seen or felt before. I had never heard of any kind of magic that could be slapped on a spirit or a mortal with the same results. I wouldn't have thought it possible. How was it being done?

More to the point, who was doing it? Or *what*?

I sat there shivering and alone and aching. I was starting to take this business personally. Malone was an ally, someone who had stood up to the bad guys beside me. The more I thought about it, the more angry and the more certain I became.

I would find this Nightmare, this thing that had crossed over, and destroy it.

And then I would find whoever or whatever had created it.

Unless, Harry, I thought to myself, *they find you first.*

Chapter 14

"No," I said into the phone. I tossed my coat onto a chair and then sprawled out on the couch. My apartment lay covered in shadows, sunlight filtering in through the sunken windows high up on the walls. "I haven't gotten the chance yet. I lost a couple of hours detouring to pull a spell off of Micky Malone, from S.I. Someone had wrapped barbed wire around his spirit."

"Mother of God," Michael said. "Is he all right?"

"Will be. But it's four hours of daylight lost." I filled him in on Mort Lindquist and his diaries, as well as the events at Detective Malone's house.

"There isn't much more time to find this Lydia, Harry," Michael agreed. "Sundown's in another six hours."

"I'm working on it. And after I get Bob out the door looking, I'll see if I can hit the streets myself. I got the *Beetle* back."

He sounded surprised. "It's not impounded?"

"Murphy fixed it for me."

"Harry," he said, disappointed. "She broke the law to get you your car back?"

"Darn tootin' she did," I said. "She owed me a favor. Hey man, the Almighty doesn't arrange for *me* to be anywhere on time. I need wheels."

Michael sighed. "There isn't time to debate this right now. I'll call you if I find her—but it doesn't look good."

"I just can't figure it. What would this thing have to do with that girl? We need to find her and work out the connection."

"Could Lydia be responsible for the recent disturbances?"

"I don't think so. That spell I ran into today—I've never seen anything like it. It was . . ." I shivered, remembering. "It was wrong, Michael. Cold. It was—"

"Evil?" he suggested.

"Maybe. Yeah."

"There is such a thing as evil, Harry, in spite of what many people say. Just remember that there's good, too."

I cleared my throat, uncomfortable. "Murphy put out the word to the folks in blue—so if one of her friends on patrol sees a girl matching Lydia's description, we'll hear about it."

"Outstanding," Michael said. "You see, Harry? This detour of yours to help Detective Malone is going to help us a great deal. Isn't that a very positive coincidence?"

"Yeah, Michael. Divine fortune, yadda, yadda. Call me."

"Don't *yadda yadda* the Lord, Harry. It's disrespectful. God go with you." And he hung up.

I put my coat away, got out my nice, heavy flannel robe and slipped into it, then went over to the rug against the south wall. I dragged it away from the floor, and the hinged door there, then swung the door open. I fetched a kerosene lamp, lit it up and dialed the wick up to a bright flame, then got ready to descend the folding wooden ladder into the sub-basement.

The telephone rang again.

I debated ignoring it. It rang again, insistent. I sighed, closed the door, put the rug back in place, and got to the phone on the fifth ring.

"What?" I said, uncharitably.

"I have to hand it to you, Dresden," Susan said. "You certainly know how to charm a girl the morning after."

I let out a long breath. "Sorry, Susan. I've been working and . . . it's not going so well. Lots of questions and no answers."

"Ouch," she said back. Someone said something to her in the background, and she murmured a response. "I don't want to add to your day, but do you remember the name of that guy you and Special Investigations took down a couple months ago? The ritual killer?"

"Oh, right. Him . . ." I closed my eyes, and grubbed about in my memory. "Leo something. Cravat, Camner, Conner. Kraven the Hunter. I didn't really get his name. I tracked him down by the demon he was calling up and nailed him that way. Michael and I didn't hang around for the paperwork afterwards, either."

"Kravos?" Susan asked. "Leonid Kravos?"

"Yeah, that might have been it, I think."

"Great," she said. "Super. Thank you, Harry." Her voice sounded a little tense, excited.

"Uh. Do you mind telling me what's going on?" I asked her.

"It's an angle I'm working on," she said. "Look, all I've got right now are rumors. I'll try to tell you more as soon as I've got something concrete."

"Fair enough. I'm sort of focused on something else right now, anyway."

"Anything you need help with?"

"God, I hope not," I said. I shifted the phone a little closer to my ear. "Did you sleep all right, last night?"

"Maybe," she teased. "It's hard to get really relaxed, when I'm that unsatisfied, but your apartment's so cold it's kind of like going into hibernation."

"Yeah, well. Next time I'll make sure it's a hell of a lot colder."

"I'm shivering already," she purred. "Call you tonight if I can?"

"Might not be here."

She sighed. "I understand. Potluck, then. Thanks again, Harry."

"Any time."

We said goodbye, hung up, and I went back to the stairs leading down into the sub-basement. I uncovered the trap door, opened it, got my lantern, and clumped on down the steep, folding staircase.

My lab never got any less cluttered, no matter how much more organization I imposed on it. The contents only grew denser. Counters and shelves ran along three walls. A long table ran down the center of the room, with enough space for me to slip sideways down its length on either side. Next to the ladder, a kerosene heater blunted the worst of the subterranean chill. On the far side of the table, a brass ring had been set into the floor—a summoning circle. I'd had to learn the hard way to keep it clear of the other debris in the lab.

Debris. Technically, everything in the lab was useful, and served some kind of purpose. The ancient books with their faded, moldering leather covers and their all-pervasive musty smell, the plastic containers with resealable lids, the bottles, the jars, the boxes—they all had something in them I either needed or had needed at one time. Notebooks, dozens of pens and pencils, paper clips and staples, reams of paper covered in my restless, scrawling handwriting, the dried corpses of small animals, a human skull surrounded by paperback novels, candles, an ancient battle axe, they all had some significance. I just couldn't remember what it was for most of them.

I took the cover off the lamp and used it to light up about a dozen candles around the room, and then the kerosene heater. "Bob," I said. "Bob, wake up. Come on, we've got work to do." Golden light and the smell of candle flames and hot wax filled the room. "I mean it, man. There's not much time."

Up on its shelf the skull quivered. Twin points of orangish flame flickered up in the empty eye sockets. The white jaws parted in a pantomime yawn, an appropriate sound coming out with it. "Stars and Stones, Harry," the skull muttered. "You're inhuman. It isn't even sundown yet."

"Stop whining, Bob. I'm not in the mood."

"Mood. I'm exhausted. I don't think I can help you out anymore."

"Unacceptable," I said.

"Even spirits get tired, Harry. I need rest."

"Time enough for rest when I'm dead."

"All right then," Bob said. "You want work, we make a deal. I want to do a ridealong the next time Susan comes over."

I snorted at him. "Hell's bells, Bob, don't you ever think about anything besides sex? No. I'm not letting you into my head while I'm with Susan."

The skull spat out an oath. "There should be a union. We could renegotiate my contract."

I snorted. "Any time you want to head back to the homeland, Bob, feel free."

"No, no, no," the skull muttered. "That's all right."

"I mean, there's still that misunderstanding with the Winter Queen, but—"

"All right, I said."

"You probably don't need my protection anymore. I'm sure she'd be willing to sit down and work things out, rather than putting you in torment for the next few hundred—"

"All *right,* I said!" Bob's eyelights flamed. "You can be such an asshole, Dresden, I swear."

"Yep," I agreed. "You awake yet?"

The skull tilted to one side in a thoughtful gesture. "You know," it said. "I am." The eye sockets focused on me again. "Anger really gets the old juices flowing. That was pretty sneaky."

I got out a relatively fresh notepad and a pencil. It took me a moment to clear off a space on the central table. "I've run into some new stuff. Maybe you can help me out. And we've got a missing person I need to look for."

"Okay, hit me."

I took a seat on the worn wooden stool and drew my warm robe a little closer about me. Trust me, wizards don't wear robes for the dramatic effect. They just can't get *warm* enough in their labs. I knew some guys in Europe who still operated out of stone towers. I shudder to think.

"Right," I said. "Just give me whatever you can." And I outlined the events, starting with Agatha Hagglethorn, through Lydia and her disappearance, through my conversation with Mort Lindquist and his mention of the Nightmare, to the attack on poor Micky Malone.

Bob whistled, no mean trick for a guy with no lips. "Let me get this straight. This creature, this thing, has been torturing powerful spirits for a couple of weeks with this barbed-wire spell. It tore up a bunch of stuff on consecrated ground. Then it blew through somebody's threshold and tore his spirit apart, and slapped a torture-spell on him?"

"You got it," I said. "So. What kind of ghost are we dealing with, and who could have called it up? And what is this girl's connection to it?"

"Harry," Bob said, his tone serious. "Leave this one alone."

I blinked at him. "What?"

"Maybe we could go on a vacation—Fort Lauderdale. They're having this international swimsuit competition there, and we could—"

I sighed. "Bob, I don't have time for—"

"I know a guy who's possessed a travel agent for a few days, and he could get us tickets cut rate. What do you say?"

I peered at the skull. If I didn't know any better, I would think that Bob sounded . . . nervous? Was that even possible? Bob wasn't a human being. He was a spirit, a being of the Nevernever. The skull was his habitat, his home away from home. I let him stay in it, protected him, and bought him trashy romance novels on occasion in exchange for his help, his prodigious memory, and his affinity for the laws of magic. Bob was a records computer and personal assistant all rolled into one, provided you could keep his mind on the issue at hand. He knew thousands of beings in the Nevernever, hundreds of spell recipes, scores of formulae for potions and enchantments and magical constructions.

No spirit could have that kind of knowledge without it translating into considerable power. So why was he acting so scared?

"Bob. I don't know why you're so upset, but we need to stop wasting time. Sundown's coming in a few hours, and this thing is going to be able to cross over from the Nevernever and hurt someone else. I need to know what it is, and where it might be going, and how to kick its ass."

"You humans," Bob said. "You're never satisfied. You always want to find out what's behind the next hill, open the next box. Harry, you've got to learn when you know too much."

I stared up at him for a moment, then shook my head. "We'll start with basics and work our way through this step by step."

"Dammit, Harry."

"Ghosts," I said. "Ghosts are beings that live in the spirit world. They're impressions left by a personality at the moment of death. They aren't like people, or sentient spirits like you. They don't change, they don't grow—they're just *there,* experiencing whatever it is they were feeling when they died. Like poor Agatha Hagglethorn. She was loopy."

The skull turned its eye sockets away from me and said nothing.

"So, they're spirit-beings. Usually, they aren't visible, but they can make a body out of ectoplasm and manifest in the real world when they want to, if they're strong enough. And sometimes, they can just barely have any physical existence at all—just kind of exist as a cold spot, or a breath of wind, or maybe a sound. Right?"

"Give it up, Harry," Bob said. "I'm not talking."

"They can do all kinds of things. They can throw things around and stack furniture. There have been documented incidents of ghosts blotting out the sun for a while, causing minor earthquakes, all sorts of stuff—but it isn't ever random. There's always some purpose to it, something related to their deaths."

Bob quivered, about to add something, but clacked his bony teeth shut again. I ginned at him. It was a puzzle. No spirit of intellect could resist a puzzle.

"So, if someone leaves a strong enough imprint when they go, you got yourself a strong ghost. I mean, badass. Maybe like this Nightmare."

"Maybe," Bob admitted, grudgingly, then spun his skull to face wholly away from me. "I'm still not talking to you, Harry."

I drummed my pencil on the blank piece of paper. "Okay. We know that this thing is stirring up the boundary between here and the Nevernever. It's making it easier for spirits to come across, and that's why things have been so busy, lately."

"Not necessarily," Bob chirped up. "Maybe you're looking at it from the wrong angle."

"Eh?" I asked.

He spun to face me again, eyelights glowing, voice enthusiastic. "Someone *else* has been stirring these spirits, Harry. Maybe they started torturing them in order to make them jump around in the pool and start causing waves."

There was a thought. "You mean, prodding the big spirits into moving so that they create the turbulence."

"Exactly," Bob said, nodding. Then he caught himself, mouth still open. He turned the skull toward the wall and started banging the bony forehead against it. "I am such an idiot."

"Stirring up the Nevernever," I said thoughtfully. "But who would do that? And why?"

"You got me. Big mystery. We'll never know. Time for a beer."

"Stirring up the Nevernever makes it easier for something to cross over," I said. "So . . . whoever laid out those torture spells must have wanted to pave the way for something." I thought of dead animals and smashed cars. "Something big." I thought of Micky Malone, quivering and mad. "And it's getting stronger."

Bob looked at me again, and then sighed. "All right," he said. "Gods, do you ever give up, Harry?"

"Never."

"Then I might as well help you. You don't know what you're dealing with, here. And if you walk into this with your eyes closed, you're going to be dead before the sun rises."

Chapter 15

"Dead before the sun rises," I said. "Stars, Bob, why don't you just go all the way over the melodramatic edge and tell me that I'm going to be sleeping with the fishes?"

"I'm not sure that much of you would be left," Bob said, seriously. "Harry, look at this thing. Look at what it's done. It crossed a threshold."

"So what?" I asked. "Lots of things can. Remember that toad demon? It came over my threshold and trashed my whole place."

"In the first place, Harry," Bob said, "you're a bachelor. You don't have all that much of a threshold to begin with. This Malone, though—he was a family man."

"So?"

"So it means his home has a lot more significance. Besides which—the toad demon came in and everything after that was pure physical interaction. It smashed things, it spat out acid saliva, that kind of thing. It *didn't* try to wrench your soul apart or enchant you into a magical sleep."

"This is getting to be a pretty fine distinction, Bob."

"It is. Did you ask for an invitation before you went into the Malone's house?"

"Yeah," I said. "I guess I did. It's polite, and—"

"And it's harder for you to work magic in a home you haven't been invited into. You cross the threshold without an invitation, and you leave a big chunk of your power at the door. It doesn't affect you as much because you're a mortal, Harry, but it still gets you in smaller ways."

"And if I was an all-spirit creature," I said.

Bob nodded. "It hits you harder. If this Nightmare is a ghost, like you say, then the threshold should have stopped it cold—and even if it had gone past it, then it shouldn't have had the kind of power it takes to hurt a mortal that badly."

I frowned, drumming my pencil some more, and made some notes on the paper, trying to keep everything straight. "And certainly not enough to lay out a spell that powerful on Malone."

"Definitely."

"So what *could* do that, Bob? What are we dealing with, here?"

Bob's eyes shifted restlessly around the room. "It could be a couple of things from the spirit world. Are you sure you want to know?" I glared at him. "All right, all right. It could be something big enough. Something so big that even a fraction of it was enough to attack Malone and lay that spell on him. Maybe a god someone's dug up. Hecate, Kali, or one of the Old Ones."

"No," I said, flatly. "Bob, if this thing was so tough, it wouldn't be tearing up people's cars and ripping kitty cats apart. That's not my idea of a godlike evil. That's just pissed off."

"Harry, it went through the threshold," Bob said. "Ghosts don't *do* that. They *can't*."

I stood up, and started pacing back and forth on the little open space of floor of my summoning circle. "It isn't one of the Old Ones. Guardian spells all over the world would be freaking out, alerting the Gatekeeper and the Council of something like that. No, this is local."

"Harry, if you're wrong—"

I jabbed a finger at Bob. "If I'm *right,* then there's a monster out there messing with my town, and I'm obliged to do something about it before someone else gets hurt."

Bob sighed. "It blew through a threshold."

"So . . ." I said, pacing and whirling. "Maybe it had some other way to get around the threshold. What if it had an invitation?"

"How could it have gotten that?" Bob said. "Ding-dong, Soul Eater Home Delivery, may I come in?"

"Bite me," I said. "What if it took Lydia? Once she was out of the church, she could have been vulnerable to it."

"Possession?" Bob said. "Possible, I guess—but she was wearing your talisman."

"If it could get around a threshold, maybe it could get around that too. She goes to Malone's, looks helpless, and gets an invite in."

"Maybe." Bob did a passable imitation of scrunching up his

eyes. "But then why were all those little animals torn up outside? We are going way out on a branch here. There are a lot of maybes."

I shook my head. "No, no. I've got a feeling about this."

"You've said that before. You remember the time you wanted to make 'smart dynamite' for that mining company?"

I scowled. "I hadn't had much sleep that week. And anyway, the sprinklers kicked in."

Bob chortled. "Or the time you tried to enchant that broomstick so that you could fly? Remember *that*? I thought it would take a year to get the mud out of your eyebrows."

"Would you focus, please," I complained. I pushed my hands against either side of my head to keep it from exploding with theories, and whittled them down to the ones that fit the facts. "There are only a couple of possibilities. A, we're dealing with some kind of godlike being in which case we're screwed."

"And the Absurd Understatement Award goes to Harry Dresden."

I glared at him. "Or," I said, lifting a finger, "B, this thing is a spirit, something we've seen before, and it's using smoke and mirrors within the rules we already know. Either way, I think Lydia knows more than she's admitting."

"Gee, a woman taking advantage of Captain Chivalry. What are the odds."

"Bah," I said. "If I can find her and find out what she knows, I could nail it today."

"You're forgetting the third possibility," Bob said amiably. "C, it's something new that neither of us understand and you're sailing off in ignorance to plunge into the mouth of Charybdis."

"You're so encouraging," I said, fastening on the bracelet, and slipping on the ring, feeling the quiet, humming power in them both.

Bob somehow waggled his eyebrow ridges. "Hey, you never went out with Charybdis. What's the plan?"

"I loaned Lydia my Dead Man's Talisman," I said.

"I still can't believe after all the work we did, you gave it to the first girl to wiggle by."

I scowled at Bob. "If she's still got it, I should be able to work up a spell to home in on it, like when I find people's wedding rings."

"Great," Bob said. "Give 'em hell, Harry. Have fun storming the castle."

"Not so fast," I said. "She might not have it with her. If she's in on this with the Nightmare, then she could have dumped it once she had it away from me. That's where you come in."

"Me?" Bob squeaked.

"Yes. You're going to head out, hit the streets, and talk to all of your contacts, see if we can get to her before sundown. We've only got a couple of hours."

"Harry," Bob pointed out, "the sun's up. I'm exhausted. I can't just flit around like some kinda dewdrop fairy."

"Take Mister," I said. "He doesn't mind you riding around. And he could use the exercise. Just don't get him killed."

"Hooboy," Bob said. "Once more into the breech, dear friends, eh? Harry, don't quit your job to become a motivational speaker. I have your permission to come out?"

"Yep," I said, "for the purposes of this mission only. And don't waste time prowling around in women's locker rooms again."

I put out the candles and the heater and started up the stepladder. Bob followed, drifting out of the eye sockets of the skull as a glowing, candleflame-colored cloud, and flowed up the steps past me. The cloud glided over to where Mister dozed in the warm spot near the mostly dead fire, and seeped in through the cat's grey fur. Mister sat up and blinked his yellow-green eyes at me, stretched his back, and flicked his stump of a tail back and forth before letting out a reproachful meow.

I scowled at Mister and Bob, shrugging into my duster, gathering up my blasting rod and my exorcism bag, and old black doctor's case full of stuff. "Come on, guys," I said. "We're on the trail. We have the advantage. What could possibly go wrong?"

Chapter 16

Finding people is hard, especially when they don't want to be found. It's so difficult, in fact, that estimates run up near seven-digit figures on how many people disappear, without a trace, every year in the United States. Most of these people aren't ever found.

I didn't want Lydia to become one of these statistics. Either she was one of the bad guys and had been playing me for a sucker, or she was a victim who was in need of my help. If the former, then I wanted to confront her—I have this thing about people who lie to me and try to get me into trouble. If the latter, then I was probably the only one in Chicago who could help her. She could be possessed by one very big and very brawny spirit who needed to get some, pardon the pun, exorcise.

Lydia had been on foot when she left Father Forthill, and I don't think she'd had much cash. Assuming she hadn't come into any more resources, she'd likely still be in the Bucktown/Wicker Park area, so I headed the *Blue Beetle* that way. The *Beetle* isn't really blue any more. Both doors had to be replaced when they'd gotten clawed to shreds, and the hood had been slagged, with a big old hole melted in it. My mechanic, Mike, who can keep the *Beetle* running most days, hadn't asked any questions. He'd just replaced the parts with pieces of other Volkswagens, so that the *Blue Beetle* was technically blue, red, white, and green. But my appellation stuck.

I tried to keep my cool as I drove, at least as best as I could. My wizard's propensity for blowing out any kind of advanced technology seems to get worse when I'm upset, angry, or afraid.

Don't ask me why. So I did my best to Zen out until I got to my destination—parking strips alongside Wicker Park.

A brisk breeze made my duster flap as I got out. On one side of the street, tall town houses and a pair of apartment buildings gleamed as the sun began to go down over the western plains. The shadows of the trees in Wicker Park, meanwhile, stretched out like black fingers creeping toward my throat. Thank God my subconscious isn't too symbolically aware or anything. The park had a bunch of people in it, young people, mothers with kids, while on the streets, business types began arriving in their business clothes, heading for one of the posh restaurants, pubs, or cafes that littered the area.

I got a lump of chalk and a tuning fork out of my exorcism bag. I glanced around, then squatted down on the sidewalk and drew a circle around myself, willing it closed as the chalk marks met themselves on the concrete. I felt a sensation, a crackling tension, as the circle closed, encasing the local magical energies, compressing them, stirring them.

Most magic isn't quick and dirty. The kind of stunts you can pull off when some nasty thing is about to jump up in your face are called evocations. They're fairly limited in what they can do, and difficult to master. I only had a couple of evocations that I could do very well, and most of the time I needed the help of artificial foci, such as my blasting rod or one of my other enchanted doodads, to make sure that I don't lose control of the spell and blow up myself along with the slobbering monster.

Most magic is a lot of concentration and hard work. That's where I was really good—thaumaturgy. Thaumaturgy is traditional magic, all about drawing symbolic links between items or people and then investing energy to get the effect that you want. You can do a lot with thaumaturgy, provided you have enough time to plan things out, and more time to prepare a ritual, the symbolic objects, and the magical circle.

I've yet to meet a slobbering monster polite enough to wait for me to finish.

I slipped my shield bracelet off of my wrist and laid it in the center of the circle—that was my channel. The talisman I'd passed off to Lydia had been constructed in a very similar manner, and the two bracelets would resonate on the same pitches. I took the tuning fork and laid it down beside the bracelet, with the two ends of the shield bracelet touching either tine, making a complete circle.

Then I closed my eyes, and drew upon the energy gathered in the circle. I brought it into me, molded it, shaped it into the effect I was looking for with my thoughts, fiercely picturing the talisman I'd given Lydia while I did. The energy built and built, a buzzing in my ears, a prickling along the back of my neck. When I was ready, I spread my hands over the two objects, opened my eyes and said, firmly, *"Duo et unum."* At the words, the energy poured out of me in a rush that left me a little light-headed. There were no sparks, no glowing luminescence or anything else that would cost a special effects budget some money—just a sense of completion, and a tiny, almost inaudible hum.

I picked up the bracelet and put it back on, then took up the tuning fork and smudged the circle with my foot, willing it broken. I felt the little *pop* of the residual energies being released, and I rose up and fetched my exorcism bag from the *Beetle.* Then I walked away, down the sidewalk, holding my tuning fork out in front of me. After I'd taken several paces away, I turned in a slow circle.

The fork remained silent until I'd turned almost all the way around—then it abruptly shivered in my hand, and emitted a crystalline tone when I had it facing vaguely northwest. I looked up and sighted along the tines of the fork, then walked a dozen paces farther and triangulated as best I could. The direction change on the way the fork faced when it toned the second time was appreciable, even without any kind of instruments—Lydia must have been fairly close.

"Yes," I said, and started off at a brisk walk, sweeping the tuning fork back and forth, setting my feet in the direction that it chimed. I kept on like that to the far side of the park, where the tuning fork pointed directly at a building that had once been some kind of manufacturing facility, perhaps, but now stood abandoned.

The lower floor was dominated by a pair of garage doors and a boarded-up front door. On the lower two floors, most of the windows had been boarded up. On the third floor, truly bored or determined vandals had pitched stones through those windows, and their shattered edges stood sharp and dusty against the blackness behind them, like dirty ice.

I took two more readings, from fifty feet on either side of the first. All pointed directly to the building. It glowered down at me, silent and spooky.

I shivered.

I would be smart to call Michael. Maybe even Murphy. I could get to a phone, try to get in touch with them. It wouldn't take them long to get here.

Of course, it would be after sundown. The Nightmare, if it was inside Lydia, would be free to leave her then, to roam abroad. If I could get to her, exorcise this thing now, I could end the spree of destruction it was on.

If, if, if. I had a lot of ifs. But I didn't have much time. The sun was swiftly vanishing. I reached inside my duster and got out my blasting rod, transferring my exorcism bag to the same hand as the tuning fork. Then I headed across the street, to the garage doors of the building. I tested one, and to my surprise it rolled upwards. I glanced left and right, then slipped inside into the darkness, shutting the door behind me.

It took a moment for my eyes to adjust. The room was lit only by the fading light that slipped its fingers beneath the plyboard over the windows, the edges of the garage doors. It was a loading dock that encompassed almost the entire first floor, I judged. Stone pillars held the place up. Water dripped somewhere, from a broken pipe, and there were pools of it everywhere on the floor.

A brand-new side-panel van, its engine still ticking, cooling off, stood parked at the far side of the loading dock, next to a five-foot-high stone abutment, where trucks would once have backed up to load and unload goods. A sign hanging by one hinge, over the van, read SUMNER'S TEXTILES MFG.

I approached the van slowly, my blasting rod held loosely at my side. I swept the tuning fork, and my eyes, around the shadowed chamber. The fork hummed every time it swept past the van.

The white van all but glowed in the half-light. Its windows had been tinted, and I couldn't see inside of them, even when I came within ten feet or so.

Something, some sound or other cue that I hadn't quite caught on the conscious level made the hair on the back of my neck prickle up. I spun to face the darkness behind me, the tip of my blasting rod rising up, my bruised fingers wrapped tight around its haft. I focused my senses on the darkness, and listened, honing my attention to the area around me.

Darkness.

Drip of water.

Creak of building, above me.

Nothing.

I put the tuning fork in my duster pocket. Then I turned back to the van, closed the distance quickly, and hauled open the side door, leveling my rod on the inside.

A blanket-wrapped bundle, approximately Lydia-sized, lay inside the van. One pale hand lay limp outside of it, my talisman, scorched-looking and bloodstained, wrapped around the slender wrist.

My heart leapt into my throat. "Lydia?" I asked. I reached out and touched her wrist. Felt the dull, slow throb of pulse. I let out a breath of relief, pulled the blankets from her pale face. Her eyes were open, staring, the pupils dilated until there was barely any color left in them at all. I waved my hand in front of her eyes and said again, "Lydia." She didn't respond. Drugged, I thought.

What the hell was she doing here? Laying in a van, covered up in blankets drugged and placed as neatly as could be. It didn't make sense, unless she was . . .

Unless she was a distraction. The bait for a trap.

I turned, but before I got halfway around that cold energy I'd felt the night before flooded over the side of my face, my throat. Something blonde and incredibly swift slammed into me with the force of a rushing bull, throwing me off my feet and into the van. I spun around onto my elbows to see the vampire Kyle Hamilton coming for me, his eyes black and empty, his face screwed up into a grimace of hunger. He still wore his tennis whites. I kicked at his chest, and superhuman strength or no, it lifted him up off the ground for a second, brought me a half-breath of life. I lifted my right hand, the silver ring there gleaming, and cried, *"Assantius!"*

The energy stored in the ring, all kinetic stuff that it saved back a little every time I moved my arm, unloaded in a flood, right in the vampire's face, an unseen fury of motion. The raw force split his lips—but no blood flowed out. It dug into the corners of his eyes and tore the skin away, but there was still no blood. It ripped the skin from his cheekbones, all rubbery black beneath the Anglo-Saxon pink, strips of flesh flapping back in the wave of force like flags in a high wind.

The vampire's body flew back and up. It thudded hard against the ceiling and then fell to the floor with a thump. I struggled out of the van, my chest aching with a dull sort of pain. I left the doctor's bag behind, shook out the shield bracelet and extended my left arm in front of me.

Kyle stirred for a moment and then flung himself to all fours, his body weirdly contorted, shoulders standing up too much, his back bent at a crooked angle. Shreds of flesh dangled from his face, slick-looking, rubbery black beneath them. His eyes also had the skin torn away from them, like pieces of a rubber mask, and bulged out black and huge and inhuman. His jaws parted, showing dripping fangs, saliva pattering to the damp floor.

"You," the vampire hissed, his voice calm, normal, disconcerting.

"Whoah, that was original," I muttered, drawing in my will. "Yeah, me. What the hell are you doing here? Where do you think you're going with Lydia?"

His inhuman expression flickered. "Who?"

My chest panged, hard, sharp, hot, as if something was broken. Broken badly. I remained standing, though, not letting him see weakness. "Lydia. Bad dye job, sunken eyes, in your van, wearing my talisman on her wrist."

He hissed out a dripping runnel of laughter. "Is that what she told you her name was? You've been used, Dresden."

I got a shivery feeling again, and narrowed my eyes. I didn't have any warning but instinct to make me throw myself to one side in an abrupt leap.

The vampire's sister, Kelly, as blonde and pretty as he had been a moment before, landed in the space I had occupied. She too dropped to her knees with a drooling hiss, fangs showing, eyes bulging. She wore a white cat suit, clinging tight to her curves, along with white boots and gloves, and a short white cape with a deep hood. Her clothing was smudged, imperfect, spotted with flecks of scarlet, and her blonde hair in disarray. Blood stained her mouth, like smeared lipstick, or a child with a big cup of juice. A blood mustache. Hells bells.

I kept my blasting rod trained on Kelly, my left hand thrust out before me. "So you two are putting the snatch on Lydia, eh? Why?"

"Let me kill him," moaned the female, her eyes all black, empty and hungry. "*Kyle.* I'm *hungry.*"

So sue me, I weird out when someone starts talking about *eating* me. I swung the blasting rod right at Kelly's face and started sending power into it, setting the tip to glowing. "Yeah, Kyle," I said. "Let her try."

Kyle *rippled,* beneath his skin, and it was enough to make my stomach turn. Something like that just ain't right, even when you know what's underneath. "This affair is none of yours, wizard."

"The girl is under my protection," I said. "You two clear out, now, and I won't have to get rough with you."

"That will not happen," Kyle said, his voice deadly quiet.

"Kyle," the female moaned again. More drool slithered out of her mouth, dripping to the floor. She started shaking, quivering, as if she were about to fly apart. Or at me. My mouth went dry, and I got ready to blast her.

I saw Kyle move out of the corner of my eye. I lifted the shield bracelet toward him, transferred my will to it, but in time only to partially deflect the broken chip of concrete that he threw at my head. It slammed against my temple and sent me spinning. I saw Kelly blur toward me, white cape flying, and I lifted the blasting rod toward her, shouting, *"Fuego!"*

Fire slammed out the end of the rod, missing Kelly by at least a foot, but still hot enough to set the hem of her cloak ablaze. The flame slewed in an arch across the ceiling and down the wall as I started falling, cutting through wood and brick and stone like an enormous arc-welder.

She flung herself atop me, straddling my hips with her thighs, moaning in excitement. I thrust the blasting rod toward her, but she batted it aside, laughing in a wild, hysterical tone, throwing her smoldering cloak off with the other hand. She plunged toward my throat, but I lifted my hands to catch at her mane of hair. I knew it was a futile gesture—she was just too damned strong. I wouldn't be able to hold her off of me for long, a few seconds at most. My heart pounded in my burning chest, and I struggled, gasping in air.

And then droplets of her spittle fell onto my throat, my cheek, into my mouth. And none of it mattered any more.

It was a glorious sensation, that spread over me—warmth, security, peace. Ecstasy began at my skin and spread through me, easing all the horrid tension from my muscles. My fingers slackened in Kelly's lovely hair, and she purred, her hips writhing against mine. She lowered her mouth toward me, and I felt her breath on my skin, her breasts press against me through the thin material of her bodysuit.

Something, some nagging thought, bothered me for a moment. Perhaps it was something about the perfect, lightless depths of her eyes, or the way her fangs rubbed against my throat—no matter how good it felt. But then I felt her lips on my skin, felt her draw in her breath in shivering anticipation, and it stopped mattering. I just wanted *more.*

Then there was a roaring sound, and I dimly perceived the west wall of the building collapsing, falling away in great, flaming sections of wood and brick. The blast I had sent spewing at Kelly had sliced through the ceiling, walls, and support beams. It must have weakened the structure of the entire building as it had.

Oops.

Sunlight flooded in, through the falling bricks and clouds of dust, the last rays of daylight, warm and golden on my face, painfully bright in my eyes.

Kelly screamed and, wherever her skin wasn't covered by cloth, from her chin up, mostly—she burst into flame. The light hit her like a physical blow, hurling her away from me. I became aware of a dull pain, uncomfortable heat on my cheek, my throat, where her saliva had coated my skin.

Everything was light and heat and pain for a few moments, and someone was screaming. I struggled up a moment later, peering around the inside of the building. Fire spread, a dull chewing sound on the floors above me, and through the missing section of wall I could hear sirens in the distance. There were smears of something black and greasy on the concrete floor, leading to the white van. The sunlight barely touched the back window of the vehicle. The side door stood wide open, and Kyle, his face still hanging in ragged strips, hauled something grotesque—his sister, her true form no longer shrouded by its mask of flesh. The vampire girl made keening sounds of agony while her brother pitched her into the back of the van. He slammed the door shut, a snarl rippling his split lips. He took a step toward me, then clenched his jaws in frustration, stopping just short of the sunlight.

"Wizard," he hissed. "You'll pay. I'll make you pay for this." Then he spun back to the van, with its dark-tinted windows, and leapt in. A moment later, the engine roared to life, and the van sped toward the garage doors, plowed through one of them, sending shards of wood flying, jounced into the street, and vanished from sight, engine racing.

I remained in place, stunned, burnt, hurting, my brain clouded. Then I stumbled to my feet, and staggered toward the hole in the wall, and out into the fading daylight. Sirens got closer.

"Damn," I mumbled, looking back at the spreading fires. "I'm kinda hard on buildings."

I shook my head, trying to clear my thoughts. Dark. It was getting dark. Had to get home. Vampires could come out after dark. Home, I thought. Home.

I started stumbling back toward the *Beetle.*

Behind me, as I did, the sun sank beneath the horizon—freeing all the things that go bump in the night to come out and play.

Chapter 17

I don't remember how I managed to get home again. I have a vague image of all the cars around me going way too fast, and then of Mister's rumbling purr greeting me as I got into my apartment and locked the door behind me.

The vampire's narcotic saliva had soaked in through my skin in a matter of a second or three, spreading into my system in short order after that. I felt numb, light, all over. The room wasn't quite whirling, but when I moved my eyes, things almost seemed to blur a little, then to settle when I focused on something. I throbbed. Every time my heart beat, my entire body pulsed with a slow, gentle pang of pleasant sensation.

Something inside me couldn't help but love every second of it. Even counting the times I'd been juiced up in a hospital, it was the best drug I'd ever had.

I stumbled to my narrow bed and dropped onto it. Mister came and prowled around my face, waiting for me to get up and feed him. "Go away," I heard myself mumble. "Stupid furball. Go on." He put one paw on my throat, and touched the area of burned skin where the sunlight had struck the smear of Kelly Hamilton's saliva. Pain flared through me, and I groaned, forcing myself into the kitchen. I got some cold cuts out of the icebox and dropped them onto Mister's plate. Then I stumbled into the bathroom and flicked on the light.

It hurt.

I shielded my eyes and studied myself in the mirror. My pupils had dilated out nice and big. The skin on my throat, my cheek, was red and glowing, as though from falling asleep outside on a summer afternoon—painful, but not dangerous. I couldn't find any marks on my throat, so the vampire hadn't bitten me. I was pretty sure that was a good thing. Something about a bite being a link to a victim. If she'd bitten me, she could have gotten into my head. Usual mind-control enchantment. Breaking one of the Laws of Magic.

I stumbled back to my bed and sank down onto it, trying to sort out my thoughts. My lovely, throbbing body made this fairly difficult. Mister came nosing around again, but I shoved him away with one hand and forced myself to ignore him.

"Focus, Harry," I mumbled to myself. "Got to have focus."

I'd learned to block out pain, when necessary. Studying under Justin, it had been a practical necessity. My teacher hadn't believed in sparing the rod and spoiling the potential wizard. You learn very quickly not to make mistakes given the correct incentive to avoid them.

Blocking out pleasure was a more difficult exercise, but I somehow managed. The first thing I had to do was separate my sense of enjoyment. It took me a while, but I slowly marked out the boundaries of the parts of me that liked all the wonderful, warm sensations, and walled them away. Then the actual pounding happiness itself. I found my heart rate and slowed it a bit, though it was already going too slowly, then started shutting down perception of my limbs, pushing them behind the walls with the rest of me that wasn't doing any good. Giddy delight went next, leaving only a dull fuzz across my thinking, chemically unavoidable.

I closed my eyes and breathed, and tried to sort through things.

Lydia had fled the shelter of the church, and Father Forthill's protection. Why? I thought back, over the details of everything I knew about her. Her sunken eyes. The tingle of touching her aura. Had her hands been shaking, just a little? I think they had, in retrospect. I thought of what I had seen of her in the van, of the bracelet on her wrist. Her beating pulse. Had it been slow? I'd thought so, at the time—but then my own had been racing. I focused on the moment I'd been touching her.

Sixty, I thought. She'd been around sixty beats per minute. My own heart rate was about a sixth of that at the moment. Had been half that, before I'd slowed it down to quiet the song of the drug in my blood.

(Song, pretty song, why the hell did I have it shut away, when I could just lower the walls, listen to the music, lay here all happy and quiet and just *feel,* just *be* . . .)

I took a moment to prop the walls up again. Lydia's heart rate had been at human normal, nominally. But she'd been laying limp and still, much as I was, now. Kyle and Kelly had poisoned her, as they had me, I was sure of it. Then why had her heart been beating so quickly, in comparison?

She left the church and had been taken, perhaps, by the Nightmare. Then gone to Malone's house under its guidance, and gotten an invitation in. But why go to Malone's house? What did he have to do with anything?

Malone and Lydia. They'd both been attacked by the Nightmare. What was the connection? What linked them together?

More questions. What did the vampires want with her? If Kyle and his sister had been after Lydia, that meant that Bianca wanted her. Why? Was Bianca in league with the Nightmare? If she was, why the hell would she need to use her most powerful goons to kidnap the girl, if she was possessed by Bianca's ally?

And how the hell had the Nightmare gone through the threshold? An even better question, how had it gotten through the protection offered to Lydia by my Dead Man's talisman? No ghost should have been able to offer her any direct harm or contact through that thing. It didn't make any sense.

(Why should it? Why should anything need to mean anything at all? Just sit back, Harry, lay back and feel good and relax and let your blood sing, let your heart beat, just ease down into the wonderful, warm, spinning dark and stop worrying, stop caring, drift and float and . . .)

The walls started to crumble.

I struggled, but sudden fear made my heartbeat quicken. I fought against the pull of the poison in my blood, but that struggle only made me more vulnerable, more susceptible. I couldn't fail, now. I *couldn't.* People were depending upon me. I had to fight—

The walls fell, and my blood surged up with a roar.

I drifted.

And it was nice.

Drifting turned into sleep. Gentle, dark sleep. And sleep, in time, turned into dreams.

In my dream, I found myself back at the warehouse down by Burnham Harbor. It was night, beneath a full moon. I was wearing my duster, my black shirt and jeans, my black sneakers, which were better for . . . well. Sneaking. Michael stood beside me, his breath steaming in the winter air, dressed in his cloak, his full mail, his bloodred surcoat. *Amoracchius* rode his hip, a source of quiet, constant power. Murphy and the other members of Special Investigations all wore dark, loose clothing and their flack vests, and everyone had a gun in one hand and something else—like vials of holy water or silver crucifixes—in the other.

Micky Malone glanced up at the moon and shifted the shotgun in both hands—he was the only person relying upon raw, shredding firepower. Hey, the guy had a point. "All right," he said. "We go in and then what?"

"Here's the plan," Murphy said. "Harry thinks that the killer's followers will be drugged out and dozing. We round them up, cuff them up, and move on." Murphy grimaced, her blue eyes sparkling in the silver light. "Tell them what's next, Harry."

I kept my voice quiet. "The guy we're after is a sorcerer. It's sort of like being a wizard, only he spends all his energy doing things that are mostly destructive. He isn't good at doing anything that doesn't fuck someone up."

"Which makes him a badass as far as we're concerned," Malone growled.

"Pretty much," I confirmed. "The guy's got power, but no class. I'm going to go in and lock down his magic. We think he might have a demon on a string—that's what the murders have been for. They're part of his payment to get the demon to work for him."

"Demon," breathed Rudolph. "Jesus, can you believe this shit?"

"Jesus did believe in demons," Michael said, his voice quiet. "If the creature is there, do not get close to it. Don't shoot at it. Leave it to me. If it gets past me, throw your holy water at the thing and run while it screams."

"That's pretty much the plan," I confirmed. "Keep any human flunkies with knives from giving them to me or Michael. I'll take Kravos's powers out, and you guys grab him as soon as we're sure the demon won't eat us. I deal with any other supernatural stuff. Questions?"

Murphy shook her head. "Let's go." She leaned out and pumped her arm in the air, signaling the rest of the S.I. team, and we headed into the warehouse.

Everything went according to plan. In the front of the warehouse, a dozen young people, all with that lost, lonely look to them, lay dozing amidst fumes that made me dizzy. The remnants of a serious party lay all over the place—beer cans, clothes, roaches, empty needles, you name it. The cops fell on the kids in a dark-clad swarm and had them cuffed and hauled out into a waiting wagon in under ninety seconds.

Michael and I moved forward, toward the back of the warehouse, through stacks of boxes and shipping crates. Murphy, Rudy, and Malone followed hard on our heels. I cracked the door at the back wall and peered through it.

I saw a circle of black, smoking candles, a red-lit figure dressed in feathers and blood kneeling beside it, and something dark and horrible crouching within.

"Bingo," I whispered. I turned to Michael. "He's got the demon in there with him."

The Knight simply nodded, and loosened his sword in its sheath.

I drew the doll out of my duster's pocket. It was a Ken doll, naked, and not anatomically correct, but it would work. The single hair that forensics had recovered from the last victim's crime scene had been carefully Scotch-taped to the doll's head, and I had attired Ken in the general garb of someone delving into black magic—reversed pentagrams, some feathers, and some blood (from a hapless mouse Mister had nabbed).

"Murphy," I hissed. "Are you absolutely sure about this hair? That it belongs to Kravos?" If it didn't, the doll wouldn't do diddly to the sorcerer, unless I managed to throw it into his eye.

"We're reasonably sure," she whispered, "yes."

"Reasonably sure. Great." But I knelt down, and marked out the circle around me, then another around the Ken doll, and wrought my spell.

The hair was Kravos's. He became aware of the spell taking effect a few seconds before it could close off his power altogether—and with those few seconds he had, he reached out and broke the circle around the demon with his will and his hand, then in a screaming rage compelled it to attack.

The demon leapt toward us, all writhing darkness and shadows and glowing red eyes. Michael stepped into the doorway and drew *Amoracchius,* the sudden blaze of light and magical fury like a gale in that darkness.

In real life, I had completed the spell and shut Kravos away from his powers. Michael had carved the demon into chutney. Kravos had made a run for it, but Malone, at fairly long range, had fired his shotgun at the ground and at Kravos's feet, and done it perfectly, sweeping the man's legs out from beneath him and leaving him writhing, bleeding, but alive. Murphy had wrestled the knife out of the sorcerer's hands, and the good guys had won the day.

In my dream, it didn't happen that way.

I felt the fabric of the spell closing around Kravos start to slip. One minute, he was there, in the weaving I was spinning around him—the next, he was simply gone, the spell collapsing of its own unsupported weight.

Michael screamed. I looked up, to see him lifted high in the air, his sword sweeping through the shadows and darkness before him in impotent futility. Dark hands, fingers nightmarishly long, grabbed Michael's head, covering his face. There was a twist, a wet, crackling sound, and the Knight's neck broke cleanly. His body jerked, then went limp. *Amoracchius's* light died out. The demon screamed, a tinny, high-pitched sound, and let the body fall to the ground.

Murphy shouted and hurled her jar of holy water at the demon. The liquid flared into silver light as it struck something in that writhing darkness that was the demon. The shape turned toward us. Claws flashed out, and Murphy stumbled back, her eyes wide with shock where the talons had carved through her kevlar jacket, her shirt, her skin, leaving her belly torn open. Blood and worse rushed out, and she let out a weak gasp, pressing both hands against her own ruined side.

Malone started pumping rounds out of the shotgun. The demon-darkness turned toward him, a red-fanged leer spreading over it, and waited until the gun clicked empty. Then it simply laughed, grabbed the end of the shotgun, and slammed Malone against a wall, shoving the hardwood stock against the man's belly until he screamed, until the flesh began to rip, until ribs started crackling, and then shoved harder, until I could clearly hear, even above the sound of Malone's retching, the bones in his spine start to splinter and break. Malone, too, fell to the ground, dying.

Rudolph screamed, pasty-faced and white, and ran away.

Leaving me alone with the demon.

My heart rushed with terror and I shook like a leaf before the creature. I was still inside of the circle. I still had the circle protecting me. I struggled to reach out for my power, to summon a strike that would annihilate this thing.

And found something in my way. A wall. The same spell I'd meant to lay on Kravos.

The demon stalked over to me and, as though my circle wasn't even there, reached out and backhanded me into the air. I landed with a thud upon the ground.

"No," I stammered, and tried to struggle back from the thing. "No, this isn't happening. This isn't the way it happened!"

The demon's red eyes glowed. I lifted my blasting rod toward it, pointed, and shouted, "Fuego!"

There was no stirring of heat. No fitful crackling of energy. Nothing.

The demon laughed again, reaching down toward me, and I felt myself lifted into the air.

"This is a dream!" I shouted. With that awareness, I started struggling to reach out to the fabric of the dream, to alter it—but I'd made no preparations before I'd slept, and was already too panicked, too distracted to focus. "This is a dream! This isn't the way it happened!"

"That was then," the demon purred, its voice silken. "This is now." Then its maw opened up and closed over my belly, horrible fangs sinking in, worrying me, stretching my guts. It shook its head, and I exploded, shreds of meat flying out of me, into it, my blood rushing out while I strained and struggled helplessly, screaming.

And then a grey tabby with a bobtail bounded out of nowhere and whipped one paw at me, lashing it across my nose, claws slashing like fire.

I screamed again and found myself in the far corner of my bedroom, back in my apartment, curled into a fetal ball. I had been puking my guts out. Mister hovered over me and then, almost judiciously, delivered another scratch to my cheek. I heard myself cry out and flinch from the blow.

Something rippled along my skin. Something cold and dark and nauseating. I sat up, blinking sleep from my eyes, struggling through the remnants of the vampire's poison and sleep to focus on the presence—but it was gone.

I shook, violently. I was terrified. Not frightened, not apprehensive—viciously and unremittingly terrified. Mindless, brain-stem terror, the kind that quite simply bypasses rational thought and heads straight for your soul. I felt horribly violated, somehow, used. Helpless. Weak.

I crawled down to my lab, fumbling in the dark. Dimly, I was aware of Mister coming along behind me. It was dark down here, dark and cold. I stumbled across the room, knocking things down left and right, to the summoning circle built into the floor. I threw myself into it, sobbing, fumbled with tingling fingers at the floor until I located the ring. Then I willed the circle closed. It struggled, resisted, and I pushed harder, forced myself on it harder, until finally I felt it snap shut around me in an invisible wall.

I curled on my side, keeping every part of myself within that circle, and wept.

Mister prowled around the circle, a rumbling, reassuring purr in his throat. Then I heard the big grey cat hop up onto the work table, and over to one of the shelves. His dim shadow curled up by the pale bone of the skull. Orange light began to glide out of his mouth, into the skull's eye sockets, until Bob's candleflame eyes blinked, and the skull turned to focus on me.

"Harry," Bob said, his voice quiet, solemn. "Harry, can you hear me?"

Shaking, I looked up, desperately grateful to hear a familiar voice.

"Harry," Bob said gently. "I saw it, Harry. I think I know what went after Malone and the others. I think I know how it did it. I tried to help you, but you wouldn't wake up."

My mind whirled, confused. "What?" I asked. My voice came out a whimper. "What are you talking about?"

"I'm sorry, Harry." The skull paused, and though its expression couldn't really change, it somehow looked troubled. "I think I know what just tried to eat you."

Chapter 18

"Eat me," I whispered. "I don't . . . I don't understand."

"This thing you've been chasing, I think. The Nightmare. I think it was here."

"Nightmare," I said. I lowered my head and closed my eyes. "Bob, I can't . . . I can't think straight. What's going on?"

"Well. You came in about five hours ago drugged to the gills on vampire spit, and muttering like a madman. I think you didn't realize that I was inside Mister. Do you remember that part?"

"Yeah. Sort of."

"What happened?"

I relayed my experience with Kyle and Kelly Hamilton to Bob. Speaking seemed to help things stop spinning, my guts to settle. My heartbeat slowly eased down to something less than that of a terrified rabbit.

"Sounds weird," Bob said. "Got to be something important to make them risk going out in daylight like that. Even in a specially equipped van."

"I realize that, Bob," I said, and mopped at my face with one hand.

"You any steadier?"

"I . . . I guess."

"I think you got torn up pretty good, spirit-wise. It's lucky you started screaming. I came as quick as I could, but you didn't want to wake up. The poison, I think."

I sat up, cross-legged, staying inside the circle. "I remember that I had a dream. God, it was a terrible dream." I felt my guts turn to water, and I started shaking again. "I tried to change it, but I wasn't ready. I couldn't."

"A dream," Bob said. "Yeah, that figures."

"Figures?" I asked.

"Sure," Bob said.

I shook my head, rested my elbows on my knees, and put my face in my hands. I did not want to be doing this. Someone else could do it. I should go, leave town. "It was a spirit that jumped me?"

"Yeah."

I shook my head. "That doesn't make any sense. How did it get past the threshold?"

"Your threshold isn't so hot to begin with, Bachelor Man."

I worked up enough courage to scowl at Bob. "The wards, then. I've got all the doors and windows warded. And I don't have any mirrors it could have used."

If Bob had any hands, he would have been rubbing them together. "Exactly," he said. "Yes, exactly."

My stomach quailed again, and a fresh burst of shuddering made me put my hands in my lap. I felt like sprawling somewhere, crying my eyes out, puking up whatever shreds of dignity remained in my stomach, and then crawling into a hole and pulling it in after me. I swallowed. "It . . . it never came in to me, then, is what you're saying. It never had to cross those boundaries."

Bob nodded, eyes burning brightly. "Exactly. You went out to it."

"When I was dreaming?"

"Yes, yes, yes," Bob bubbled. "It makes sense now—don't you see?"

"Not really."

"Dreams," the skull said. "When a mortal dreams, all kinds of strange things can happen. When a wizard dreams, it can be even weirder. Sometimes, dreams can be intense enough to create a little, temporary world of their own. Kind of a bubble in the Nevernever. Remember how you told me Agatha Hagglethorn was a strong enough ghost to have had her own demesne in the Nevernever?"

"Yeah. It looked kind of like old Chicago."

"Well, people can do the same, at times."

"But I'm not a ghost, Bob."

"No," he said. "You're not. But you've got everything it takes to make a ghost inside you except for the right set of circumstances. Ghosts are only frozen images of people, Harry, last impressions made by a personality." Bob paused, reflectively. "People are almost always more trouble than anything you run into on the Other Side."

"I hadn't noticed," I said. "All right. So you're saying that any time I dream, it creates my own little rent-by-the-hour demesne in the Nevernever."

"Not every time," Bob said. "In fact, not even most times. Only really intense dreams, I suspect, bring the necessary energy out of people. But, with the border being so turbulent and easy to get through . . ."

"More people's dreams are making bubbles on the other side. That must have been how it got to poor Micky Malone, then. While he was sleeping. His wife said he'd had insomnia that night. So the thing hangs around outside his house waiting for him to fall asleep and starts killing fuzzy animals to fill up the time."

"Could be," Bob said. "Do you remember your dream?"

I shuddered. "Yeah. I . . . I remember it."

"The Nightmare must have got inside with you."

"While my spirit was in the Nevernever?" I asked. "It should have ripped me to shreds."

"Not so," Bob beamed. "Your spirit's demesne, remember? Even if only a temporary one. Means you have the home field advantage. It didn't help, since it got the drop on you, but you had it."

"Oh."

"Do you remember anything in particular, any figure or character in the dream that wouldn't have been acting the way you thought it should have?"

"Yeah," I said. My shaking hands went to my belly, feeling for tooth marks. "Hell's bells, yeah. I was dreaming of that bust a couple of months back. When we nailed Kravos."

"That sorcerer," Bob mused. "Okay. This could be important. What happened?"

I swallowed, trying not to throw up. "Um. Everything went wrong. That demon he'd called. It was stronger than it had been in life."

"The demon was?"

I blinked. "Bob. Is it possible for something like a demon to leave a ghost?"

"Oh, uh," Bob said, "I don't think so—unless it had actually died there. Eternally perished, I mean, not just had its vessel dispersed."

"Michael killed it with *Amoracchius,*" I said.

Bob's skull shuddered. "Ow," he said. "*Amoracchius.* I'm not sure, then. I don't know. That sword might be able to kill a demon, even through a physical shell. That whole faith-magic thing is awfully strong."

"Okay, so. We could be dealing with the ghost of a demon, here," I said. "A demon that died while it was all fired up for a fight. Maybe that's what makes it so . . . so vicious."

"Could be," Bob agreed, cheerily.

I shook my head. "But that doesn't explain the barbed-wire spells we've been finding on those ghosts and people." I grabbed onto the problem, the tangled facts, with a silent kind of desperation, like a man about to drown who has no breath to waste on screaming. It helped to keep me moving.

"Maybe the spells are someone else's work," Bob offered.

"Bianca," I said, suddenly. "She and her lackeys are all messed up in this somehow—remember that they put the snatch on Lydia? And they were waiting for me, that first night, when I came back from being arrested."

"I didn't think she was that big time a practitioner," Bob said.

I shrugged. "She's not, horribly. But she just got promoted, too. Maybe she's been studying up. She's always had a little more than her share of freaky vampire tricks—and if she was over in the Nevernever when she did it, it would have made her stronger."

Bob whistled through his teeth. "Yeah, that could work. Bianca stirs things up by torturing a bunch of spirits, gets all the turbulence going so that she can prod this Nightmare toward you. Then she lets it loose, sits back, and enjoys the fun. She got a motive?"

"Regret," I said, remembering a note I'd read more than a year ago. "She blames me for the death of one of her people. Rachel. She wants to make me regret it."

"Neat," Bob said. "And she could have been everywhere in question?"

"Yeah," I said. "Yeah, she could have been."

"Means, opportunity, motive."

"Damn shaky logic, though. Nothing I could justify to the Council in order to get their back-up, either. I don't have any proof."

"So?" Bob said. "Hat up, go kill her. Problem solved."

"Bob," I said. "You can't just go around killing people."

"I know. That's why you should do it."

"No, no. *I* can't go around killing people, either."

"Why not? You've done it before. And you've got a new gun and everything."

"I can't arbitrarily end someone's life because of something they may have done."

"Bianca's a vampire," Bob pointed out cheerfully. "She's not alive in the classic sense. I'll get Mister and go fetch the bullets and you—"

I sighed. "No, Bob. She's got lots of people around her, too. I'd probably have to kill some of them to get to her."

"Oh. Damn. This is one of those right and wrong issues again, isn't it."

"Yeah, one of those."

"I'm still confused about this whole morality thing, Harry."

"Join the club," I muttered. I took a shaking breath and leaned forward to put my hand over the circle, and will it broken. I almost cringed when its protective field faded from around me, but forced myself not to. I was as recovered as I was going to get. I needed to focus on work.

I stood up and walked to my work table, my eyes by now adjusted to the dimness. I reached for the nearest candle, but there weren't any matches handy. So, I pointed my finger at it, frowned, and muttered the words, *"Flickum bicus."*

My spell, a tiny one I had used thousands of times, stuttered and coughed, the energy twitching instead of flowing. The candle's wick smoked, but did not flicker to life.

I frowned, then closed my eyes, made a little bit of an effort, and repeated the spell. This time, I felt a little surge of dizziness, and the candle flickered to life. I braced one hand on the edge of the table.

"Bob," I asked. "Were you watching that?"

"Yeah," Bob said, a frown in his voice.

"What happened?"

"Um. You didn't put enough magic into the spell, the first time around."

"I put as much as I always do," I protested. "Come on, I've done that spell a million times."

"Seventeen hundred and fifty-six, that I've seen."

I gave him a pale version of my usual glower. "You know what I mean."

"Not enough power," Bob said. "I call 'em like I see 'em."

I stared at the candle for a second. Then muttered, to myself, "Why did I have to work to make that thing light up?"

"Probably because the Nightmare took a big bite out of your powers, Harry."

I turned around, very slowly, to blink at Bob. "It . . . it did what?"

"When it attacked you, in your dream, did it go after a specific place on your body?"

I put my hand to the base of my stomach, pressing there, and felt my eyes go wide.

Bob winced. "Oooooo, chakra point. That isn't good. Got you right in the chi."

"Bob," I whispered.

"Good thing he didn't go after your mojo though, right? I mean, you have to look on the bright side of these—"

"Bob," I said, louder. "Are you saying it . . . it *ate* my magic?"

Bob got a defensive look on his face. "Not *all* of it. I woke you up as quick as I could. Harry, don't worry about it, you'll heal. Sure, you might be down for a couple of months. Or, um, years. Well, decades, possibly, but that's only a very outside chance—"

I cut him off with a slash of my hand. "He ate part of my power," I said. "Does that mean that the Nightmare is stronger?"

"Well, naturally, Harry. You are what you eat."

"Dammit," I snarled, pressing one hand against my forehead. "Okay, okay. We've really got to find this thing now." I started pacing back and forth. "If it's using my power, it makes me responsible for what it does with it."

Bob scoffed. "Harry, that's irrational."

I shot him a look. "That doesn't make it any less true," I snapped.

"Okay," Bob said, meekly. "We have now left Reason and Sanity Junction. Next stop, Looneyville."

"Grrrr," I said, still pacing. "We have to figure out where this thing is going to hit next. It's got all night to move."

"Six hours, thirteen minutes," Bob corrected me. "Shouldn't be hard. I've been reading those journals you got from the ectomancer, while you were sleeping. The thing can show up in nightmares, but there's going to be commonality between all of it. Ghosts can only have the kind of power this Nightmare has while they are acting within the parameters of their specific baliwick."

"Baili-what?"

"Look at it this way, Harry. A ghost can only affect something that relates directly to its death somehow. Agatha Hagglethorn couldn't have terrorized a Cubs game. That wasn't where her power was. She could mess with infants, with abusive husbands, maybe with abused wives—"

"And meddling wizards," I mumbled.

"You put yourself in the line of fire, sure," Bob said. "But Agatha couldn't just run somewhere willy-nilly and wreak havoc."

"The Nightmare's got to have a personal beef in this," I said. "That's what you're saying."

"Well. It has to be related to its demise, somehow. So, yeah. I guess that is what I'm saying. More specifically, it's what Mort Lindquist was saying, in his journals."

"Me," I said. "And Lydia. And Mickey Malone. How the hell do all of those relate? I never saw Lydia before in my life." I frowned. "At least, I don't think I have."

"She's kind of an oddball," Bob agreed. "Leave her out of the equation for a minute?"

I did, and it came to me as clearly as a beam of sunlight. "Dammit," I said. I turned and ran toward the stairs on my unsteady legs, started hauling myself up them and toward the phone.

"What?" Bob called after me. "Harry, what?"

"If that thing is the demon's ghost, I know what it wants. Payback. It's after the people that took it down." I yelled back down the stairs, "I've got to find Murphy.

Chapter 19

There's a kind of mathematics that goes along with saving people's lives. You find yourself running the figures without even realizing it, like a medic on a battlefield. This patient has no chance of surviving. That one does, but only if you let a third die.

For me, the equation broke down into fairly simple elements. The demon, hungry for its revenge, would come after those who had struck it down. The ghost would only remember those who had been there, whom it had focused on in those last moments. That meant that Murphy and Michael would be its remaining targets. Michael had a chance of protecting himself against the thing—hell, maybe a better chance than me. Murphy didn't.

I got on the phone to Murphy's place. No answer. I called the office, and she answered with a fatigue-blurred, "Murphy."

"Murph," I said. "Look, I need you to trust me on this one. I'm coming down there and I'll be there in about twenty minutes. You could be in danger. Stay where you are and stay awake until I get to you."

"Harry?" Murphy asked. I could hear her starting to scowl. "You telling me you're going to be late?"

"Late? No, dammit. Look, just do what I said, all right?"

"I do not appreciate this crap, Dresden," Murphy growled. "I haven't slept in two days. You told me you'd be here in ten minutes, and I told you I'd wait."

"Twenty. I said twenty minutes, Murph."

I could feel her glare over the phone. "Don't be an asshole, Harry. That's not what you said five minutes ago. If this is some kind of joke, I am not amused."

I blinked, and a cold feeling settled into my gut, into the hollow place the Nightmare had torn out of me. The phone line snapped, crackled, and popped, and I struggled to calm down before the connection went out. "Wait, Murphy. Are you saying you talked to me five minutes ago?"

"I am about two seconds short of killing the next thing that pisses me off, Harry. And everything keeping me out of bed is pissing me off. Don't get added to the list." She hung up on me.

"Dammit!" I yelled. I hung up the phone and dialed Murphy's number again, but only got a busy signal.

Something had talked to Murphy and convinced her she was talking to me. The list of things that could put on someone else's face was awfully long, but the probabilities were limited: either another supernatural beastie had wandered onto the stage or, I gulped, the Nightmare had taken a big enough bite of me that it could put on a convincing charade.

Ghosts could take material form, after all—if they had the power to form a new shape out of material from the Nevernever, and if they were familiar enough with the shape. The Nightmare had eaten a bunch of my magic. It had the power it needed. And it had the familiarity it needed.

Hell's bells, it was pretending to be me.

I hung up the phone and tore around the house frantically, collecting car keys and putting together an improvised exorcism kit from stuff in my kitchen: Salt, a wooden spoon, a table knife, a couple of storm candles and matches, and a coffee cup. I stuffed them all into an old Scooby-Doo lunch box, then, as an afterthought, reached into a bag of sand that I keep in the kitchen closet for Mister's litter box, and tossed a handful into a plastic bag. I added the scorched staff and blasting rod to the accumulating pile of junk in my arms. Then I ran for the door.

I hesitated, though. Then went to the phone and dialed Michael's number, fingers dancing over the rotary. It was also busy. I let out a shriek of purest frustration, slammed down the phone, and ran out the door to the *Blue Beetle.*

It was late. Traffic could have been worse. I got there in less than the twenty minutes I'd promised Murphy and parked the car in one of the visitor's parking spaces.

The district station Murphy worked in crouched down amongst taller buildings that surrounded it, solid and square and a bit battered, like a tough old sergeant amongst a forest of tall, young recruits. I ran up the stairs, taking my blasting rod with me, with my Scooby-Doo lunch box in my right hand.

The grizzled old sergeant behind the desk blinked at me as I came panting through the doorway. "Dresden?"

"Hi," I panted. "Which way did I go?"

He blinked. "What?"

"Did I come through here a minute ago?"

His thick, grey moustache twitched in nervous little motions. He took a look at his clipboard. "Yeah. You went up to see Lieutenant Murphy just a minute ago."

"Great," I said. "I need to see her again. Buzz me through?"

He peered at me, a little closer, then reached forward to buzz me through. "What's going on here, Mr. Dresden?"

"Believe me," I said, "As soon as I work that out, I'll be sure to tell you." I opened the door and headed through, up the stairs, and toward the S.I. offices on the fourth floor. I pounded through the doors and sprinted down the rows of desks toward Murphy's office. Stallings and Rudolph both started up from their chairs, blinking as I went past.

"What the hell?" Rudy blurted, his eyes widening.

"Where's Murphy?" I shouted.

"In her office," Stallings stammered, "with you."

Murphy's office stood at the back of the room, with cheap walls and a cheap door that finally bore a genuine metallic nameplate with her name and title on it. I leaned back and drove my heel at the doorknob. The cheap door splintered, but I had to kick it again to send it swinging open.

Murphy sat at her desk, still wearing the clothes I'd last seen her in. She'd taken her hat off, and her short blonde hair was mussed. The circles beneath her eyes were almost as dark as bruises. She sat perfectly still, staring forward with her blue eyes set in an expression of horror.

I stood behind her, all in black—the same outfit I'd worn the night we'd stopped Kravos and his demon. The Nightmare looked like me. Its hands rested on either side of her face, fingertips on her temples—except that they had, somehow, pressed *into* her head, reaching down through skin and bone as though gently massaging her brain. The Nightmare was smiling, leaning down a bit toward her, head canted as though listening to music. I didn't know my face was capable of making an expression like that—serene and malicious and frightening.

I stared for a second in sheer horror at the weirdness of the sight. Then blurted, "Get the hell off of her!"

The Nightmare's dark eyes snapped up, sparkling with a cold, calm intelligence. It lifted its lips away from its teeth in an abrupt snarl. "Be thou silent, wizard," it murmured, steel and razor blades in its words. "Else I will tear thee apart, as I already have this night."

A little gibbering shriek of terror started somewhere down in my quivering belly, but I refused to give it a voice. I heard Rudy and Stallings coming behind me. I lifted the blasting rod and leveled it at the Nightmare's head. "I said to get off of her."

The Nightmare's mouth twisted into a smile. It lifted its hands away from Murphy, fingers just sliding out of her skin as though from water, and showed me its palms. "There is something thou hast forgotten, wizard."

"Yeah?" I asked. "What's that?"

"I have partaken of thee. I am what thou art," the Nightmare whispered. He flicked his wrists toward me. "*Ventas servitas.*"

Wind roared up in a sudden fury and hurled me from my feet, back into the air. I collided with Rudolph and Stallings as they ran forward. We all went down in a heap upon the ground.

I lay there stunned for a moment. I heard the Nightmare walk out. It just walked past us, footsteps calm and quiet, and left the room. We gathered ourselves together slowly, sitting up.

"What the hell?" Rudolph said.

My head hurt, in back. I must have slammed it into something. I pressed a hand against my skull, and groaned. "Oh, stars," I muttered. "I should have known better than to give him a straight line like that."

Stallings had blood running out his nose and into his greying moustache. Flecks of red spotted his white dress shirt. "That . . . Good Lord, Dresden. What was that thing?"

I pushed myself to my feet. Everything wobbled for a moment. My whole body shook, and I felt like I might just fall over and start crying like a baby. It had used my magic. It had stolen my face and my magic and used them both to hurt people. It made me want to start screaming, to tear something apart with my bare hands.

Instead, I staggered toward Murphy's office. "It's what got Malone," I told Stallings. "It's kind of complicated."

Murphy still sat in her chair, her eyes wide and staring and horrified, her hands folded into her lap. "Murph?" I asked. "Karrin? Can you hear me?"

She didn't move. But her breath came out with a little edge to it, as though she had tried to speak. She breathed. Thank God. I knelt down and took her hands in mine. They felt ice cold.

"Murph," I whispered. I waved my hand in front of her eyes, and snapped my fingers sharply. She didn't so much as blink.

Rudolph's handsome face was pale. "I'll call downstairs. Tell them not to let him out." I heard him go to the nearest phone and start calling down to the desk. I didn't bother to tell him that it wouldn't do any good. The Nightmare could walk out through the walls if it needed to.

Stallings joined me in the room, looking shaken and a little grey. He stared at Murphy for a long moment, and then asked, "What is it? What's wrong with her?"

I peered at her eyes. They were dilated wide. I braced myself, and looked deeper into her eyes. When a wizard looks into your eyes, you cannot hide from him. He can see deep down into you, see the truest parts of your character, the dark places and the light—and you see him in return. Eyes are the windows to the soul. I searched for Murphy behind all of that terror, and waited for the soulgaze to begin.

Nothing happened.

Murphy just sat there, staring ahead. Another low breath rattled out, not quite making a sound—but I recognized the effort she was making for what it was.

Murphy was screaming.

I had no idea what she was seeing, what horrors the Nightmare had set before her eyes. What it had taken from her. I touched her throat with gentle fingertips, but I couldn't feel the bone-chilling cold of the torment-spell like the one upon Malone. At least there was that much. But if I couldn't see inside of her, then Murphy was in another place. The lights were on, but no one was home.

"She's . . . This thing has messed with her head. I think it's making her see things. Things that aren't here. I don't think she knows where she is, and she can't seem to move."

"Christ preserve," Stallings whispered. "What can we do?"

"John," I said, quietly. "I need you to pull the evidence files from the Kravos case. I need that big leather book that we found at his apartment."

Stallings started, and then stared at me. "You need what?"

I repeated my request.

He closed his eyes. "Jesus, Dresden. I don't know. I don't know if I could get it. There's been some stuff come up lately."

"I need that book," I said. "The thing that's doing this is a kind of demon. Kravos will have that demon's name written down in his spell book. If I can get that name, I can catch this thing and stop it. I can make it tell me how to help Murph."

"You don't understand. It isn't going to be that easy for me. This has gotten complicated, and I'm not going to be able to just walk into storage and get the damn thing for you, Dresden." He studied Murphy with worried eyes. "It could cost me my job."

I set my Scooby-Doo lunch box on the floor and opened it up. "Listen to me," I said. "I'm going to try to help Murphy. I need someone to stay with her until dawn and then to take her back to her house—or better yet, to Malone's house."

"Why?" Stallings asked. "What are you doing?"

"I think this thing is making her live through some messed up stuff—like in a nightmare. I'm pretty sure I can stop it, but she'll still be vulnerable. So I'm going to set up a protection around her so that she'll be safe until dawn." Once morning rolled around, the Nightmare would be trapped in whatever mortal body it possessed, or else would have to flee to the Nevernever. "Someone will need to watch her, in case she wakes up."

"Rudolph can do it," Stallings said, and rose to his feet. "I'll talk to him."

I looked up at him. "I need that book, John."

He frowned, studying the ground in front of me. "Are we going to be able to catch this thing, Dresden?" *We* meaning the police. I could hear that much in his voice.

I shook my head.

"If I get the book for you," he said, "can you help the lieutenant?"

I nodded at him.

He closed his eyes and let out a breath. "All right," he whispered. Then he walked out. I heard him talking to Rudolph a moment later.

I turned back to Murphy, taking the plastic sack of sand out of the lunch box. I got out a piece of chalk and pushed Murphy's chair back from the desk so that I could draw a circle around us both and will it closed. It took more effort than it usually did, leaving me dizzy for a second.

I swallowed and began to gather up energy, to focus it as carefully and precisely as I could. It built slowly, while Murphy continued to inhale, and to exhale whispered screams. I put my hand on her cold fingers, and thought about all the stuff we'd been through, the bond of friendship that had grown between us. Good times and bad, Murph's heart had always been in the right place. She didn't deserve this kind of torment.

A great fury began to stir in me—not some vaporous, swiftly dissipated flash of anger, but something deeper, darker, more calm and more dangerous. Rage. Rage that this sort of thing should happen to someone as selfless and caring as Murphy. Rage that the creature had used my power, my face, to trick its way close to her and to hurt her.

From that rage came the power I needed. I gathered it up carefully and shaped it with my thoughts into the softest-edged spell I could conceive. Gently, I sent the power coursing down my arm into the grains of sand I pinched between a single fingertip. Then I slowly lifted my arm, the spell holding in a precarious balance as I sprinkled a bit of sand over each of her eyes. *"Dormius, dorme,"* I whispered. "Murphy, *dormius.*"

Power coursed out of me, flowed down my arm like water. I felt it fall with the grains of sand. Murphy let out a long, shivering breath, and her staring eyes began to flutter closed. Her expression slackened, from horror to deep, silent sleep, and she slumped into her chair.

I let out my breath as the spell took hold, and bowed my head, trembling. I reached out and stroked my hand over Murphy's hair. Then I composed her into something that looked a little more comfortable. "Down where there's no dreams," I whispered to her. "Just rest, Murph. I'll nail this thing for you."

With an effort of will, I smudged the circle and broke it. Then I stepped outside it, used the chalk to close it again and willed it closed around Murphy. I had to strain, this time, more than I'd ever needed to since I was barely more than a child. But the circle closed around her, sealing her in. A small haze, only an inch or two high, danced around the chalk lines, like heat waves rising from summer roads. The circle would keep out anything from the Nevernever—and the enchanted sleep would hold until the dawn came, keep her from dreaming and giving the Nightmare a way to further harm her.

I shambled out of her office, to the nearest phone. Rudolph watched me. Stallings wasn't in evidence. I dialed Michael's number. It was still busy.

I wanted to crawl home and drop a sleep spell on myself. I wanted to hide somewhere warm and quiet and get some rest. But the Nightmare was still out there. It was still after its vengeance, after Michael. I had to get to it, find it, stop it. Or at least warn him.

I put the phone down and started gathering my stuff together. Someone touched my shoulder. I looked up at Rudolph. He looked uncertain, pale.

"You'd better not be a fake, Dresden," he said, quietly. "I'm not really sure what's going on here. But so help me God, if something happens to the lieutenant because of you . . ."

I studied his face numbly. And then nodded. "I'll call back for Stallings. I need that book."

Rudolph's expression was serious, earnest. He'd never much liked me, anyway. "I mean it, Dresden. If you let Murphy get hurt, I'll kill you."

"Kid, if anything happens to Murphy because of me . . ." I sighed. "I think I'll let you."

Chapter 20

I wouldn't have thought you could find a peaceful, suburbanish neighborhood in the city of Chicago. Michael had managed, not too far west of Wrigley Field. Ancient old trees lined either side of the street in stately splendor. The homes were mostly old Victorian affairs, restored after a fluctuating economy and a century of wear and tear had reduced them to trembling firetraps. Michael's house looked like it was made of gingerbread. Fancy trim, elegant paint in ivory and burgundy—and, perhaps inevitably, a white picket fence around the house and its front yard. The porch light cast a circle of white radiance out onto the front lawn, almost to the edge of the property.

I slewed the *Beetle* up onto the curb in front of the house and pushed my way through the swinging gate, clomping up the stairs to rattle the knocker against the front door. I figured that it would take Michael a minute to stagger out of bed and come down the stairs, but instead I heard a thump, a pair of long steps, and then the curtains of the window beside the door stirred. A second later, the door opened, and Michael stood there, blinking sleep out of his eyes. He wore a pair of jeans and a T-shirt with JOHN 3:16 across his chest. He held one of his kids in his brawny arms, one I hadn't seen yet—maybe a year old, with a patch of curly, golden hair, her face pressed against her daddy's chest as she slept.

"Harry," Michael said. His eyes widened. "Merciful Father, what's happened to you?"

"It's been a long night," I said. "Have I been here yet?"

Michael peered at me. "I'm not sure what you mean, Harry."

"Good. Then I haven't. Michael, you've got to wake your family up, *now.* They could be in danger."

He blinked at me again. "Harry, it's late. What on earth—"

"Just listen." In terse terms, I outlined what I'd learned about the Nightmare, and how it was getting to its victims.

Michael stared at me for a minute. Then he said, "Let me get this straight. The ghost of a demon I killed two months ago is rampaging around Chicago, getting into people's dreams, and eating their minds from the inside."

"Yeah," I said.

"And now it's taken a part of you, manifested a body that looks like you, and you think it's coming here."

"Yes," I said. "Exactly."

Michael pursed his lips for a moment. "Then how do I know that you aren't this Nightmare, trying to get me to invite you in?"

I opened my mouth. Closed it again. Then said, "Either way, it's better if I stay out here. Charity would probably gouge out my eyes for showing up at this hour."

Michael nodded. "Come on in, Harry. Let me put the baby to bed."

I stepped inside, into a small entry hall with a polished hardwood floor. Michael nodded toward his living room, to the right, and said, "Sit down. I'll be back in a second."

"Michael," I said. "You should wake your family up."

"You said this thing is in a solid body, right?"

"It was a few minutes ago."

"Then it's not in the Nevernever. It's here, in Chicago. It can't get into people's dreams from here."

"I don't *think* so, but—"

"And it's going to be after the people who were near it when it died. It's going to come after me."

I chewed on my lip for a second. Then I said, "It's got a part of me in it, too."

Michael frowned at me.

"If I was going to come after you, Michael," I said. "I wouldn't start with you."

He looked down at the child he carried. His face hardened, and he said, in a very soft voice, "Harry. Sit. I'll be down in a moment."

"But it might—"

"I'll see to it," he said in that same soft, gentle voice. It scared me. I sat down. He took the child, walking softly, and vanished up a stairway.

I sat for a moment in a big, comfortable easy chair, the kind that rocks back and forth. There was a towel and a half-emptied bottle off to my left, on the lamp table. Michael must have been rocking the little girl to sleep.

Beside the bottle was a note. I leaned forward and picked it up, reading:

Michael. Didn't want to wake you and the baby. The little one is demanding pizza and ice cream. I'll be back in a few minutes—probably before you wake up and read this. Love, Charity.

I stood up, and started toward the stairs. Michael appeared at the top of them, his face pale. "Charity," he said. "She's gone."

I held up the note. "She went to the store for pizza and ice cream. Pregnant cravings, I guess."

Michael came down the stairs and brushed past me. Then he reached into the entry hall closet and pulled out a blue Levi's jacket and *Amoracchius* in its black scabbard.

"What are you waiting for, Harry? Let's go find her."

"But your kids—"

Michael rolled his eyes, took a step to the door, and jerked it open without looking away from me. Father Forthill stood on the other side, his thinning hair windblown, his bright blue eyes surprised behind his wire-rimmed spectacles. "Oh. Michael. I didn't mean to stop by so late, but my car stalled only a block from here on the way back from taking Mrs. Hamish home, and I thought I might borrow—" He paused, looking from me to Michael and then back to me again. "You need a baby-sitter again, don't you."

Michael shrugged into his jacket and slung the sword belt over his shoulder. "They're already asleep. Do you mind?"

Father Forthill stepped in. "Never." He made the Cross over each of us again and murmured, "God go with you."

We started out of the house and to Michael's truck. "You see, Harry?"

I scowled. "Handy fringe benefit."

Michael drove, the big white truck rumbling down the local streets toward a corner grocery on Byron Street, within a long sprint of the famous Graceland Cemetery. The lowering clouds rumbled and started dumping a steady, heavy rain down onto the city, giving all the lights golden halos and casting ghostly reflections on the wet streets.

"This time of night," Michael said, "Walsham's is the only place open. She'll be there." Thunder rumbled again in growling punctuation to the statement. I drummed my fingers on my scorched staff, and made sure that my blasting rod was hanging loosely by its thong around my wrist.

"There's her van," Michael said. He pulled the truck up into the row of parking spots in front of the grocery, next to the white Suburban troop transport. He barely took the time to take his keys with him—instead just snatching out *Amoracchius* and loosening the great blade in its sheath as he strode toward the store's front doors, his eyes narrowed, his jaw set. The rain pasted his hair down to his head after a few steps, soaking his Levi's jacket dark blue. I followed him, wincing at the damage to my leather duster, and reflecting that the old canvas job would have fared better in this weather.

Michael slammed the heel of his hand into the door, and it swept open with a jangling of tinny bells. He strode into the store, swept his eyes around the visible displays and the cash registers, and then bellowed, "Charity! Where are you?"

A couple of teenage cashiers blinked at him, and an elderly woman perusing the vitamins turned to gawk at him through her spectacles. I sighed, then nodded to the nearest cashier, a too-skinny, too-blonde girl who looked as though she were impatient for her cigarette break. "Uh, hi," I said. "Did you see me come in here a minute ago?"

"Or a pregnant woman," Michael said. "About this high." He stuck his hand out flat about at the level of his own ear.

The female cashier traded a look with her counterpart. "Seen you, mister?"

I nodded. "Another guy, like me. Tall, skinny, all in black—jacket like mine, but all black clothes underneath."

The girl licked her lips and gave us a calculating look. "Maybe I have," she said. "What's in it for me?"

Michael rolled forward a step, a growl bubbling up out of his throat. I grabbed at his shoulder and leaned back. "Whoah, whoah, Michael," I yelped. "Slow down, man."

"There isn't *time* to slow down," Michael muttered. "You detect. I'm looking." With that, he turned and strode off deeper into the store, casually carrying the sword in his left hand, his right upon the weapon's grip. "Charity!"

I muttered something unflattering under my breath, then turned back to the cashier. I fumbled in my pockets for my billfold, and managed to produce a sorry trio of wrinkled fives. I held them up and said, "Okay. My evil twin or else a pregnant woman. You seen either one?"

The girl looked at the bills and then back at me and rolled her eyes. Then she leaned out from her counter and plucked them from my hands. "Yeah," she said. "She went down aisle five a few minutes ago. Back toward the freezer section."

"Yeah?" I asked. "Then what?"

She smiled. "What? Is this your brother or something, running around with your woman? Am I going to see this on Larry Fowler tomorrow?"

I narrowed my eyes. "It's complicated," I said. "What else did you see?"

She shrugged. "She paid for some stuff, and went to that van out there. It wouldn't start. I saw you—or the guy that looks like you, come up to her and start talking to her. She looked pretty pissed at him, but she walked off with him. I didn't think anything of it."

My stomach gave a little lurch. "Walked off?" I said. "Which way?"

The cashier shrugged. "Look, mister, she just looked like she was getting a ride somewhere. She wasn't fighting or nothing."

"Which way!" I thundered. The cashier blinked, and her jaded exterior wobbled for a moment. She pointed down the street—toward Graceland.

"Michael!" I shouted. "Come on!" Then I turned around and banged my way back outside and into the rain and the dark. I stopped at Charity's van for a second, and tapped at the hood. It wobbled up without resistance, to reveal a mess of torn wires and shredded belts and broken pieces of metal. I winced, and shielded my eyes from the rain, trying to scan down the street toward the cemetery.

In the far distance, just barely, I saw two figures—one ungainly, with long hair. The other stood tall over her, slender, walking toward the cemetery holding her firmly by the hair.

They vanished into the shadows at the base of the stone wall around Graceland. I gulped, and looked around. "Michael!" I shouted again. I peered through the grocery's windows, but I couldn't see him anywhere.

"Dammit!" I said, and kicked at the front bumper of the van.

I was in no shape to go after the Nightmare on my own. It was full of power it had stolen from me. It had the booga booga factor going for it. And it had my friend's wife and unborn child as hostages.

Hell's bells, all I had was a headache, an hourglass quickly running out of sand, and a case of the shakes. Chicago's biggest cemetery, on a dark, rainy night, when the border between here and the spirit world was leaking like a sieve. It would be full of spooks and crawlies, and I would be alone.

"Yeah," I muttered. "That figures."

I sprinted for the darkness into which I had seen the Nightmare disappear with Charity.

Chapter 21

I've done smarter things in my life. Once, for example, I threw myself out of a moving car in order to take on a truckload of lycanthropes singlehandedly. That had been nominally smarter. At least I had been fairly certain that I could kill them, if I had to, at the time.

Which put me one step ahead of where I was, now. I had already killed the Nightmare—or helped to kill it, at least. Something about that just didn't seem fair. There should be some kind of rule against needing to kill anything more than once.

Rain fell in sheets rather than drops, sluicing down into my eyes. I had to keep on wiping my brow, sweeping water away, only to have it fill my vision again. I started to give serious thought to what it might be like to drown, right there on the sidewalk.

I cut across the street toward the cemetery fence. Seven feet of red brick, the fence rose in a jagged stair-step fashion every hundred feet or so, keeping up with the slow slope of the street along its southern perimeter as it moved west. At one point, a gaping slash of darkness marred the fence's exterior, and I slowed as I approached it. The bricks had been torn like paper, and lay in rubble two feet deep around the hole in the wall. I tried to peer beyond it, and saw only more rain, green grass, the shadows of trees cast over the carefully tended grounds.

I paused, outside the graveyard. A dull, restless energy pressed against me, like when weariness and caffeine mix around three-thirty in the morning. It rolled against my skin, and I heard, actually *heard* whispering voices, through the rain, dozens, hundreds of whispers, ghostly sussurance. I put my hand on the wall, and felt the tension there. There are always fences around cemeteries. Always, whether stone or brick or chain-link. It's one of those unwritten things that people don't really notice, they just do it by reflex. Any kind of wall is a barrier in more than merely a physical sense. Lots of things are more than what they seem in a purely physical sense.

Walls keep things out. Walls around cemeteries keep things in.

I looked back, hoping that Michael had followed me, but I didn't or couldn't see him in the rain. I still felt weak, shaken. The voices whispered, clustering around the weak point in the wall, where the Nightmare had torn its way in. Even if only one death in a thousand had produced a ghost (and more than that did) there might be dozens of restless spirits wandering the grounds, some even strong enough for non-practitioners of the Art to experience.

Tonight, there weren't dozens. Dozens would have been a happy number. I closed my eyes and could feel the power they stirred up, the way the air wavered and shook with the presence of hundreds of spirits, easily crossed over from the turbulent Nevernever. It made my knees shake, my belly quiver—both from the wounds that had been inflicted on me by the Nightmare and from simple, primitive fear of darkness, the rain, and a place of the dead.

The inmates of Graceland felt my fear. They pressed close to the break in the wall, and I began to hear actual, physical moans.

"I should wait here," I muttered to myself, shaking in the rain. "I should wait for Michael. That would be the smart thing to do."

Somewhere, in the darkness of the cemetery, a woman screamed. Charity.

What I wouldn't have given to have my Dead Man's talisman back, now. Son of a bitch.

I gripped my staff, knuckles white, and got out my blasting rod. Then I clambered through the break in the wall and headed into the darkness.

I felt them the moment I crossed into the cemetery, the second my shoes hit the ground. Ghosts. Shades. Haunts. Whatever you want to call them, they were dead as hell and they weren't going to take it anymore. They were weak spirits, each of them, something that would barely have given me a passing shiver on a normal night—but tonight wasn't.

A chill fell over me, abrupt as winter's first wind. I took a step forward and felt a resistance, but not as though someone was trying to keep me out. It felt more like those movies I've seen with tourists struggling through crowds of beggars in dusty Middle Eastern cities. That's what I experienced, in a chilling and spectral kind of way—people pushing against me, struggling to get something from me, something that I wasn't sure I had and that I didn't think would do any good even if I gave it to them.

I gathered in my will and slipped my mother's amulet from around my neck. I held it aloft in the smothering, clammy darkness, and fed power into it.

The blue wizard light began to glow, to cast out a dim radiance, not so bright as usual. The silver pentagram within the circle was the symbol of my faith, if that's what you wanted to call it, in magic. In the concept of power being controlled, ordered, used for constructive purpose. I wondered, for a minute, if the dimness was a reflection of my injuries or if it said something about my faith. I tried to think of how often I'd had to set something on fire, the past few years, how many times I'd had to blow something up. Or smash a building. Or otherwise wreak havoc.

I ran out of fingers and shivered. Maybe I'd better start being a little more careful.

The spirits fell back from that light, but for a few who still clustered close, whispering things into my ears. I didn't pay them any attention, or stop to listen. That way lay madness. I shoved forward, more an effort of the heart than of the body, and started searching.

"Charity!" I shouted. "Charity, where are you?"

I heard a short sound, a call, off to my right, but it cut off swiftly. I turned toward it and began moving forward at a cautious lope, glowing pentacle held aloft like Diogenes's lamp. Thunder rumbled again. The rain had already soaked the grass, made the dirt beneath my feet soft and yielding. A brief, disturbing image of the dead tearing their way up through the softened earth brought me a brief chill and a dozen spirits clustering close as though to feed from it. I shoved both fear and clutching, unseen fingers aside, and pressed forward.

I found Charity laying upon a bier within a marble edifice that looked like nothing so much as a Greek temple, the roof open to the sky. Michael's wife lay upon her back, her hands clutched over her swollen belly, her teeth bared in a snarl.

The Nightmare stood over her, with my dark hair plastered to its head, my dark eyes reflecting the gleam of my pentacle. It held one hand in the air over Charity's belly, its other over her throat. It tilted its head and watched me approach. In the edges of my wizard's light, shapes moved, flitted, spirits swirling around like moths.

"Wizard," the Nightmare said.

"Demon," I responded. I wasn't feeling much like any snapper patter.

It smiled, teeth showing. "Is that what I am," it said. "Interesting. I wasn't sure." It lifted its hand from Charity's throat, pointed a finger toward me, and murmured, "Goodbye, wizard. *Fuego.*"

I felt the surge of power before any fire rose up and swept toward me through the rain. I lifted my staff in my left hand in front of me, horizontally, and slammed power recklessly into a shield. *"Riflettum!"*

Fire and rain met in a furious hiss and a cloud of steam a foot in front of my outstretched staff. The rain helped, I think. I would never have been stupid enough to try for a gout of flame in a downpour like this. It was too easily defeated.

Charity moved, the instant the Nightmare's attention was distracted. She spun her feet toward it and, with a furious cry, planted both her heels high in the thing's chest with a vicious shove.

Charity wasn't a weak woman. The thing grunted and flew back, away from her, and at the same time the motion pushed Charity's body off the bier. She fell to the other side, crying out, curling her body around her unborn child to protect it.

I sprinted forward. "Charity," I shouted. "Get out! Run!"

She turned her head toward me and I saw how furious she was. She bared her teeth at me for a moment, but her face clouded with confusion. "Dresden?" she said.

"No time!" I shouted. On the other side of the bier, the Nightmare rose to its feet again, dark eyes gone now, instead blazing with scarlet fury. I didn't have time to think about it, running forward. "Run, Charity!"

I knew it would be suicide to wrestle with something that had torn down a brick wall a few minutes ago—but I had a sinking feeling that I was outclassed in the magic department. If he got another spell off, I didn't think I could counter it. I held my staff in both hands, planted it at the base of the bier and vaulted up, swinging my feet toward the Nightmare's face.

I had speed and surprise on my side. I hit it hard and it staggered back. My staff spun out of my hands and my hip struck painfully on the edge of the bier and scraped along my ribs as I continued forward, riding the thing into the marble flooring. My concentration gone, the blue wizard light died out and I fell in darkness.

I hit the ground with a wheeze, and scrambled back. If the Nightmare got hold of me, that would be it. I had just reached the edge of the bier when something seized my leg, right below the knee, a grip like an iron band around me. I struggled to draw myself back, but there was nothing to grab onto but rain-slicked marble.

The Nightmare stood up, and a flash of lightning somewhere overhead showed me its dark eyes, its face like mine. It was smiling. "And so it ends, wizard," it said. "I am rid of thee at last."

I tried to get away, but the Nightmare simply whirled me by one leg, whipping me into a circle in the air. Then I flew upwards and saw one of the columns coming toward me.

Then there was a flash of light and a sharp pain in the center of my forehead. The impact with the ground came as a secondary sensation, relatively pleasant compared with the first.

Unconsciousness would have been a mercy. Cold rain instead kept me awake enough to experience every agonizing second of expanding pain in my skull. I tried to move my limbs and couldn't, and for a second I thought that my neck must have broken. Then, in the corner of my vision, I saw my fingers twitch, and thought with a flash of depression that I wasn't out of the fight yet.

A major effort got my hand down onto the ground. Another major effort pushed me up and made my head spin, my stomach heave. I leaned back against the column, gasping for breath through the rain, and tried to gather my strength.

It didn't take long—there just wasn't all that much strength left to gather. I opened my eyes, slowly focused them. I felt a sharp tang in my mouth. I touched my hand to my mouth, my cheek, and my fingers came away stained with something warm and dark. Blood.

I tried to rise up and couldn't. Just couldn't. Everything spun too much. Water coursed down over me, chilling me, pooling at the base of the little hill the Greek temple-cum-mausoleum stood upon, running a stream down toward another creek.

"So much water," purred a female voice beside me. "So many things flowing down, away. I wonder if some of them are not being wasted."

I rolled my head enough to see my godmother standing beside me in her green dress. Lea's skin had evidently recovered from the ghost dust I'd dumped upon her in Agatha Hagglethorn's demesne. Her golden cat-eyes studied me with their old, familiar warmth, her hair spilling around her in a mane that seemed unaffected by the rain. She didn't seem to mind it soaking her dress, though. It clung to the curves of her body, showed the perfection of her breasts, their tips clearly showing through the silken fabric as she knelt down beside me.

"What are you doing here?" I muttered.

She smiled, reached out a finger, and ran it over my forehead, then drew it back to her mouth and slipped it between her lips and suckled, gently, upon it. Her eyes closed, and she let out a long and shivering sigh. "Such a sweet boy. You always were such a sweet boy."

I tried to push myself to my feet and couldn't. Something in my head seemed broken.

She watched me with that same, benign smile. "Thy strength is fading, my sweet. Here in the place of the dead, it may fail thee altogether."

"This isn't the Nevernever, godmother," I rasped. "You don't have any power here."

She pursed her lips in what would have been a seductive pout on a human. My blood had stained them even darker. "My sweet. You know it is not true. I simply only have what I am given, here. What I have fairly traded for."

I bared my teeth at her. "You're going to kill me, then."

She threw back her head in a rich laugh. "Kill you? I *never* intended to kill you, my sweet, barring moments of frustration. Our bargain was for your life—not your death." One of her hounds appeared out of the darkness, and crouched beside her, fastening its dark eyes upon me. She laid a fond hand upon its broad head, and it shivered in pleasure.

I felt myself grow colder, at that, staring at the hound. "You don't want me dead. You want me . . ." I couldn't finish the sentence.

"Tamed." Lea smiled. She scratched the dog's ears, fondly. "But not like this." Her mouth twisted into a contemptuous smirk. "Not as you are. Pathetic. Really, Harry, allowing yourself to be *eaten,* so. Justin and I taught you better than that."

Somewhere close, Charity shouted again. Thunder rolled overhead.

I groaned and struggled to push myself up. Lea watched me through golden, cat-slitted eyes, interested and uncaring. I managed to get to my feet, my back and most of my weight leaning against the column. In the rain, I could dimly see Charity on her knees. The Nightmare stood over her, one hand clutching her hair. It pushed the other toward her head. She fought it, uselessly, shuddering in the rain. Its fingers sunk into her skull, and Charity's struggles abruptly ceased.

I groaned and pushed myself forward, to get closer, to do something. Everything spun around and I fell to the earth again, hard.

"Sweet boy." Lea sighed. "Poor child." She knelt down beside me again, and stroked my hair. It felt nice, through my nausea and pain. I think the nausea and pain definitely cut down on the seductive potential of it, though. "Would you like me to help you?"

I managed to look up at her lovely face. "Help me?" I asked. "H-how?"

Her eyes sparkled. "I can give you what you need to save the White Knight's Lady."

I stared up at her. All the pain, the terror, the stupid, rainy cold made me ache horribly. I heard Charity whimper. I had tried. Dammit, I had done my best to help the woman. She didn't even like me. It wasn't my fault if she died, right? I had done everything in my power.

Hadn't I?

I swallowed down the sickly taste of bile and acid and asked, "What do you want, Godmother?"

She shivered and drew in a swift breath. "What I have always wanted, sweet boy. This bargain is no different than the one we made years ago. It is, in fact, a part of the same. I give you power. And in return, I get you." Her eyes flashed. "I want your promise, wizard. I want your promise that when the woman is safe, you will come to me. You will take my hand. Here, tonight."

"You want me to go back with you," I whispered. "But you don't want me like this, Godmother. All torn up. I'm empty inside."

She smiled, and stroked the hellhound's head. "Yes. In time, you will heal. And I will make that time pass swiftly, my sweet." She leaned closer to me, golden eyes burning. "Such pleasures I will teach you. No man could wish for a merrier passing." She looked up again, over the bier that hid my view of Charity and the Nightmare. "The White Knight's Lady sees such things, now. Soon, she will be trapped, as is the police woman."

"How did you know about Murphy?" I demanded.

"I know many things. I know that you may die, if you do nothing, my sweet. You may die here cold and alone."

"I don't care about that," I said. "I . . ."

Charity let out a choking, sobbing sound nearby. Lea smiled, and murmured, "Time is fleeting, child. It waits for no one, not man nor sidhe nor wizard."

Lea already had me over a barrel. If I deepened our pact, reconfirmed it, I'd be letting her nail it closed with me inside. But I couldn't get up. I couldn't do a damned thing to save Charity without getting some help.

I closed my eyes, and saw Michael's little daughter. I thought of her growing up without a mother.

Damn it.

"I accept your bargain, Godmother." When I spoke the words, I felt something stir against me, something that sealed closed.

Lea gasped, eyes closing as she shuddered again, then opening with a feral glow. She leaned down and murmured, "The answer, my sweet, is all around you." Then she kissed my forehead and was gone in a flicker of shadows.

I found myself thinking clearly again. It still hurt to move—stars, did it hurt, but I managed it. I clambered to my feet, leaned against the bier, and looked up to let the rain wash the blood from my eyes.

The answer was all around me. What the hell kind of idiotic advice was that? I glared around, but saw nothing but rolling lawns, trees, and graves. Lots of graves. Plain tombstones and marble markers, graves with ponds beside them, graves with lights, graves with small fountains. Dead people. That's what was all around.

I focused my eyes on Charity and the Nightmare, and felt cold anger inside. I moved around the edge of the bier, gaining a little stability and balance as I went, and shouted, "Hey! You! Ugly!"

The Nightmare turned its head to blink in my direction, surprised. Then it smiled again and said, "Thou art not yet dead. How interesting." It released Charity, fingers gliding out of her as they had from Murphy, and she fell limply to her side. "I can finish that one at leisure. But thou, wizard, I will make an end to at once."

"Yadda yadda yadda," I muttered. I bent down and recovered my staff, standing again with it in both hands. "People don't *talk* like that anymore. All those thous and thees. Hells bells, at least the faeries can keep up with the dialect."

The Nightmare frowned at me, and started walking toward me. "Dost thou not realize it, fool? This is thy death come upon thee."

A boot planted itself heavily on the marble beside me. Then

another. *Amoracchius* cast a glowing white light upon my shoulder, and Michael said, "I think not."

I glanced aside at Michael. "You," I groaned, "have very good timing."

He bared his teeth in an unpleasant, fierce expression. "My wife?"

"She's alive," I said. "But we'd better get her out of here."

He nodded. "I'll kill it again," he said. He passed me something hard and cool—a crucifix. "You get her. Give her this."

The Nightmare came to a halt, its eyes narrowing upon the pair of us. "Thou," it said to Michael. "I knew it would come to this."

"Oh, shut *up*!" I shouted, exasperated. "Michael, killing this thing already!"

Michael started forward, the sword's white fire lighting the night like a halogen torch. The Nightmare screamed in fury and threw itself to one side, avoiding the blade, then rushed back in toward Michael, fingers raking like claws. Michael ducked under them, planted a shoulder in the thing's gut, and shoved it away, spun, and whipped the sword at it. *Amoracchius* cut into the Nightmare's midsection, and white fire erupted from the wound.

I hurried forward, around Michael's back to Charity. Already, she was stirring, trying to sit up. "Dresden," she whispered to me. "My husband?"

"He's busy kicking ass," I said, and pressed the crucifix into her fingers. "Here. Take this. Can you walk?"

"Mind your tongue, Mr. Dresden." She grasped the crucifix and bowed her head for a second. "I don't know," she said. "Oh, Lord help me. I think—" Her whole body tightened, and she let out a low gasp, pressing her hand against her belly.

"What?" I said. Had she been injured? Behind me, I could hear Michael grunting, see the sweep of *Amoracchius's* white fire making shadows dance. "Charity, what is it?"

She let out a low groan. "The baby," she said. "Oh, I think . . . I think my water broke earlier. When I fell." Her face twisted up, flushing bright red, and she groaned again.

"Oh," I said. "Oh. Oh, no. No, this is *not* happening." I put the heel of my hand to my forehead. "This is just *wrong*." I shot an accusing glance skywards. "Someone up there has a *sick* sense of humor."

"Nnngggrhhh!" Charity groaned. "Oh, Lord preserve. Mr. Dresden, I don't have much time."

"No." I sighed. "Naturally not." I bent down to pick her up and all but fell on my face. I managed to keep from sprawling onto her, but wobbled as I stood up again. Charity was not a dainty flower. There was no way I could carry her out of there.

"Michael!" I shouted. "Michael, we've got a problem!"

Michael threw himself behind one of the biers as a stone whistled out of the darkness and shattered to powder against it. "What?"

"Charity!" I shouted. "Her baby's coming!"

"Harry!" Michael shouted. "Look out!"

I turned and the Nightmare appeared from the darkness behind me, moving almost more swiftly than I could see. It reached down and simply tore a marble headstone from the earth, lifting it high. I threw myself between it and Charity, but even as I did, I knew it would be a futile gesture—it was strong enough to crush her right through me. But I did it anyway.

"Now!" screamed the Nightmare. "Put down your sword, Knight! Put it down, or I crush them both!"

Michael started towards us, his face pale. "Not a step closer," the Nightmare snarled. "Not an inch."

Michael stopped. He stared at Charity, who groaned again, panting, eyes forced shut. "H-Harry?" he said.

I could get out of the thing's way. I could draw its fire, maybe. But if I moved, it could simply crush Charity. She'd have no chance at all.

"The sword," the Nightmare said, voice cool. "Drop it."

"Oh Lord," Michael whispered.

"Don't do it, Michael," I said. "It's only going to kill us anyway."

"Be thou silent," the Nightmare said. "My quarrel is with thee, wizard, and with the knight. The woman and her child are nothing to me, so long as I have both of you."

Rain sleeted down for a long and otherwise silent moment. Then Michael closed his eyes. "Harry," he said. He lowered the great sword. Then gave it a gentle toss to one side, letting it fall on the ground. "I'm sorry. I can't do it."

The Nightmare met my eyes with its own, glowing faint scarlet, and its lips curled up into a gleeful smile. "Wizard," it said, in a whisper. "Thy friend should have listened to thee." I saw the gravestone start to come down toward me.

Charity's arm abruptly swept up, the crucifix I'd passed her held in it. The symbol flickered, and then kindled with white fire that threw harsh, horror-movie shadows up over the Nightmare's face. It twisted and recoiled from that light, screaming, and the tombstone crashed down to the earth, rending the damp, vulnerable soil.

Everything slowed down and came into crystalline focus. I could clearly see the grounds, the shadows of the trees. I could hear Charity beside me, uttering something in harsh Latin, and out of the corner of my eye, could see the restless shades moving about the cemetery. I could feel the cold sharpness of the rain, feel it coursing down over me, flowing down the gentle slopes to run in rivulets and streams to the nearby pond.

Running water. The answer was all around me.

I moved forward, toward the Nightmare. It swung at me with one flailing arm, and I felt it clip my shoulder as it swept down. Then I threw myself into the Nightmare's body, hit it hard. We tumbled together down the slope, toward the newly forming stream.

You ever hear the Legend of Sleepy Hollow? Remember the part with poor old Ichabod riding like blazes for the covered bridge and safety? Running water grounds magical energies. Creatures of the Nevernever, spirit bodies, cannot cross it without losing all the energy required to keep those bodies here. That was the answer.

I rolled down the slope with the Nightmare, and felt its hands tearing at me. We went down into the stream together, as one of its hands clenched my throat and shut off my breath.

And then it began to scream. It jerked and twisted atop me in eight or nine inches of running water, shrieking. The thing's body just started melting away, like sugar in water, starting at its feet and moving up. I watched it, watched myself dissolve with a morbid kind of fascination. It writhed, it bucked, it thrashed.

"Wizard," it said, voice bubbling. "This is not over. Not over. When the sun sets again, wizard, I will be back for thee!"

"Melt already," I mumbled. And, seconds later, the Nightmare vanished, leaving only sticky gook behind, on my coat, my throat.

I stood up out of the water, drenched and shivering, and slogged my way back up the little hill. Michael had gone to his wife and crouched down beside her. He got his arms underneath her and lifted her as though she were a basket of laundry. Like I said before, Michael's buff.

"Harry," he said. "The sword."

"I got it," I replied. I trudged up to where he'd let *Amoracchius* fall and picked it up. The great blade weighed less than I would have thought, and it fairly hummed with power, vibrating in my fingers. I didn't have a sheath for it, so I just slung it up on one shoulder and hoped I wouldn't fall and cut my head off or something. I recovered my other stuff, too, and turned to walk out with Michael.

That was when Lea arrived, appearing before me with a trio of her hellhounds around her. "My sweet," she said. "It is time to fulfill your bargain."

I yelped and jumped back from her. "No," I said. "No, wait. I beat this thing, but it's still loose. It will be able to come back from the Nevernever tomorrow night."

"That is of no concern to me," Lea said, and shrugged. "Our bargain was for you to save the woman with what I gave you."

"You didn't give me *anything,*" I said. "You just blanked out some of the pain. It isn't as though you made the water, Godmother."

She shrugged, smiling. "Semantics. I pointed it out to you, did I not?"

"I would have realized it on my own," I said.

"Perhaps. But we have a bargain." She lowered her face, eyes gleaming gold and dangerous. "Are you going to attempt to escape it once more?"

I'd given my word. And broken promises add up to trouble. But the Nightmare hadn't been defeated. Driven back, sure, but it would only be back the next night.

"I'll go with you," I said. "When I've beaten the Nightmare."

"You'll go now." Lea smiled. "This instant. Or pay the price." The three hellhounds took a pace toward me, baring their teeth in a silent snarl.

I fumbled everything out of my grasp but the sword, and gripped it tightly. I don't know a thing about broadswords, but it was heavy and sharp, and even without its vast power, I was pretty sure I could stick the pointy part into one of those hounds. "I can't do that," I said. "Not yet."

"Harry!" Michael shouted. "Wait! It can't be used like that!"

One of the hounds leapt toward me, and I lifted the blade. Then there was a flash of light and a jolt of pain that lanced up through my hands and arms. The blade twisted in my grasp, fell out of it and spun to the ground. The hellhound snapped at me, and I stumbled back, my hands gone numb and useless.

Lea's laughter rang out through the graves like silver bells. "Yes!" she caroled, stepping forward. She bent and with a casual motion picked up the great sword. "I knew you would try to cheat me again, sweet boy." She smiled at me, a flash of dainty canines. "I must thank you, Harry. I would never have been able to touch this had not the one who held it betrayed its purpose."

I felt a flash of anger at my own stupidity. "No," I stammered. "Wait. Can't we talk about this, Godmother?"

"We'll talk again, sweet boy. I'll see you both very soon." Lea laughed again, eyes gleaming. And then she turned, her hellhounds gathering at her feet, and took a step forward, vanishing into the night. The sword went with her.

I stood there in the rain, feeling tired and cold and stupid. Michael stared at me for a second, his expression shocked, eyes wide. Charity curled against him, shuddering and moaning quietly.

"Harry," Michael whispered. I think he was crying, but I couldn't see the tears in the rain. "Oh my God. What have you done?"

Chapter 22

All hospital emergency rooms have the same feel to them. They're all decorated in the same dull, muted tones and softened edges, which are meant to be comforting and aren't. They all have the same smell too: one part tangy antiseptics, one part cool dispassion, one part anxiety, and one part naked fear.

They wheeled Charity away first, Michael at her side. Triage being what it is, I got bumped to the front of the line. I felt like apologizing to the five-year-old girl holding a broken arm. Sorry, honey. Head trauma before fractured limbs.

The doctor who examined me wore a nameplate that read SIMMONS. She was broadly built and tough-looking, hair going grey in sharp contrast to her rich, dark skin. She sat down on a stool in front of me and leaned over, putting her hands on either side of my head. They were large, warm, strong. I closed my eyes.

"How are you feeling?" she asked, releasing me after a moment, and reaching for some supplies on a table next to her.

"Like a supervillain just threw me into a wall."

She let out a soft chuckle. "More specifically. Are you in pain? Dizzy? Nauseous?"

"Yes, no, and a little."

"You hit your head?"

"Yeah." I felt her start to daub at my forehead with a cold cloth, cleaning off grime and dried blood, though there wasn't much left, thanks to the rain.

"Mmmm. Well. There's some blood here. Are you sure it's yours?"

I opened my eyes and blinked at her. "Mine? Whose else would it be?"

The doctor lifted an eyebrow at me, dark eyes glittering from behind her glasses. "You tell me, Mister . . ." she checked her charts. "Dresden." She frowned and then peered up at me. "Harry Dresden? The wizard?"

I blinked. I'm not really famous, despite being the only wizard in the phone book. I'm more infamous. People don't tend to spontaneously recognize my name. "Yeah. That's me."

She frowned. "I see. I've heard of you."

"Anything good?"

"Not really." She let out a cross sigh. "There's no cut here. I don't appreciate jokes, Mister Dresden. There are people in need to attend to."

I felt my mouth drop open. "No cut?" But there had been a nice, flowing gash in my head at some point, pouring blood into my eyes and mouth. I could still taste some of it, almost. How could it have vanished?"

I thought of the answer and shivered. Godmother.

"No cut," she said. "Something that might have been cut a few months ago."

"That's impossible," I said, more to myself than to her. "That just can't be."

She shone a light at my eyes. I winced. She peered at each eye (mechanically, professionally—without the intimacy that triggers a soulgaze) and shook her head. "If you've got a concussion, I'm Winona Ryder. Get off that bed and get out of here. Make sure to talk to the cashier on the way out." She pressed a moist towelette into my hand. "I'll let you clean up this mess, Mister Dresden. I have enough work to do."

"But—"

"You shouldn't come into the emergency room unless it's absolutely necessary."

"But I didn't—"

Dr. Simmons didn't stop to listen to me. She turned around and strode off, over to the next patient—the little girl with the broken arm.

I got up and made my bruised way into the bathroom. My face was a mess of faint, dried blood. It had settled mostly into the lines and creases, making me look older, a mask of blood and age. I shivered and started cleaning myself off, trying to keep my hands from shaking.

I felt scared. Really, honestly scared. I would have been much happier to have needed stitches and painkillers. I wiped away blood and peered at my forehead. There was a faint, pink line beginning about an inch below my hair and slashing up into it at an angle. It felt very tender, and when I accidentally touched it with the rag, it hurt so much that I almost shouted. But the wound was closed, healed.

Magic. My godmother's magic. That kiss on the forehead had closed the wound.

If you think I should have been happy about getting a nasty cut closed up, then you probably don't realize the implications. Working magic directly on a human body is difficult. It's *very* difficult. Conjuring up forces, like my shield, or elemental manifestations like the fire or wind is a snap compared to the complexity and power required to change someone's hair a different color—or to cause the cells on either side of an injury to fuse back together, closing it.

The healing cut was a message for me. My godmother had power over me on earth now, too, as well as in the Nevernever. I'd made a bargain with one of the Fae and broken it. That gave her power over me, which she demonstrated aptly by the way she'd wrought such a powerful and complex working on me—and I'd never even felt it happening.

That was the part that scared me. I'd always known that Lea had outclassed me—she was a creature with a thousand years or more of experience, knowledge, and she had been born to magic like I had been born to breathing. So long as I remained in the real world, though, she'd had no advantage over me. Our world was a foreign place to her, just as hers was to me. I'd had the home field advantage.

Had being the operative word. Had.

Hell's bells.

I gave up and let my hands shake while I wiped off my face. I had a good reason to be afraid. Besides, my clothes were soaked from the rain and I felt desperately cold. I finished washing the blood away, and went to stand in front of the electric hand dryer. I had to slam the button a dozen times before it started.

I had the nozzle of the thing turned up, directing the hot air up my shirt, when Stallings came in sans, for once, Rudolph. He looked as though he hadn't slept since I'd seen him last. His suit was rumpled, his grey hair a little greyer, and his moustache was almost the same color as the bags underneath his eyes. He went to the sink and splashed cold water on his face without looking at me.

"Dresden," he said. "We got word you were in the hospital."

"Heya, John. How's Murphy?"

"She slept. We just brought her in."

I blinked at him. "Christ. Is it dawn already?"

"About twenty minutes ago." He moved over to the dryer next to mine. His started on the first slap of the button. "She's sleeping, still. The docs are arguing about whether she's in a coma or on some kind of drug."

"You tell them what happened?" I asked.

He snorted. "Yeah. I'll just tell them that a wizard put her under a spell, and she's sleepy." He glanced over at me. "So when's she going to wake up?"

I shook my head. "My spell won't hold her for long. Maybe a couple more days, at the most. Each time the sun comes up, it's going to degrade it a little more."

"What happens then?"

"She starts screaming. Unless I find the thing that got her and figure out how to undo what it did."

"That's what you want Kravos's book for," Stallings said.

I nodded. "Yeah."

He reached into his pocket and produced the book—a little journal, thick but not broad, bound in dark leather. It was sealed in a plastic evidence bag. I reached for it, but Stallings pulled it away.

"Dresden. If you touch this, if you open it up, you're going to be leaving your prints on it. Skin cells. All sorts of things. Unless it disappears."

I frowned at him. "What's the big deal? Kravos is all but put away, right? Hell, we caught him with the murder weapon, with a body at the scene. There isn't anything in the journal to beat that, is there?"

He grimaced. "If it was just his trial, it wouldn't be a problem."

"What do you mean?"

He shook his head. "Inside shit. I can't talk about it. But if you take this book, Dresden, it's got to vanish."

"Fine," I said, reaching for it. "It's gone."

He pulled it away again. "I mean it," he said. "Promise."

Something about the quiet intensity of his words touched me. "All right," I said. "I promise."

He stared at the book for a second, then slapped it into my palm. “Hell with it,” he said. “If you can help Murph, do it.”

“John,” I said. “Hey, man. If I didn’t think I needed it . . . What’s going on here?”

“Internal Affairs,” Stallings said.

“Looking at S.I.? Again? Don’t they have anything better to do? What set them off this time?”

“Nothing,” Stallings lied. He turned to go.

“John,” I said. “What aren’t you telling me here?”

He paused at the door and grimaced. “They’re interested in the Kravos case. That’s all I can say. You should hear word in the next day or so. You’ll know it when you hear it.”

“Wait,” I said. “Something happened to Kravos?”

“I’ve got to go, Harry. Good luck.”

“Wait, Stallings—”

He headed out the door. I cursed and started after him, but he lost me. I wound up standing in the hallway, shivering like a wet puppy.

Dammit. Cops were tight, a special kind of brotherhood. They’d work with you, but if you weren’t a cop, you were on the outside in a billion subtle ways—one of which was that they didn’t let you in on the department’s secrets. What could have happened to Kravos? Something serious. Hell, maybe the Nightmare had taken out a little vengeance on him, as well, as long as it was out and about. Served him right, though, if it had happened.

I stood there for a minute, trying to work out what to do. I had no money on me, no car, no way to get either.

I needed Michael.

I asked someone for directions and headed for Maternity. I took a long route around, staying away from anything that looked technical or expensive. The last thing I wanted was to blow up grandpa’s iron lung.

I found Michael standing in a hallway. His hair had dried, all curled and mussed. There seemed to be more grey in it, this way, than usual. His beard had a rough, untrimmed look to it. His eyes were sunken. Mud spattered his boots and his jeans to the knee. *Amoracchius’s* black scabbard hung over his shoulder, empty.

Michael stood in front of a big picture window. Rows of little people in rolling cradles faced the window, heat lamps making sure that they didn’t get chills. I stood there quietly with him, looking at the babies for a time. A nurse looked up, and then did a double take, staring at us, before hurrying out of the room.

"Aha," I said. "That nurse recognizes us. I didn't realize we were back down at Cook County. Didn't recognize the place without something being on fire."

"Charity's doctor is here."

"Uh-huh," I said. "So. Which one is the newest little Carpenter?"

Michael remained silent.

I got a sick little feeling, and glanced aside at him. "Michael?"

When he spoke, his voice was exhausted, numb. "The labor was complicated. She was cold, and might have been getting sick with something. Her water did break, back at the graveyard. I guess it makes it a lot harder on the baby."

I just listened to him, feeling sicker.

"They had to go ahead and do a C-section. But . . . they think there might be damage. She got hit in the stomach at one point, they think. They don't know if she'll be able to have children again."

"The baby?"

Silence.

"Michael?"

He stared at the infants and said, "The doctor says that if he lasts thirty-six hours, he might have a chance. But he's weakening. They're doing everything they can." Tears started at his eyes and rolled down his cheeks. "There were complications. Complications."

I tried to find something to say, and couldn't. Dammit. Tired frustration stirred my already unsteady belly. This shouldn't have happened. If I'd been faster, or smarter, or made a better decision, maybe I could have stopped Charity from getting hurt. Or the baby. I put my hand on Michael's shoulder and squeezed tight. Just trying to let him know that I was there. For all the good I'd done.

He took in a breath. "The doctor thinks I beat her. That's how she got the bruises. He never said anything, but . . ."

"That's ridiculous," I said, at once. "Stars and stones, Michael, that's the stupidest thing I've ever heard."

His voice came out hard, bitter. He stared at his faint reflection in the glass. "It might as well have been me, Harry. If I hadn't gotten myself involved, this demon wouldn't have gone after her." I heard his knuckles pop as he clenched his fists. "It should have come after me."

"You're right," I said. "Holy hell, Michael, you're right."

He shot me a look. "What are you talking about?"

I rubbed my hands together, trying to sort through the ideas flashing across my brain in neon lights. "It's a demon, this thing we're after, right? It's a demon's ghost." An orderly, walking by pushing a tray, gave me an odd look. I smiled at him, feeling rather manic. He hurried along.

"Yes," Michael said.

"Demons are tough, Michael. They're dangerous and they're scary, but they're really kind of clueless in a lot of ways."

"How so?"

"They just don't get it, about people. They understand things like lust and greed and the desire for power, but they just don't get things like sacrifice and love. It's alien to most of them—doesn't make any sense at all."

"I don't understand what you're driving at."

"Remember what I said, about how I knew the worst way to get to you would be through your family?"

His frown darkened, but he nodded.

"I know that because I'm human. I know what it's like to care about someone other than myself. Demons don't—especially the thug-type demons who make pacts with two-bit sorcerers like Kravos. Even knowing that I thought the best way to get to you would be through someone close to you, I don't think a demon would have understood the context of that information."

"So what you're saying is that this demon would have had no reason to go after my wife and child."

"I'm saying it's inconsistent. If it was just a question of a demon's ghost going after the people who had killed it, then it should have just hammered on us all until we died and been done with it. I don't think it ever would have occurred to it to take a shot at someone that we care about—even if it did have my knowledge about you. There's got to be something else going on here."

Michael's eyes widened a bit. "The Nightmare is a cat's-paw," he said. "Someone else is using it to hit at us."

"Someone who can cast those barbed-wire torment spells," I said. "And we've been chasing around after the tool instead of going after the hand that's wielding it."

"Blood of God," Michael swore. It was about the secondmost powerful oath he used. "Who could it be?"

I shook my head. "I don't know. Someone who has us both in common, I guess. How many enemies do we share?"

He wiped his eyes on his sleeve, expression intent. "I'm not sure. I've made enemies with pretty much every creature in the country."

"Ditto," I said, morosely. "Even some of the other wizards wouldn't mind seeing me fall down a few flights of stairs. Not knowing our attacker's identity doesn't bother me as much as something else, though."

"What's that?"

"Why he hasn't taken us out already."

"They want to hurt us, first. Vengeance." His brow beetled. "Could your godmother be behind this?"

I shook my head. "I don't think so. She's a faerie. They aren't usually this methodical or organized. And they aren't impatient, either. This thing's been active every night, like it couldn't wait to get going."

Michael looked at me for a moment. Then he said, "Harry, you know that I don't think it's my place to judge another person."

"I hear a 'but' coming."

He nodded. "But how did you get mixed up with the likes of that faerie? She's bad, Harry. Some of them are merely alien, but that one is . . . malevolent. She enjoys causing pain."

"Yeah," I said. "I didn't exactly pick her."

"Who did?"

I shrugged. "My mother, I think. She was the one with power. My father wasn't a wizard. Wasn't into their world."

"I don't understand why she would do that to her child."

Something inside me broke with a little snapping sensation, and I felt tears at my eyes. I scowled. They were a child's tears, to go with a child's old pain. "I don't know," I said. "I know that she was mixed up with some bad people. Bad beings. Whatever. Maybe Lea was one of her allies."

"Lea. It's short for Leanandsidhe, isn't it."

"Yeah. I don't know her real name. She takes blood from mortals and gives them inspiration in return. Artists and poets and things. That's how she amassed most of her power."

Michael nodded. "I've heard of her. This bargain you have with her. What is it?"

I shook my head. "It isn't important."

Something shifted in Michael, became harder, more resolute. "It is important to me, Harry. Tell me."

I stared at the babies for a minute, before I said, "I was a kid. Things fell out with my old teacher, Justin. He sent a demon to kill me, and I went on the run. I made a bargain with Lea. Enough power to defeat Justin in exchange for my service to her. My loyalty."

"And you broke faith with her."

"More or less." I shook my head. "She's never pushed it before now, and I've been careful to stay out of her way. She doesn't usually get this involved with mortal business."

Michael moved his hand to *Amoracchius's* empty scabbard. "She did take the sword though."

I winced. "Yeah. I guess that was my fault. If I hadn't have tried to use it to weasel out of the deal . . ."

"You couldn't have known," Michael said.

"I should have," I said. "It isn't as though it as a tough one to figure out."

Michael shrugged, though his expression was less casual than the gesture. "What's done is done. But I don't know how much help to you I can be without the sword."

"We'll get it back," I said. "Leah can't help herself. She makes deals. We'll figure out a way to get it back from her."

"But will we do it in time," Michael said. He shook his head, grim. "The sword won't stay in her hands forever. The Lord won't allow that. But it may be that my time to wield it has passed."

"What are you talking about?" I asked.

"Perhaps it was a sign. Perhaps that I am no longer worthy to serve Him in this way. Or that the burden of it has passed on to someone else." He grimaced, staring at the glass, the infants. "My family, Harry. Perhaps it's time they had a full-time father."

Oh, great. All I needed, now, was a crisis of faith and bad case of career doubt from the Fist of God. I needed Michael. I needed someone to watch my back, someone who was used to dealing with the supernatural. Sword or no sword, he had a steady head, and his faith had a subtle power of its own. He could be the difference between me getting killed and defeating whoever was out there.

Besides, he had wheels.

"Let's get going. Time's a-wasting."

He frowned. "I can't. I'm needed here."

"Michael, look. Is someone with your kids at home?"

"Yes. I called Charity's sister last night. She went over. Father Forthill was going to get some sleep, and then stay on."

"Is there anything more you can do for Charity here?"

He shook his head. "Only pray. She's resting, now. And her mother is on the way here."

"Okay, then. We've got work to do."

"You expect me to leave them again?"

"No, not leave them. But we need to find the person behind the Nightmare and take care of them."

"Harry. What are we going to do? Kill someone?"

"If we have to. Hell's bells, Michael, they might have murdered your son."

His face hardened, and I knew then that I had him, that he'd followed me into Hell to get at whoever had hurt his wife and child. I had him all right—and I hated myself for it. Way to go, Harry. Jerk those heartstrings like a fucking puppeteer.

I held up the book. "I think I've got a line on the Nightmare's name. I'll bet you anything that Kravos recorded it in his book of shadows, here. If I'm right, I might be able to use it to make contact with the Nightmare and then trace his leash back to whoever's holding it."

Michael stared at the glass, at the kids beyond it.

"I need you to drive me home. From my lab, I might be able to sort out what's going on before things get any more out of hand. Then we go handle it."

He didn't say anything.

"Michael."

"All right," he said, voice quiet. "Let's go."

Chapter 23

Back in my lab, it felt a little creepy to be working by candlelight. Intellectually, I knew that it was still full daylight outside, but last night had brought out the instinctive fear of the dark that is a part of being human. I had been wounded. Everything, every shadow, every small sound made me twitch and jerk and look aside.

"Steady, Harry," I told myself. "You have time before sundown. Just relax and get it over with."

Good advice. Michael and I had driven around most of the morning, collecting what I would need for the spell. I'd read through Kravos's journal while Michael drove. Sick stuff. He'd been careful about listing out every step of his rituals, complete with notes on the physical ecstasy he'd experienced during the killings—nine in all. Most of them had been women or children he'd killed with a cruelly curved knife. He'd roped a bunch of young people into his fold with drugs and blackmail, and then thrown orgies where he'd either participate or else channel the energy raised by all that lust into his magic. That seemed to be standard operating procedure for guys like Kravos. Win-win situation.

A thorough man. Thorough in his efforts to kill and corrupt lives to acquire more power, thorough in the documentation of his sick pleasures—and thorough in the listing of his efforts to secure a familiar demon by the name of Azorthragal.

The name had been carefully written, each syllable marked for specific emphasis.

Magic is a lot like language: it's all about stringing things together, linking one thing with another, one idea with another. After you establish links, then you pour power into them and make something happen. That's what we call thaumaturgy in the business—creating links between small things and big things. Then, you make something happen on the small scale and it happens on the large scale, too. Voodoo dolls are the typical example for that one.

But simulacra, like a voodoo doll, aren't the only way to create links. A wizard can use fingernail clippings, or hair, or blood, if it's fresh enough, or just about any other body part to create a link back to the original being.

Or you can use its name. Or maybe I should say, its Name.

Names have power. Everyone's Name says something about them, whether they're aware of it or not. A wizard can use that Name to forge a link to someone. It's difficult with people. People's self-concepts are always changing, evolving, so even if you get someone to tell you their full name, if you try to establish the link when they're in a radically different mood, or after some life-changing event that alters the way they see themselves, it might not work. A wizard can get a person's name only from their own lips, but if he doesn't use it fairly quickly, it's likely to get stale.

Demons, however, are a different matter. Demons aren't people. They don't have the problem of having a soul, and they don't worry about silly things like good and evil, or right and wrong. Demons are. If a demon is going to be inclined to eat your face, it's going to eat your face then, and now, and a thousand years from now.

It's almost comforting, in a way—and it makes them vulnerable. Once you know a demon's Name, you can get to it whenever you want to. I had Azorthragal's Name. Even though it was a ghost now, instead of a demon, it ought to respond to the memory of its Name, if nothing else.

Time to get to it.

Five white candles surrounded my summoning circle, the points of an invisible pentacle. White for protection. And because they're the cheapest color at Wal-Mart. Hey, being a wizard doesn't make money grow on trees.

Between each candle was an object from someone the Nightmare had touched. My shield bracelet was there. Michael had given me his wedding ring, and Charity's. I'd gone by the station, and grabbed the hand-lettered nameplate Murphy had kept stubbornly on her office door until the publicity last year had driven the municipal politicians into getting her a real one. It lay on the floor beside them. A visit to a grateful Malone household had turned up Micky's retirement watch. It completed the circle, between the last pair of candles.

I drew in a breath, and checked my props. You don't need all the candles and knives and whatnot to work magic. But they help. They make it easier to focus. In my weakened condition, I needed all the help I could get.

So I lit the incense and paced around the outside of the summoning circle, leaving myself enough room to work with inside the circle of incense and outside the circle of copper. I put out a little willpower as I did, just enough to close the circle, and felt the energy levels rise as random magic coalesced.

"Harry," Michael called down from the room above. "Are you finished?"

I suppressed a flash of irritation. "Just getting started."

"Forty-five minutes until sundown," he said.

I couldn't keep the annoyance out of my voice. "Gee, thanks. No pressure, Michael."

"Can you do it or not, Harry? Father Forthill is staying at my house with the children. If you can't stop this thing now, I've got to go back to Charity."

"I sure as hell can't do it with you breathing down my neck. Hell's bells, Michael, get out of the way and let me work."

He growled something to himself about patience or turning the other cheek or something. I heard his feet on the floor above as he retreated from the door leading down to my lab.

Michael didn't come down into the lab with me because the whole concept of using magic without the Almighty behind it didn't sit well with him, regardless of what we'd been through together. He could tolerate it, but not approve of it.

I got back to work, closing my eyes and forcing myself to clear my thoughts, to focus on the task at hand. I started to draw my concentration toward the copper circle. The incense smoke tickled at my senses, and swirled about inside the perimeter of the outer circle, not leaving it. The energy grew slowly, as I concentrated, and then I picked up the knife in my right hand, and a handful of water from a bowl on my left.

Now for the three steps. "Enemy, mine enemy," I spoke, slipping power into the words, "I seek you." I passed the knife over the copper circle, straight down. I couldn't see it, without opening my Sight, but could feel the silent tension as I cut a slit between the mortal world and the Nevernever.

"Enemy, mine enemy," I spoke again. "I search for you. Show me your face." I cast the water up, over the circle, where the energy of the spell atomized it into a fine, drifting mist, filled with rainbows from the surrounding candles, shifting shapes and colors.

Now for the hard part. "Azorthragal!" I shouted, "Azorthragal, Azorthragal! *Appare!*" I used the knife to cut my finger, and smeared the blood onto the edge of the copper circle.

Power surged out of me, into the circle, through the rent in the fabric of reality, and as it did, the circle sprang up like a wall around the band of copper in the floor. I felt the cut as an acute, vicious pain, enough to make me blink tears out of my eyes as the power quested out, fueled by the energy of the circle, guided by the articles spread around it.

The spell quested about in the Nevernever, like the blind tentacle of the Kraken scouring the deck, looking for some hapless soul to grab. It shouldn't have happened like that. It should have zipped to the Nightmare like a lariat and brought it reeling in. I reached out and put more power into the spell, picturing the thing that I had been fighting, the results of its work, trying to give the spell more guidance. It wasn't until I hit upon the *sense* of the Nightmare, for lack of a better word, the terror it had inspired that the spell latched onto something. There was a moment of startled stillness, and then a wild, bucking energy, a resistance, that made my heart pound in my chest, the cut in my finger burn as though someone had poured salt over it.

"Appare!" I shouted, forcing will into my voice, reeling back in on the spell. "I command thee to appear!" I slip into the archaic at dramatically appropriate moments. So sue me.

The swirling mist of rainbows swayed and wavered, as though some kind of half-solid thing were stirring the air within the summoning circle. It struggled like a maddened bull, trying to tear away from my spell. *"Appare!"*

Upstairs, the telephone rang. I heard Michael walk across the floor while I struggled through several silent, furious seconds, the Nightmare trying to escape the web of my concentration.

"Hello," Michael said. He'd left the door open and I heard him clearly.

"Appare!" I grated again. I felt the thing slip, and I jerked it closer in vicious triumph. The mists and lights swirled, began to take on shape, vaguely humanoid.

"Oh. Yes, but he's . . . a little busy," Michael said. "Uh-huh.

No, not exactly. I think—Yes, but—" Michael sighed. "Just a minute." I heard his feet cross to the trap door again.

"Harry," Michael called. "Susan's on the phone. She says she needs to talk to you."

I all but screamed, struggling to hold onto the Nightmare. "I'll call her back," I managed to gasp.

"She says it's really important."

"Michael!" I half-screamed. "I'm a little *busy* here!"

"Harry," Michael said, his voice serious. "I don't know what you're doing down there, but she sounds very upset. Says she's been trying to get in touch with you for a while without any luck."

The Nightmare started slipping away from me. I gritted my teeth and hung on. "Not now!"

"All right," Michael said. He retreated from the door down to the lab, and I heard him speaking quietly on the phone again.

I blocked it out, blocked out everything but my spell, the circle, and the thing on the other end of it. I was tiring, but so was it. I had all the props, the power and focus of the circle—it was strong, but I had the leverage on it, and after another minute, minute and a half, I shouted, *"Appare!"* for the last time.

The mist in the circle swirled and trembled, taking on a vaguely humanoid shape. The shape screamed, a faint and bubbly sound, still trying to escape.

"You can't get away!" I shouted at it. "Who brought you over! Who sent you!"

"Wizard," the thing screamed. "Release me!"

"Yeah, right. Who sent you!" I forced more energy into my voice, compulsion.

It screamed, a distorted sound, like a radio getting interference. The shape refused to clarify or solidify anymore. "No one!"

"Who sent you!" I said, hammering on the spell and the Nightmare, with my will. "Who has compelled you to harm these people? Hell's bells, you *will* answer me!"

"No one," the Nightmare snarled. Its struggling redoubled, but I grabbed on tightly.

And then I felt it—a third party, intruding from the other side. I felt that cold, horrible power that had been behind the torment-spell on Micky Malone and on Agatha Hagglethorn's ghost. It poured into the Nightmare like nitrous into an engine, supercharging it. The Nightmare went from raging bull to frenzied elephant, and I felt it begin to tear free of my spell, to get loose.

"Wizard!" it howled in triumph. "Wizard, the sun is sinking!

I will tear out thy heart! I will hunt thy friends and their children! I will slay them all!"

"It's thine heart," I muttered. "And no you won't." I lifted my left hand and slashed it at the sparkling mist, sprinkling droplets of blood at it. "Bound, thou art," I snarled. I reached out toward the thing, and found the part of me that was still inside of it, a warm sensation, like coming home again after a long trip. I could only barely brush it, but it was enough for what I wanted to do. "No other souls wilt thou harm, no other blood wilt thou spill. Thy quarrel is now with *me*. Bound, I make thee! Bound!" And with the third repetition of the word, I felt the spell lock, felt it settle around the Nightmare like steel coils. I couldn't keep it from getting away, I couldn't forbid it from the mortal world altogether, but I could damn well make sure that the only person it could mess with would be me. "Now let's see how you do in a fair fight, asshole."

It screamed, all but bursting the bonds of my spell, the sound reverberating through the room. I lifted the knife in my other hand and ripped it at the air over the circle, releasing the holding spell, pouring everything I had left into the strike. I saw the magic lance out into the circle, even as the Nightmare faded. It split the rainbow mist like the sweep of some invisible woodsman's axe, and once more, the Nightmare screamed.

Then the mist gathered together in a horrible rush, an implosion of space, and the creature was gone. A handful of water splattered the ground, and the candles went out.

I collapsed forward, to my forearms, wheezing and gasping for breath, my muscles shaking. I'd hurt the bastard. It wasn't invincible. I'd hurt it. Maybe nothing much more inconvenient than the cut on my finger, or a slap in the face, but it hadn't expected that.

I hadn't been able to get to the person behind it, but I'd felt something—I'd sensed their presence, gotten a clear whiff of their perfume, in a metaphysical sense. Maybe I could use that.

"Take that, jerk," I mumbled. I lay there gasping for several minutes, my head spinning from the effort of the spell. Then I put my things away and shambled up out of my lab, into the room above.

Michael helped me to a seat. He'd built up the fire, and I soaked in its warmth gratefully. He went to the kitchen and brought me a Coke, a sandwich. I drank and ate greedily. Only after I'd finished the last of the drink did he ask, "What happened?"

"I called it up. The Nightmare. Someone helped it get away, but not before I laid a binding on it."

He frowned at me, grey eyes studying my face. "What kind of binding?"

"I kept it from going after you. Or Murphy. Or your family. I couldn't keep it out, but I could limit its targets."

Michael blinked at me for a moment. Then said, slowly, "By making it come after you."

I grinned at him, a fierce show of teeth, and nodded. A touch of pride filled my voice. "I had to do it at the last second, on the fly. I hadn't really planned it, but it worked. So long as I'm alive, it can't mess with anyone else."

"So long as you're alive," Michael said. He frowned, and leaned his thick forearms on his knees, pressing his palms together. "Harry?"

"Yeah?"

"Doesn't that mean it's certainly going to try to kill you? No torment, no sadistic tortures—just flat-out mayhem and death."

I nodded, sobering. "Yeah."

"And . . . whatever person is behind the Nightmare, whoever helped it escape—that means that you've just put yourself in their way. They can't use their weapon until they've removed you."

"Yeah."

"So . . . if they didn't need you dead before, they're going to stop at nothing else now."

I was quiet for a moment, thinking about that. "I made my choice, man," I said, finally. "But hell, I'm already in water so deep, it doesn't matter if it gets any deeper. Let the Nightmare and my godmother duke it out for who gets to be first in line."

His eyes flickered up at mine. "Oh, Harry. You shouldn't have done that."

I scowled at him. "Hey. It's better than anything else we've managed, so far. You'd have done the same thing, if you could."

"Yes," Michael said. "But my family is well provided for." He paused, and then added, in a gentle voice, "And I'm sure of my soul's destination, when it's time for me to go."

"I'll worry about Hell later. Besides, I think I have a plan."

He grimaced. "You aren't concerned about your soul, but you have a plan."

"I don't intend to get killed just yet. We've got to take the offensive, Michael. If we just sit back and wait, it's going to be able to take us apart."

"Take *you* apart, you mean," he said. His expression grew more troubled. "Harry, without *Amoracchius* . . . I'm not sure how much help I'll be to you."

"You know what you're doing, Michael. And I don't think the Almighty is going to quit the team just because we fumbled the ball, right?"

"Of course not, Harry. He is ever faithful."

I leaned toward him, put a hand on his shoulder, and looked him right in the eyes. I don't do that to people very often. There aren't many I can. "Michael. This thing is big, and it's bad, and it scares the hell out of me. But I might be the only one who can stop it, now. I need you. I need your help. Hell, man. I need to know that you're at my back, that you believe in what I'm doing here. Are you with me or not?"

He studied my face. "You've lost much of your power, you say. And I don't have the sword anymore. Our enemies know it. We could both be killed. Or worse."

"If we stay here doing nothing, we're going to get killed anyway. And maybe Murphy and Charity and your kids with us."

He bowed his head, and nodded. "You're right. There's not really any choice." His hand covered mine for a moment, big and calloused and strong, and then he stood up again, his back straight and his shoulders squared. "We just have to have faith. The good Lord wouldn't give us more than we could bear."

"I hope you're right," I said.

"So what's the plan, Harry? What are we going to do?"

I got up and went to the mantel over the fire, but what I needed wasn't there. I frowned, looking around the room, and spied it on the coffee table. I bent down and plucked up the white envelope, taking the gold-lettered invitation Kyle and Kelly Hamilton had delivered.

"We're going to a party."

Chapter 24

Michael parked his truck on the street outside Bianca's mansion. He put the keys in his leather belt pouch, and buttoned it with the silver cross button. Then he straightened the collar of his doublet, which showed through the neck of the mail, and reached behind the seat for the steel helmet that slipped on over his head. "Tell me again, Harry, why this is a good idea. Why are we going to a masquerade ball with a bunch of monsters?"

"Everything points us this way," I said.

"How?"

I took a breath, trying to be patient, and passed him the white cloak. "Look. We know that someone's been stirring up the spirit world. We know that they did it in order to create this Nightmare that's been after us. We know that the girl, Lydia, was connected to the Nightmare somehow."

"Yes," Michael said. "All right."

"Bianca," I said, "sent out her thugs to take Lydia. And Bianca's hosting a party for the nastiest bad guys in the region. Stallings told me that people have been going missing off the streets. They've probably been taken for food or something. Even if Bianca isn't behind it, and I'm not saying she isn't, chances are that anyone who could be is going to be at the party tonight."

"And you think you'll be able to spot them?" Michael asked.

"Pretty sure," I responded. "All I'll have to do is get close enough to touch them, to feel their aura. I felt whoever was backing the Nightmare when they helped it get away from me. I should be able to tell when I feel them again."

"I don't like it," Michael said. "Why didn't the Nightmare come after you the minute the sun went down?"

"Maybe I scared it. I cut it up a little."

Michael frowned. "I still don't like it. There are going to be dozens of things in there that have no right to exist in this world. It will be like walking into a roomful of wolves."

"All you have to do," I said, "is keep your mouth shut and watch my back. The bad guys have to play by the rules tonight. We've been given the protection of the old laws of hospitality. If Bianca doesn't respect that, it's going to kill her reputation in front of her guests and the Vampire Court."

"I will protect you, Harry," Michael said. "As I will protect anyone who these . . . things threaten."

"We don't need any fights, Michael. That's not why we're here."

He looked out the truck window and set his jaw.

"I mean it, Michael. It's their turf. There's probably going to be bad stuff inside, but we have to keep the big picture in focus here."

"The big picture," he said. "Harry, if there's someone in there that needs my help, they're getting it."

"Michael! If *we* break the truce first, we're open game. You could get us both killed."

He turned to look at me, and his eyes were granite. "I am what I am, Harry."

I threw my arms up in the air, and banged my hands on the roof of the truck. "There are people who could get killed if we mess this up. It isn't only our own lives we're talking about, here."

"I know," he said. "My family are some of them. But that doesn't change anything."

"Michael," I said. "I'm not asking you to smile and chat and get cozy. Just keep quiet and stay out of the way. Don't shove a crucifix down anyone's throat. That's all I'm asking."

"I won't stand by, Harry," he said. "I can't." He frowned and said, "I don't think you can, either."

I glared at him. "Hell's bells, Michael. I don't want to die, here."

"Nor do I. We must have faith."

"Great," I said. "That's just great."

"Harry, will you join me in prayer?"

I blinked at him. "What?"

"A prayer," Michael said. "I'd like to talk to Him for a moment." He half smiled at me. "You don't have to say anything. Just be quiet and stay out of the way." He bowed his head.

I squinted out the window of the truck, silent. I don't have anything against God. Far from it. But I don't understand Him. And I don't trust a lot of the people that go around claiming that they're working in His best interests. Faeries and vampires and whatnot—those I can fathom. Even demons. Sometimes, even the Fallen. I can understand why they do what they do.

But I don't understand God. I don't understand how he could see the way people treat one another, and not chalk up the whole human race as a bad idea.

I guess he's just bigger about it than I would be.

"Lord," Michael said. "We walk into darkness now. Our enemies will surround us. Please help to make us strong enough to do what needs to be done. Amen."

Just that. No fancy language, no flashy beseeching the Almighty for aid. Just quiet words about what he wanted to get done, and a request that God would be on his side—on our side. Simple words, and yet power surrounded him like a cloud of fine mist, prickling along my arms and my neck. Faith. I calmed down a little. We had a lot going for us. We could do this.

Michael looked up at me and nodded. "All right," he said. "I'm ready."

"How do I look?" I asked him.

He smiled, white teeth showing. "You're going to turn heads. That's for sure."

I had to smile back at him. "Okay," I said. "Let's party."

We got out of the truck, and started walking toward the gates around Bianca's estate. Michael buckled on the white cloak with its red cross as he went. He had a matching surcoat, boots, and armored guards on his shoulders. He had a pair of heavy gauntlets tucked through his boots, and wore a pair of knives on his belt, one on either side. He smelled like steel and he clanked a little bit when he walked. It sounded comforting, in a friendly, dreadnought kind of way.

It would have been more stylish to drive up through the gates and have a valet park the truck, but Michael didn't want to hand over his truck to vampires. I didn't blame him. I wouldn't trust a bloodsucking, night stalking, fiend of the shadows valet, either.

The gate had an honest-to-goodness guard house, with a pair of guards. Neither one of them looked like they were carrying guns, but they held themselves with an armed arrogance that neither myself nor Michael missed. I held up the invitation. They let us in.

We walked up the drive to the house. A black limo pulled up along the drive as we did, and we had to step off to the side to let it past. When we got to the front of the house, the occupants were just getting out of the car.

The driver came around to the rear door of the limo and opened it. Music washed out, something loud and hard. There was a moment's pause, and then a man glided out of the limo.

He was tall, pale as a statue. Sable hair fell in tousled curls to his shoulders. He was dressed in a pair of opalescent butterfly wings that rose from his shoulders, fastened to him by some mysterious mechanism. He wore white leather gloves, their gauntlet cuffs decorated in winding silver designs, and similar designs were set around his calves, down to his sandals. At his side hung a sword, delicately made, the handle wrought as though out of glass. The only other thing he had on was a loincloth of some soft, white cloth. He had the body for it. Muscle, but not too much of it, good set of shoulders, and the pale skin wasn't darkened anywhere by hair. Hell's bells, *I* noticed how good he looked.

The man smiled, bright enough for a toothpaste commercial, and then reached a hand back down to the car. A pair of gorgeous legs in pink high heels slid out of the car, followed by a slender and scrumptious girl barely covered in flower petals. She had a short, tight skirt made out of them, and more petals cupped her breasts like delicate hands. Other than that, and the baby's breath woven into the tumbled mass of her black hair, she wore nothing. And she wore it well. In the heels, she might have been five-seven, and she had a face that made me think that she was both lovely and sweet. Her cheeks were flushed in a delicate pink blush, vibrant and alive, her lips parted, and she had a look to her eyes that told me she was on something.

"Harry," Michael said. "You're drooling."

"I'm not drooling," I said.

"That girl can't be nineteen years old."

"I'm not drooling!" I scowled, gripped my cane in hand, and stalked on up the driveway to the house. And wiped at my mouth with my sleeve. Just in case.

The man turned toward me, and both his eyebrows lifted. He looked me and my costume up and down, and burst out into a rich, rolling laugh. "Oh, my," he said. "You must be Harry Dresden."

That got my hackles up. It always bugs me when someone knows me and I don't know them. "Yeah," I said. "That's me. Who the hell are you?"

If the hostility bothered him, it didn't bother his smile. The girl with him slipped beneath his left arm and nestled against him, watching me with stoned eyes. "Oh, of course," he said. "I forget that you probably know very little of the intricacies of the Court. My name is Thomas, of House Raith, of the White Court."

"White Court," I said.

"Three vampire Courts," Michael supplied. "Black, Red, and White."

"I knew that."

Michael shrugged one shoulder. "Sorry."

Thomas smiled. "Well. Only two, for all practical purposes. The Black Court has fallen on hard times of late, the poor darlings." His tone of voice suggested muted glee rather than pity. "Mister Dresden, allow me to introduce Justine."

Justine, the girl beneath his arm, gave me a sweet smile. I half-expected her to extend her hand to me to be kissed, but she didn't. She just molded her body to Thomas's in what looked like a most pleasant fashion.

"Charmed," I said. "This is Michael."

"Michael," Thomas mused, and studied the man up and down. "Dressed as a Knight Templar."

"Something like that," Michael said.

"How ironic," Thomas said. His eyes returned to me, and that smile widened. "And you, Mister Dresden. Your costume is . . . going to make quite a stir."

"Why, thank you."

"Shall we go inside?"

"Oh, let's." We all trouped up the front stairs, affording me an uncomfortably proximate view of Justine's legs along the way, lean and lovely and made for doing things that had nothing to do with locomotion. A pair of tuxedo-clad doormen who looked human swung open the mansion's doors for us.

The entry hall to Bianca's mansion had been redecorated since the last time I'd been there. The old-style decor had been lavishly restored. She'd had marble laid out instead of gleaming hardwood. All the doorways stood in graceful arches rather than stolid rectangles. Alcoves every ten feet or so sported small statuary and other pieces of art. It was lit only by the spots on each alcove, creating deep pools of shadow in between.

"Rather tacky," Thomas sniffed, his butterfly wings quivering. "Have you been to any Court functions before, Mister Dresden? Are you aware of the etiquette?"

"Not really," I said. "But it had better not involve anyone drinking anyone's bodily fluids. Particularly mine."

Thomas laughed, richly. "No, no. Well," he admitted, "not formally, in any case, though there will be ample opportunity to indulge, if you wish." His fingers caressed the girl's waist again, and she focused her eyes on me in a disconcertingly intent fashion.

"I don't think so. What do I need to know?"

"Well, we're all outsiders, not being members of the Red Court, and this is a Red function. First, we'll be presented to the company and they'll have the chance to come meet us."

"Mingle, eh?"

"Just so. Afterwards, we'll be presented to Bianca herself, and she, in turn, will give us a gift."

"A gift?" I asked.

"She's the hosting party. Of course she'll be giving gifts." He smiled at me. "It's only civilized."

I eyed him. I wasn't used to vampires being so chatty. "Why are you being so helpful?"

He laid his fingers upon his chest, lifting his eyebrows in a perfectly executed "who me?" expression. "Why, Mister Dresden. Why should I not help you?"

"You're a vampire."

"So I am," he said. "But, I'm afraid, I'm not a terribly good one." He gave me a sunny smile and said, "Of course, I could also be lying."

I snorted.

"So, Mister Dresden. Rumor had it you had refused Bianca's invitation."

"I had."

"What changed your mind?"

"Business."

"Business?" Thomas asked. "You're here on business?"

I shrugged. "Something like that." I stripped off my gloves, trying to look casual, and offered him my hand. "Thanks again."

His head tilted to one side and he narrowed his eyes. He looked down at my hand and then back up at me, his gaze calculating, before trading grips with me.

There was a faint, flickering aura about him. I felt it dance and glide over my skin like a soft, cool wind. It felt odd, different than the energy that surrounded a human practitioner—and nothing like the sense of whatever had been pumping up the Nightmare.

Thomas wasn't my man. I must have relaxed visibly, because he smiled and said, "I pass the test, eh?"

"I don't know what you're talking about."

"Whatever you say. You're an odd duck, Harry Dresden. But I like you." And with that, he and his escort turned and glided together down the length of the entry hall, and through the curtained doors at the far end.

I glowered after them.

"Anything?" Michael asked.

"He's clean," I said. "Relatively speaking. Must be someone else here."

"You'll get the chance to do some handshaking, it sounds like," Michael said.

"Yeah. You ready?"

"Lord willing," Michael said.

We started together down the hall, and through the curtained doorway, and emerged into Vampire Party Central.

We stood on a concrete deck, elevated ten feet off the rest of a vast, outdoor courtyard. Music flowed up from below. People crowded the courtyard in a blur of color and motion, talk and costume, like some kind of Impressionist painting. Glowing globes rested on wire stands, here and there, giving the place a sort of torch-lit mystique. A dias, opposite the entryway we stood in, rose up several feet higher in the air, a suspiciously throne-like chair upon it.

I had just started to take in details when a brilliant white light flooded my eyes, and I had to lift a hand against it. The music died down a bit, and the chatter of people quieted some. Evidently, Michael and I had just become the center of attention.

A servant stepped forward and asked, calmly, "May I have your invitation, sir?" I passed it over, and a moment later heard the same voice, over a modest public address system.

"Ladies and gentlemen of the Court. I am pleased to present Harry Dresden, Wizard of the White Council, and guest."

I lowered my hands, and the voices fell completely silent. From either side of the throne opposite, a pair of spotlights glared at me.

I shrugged my shoulders to get my cape to fall into place correctly, tattered red lining flashing against the black cotton exterior. The collar of the thing came up high on either side of my face.

The spot glared off of the painted gold plastic medallion I wore at my throat. The worn powder-blue tux beneath it could have made an appearance at someone's prom, in the seventies. The servants at the party had better tuxes than I did.

I made sure to smile, so that they could see the cheap plastic fangs. I suppose the spotlight must have bleached my face out to ghostly whiteness, especially with the white clown makeup I had on. The fake blood drooling out the corners of my mouth would be standing out bright red against it.

I lifted a white-gloved hand and said, slurring a little through the fangs. "Hi! How are you all doing?"

My words rang out on deathly silence, from below.

"I still can't believe," Michael said, sotto voce, "that you came to the Vampires' Masquerade Ball dressed as a vampire."

"Not just a vampire," I said, "a *cheesy* vampire. Do you think they got the point?" I managed to peer past the spotlights enough to make out Thomas and Justine at the foot of the stairs. Thomas was staring around at the courtyard with undisguised glee, then flashed me a smile and a thumbs-up.

"I think," Michael said, "that you've just insulted everyone here."

"I'm here to find a monster, not make nice with them. Besides, I never wanted to come to this stupid party in the first place."

"All the same. I think you've peeved them off."

"Peeved? Come on. How bad could that be? Peeved."

From the courtyard below came several distinctive sounds: A few hisses. The rasp of steel as several someones drew knives. Or maybe swords. The nervous *click-clack* of someone with a semi-automatic working the slide.

Michael shrugged in his cloak, and I sensed, more than saw him put his hand on the hilt of one of his knives. "I think we're about to find out."

Chapter 25

Silence lay heavy over the courtyard. I gripped my cane and waited for the first gunshot, or whistle of a thrown knife, or blood-curdling scream of fury. Michael was a steel-smelling presence beside me, silent and confident in the face of the hostility. Hell's bells. I'd meant to give the vamps a little thumb of the nose with the costume, but wow. I didn't think I'd net *this* much of a reaction.

"Steady, Harry," Michael murmured. "They're like mean dogs. Don't flinch or run. It will only set them off."

"Your average mean dog doesn't have a gun," I murmured back. "Or a knife. Or a sword." But I remained where I stood, my expression bland.

The first sound to ring out was neither gunshot nor battle cry, but rich, silvery laughter. It drifted up, masculine, somehow merry and mocking, bubbling and scornful all at once. I squinted down through the lights, to see Thomas, posed like some bizarre post-chrysalis incarnation of Errol Flynn, one foot up on the stairs, hand braced, his other hand on the crystalline hilt of his sword. His head was thrown back, every lean line of muscle on him displayed with the casual disregard of skilled effort. The butterfly wings caught the light at the edges of the spots and threw them back in dazzling colors.

"I've always heard," Thomas drawled, his voice loud enough to be heard by all, artfully projected, "that the Red Court gave its guests a warm welcome. I hadn't thought I'd get such a picturesque demonstration, though." He turned toward the dias and bowed. "Lady Bianca, I'll be sure to tell my father all about this dizzying display of hospitality."

I felt my smile harden, and I peered past the spotlights to the dias. "Bianca, dear, there you are. This *was* a costume party, was it not? A masquerade? And we were all supposed to come dressed as something we weren't? If I misread the invitation, I apologize."

I heard a woman's voice murmur something, and the spotlights flicked off. I was left in the dark for a minute, until my eyes could adjust, and I could regard the woman standing across from me, upon the dias.

Bianca wasn't tall, but she was statuesque in a way you only find in erotic magazines and embarrassing dreams. Pale of skin, dark of hair and eye, full of sensuous curves, from her mouth to her hips, everything possessed of luscious ripeness coupled with slender strength that would have caught the eye of any man. She wore a gown of flickering flame. I don't mean that she wore a red dress—she *wore* flame, gathered about her in the shape of an evening gown, blue at its base fading through the colors of a candle to red as it cupped her full, gorgeous breasts. More flame danced and played through the elegant piles of her dark hair, flickering over her like a tiara. She had on a pair of real heels at least, adding several inches to her rather unimpressive height. The shoes did interesting things to the shape of her legs. The curve of her smile promised things that were probably illegal, and bad for you, and would carry warnings from the Surgeon General, but that you'd still want to do over and over again.

I wasn't interested. I had seen what was underneath her mask, once before. I couldn't forget what was there.

"Well," she purred, her voice carrying over the whole of the courtyard. "I suppose I shouldn't have expected any more taste from you, Mister Dresden. Though perhaps we will see about your taste, later in the evening." Her tongue played over her teeth, and she gave me a dazzling smile.

I watched her, watched behind her. A pair of figures in black cloaks, hardly more than vague shapes behind her stood quietly, as though ready to attack if she snapped a finger. I suppose every decent flame casts shadows. "I think you'd better not try it."

Bianca laughed again. Several in the courtyard joined in with her, though it was a nervous thing. "Mister Dresden," she said. "Many things can change a man's mind." She crossed her legs, slowly, flashing naked skin up to her taut, silky thigh as she did. "Perhaps we'll find something that changes yours." She waved her hand, lazy and arrogant. "Music. We are here to celebrate. Let us do so."

The music began again while I sorted out the meaning behind what Bianca had just said. She had given her tacit permission for her people to try to get to me. They couldn't just walk up and bite me, maybe, but yeesh. I'd have to be on my guard. I thought of Kelly Hamilton's narcotic kisses on my throat, the glowing warmth that had surrounded me, infused me, and shivered. Some part of me wondered what it might be like to let the vamps catch me, and if it would be all that bad. Another chewed furiously over everything I'd seen so far that evening—Bianca clearly had something in mind.

I shook my head and glanced back at Michael. He nodded to me, a slight motion beneath the great helm, and we both descended the stairs. My legs were shaking, making the trip down unsteady. I prayed that none of the vamps noticed it. Wouldn't do to let them see weakness. Even if I was as nervous as a bird in a coal mine.

"Do what you need to do, Harry," Michael said, low. "I'll be a couple steps behind you, to your right. I'll watch your back."

Michael's words steadied me, calmed me, and I felt profoundly grateful for them.

I expected the vamps to descend on me in a charming and dangerous cloud when I reached the courtyard, but they didn't. Instead, Thomas was waiting for me with one hand on the hilt of his sword, his pale body on shameless display. Justine stood a bit behind him. His face practically glowed with glee.

"Oh, *my,* that was marvelous, Harry. May I call you Harry?"

"No," I said. I caught myself, though, and tried to soften the answer. "But thanks. For what you said, when you did. Things might have gotten ugly."

Thomas's eyes danced. "They still might, Mister Dresden. But we couldn't have it descending into a general brawl, now could we?"

"We couldn't?"

"No, of course not. There would be far fewer opportunities to seduce and deceive and backstab."

I snorted. "I suppose you've got a point."

The tip of his tongue touched his teeth when he smiled. "I usually do."

"Um, thanks, Thomas."

He glanced aside, and frowned. I followed his gaze. Justine had drifted away from him, and now stood with a bright smile on her sweet face as she spoke to a lean, smiling man dressed in a scarlet tux and a domino mask. While I watched, the man reached out and stroked his fingers over her shoulder. He made some comment that made the lovely girl laugh.

"Excuse me," Thomas said with distaste. "I can't abide poachers. Do enjoy the party, Mister Dresden."

He drifted off toward them, and Michael stepped up to me. I half-turned my head toward him, to hear him murmur, "They're surrounding us."

I looked around. The courtyard was full of people. Many of them were young, pretty folk, dressed in all manner of black, poster children for the Goth subculture. Leather, plastic, and fishnet seemed to be the major themes in display, complete with black domino masks, heavy hoods upon cloaks, and a variety of different kinds of face paint. They talked and laughed, drank and danced to the music. Some of them wore a band of scarlet cloth about their arm, or a bloodred choker around their throats.

While I watched, I saw a too-lean young man bend over a table to inhale something through one nostril. A trio of giggling girls, two blondes and a brunette, all dressed up like Dracula's cheerleading squad, complete with black-and-red pom-poms, counted to three together and washed down a pair of pills with glasses of dark wine. Other young people pressed together in sensual motion, or simply sat or stood kissing, touching. A few, already partied out, lay upon the courtyard, smiling dreamily, their eyes closed.

I scanned the crowd with my eyes, and picked out the differences at once. Drifting among the young people clad in black were lean figures in scarlet—perhaps two or three dozen, in all. Male and female, of a variety of appearances and costumes, all shared the scarlet clothes, beauty, and a confident, stalking kind of motion that marked them as predators.

"The Red Court," I said. I licked my lips, and looked around some more. The vampires were being casual about it, but they had wandered into a ring around us. If we remained there any longer, we wouldn't be able to walk out of the courtyard without coming within a few feet of one of them. "The kids with the red bands are what? Junior vampires?"

"Marked cattle, I'd say," Michael rumbled. There was anger in it, steady and slow anger.

"Easy, Michael. We need to move around a little. Make it harder for them to hem us in."

"Agreed." Michael nodded toward the drink table, and we

headed that way, our pace brisk. The vamps tried to adjust to follow us, but they couldn't make it look casual.

A couple in red moved to intercept us, meeting Michael and me just before we reached the table. Kyle Hamilton wore a harlequin's outfit, all in shades of scarlet. Kelly followed along with him, dressed in a scarlet body stocking that left nothing to the imagination, but with a long cloak covering her shoulders and collarbones, the hood up high around her face. A scarlet mask hid her features, except for her chin and luscious mouth. I thought I could see a puckering of the skin at one side of her mouth—perhaps the burns she'd suffered.

"Harry Dresden." Kyle greeted me in a too-loud voice, with a too-wide smile. "How pleasant to see you again."

I chucked him boisterously on the shoulder, making his balance waver. "I wish it was mutual."

The smile became brittle. "And of course you remember my sister, Kelly."

"Sure, sure," I said. "Hit that tanning bed a little too long, did we?"

I expected her to snarl or hiss or go for my throat. But instead she turned to the table, collected a silver goblet and a crystal wineglass from the attendant there, and offered them to us with a smile that mirrored her brother's. "It's so pleasant to see you, Harry. I'm sorry that we didn't get to see the lovely Miss Rodriguez tonight."

I accepted the goblet. "She had to wash her hair."

Kelly turned to Michael and offered him the glass. He accepted it with an inclination of his head, stiffly polite. "I see," she purred. "I had no idea you were into men, Mister Dresden."

"What can I say? They're just so big and strong."

"Of course," Kyle said. "If I was surrounded by people who wanted to kill me as badly as I want to kill you, I'd want a bodyguard about, too."

Kelly sidled up to Michael, her breasts thrust forward, straining the sheer fabric of the body stocking. She walked in a slow circle around him, while Michael remained standing just as he was. "He's gorgeous," she purred. "May I give him a kiss, Mister Dresden?"

"Harry," Michael said.

"He's married, Kelly. Sorry."

She laughed, pressing close to Michael, and tried to catch his eyes. Michael frowned, and stared at nothing, avoiding her. "No?" she asked. "Well. Don't worry, pretty man. You'll love it.

Everyone wants to party like it's their last night on earth." She flashed a wicked smile up at him. "Now you get to."

"The young lady is too kind," Michael said.

"So stiff. I admire that in a man." She shot me a glance from behind her mask. "You really shouldn't drag poor defenseless mortals into these things, Mister Dresden." She looked Michael up and down again, admiring. "This one will be delicious, later."

"Don't bite off more than you can chew," I advised her.

She laughed, as though delighted. "Well, Mister Dresden. I see his crosses, but we all know the value of them to most of the world." She reached her hand toward Michael's arm, possessively. "For a moment, you almost had me thinking that he might be a true Knight Templar."

"No," I said judiciously. "Not a Knight Templar."

Kelly's hand touched Michael's steel-clad arm—and erupted into sudden, white flame, as brief and violent as a stroke of lightning. She screamed, a piercing wail, and fell back from him to the ground. She lay there, curled helplessly around her blackened hand, struggling to get enough breath back to scream. Kyle flew to her side.

I looked at Michael and blinked. "Wow," I said. "Color me impressed."

Michael looked vaguely embarrassed. "It happens like that sometimes," he said, apologetically.

I nodded and took that in stride. I turned my gaze back to the vampire twins. "Let that be a lesson to you. Hands off the Fist of God."

Kyle shot me a murderous look, his face rippling.

My heart sped up, but I couldn't let the fear show. "Go ahead, Kyle," I dared him. "Start something. Break the truce your own leader set up. Violate the laws of hospitality. The White Council will burn this place down so fast, people will call it Little Pompeii."

He snarled at me, and picked Kelly up. "This isn't over," he promised. "One way or another, Dresden. I'll kill you."

"Uh-huh." I flicked my wrist at him, my hand right in his face. "Shoo, shoo. I have to mingle."

Kyle snarled. But the pair withdrew, and I turned my gaze slowly around the courtyard. Everything in the immediate vicinity had stopped while people, black- and red-clad alike, stared at us. Some of the vampires in scarlet looked at Michael, swallowed, and took a couple of steps back.

I grinned, as cocky and as confident as I could appear, and lifted my glass. "A toast," I said. "To hospitality."

They were quiet for a moment, then hurriedly mumbled an echo to my toast and sipped from their drinks. I drained my goblet in a single gulp, hardly noticing the delightful flavor of it, and turned to Michael. He lifted his glass to the mouth of his helm in a token sip, but didn't take any.

"All right," I said. "I got to touch Kyle. He's out, too, though I didn't expect him to be our man. Or woman. Or monster."

Michael looked slowly around as the scarlet-clad vampires continued to withdraw. "It looks like we've cowed them for now."

I nodded, still uneasy. The crowd parted at one side, and Thomas and Justine came to us, blazes of pale skin and brilliant color amidst the scarlet and black. "There you are," Thomas said. He glanced down at my goblet and let out a sigh. "I'm glad I found you in time."

"In time for what?" I asked.

"To warn you," he said. He flicked a hand at the refreshments table. "The wine is poisoned."

Chapter 26

"Poisoned?" I said, witlessly.

Thomas peered at my face and then down at my goblet. He leaned over it enough to see that it was empty and said, "Ah. Oops."

"Harry." Michael stepped up beside me, and set his own glass aside. "I thought you said that they couldn't try anything so overt."

My stomach kept churning. My heart beat more quickly, though whether this was from the poison or the simple, cold fear that Thomas's words had brought to me, I couldn't say. "They can't," I said. "If I pitch over dead, the Council would know what happened. I sent word in today that I was coming here tonight."

Michael shot Thomas a hard look. "What was in the wine?"

The pale man shrugged, slipping his arm around Justine once more. The girl leaned against him and closed her eyes. "I don't know what they put in it," he said. "But look at these people." He nodded to those black-clad folk who were already stretched out blissfully upon the ground. "They all have wineglasses."

I looked a bit closer and it was true. The servants moved about the courtyard, plucking up glasses from the fallen. As I watched, another young couple, dancing slowly together, sank down to the ground in a long, deep kiss that faded away into simple stillness.

"Hell's bells," I swore. "That's what they're doing."

"What?" Michael asked.

"They don't want me dead," I said. "Not from this." I didn't have much time. I stalked past the refreshments table to a potted fern and bent over it. I heard Michael take up a position behind me, guarding my back. I shoved a finger down my throat. Simple, quick, nasty. The wine burned my throat coming back up, and the fern's fronds tickled the back of my neck as I spat it back out into the base of the plant. My head spun as I sat back up again, and when I looked back toward Michael, everything blurred for a moment before it snapped back into focus. A slow, delicious numbness spread over my fingers.

"Everyone," I mumbled.

"What?" Michael knelt down in front of me and gripped my shoulder with one arm. "Harry, are you all right?"

"I'm fuzzy," I said. Vampire venom. Naturally. It felt good to have it in me again, and I wondered, for a moment, what I was so worried about. It was just that nice. "It's for everyone. They're drugging everyone's wine. Vamp venom. That way they can say they weren't just targeting me." I wobbled, and then stood up. "Recreational poisoning. Put everyone in the party mood."

Thomas mused. "Rather ham-handed, I suppose, but effective." He looked around at the growing numbers of young people joining the first few upon the ground in ecstatic stupor. His fingers stroked Justine's flank absently, and she shivered, pressing closer to him. "I suppose I'm prejudiced. I prefer my prey a little more lively."

"We've got to get you out of here," Michael said.

I gritted my teeth, and tried to push the pleasant sensations aside. The venom had to have an enormously quick absorption rate. Even if I'd brought the wine back up, I must have gotten a fairly good dose. "No," I managed after a moment. "That's what they want me to do."

"Harry, you can barely stand up," Michael objected.

"You are looking a bit peaked," Thomas said.

"Bah. If they want me incapacitated, it means they've got something to hide."

"Or just that they want you to get killed," Michael said. "Or drugged enough to agree to let one of them feed on you."

"No," I disagreed. "If they wanted to seduce me, they'd have tried something else. They're trying to scare me off. Or keep me from finding something out."

"I hate to point out the obvious," Thomas said, "but why on earth would Bianca invite you if she didn't want you to be here?"

"She's obligated to invite the Council to witness. That means me, in this town. And she didn't expect me to actually show—pretty much everyone was surprised to see me at all."

"They didn't think you'd come," Michael murmured.

"Yeah. Ain't I a stinker." I took a couple of deep breaths and said, "I think the one we're after is here, Michael. We've got to stick this out for a little while. See if I can find out exactly who it is."

"Exactly who is what?" Thomas asked.

"None of your beeswax, Thomas," I said.

"Has anyone ever told you, Mister Dresden, that you are a thoroughly annoying man?" That made me grin, to which he rolled his eyes. "Well," he said, "I'll not intrude on your business any further. Let me know if there's anything I can do for you." He and Justine sauntered off into the crowd.

I watched Justine's legs go, leaning on my cane a bit to help me balance. "Nice guy," I commented.

"For a vampire," Michael said. "Don't trust him, Harry. There's something about him I don't like."

"Oh, I like him," I said. "But I sure as hell don't trust him."

"What do we do now?"

"Look around. So far we've got food in black, the vampires in red, and then there's you and me, and a handful of other people in different costumes."

"The Roman centurion," Michael said.

"Yeah. And some Hamlet-looking guy. Let's go see what they are."

"Harry," Michael asked. "Are you going to be okay?"

I swallowed. I felt dizzy, a little sickened. I had to fight to get clear thoughts through, bulldogging them against the pull of the venom. I was surrounded by things that looked at people like we look at cows, and felt fairly sure that I was going to get myself killed if I stayed.

Of course, if I didn't stay, other people could get killed. If I didn't stay, the people who had already been hurt remained in danger: Charity. Michael's infant son. Murphy. If I didn't stay, the Nightmare would have time to recuperate, and then it and its corporate sponsor, who I thought was here at this party, would feel free to keep taking pot shots at me.

The thought of remaining in that place scared me. The thought of what could happen if I gave up now scared me a lot more.

"Come on," I said. "Let's get this over with."

Michael nodded, looking around, his grey eyes dark, hard. "This is an abomination before the Lord, Harry. These people.

They're barely more than children . . . what they're doing. Consorting with these *things*."

"Michael. Chill *out*. We're here to get information, not bring the house down on a bunch of nasties."

"Samson did," Michael said.

"Yeah, and look how well things turned out for him. You ready?"

He muttered something, and fell in behind me again. I looked around and oriented on the man dressed as a Roman centurion, then headed toward him. A man of indefinite years, he stood alone and slightly detached from the rest of the crowd. His eyes were an odd color of green, deep and intense. He held a cigarette between his lips. His gear, right down to the Roman short sword and sandals, looked awfully authentic. I slowed a little as I approached him, staring.

"Michael," I murmured, over my shoulder. "Look at his costume. It looks like the real thing."

"It *is* the real thing," said the man in a bored tone of voice, not looking at me. He exhaled a plume of smoke, then put the cigarette back between his lips. Michael would have barely been able to hear my question. This guy had picked it right out. Gulp.

"Interesting," I said. "Must have cost you a fortune to put together."

He glanced at me. Smoke curled from the corners of his mouth as he gave me a very slight, very smug smirk. And said nothing.

"So," I said, and cleared my throat. "I'm Harry Dresden."

The man pursed his lips and said, thoughtfully and precisely, "Harry. Dresden."

When someone, anyone, says your name, it touches you. You almost feel it, that sound that stands out from a crowd of others and demands your attention. When a wizard says your Name, when he says it and *means* it, it has the same effect, amplified a thousandfold. The man in the centurion gear said my part of my Name and said it exactly right. It felt like someone had just rung a tuning fork and pressed it against my teeth.

I staggered, and Michael caught my shoulder, keeping me upright. Dear God. He had just used one *part* of my full name, my true Name, to reach out to me and casually backhand me off my feet.

"Hell's bells," I whispered. Michael propped me back up. I

planted my cane, so that I would have an extra support, and just stared at the man. "How the hell did you *do* that?"

He rolled his eyes, took the cigarette in his fingers and blew more smoke. "You wouldn't understand."

"You're not White Council," I said.

He looked at me as though I had just stated that objects fall toward the ground; a withering, scathing glance. "How very fortunate for me."

"Harry," Michael said, his voice tense.

"Just a minute."

"Harry. Look at his cigarette."

I blinked at Michael. "What?"

"Look at his cigarette," Michael repeated. He was staring at the man with wide, intent eyes, and one hand had fallen to the hilt of a knife.

I looked. It took me a minute to realize what Michael was talking about.

The man blew more smoke out of the corner of his mouth, and smirked at me.

The cigarette wasn't lit.

"He's," I said. "He's, uh."

"He's a dragon," Michael said.

"A what?"

The man's eyes flickered with interest for the first time, and he narrowed his focus—not upon me, but upon Michael. "Just so," he said. "You may call me Mister Ferro."

"Why don't I just call you Ferrovax," Michael said.

Mister Ferro narrowed his eyes, and regarded Michael with a dispassionate gaze. "You know something of the lore, at least, mortal."

"Wait a minute," I said. "Dragons . . . dragons are supposed to be *big.* Scales, claws, wings. This guy isn't big."

Ferro rolled his eyes and said, impatient, "We are what we wish to be, Master Drafton."

"Dresden," I snapped.

He waved a hand. "Don't tempt me to show you what I can do by speaking your name and making an effort, mortal. Suffice to say that you could not comprehend the kind of power I have at my command. That my true form here would shatter this pathetic gathering of monkey houses and crack the earth upon which I stand. If you gazed upon me with your wizard's sight, you would see something that would awe you, humble you, and quite probably destroy your reason. I am the eldest of my kind, and the strongest. Your life is a flickering candle to me, and your civilizations rise and fall like grass in the summer."

"Well," I said. "I don't know about your true form, but the weight of your ego sure is pushing the crust of the earth toward the breaking point."

His green eyes blazed. "What did you say?"

"I don't like bullies," I said. "You think I'm going to stand here and offer you my firstborn and sacrifice virgins to you or something? I'm not that impressed."

"Well," Ferro said. "Let's see if we can't make an impression."

I clutched my cane and gathered up my will, but I was way, way too slow. Ferro just waved a hand vaguely in my direction, and something crushed me down to the earth, as though I suddenly had gained about five thousand pounds. I felt my lungs strain to haul in a breath, and my vision clouded over with stars and went black. I tried to gather up my magic, to thrust the force away from me, but I couldn't focus, couldn't speak.

Michael looked down at me dispassionately, then said, to Ferro, "Siriothrax should have learned that trick. It might have kept me from killing him."

Ferro's cold regard swept back to Michael, bringing with it a tiny lessening in the pressure—not much, but enough that I could gasp out, *"Riflettum,"* and focus my will against it. Ferro's spell cracked and began to flake apart. I saw him look at me, sensed that he could have renewed the effort without difficulty. He didn't. I climbed back to my feet, gasping quietly.

"So," Ferro said. "You are the one." He looked Michael up and down. "I thought you'd be taller."

Michael shrugged. "It wasn't anything personal. I'm not proud of what I did."

Ferro tapped a finger against the hilt of his sword. Then said, quietly, "Sir Knight. I would advise you to be more humble in the face of your betters." He cast a disdainful glance at me. "And you might consider a gag for this one, until he can learn better manners."

I tried for a comeback, but I still couldn't breathe. I just leaned against my cane and wheezed. Ferro and Michael exchanged a short nod, one where neither of them looked away from the other's eyes. Then Ferro turned and . . . well, just vanished. No flicker of light, no puff of flame. Just gone.

"Harry," Michael chided. "You're not the biggest kid on the block. You've got to learn to be a little more polite."

"Good advice," I wheezed. "Next time, you handle any dragons."

"I will." He looked around and said, "People are thinning out, Harry." He was right. As I watched, a vampire in a tight red dress tapped the arm of a young man in black. He glanced over to her and met her eyes. They stared at one another for a while, the woman smiling, the man's expression going slowly slack. Then she murmured something and took his hand, leading him out into the darkness beyond the globes of light. Other vamps were drawing more young people along with them. There were fewer scarlet costumes around, and more people blissed out on the ground.

"I don't like the direction this is going," I said.

"Nor do I." His voice was hard as stone. "Lord willing, we can put a stop to this."

"Later. First, we talk to the Hamlet guy. Then there's just Bianca herself to check."

"Not one of the other vampires?" Michael asked.

"No way. They're all subordinate to Bianca. If they were that strong, they'd have knocked her off by now, unless they were in her inner circle. That's Kyle and Kelly. She doesn't have the presence of mind for it, and he's already out. So if it's not a guest, it's probably Bianca."

"And if it's not her?"

"Let's not go there. I'm floundering enough as it is." I squinted around. "Do you see Hamlet anywhere?"

Michael squinted around, taking a few paces to peer around another set of ferns.

I saw the flash of red out of the corner of my eye, saw a form in a red cloak heading for Michael's back, from around the ferns. I turned toward Michael and threw myself at his attacker.

"Look out!" I shouted. Michael spun, a knife appearing in his hand as though conjured. I grabbed the red cloaked-figure and whirled it around to face me.

The hood fell back from Susan's face, revealing her startled dark eyes. She'd pulled her hair into a ponytail. She wore a low-cut white blouse and a little pleated skirt, complete with white knee socks and buckle-down shoes. White gloves covered her hands. A wicker basket dangled in the crook of her elbow, and round, mirror-toned spectacles perched upon the bridge of her slender nose.

"Susan?" I stammered. "What are you doing here?"

She let out a breath, and drew her arm out of my hand. "God, Harry. You scared me."

"What are you *doing* here?" I demanded.

"You know why I'm here," she said. "I came to get a story. I tried to call you and talk you into it, but *no,* you were way too busy doing whatever you were doing to even spare five minutes to talk to me."

"I don't believe this," I muttered. "How did you get in here?"

She looked at me coolly and flicked open her basket. She reached inside and came out with a neat white invitation, like my own. "I got myself an invitation."

"You *what*?"

"Well. I had it made, in any case. I didn't think you'd mind me borrowing yours for a few minutes."

Which explained why the invitation hadn't been on the mantel, back at my apartment. "Hell's bells, Susan, you don't know what you've done. You've got to get out of here."

She snorted. "Like hell."

"I mean it," I said. "You're in danger."

"Relax, Harry. I'm not letting anyone lick me, and I'm not looking anyone in the eyes. It's kind of like visiting New York." She tapped her specs with a gloved finger. "Things have gone all right so far."

"You don't get it," I said. "You don't understand."

"Don't understand what?" she demanded.

"You don't understand," purred a dulcet voice, behind me. My blood ran cold. "By coming uninvited, you have waived any right you had to the protection of the laws of hospitality." There came a soft chuckle. "It means, Little Red Riding Hood, that the Big, Bad Wolf gets to eat you all up."

Chapter 27

I turned to find Lea facing me, her hands on her hips. She wore a slender, strapless dress of pale blue, which flowed over her curves like water, crashing into white foamy lace at its hem. She wore a cape of some material so light and sheer that it seemed almost unreal, and it drifted around her, catching the light in an opalescent sheen that trapped little rainbows and set them to dancing against her pale skin. When people talk about models or movie stars being glamorous, they take it from the old word, from *glamour,* from the beauty of the high sidhe, faerie magic. Supermodels wish they had it so good as Lea.

"Why, Godmother," I said, "what big eyes you have. Are we straining the metaphor or what?"

She drifted closer to me. "I don't make metaphors, Harry. I'm too busy being one. Are you enjoying the party?"

I snorted. "Oh, sure. Watching them drug and poison children and getting roughed up by every weird and nasty thing in Chicagoland is a real treat." I turned to Susan and said, "We have to get you out of here."

Susan frowned at me and said, "I didn't come here so that you could hustle me home, Harry."

"This isn't a game, Susan. These thing are dangerous." I glanced over at Lea. She kept drawing closer. "I don't know if I can protect you."

"Then I'll protect myself," Susan said. She laid her hand over the picnic basket. "I came prepared."

"Michael," I said. "Would you get her out of here?"

Michael stepped up beside us, and said, to Susan, "It's dangerous. Maybe you should let me take you home."

Susan narrowed her dark eyes at me. "If it's so dangerous, then I don't want to leave Harry here alone."

"She has a point, Harry."

"Dammit. We came here to find out who's behind the Nightmare. If I leave before I do that, we might as well never have come. Just go, and I'll catch up with you."

"Yes," Lea said. "Do go. I'll be sure to take good care of my godson."

"No," Susan said, her tone flat. "Absolutely not. I'm not some kind of child for you to tote around and make decisions for, Harry."

Lea's smile sharpened, and she reached a hand toward Susan, touching her chin. "Let me see those pretty eyes, little one," she purred.

I shot my hand toward my godmother's wrist, jerking it away from Susan before the faerie could touch her. Her skin was silk-smooth, cool. Lea smiled at me, the expression stunning. Literally. My head swam, images of the faerie sorceress flooding my thoughts: those berry-sweet lips pressing to my naked chest, smeared with my blood, rose-tipped breasts bared by the light of fire and full moon, her hair a sheet of silken flame on my skin.

Another flash of image came then, accompanied by intense emotion: myself, looking up at her as I lay at her feet. She stretched out her hand and lightly touched my head, an absently fond gesture. An overwhelming sense of well-being filled me like shining, liquid light, poured into me and filled every empty place within me, calmed every fear, soothed every pain. I almost wept at the simple relief, at the abrupt release from worry, from hurt. My whole body trembled.

I was just so damned tired. So tired of hurting. Of being afraid.

"So it will be when you are with me, poor little one, poor lonely child." Lea's voice coursed over me, as sweet as the drug already within me. I knew she spoke the truth. I knew it on a level so deep and simple that a part of me screamed at myself for struggling to avoid her.

So easy. It would be so easy to lay down at my lady's feet, now. So easy to let her make all the bad things go away. She would care for me. She would comfort me. My place would be there, in the warmth at her feet, staring up at her beauty—

Like a good dog.

It's tough to say no to peace, to the comfort of it. All through history, people have traded wealth, children, land, and lives to buy it.

But peace can't be bought, can it, chief, prime minister? The only ones offering to sell it always want something more. They lie.

I shoved the feelings away from me, the subtle glamour my godmother had cast. I could have taken a cheese grater to my own skin with less pain. But my pain, my weariness, my worries and fear—they were at least my own. They were honest. I gathered them back to me like a pack of mud-spattered children and stared at Lea, hardening my jaw, my heart. "No," I said. "No, Lea."

Surprise touched those delicate features. Dainty copper brows lifted. "Harry," she said, her voice gentle, perplexed, "the bargain is already made. So mote it be. There is no reason for you to go on hurting."

"There are people who need me," I said. My balance wavered. "I still have a job to do."

"Broken faiths weaken you. They bind you tighter, lessen you every time you go against your given oath." She sounded concerned, genuinely compassionate. "Godson, I beg of you—do not do this to yourself."

I said, struggling to be calm, "Because if I do that, there will be less for you to eat, yes? Less power for you to take."

"It would be a terrible waste," she assured me. "No one wants that."

"We're under *truce* here, Godmother. You're not allowed to work magic on me without violating hospitality."

"But I didn't," Lea said. "I've not worked any magic on you this night."

"Bullshit."

She laughed, silver and merry. "Such language, and in front of your lover too."

I stumbled. Michael was there at once, supporting my weight with his shoulder, drawing my arm across it. "Harry," he said. "What is it? What's wrong?"

My head kept on spinning and my limbs started to shake. The drug already coursing through me, plus this new weakness, almost took me out. Blackness swam in front of my eyes and it was only with an effort of will that I kept myself from drowning in that darkness or giving in to the mad desire to throw myself down at Lea's feet. "I'm okay," I stammered. "I'm fine."

Susan moved to my other side, her anger pouring off of her like heat from a desert highway. "What have you done to him?" she snapped at Lea.

"Nothing," Lea replied in a cool voice. "He has done this to himself, the poor little one. One always risks dire consequences should one not keep a bargain with the sidhe."

"What?" Susan said.

Michael grimaced, and said, "Aye. She's telling the truth. Harry made a bargain last night, when we fought the Nightmare and drove it away from Charity."

I struggled to speak, to warn them not to let Lea trick them, but I was too busy trying to sort out where my mouth was, and why my tongue wasn't working.

"That doesn't give her the right to put a spell on him," Susan snapped.

Michael rumbled, "I don't think she has. I can usually feel it, when someone's done something harmful."

"Of course I haven't," Lea said. "I have no need to do so. He's already done it himself."

What? I thought. *What was she talking about?*

"What?" Susan said. "What are you talking about?"

Lea's voice took on a patient, faux-sympathetic tone. "Poor little poppet. All of your efforts to learn and you still know so little. Harry made a bargain with me long ago—and broke it, once then, and once a few nights past. He swore to uphold it again, last night, and broke it thrice. Now he reaps the consequences of his actions. His own powers turn against him, the poor dear, to encourage him to fulfill his word, to keep his promise."

"They weren't doing it a minute ago," Susan said. "Only when you came up to him."

Lea laughed, warmly. "It's a party, dear poppet. We're here to mingle, after all. And I have lifted no weapon or spell against him. This is of his own doing."

"So back off," Susan said. "Leave him alone."

"Oh, this won't ever leave hm alone, poppet. It's a small thing now, but it will grow, in time. And destroy him, the poor, dear boy. I'd hate so much for that to happen."

"So stop it!"

Lea focused her eyes on Susan. "Do you offer to purchase his debt away from me? I don't think you could afford it, dear poppet . . . though I think surcease could be arranged."

Susan shot a quick glance at me, and then Michael. "Surcease? Purchase?"

Michael watched Lea, grimly. "She's a faerie—"

Lea's voice crackled with irritation. "A *sidhe*."

Michael looked at my godmother and continued, "A faerie, Miss Rodriguez, and they're prone to making bargains. And to getting the better of mortals when they do."

Susan's mouth hardened. She was silent for a moment, and then said, "How much, witch? How much for you to make this stop hurting Harry?"

I struggled to say something, but my mouth didn't work. Things spun faster instead of slowing down. I sagged more, and Michael labored to keep me on my feet.

"Why, poppet," Lea purred. "What do you offer?"

"I don't have much money," Susan began.

"Money. What is money." Lea shook her head. "No, child. Such things mean nothing to me. But let me see." She walked in a slow circle around Susan, frowning at her, looking her up and down. "Such pretty eyes, even though they are dark. They will do."

"My *eyes*?" Susan stammered.

"No?" Lea asked. "Very well. Your Name, perhaps? Your whole Name?"

"Don't," Michael said at once.

"I know," Susan answered him. She looked at Lea and said, "I know better than that. If you had my Name, you could do anything you wanted."

Lea thrust out her lip. "Her eyes and her Name are too precious to allow her beloved to escape his trap. Very well, then. Let us ask of her a different price." Her eyes gleamed and she leaned toward Susan. "Your love," she murmured. "Give me that."

Susan arched her brows and peered over her spectacles. "Honey, you want me to love you? You've got a lot of surprises coming, if you think it works like that."

"I didn't ask you to love me," Lea said, her tone offended. "I asked for your love. But well enough, if that is also too steep a price, perhaps memory will do instead."

"My memory?"

"Not all of it," Lea said. She tilted her head to one side and purred, "Indeed. Only some. Perhaps the worth of one year. Yes, I think that would suffice."

Susan looked uncertain. "I don't know . . ."

"Then let him suffer. He won't live the night, with those arrayed against him. Such a loss." Lea turned to leave.

"Wait," Susan said, and clutched at Lea's arm. "I . . . I'll make the trade. For Harry's sake. One year of my memory, and you make whatever is happening stop."

"Memory for relief. Done," Lea purred. She leaned forward and placed a gentle kiss upon Susan's forehead, then shivered, drawing in her breath in a swift inhalation, the tips of her breasts hardening against the silky fabric of her dress. "Oh. Oh, sweet poppet. What a dear thing you are." Then she turned and slapped me across the face with a sharp sound of impact, and I tumbled down to the ground despite Michael's best efforts.

My head abruptly cleared. The narcotic throb of the vampire venom lessened a bit, and I found my thoughts running again, slowly, like a train gathering momentum.

"Witch," Michael hissed up at Lea. "If you hurt either of them again—"

"For shame, Sir Knight," Lea said, her voice dreamy. " 'Tis no fault of mine that Harry made the agreement he did, nor fault of mine that the girl loves him and would give anything for him. Nor was it my doing that the Sword fell ownerless to the ground before me and that I picked it up." She fixed Michael with that dazzling smile. "Should you wish to bargain to have it returned to you, you have only to ask."

"Myself, for the Sword," Michael said. "Done."

She let her head fall back and laughed. "Oh, oh my, dear Knight, no. For once the Redeemer's blade was in your hands again, you would find the shattering of our pact a simple enough matter." Her eyes glittered again. "And you are, in any case, far too . . . restricted, for my tastes. You are set in your ways. Unbendable."

Michael stiffened. "I serve the Lord as I may."

Lea made a face. "Faugh. Just so. Holy." Her smile turned sly again. "But there are others whose lives you hold and can bargain with. You have children, do you not?" She shivered again and said, "Mortal children are so sweet. And can be bent and shaped in so many, many ways. Your eldest daughter, I think, would—"

Michael didn't snarl, didn't roar, didn't make any sounds at all. He simply seized the front of Lea's dress and lifted her clear off the ground by it. His voice came out in a vicious growl. "Stay away from my family, faerie. Or I will set such things in motion against you as will destroy you for all time."

Lea laughed, delighted. " 'Vengeance is mine, saith the Lord,' is how the phrase runs, is it not?" There was a liquid shimmering in the air, and she abruptly stood upon the ground again, facing Michael, out of his grasp. "Your power weakens with rage, dear man. You will not bargain—but I suppose I had plans for the Sword in any case. Until then, good Knight, adieu." She gave me one last smile and a mocking laugh. Then she vanished into the shadows and the darkness.

I gathered myself back to my feet, and mumbled, "That could have gone better."

Michael's eyes glittered with anger beneath his helmet. "Are you all right, Harry?"

"I'm better," I said. "Stars and stones, if this is some kind of self-inflicted spell . . . I'll have to talk to Bob about this one, later." I rubbed at my eyes and asked, "What about you, Michael? Are you all right?"

"Well enough," Michael said. "But we still don't have a culprit, and it's getting late. I've got a bad feeling that we're going to run into trouble if we don't get out of this place soon."

"I've got a feeling you're right," I said. "Susan? Are you okay? You ready to get out of here?"

Susan brushed her hair idly back from her face with one hand, and turned to stare at me, frowning slightly.

"What?" I asked. "Look, you didn't have to do what you did, but we can work on getting it taken care of. Let's just get out of here. Okay?"

"Okay," she said. Then her frown deepened and she peered at me. "This is going to sound odd, but—do I know you?"

Chapter 28

I stared at Susan in mute disbelief.

She looked apologetic. "Oh, I'm sorry. I mean. I didn't mean to upset you, Mister . . ."

"Dresden," I supplied in a whisper.

"Mister Dresden, then." She frowned down at herself, and smoothed a hand uncomfortably over the skirt, then looked around her. "Dresden. Aren't you the guy who just opened a business as a wizard?"

Anger made me clench my teeth. "Son of a—"

"Harry," Michael said. "I think we need to leave, rather than stand about cursing."

My knuckles whitened as I tightened my fingers on my cane. No time for anger. Not now. Michael was right. We had to move, and quickly. "Agreed," I said. "Susan, did you drive here?"

"Hey," she said, squaring off against me. "I don't know you, okay? My name is Miss Rodriguez."

"Look, Su—Miss Rodriguez. My faerie godmother just stole a year's worth of your memory."

"Actually," Michael put in, "you traded it away to her to keep some kind of spell from leaving Harry helpless."

I shot him a glare and he subsided. "And now you don't remember me, or I guess, Michael."

"Or this faerie godmother, either," Susan said, her face and stance still wary.

I shot Lea a look. She glanced over at me and her lips curved up into a smirk, before she turned back to her conversation with Thomas. "Oh, damn. She's such a bitch."

Susan rolled her eyes a little. "Look, guys. It's been nice chatting with you, but this has got to be the lamest excuse for a pick-up line I've ever heard."

I reached a hand toward her again. Her own flashed down into the picnic basket and produced a knife, a G.I.-issue weapon from the last century, its edge gleaming. "I told you," she said calmly, "I don't know you. Don't touch me."

I drew my hand back. "Look. I just want to make sure you're all right."

Susan's breathing was a little fast, but other than that she concealed her tension almost completely. "I'm perfectly fine," she said. "Don't worry about me."

"At least get out of here. You're not safe here. You came in on an invitation you had made up. Do you remember that?"

She screwed up her face into a frown. "How did you know that?" she asked.

"You told me so about five minutes ago," I said, and sighed. "That's what I'm trying to tell you. You've had a bunch of your memories taken."

"I remember coming here," Susan said. "I remember having the counterfeit invitation made."

"I know," I said. "You got it off of my living room table. Do you remember that?"

She frowned. "I got it . . ." Her expression flickered, and she swallowed, glancing around. "I don't remember where I got it."

"There," I said. "Do you see? Do you remember driving out to bail me out of jail a couple of nights ago?"

She'd lowered the knife by now. "I . . . I remember that I went down to the jail. And paid the bail money, but . . . I can't think . . ."

"Okay, okay," I said. My head hurt, and I pinched the bridge of my nose between my thumb and forefinger. "It looks like she took all of your memories that had me directly in them. Or her. What about Michael, do you remember him?"

She looked at Michael and shook her head.

I nodded. "Okay. Then I need to ask you to trust me, Miss Rodriguez. You've been affected by magic and I don't know how we can get it fixed yet. But you're in danger here and I think you should leave."

"Not with you," she said at once. "I have no idea who you are. Other than some kind of psychic consultant for Special Investigations."

"Okay, okay," I said. "Not with me. But at least let us walk you out of here, so that we can make sure you get out okay. You can't swing a cat without hitting a vampire in here. So let us get you out to your car and then you can go wherever you like."

"I didn't get my interview," she said. "But . . . I feel so strange." She shook her head, and replaced her knife in her picnic basket. I heard the click of a tape recorder being switched off. "Okay," she said. "I guess we can go."

I nodded, relieved. "Wonderful. Michael, shall we?"

He chewed on his lip. "Maybe I should stay, Harry. If your godmother's here, the Sword might be here too. I might get the chance to take it back."

"Yeah. And you might get the chance to get taken from behind without someone here to cover for you. There's too much messed up stuff here, man. Even for me. Let's go."

Michael fell in behind me, to my right. Susan walked beside him, on my left, keeping us both in careful view, and one hand still inside her picnic basket. I briefly wondered what kind of goodies she'd been bringing in case the big, bad wolf tried to head her off from grandma's house.

We reached the foot of the stairs that led back up into the house. Something prickled the hairs at the back of my neck, and I stopped.

"Harry?" Michael asked. "What is it?"

"There's someone . . ." I said, and closed my eyes. I brought up my Sight, just for a moment, and felt the pressure just a little above the spot between my eyebrows. I looked up again. The Sight cut through the enchantment in front of me like sunlight through a wispy cloud. Behind me, Michael and Susan both took in sharp breaths of surprise.

The Hamlet lookalike stood three stairs up, half smiling. I realized only then that the figure was a woman rather than a man, the slender shape of her slim hips and breasts obscured by the sable doublet she wore, giving her an odd, androgynous appearance. Her skin was pallid—not pale, not creamy. Pallid. Translucent. Almost greyish. Her lips were tinged very faintly blue, as though she'd been recently chilled. Or dead. I shivered, and lowered the Sight before it showed me something that I didn't want to keep with me.

It didn't change her appearance one bit. She wore a cap, which hid her hair completely, one of those puffy ones that fell over to one side, and stood with one hip cocked out, a rapier hanging from her belt. She held a skull in her other hand—it was a real one. And the bloodstains on it couldn't have been more than a few hours old.

"Well done, wizard," she said. Her voice sounded raspy, a quiet, hissing whisper, the kind that comes from throats and mouths which are perfectly dry. "Very few can see me when I do not wish to be seen."

"Thank you. And excuse me," I said. "We were just leaving."

Bluish lips curved into a chill little smile. Other than that, she didn't move. Not an inch. "Oh, but this is the hour for all to mingle and meet. I have a right to introduce myself to you and to hear your names and exhange pleasantries in return." Her eyes fastened calmly on my face, evidently not fearing to meet my gaze. I figured that whatever she was, she probably had an advantage on me in the devastating gaze department. So I kept my own eyes firmly planted on the tip of her nose, and tried very hard not to notice that her eyes had no color at all, just a kind of flaccid blue-grey tinge to them, a filmy coating like cataracts.

"And what if I don't have time for the pleasantries?" I said.

"Oh," she whispered. "Then I might be insulted. I might even be tempted to call for satisfaction."

"A duel?" I asked, incredulous. "Are you kidding me?"

Her eyes drifted to my right. "Of course, if you would rather a champion fought in your place, I would gladly accept."

I glanced back at Michael, who had his eyes narrowed, focused on the woman's doublet or upon her belt, perhaps. "You know this lady?"

"She's no lady," Michael said, his voice quiet. He had a hand on his knife. "Harry Dresden, Wizard of the White Council, this is Mavra, of the Black Court of Vampires."

"A real vampire," Susan said. I heard the click of her tape recorder coming on again.

"A pleasure," Mavra whispered. "To meet you, at last, wizard. We should talk. I suspect we have much in common."

"I'm failing to see anything we might possibly have in common, ma'am. Do you two know each other?"

"Yes," Michael said.

Mavra's whisper became chill. "The good Knight here murdered my children and grandchildren, some small time ago."

"Twenty years ago," Michael said. "Three dozen people killed in the space of a month. Yes, I put a stop to it."

Mavra's lips curved a little more, and showed yellowed teeth. "Yes. Just a little time ago. I haven't forgotten, Knight."

"Well," I said. "It's been nice chatting, Mavra, but we're on our way out."

"No you're not," Mavra said, calmly. But for her lips and her eyes, she still hadn't moved. It was an eerie stillness, not real. Real things move, stir, breathe. Mavra didn't.

"Yes, we are."

"No. Two of you are on your way out." Her smile turned chilly. "I know that the invitations said only one person could be brought with you. Therefore, one of your companions is not under the protection of the old laws, wizard. If the Knight is unprotected, then he and I will have words. A pity you do not have *Amoracchius* with you, Sir Knight. It would have made things interesting, at least."

I got a sinking feeling in my gut. "And if it isn't Michael?"

"Then you keep offensive company, wizard, and I am displeased with you. I will demonstrate my displeasure decisively." Her gaze swept to Susan. "By all means. Choose which two are leaving. Then I will have a brief conversation with the third."

"You mean you'll kill them."

Mavra shrugged, finally breaking her stillness. I thought I heard a faint crackling of tendons, as though they'd protested moving again. "One must eat, after all. And these little, dazzled morsels the Reds brought tonight are too sweet and insubstantial for my taste."

I took a step back, and turned to Michael, speaking in a whisper. "If I get Susan out of here, can you take this bitch?"

"You might as well not whisper, Harry," Michael said. "It can hear you."

"Yes," Mavra said. "It can."

Way to go, Harry. Endear yourself to the monsters, why don't you. "Well," I asked Michael. "Can you?"

Michael looked at me for a moment, his lips pressed together. Then he said, "Take Susan and go. I'll manage here."

Mavra laughed, a dry and raspy sound. "So very noble. So pure. So self-sacrificing."

Susan stepped around me, to close a triangle with Michael and me. As she did, I noticed that Mavra leaned back from her, just slightly. "Now just a minute," Susan said. "I'm a big girl. I knew the risks when I came here."

"I'm sorry, Miss Rodriguez," Michael said, his tone apologetic. "But this is what I do."

"Save me from chauvinist pigs," Susan muttered. She turned

her head around to me. "Excuse me. What do you think you're doing?"

"Looking in your pick-a-nick basket," I responded, as I flipped open one cover. I whistled. "You came armed for bear, Miss Rodriguez. Holy water. Garlic. Two crosses. Is that a thirty-eight?"

Susan sniffed. "A forty-five."

"Garlic," Michael mused.

Above us on the stairs, Mavra hissed.

I glanced up at her. "The Black Court was nearly wiped out, Thomas said. I wonder if that's because they got a little too much publicity. Do you mind, Miss Rodriguez?" I reached into the basket and produced a nice, smelly clove of garlic, then idly flicked it through the air, toward Mavra.

The vampire didn't retreat—she simply blurred, and then stood several steps higher than she had been a moment before. The garlic clove bounced against the stairs where she'd been, and tumbled back down toward us. I bent down and picked it up.

"I'd say that's a big yes." I looked up at Mavra. "Is that what happened, hmm? Stoker published the *Big Book of Black Court Vampire Slaying*?"

Those drowned-blue lips peeled back from her yellowed teeth. No fangs. "It matters little. You are beings of paper and cotton. I could tear apart a dozen score of your kind."

"Unless they'd had an extra spicy pizza, I guess. Let's get out of here, guys." I started up the stairs.

Mavra spread her hands out to either side, and gathered darkness into her palms. That's the only way I can explain it. She spread out her hands, and blackness rushed in to fill them, gathering there in a writhing mass that shrouded her hands to the wrists. "Try to force your way past me with that weapon, wizard, and I will take it as an attack upon my person. And defend myself appropriately."

Cold washed over me. I extended my senses toward that darkness, warily. And it felt familiar. It felt like frozen chains and cruel twists of thorny wire. It felt empty and black, and like everything that magic isn't.

Mavra was our girl.

"Michael," I said, my voice strangled. Steel rasped as he drew one of his knives.

"Um," Susan said. "Why are her hands doing that? Can vampires do that?"

"Wizards can," I said. "Get behind me."

They both did. I lifted my hand, my face creasing in concentration. I reached out and tried to call in my will, my power. It felt shaky, uncertain, like a pump that has lost its prime. It came to me in dribs and drabs, bit by bit, stuttering like a nervous yokel. But I gathered it around my upraised hand, in a crystalline azure glow, beautiful and fragile, casting harsh shadows over Mavra's face.

Her dead man's eyes looked down at me, and I had an abrupt understanding of why Michael had called her "it." Mavra wasn't a woman anymore. Whatever she was, she wasn't a person. Not like I understood people, in any case. Those eyes pulled at mine, pulled at me with a kind of horrid fascination, the same sickly attraction that makes you want to see what's under the blanket in the morgue, to turn over the dead animal and see the corruption beneath. I fought and kept my eyes away from hers.

"Come, wizard," Mavra whispered, her face utterly without expression. "Let us test one another, thou and I."

I hardened the energy I held. I wouldn't have enough juice to take two shots at her. I'd have to take her out the first time or not at all. Cold radiated off of her, little wisps of steam curling up as ice crystals formed on the steps at her feet.

"But you won't take the first shot, will you." I didn't realize I'd spoken my thoughts aloud until after I had. "Because then you'd be breaking the truce."

I saw an emotion in that face, finally. Anger. "Strike, wizard. Or do not strike. And I will take the mortal of your choice from you. You cannot claim the protection of hospitality to them both."

"Get out of the way, Mavra. Or don't get out of the way. If you try to stop us from leaving, if you try to hurt anyone under my protection, you'll be dealing with a Wizard of the Council, a Knight of the Sword and a girl with a basket full of garlic and holy water. I don't care how big bad and ugly you are, there won't be anything left of you but a greasy spot on the floor."

"You dare," she whispered. She blurred and came at me. I took a breath, but she'd caught me on the exhale, and I had no time to unleash the crystalline blast I'd prepared.

Michael and Susan moved at the same time, hands thrusting past me. She held a wooden cross, simple and dark, while he clutched his dagger by its blade, the crusader-style hilt turned up into a cross as well. Both wood and steel flared with a cold white light as Mavra closed, and she slammed into that light as if it were a solid wall, the shadows in her hand scattering and falling away like sand between her fingers. We stood facing her, my azure power and two blazing crosses, which burned with a kind of purity and quiet power I had never seen before.

"Blood of the Dragon, that old Serpent," Michael said, quietly. "You and yours have no power here. Your threats are hollow, your words are empty of truth, just as your heart is empty of love, your body of life. Cease this now, before you tempt the wrath of the Almighty." He glanced aside at me and added, probably for my benefit, "Or before my friend Harry turns you into a greasy spot on the floor."

Mavra walked slowly back up the steps, tendons creaking. She bent and gathered up the skull she'd dropped at some point during the discussion. Then turned back to us, looking down with a quiet smile. "No matter," she said. "The hour is up."

"Hour?" Susan asked me, in a tight whisper. "What hour is she talking about, Dresden?"

"The hour of socialization," Mavra whispered back. She continued up to the top of the stairs, and gently shut the doors leading out. They closed with an ominous boom.

All the lights went out. All but the blue nimbus around my hand, and the faded glory of the two crosses.

"Great," I muttered.

Susan looked frightened, her expression hard and tightly controlled. "What happens now?" she whispered, her eyes sweeping around in the dark.

Laughter, gentle and mocking, quiet, hissing, thick with something wet and bubbling, came from all around us. When it comes to spooky laughter, it's tough to beat vampires. You're going to have to trust me on this one. They know it well.

Something glimmered in the dark, and Thomas and Justine appeared in the glow of the power gathered in my hand. He lifted both hands at once, and said, "Would you mind terribly if I stood with you?"

I glanced at Michael, who frowned. Then at Susan, who was looking at Thomas in all his next-to-naked glory . . . somewhat intently. I nudged her with my hip and she blinked and looked at me. "Oh. No, not at all. I guess."

Thomas took Justine's hand, and the two of them stood off to my right, where Michael kept a wary eye on them. "Thank you, wizard. I'm afraid I'm not well loved here."

I glanced over at him. There was a mark on his neck, black

and angry red, like a brand, in the shape of lovely, feminine lips. I would have thought it lipstick, but I sensed a faint odor of burnt meat in the air.

"What happened to your neck?"

His face paled a few shades. "Your godmother gave me a kiss."

"Damn," I said.

"Well put. Are you ready?"

"Ready for what?"

"For Court to be held. To be given our gifts."

The tenuous hold I had on the power faltered, and I lowered my trembling hand, let go of the tension gently, before I lost control of it. The last light flickered and went out, leaving us in a darkness I wouldn't have believed possible.

And then the darkness was shattered by light—the spotlights again, shining up on the dias, upon the throne there, and Bianca in her flaming dress upon it. Her mouth and throat and the rounded slopes of her breasts were smeared in streaks of fresh blood, her lips stained scarlet as she smiled, down at the darkness, at the dozens of pairs of glowing eyes in it, gazing up at the dias in adoration, or terror, or lust, or all three.

"All rise," I whispered, as soft whispers and moans, rustled up out of the darkness around us, not at all human. "Vampire Court is now in session."

Chapter 29

Fear has a lot of flavors and textures. There's a sharp, silver fear that runs like lightning through your arms and legs, galvanizes you into action, power, motion. There's heavy, leaden fear that comes in ingots, piling up in your belly during the empty hours between midnight and morning, when everything is dark, every problem grows larger, and every wound and illness grows worse.

And there is coppery fear, drawn tight as the strings of a violin, quavering on one single note that cannot possibly be sustained for a single second longer—but goes on and on and on, the tension before the crash of cymbals, the brassy challenge of the horns, the threatening rumble of the kettle drums.

That's the kind of fear I felt. Horrible, clutching tension that left the coppery flavor of blood on my tongue. Fear of the creatures in the darkness around me, of my own weakness, the stolen power the Nightmare had torn from me. And fear for those around me, for the folk who didn't have the power I had. For Susan. For Michael. For all the young people now laying in the darkness, drugged and dying, or dead already, too stupid or too reckless to have avoided this night.

I knew what these things could do to them. They were predators, vicious destroyers. And they scared the living hell out of me.

Fear and anger always come hand in hand. Anger is my hiding place from fear, my shield and my sword against it. I waited for the anger to harden my resolve, put steel into my spine. I waited for the rush of outrage and strength, to feel the power of it coalesce around me like a cloud.

It never came. Just a hollow, fluttering sensation, beneath my belt buckle. For a moment, I felt the fangs of the shadow demon from my dream once again. I started shaking.

I looked around me. All around, the large courtyard was surrounded by high hedges, cut with crenelated squares, in imitation of castle walls. Trees rose up at the corners, trimmed to form the shapes of the guard towers. Small openings in the hedge led out into the darkness of the house's grounds, but were closed with iron-barred doors. The only other way out that I saw was at the head of the stairs, where Mavra leaned against the doors leading back into the manor and out front. She looked at me with those corpse-milk eyes and her lips cracked as she gave me a small, chill smile.

I gripped my cane with both hands. A sword cane, of course—one made in merry old Jack the Ripper England, not a knock-off from one of those men's magazines that sells lava lamps and laser pointers. Real steel. Clutching it didn't do much to make me feel better. I still shook.

Reason. Reason was my next line of defense. Fear is bred from ignorance. So knowledge is a weapon against it, and reason is the tool of knowledge. I turned back to the front as Bianca started speaking to the crowd, some vainglorious bullshit I didn't pay any attention to. Reason. Facts.

Fact one: Someone had engineered the uprising of the dead, the torment of the restless souls. Most likely Mavra had been the one to actually work the magic. The spiritual turbulence had allowed the Nightmare, the ghost of a demon Michael and I had slain, to cross over and come after me.

Fact two: The Nightmare was out to get me and Michael, personally, by taking shots at us and all of our friends. Mavra might even have been directing it, controlling it, using it as a cat's-paw. Optionally, Bianca could have been learning from Mavra, and used it herself. Either way, the results had been the same.

Fact three: It hadn't come after us at sundown, the way we'd half expected.

Fact four: I was surrounded by monsters, with only the strength of a centuries-old tradition keeping them from tearing my throat out. Still, it seemed to be holding. For now.

Unless . . .

"Hell's bells," I swore. "I hate it when I don't figure out the mystery that it's too late."

Dozens of gleaming red eyes turned toward me. Susan jabbed her elbow into my ribs. "Shut *up,* Dresden," she hissed. "You're making them look at us."

"Harry?" Michael whispered.

"That's their game," I said, quietly. "We've been set up."

Michael grunted. "What?"

"This whole thing," I said. The facts started falling into place, about two hours too late. "It's been a setup from the very beginning. The ghosts. The Nightmare demon. The attacks on our family and friends. All of it."

"For what?" Michael whispered. "What's it a setup for?"

"She meant to force us to show here from the very beginning. She's getting set to take a lesson from history," I said. "We have to get out of here."

"A lesson from history?" Michael said.

"Yeah. Remember what Vlad Tepesh did at his inauguration?"

"Oh Lord," Michael breathed. "Lord preserve us."

"I don't get it," Susan said, voice quiet. "What did this guy do?"

"He invited all of his political and personal enemies to a feast. Then he locked them in and burned them all alive. He wanted to start off his administration on a high note."

"I see," Susan said "And you think this is what Bianca's doing?"

"Lord preserve us," Michael murmured again.

"I'm told that He helps those who help themselves," I said. "We've got to get out of here."

Michael's armor clinked as he looked around. "They've blocked the exits."

"I know. How many of them can you handle without the Sword?"

"If it was only a question of holding them off . . ."

"But it isn't. We may have to punch a hole through them."

Michael shook his head. "I'm not sure. Maybe two or three, Lord willing."

I grimaced. Only one vampire guarded each way out, but there were another two or three dozen in the courtyard—not to mention my godmother or any of the other guests, like Mavra.

"We'll head for that gate," Michael said, nodding toward one of the gates in the hedges.

I shook my head. "We'd never make it."

"You will," he said. "I think I can manage that much."

"Ixnay on that upidstay anplay," I said. "We need an idea that gets us all out alive."

"No, Harry. I'm supposed to stand between people and the harm things like these offer. Even if it kills me. It's my job."

"You're supposed to have the Sword to help. It's my fault that it's gone, so until I get it back for you, ease off on the martyr throttle. I don't need anyone else on my conscience." Or, I thought, a vengeful Charity coming after me for getting her children's father killed. "There's got to be a way out of this."

"Let me get this straight," Susan said, quietly, as Bianca's speech went on. "We can't leave now because it would be an insult to the vampires."

"And all the excuse they would need to call for instant satisfaction."

"Instant satisfaction," Susan said. "What's that?"

"A duel to the death. Which means that one of them would tear my arms off and watch me bleed to death," I said. "If I'm lucky."

Susan swallowed. "I see. And what happens if we just wait around?"

"Bianca or one of the others finds a way to make us cross the line and throw the first punch. Then they kill us."

"And if we don't throw the first punch?" Susan asked.

"I figure she'll have a backup plan to wipe us out with, just in case."

"Us?" Susan asked.

"I'm afraid so." I looked at Michael. "We need a distraction. Something that will get them all looking the other way."

He nodded and said, "You might be better for that than me, Harry."

I took a breath and looked around to see what I had to work with. We didn't have much time. Bianca was bringing her speech to a close.

"And so," Bianca said, her voice carrying ably, "we stand at the dawn of a new age for our kind, the first acknowledged Court this far into the United States. No longer need we fear the wrath of our enemies. No longer shall we meekly bow our heads and offer our throats to those who claim power over us." At this point, her dark eyes fastened directly upon me. "Finally, with the strength of the entire Court behind us, with the Lords of the Outer Night to empower us, we will face our enemies. And bring them to their knees." Her smile widened, curving fangs, blood red.

She trailed a fingertip across her throat, then lifted the blood to her mouth to suckle it from her finger. She shivered. "My dear subjects. Tonight, we have guests among us. Guests brought here to witness our ascension to real power. Please, my friends. Help me welcome them."

The spotlights swivelled around. One of them splashed onto my little group; me, Michael, Susan, with Thomas and Justine just a little apart. A second illuminated Mavra, at the head of the stairs, in all her stark and unearthly pallor. A third settled upon my godmother, who glowed with beauty in its light, casually tossing her hair back and casting a glittering smile around the courtyard. At my godmother's side was Mister Ferro, unlit cigarette still between his lips, smoke dribbling out his nostrils, looking martial and bland in his centurion gear, and utterly unconcerned with everything that was going on.

Applause, listless and somehow sinister, came out of the dark around us. There should be some kind of law. Anything that is so bad that its *applause* is sinister should be universally banned or something. Or maybe I was just that nervous. I coughed, and waved my hand politely.

"The Red Court would like to take this opportunity to present our guests with gifts at this time," Bianca said, "so that they may know how very, very deeply we regard their goodwill. So, without further ado, Mister Ferro, would you honor me by stepping forward and accepting this token of the goodwill of myself and my Court."

The spotlight followed Ferro as he walked forward. He reached the foot of the dias, inclined his head in a shallow but deliberate nod, then ascended to stand before Bianca. The vampire bowed to him in return, and made a gesture with one hand. One of the hooded figures behind her stepped forward, holding a small cask, about as big as a breadbox. The figure opened it, and the lights gleamed on something that sparkled and shone.

Ferro's eyes glittered, and he stretched his hand down into the cask, sinking it to the wrist. A small smile stretched his lips, and he withdrew his hand with slow reluctance. "A fine offering," he murmured. "Especially in this age of paupers. I thank you."

He and Bianca exchanged bows where she dipped her head just a fraction lower than his own. Ferro closed the cask and took it beneath one arm, withdrawing a polite step before turning and descending the stairs.

Bianca smiled and faced the courtyard again. "Thomas, of House Raith, of our brothers and sisters in the White Court. Please step forward, that I may give you a token of our regard."

I glanced over at Thomas. He took a slow breath and then said, to me, "Would you stand with Justine for me, while I'm up there."

I glanced at the girl. She stood looking up at Thomas, one hand on his arm, her eyes worried, one sweet little lip between her teeth. She looked small, and young, and frightened. "Sure," I said.

I held out a rather stiff arm. The girl's hands clutched at my forearm, as Thomas turned with a brilliant smile, and swaggered into the spotlight and up the steps. She smelled delicious, like flowers or strawberries, with a low, heady musky smell underneath, sensual and distracting.

"She hates him," Justine whispered. Her fingers tightened on my arm, through my sleeve. "They all hate him."

I frowned and glanced down at the girl. Even worried, she was terribly beautiful, though her proximity to me lessened the impact of her outfit. Or lack thereof. I focused on her face and said, "Why do they hate him?"

She swallowed, then whispered, "Lord Raith is the highest Lord of the White Court. Bianca extended her invitation to him. The Lord sent Thomas in his stead. Thomas is his bastard son. Of the White Court, he is the lowest, the least regarded. His presence here is an insult to Bianca."

I got over my surprise that the girl had spoken that many words all together. "Is there some kind of grudge between them?"

Justine nodded, as on the dias, Thomas and Bianca exchanged bows. She presented him with an envelope, speaking too quietly for the crowd to hear. He responded in kind. Justine said, "It's me. It's my fault. Bianca wanted me to come be hers. But Thomas found me first. She hasn't forgiven him for it. She calls him a poacher."

Which made sense, in a way. Bianca had risen to where she was by being Chicago's most infamous Madame. Her Velvet Room provided the services of girls most men only got to daydream about, for a hefty price. She had enough dirt and political connections that she could protect herself from legal persecution, even without counting any of her vampire tricks, and she'd always had more than her share of those. Bianca would want someone like Justine—sweet looking, gorgeous, unconsciously sexy. Probably dress her up in a plaid skirt and a starched white shirt with—

Down, Harry. Hell's bells. "Is that why you stay with him?" I asked her. "Because you feel that it's your fault he has enemies?"

She looked up at me, for a moment, and then away, her expression more sad than anything. "You wouldn't understand."

"Look. He's a vampire. I know that they can affect people, but you could be in danger—"

"I don't need rescuing, Mr. Dresden," she said. Her lovely eyes sparkled with something hard, determined. "But there is something you can do for me."

I got an edgy feeling and watched the girl warily. "Yeah? Like what?"

"You can take Thomas and me with you when you leave."

"You guys showed up in a limo, and you want a ride home with me?"

"Don't be coy, Mr. Dresden," she said. "I know what you and your friends were talking about."

I felt my shoulders creak with tension. "You heard us. You aren't human, either."

"I'm very human, Mister Dresden. But I read lips. Will you help him or not?"

"It isn't my business to protect him."

Her soft mouth compressed into a hard line. "I'm making it your business."

"Are you threatening me?"

Her face flushed as pink as the dress she was almost wearing, but she stood her ground. "We need friends, Mister Dresden. If you won't help us, then I'll try to buy Bianca's favor by exposing your plans to escape and claiming that I heard you talking about killing her."

"That's a lie," I hissed.

"It's an exaggeration," she said, her voice gentle. She lowered her eyes. "But it will be enough for her to call duel. Or to force you to shed blood. And if that happens, you will die." She took a breath. "I don't want it to be like that. But if we don't do something to protect ourselves, she'll kill him. And make me into one of her pet whores."

"I wouldn't let that happen to you," I said. The words poured out of my mouth before I'd had time to run them past the thinking part of my brain, but they had that solid, certain ring of truth. Oh, hell.

She looked up at me, uncertain again, catching one of those soft lips between her teeth. "Really?" she whispered. "You really mean that, don't you."

I grimaced. "Yeah. Yeah, I guess I do."

"Then you'll help me? You'll help us?"

Michael, Susan, Justine, Thomas. Before long, I was going to need a secretary just to keep track of everyone I was supposed to be looking out for. "You. But Thomas can look out for himself."

Justine's eyes filled with tears. "Mister Dresden, please. If there's anything I can do or say to convince you, I—"

"Dammit," I swore, earning a glare from Michael. "Dammit, dammit, dammit, woman. All women, for that matter." That earned me a glare from Susan. "He's a *vampire,* Justine. He's *eating* you. Why should you care if something happens to him?"

"He's also a person, Mister Dresden," Justine said. "A person who's never done you any harm. Why shouldn't you care what happens to him?"

I hate it when a woman asks me for help and I witlessly decide to go ahead and give it, regardless of dozens of perfectly good reasons not to. I hate it when I get threatened and strong-armed into doing something stupid and risky. And I hate it when someone takes the moral high ground on me and wins.

Justine had just done all three, but I couldn't hold it against her. She just looked too sweet and helpless.

"All right," I said, against my better judgment. "All right, just stay close. You want my protection, then you do what I say, when I say, and maybe we can all get out of this alive."

She let out a little shudder that ran through her most attractively, and then she pressed herself against me. "Thank you," she murmured, nuzzling her face into the hollow of my throat so that little lightning-streaks of sensation flickered down my spine. "Thank you, Mister Dresden."

I coughed, uncomfortably, and firmly shoved back any ideas of extracting a more thorough thanks from her later, despite the clamoring of my sex drive. Probably the vampire venom, I reasoned, making me notice things like that even more. Sure. I pushed Justine gently away, and looked up to see Thomas returning from his visit to the dias, holding an envelope in his hand.

"Well," I greeted him quietly, as he returned. "That looks like it went well enough."

He gave me a rather pallid smile. "It . . . she can be rather frightening, when she wishes, can't she."

"Don't let her get to you," I advised him. "What did she give you?"

Thomas accepted Justine into the circle of his arm, and she

pressed her body to his as though she wanted to wallow in him and leave one of those angel shapes. He lifted the envelope and said, "A condo in Hawaii. And a ticket there, on a late flight tonight. She suggested that I might want to leave Chicago. Permanently."

"One ticket," I said, and glanced at Justine.

"Mmmm."

"Friendly of her," I commented. "Look, Thomas. We both want to get out of here tonight. Just stay close to me and follow my lead. All right?"

He frowned a bit, and then shot Justine a reproachful look. "Justine. I asked you not to—"

"I had to," she said, her face earnest, frightened. "I had to do something to help you."

He coughed. "I apologize, Mister Dresden. I didn't want to involve anyone else in my problems."

I rubbed at the back of my neck. "It's okay. We can help each other, I guess."

Thomas closed his eyes for a moment. Then he said, very simply and very openly, "Thank you."

"Sheesh," I said. I glanced up at Bianca, who was in converse with one of the robed and hooded shadows. The pair of them vanished to the back of the dias while Bianca watched, and then returned, lugging something that evidently weighted a good deal. They settled the fairly large object, hidden beneath a dark red cloth, on the dias beside Bianca.

"Harry Dresden," Bianca purred. "Old and esteemed acquaintance, and wizard of the White Council. Please come forward so that I can give you some of what I've been longing to for so long."

I gulped, and shot a glance back at Michael and Susan. "Look sharp," I said. "If she's going to do something, I guess it will be now, when we're separated."

He put his hand on her shoulder, and said, "God go with you, Harry." Energy thrummed along my skin, and the nearest vampires shifted about uneasily and took a few steps away. He saw me notice, and gave me a small, sheepish smile.

"Be careful, Mister Dresden," Susan said.

I bobbed my eyebrows at them, nodded to Thomas and Justine, and then walked forward, my cane in one hand, my cheesy cape flowing in the night air as I mounted the stairs to the dias. A bit of sweat stung in the corner of my eye, smearing my makeup, probably. I ignored it, meeting Bianca's gaze as I came level with her.

Vampires don't have souls. She didn't have to fear my gaze. And she wasn't good enough to sucker me into her eyes. Or at least, she hadn't been, a couple years ago. She met my gaze, steady, her eyes dark and lovely and so very, very deep.

I took the better course of valor, and focused upon the tip of her perfectly upturned nose. I saw her breasts rise and fall in pleasure beneath the flames that gowned her, and she let out a small, purring sound of satisfaction. "Oh, Harry Dresden. I had looked forward to seeing you tonight. You are a very handsome man, after all. But you look utterly ridiculous."

"Thanks," I said. No one, except maybe the pair of robed attendants at the back of the dias, could hear us. "How did you plan on killing me?"

She fell quiet for a moment, thoughtful. Then she asked me, as she formally inclined her head, for the benefit of the crowd below, "Do you remember Paula, Mister Dresden?"

I returned the gesture, only more shallowly, just to throw the little zing of insult into it. "I remember. She was pretty. Polite. I didn't really get to meet her much."

"No. She was dead within an hour of you setting foot in my house."

"I thought she might have gone that way," I said.

"That you might have killed her, you mean?"

"Isn't my fault if you lost control and ate her, Bianca."

She smiled, teeth blinding white. "Oh, but it *was* your fault, Mister Dresden. You'd come to my house. Provoked me to near madness. Forced me to go along with you under threat of my destruction." She leaned forward, giving me a glimpse down the flame-dress. She was naked beneath. "Now I get to return the favor. I'm not someone you can simply walk over, slap around, whenever you have a need. Not anymore." She paused and then said, "In a way, I'm grateful to you, Dresden. If I hadn't wanted so very badly to kill you, I would never have amassed the power and the contacts that I have. I never would have been elevated to the Court." She gestured to the crowd of vampires below, the courtyard, the darkness. "In a way, all of this is your doing."

"That's a lie," I said, quiet. "I didn't make you rope Mavra into working for you. I didn't make you order her to torture those poor ghosts, stir up the Nevernever and bring Kravos's pet demon back across to send after a bunch of innocents while you tried to get to me."

Her smile widened. "Is *that* what you think happened? Oh,

my, Mister Dresden. You have an unpleasant surprise awaiting you."

Anger made me lift my eyes to meet her gaze, gave me the strength not to get pulled in by it—no mistaking. She had grown stronger in the past couple of years. "Can we just get this over with."

"Anything worth doing is worth doing slowly," she murmured, but she reached out a hand and tugged on the dark red cloth, uncovering the object there. "For you, Mister Dresden. With all of my most fervent sincerities."

The cloth slid away from a white marble tombstone, set with a pentacle of gold in its center. Block letters carved into it read HERE LIES HARRY DRESDEN, above the pentacle. Below it, they read HE DIED DOING THE RIGHT THING. An envelope had been taped to the side of the tombstone.

"Do you like it?" Bianca purred. "It comes complete with your own plot at Graceland, near to dear little Inez. I'm sure you'll have ever so much to talk about. When your time comes, of course."

I looked from the tombstone back up to her. "Go ahead," I said. "Make your move."

She laughed, a rich sound that spilled back down into the crowd below. "Oh, Mister Dresden," she said, lowering her voice. "You really don't understand, do you. I can't openly strike you down. Regardless of what you may have done to me. But I can defend myself. I can stand by while my guests defend themselves. I can watch you die. And if things are hectic and confusing enough, and a few others die along with you, well. That's hardly to be blamed upon me."

"Thomas," I said.

"And his little whore. And the Knight, and your reporter friend. I'm going to enjoy the rest of the evening, Harry."

"My friends call me Harry," I said. "Not you."

She smiled, and said, "Revenge is like sex, Mister Dresden. It's best when it comes on slow, quiet, until it all seems inexorable."

"You know what they say about revenge. I hope you got a second tombstone, Bianca. For the other grave."

My words stung her, and she stiffened. Then she beckoned the attendants forward, to lift my tombstone in their gloved hands and carry it back. "I'll have it delivered to Graceland, Mister Dresden. They'll have your bed all ready for you, before the sun rises." She flicked her wrist at me, curt dismissal.

I bowed my head, a bare, stark motion, cold. "We'll see."

How's that for a comeback? Then I turned and descended the stairs, my legs shaking a little, my back rigid and straight.

"Harry," Michael said, as I drew close. "What happened?"

I held up my hand and shook my head, trying to think. The trap was already closing around me. I could feel that much. But if I could figure out Bianca's plan, see it coming, maybe I could think my way out ahead of her.

I trusted Michael and the others to keep an eye out for trouble while I furiously pondered, tried to work through Bianca's logic. My godmother glided forward at Bianca's bidding, and I paused for a moment, to glance up to the dias.

Bianca presented her with a small black case. Lea opened it, and a slow tremble ran down her body, made her flame-red hair shift and glisten. My godmother closed it again and said, "A princely gift. Happily, as is the custom of my people, I have brought a matter of equal worth, to exchange with you."

Lea beckoned the attendant forward, and was given a long, dark case. She opened it, displaying it for a moment to Bianca, and then turned, showing it to the gathered Court.

Amoracchius. Michael's sword. It lay gleaming in the dark box, casting back the ruddy light with a pure, argent radiance. Michael went stiff beside me, stifling a shout.

A murmur went up from the assembled vampires and sundry creatures. They recognized the sword as well. Lea basked in it for a moment, until she folded the case closed and passed it over to Bianca. Bianca settled it across her lap, and smiled down at me and, I thought, at Michael.

"A worthy reply to my gift," Bianca said. "I thank you, Lady Leanandsidhe. Let Mavra of the Black Court come forward."

My godmother retreated. Mavra glided out of the night and onto the dias.

"Mavra, you have been a most gracious and honorable guest in my house," Bianca said. "And I trust that you have found your treatment here fair and equitable."

Mavra bowed to Bianca, silent, her rheumy eyes gleaming, glancing down towards Michael.

"Oh, Jesus," I whispered. "Son of a *bitch*."

"He didn't mean it, Lord," Michael said. "Harry? What did you mean?"

I clenched my teeth, eyes flickering around. Everyone was watching me, all the vampires, Mister Ferro, everyone. They all knew what was coming. "The tombstone. It was written on my damned tombstone."

Bianca watched the realization come over me, still smiling. "Then please, Mavra, accept these minor tokens of my goodwill, and with them my hopes that vengeance and prosperity will belong to you and yours." She offered forth the case, containing the sword, which Mavra accepted. Bianca then beckoned to the background, and the attendants brought out another covered bundle.

The attendants jerked the cover off of the bundle—Lydia. Her dark, tousled hair had been trimmed into an elegant cut, and she wore a halter and shorts of black Lycra that emphasized her hips, the beauty of her pale limbs. Her eyes stared into the lights, glazed, drugged, and she sagged helplessly between the attendants.

"My God," Susan said. "What are they going to do with that girl?"

Mavra turned to Lydia, reaching into the case as she did. "Sweet," her hissing voice rasped. Her eyes went to Michael again. "Now to open my gift. It may tarnish the steel a bit, but I'm sure I'll get over it."

Michael drew in a sudden breath.

"What's going on?" Susan blurted.

"The blood of innocents," he snarled. "The Sword is vulnerable. She means to unmake it. Harry, we cannot allow it."

All around me, vampires dropped their wineglasses, slid out of their jackets, bared their scarlet-smeared fangs in slow smiles to me. Bianca started laughing, up above me, as Mavra opened the case and withdrew *Amoracchius*. The sword seemed to almost chime with an angry sound as the vampire touched it, but Mavra only sneered down at the blade as she lifted the sword.

Thomas moved closer to us, pushing Justine behind him as he drew his sword. "Dresden," he hissed. "Dresden, don't be a fool. It's only one life—one girl's life and a sword balanced against all of us. If you act now, you condemn us all."

"Harry?" Susan asked, her voice shaking.

Michael too turned to look at me, his expression grim. "Faith, Dresden. Not all is lost."

All looked pretty damned lost to me. But I didn't have to do anything. I didn't have to lift a finger. All I had to do, to get out of here alive, was to sit still. To do nothing. All I had to do was stand here and watch while they murdered a girl who had come to me a few days before, begging me for protection. All I had to do was ignore her screams as Mavra gutted her. All I had to do was let the monsters destroy one of the major bastions standing against them. All I had to do was let Michael go to his death, claim the protection of the laws of hospitality upon Susan, and I could walk away.

Michael nodded at me, then drew both knives and turned toward the dias.

I closed my eyes. *God forgive me for what I'm about to do.*

I grabbed Michael's shoulder before he could start walking. Then I drew the sword blade forth from the cane, holding the cane in my left hand, reversing it in my grip as I drew in my will, sent it coursing down the haft of the cane, caused blue-white light to flare in the runes etched there.

Michael flashed me a fighting grin and took position at my right. Thomas took one look at me and whispered, "We're dead." But he fell in at my left, crystalline sword glittering in his hand. A howl went up from the vampires, a sudden wave of deafening sound. Mavra turned her eyes to us, gathering night into the fingers of her free hand again. Bianca slowly rose, dark eyes glowing in triumph. Over to one side, Lea laid her hand on Mister Ferro's arm, frowning faintly, standing well out of the way.

Mavra hissed, lifting *Amoracchius* up high.

"Harry?" Susan asked. Her shaking hand touched my shoulder. "What are we going to do?"

"Stay behind me, Susan." I clenched my teeth. "I guess I'm going to do the right thing."

Even if it kills me, I thought. *And all of you, too.*

Chapter 30

In games and history books and military science lectures, teachers and old warhorses and other scholarly types lay out diagrams and stand up models in neat lines and rows. They show you, in a methodical order, how this division forced a hole in that line, or how these troops held their ground when all others broke.

But that's an illusion. A real struggle between combatants, whether they number dozens or thousands, is something inherently messy, fluid, difficult to follow. The illusion can show you the outcome, but it doesn't impress upon you the surge and press of bodies, the screams, the fear, the faltering rushes forward or away. Within the battle, everything is wild motion and sound and a blur of impressions that flash by almost before they have time to register. Instinct and reflex rule everything—there isn't time to think, and if there's a spare second or two, the only thought in your head is "How do I stay alive?" You're intensely aware of what is happening around you. It's an obscure kind of torture, an acute and temporary hell—because one way or another, it doesn't last long.

A tide of vampires came toward us. They rushed in, animal-swift, a blur of twisted, bulging faces and staring black eyes. Their jaws hung too far open, fangs bared, hissing and howling. One of them held a long spear and shoved it toward Thomas's pale belly. Justine screamed. Thomas swept the crystalline sword he bore down in an arc, parrying the spear's tip aside and cutting through the haft.

Undeterred, the spear-wielding vampire came on, and sank its fangs into Thomas's forearm. Thomas shoved the vamp back, but it held firm. Thomas switched tactics, abruptly lifting the vampire up and clear of the ground, and then rolled the sword's blade around its belly, splitting it open in a welter of gore. The vampire fell to the ground, a sound bubbling up from his throat that was one part fury and one part agony.

"Their bellies!" Thomas shouted. "Without the blood they're too weak to fight!"

Michael caught a descending machete's blade on the metal guard around his forearm, and whipped one of his knives across the belly of the vamp who held it. Blood splattered out of the vamp, and it went down in convulsions. "I know," Michael snapped back, flashing Thomas an irritated look.

And then he was buried in a swarm of red-clad bodies.

"Michael!" I shouted. I tried to push toward him, but found myself jostled aside. I saw him struggle and drop to one knee, saw the vampires shoving knives at him, and fangs, teeth tearing and worrying, and if any of them were burning, like before, I couldn't see it.

Kyle Hamilton appeared, across the dogpile over the fallen knight. He bared his fangs at me, and lifted a semiautomatic, one of the expensive models. Gold-plated. "Fare thee well, Dresden."

I lifted the cane, its runes shimmering blue and white, and snapped. *"Venteferro!"*

The magic whispered silently out through the runes on the cane. Earth magic isn't really my forte, but I like to keep my hand in. The runes and the power I willed into the staff reached out and caught the gun in invisible waves of magnetism. I had been worried that the spells I'd laid on the cane might have gone stale, but they were still hanging in there. The gun flew from Kyle's hands.

I whipped it through the air, into the face of another vamp coming toward Justine. It hit at something just this side of the speed of sound, and sent the thing flying back into the darkness. Justine whirled, as a second vampire came at her, only to have its legs literally scythed out from beneath it by Thomas's blade.

"Iesu domine!" Michael's voice rang out from beneath the vampires like a brass army bugle, and with a sudden explosion of pressure and unseen force, bodies flew back and up, away from him, flesh ripped and torn from them, hanging in ragged, bloodless strips like cloth, showing gleaming, oily black flesh beneath. *"Domine!"* Michael shouted, rising, slewing gutted vamps off of him like a dog shakes off water. *"Lava quod est sordium!"*

"Come on!" I called, and strode forward, toward the stairs

leading up to the dias. Michael had parted the scarlet sea, as it were—stunned vampires gathered themselves from the ground or slowed their attack, hovering several feet away, hissing. Susan and Justine caught one of them starting to creep in closer, and discouraged the others from following its example by splattering it with holy water from Susan's basket. The thing howled and fell back, clawing at its eyes, flopping and wriggling like a half-crushed bug.

"Bianca!" Thomas shouted. "Our only chance is to take out their leader!" A knife flew out of the dark, too fast for me to see. But Thomas did. He reached out and flicked the blade of his sword across its path with a contemptuous swat, deflecting it out.

We reached the foot of the stairs. "Thomas, hold them here. Michael, we go up." I didn't wait to see who was listening—I just turned and headed up the stairs, sword and cane out and ready, my stomach sinking. There was no way we would be in time to save Lydia.

But we were. The carnage had evidently drawn Mavra's attention, and she stared at the blood, withered lips pulled back from yellow teeth. She looked at me, and her expression twisted in malice. She spun back to Lydia, sword held high.

"Michael," I snapped, and stretched out my cane. *"Venteferro!"*

Amoracchius burst into conflicting shades of blue and golden light, as my power wrapped around it, a coruscation of sparks that made Mavra howl in surprise and pain. The vampire retreated, but kept her pale hands clenched on the blade.

"Suit yourself, sparky," I muttered. I gritted my teeth as the cane smoked and shook in my hand. *"Vente! Venteferro!"* I whipped the cane in a wide arc, and with a hiss the vampire found herself lifted clear of the ground by her grip on the sword, and flung like a beach ball toward the courtyard below. She smacked into the stones of the courtyard hard, brittle popping sounds a gruesome accompaniment. The sword exploded in another cloud of vengeful argent sparks and went spinning away from Mavra, the blade flashing where hit the ground.

A wave of exhaustion and dizziness swept over me, and I nearly fell. Even using a focus, the rune-etched cane, that effort had nearly been more than I could manage. I had to clench my teeth and hope I wouldn't simply pitch to one side. I was getting down to the bottom of the barrel, as far as magic went.

"Harry!" Michael shouted. "Look out!"

I looked up to see Mavra bound up onto the dias again, not

bothering to take the stairs, landing a few feet from me. Michael strode forward, one hand holding a dagger up reversed, point down, a cross extended toward Mavra. The vampire flung her hands at Michael, and darkness spilled out of them like oil, splattering toward the knight. It sizzled and spat against him, going up in puffs of steam, and Michael came on forward through it, white fire gathering around the upheld cross. Mavra let out a dusty, hissing scream and fell back from him, forced away from me.

"Harry," Thomas shouted up the stairs, "hurry up! We can't last much longer!"

My eyes swept the dias, but I could see no sign of Bianca or her attendants in the shadows cast by the halogen-brightness of Michael's blazing cross. I hurried to Lydia, sheathing my slender blade before scooping her up. "Longer? I'm amazed we're still alive now!"

"Light shines brightest in the deepest dark!" Michael shouted, a fierce joy on his face, his eyes alight with a passion and a vengeance I had never seen in him. He kept forcing Mavra back before the paralyzing fire of the cross, until with a scream she fell from the dias. "Let come the forces of night! We will stand!"

"We will get the hell out of here is what we will do," I muttered, but louder I said, "back down the stairs. Let's go!"

I turned to see Thomas, Susan, and Justine holding off a ring of vampires, at the base of the stairs to the dias, between the pair of spotlights. Only scraps of skin and cloth clung to the vampires. Some of the Red Court still had partially human faces, but most stood naked, now, free of the flesh masks they wore. Black, flabby creatures, twisted, horrible faces, bellies bulging, mostly, tight with fresh blood. Black eyes, empty of anything but hunger, glittered in the light. Long, skinny fingers ended in black claws, as did the grasping toes of their feet. Membranes stretched between their arms and flanks, horribly slime-covered, the beautiful bodies and shapes of before given way to the horror beneath.

A vampire lurched toward Thomas, while another reached out to grasp Susan. She thrust her cross in its face, but unlike with Mavra, the wood did not blaze to light. Faith magic isn't always easy to work, even on vampires, and the Red Court, creatures with a more solid hold on reality than the more magical denizens of the Black, were not so easily repelled. The vampire howled, mouth yawning open, foaming slaver spattering Susan's red hood.

She twisted and fought, and with her other hand swept up another baby food jar of holy water—not at the vampire, but at the spotlight beside them. With a screaming hiss, the water vaporized against the heat of the light, bursting out in a sudden cloud of steam that enfolded the vampire completely. It let out a screech that swept upward through the range of human hearing, vanishing above it, and fell away from Susan, its skin sloughing off, the black, stringy muscles and bones beneath showing through.

Susan fumbled her basket open and drew her gun. She fired for the vampire's belly, the rapid *thump-thump-thump* of panic fire, and the vampire's abdomen ruptured, blood spraying out in a cloud. The vamp fell to the ground, and I remember thinking that she'd just killed the thing—really and truly taken one of them out. A fierce pride shot through me, and I headed down the stairs.

And then our streak of luck ended.

Justine took a step too far to one side, and Bianca appeared out of nowhere, seizing the girl by the hair and dragging her away from Thomas. Thomas whirled, but too late. Bianca held the girl's back against her front, her fingers wound with deceptive gentleness around Justine's throat. With the other hand, Bianca, still quite human-seeming and calm, caressed the girl's belly. Justine struggled, but Bianca simply turned her head to one side and drew her tongue slowly, sensuously over Justine's throat. The girl's eyes widened, panicked. Then they grew heavy. She shuddered, her body relaxing toward Bianca, arching slowly. Bianca's rich mouth quirked, and she murmured something into Justine's ear that made the girl whimper.

"Enough," Bianca said. And as quickly as that, the courtyard grew silent. Michael and I stood on the stairs a bit above Thomas and Susan. The vampires ringed them in, just out of reach of Thomas's sword. I held Lydia unmoving in my arms. Bianca looked up at me and said, "The game has ended, wizard."

"You haven't taken us down yet," I shot back. "Smart for you and your people to get out of my way, before I get cranky."

Bianca laughed, idly plucking some of the petals from Justine's top, baring a bit more of her breasts. "Surely you don't think me so stupid as to be bluffed now, Dresden. You have already had a measure of your strength taken. What remains barely keeps you standing. If you could force your way out, you'd have done it already." Her eyes moved to Michael. "And you, Sir Knight. You will die gloriously and take many of the horrid creatures of the night with you. But you are outnumbered and alone, and without the sword. You will die."

I glanced at Thomas and Susan and said, "Well, then. I guess it's a good thing we brought help. Your whole Court, Bianca, and you couldn't take us down." I swept my eyes back and forth over the vampires below, and said, "All of your little minions here have eternity laid out before them. Eternity is a bad thing to lose. And maybe you would get us, eventually. But whichever one of you would like to lose eternity first, please. Just go ahead and step on up."

Silence reigned over the courtyard for a moment. I allowed a bit of hope to seep into my pounding heart. Kenny Rogers, eat your heart out. If this bluff worked, I'd be more of a gambler than he'd ever dreamed.

Bianca only smiled, and said, to Thomas, "She's so beautiful, my cousin of the White Court. I've wanted her ever since the moment I saw her." Bianca licked her lips. "What would you say to a bargain?"

I sneered. "You think we would do business with you?"

Thomas glanced back up at me. Incredibly, he was clean—but for a sprinkling of scarlet droplets on his pale flesh, unmarred, loincloth, wings, and all. "Go ahead," he said. "I'm listening."

"Give them to us, Thomas Raith," Bianca said. "Give us these three, and take the girl as your own, uncontested. I will have as many little pets as I wish, now. What is one over another?"

"Thomas," I said. "I know we just met, but don't listen to her. She set you up to get killed already."

Thomas glanced back and forth between us. He met my eyes for a moment—almost long enough to let me see inside him. Then looked away. I had the impression that he was trying to tell me something. I don't know what. His expression seemed apologetic, maybe. "I know, Mister Dresden," he said. "But . . . I'm afraid the situation has changed." He didn't kick Susan, so much as he simply planted his sandaled foot against her and shoved her into the crowd of vampires. She let out a short, startled scream, and then they took her, and dragged her into the darkness.

Thomas lowered his sword and turned toward me, his back to the vampires. Leering, hissing, they crept closer to Michael and me, around Thomas, one of them rubbing up against his legs. His mouth twisted in distaste, and he sidestepped. "I'm sorry, Mister Dresden. Harry. I do like you quite a bit. But I'm afraid that I like myself a whole lot more."

Thomas faded back, while the vampires crowded around the bottom of the stairs. Somewhere, in the dark, Susan let out a short, terrified scream. And then it faded to a moan. And then silence.

Bianca smiled sweetly at me, over Justine's lolling head. "And so, wizard, it ends. The pair of you will die. But don't worry. No one will ever find the bodies." She glanced back, toward where Thomas had faded into the background and said, aside, "Kyle, Mavra. Kill the white-bellied little bastard, too."

Thomas's head whipped around toward Bianca and he snarled, "You bitch!"

My mouth worked and twisted, but no words came out. How could they? Words couldn't possibly contain the frustration, the rage, the fear that poured through me. It cut through my weariness, sharp as thorns and barbed wire. It wasn't fair. We'd done everything we could. We'd risked everything.

Not we. The choices had been mine.

I'd risked everything.

And I'd lost.

Michael and I couldn't possibly fight them all alone. They'd taken Susan. The help we thought we'd found had turned against us.

They had Susan.

And it was my fault. I hadn't listened to her, when I should have. I hadn't protected her. And now she was going to die, because of me.

I don't know how that realization would make someone else feel. I don't know if the despair, and the self-loathing and the helpless fury would crumble them like too-brittle concrete, or melt them like dirty lead, or shatter them like cheap glass.

I only know what it did to me.

It set me on fire.

Fire in my heart, in my thoughts, in my eyes. I burned, burned down deep in my gut, burned in places I hadn't known I could hurt.

I don't remember the spell, or the words I said. But I remember reaching for that pain. I remember reaching for it, and thinking that if we had to go, then so help me God, weakened or not, hopeless or not, I was going to take these murdering, bloodsucking sons of bitches with me. I would show them that they couldn't play lightly with the powers of creation, of life itself. That it wasn't smart to cross a wizard of the White Council when someone has stolen his girlfriend.

I think Michael must have sensed something and taken the girl from my arms, because the next thing I remember is thrusting my hands toward the night sky and screaming, "*Fuego! Pyrofuego*! Burn, you greasy bat-faced bastards! Burn!"

I reached for fire—and fire answered me.

The tree-towers of the topiary castle exploded into blazes of light, and the hedge-walls, complete with their crenelated tops, went up with them. Fire leapt up into the air, forty, fifty feet, and the sudden explosion of it lifted everyone but me up and off the ground, sent wind roaring around us in a gale.

I stood amidst it, my mind brilliantly lit by the power coursing through me. It burned me, and some part of me screamed out in joy that it did. My cloak flapped and danced in the gale, spreading out around me in a scarlet and sable cloud. The abrupt glare fell on the scene of the vampires' revelry, lighting it harshly. The young people of earlier lay about, out in the darkness near the hedges, near the fires, pathetic little lumps. Some of them twitched. Some of them breathed. A few whimpered and tried to crawl away from the heat—but most lay dreadfully, perfectly still.

Pale. Pretty.

Dead.

The fury in me grew. It swelled and burned and I reached out to the fires again. Flames flew out, caught one of the more cowardly of the vampires, huddled at the back, scrabbling to slip his flesh mask back over his squashed bat face. The fire touched him and then twined about him, searing and blackening his skin, then dragging him back, winding and rolling him toward the blaze.

The magic danced in my eyes, my head, my chest, flying wild and out of control. I couldn't follow everything that happened. More vampires got too close to the flames, and began screaming. Tendrils of fire rose up from the ground and began to slither over the courtyard like serpents. Everything exploded into motion, shadows flashing through the brightness, seeking escape, screaming.

I felt my heart clench in my chest and stop beating. I swayed on my feet, gasping. Michael got to me, Lydia slung over his shoulder in a fireman's carry. He'd torn his cloak off, and it lay to one side, burning. He dragged my arm across his shoulder, and half carried me down the stairs.

Smoke gathered on us, thick and choking. I coughed and retched, helpless. The magic coursed through me, slower now, a trickle—not because the floodgates had closed, but because I had nothing left to pour out. I hurt. Fire spread out from my heart, my arms and legs clenching and twitching. I couldn't get a breath, couldn't think, and I knew, somewhere amidst all that pain, that I was about to die.

"Lord!" Michael coughed. "Lord, I know that Harry hasn't

always done what You would have done!" He staggered forward, carrying me, and the girl. "But he's a good man! He's fought against Your foes! He deserves better than to die here, Lord! So if you could be kind enough to show me how to get us out of here, I'd really appreciate it."

And then, abruptly, the smoke parted, and sweet, untainted air hit us in the face like a bucket of ice water.

I fell to the ground. Michael dropped the girl somewhere near me and tore the cheap tuxedo open. He laid his hand over my heart and let out a short cry. After that, I don't remember much more than pain, and a series of dull, hard thumps on my chest.

And then my heart lurched and began to beat again. The red haze of agony receded.

I looked up.

The smoke had parted in a tunnel, as though someone had shoved a glass tube of clean air through it and around us. At the far end of the tunnel stood a slender, willowy figure, tall, feminine. Something like wings spread out behind the figure, though that might have been an illusion, light falling on it from many angles, so that it was all shadow and color.

"I thought He wasn't so literal," I choked.

Michael drew back from me, his soot-stained face breaking into a brief smile. "Are you complaining?"

"H—Heck, no. Where's Susan?"

"I'll come back in for her. Come on." Too tired to argue, I let him haul me back to my feet. He picked up Lydia, and we staggered forward and out, to the figure at the tunnel's far end.

Lea. My faerie godmother.

We both drew up short. Michael fumbled for his knife, but it was gone.

Lea quirked one delicate brow at us. Her dress, still blue, unsoiled, flowed around her, and her silken mane matched the bloody fires consuming the courtyard. She looked almost good enough to drink, and she still held the black box Bianca had given her beneath one slender arm.

"Godmother," I said, startled.

"Well, fool? What are you waiting for. I took the trouble to show you a way to escape. Do it."

"*You* saved us?" I coughed.

She sighed and rolled her eyes. "Though it pains me in ways I could not explain, yes, child. How am I supposed to have you if I let this Red Court hussy kill you? Stars above, wizard, I thought you had better sense than this."

"You saved me. So *you* could get me."

"Not like *this,*" Lea said, holding a silken cloth to her nose, delicately. "You're a husk, and I want the whole fruit. Go rest, child. We will speak again soon enough."

And then she withdrew and was gone.

Michael got me out of the house. I remember the smell of his old truck, sawdust and sweat and leather. I felt its worn seat creak beneath me.

"Susan," I said. "Where's Susan?"

"I'll try."

Then I drifted in darkness for a while, dimly conscious of a lingering pain in my chest, of Lydia's warm skin pressed against my hand. I tried to move, to make sure the girl was all right, but it was too much effort.

The truck door opened and slammed closed. Then came the rumble of its engine.

And then everything went mercifully black.

Chapter 31

The darkness swallowed me and kept me for a long time. There was nothing but silence where I drifted, nothing but endless night. I wasn't cold. I wasn't warm. I wasn't anything. No thought, no dreams, no anything.

It was too good to last.

The pain of the burns came to me first. Burns are the worst injuries in the world. I'd been scorched on my right arm and shoulder, and it throbbed with a dull persistence that dragged me out of the peace. All the other assorted scrapes and bruises and cuts came back to me. I felt like a collection of complaints and malfunctions. I ached everywhere.

Memory came through the haze next. I started remembering what had happened. The Nightmare. The vampire ball. The kids who had been seduced into being there.

And the fire.

Oh, God. What had I done?

I thought of the fire, towering up in walls of solid flame, reaching out with hungry arms to drag the vampires screaming back into the pyre I had made of the hedges and the trees.

Stars and stones. Those children had been helpless in that. In the fire and the smoke that I'd needed a major sidhe sorceress's assistance to escape. I had never stopped to think about that. I had never even considered the consequences of unleashing my power that way.

I opened my eyes. I lay in my bed in my room. I stumbled out of the bed and into my bathroom. Someone must have fed me soup at some point, because when I started throwing up, there was something left to come out.

Killed them. I killed those kids. My magic, the magic that was the energy of creation and life itself had reached out and burned them to death.

I threw up until my belly ached with the violence of it, wild grief running rampant over me. I struggled, but I couldn't force the images out of my head. Children burning. Justin burning. Magic defines a man. It comes from down deep inside you. You can't accomplish anything with magic that isn't in you, somewhere, to do.

And I had burned those children alive.

My power. My choice. My fault.

I sobbed.

I didn't come to myself until Michael came into the bathroom. By the time he did, I lay on my side, curled up tight, the water of the shower pouring down over me, the cold making me shiver. Everything hurt, inside and out. My face ached, from being twisted up so tightly. My throat had closed almost completely as I wept.

Michael picked me up as though I weighed no more than one of his children. He dried me with a towel and shoved me into my heavy robe. He had on clean clothes, a bandage on his wrist and another on his forehead. His eyes looked a little more sunken, as though short on sleep. But his hands were steady, his expression calm, confident.

I gathered myself again, very slowly. By the time he was finished, I lifted my eyes to his.

"How many?" I asked. "How many of them died?"

He understood. I saw the pain in his eyes. "After I got the pair of you out, I called the fire department and let them know that people needed a rescue. They got there pretty quickly, but—"

"How many, Michael?"

He drew in a slow breath. "Eleven bodies."

"Susan?" My voice shook.

He hesitated. "We don't know. Eleven was all they found. They're checking dental records. They said the heat was so intense that the bones hardly look human."

I let out a bitter laugh. "Hardly human. There were more kids than that there—"

"I know. But that's all they found. And they rescued a dozen more, alive."

"It's something, at least. What about the ones unaccounted for?"

"They were gone. Missing. They're . . . they're presumed dead."

I closed my eyes. Fire had to burn hot to reduce bones to ash. Had my spell been that powerful? Had it hidden most of the dead?

"I can't believe it," I said. "I can't believe I was so stupid."

"Harry," Michael said. He put his hand on my shoulder. "We've no way to know. We just don't. They could have been dead before the fires came. The vampires were feeding from them indiscriminately, where we couldn't see."

"I know," I said. "I know. God, I was so arrogant. Such an *idiot* to go walking in there like that."

"Harry—"

"And those poor, stupid kids paid the price. Dammit, Michael."

"A lot of the vampires didn't make it out, either, Harry."

"It isn't worth it. Not if it wiped out all the vamps in Chicago."

Michael fell quiet. We sat that way for a long time.

Finally, I asked him, "How long have I been out?"

"More than a day. You slept through last night and yesterday and most of tonight. The sun will rise soon."

"God," I said. I rubbed at my face.

I could hear Michael's frown. "I thought we'd lost you for a while. You wouldn't wake up. I was afraid to take you to the hospital. Any place where there'd be a record of you. The vampires could trace it."

"We need to call Murphy and tell her—"

"Murphy's still sleeping, Harry. I called Sergeant Stallings, last night, when I called the fire department. S.I. tried to take over the investigation, but someone up the line called the police department off of it altogether. Bianca has contacts in City Hall, I guess."

"They can't stop the missing persons investigations that are going to start cropping up as soon as people start missing those kids. But they can stick a bunch of things in the way of it. Crap."

"I know," Michael said. "I tried to find Susan, the girl Justine, and the sword, after. Nothing."

"We almost pulled it off. Sword and captives and all."

"I know."

I shook my head. "How's Charity? The baby?"

He looked down. "The baby—they still don't know about him.

They can't find out what's wrong. They don't have any idea why he is getting weaker."

"I'm sorry. Is Charity—?"

"She's stuck in bed for a while, but she'll be fine. I called her yesterday."

"Called. You didn't go see her?"

"I guarded you," Michael said. "Father Forthill was with my family. And there are others who can watch them, when I'm away."

I winced. "She didn't like that, did she. That you stayed with me."

"She's not speaking to me."

"I'm sorry."

He nodded. "So am I."

"Help me up. I'm thirsty."

He did, and I only swayed a little as I stood. I tottered out into the living area of my apartment. "What about Lydia?" I asked.

Michael remained silent, and my eyes answered my own question a few seconds later. Lydia lay on the couch in my living room, under a ton and a half of blankets, curled up, her eyes closed and her mouth a little open.

"I recognize her," Michael said.

I frowned. "From where?"

"Kravos's lair. She was one of the kids they hauled away, early on."

I whistled. "She must have known him. Known what he was going to do, somehow."

"Try not to wake her up," Michael said, his voice soft. "She wouldn't sleep. I think they'd drugged her. She was panicky, gabbling. I just got her quieted down half an hour ago."

I frowned a little and went into the tiny kitchen. Michael followed. I got a Coke out of the icebox, thought better of it with my stomach the way it was, and fetched a glass of water instead. I drank unsteadily. "I've got hell to pay now, Michael."

He frowned at me. "How do you mean?"

"What you do comes back to you, Michael. You know that much. Roll a stone and it rolls back upon you. Sow the wind and reap the whirlwind."

Michael lifted his eyebrows. "I didn't realize you'd read much of the Bible."

"Proverbs always made a lot of sense to me," I said. "But with magic, things like that come a lot sharper and cleaner than with other things. I killed people. I burned them. It's going to come back to haunt me."

Michael frowned, and looked out at Lydia. "The Law of Three, eh?"

I shrugged.

"I thought you told me once that you didn't believe in that."

I drank more water. "I didn't. I don't. It's too much like justice. To believe that what you do with magic comes back to you threefold."

"You've changed your mind?"

"I don't know. All I know is that there's going to be justice, Michael. For those kids, for Susan, for what's happened to Charity and your son. If no one else is going to arrange it, I'll damn well do it myself." I grimaced. "I just hope that if I'm wrong, I can dodge karmic paybacks long enough to finish this."

"Harry, the ball was the whole point. It was Bianca's chance to put you down while staying within the terms of the Accords. She laid her trap and missed. Do you think she's going to keep pushing it?"

I gave him a look. "Of course. And so do you. Or you wouldn't have played watchdog here for the past day."

"Good point."

I raked my fingers through my hair, and reached for the Coke, my stomach be damned. "We just have to decide what our next move is going to be."

Michael shook his head. "I don't know. I need to be with Charity. And my son. If he's . . . if he's sick. He needs me near him."

I opened my mouth to object, but I couldn't. Michael had already risked his neck for me more than once. He'd given me a lot of good advice that I hadn't listened to. Especially about Susan. If I'd only paid more attention, told her what I felt, maybe . . .

I cut off that line of thought before the hysterical sob that rose in my throat became more than a blur of tears in my eyes. "All right," I said. "I . . . thank you. For your help."

He nodded, and looked down, as though ashamed. "Harry. I'm sorry. I've done all that I could. But I'm not as young as I used to be. And . . . I lost the sword. Maybe I'm not the one to hold it anymore after all. Maybe this is how He is telling me that I need to be at home now. Be there for my wife, my children."

"I know," I said. "It's all right. Do what you think is best."

He touched the bandage on his forehead, lightly. "If I had the sword, maybe I'd feel differently." He fell quiet.

"Go on," I said. "Look, I'll be all right, here. The Council will probably give me some help." If they didn't hear about the people who'd died in the fire, that is. If they heard about that, that I'd broken the First Law of Magic, they'd take my head off my neck faster than you could say "capital offense." "Just go, Michael. I'll take care of Lydia."

"All right," he said. "I'll . . ."

A thought occurred to me, and I didn't hear what Michael said next.

"Harry?" he asked. "Harry, are you all right?"

"I'm having a thought," I said. "I . . . something feels *off* about this to me. Doesn't it to you?"

He just blinked at me.

I shook my head. "I'll think about it. Make some notes. Try to sort this mess out." I started toward the door. "Come on. I'll let you out."

Michael followed me to the door, and I had my hand on the knob when the door abruptly rattled under several rapid blows that could only loosely be construed as knocking. I shot him a glance over my shoulder, and without a word, he retreated to the fireplace and picked up the poker that had been laying against some of the logs. The tip glowed orange-red.

When a fresh barrage hammered against my door, I jerked it open, slipping to one side.

A slender figure of medium height stumbled into the room. He wore a leather jacket, jeans, tennis shoes, and a Cubs ball cap. He carried a rifle case made of black plastic, and he smelled of sweat and feminine perfume.

"You," I snarled. I grabbed the man's shoulder before he could get his balance and spun his shoulders hard, sending him back against the wall. I drove my fist hard at his mouth, felt the bright *smack-thud* of impact on my knuckles. I grabbed the front of his jacket in both hands, and with a snarl hurled him away from the wall, to the floor of my living room.

Michael stepped forward, put his work boot on the back of the intruder's neck, and pressed the glowing tip of the poker close to his eyes.

Thomas released the rifle case and jerked his hands up, pale fingers spread. "Jesus!" he gasped. His full lower lip had split, and was smeared with something pale and pinkish, not much like human blood. I glanced down at my knuckles, and they were smeared with the same substance. It caught the light of the fire and refracted in an opalescent sheen. "Dresden," Thomas stammered. "Don't do anything hasty."

I reached down and plucked the hat off of his head, letting his dark hair spill out and down in an unkempt mane. "Hasty? Like, maybe, turn traitor on you all of a sudden and let a bunch of monsters eat your girlfriend?"

His eyes rolled back to Michael and then over to me. "God, wait. It wasn't like that. You didn't see all that happened afterwards. At least shut the door and listen to me."

I glanced over at the open doorway, and after a hesitation shut it. No sense in leaving my back open just to be contrary. "I don't want to listen to him, Michael."

"He's a vampire," Michael said. "And he betrayed us. He's probably come here to try to trick us again."

"You think we should kill him?"

"Before he hurts someone," Michael said. His tone was flat, disinterested. Scary, actually. I shivered a little, and drew my robe closed around me a little more tightly.

"Look, Thomas," I said. "I've had a really bad day, and I only woke up half an hour ago. You're adding to it."

"We're all having a bad day, Dresden," Thomas said. "Bianca's people were after me all day and all night, too. I just barely got here without getting myself torn to pieces."

"The night is young," I said. "Give me one good reason why I shouldn't kill you like the lying, treacherous vampire sleaze you are?"

"Because you can trust me," he said. "I want to help you."

I snorted. "Why the hell should I believe you?"

"You shouldn't," he said. "Don't. I'm a good liar. One of the best. I'm not asking you to believe me. Believe the circumstances. We have a common interest."

I scowled. "You're kidding me."

He shook his head, and offered me a wry smile. "I wish I was. I thought I would get the chance to help you out once Bianca had taken her eyes off me, but she double crossed me."

"Well, Thomas. I don't know how new you are to all of this, but Bianca is what we colloquially refer to as a 'bad guy.' They do that. That's one way you can tell they're bad guys."

"God save me from idealists," Thomas muttered. Michael growled, and Thomas shot him a hopeful, puppy-like smile. "Look, both of you. They have Dresden's woman."

I took a step forward, my heart fluttering. "She's alive?"

"For now," Thomas said. "They've got Justine, too. I want her back. You want Susan back. I think we can make a deal. Work together. What do you say?"

Michael shook his head. "He's a liar, Harry. I can tell just by being this close to him."

"Yes, yes, yes," Thomas said. "I confess to it. But at the moment, it isn't a part of my agenda to lie to anyone. I just want her back."

"Justine?"

Thomas nodded.

"So he can keep on draining the life out of her," Michael said. "Harry, if we aren't going to kill him, let's at least put him out."

"If you do," Thomas said. "You'll be making a huge mistake. And I swear to you, by my own stunning good looks and towering ego, that I'm not lying to you."

"Okay," I said to Michael. "Kill him."

"Wait!" Thomas shouted. "Dresden, please. What do you want me to pay you? What do you want me to do? I don't have anywhere else to go."

I studied Thomas's expression. He looked weary, desperate, beneath the cool facade he was barely holding onto. And beneath the fear, he looked resigned. Determined.

"Okay," I said. "It's all right, Michael. Let him up."

Michael frowned. "You sure?"

I nodded. Michael fell back from Thomas, but he kept the poker gripped loosely in one hand.

Thomas sat up, running his fingers lightly over his throat, where Michael's boot had left a dark mark, and then touched his split lip, and winced. "Thank you," he said, quietly. "Look in the case."

I glanced at the black rifle case. "What's in it?"

"A deposit," he said. "A down payment, for your help."

I quirked an eyebrow and leaned over the case. I ran my fingertips lightly over it. There was no spiny buzz of energy around it to herald a sorcerous booby trap, but a good one would be hard to notice. There was something inside, though. Something that hummed quietly, a silent vibration of power that ran through the plastic and into my hand. A vibration I recognized.

I flicked open the latches on the rifle case, fumbling in my hurry, and swung it open.

Amoracchius lay gleaming against the grey foam inside the case, unmarked from the inferno at Bianca's town house.

"Michael," I said, quietly. I reached out and touched the blade's hilt, again. Still, it buzzed with that quiet, deep power, at once reassuring and intimidating. I withdrew my fingers.

Michael paced over to the case and leaned down, staring at the sword. His expression wavered and became difficult to read. His eyes filled with tears, and he reached a broad, scarred hand down to the weapon's hilt. He took it in hand and closed his eyes.

"It's all right," he said. "They didn't hurt it." He blinked his eyes open, and looked upwards. "I hear you."

I glanced up toward my ceiling and said, "I hope you meant that in a figurative sense. Because I didn't hear anything."

Michael smiled and shook his head. "I was weak for a while. The swords are a burden. A power, yes, but at a price. I thought that perhaps the loss of the sword was His way of telling me it was time to retire." He ran his other hand over the twisted metal nail set into the blade at the weapon's crossguard. "But there's still work to be done."

I glanced up, at Thomas. "You say they've got Susan and Justine, huh? Where?"

He licked his lips. "The town house," he said. "The fire ruined the back of the house, but only the exterior. The inside was fine, and the basement was untouched."

"All right," I said. "Talk."

Thomas did, laying out facts in rapid order. After the havoc of the fire, Bianca and the Court had retreated into the mansion. Bianca had ordered the other vampires to each carry one of the helpless mortals out. One of them had brought Susan. When the police and fire crews had arrived, most of the action was over, and the fire marshal had been worked up into a lather over the deaths. He'd gone inside to speak to Bianca, and come out calm and collected, and ordered everyone to pack up and leave, that he was satisfied that it had been a terrible accident and that everything was over.

After that, the vampires had been able to relax and enjoy their "guests."

"I think they're turning some of them," Thomas said. "Bianca has the authority to allow it, now. And they lost too many in the fight and the fire. I know Mavra took a couple and took them with her when she left."

"Left?" I asked.

Thomas nodded. "She skipped town just after sunset, word is. Couple of hungry new mouths to feed, you know?"

"And how do you know all of this, Thomas? The last I heard, Bianca's people were trying to kill you."

He shrugged. "There's more to a good liar than meets the eye, Dresden. I was able to keep an eye on things for a while."

"Okay," I said. "So they've got our people at the manor house. We just need to get inside, get them, and get out again."

Thomas shook his head. "We need something else. She's brought in mortal security. Guards with machine guns. It would be a slaughter."

"That's the spirit," I said, with a grim smile. "Where in the house are they keeping the captives?"

Thomas looked at me rather blankly for a moment. Then he shook his head. "I don't know."

"You've known everything so far," Michael said. "Why are you drying up on us now?"

Thomas gave the Knight a wary look. "I'm serious. I haven't seen any more of that house than you two."

Michael frowned. "Even if we do get in, we can't go blundering around checking every broom closet. We need to know about the inside of the house."

Thomas shrugged. "I'm sorry. I'm tapped."

I waved a hand. "Don't worry. We just need to talk to someone who *has* seen the inside of the house."

"Capture a prisoner?" Michael asked. "I don't know how much luck we'd have with that."

I shook my head, and glanced over at the sleeping figure of Lydia, who hadn't stirred in all that time. "We just need to talk to her. She was inside. She might have some useful insights for us, in any case. She's got a gift for it."

"Gift?"

"Cassandra's Tears. She can see bits of the future."

I got dressed, and we gave Lydia another hour or so. Thomas went into the bathroom to shower, while I sat out in the living room with Michael. "What I can't figure," I said, "is how we managed to get out of there so easily."

"You call that easy?" Michael said.

I grimaced. "Maybe. I would have expected them to come after us by now. Or to have sent the Nightmare to get us."

Michael frowned, rolling the hilt of the sword between his two hands as though it were a golf club. "I see what you mean." He was quiet for a minute, and then said, "You really think the girl will be of help?"

"I hope so."

At that moment, Lydia started coughing. I moved to her side, and helped her drink some water. She seemed groggy, though she started to stir. "Poor kid," I commented to Michael.

"At least she got a little sleep. I don't think she'd had any for days."

Michael's words froze me solid.

I started to push myself away from Lydia, but her fingers reached out and dug into the sweater I was wearing. I jerked against them, but she held me, easily, not at all moved. The pale girl opened her sunken eyes, and they were flooded with blood, all through the whites, scarlet. She smiled, slow and malicious. She spoke, and her voice came out in a low, harsh sound totally unlike her natural tones, alien and malevolent. "You should have kept her from sleeping. Or killed her before she woke."

Michael started to his feet. Lydia rose, and with one arm she lifted me clear of the ground, bloody eyes glaring up at me with wicked exultation. "I've waited long enough for this," the alien voice, that of the Nightmare, purred. "Goodbye, wizard." And the slender girl flung me like a baseball at the stone of my fireplace.

Some days, it just doesn't pay to get out of bed.

Chapter 32

I flailed my arms and legs and watched the fireplace get closer to breaking open my head. At the last second, I saw a blur of white and pink, and then I slammed into Thomas, driving him into the stones of the fireplace. He let out a grunt, and I bounced off of him, and back to the floor, momentarily breathless. I shoved myself up to my hands and knees and looked at him. He'd wrapped a pink bath towel around his hips, but either the sheer speed of his movement or else the impact had knocked it mostly askew. His ribs jutted out on one side, oddly misshapen.

Thomas looked up at me, his face twisted into a grimace. "I'll be all right," he said. "Look out."

I looked up to find Lydia stalking toward me. "Idiot," she seethed at Thomas. "What did you think you could accomplish? So be it. You just got added to the list."

Michael slipped in between the possessed girl and me, the sword glittering in the low light of the room. "That's far enough," he said. "Get back."

I struggled back to my feet, and wheezed, "Michael, be careful."

Lydia let out another twisted laugh, and leaned forward, pressing her sternum against *Amoracchius's* tip. "Oh yes, Sir Knight. Get back or what? You'll murder this poor child? I don't think so. I seem to remember, there was something about this sword not being able to draw innocent blood, wasn't there?"

Michael blinked, and darted a glance back at me. "What?"

I got to my feet. "This is really Lydia. It isn't a magical construct, like we saw before. The Nightmare is possessing her.

Anything we do to Lydia's body, she's going to have to live with, later."

The girl ran a hand over her breasts, beneath the taut Lycra, licking her lips and staring at Michael with bloody eyes. "Yes. Just a sweet little innocent lamb, wandered astray. You wouldn't want to hurt her, would you, Knight?"

"Harry," Michael said, "how do we handle this?"

"You die," Lydia purred. She rushed Michael, one hand reaching out to strike the sword's blade aside.

When she rushed me, I just got grabbed. But Michael had training, experience. He let the sword fall to the floor and rolled back with Lydia's rush. He grabbed her forearms as she reached for his throat, whirled, and sent her tumbling into the couch, knocking it over backwards and sending her into a sprawl on the far side.

"Keep her busy!" I shouted to him. "I can get it out of her!" And then I rushed back into my bedroom, searching for the ingredients for an exorcism. My room was a mess. I scrambled through it, while out in the living room, Lydia screamed again. There was another thump, this one rattling the wall beside the bedroom door, and then the sounds of panting, scuffling.

"Hurry up, Harry!" Michael gasped. "She's strong!"

"I know, I know!" I jerked open the door to my closet and started knocking things off the shelves, rather than hunt through them.

Behind the spare cans of shaving cream, I located five trick birthday candles, the kind that you can't blow out, and a five-pound bag of salt. "Okay!" I called. "I'm coming!"

Michael and Lydia lay on the floor, his legs wrapped around hers, while his arms pinned hers back behind her in some kind of modified full Nelson hold.

"Hold her there!" I shouted. I rushed in a circle around them, shoving back a chair and a footrest, kicking rugs and carpets aside, finally jerking the last one out from beneath Michael. Lydia fought him, twisting like an eel and screaming at the top of her lungs.

I tore open the salt and ran about the pair of them, dumping it out into a white mound in a circle. Then I ran about again, setting the candles down, piling up enough salt around them to keep them from being turned over. Lydia saw what I was doing and screamed again, redoubling her efforts.

"Flickum bicus!" I shouted, shoving a hurried effort of will

into the little spell. The effort made me dizzy for a moment, but the candles burst to light, the circle of candles and salt gathering power.

I rose, reaching out my right hand and feeding more energy into the circle, setting it up in a spinning vortex winding about the three beings inside it—Lydia, Michael, and the Nightmare. Energy gathered in the circle, spinning around, whirling magic down into the earth, grounding and dispersing it. I could almost see the Nightmare clutching tighter to Lydia, holding on. All I needed was the right move to stun the Nightmare, to lock it up for a second, so that the exorcism could sweep it away.

"Azorthragal!" I shouted, bellowing out the demon's name. "Azorthragal! Azorthragal!" I stretched out my right hand again, concentrating fiercely. "Begone!"

Energy rushed out of my body as I completed the spell, swept toward the Nightmare within Lydia like a wave lifting a sleeping seal off a rock—

—and passed over, leaving it untouched.

Lydia began to laugh wildly, and managed to catch one of Michael's hands in hers. She gave a twist, and bones snapped with sharp pops and crackles. Michael let out an agonized scream, twisting and jerking. He knocked the circle of salt askew, and Lydia escaped him, rising to face me.

"Such a *fool,* wizard," she said. I didn't banter. I didn't even stand there, stunned that my spell had failed so miserably. I wound back a hand and threw a punch at her as hard as I could, hoping to stun the body the demon was riding in, to keep it from reacting.

The possessed Lydia glided from the path of my punch, caught my wrist, and dumped me onto my back. I started to push myself up, but she threw herself astride me, and slammed my head back against the floor, twice. I saw stars.

Lydia stretched above me, purring, and thrusting her hips down against mine. I tried to escape during the moment of gloating, but my arms and legs just didn't respond. She reached down, laying both of her hands almost delicately on my throat, and murmured, "Such a shame. All this time, and you didn't even know who it was after you. You didn't even know who else wanted revenge."

"I guess sometimes you find out the hard way," I slurred.

"Sometimes," Lydia agreed, smiling And then her hands closed over my throat, and I didn't have any more air.

Sometimes, when you're facing death, it feels like everything slows down. Everything stands out sharply in detail, almost freezes. You can see it all, feel it all, as though your brain has decided, in sheer defiance, to seize the last few moments of life and to squeeze them for every bit of living left.

My brain did that, but instead of showing me my trashed apartment and how I really needed a new coat of paint on the ceiling, it started frantically shoving puzzle pieces together. Lydia. The shadow demon. Mavra. The torment spells. Bianca.

One thing stood out in my mind, a piece that didn't fit anywhere. Susan had been gone for a day or two, where I had barely been able to talk to her. She'd said she was working on something. That something was happening. It fit, somehow, somewhere.

Stars swam in my vision and fire started to spread through my lungs. I struggled to pry her arms off of me, but it was no use—possessed, she was simply too strong to deal with.

Susan had been asking me about something, some insignificant part of the phone conversation we had, between sexual innuendos. What had it been?

I heard myself making a very slight sound, something like, "Gaghk. Aghk." I tried to lever Lydia's weight up and off of me, but she simply rolled with me, taking my weight onto her and then continuing the motion, slamming me to the floor again. My vision began to darken, though I opened my eyes wide. It was like staring down a dark tunnel, looking up at Lydia's blood-filled eyes.

I saw Michael struggle to his knees, his face white as a fresh dusting of snow. He moved toward Lydia, but she turned her head slightly and kicked him, lashing out with one heel. I heard something else snap as the force of the kick drove Michael back.

Murphy had been distracted about something, too. Something she'd hurriedly changed subjects on. Intuition drew a line between them. And then an equal sign.

And then I had it: the last piece of the puzzle. I knew what had happened, where the Nightmare had come from, why it was after me, in particular. I knew how to stop it, knew what its limits were, how Bianca had enlisted it, and why my spells had been so hard-pressed to affect it.

Almost a pity, really. I'd figured things out just in time to die.

Vision faded altogether.

And a moment later, so did the pain in my throat.

Instead of drifting off into whatever lay beyond, though, I sucked in a breath of air, choking and gasping. My vision became red for a moment, as blood rushed back through my head, and then started to clear.

Lydia still crouched over me, up on her knees, straddling me—but she'd released my throat. Instead, she had arched her arms up and back, over her head, to caress Thomas's naked shoulders.

The vampire had pressed up against Lydia's back. His mouth nuzzled her throat, slow kisses, strokes of his tongue that made the girl shudder and quiver. His hands roamed slowly over her body, always touching skin, fingers roaming up beneath the brief Lycra top to caress her breasts. Lydia gasped, blood-filled eyes distant, unfocused, body responding with a slow, sensual grace.

Thomas looked past her, through the dark fall of his hair, to me. His eyes weren't blue-grey anymore. They were empty, white, no color to them at all. I felt cold coming off of him, something I sensed more than felt on my skin, a horrible and seductive cold. He continued, spreading a line of kisses up Lydia's neck, to her ear, making her whimper and shake.

I swallowed, and crawled back on my elbows, dragging my hips and legs out from beneath the pair of them.

Thomas murmured, so softly that I wasn't sure I'd heard him. "I don't know how long I can distract her, Dresden. Quit gawking and do something. I'll put on afternoon theater for you later, if you want to watch that bad." Then his mouth covered the girl's, and she stiffened, eyes flying open wide before they languidly closed, deepening the kiss.

I flushed at Thomas's words, which made my head pound painfully. I rooted around the floor and recovered the candles, still lit, and the bag of salt. I spread the salt in a circle around Lydia and Thomas, as Lydia drew the Lycra shorts down and reached back to grasp at Thomas, to urge him toward her.

Thomas let out a groan of pure anguish and said, "Dresden. *Hurry.*"

I settled the candles into place and gathered up whatever power I had left to close the circle and to begin the vortex again. If I was right, I would free Lydia, maybe permanently. If I was wrong, this was the last of my energy, and I'd dump it into the earth for nothing. The Nightmare would presumably kill us—and I didn't think any of us were in shape to do anything about it.

Energy gathered in the circle, rising in a growing whirl of invisible, tingling power. I stretched out my hand and willed more energy into it, feeling dizzy.

The Nightmare finally seemed to take notice of what was around it again. Lydia shivered and leaned a little away from

Thomas, breaking some of the contact between them—then the bloodred eyes snapped open, and focused on me. Lydia began to rise, but Thomas clutched onto her hard, holding her.

The power rose again, a second vortex whirling around the pair of them, tugging at spiritual energies within. Lydia screamed.

"Leonid Kravos!" I thundered. I repeated the name, and saw Lydia's eyes fly open wide in shock. "Begone, Kravos! You secondrate firecaller! Begone! Begone!" And with the last word, I stamped my foot down, releasing the power of the exorcism down, into the earth.

Lydia screamed, her body arching, her mouth dropping open wide. Within the whirling vortex, glittering motes of silver and gold light gathered into a funnel, centered on Lydia's gaping mouth. Scarlet energy flooded out of her screaming mouth, and for a moment there was an unnerving overlap of screams—one high-pitched, young, feminine, terrified, while the other was inhuman, otherworldly. More scarlet light lashed forth from Lydia's eyes, stolen away by the vortex's power.

And then with a rush and an implosion of suddenly empty air, the vortex swirled into an infinitely thin line and vanished, dropping down into the floor, lower, deep into the earth.

Lydia let out a low, exhausted cry, and dropped limply to the floor. Thomas, still clutching her, tumbled down with her. Silence fell on the room, but for the four of us, gasping for breath.

Finally, I managed to sit up. "Michael," I called, my voice hoarse. "Michael. Are you okay?"

"Did you stop it?" he asked. "Is the girl all right?"

"I think so."

"Thank God," he said. "It kicked me, got one of my ribs. I'm not sure I can sit up."

"Don't," I said, and mopped sweat from my brow. "Broken ribs could be bad. Thomas? Are you— Hey! What the hell do you think you're doing?"

Thomas lay with his arms around Lydia, his pale, naked body pressed against hers, his lips nuzzling her ear. Lydia's eyes were open, colored naturally again, but not focused on anything. She didn't look conscious, but she was making tiny, aroused motions of her body, her hips, leaning back to him. Thomas blinked up at me when I spoke, eyes still empty and white.

"What?" he asked. "She's not unwilling. She's probably just grateful to me, for my help."

"Get away from her," I snapped.

"I'm *hungry,*" he said. "It won't kill her, Dresden. Not the first time. You'd be dead right now without me. Just let me—"

"No," I said.

"But—"

"No. Get off of her, or you and I are going to have words."

A snarl split the air between us, Thomas's full lips peeling back from his teeth. They looked like human teeth, not vampire fangs. Whiter and more perfect than human teeth, but other than that, normal.

I returned his stare coolly.

Thomas looked away first. He closed his eyes for a moment, and when he opened them again, there were pale rings of color in them once more, slowly darkening. He released Lydia and rolled away from her. His ribs still looked dented, but not as much as before. He got to his feet and wrapped the towel around his hips again, then stalked back toward the bathroom without another word.

I checked Lydia's pulse, blushed, and tugged her shorts back into place. Then I righted the couch and put her back onto it, beneath the blankets. After that, I went to Michael.

"What was that all about?" he asked.

I told him what had happened, in terms as PG rated as possible. He scowled, flicking a glance back toward the bathroom. "They're like that. The White Court. Seducers. They feed on lust, fear, hatred. Emotions. But they always use lust to seduce their victims. They can force them to feel it, indulge in sex. It's how they feed."

"Sex vampires, I know," I muttered. "Still. It's interesting."

"Interesting?" Michael sounded skeptical. "Harry, I wouldn't call it *interesting*."

"Why not?" I said. I squinted after Thomas, thoughtfully. "Whatever he used, it worked on the Nightmare. Caught it up. That means that it's either some kind of ambient magic, maybe that cold I felt, that works on everything around, or else it's something chemical—like Red Court venom. Something that got to Lydia's body and bypassed the Nightmare's control of her mind, altogether. Pheromones, maybe."

"Harry," Michael said, "I really don't mean to discourage your scholarly pursuits, but would you mind, very much, helping me with these broken ribs."

We took inventory. I had some nasty bruises on my throat, but nothing more. Michael had one rib that was definitely broken, and one more than might have been cracked, tender as it was. I got him wrapped up pretty well. Thomas came out of my room, dressed in some of my spare jogging clothes. They hung off of him, and he had to roll the sleeves and legs of the sweatpants up. He slouched into a chair, his gaze settling on Lydia's sleeping form with a rather disconcerting intensity.

"It all fits now," I told them. "I know what's going on, so I can finally do something about it. I'm going to go to the town house, and get everyone out."

Michael frowned at me. "What fits?"

"It wasn't the demon that crossed over, Michael. We were never fighting the demon. It was Kravos himself. Kravos is the Nightmare."

Michael blinked at me. "But we didn't kill Kravos. He's still alive."

"Dollars to donuts he isn't. I figure the night before the Nightmare's attacks started, he puts together a ritual and takes himself out."

"Why would he do that?"

"To come back as a ghost. To get revenge. Think about it—that's all the Nightmare has been doing. It's been rampaging around, avenging Kravos."

"Could he *do* that?" Michael asked.

I shrugged. "I don't see why he couldn't, if he had raised a bunch of power, and if he was focused on getting his vengeance and turning himself into a ghost. Especially . . ."

". . . with the border to the Nevernever as turbulent as it was," Michael finished.

"Exactly. Which means that Mavra and Bianca helped him out, specifically. Hell, they probably put together the ritual that he used. And if someone in federal custody here in Chicago suddenly turned up suicided in his cell, it would cause a big stir in local police—and would be serious news for the media. Which is why Murphy was being so hush-hush, and Susan was so distracted. She was working on a story, finding out what happened. Following up a rumor, maybe."

Thomas frowned. "Let me get this straight. This Nightmare is the ghost of the sorcerer Kravos. The cult murderer in the news several months ago."

"Yeah. The turbulence in the Nevernever let him get made into a badass ghost."

"Turbulence?" Thomas said.

I nodded. "Someone began binding the local spooks with torment spells. They went wild and started stirring the border between the real world and the Nevernever. I figure it was Mavra, working with Bianca. That same turbulence let Kravos hit everyone he could in their dreams. It's how he got to me, and how he got to poor Malone, and how he got to Lydia just now. Lydia knew what he was doing. That's why she never wanted to go to sleep. I didn't see it coming, when he hit me in my dreams. I wasn't ready for a fight, and he kicked my ass."

"But now you can defeat him?" Michael asked.

"I'm ready for him now. I beat this punk when he was alive. Now that I know what I'm dealing with, I can do it to his shade, too. I'll go to the house, take out the Nightmare, Bianca if I have to, and get everyone out."

"Did you get hit on the head when I wasn't looking?" Thomas asked. "Dresden, I told you about the guards. The machine guns. I did mention the machine guns, didn't I?"

I waved a hand. "I'm already past the point where a sane man would be afraid. Guards and machine guns, whatever. Look, Bianca has Susan, plus Justine, and maybe twenty or thirty kids being held captive, or getting set to get turned into fresh vampires. The police's hands are tied on this. Someone has to do something, and I'm the only one in a position to—"

"Get riddled with bullets," Thomas interjected, his tone dry. "My, how very helpful that will be toward attaining our mutual goals."

"Oh ye of little faith," Michael said, from his place in my easychair. He swung his head back toward me. "Go ahead, Harry. What do you have in mind?"

I nodded. "All right. I figure Bianca will have security all over the outside of the house. She'll cover all the approaches to it, any cars that go in are going to get searched, and so on."

"Exactly," Thomas said. "Dresden, I thought maybe we could pool our resources. Work something out with our contacts and spies. Perhaps disguise ourselves as caterers and sneak in." He paused. "Well. *You* could pass for a caterer, in any case. But if we simply assault her house, we'll all be killed."

"If we walk up where they can see us."

Thomas frowned. "You have something else in mind? I doubt we could veil ourselves with magic. In familiar surroundings, she's going to be difficult to fool with those kinds of glamour."

I lifted an eyebrow at the vampire. "You're right. I had something else in mind."

* * *

I came through the rift between the mortal world and the Nevernever last. I bore my staff and rod, and wore my leather duster, my shield bracelet and a copper ring upon my left hand matched by another upon my right.

The Nevernever, near my apartment, looked like . . . my apartment. Only a bit cleaner and brighter. Deep philosophical statement about the spirituality of my little basement? Maybe. Shapes moved in the shadows, scurrying like rats, or gliding over the floor like snakes—spirit-beings that fed on the crumbs of energy that spilled over from my place in the real world.

Michael bore *Amoracchius* in his hand, its blade glowing with a pearly luminescence. As soon as he had picked up the blade, his face had regained color, and he had moved as though his bandaged ribs no longer pained him. He wore denim and flannel and his steel-toed work boots.

Thomas, dressed in my castoffs and carrying an aluminum baseball bat from my closet, looked about the place, amused, his dark hair still damp and curling wetly over his shoulders.

In a sack made of fishnet, Bob's skull hung from my fist, the orange skull-lights glowing dimly, like candles. "Harry," Bob asked. "Are you sure about this? I mean, I don't really want to get caught in the Nevernever if I can avoid it. A few old misunderstandings, you see."

"You aren't any more worried about it than I am. If my godmother catches me here, I've had it. Take it easy, Bob," I said. "Just guide us through the shortest path to Bianca's place. Then I tear a hole back over to our side, into her basement, we get everyone and get them out again, and bring them home."

"There is no shortest path, Harry," Bob said. "This is the spirit world. Things are linked together by concepts and ideas and don't necessarily adhere to physical distance like—"

"I know the basics, Bob," I told him. "But the bottom line is that you know your way around here a lot better than I do. Get us there."

Bob sighed. "All right. But I can't guarantee we'll be in and out before sundown. You might not even be able to make a hole through, while the sun's still up. It tends to diffuse magical energies that—"

"Bob. Save the lecture for later. Leave the wizarding to me."

The skull swung around to Michael and Thomas. "Excuse me. Have either of you told Harry what a brainless plan this is?"

Thomas raised his hand. "I did. It didn't do much good."

Bob rolled his eyelights. "It never does. So help me, Dresden, if you die I'm going to be very annoyed. You'll probably roll me under a rock at the last minute, and I'll be stuck there for ten thousand years until someone finds me."

"Don't tempt me. Less talk, more guide."

"Sí, memsahib," Bob said, seriously. Thomas snickered. Bob turned his eyelights toward the stairs leading out of the Nevernever version of my apartment. "That way," he said.

We passed out of the apartment, and into a sort of vague representation of Chicago, which looked like a stage set—flat building faces with no real substance to them, vague light that could have come from sun or moon or streetlights, plus a haze of grey-brown fog. From there, Bob guided us down a sidewalk, then turned into an alley, and opened a garage door, which led to a stone-carved staircase, winding down into the earth.

We followed his lead, into the darkness. At times, the only light we had was the orange glow of the skull's eyelights. Bob turned his head in the direction required, and we passed through a subterranean region that was mostly blackness and low ceilings, eventually rising up a slope that emerged in the center of a ring of standing dolmens atop a long hill. Stars shone overhead in a fierce blaze, and lights danced in the woods at the base of the hill, skittering around like manic fireflies.

I stiffened in my boots. "Bob," I said. "Bob. You blew it, man. This is Faerie."

"Of course it is," Bob said. "It's the biggest place *in* the Nevernever. You can't get to anywhere without crossing through Faerie at one place or another."

"Well hurry up and cross us out," I said. "We can't stay here."

"Believe me, I don't want to hang here, either. Either we get the Disney version of Faerie, with elves and tinkerbell pixies and who knows what sugary cuteness, or we get the wicked witch version, which is considerably more entertaining, but less healthy."

"Even the Summer Court isn't all sweetness and light. Bob, shut up. Which way?"

The skull turned mutely toward what seemed to be the westernmost side of the hill, and we descended down it.

"It's like a park," Thomas commented. "I mean, the grass should be over our knees. Or no, maybe like a good golf course."

"Harry," Michael said, quietly. "I'm getting a bad feeling."

The skin on my neck started to crawl, and I looked back to Michael, nodding. "Bob, which way out?"

Bob nodded ahead, as we rounded a stand of trees. An old, colonial-style covered bridge arched up over a ridiculously deep chasm. "There," Bob said. "That's the border. Where you're wanting isn't too far past that."

In the distance, came the notes of a hunting horn, dark and clear—and the baying of hounds.

"Run for the bridge," I snapped. Thomas sprinted beside me without apparent effort. I glanced at Michael, who had reversed his grip on the sword and held it pommel-first, the blade laying against his forearm as he ran. His face was twisted up in effort and pain, but he kept pace.

"Harry," Bob commented. "If it's all the same, you might want to run a bit faster. There's a hunt coming."

The horn belled again, backed up by the dolmens, and the cries of the pack rang out sharp and clear. Thomas whirled to look, running a few paces backward, before turning again. "I could have sworn they were miles away a moment ago."

"It's the Nevernever," I panted. "Distance, time. It's all fucked up here."

"Wow," Bob commented. "I hadn't realized that they *grew* hellhounds that big. And look, Harry, it's your godmother! Hi, Lea!"

If Bob had a body, he'd have been jumping up and down and waving his fingers at her. "Don't be so enthusiastic, Bob. If she catches me, I get to join the pack."

Bob's eyelights swung toward me and he gulped. "Oh," he said. "There's been a falling out, then. Or a falling further out, at any rate, since you weren't on such great terms to begin with."

"Something like that," I panted.

"Um. Run," Bob said. "Run faster. You really need to run faster, Harry."

My feet flew over the grass.

Thomas reached the bridge first, his feet thumping out onto it. Michael got there a pace later. With a broken rib and twenty years on me, he still outran me to that damn bridge. I've got to work out more.

"Made it!" I shouted, taking a last long step toward the bridge.

The lariat hit me about the throat before my feet had quite touched down, and jerked me back through the air with a snap. I lay on the ground, stunned, choking for the second time in two hours.

"Uh-oh," Bob said. "Harry. Whatever you do, don't drop me. Especially under a rock."

"Thanks a lot," I gasped, reaching up to jerk the rope from its constricting hold on my throat.

Heavy hooves sank into the turf on either side of my head. I gulped, and looked up at a night-black steed with black and silver tack. Its hooves were shod with bladed shoes of some silvery metal. It wasn't iron or steel. There was blood on those shoes, as though the horse had trampled some poor, trapped thing to death. Or else sliced it apart.

My gaze slid on up past the horse, to its rider. Lea rode the beast sidesaddle, perfectly relaxed and confident, wearing a dress of sable and midnight blue, her hair caught back in a loose braid of flame. Her eyes gleamed in the starlight, the other end of the lariat held in one lovely hand. The hellhounds crowded around her steed, all of them focused on yours truly. Call it a wild impression of the moment, but they looked hungry.

"Feeling better, are we?" Lea asked, with a slow smile. "That's wonderful. We can finally conclude our bargain."

Chapter 33

It only takes a couple of these rough little episodes of life to teach a man a certain amount of cynicism. Once a rogue wizard or three has tried to end your life, or some berserk hexenwolves have worked really hard to have your throat torn out, you start to expect the worst. In fact, if the worst doesn't happen, you find yourself somewhat disappointed.

So really, it was just as well that Godmother had caught up to me, in spite of my best efforts to avoid her. I'd hate to find out that the universe really wasn't conspiring against me. It would jerk the rug out from under my persecution complex.

Therefore, working on the assumption that some sadistic higher power would make sure my evening got as complicated as it possibly could, I had formed a plan.

I jerked the lariat from about my throat and croaked, "Thomas, Michael. Now."

The pair of them produced small cardboard boxes from their pockets, palm-sized and almost square. With a shake, Michael cast the contents of the first box forward, slewing the box left and right, like a man scattering seeds. Thomas followed his lead, on the other side of my body, so that objects began to rain down atop and nearby me.

The faerie hounds let out startled yelps and leapt away. My godmother's horse let out a scream and pranced back several steps, putting distance between us.

I scrunched up my face and did my best to shield my eyes from the scattering nails. They fell over me in a sharp-toothed shower, prickling as they struck, and settled around me.

Godmother had to let out on the rope that had looped about my throat as her horse backed away, giving me a bit of slack.

"Iron," hissed my godmother. Her lovely face turned livid, furious. "You *dare* defile the Awnsidhe soil with iron! The Queen will rip your eyes from your skull!"

"No," Thomas said. "They're aluminum. No iron content. That's a lovely horse you have. What's its name?"

Lea's eyes flashed to Thomas, and then at the nails all over the ground. While she did, I dipped a hand into my pocket, palmed my contingency plan, and popped it into my mouth. Two or three chews and a swallow and I was finished.

I tried not to let the abrupt surge of terror show.

"Not steel?" Lea said. She beckoned sharply at the ground, and one of the nails leapt up to her hand. She gripped it, frowning, her expression abruptly wary. "What is the meaning of this?"

"It's meant to be a distraction, Godmother," I said. I coughed, and patted my chest. "I just had to eat something."

Lea laid a hand on her horse's neck, and the savage beast calmed. One of the shadowy hounds nosed forward, nudging one of the nails with its snout. Lea gave the rope a little jerk, taking up the slack again, and said, "It will do you no good, wizard. You cannot escape this rope. It is bound to hold you. You cannot escape my power. Not here, not in Faerie. I am too strong for you."

"All true," I agreed, and got to my feet. "So let's get cracking. Turn me into a doggie and show me which trees I can pee on."

Lea stared at me as though I'd gone mad, her expression wary.

I took hold of the rope and shook it impatiently. "Come on, Godmother. Make with the magic already. Do I get to pick my color? I don't think I want to be that charcoal grey. Maybe you could do a nice sandy pelt for me. Or oh, I know, winter white. With blue eyes, I always wanted blue eyes, and—"

"Be silent!" Lea snarled, and shook the rope. There was a sharp, stinging sensation, and my tongue literally stuck to the roof of my mouth. I tried to keep talking, but it made my throat buzz as though bees were in it, angry, stinging. I kept silent.

"Well," Thomas said. "I'd like to see this. I've never seen an external transformation before. Do proceed, madame." He waved his hand impatiently. "Dog him, already!"

"This is a trick," Lea hissed. "It will avail you naught, wizard. No matter what hidden powers your friends are preparing to cast at me—"

"We're not," Michael put in. "I swear it on the Blood of Christ."

Lea sucked in a breath, as though the words had brought a sudden chill over her. She rode the horse up to me, close, so that the animal's shoulder pressed against mine. She reeled in on the braided leather of the lariat as she did, until she held it by a length of no more than six inches, jerking hard against my throat, hauling me almost off balance. She leaned down close to me and whispered, "Tell me, wizard. What are you hiding from me?"

My tongue loosened again, and I cleared my throat. "Oh. Nothing much. I just wanted a bite to eat before we left."

"A bite," Lea murmured. Then she jerked me over toward her and leaned down close, dainty nostrils flaring. She inhaled, slow, the silken mass of her hair brushing against my cheek, her mouth almost nuzzling mine.

I watched her face, her expression changing to slow surprise. I spoke to her in a quiet voice. "You recognize the smell, yes?"

The whites showed around her emerald eyes as they opened wider. "Destroying Angel," she whispered. "You have taken death, Harry Dresden."

"Yep," I agreed. "Toadstool. *Amanita virosa.* Whatever. The amantin toxin is going to show up in my blood in about two minutes. After that, it will start tearing apart my kidneys and liver. A few hours from now, I'll collapse, and if I don't die then, then I'll apparently recover for a few days while my innards fall apart, and then drop into arrest and die." I smiled. "There's no specific antidote for it. And I kind of doubt even you could use magic to put me back together again. Stitching closed a wound is a lot different from major internal transmutation. So, shall we?" I started walking in the direction Lea had come from. "You should be able to enjoy tormenting me for a few hours before I start vomiting blood and die."

She jerked the lariat tight, halting me. "This is a trick," she hissed. "You are lying to me."

I looked up at her with a lopsided grin. "Now, Godmother," I said. "You know I'm a terrible liar. Do you think I could really lie to you? Do you not smell it yourself?"

She stared at me, her face twisting slowly into an expression of horror. "Merciless winds," she breathed. "You have gone mad."

"Not mad," I assured her. "I know precisely what I'm doing." I turned to glance back at the bridge. "Goodbye Michael. Goodbye Thomas."

"Harry," Michael said. "Are you sure we shouldn't—"

"Shhh," I said, shooting him a look. "Ixnay."

Lea's eyes flickered back and forth between us. "What?" she demanded. "What is it?"

I rolled my eyes, and gestured at Michael.

"Well," Michael said. "As it happens, I have something here that might help."

"Something?" Lea demanded. "What?"

Michael reached into the pocket of his jacket and produced a small vial, capped at one end. "It's extract of St. Mary's Thistle," he said. "They use it in a lot of hospitals in Europe, for mushroom poisoning. Theoretically, it should do quite a bit to help a poisoning victim survive. Provided it's taken in time, of course."

Lea's eyes narrowed. "Give it to me. Now."

I *tsked*. "Godmother. As your faithful pet and companion, I feel I should warn you about how *dangerous* it is for one of the high sidhe to accept gifts. It could bind you to the giver if you don't return a gift in kind."

Lea's face slowly flushed scarlet, sweeping up from the creamy skin of her collarbones and throat over her chin and cheeks and up into her hair. "So," she said. "You would drive a bargain with me. You would take deadly toadstool to force me to release you."

I lifted my eyebrows and nodded, with a smile. "Essentially, yes. You see, I figure it's like this. You want me alive. I'm not of any use to you dead. And you won't be able to undo the poisoning with magic."

"I *own* you," she snarled. "You are *mine* now."

"Beg to differ," I said. "I'm yours for the next couple of days. After that, I'm dead, and I won't be doing you any more good."

"No," she said. "I will not set you free in exchange for this potion. I too can find the thistle."

"Maybe," I admitted. "Maybe you can even do it in time. Maybe not. Either way, without a trip to the hospital, there's not much chance of me living, even with the extract. And none at all, really, if I don't get it soon."

"I will not trade you away! You have given yourself to me!"

Michael shrugged one shoulder. "I believe that you wrought a bargain with a foolish young man caught in the heat of the moment. But we aren't asking you to undo it altogether."

Lea frowned. "No?"

"Naturally not," Thomas said. "The extract only offers Harry a chance at life. That's all we'd ask from you. You'd be obliged to let him go—and bound for a year and a day to do no harm to him or his freedom so long as he remains in the mortal world."

"That's the deal," I said. "As a faithful pet, I should point something out: If I die, you *never* get me, Godmother. If you let me go now, you can always give it a shot another night. It isn't as though you have a limited number of them, is it. You can afford to be patient."

Lea fell silent, staring at me. The night fell silent as well. We all waited, saying nothing. The quiet panic I already felt, after eating the toadstool, danced about my belly, making it twitch and jerk.

"Why?" she said, finally, her voice very quiet, pitched only for me. "Why would you do this to yourself, Harry? I don't understand."

"I didn't think you would," I said. "There are people who need me. People who are in danger because of me. I have to help them."

"You cannot help them if you are dead."

"Nor if I am taken by you."

"You would give your own life in place of theirs?" she asked, her tone incredulous.

"Yes."

"Why?"

"Because no one else can do this. They need me. I owe it to them."

"Owe them your life," Lea mused. "You are mad, Harry Dresden. Perhaps it comes of your mother."

I frowned. "What's that supposed to mean?"

Lea shrugged. "She spoke as you do. Near the end." She lifted her eyes to Michael and straightened on the horse. "A dangerous play, you made tonight, wizard. A bold play. You cut the traditions of my people very close to the bone. I accept your bargain."

And then, with a casual flick, she removed the lariat from me. I stumbled back, away from her, gathered up my fallen staff and rod, and Bob in his net sack, and made my way to the bridge. Once there, Michael gave me the vial. I unstoppered it and drank. The liquid within tasted gritty, a little bitter. I closed my eyes and took a deep breath, after swallowing it down.

"Harry," Michael said, watching Lea. "Are you sure you'll be all right?"

"If I get to the hospital soon," I said. "I've got somewhere between six and eighteen hours. Maybe a little longer. I drank all that pink stuff before we left to line my stomach. It might slow down the rate of digestion on the mushroom, give the extract a chance to beat it to my guts."

"I don't like this," Michael muttered.

"Hey. I'm the one who ate the deadly poison, man. I don't much care for it myself."

Thomas blinked at me. "You mean, you were telling her the truth?"

I glanced at him, nodding. "Yeah. Look, I figure we'll be in there and out again in an hour, tops. Or else we'll be dead. Either way, it will happen in plenty of time before the first round of symptoms sets in."

Thomas just stared at me for a moment. "I thought you were lying," he said. "Bluffing."

"I don't bluff if I can help it. I'm not too good at it."

"So you really could die. Your godmother is right, you know. You are mad as a hatter. Nutty as a fruitcake."

"Crazy like a fox," I said. "All right. Bob, wake up." I shook the skull, and its empty eye sockets kindled with orange-red lights, somehow too far back inside them.

"Harry?" Bob said, surprised. "You're alive."

"For a while," I said. I explained to him how we'd gotten me away from my godmother.

"Wow," Bob said. "You're dying. What a great plan."

I grimaced. "The hospital should be able to take care of it."

"Sure, sure. In some places, the survival rate is as high as fifty percent, in the case of amantin poisoning."

"I took extract of milk thistle," I said, a little defensive.

Bob coughed, delicately. "I hope you got the dosage right, or it could do more harm than good. Now, if you'd come to me about this to begin with—"

"Harry," Michael said, sharply. "Look."

I turned to look at my godmother, who had ridden a little way off and sat still upon her dark steed. She raised in her hand something dark and gleaming, maybe a knife. She waved it to the four corners, north, west, south, east. She said something in a twisting, slippery tongue, and the trees began to moan as the wind rose, washing through them. Power washed out from the sidhe sorceress, from the dark knife in her hand, and raised the hairs on my arms, the nape of my neck.

"Wizard!" she called to me. "You have made bargain with me tonight. I will not seek you. But you have made no such bargain with others." She threw back her head in a long, loud cry, somehow terrifying and beautiful at once. It echoed over the rolling land, and then was answered. More sounds came drifting back, high-pitched howls, whistling shrieks, and deep, throaty coughing roars.

"Many there are who owe me," Lea sneered. "I will not be cheated of you. You have had the potion. You would not have placed your life in such jeopardy without a cure to hand. I will raise no hand against you—but they will bring you to me. One way or another, Harry Dresden, you will be mine this night."

The wind continued to rise, and overhead sudden clouds began to blot out the stars. The howls and calls came closer, carried on the rising wind.

"Shit," I said. "Bob, we have to get out of here. Now."

"It's still a pretty good walk to the spot you showed me on the map," Bob said. "A mile, maybe two, in subjective terms."

"Two miles," Michael noted, clinically. "I can't run that far. Not with my ribs like they are."

"And I can't carry you," Thomas said. "I'm amazing and studly, but I have limits. Let's go, Harry. It's just me and you."

My mind raced, and I struggled to put together a plan. Michael couldn't keep up. He had managed the sprint before, but his face looked a little greyish, now, and he carried himself stiffly, as though in pain. I trusted Michael. I trusted him at my side, and at my back. I trusted him to be able to take care of himself.

But alone, against a wrathful faerie posse, how would he do? I couldn't be sure—even with the sword, he was still a man. He could still lose his life. And I didn't want another life on my conscience.

I glanced over at Thomas. The handsome vampire managed to wear my castoff clothes and make them look like some kind of fashion statement. Slouch nouveau. He returned my glance with a perfect, shining smile, and I thought about what he had said, about what a good liar he was. Thomas had sided with me. Mostly. He'd been friendly enough. He even, apparently, had every reason to want to help me and work with me to get Justine back.

Unless he was lying to me. Unless she hadn't been taken at all.

I couldn't trust him.

"The two of you are staying here," I said. "Hold the bridge. You won't have to do it for long. Just slow them down. Make them go around."

"Oooo," Bob said. "Good plan. That should make it a real pain for them, Harry. I mean, until they kill Michael and Thomas and come after you. But that could take minutes! Hours, even!"

I glanced at the skull, and then at Michael. He shot Thomas a look, and then nodded to me.

"If there's trouble, you'll need me to protect you," Thomas objected.

"I can watch out for myself," I told him. "Look, this whole plan is based on surprise and speed and quiet. I can be quiet better alone. If it turns out that fighting has to be done, one or two people wouldn't make a difference. If we have to fight, this whole thing is over."

Thomas grimaced. "So you want us to stay here and die for you, is that it?"

I glared. "Hold the bridge until I can make it out of the Nevernever. After that, they shouldn't have any reason to come after you."

The wind rose to a howl, and shapes began to crest the top of the hill with the dolmens, dark things, moving swift and close to the ground.

"Harry, go," Michael said. He took *Amoracchius* into his hands. "Don't worry. We'll keep them off of your back."

"Are you sure you wouldn't rather I come with you?" Thomas asked, and took a step toward me. The shining steel of Michael's sword abruptly dropped in front of Thomas, the sharp edge of it pressing against his belly.

"I'm sure I'd rather not leave him alone with you, vampire," Michael said, his tone polite. "Do I make myself clear?"

"As water," Thomas said, sourly. He glanced at me and said, "You'd better not leave her there, Dresden. Or get killed."

"I won't," I said. "Especially that second part."

And then the first monstrous thing, like a mountain lion made all of shadows, bounded past Lea, and a set of dark talons flashed toward me. Thomas shoved me out of the way of the strike, crying out as the thing tore into his arm. Michael shouted in Latin, and his sword flared into argent light, cutting the vaguely catlike beast and dropping it into two squirming, struggling halves to the floor of the bridge.

"Go!" Michael roared. "God go with you!"

I ran.

The sounds of fighting died behind me, until I could only hear my own laboring breaths. The Nevernever changed, from sculpted, faerie-tale wilderness to dark, close forest, with cobwebs hanging down across a narrow trail through glowering trees. Eyes flashed in the shadows, things that never quite could be clearly seen, and I stumbled on.

"There!" Bob called. His orange eyelights swung to shine upon the split trunk of a dead, hollow tree. "Open a way there, and it will take us through!"

I grunted, and came to a halt, gasping. "Are you sure?"

"Yes, yes!" Bob said. "Hurry! Some of the awnsidhe will be here at any moment!"

I cast a fearful glance behind me, and then started gathering in my will. It hurt to do. I felt so weak. The poison in my belly hadn't started tearing my body apart yet, but I almost thought that I could feel it stirring, moving, licking its chops and eyeing my organs with malevolent glee. I shoved all of that out of my thoughts, and forced myself to breathe steadily, to gather in my strength and reach out to part the curtain between worlds.

"Uh, Harry," Bob said suddenly. "Wait a minute."

Behind me, something broke a branch. There was a swift, rushing sound, of something moving toward me. I ignored it and reached out a hand, sinking my fingers into the friable border substance of the Nevernever.

"Harry!" Bob said. "I really think you should hear this!"

"Not now," I muttered.

The rushing noise grew closer, the rattle of undergrowth shunted aside by something large. Behind me, a warbling bellow shook the ground. Holy brillig and slithy toves, Batman.

"Aparturum!" I shouted, thrusting out with my will and opening a way. The rent in reality shone with dim light.

I threw myself forward into it, willing the way closed behind me. Something snagged at one corner of my leather duster, but with a jerk I was free of it and through.

I tumbled forward, onto the floor, the smell of autumn air and damp stone all around me. My heart thudded painfully with the effort of both the running and the spell. I lifted my head to look around me and get my bearings.

Bob had been good to his word. He had brought me out of the Nevernever right into Bianca's mansion. I found myself on the floor at the head of a staircase down, away from the front doors and the main hall.

I also found myself surrounded by a ring of vampires, all of them in their inhuman forms, the flesh masks gone. There had to be a dozen of them there, dark eyes glittering, their noses snuffling, drool spattering out and dripping from their bared fangs to the floor while their talons clawed at the air or ran lightly over their flabby black bodies. Some of them showed burns on their rubbery hide, patches of shrunken, wrinkled, scar-like tissue.

I didn't move. Anything, I sensed, would have set them off. Any motion, any move to flee or fight or escape would have ignited a frenzy, with myself on the receiving end.

While I watched, frozen, Bianca came up the stairs dressed in a white silk nightgown that whispered around her shapely calves. She carried a single candle that bathed her in soft radiance. She smiled at me, very slowly, very sweetly, and the bottom dropped out of my stomach.

"Well," she purred. "Harry Dresden. Such a pleasant surprise to have you visit."

"I tried to tell you," Bob said, his voice miserable. "The curtain felt weak there. Like someone had just gone through it. Like they had been watching this side."

"Of course," Bianca murmured. "A guard for every door. Did you think me a fool, Mister Dresden?"

I glowered at her, despairing. There wasn't anything I could say. I saved my breath, and began to draw in my will, to throw everything I had left into taking that smug smile off of her pretty, false face.

"Dears," Bianca purred, watching me. "Bring him down."

They hit me so fast that I never saw them move. There simply came a hideous, rushing force. I have memories of being passed from claw to claw, thrown, carried into the air, toyed with. Snuffling, squashed snouts, and staring black eyes, and hissing, terrible laughter.

I was driven down, carried, tossed about, everything torn from me, Bob disappearing without a sound. They pressed me down while I struggled and screamed, all useless, my mind too full of terror to focus, to defend myself.

And there, in the dark, they tore my clothes from me. I felt Bianca press her naked flesh to me, a heated, sinuous dream-body that unraveled into a nightmare. I felt the skin split and burst apart around her true form. The sweetness of her perfume gave way to a rotten-fruit reek. Her purring voice became a whining hiss.

And their tongues. Soft, intimate, warm, moist. Pleasure that struck me like hammers while I tried to scream against it.

Chemical pleasure, animal sensation, heartless and cold, uncaring of my horror, revulsion, despair.

Darkness. Horrible, thick, sensual darkness.

Then pain.

Then nothing.

Chapter 34

I have very few memories of my father. I was about six years old when he died. What I do remember is a careworn, slightly stoop-shouldered man with kind eyes and strong hands. He was a magician—not a wizard, a stage magician. A good one. He never made it big, though. He spent too much time performing for children's hospitals and orphanages to pull down much money. He and I and his little show roamed around the country. The memories of the first several years of my life are of my bed in the backseat of the station wagon, going to sleep to the whisper of asphalt beneath the tires, secure in the knowledge that my father was awake, driving the car, and there to take care of me.

The nightmares hadn't started until just before his death. I don't remember them, specifically—but I remember waking up, screaming in a child's high-pitched shriek of terror. I'd scream in the darkness, scrambling to squeeze into the smallest space I could find. My father would come looking for me, and find me, and pull me into his lap. He would hold me, and make me warm, and soon I would fall asleep again, safe, secure.

"The monsters can't get you here, Harry," he used to say. "They can't get you."

He'd been right.

Until now. Until tonight.

The monsters got me.

I don't know where real life left off and the nightmares began, but I thrashed myself awake, screaming a scratchy, hollow scream that made little more noise than a whimper. I screamed until I ran out of breath, and then all I could do was sob.

I lay there, naked, undone. No one came to hold me. No one came to make it all better. No one had, really, since my dad died.

Breathing first, then. I forced myself to control it, to stop the wracking sobs and to draw in slow, steady breaths. Next came the terror. The pain. Humiliation. More than anything, I wanted to crawl into a hole and pull it in after me. I wanted to be not.

But I wasn't not. I hurt too much. I was very painfully, very acutely, very much alive.

The burn still hurt the most, but the sweeping nausea running through me came in a photo finish second. My hands told me that I was lying upon a floor, but the rest of me thought I had been strapped into a giant gyroscope. I ached. My throat felt tight, and burned, as though seared by some hot liquid or chemical. I didn't want to dwell too long on that.

I tested my limbs, and found them all present and functional. My belly twisted and roiled, and for a moment locked up tight, jerking me into a tight curl around it.

The sweat on my naked body went cold. The mushroom. The poison. Six to eighteen hours. Maybe a little more.

I felt thick, dry mouthed, fuzzy with the same aftereffects of the vampire venom that I'd felt before.

For a minute, I stopped fighting. I just lay there, weak and thirsty and hurting and sick, curled up into a ball. I would have started crying again if I'd had that much feeling left in me. I would have wept and waited to die.

Instead, some merciless, steady voice in my head drove me to open my eyes. I hesitated, afraid. I didn't want to open my eyes and see nothing. I didn't want to find myself in that same darkness. That darkness, with hissing things all around me. Maybe there, still, just waiting for me to awaken so that they—

Panic swept me for a moment, and gave me enough strength to shiver and push myself up into a sitting position. I took a deep breath, and opened my eyes.

I could see. Light seared at my eyes, a thin line of it surrounding a tall rectangle—a doorway. I had to squint for a moment, so used were my eyes to the darkness.

I looked around the room, wary. It wasn't big. Maybe twelve by twelve, or a little more. I lay in a corner. The smell was violently rotten. My jailors, apparently, had no problems with letting me lie in my own filth. Some of it had crusted onto me, onto my legs and arms. Vomit, I guessed. There was blood in it. An early symptom of the mushroom poisoning.

There were other shapes in the dimness. A lump of cloth in one corner, like a pile of dirty laundry. Several laundry baskets, as well. A washer and dryer, on the far wall from the door.

And Justine, dressed in as little as I, curled up and sitting with her back to the wall, her arms wrapped loosely around her drawn-up knees, watching me with dark, feverish eyes.

"You're awake," Justine said. "I didn't think you'd ever wake up."

Gone was the glamorous girl I'd seen at the ball. Her hair hung lank and greasy. Her pale body looked lean, almost gaunt, and her limbs, what I could see of them, were stained and dirty, as was her face.

Her eyes disturbed me. There was something feral in them, something unsettling. I didn't look at her for too long. Even as bad off as I was, I had enough presence of mind to not want to look into her eyes.

"I'm not crazy," she said, her voice sharp, edged. "I know what you're thinking."

I had to cough before I could talk, and it made pains shoot through my belly again. "That wasn't what I was thinking."

"Of course it wasn't," the girl snarled. She rose, all lean grace and tension, and stalked toward me. "I *know* what you were thinking. That they'd shut you in here with that stupid little *whore*."

"No," I said. "I . . . that isn't what—"

She hissed like a cat, and raked her nails across my face, scoring my cheek in three lines of fire. I cried out and fell back, the wall interrupting my retreat.

"I can always tell, when I'm like this," Justine said. She gave me an abruptly careless look, turned on the balls of her feet and walked several feet away before stretching and dropping to all fours, watching me with an absent, disinterested gaze.

I stared at her for a moment, feeling the heat of the blood welling in the scratches. I touched a finger to them, and it came away sprinkled with scarlet. I lifted my gaze to the girl and shook my head. "I'm sorry," I said. "God. What did they do to you?"

"This," she said, carelessly, thrusting out one hand. Round, bruised punctures marked her wrist. "And this." She held out the other wrist, showing another set of marks. "And this." She stretched out her thigh to one side of her body, parallel to the floor, to show more marks, along it. "They all wanted a little taste. So they got it."

"I don't understand," I said.

She smiled with too many teeth, and it made me uneasy. "They didn't do anything. I'm like this. This is the way I always am."

"Um," I said. "You weren't that way last night."

"Last night," she snapped. "Two nights ago. At least. That was because *he* was there."

"Thomas?"

Her lower lip abruptly trembled, and she looked as though she might cry. "Yes. Yes, Thomas. He makes it quieter. Inside me, there's so much trying to get out, like at the hospital. Control, they said. I don't have the kind of control other people have. It's hormones, but the drugs only made me sick. He doesn't, though. Only a little tired."

"But—"

Her face darkened again. "Shut *up,*" she snapped. "But, but, but. Idiot, asking idiot questions. Fool who did not want me when I was willing to give. Nothing does that. None of them, because they all want to take, take, take."

I nodded, and didn't say anything, as she became more agitated. It might have been politically incorrect of me, but the word LOONY all but appeared in a giant neon sign over Justine's head. "Okay," I said. "Just . . . let's just take it easy, all right?"

She glowered at me, falling silent. Then she slunk back to the space between the wall and the washing machine and sank into it. She started playing with her hair, and took no apparent notice of me.

I got up. It was hard. Everything spun around. On the floor, I found a dusty towel. I used it to sweep some of the grime off of my skin.

I went to the door and tried it. It stood firmly locked. I tested my weight against it, but the effort made a sudden fire of scarlet flash through my belly and I dropped to the floor, convulsing again. I threw up in the middle of it, and tasted blood on my mouth.

I lay exhausted for a while after that, and might have dropped off to sleep again. I looked up to find Justine holding the towel, and pushing it fitfully at my skin, the fresh mess.

"How long," I managed to ask her. "How long have I been here?"

She shrugged, without looking up. "They had you for a while. Just outside this door. I heard them taking you. Playing with you, for two hours, maybe. And then they put you in here. I slept. I woke. Maybe another ten hours. Or less. Or more. I don't know."

I kept an arm wrapped around my belly, grimacing, and nodded. "All right," I said. "We have to get out of here."

She brayed out a sharp laugh. "There is no out of here. This is the larder. The Christmas turkey doesn't get up and walk away."

I shook my head. "I . . . I was poisoned. If I don't get to a hospital, I'm going to die."

She smiled again, and played with her hair, dropping the towel. "Almost everyone dies in a hospital. You'd get to be someplace different. Isn't that better?"

"It's one of those things I could live without," I said.

Justine's expression went slack, her eyes distant, and she became still.

I stared at her, waved my hand in front of her eyes. Snapped my fingers. She didn't respond.

I sighed and stood up, then tested the door again. It was firmly bolted shut from the other side. I couldn't move it.

"Super." I sighed. "That's great. I'm never going to get out of here."

Behind me, something whispered. I spun, putting the door at my back, searching for the source of the sound.

A low mist crept out of the wall, a smoky, slithery mass that whirled itself down onto the floor like ethereal lace. The mist touched lightly at my blood on the floor where I'd thrown up, and then began to swirl and shape itself into something vaguely human.

"Great," I muttered. "More ghosts. If I get out of this alive, I've got to get a new job."

The ghost took shape before me, very slowly, very translucently. It resolved itself into the form of a young woman, attractive, dressed like an efficient secretary. Her hair was pulled up into a bun, but for a few appealing tendrils that fell down to frame her cheeks. Her ghostly wrist was crusted with congealed blood, spread around a pair of fang-punctures. Abruptly, I recognized her, the girl Bianca had fed upon until she died.

"Rachel," I whispered. "Rachel, is that you?"

As I spoke her name, she turned to me, her eyes slowly focusing on me, as though beholding me through a misty veil. Her expression turned, no pun intended, grave. She nodded to me in recognition.

"Hell's bells," I whispered. "No wonder Bianca got stuck on a vengeance kick. She literally was haunted by your death."

The spirit's face twisted in distress. She said something, but I could hear it only as a distant, muffled sound accompanying the movement of her lips.

"I can't understand you," I said. "Rachel, I can't hear you."

She almost wept, it seemed. She pressed her hand to her ghostly breast, and grimaced at me.

"You're hurt?" I guessed. "You hurt?"

She shook her head. Then touched her temple and drew her fingers slowly down over her eyes, closing them. "Ah," I said. "You're tired."

She nodded. She made a supplicating motion, holding out her hands as though asking for help.

"I don't know what I can do for you. I don't know if I can help you rest or not."

She shook her head again. Then she nodded, toward the door, and made a bottle-shaped curving gesture of her hands.

"Bianca?" I asked. When she nodded, I went on. "You think Bianca can lay you to rest." She shook her head. "She's keeping you here?"

Rachel nodded, her ghostly, pretty face agonized.

"Makes sense," I muttered. "Bianca fixates on you as you die tragically. Binds your ghost here. The ghost appears to her and drives her into a vengeance, and she blames it all on me."

Rachel's ghost nodded.

"I didn't kill you," I said. "You know that."

She nodded again.

"But I'm sorry. I'm sorry that me being in the wrong place at the wrong time set you up to die."

She gave me a gentle smile—which transformed into a sudden expression of horror. She looked past me, at Justine, and then her image began to fade, to withdraw into the wall.

"Hey!" I said. "Hey, wait a minute!"

The mist vanished, and Justine started to move. She rose, casually, and stretched. Then glanced down at herself and ran her hands appreciatively down over her breasts, her stomach. "Very nice," she said, voice subtly altered, different. "Rather like Lydia, in a lot of ways, isn't she, Mister Dresden."

I tensed up. "Kravos," I whispered.

Justine's eyes flooded with blood through the whites. "Oh yes," she said. "Yes indeed."

"Man, you need to get a life in the worst way. That was you, wasn't it. The telephone call the night Agatha Hagglethorn went nuts."

"My last call," Kravos said through Justine's lips, nodding. "I wanted to savor what was about to happen. Like now. Bianca has ordered that you should receive no visitors, but I just couldn't resist the chance to take a look at you."

"You want to look at me?" I asked. I tapped my head. "Come on in. There's a few things in here I'd like to show you."

Justine smiled, and shook her head. "It would be too much effort for too little return. Even without the shelter of a threshold, possessing even a mind so weak as this child's requires a considerable amount of effort. Effort," she added, "which was made possible by a grant from the Harry Dresden Soul Foundation."

I bared my teeth. "Leave the girl alone."

"Oh, but she's fine," Kravos said, through Justine's lips. "She's really happier like this. She can't hurt anyone, you see. Or herself. Her ranting emotions can't compel her to act. That's why the Whites love her so much. They feed on emotion, and this little darling is positively mad with it." Justine's body shivered, and arched sensuously. "It's rather exciting, actually. Madness."

"I wouldn't know," I said. "Look, if we're going to fight, let's fight. Otherwise, blow. I've got things to do."

"I know," Justine said. "You're busy dying of some kind of poisoning. The vampires tried to drink from you, but you made some of them very sick, and so they left you more or less untapped. Highly miffed, Bianca was. She wanted you to die as food for her and her new children."

"What a shame."

"Come now, Dresden. You and I are among the Wise. We both know you wouldn't want to die at the hands of a lesser being."

"I might rank among the wise," I said. "You, Kravos, are nothing but a two-bit troublemaker. You're the stupid thug of wizard land, and that you managed to live as long as you did without killing yourself is some kind of miracle in itself."

Justine snarled and lunged for me. She pinned me to the door with one hand and a casual, supernatural strength that told me she could have pushed her hand *through* me just as easily. "So self-righteous," she snarled. "Always sure that you're right. That you're in command. That you have all the power and all the answers."

I grimaced. Pain flared through my belly again, and it was suddenly all I could do not to scream.

"Well, Dresden. You're dead. You've been slated to die. You'll be gone in the next few hours. And even if you aren't, if you live through what they have planned, the poison will kill you slowly. And before you go you'll sleep. Bianca won't stop mc, this time. You'll sleep and I'll be there. I'll come into your dreams and I will make your last moments on earth a nightmare that lasts for years." She leaned up close, standing on tiptoe, and spat into my face. Then the blood rushed from Justine's eyes and her head fell loosely forward, as though she'd been a horse struggling against the reins, to find their pressure gone. Justine let out a whimper, and sank against me.

I did my best to hold her. We sort of wound up on the floor together, neither one of us in much shape to move. Justine wept. She cried piteously, like a small child, mostly quiet.

"I'm sorry," she said. "I'm sorry. I want to help. But there's too much in the way. I can't think—"

"Shhhhh," I said. I tried to stroke her hair, to soothe her before she could become agitated again. "It's going to be all right."

"We'll die," she whispered. "I'll never see him again."

She wept for some time, as the nausea and pain in my belly grew. The light outside the door never wavered. It didn't know if it was dark or light outside. Or if Thomas and Michael were still alive to come after me. If they were gone, and it was my fault, I'd never be able to live with myself in any case.

I decided that it must be night. It must be fullest, darkest night. No other time of day could possibly suit my predicament.

I rested my head on Justine's, after she fell quiet, and relaxed, as though she were falling asleep after her weeping. I closed my eyes and struggled to come up with a plan. But I didn't have anything. Nothing. It was all but over.

Something stirred, in the shadows where the laundry was piled.

Both of us looked up. I started to push Justine away, but she said, "Don't. Don't go over there."

"Why not?" I asked.

"You won't like it."

I glanced at the girl. And then got up, unsteadily, and made my way over to the piled laundry. I clutched the towel in my hand, for lack of any other weapon.

Someone lay in the piled clothing. Someone in a white shirt, a dark skirt, and a red cloak.

"Stars above," I swore. "Susan."

She groaned, faintly, as though very much asleep or drugged. I hunkered down and moved clothing off of her. "Hell's bells.

Susan, don't try to sit up. Don't move. Let me see if you're hurt, okay?"

I ran my hands over her in the dimness. She seemed to be whole, not bleeding, but her skin was blazing with fever.

"I'm dizzy. Thirsty," she said.

"You've got a fever. Can you roll over here toward me?"

"The light. It hurts my eyes."

"It did mine too, when I woke up. It will pass."

"Don't," Justine whispered. She sat on her heels and rocked slowly back and forth. "You won't like it. You won't like it."

I glanced back at Justine as Susan turned toward me, and then looked down at my girlfriend. She looked back up to me, her features exhausted, confused. She blinked her eyes against the light, and lifted a slim, brown hand to shield her face.

I caught her hand halfway, and stared down at her.

Her eyes were black. All black. Black and staring, glittering, darker than pitch, with no white to them at all to distinguish them as human. My heart leapt up into my throat, and things began to spin faster around me.

"You won't like it," Justine intoned. "They changed her. The Red Court changed her. Bianca changed her."

"Dresden?" Susan whispered.

Dear God, I thought. This can't be happening.

"Mister Dresden? I'm so thirsty."

Chapter 35

Susan let out a whimper and a groan, moving fitfully. By chance, her mouth brushed against my forearm, still stained with drying blood. She froze, completely, her whole body shuddering. She looked up at me with those dark, huge eyes, her face twisting with need. She moved toward my arm again, and I jerked it back from her mouth.

"Susan," I said. "Wait."

"What was that?" she whispered. "That was good." She shivered again and rolled to all fours, eyes slowly focusing on me.

I shot a glance toward Justine, but only saw her feet as she pulled them back to her, slipping back into the tiny space between the washing machine and the wall. I turned back to Susan, who was coming toward me, staring as though blind, on all fours.

I backed away from her, and fumbled out to my side with one hand. I found the bloodstained towel I'd been using before, and threw it at her. She stopped for a moment, staring, and then lowered her face with a groan, beginning to lick at the towel.

I scooted back on all fours, getting away from her, still dizzy. "Justine," I hissed. "What do we do?"

"There's nothing to do," Justine whispered. "We can't get out. She isn't herself. Once she kills, she'll be gone."

I flashed a glance at her over my shoulder. "Once she kills? What do you mean?"

Justine watched me with solemn eyes. "Once she kills. She's different. But she isn't quite like them until it's complete. Until she's killed someone feeding on them. That's the way the Reds work."

"So she's still Susan?"

Justine shrugged again, her expression disinterested. "Sort of."

"If I could talk to her, though. Get through to her. We could maybe snap her out of it?"

"I've never heard of it happening," Justine said. She shivered. "They stay like that. It gets worse and worse. Then they lose control and kill. And it's over."

I bit my lip. "There's got to be something."

"Kill her. She's still weak. Maybe we could, together. If we wait until she's further gone, until the hunger gives her strength, she'll take us both. That's why we're in here."

"No," I said. "I can't hurt her."

Something flickered in Justine's face when I spoke, though I couldn't decide whether it was something warm or something heated, angry. She closed her eyes and said, "Then maybe when she drinks you she'll die of the poison in you."

"Dammit. There's got to be something. Something else you can tell me."

Justine shrugged and shook her head, wearily. "We're already dead, Mister Dresden."

I clenched my teeth together and turned back to Susan. She kept licking at the towel, making frustrated, whimpering noises. She lifted her face to me and stared at me. I could have sworn I saw the bones of her cheeks and jaw stand out more harshly against her skin. Her eyes became drowning deep and pulled at me, beckoned to me to look deeper into that spinning, feverish darkness.

I jerked my eyes away before that gaze could trap me, my heart pounding, but it had already begun to fall away. Susan furrowed her brow in confusion for a moment, blinking her eyes, whatever dark power that had touched them fading, slipping unsteadily.

But even if that gaze hadn't trapped me, hadn't gone all the way over into hypnosis, it made something occur to me: Susan's memories of the soulgaze hadn't been removed. My godmother couldn't have touched those. I was such an idiot. When a mortal looks on something with the Sight, really *looks,* as a wizard may, the memories of what he sees are indelibly imprinted on him. And when a wizard looks into a person's eyes, it's just another way of using the Sight. A two-way use of it, because the person you look at gets to peer back at you, too.

Susan and I had soulgazed more than two years before. She'd

tricked me into it. It was just after that she began pursuing me for stories more closely.

Lea couldn't have taken memories around a soulgaze. But she could have covered them up, somehow, misted them over. No practical difference, for the average person.

But, hell, I'm a wizard. I ain't average.

Susan and I had always been close, since we'd started dating. Intimate time together. The sharing of words, ideas, time, bodies. And that kind of intimacy creates a bond. A bond that I could perhaps use, to uncover fogged memories. To help bring Susan back to herself.

"Susan," I said, forcing my voice out sharp and clear. "Susan Rodriguez."

She shivered as I Named her, at least in part.

I licked my lips and moved towards her. "Susan. I want to help you. All right? I want to help you if I can."

She swallowed another whimper. "But. I'm so thirsty. I can't."

I reached out as I approached her, and plucked a hair from her head. She didn't react to it, though she leaned closer to me, inhaling through her nose, letting out a slow moan on the exhale. She could smell my blood. I wasn't clear on how much of the toxin would be in my bloodstream, but I didn't want her to be hurt. No time to dawdle, Harry.

I took the hair and wound it about my right hand. It went around twice. I closed my fist over it, then grimaced, reaching out to grab Susan's left hand. I spat on my fingers and smoothed them over her palm, then pressed her hand to my fist. The bond, already something tenuously felt in any case, thrummed to life like a bass cello string, amplified by my spit upon her, by the hair in my own hands, the joining of our bodies where our flesh pressed together.

I closed my eyes. It hurt to try to draw in the magic. My weakened body shook. I reached for it, tried to piece together my will. I thought of all the times I'd had with Susan, all the things I'd never had the guts to tell her. I thought of her laugh, her smile, the way her mouth felt on mine, the smell of her shampoo in the shower, the press of her warmth against my back as we slept. I summoned up every memory I had of us together, and started trying to push it through the link between us.

The memories flowed down my arm, to her hand—and stopped, pressing against some misty and elastic barrier. Godmother's spell. I shoved harder at it, but its resistance only grew greater, more intense, the harder I pushed.

Susan whimpered, the sound lost, confused, hungry. She rose up onto her knees and pressed against me, leaning on me. She snuggled her mouth down against the hollow of my throat. I felt her tongue touch my skin, sending an electric jolt of lust flashing through me. Even close to death, hormones will out, I guess.

I kept struggling against Godmother's spell, but it held in place, powerful, subtle. I felt like a child shoving fruitlessly at a heavy glass door.

Susan shivered, and kept licking at my throat.

My skin tingled pleasantly and then started to go numb. Some of my pain faded. Then I felt her teeth against my throat, sharp as she bit at me.

I let out a startled cry. It wasn't a hard bite. She'd bitten me harder than that for fun. But she hadn't had eyes like that then. Her kisses hadn't made my skin go narcotic-numb then. She hadn't been halfway to membership in Club Vampire then.

I pushed harder at the spell, but my best efforts grew weaker and weaker. Susan bit harder, and I felt her body tensing, growing stronger. No longer did she lean against me. I felt one of her hands settle on the back of my neck. It wasn't an affectionate gesture. It was to keep me from moving. She took a deep, shuddering breath.

"In here," she whispered. "It's in here. It's good."

"Susan," I said, keeping the feeble pressure on my godmother's spell. "Susan. Please don't. Don't go. I need you here. You could hurt yourself. Please." I felt her jaws begin to close. Her teeth didn't feel like fangs, but human teeth can rip open skin just fine. She was vanishing. I could feel the link between us fading, growing weaker and weaker.

"I'm so sorry. I never meant to let you down." I said. I sagged against her. There wasn't much reason to keep fighting. But I did anyway. For her, if not for me. I held onto that link, to the pressure I had forced against the spell, to the memories of Susan and me, together.

"I love you."

Why it worked right then, why the webbing of my godmother's spell frayed as though the words had been an open flame, I don't know. I haven't found any explanation for it. There aren't any magical words, really. The words just hold the magic. They give it a shape and a form, they make it useful, describe the images within.

I'll say this, though: Some words have a power that has nothing to do with supernatural forces. They resound in the heart and mind, they live long after the sounds of them have died away, they echo in the heart and the soul. They have power, and that power is very real.

Those three words are good ones.

I flooded into her, through the link, into the darkness and the confusion that bound her, and I saw, through her thoughts, that my coming was a flame in the endless cold, a beacon flashing out against that night. The light came, our memories, the warmth of us, she and I, and battered down the walls inside her, crushed away Lea's lingering spell, tore those memories away from my godmother, wherever she was, and brought them back home.

I heard her cry out at the sudden flush of memory, as awareness washed over her. She changed, right there against me—the hard, alien tension changed. It didn't vanish, but it changed. It became Susan's tension, Susan's confusion, Susan's pain, aware, alert, and very much herself again.

The power of the spell faded away, leaving only the blurred impression of it, like lightning that crackles through the night, leaving dazzling colors in the darkness behind.

I found myself kneeling against her, holding her hand. She still held my head. Her teeth still pressed against my throat, sharp and hard.

I reached up with my other shaking hand, and stroked at her hair. "Susan," I said, gentle. "Susan. Stay with me."

The pressure lessened. I felt hot tears fall against my shoulder.

"Harry," she whispered. "Oh, God. I'm so thirsty. I want it so much."

I closed my eyes. "I know," I said. "I'm sorry."

"I could take you. I could take it," she whispered.

"Yes."

"You couldn't stop me. You're weak, sick."

"I couldn't stop you," I agreed.

"Say it again."

I frowned. "What?"

"Say it again. It helps. Please. It's so hard not to . . ."

I swallowed. "I love you," I said.

She jerked, as though I'd punched her in the pit of the stomach.

"I love you," I said again. "Susan."

She lifted her mouth from my skin, and looked up, into my eyes. They were her eyes again—dark, rich, warm brown, bloodshot, filled with tears. "The vampires," she said. "They—"

"I know."

She closed her eyes, more tears falling. "I tr-tried to stop them. I tried."

Pain hit me again, pain that didn't have anything to do with poison or injuries. It hit me sharp and low, just beneath my heart, as though someone had just shoved an icicle through me. "I know you did," I told her. "I know you did."

She fell against me, weeping. I held her.

After a long time, she whispered, "It's still there. It isn't going away."

"I know."

"What am I going to do?"

"We'll work on that," I said. "I promise. We have other problems right now." I filled her in on what had happened, holding her in the dimness.

"Is anyone coming for us?" she asked.

"I . . . I don't think so. Even if Thomas and Michael got away, they couldn't storm this place. If they ever even got out of the Nevernever. Michael could go to Murphy, but she couldn't just smash her way in here without a warrant. And Bianca's contacts could probably stall that for a while."

"We have to get you out of here," she said. "You've got to get to a hospital."

"Works in theory. Now we just have to work out the details."

She licked her lips. "I . . . can you even walk?"

"I don't know. That last spell. If there was much left in me, that spell took it out."

"What if you slept?" she asked.

"Kravos would have his chance to torture me." I paused, and stared at the far wall.

"God," Susan whispered. She hugged me, gently. "I love you, Harry. You should get to hear it t—" She stopped, and looked up at me. "What?"

"That's it," I said. "That's what needs to happen."

"What needs to happen? I don't understand."

The more I thought about it, the crazier it sounded. But it might work. If I could time it just right . . .

I looked down, taking Susan's shoulders in my hands, staring at her eyes. "Can you hold on? Can you keep it together for another few hours?"

She shivered. "I think so. I'll try."

"Good," I said. I took a deep breath. "Because I need to be asleep long enough to start dreaming."

"But Kravos," Susan said. "Kravos will get inside of you. He'll kill you."

"Yeah," I said. I took a slow breath. "I'm pretty much counting on it."

Chapter 36

My nightmares came quickly, dull cloud of poisonous confusion blurring my senses, distorting my perceptions. For a moment, I was hanging by one wrist over an inferno of fire, smoke, and horrible creatures, the steel of the handcuffs suspending me cutting into my flesh, drawing blood. Smoke smothered me, forced me to cough, and my vision blurred as I started to fade out.

Then I was in a new place. In the dark. Cold stone chilled me where I lay upon it. All around me where the whispers of things moving in the shadows. Scaly rasps. Soft, hungry hisses, together with the gleam of malevolent eyes. My heart pounded in my throat.

"There you are," whispered one of the voices. "I watched them have you, you know."

I sat up, shivering violently. "Yeah, well. That's why they call them monsters. It's what they do."

"They enjoyed it," came the whispering voice. "If only I could have videotaped it for you."

"TV will rot your brain, Kravos," I said.

Something blurred out of the darkness and struck me across the face. The blow drove me back and down. My vision blurred over with scarlet and my perceptions sharpened through a burst of pain, but I didn't drop unconscious. You don't, as a rule, in dreams.

"Jokes," the voice hissed. "Jokes will not save you now."

"Hell's bells, Kravos," I muttered, sitting up again. "Do they produce a *Cliched Lines Textbook for Villains* or something? Go for broke. Tell me that since you're going to kill me anyway, you might as well reveal your secret plan."

The dark blurred toward me again. I didn't bother trying to defend myself. It drove me to the ground, and sat on my chest.

I stared up at Kravos. Forms and shapes hung about him like misty clothes. I could see the shape of the shadow demon, around him. I could see my own face, drifting among the layers. I saw Justine there, and Lydia. And there, at the center of that distorted, drifting mass, I saw Kravos.

He didn't look much different. He had a thin, pinched face, and brown hair faded with grey. He wore a full, untrimmed beard, but it only made his head seem misshapen. He had wide, leathery shoulders, and symbols painted in blood, ritual things whose meanings I could vaguely piece together, covered his chest. He lifted his hands and delivered two more blows to my face, explosions of pain.

"Where are your gibes now, wizard?" Kravos snarled. "Where are your jokes? Weak, petty, self-righteous fool. We are going to have a very good time together, until Bianca comes to finish you."

"You think so?" I asked. "I'm not sure. It's our first date. Maybe we should take this one step at a time."

Kravos hit me again, across the bridge of my nose, and my vision blurred with tears. "You aren't funny!" he shouted. "You are going to *die*! You can't treat this as a joke!"

"Why not?" I shot back. "Kravos, I took you out with a piece of chalk and a Ken doll. You're the biggest joke of a spellslinger I've ever seen. Even I didn't expect you to drop like that; maybe the link with that doll worked so well because it was anatomically corr—"

I didn't get the chance to finish the sentence. Kravos screamed and took my dream self by the throat. It felt real. It felt completely as though he had me, his weight pinning my weakened body down, his fingers crushing into my windpipe. My head pounded. I struggled against him, futile and reflexive motions—but to no avail. He kept on choking me, the pressure increasing. Blackness covered my dream vision, and I knew that he would hold it until he was sure I was dead.

People who have near-death experiences often talk about moving toward the light at the end of the tunnel. Or ascending toward the light, or flying or floating, or falling. I didn't get that. I'm not sure what that says about the state of my soul. There was no light, no kindly beckoning voice, no lake of fire to fall into. There was only silence, deep and timeless, where not even the beating of my heart thudded in my ears. I felt an odd pressure against my skin, my face, as though I had pressed into and through a wall of plastic wrap.

I felt a dull thud on top of my chest, and a sudden lessening of the burning in my lungs. Then another thud. More easing on my lungs. Then more blows to my chest.

My heart lurched back into motion with a hesitant thunder, and I felt myself take a wheezing breath. The plastic-wrap sensation tugged at me for a moment, then lifted away.

I shuddered, and struggled to open my eyes again. When I did, Kravos, still holding my throat, blinked his eyes in shock. "No!" he snarled. "You're dead! You're dead!"

"Susan's giving his real body CPR," someone said, behind him. Kravos whipped his head around to look, just in time to catch a stiff cross to the tip of his chin. He cried out in startled fear, and fell off of me.

I sucked in another labored breath and sat up. "Hell's bells," I gasped. "It worked."

Kravos struggled to his feet and backed away, staring, his eyes flying open wide as they looked back and forth between me and my savior.

My savior was me, too. Or rather, something that looked a very great deal like me. It was my shape and coloring, and had bruises and scratches, mixed with a few burns, all over it. Its hair was a wild mess, its eyes sunken over circles of black in a pale, sickly face.

My double peered at me and said, "You know. We really look like hell."

"What's this?" hissed Kravos. "What trick is this?"

I offered myself a hand up, so I took it. It took me a moment to balance, but I said, "Hell, Kravos. As flexible as the boundaries between here and the spirit world have been, I would have expected you to figure it out by now."

Kravos looked at the two of us, and bared his teeth. "Your ghost," he hissed.

"Technically," my ghost said. "Harry actually died for a minute. Don't you remember how ghosts are made? Normally, there wouldn't be enough latent energy to create an impression like me, but with him being a wizard—a real wizard, not a petty fake like you—and with the border to the Nevernever in such a state of flux, it was pretty much inevitable."

"That was very well said," I told my ghost.

"Just be glad your theory worked. I wouldn't be very good at this, solo."

"Well, thank Kravos here. It was him and Bianca and Mavra who stirred things up enough to make this possible." We looked at Kravos. "You aren't getting to sneak attack me while I'm doped unconscious, bub. It isn't going to be like last time. Any questions?"

Kravos hurled himself at me in a fury. He overpowered me, and bore down on me, far too strong for me to overcome directly. I thrust a thumb into his eye. He screamed and bit at my hand.

And then my ghost came in. He wrapped his arms around Kravos's neck and leaned back, hard, tugging the man's body into a bow. Kravos strained and struggled, his arms flailing, strong as any maddened beast. My ghost was a little stronger than I, but he wouldn't be able to hold Kravos for long.

"Harry!" my ghost shouted. "Now!"

I gripped Kravos by the throat, letting all the frustration and fury inside well up. I held up my left hand, and my dream self's nails lengthened into glittering claws. Kravos stared at me in shock.

"You think you're the only one who can play in dreams, Kravos? If I'd been ready for you the last time, you'd have never been able to do to me what you did." My face twisted, mouth extending into a muzzle. "This time I'm ready. You're in my dream, now. And I'm taking back what's mine."

I tore into his guts. I ripped him open with my claws and wolfed into his vitals, just as he had to me. Bits of him flew free, dream-blood splashing, dream-vitals steaming.

I tore and worried and gulped down bloody meat. He screamed and fought, but he couldn't get away. I tore him to pieces and devoured him, the blood a hot, sweet rush on my tongue, his ghost-flesh hot and good, easing the ache of emptiness inside of me.

I ate him all up.

As I did, I felt power, surety, confidence, all rushing back into me. My stolen magic came raging back into me, filling me like silver lightning, a tingling, almost painful rush as I took back what was mine.

But I didn't stop there. My ghost fell away as I kept going. Kept tearing Kravos apart and gulping down the pieces. I got to his own power when I ate his heart—red, livid power, vital and primitive and dangerous. Kravos's magic had been for nothing but causing harm.

I took it. I had plenty of harm to start causing.

By the time I'd finished tearing him to shreds, the pieces were vanishing like the remnants of any foul dream. I crouched on the dream-floor as they did, shaking with the rushing energy inside of me. I felt a hand on my shoulder, and looked up.

I must have looked feral. My ghost took a step back and lifted both hands. "Easy, easy," he said. "I think you got him."

"I got him," I said quietly.

"He was a ghost," my ghost said. "He wasn't really a person any more. And even as ghosts go, he was a bad egg. You don't have anything to regret."

"Easy for you to say," I said. "You don't have to live with me."

"True," my ghost answered. He glanced down at himself. His bruised limbs grew slowly translucent, and he began vanishing. "That's the only bad thing about this gig as a ghost. Once you accomplish whatever it was that caused you to get created, you're done. Kravos—the real Kravos—is already gone. Just his shell stayed behind. And this would have happened to him, too, if he'd killed you."

"Do unto others before they do unto you," I said. "Thanks."

"It was your plan," my ghost said. "I feel like hell anyway."

"I know."

"I guess you do. Try not to get killed again, okay?"

"Working on it."

He waved one hand, and faded away.

I blinked open my eyes. Susan knelt over me, striking my face with her hand. I felt wretched—but that wasn't all. My body almost buzzed with the energy I held, my skin tingling as though I hadn't used a whit of magic in weeks. She struck me twice more before I let out a strangled groan and lifted a hand to intercept hers.

"Harry?" she demanded. "Harry, are you awake?"

I blinked my eyes. "Yeah," I said. "Yeah. I'm up."

"Kravos?" she hissed.

"I pushed his buttons and he lost control. He got me," I said. "Then I got him. You did it just right."

Susan sat back on her heels, trembling. "God. When you

stopped breathing, I almost screamed. If you hadn't told me to expect it, I don't know what I would have done."

"You did fine," I said. I rolled over and pushed myself to my feet, though my body groaned in protest. The pain felt like something happening very far away, to someone else. It wasn't relevant to me. The energy coursing through me—*that* was relevant. I had to release some of it soon or I'd explode.

Susan started to help me, and then sat back, staring at me. "Harry? What happened?"

"I got something back," I said. "It's a high. I still hurt, but that doesn't seem to be important." I stretched my arms out over my head. Then I stalked over to the dirty laundry and found a pair of boxers that fit me, more or less. I gave Susan a self-conscious glance, and slipped into them. "Get something on Justine, and we're out of here."

"I tried. She won't come out from behind the washing machine."

I clenched my jaw, irritated, and snapped my fingers while saying, *"Ventas servitas."*

There was an abrupt surge of moving air and Justine came tumbling out from behind the washing machine with a yelp. She lay there for a moment, naked and stunned, staring up at me with wide, dark eyes.

"Justine," I said. "We're leaving. I don't care how crazy you are. You're coming with me."

"Leaving?" Justine stammered. Susan helped her sit up, and wrapped the red cloak around her shoulders. It fell to mid-thigh on the girl, who rose, trembling like a deer before headlights. "But. We're going to die."

"Were," I said. "Past tense." I turned back to the door and reached into all that energy glittering through me, pointed my finger and shouted, *"Ventas servitas!"* With another roar of wind, the door exploded outwards, into a large, empty room, splinters flying everywhere and shattering one of the two lightbulbs illuminating the room beyond.

I said, voice crackling with tension and anger, "Get behind me. Both of you. Don't get in front of me unless you want to get hurt."

I took a step toward the doorway.

An arm shot around the edge of the door, followed swiftly by Kyle Hamilton's body in its masquerade costume, his flesh mask back in place. He got me by the throat, whirling me in a half circle to slam me against the wall.

"Harry!" Susan shouted.

"Got you," Kyle purred, pinning me in place with supernatural force. Behind him, Kelly followed him in, her once-pretty face twisting and bulging beneath her flesh mask, as though she could barely contain the creature inside her. Her face was warped, twisted, distorted, as though whatever was beneath it had been so horribly mangled that not even a vampire's powers of masquerade could wholly conceal its hideousness.

"Come along, sister," Kyle said. "Tainted or not, we shall tear open his heart and see what a wizard's blood tastes like."

Chapter 37

Fury surged through me, before fear or anxiety, a fury so scarlet and bright that I could scarcely believe it was mine. Maybe it wasn't. After all, you are what you eat—even if you're a wizard.

"Let go, Kyle," I grated. "You've got one chance to live through this. Walk away, right now."

Kyle laughed, letting his fangs extend. "No more bluffs, wizard," he purred. "No more illusions. Take him, sister."

Kelly came at me in a rush, but I had been waiting for that. I lifted my right hand and snarled, *"Ventas servitas!"* A furious column of wind slammed into her like a bag of sand, catching her in midair and driving her across the room, into the wall.

Kyle screamed in fury, drawing his hand back off of my throat and then driving it at me. I dodged the first blow by jerking my head to one side, and heard his hand crunch into the stone. The dodge cost me my balance, and as I teetered, he lashed out again, aiming for my neck. All I could do was watch it come.

And then Susan came between us. I didn't see her move toward us, but I saw her catch the blow in both of her hands. She spun, twisting her hips and body and shoulders, letting out a furious scream. She threw Kyle across the room, in the air the whole way, and with no noticeable trajectory. He slammed into his sister, driving them both into the wall once more. I heard Kelly scream, incoherent and bestial. The black, slime-covered bat-thing beneath the pleasant flesh mask tore its way out, shredding damply flapping skin with its talons as it started raking at Kyle. He struggled against her, shouting something that became lost in his creature-form's scream as he too tore his way free. The two of them started clawing at one another in a frenzy, fangs and tongues and talons flashing.

I snarled, and rolled my wrist, flipping my hand toward them in a gesture wholly unfamiliar to me. Words spilled from my lips in thundering syllables, *"Satharak, na-kadum!"* That scarlet, furious power I had stolen from Kravos flashed over me, following the gesture of my right hand, lashing out in a blaze of scarlet light that spun around the maddened vampires. The scarlet blaze whirled about them, winding too swiftly to be seen, a ribbon of flame that cocooned them both, burned brighter and hotter, the spell enfolding them in fire.

They screamed as they died, sounds like metal sheets tearing, and somehow also like terrified children. Heat thrummed back against us, almost singeing the exposed hairs on my legs, my chest. Greasy black smoke started to spread over the floor, and it stank.

I watched as they burned, though I could see nothing beneath the blazing flame-cocoon. Part of me wanted to dance in malicious glee, to throw my arms up in the air and crow my defiance and scorn to my enemies while they died, and to roll through their ashes when they'd cooled.

More of me grew sickened. I stared at the spell I had wrought and couldn't believe it had come from me—whether or not I'd taken the power, maybe even some primal knowledge of this spell, from Kravos's devoured spirit, the magic had come from *me.* I had killed them, as swiftly and as efficiently as with as little forethought as one gives to crushing an ant.

They were vampires, some part of me said. *They had it coming. They were monsters.*

I glanced aside, at Susan, who stood panting, her white shirt stained dark brown with blood. She stared at the fire, her eyes dark and wide, the whites filled in with black. I watched her shudder and close her eyes. When she opened them again, they were normal once more, blurred with tears.

Within the confines of my spell, the screams stopped. Now there were only cracklings. Poppings. The sound of overheated marrow boiling, bursting out of bone.

I turned away, toward the door, and said, "Let's go."

Susan and Justine followed me.

I led them through the basement. It was large and unfinished and damp. The room outside the washroom had a large drain in the center of the floor. There were corpses, there. Children from the masquerade. Others, dressed in rags and castoff clothes. The missing street people.

I stopped long enough to send my senses questing out over them, but there was no stirring of breath, no faint pulse of heartbeat. The corpses showed no lividity at all. The floor lay damp beneath our feet, and a hose still ran out a trickle of water, to one side.

Dinner had already been served.

"I hate them," I said. My voice rang out too loud, in that room. "I hate them, Susan."

She said nothing, in answer.

"I'm not going to let them keep this up. I've tried to stay out of their way before. I can't, now. Not after what I've seen."

"You can't fight them," Justine whispered. "They're too strong. There are too many of them."

I held up a hand, and Justine fell silent. I tilted my head to one side, and heard a faint thrumming, at the very edges of my magical perception. I stalked across the room, around the bodies, to an alcove in the wall.

Cheap shelving had been installed in the alcove, and on the shelves sat my shield bracelet, my blasting rod, and Bob's skull, still in its fishnet sack. Even as I approached, the skull's eyes flared to life.

"Harry," Bob said. "Stars and skies, you're all right!" He hesitated for a second, and then said, "And looking *grim.* Even dressed in boxers with yellow duckies on them."

I glanced down, and did my best to picture a vampire wearing boxers with yellow duckies. Or a wizard wearing yellow duckies, for that matter. "Bob," I said.

Bob whistled. "Wow. Your aura is different. You look a lot like—"

"Shut up, Bob," I said, my voice very quiet.

He did.

I put on my bracelet, and took up my rod. I scanned around and found my staff wedged into a corner, and took it out as well. "Bob," I asked. "What is all my stuff doing here?"

"Oh," Bob said. "That. Well. Bianca got the idea, somewhere, that your stuff might explode if anyone messed around with it."

I heard the wryness in my voice, though I didn't feel it. "She did, did she."

"I can't imagine how."

"I'm doubling your pay." I took Bob's skull and handed it back to Justine. "Carry this. Don't drop it."

Bob whistled. "Hey, cutie. That's a real nice red cloak you got there. Will you let me see the lining?"

I swatted the skull on the way past, drawing an outraged, "Ow!" from Bob.

"Stop goofing around. We're still inside Bianca's, and we still have to get out." I frowned, and glanced at Justine, then swiftly, left and right. "Where's Susan?"

Justine blinked. "She was right here behind—" She turned, staring.

Water dripped.

Silence reigned.

Justine started trembling like a leaf. "Here," she whispered. "They're here. We can't see them."

"What's this 'we' stuff, kimosabe," Bob muttered. The skull spun about in its fishnet sack. "I don't see any veils, Harry."

I swept my eyes left and right, gripping my blasting rod. "Did you see her leave? Or anyone take her?"

Bob coughed. "Well. Truth be told, I was looking at Justine's luscious little—"

"I get the point, Bob."

"Sorry."

I shook my head, irritated. "They snuck in, under a veil maybe. Grabbed Susan and went. Why the hell didn't they stick around? Just put a knife in my back? Why didn't they take Justine, too?"

"Good questions," Bob said.

"I'll tell you why. Because they weren't here. They couldn't have just carried Susan off that easy. Not now."

"Why not?" Bob asked.

"Trust me. She'd be a handful. They couldn't do it without making a fuss, which we'd notice."

"Assuming you're right," Bob said, "why would she just walk away?"

Justine glanced back at me, and licked her lips. "Bianca could make her. I've seen her do it. She made Susan walk into the laundry room on her own."

I grunted. "Looks like Bianca's been hitting the books, Bob."

"Vampire wizard," Bob said. "Black magic. Could be very tough."

"So can I. Justine, stay behind me. Keep your eyes open."

"Yes, sir," she said, her voice quiet. I strode past her, toward the stairs. Some of the energy I'd felt before had faded away. My pain and weakness grew closer to me, more noticeable. I did everything I could to shove it to the back of my mind. A swift little thrill of panic gabbled in my throat and tried to make me start screaming. I shoved that away, too. I just walked to the bottom of the stairs, and looked up them.

The doors at the top were elegant wood, and standing open. A soft breeze and the smell of night air flowed down the stairs. Late night, faint with the traces of dusty dawn. I glanced back at Justine, and she all but flinched away from me.

"Stay down here," I told her. "Bob, some things are going to start flying. Give her whatever help you can."

"All right, Harry," Bob said. "You know that door's been opened for you. They're going to be waiting for you to walk up there."

"Yeah," I said. "I'm not getting any stronger. Might as well do it now."

"You could wait until dawn. Then they'd—"

I cut him off, short. "Then they'd force their way down here to escape the sunlight. And it would still be a fight." I glanced at Justine and said, "I'll get you out, if I can."

She chanced a swift glance at my face, and back down. "Thank you, Mister Dresden. For trying."

"Sure, kid." I flexed my left hand, feeling the cool silver of the shield bracelet there. I gripped my staff tight. Then rolled the blasting rod through my fingers, feeling the runes carved into the wood, formulae of power, fire, force.

I put one foot on the stairs. My bare foot made little sound, but the board creaked beneath my weight. I squared my shoulders, and went up the next stair, and the next. Resolute, I guess. Terrified, certainly. Seething with power, with a simmering anger ready to boil over again.

I tried to clear my mind, to hang onto the anger and to dismiss the fear. I had limited success, but I made it up the stairs.

At the top, Bianca stood at one end of the great hall through the open doors. She wore the white gown I'd seen her in before, the soft fabric draping and stretching in alluring curves, creating shadows upon her with an artist's conviction. Susan knelt beside her, shaking, her head bowed. Bianca kept one hand on her hair.

Spread out around and behind Bianca were a dozen vampires; skinny limbs, flabby black bodies and drooling fangs, the flaps of skin between arm and flank and thigh stretched out, here and there, like half-functional wings. Some of the vampires had climbed up the walls and perched there, like gangly black spiders. All of them, even Susan, had huge, dark eyes. All of them stood looking at me.

In front of Bianca knelt a half-dozen men in plain suits that bulged in odd places. They held guns in their hands. Great big guns. Some kind of assault weapons, I thought. Their eyes looked a little vague, like they'd only been allowed to see some of what was in the room. Just as well.

I looked back at them and leaned on my staff. And I laughed. It came out a wheezing cackle, that echoed around the great hall, and caused the vampires to stir restlessly.

Bianca let her lips curve into a slow smile. "And what do you find so amusing, my pet?"

I smiled back. There was nothing friendly in it. "All of this. For a guy with two sticks and a pair of yellow ducky boxer shorts, you must think I'm a real dangerous man."

"As a matter of fact, I do," Bianca said. "Were I you, I would consider it flattery."

"Would you?" I asked.

Bianca let her smile widen. "Oh. Oh, yes. Gentlemen," she said, to the men with guns. "Fire."

Chapter 38

I lifted my left hand before me, pouring energy into the shield bracelet, and shouted, *"Riflettum!"*

The guns roared with fire and thunder. Sparks showered off of a barrier less than six inches away from my hand. The bracelet grew warm as the security men poured a hail of gunfire at me. It stopped, just short, and bullets shot aside, chewing through the expensive woodwork and bouncing wildly around the room. One of the vampires let out a yowl and dropped from the wall to splat on the ground like a fat bug. One of the security men's guns suddenly jumped and twisted, and he cried out in pain, reeling back, blood streaming from his hands and the ruins of his face.

Technology doesn't tend to work too well around magic. Including the feeding mechanisms of automatic weapons.

Two of the guns jammed before dumping their full clips, and the others fell silent, spent. I still stood, one hand extended. Bullets lay all over the floor in front of me, misshapen slugs of lead. The security men stared, and stumbled away from me, behind Bianca and the vampires, and out the door. I don't blame them. If all I had was a gun, and it had just been that useless, I would run, too.

I took a step forward, scattering bullets with my bare feet. "Get out of my way," I said. "Let us out. No one else has to get hurt."

"Kyle," Bianca said, stroking Susan's hair. "Kelly. She was quite mad in any case. Not all of them make the transition well." Her gaze traveled down to Susan.

The smile I wore sharpened. "Last chance, Bianca. Let us out peacefully, and you walk away alive."

"And if I say no?" she asked, very mild.

I snarled, my temper snapping. I lifted the blasting rod, whirled it around my head as I drew in my will, and snarled, *"Fuego!"* Power exploded from the rod, circular coruscations following a solid scarlet column of energy that lanced forward, toward the vampire's head.

Bianca kept smiling. She lifted her left hand, mumbled some gibberish, and I saw cold darkness gather before her, a concave disk that met my energy lance and absorbed it, scattered it, sent smaller bolts of fire darting here and there, splashing on the floor in small, blazing puddles.

I just stared at her for a moment. I knew that she'd known some tricks, maybe a veil or two, a glamour or two, maybe how to whip up a fascination. But that kind of straightforward deflection wasn't something just anyone could do. Some of the people on the White Council couldn't have stopped that shot without help.

Bianca smiled at me, and lowered her hand. The vampires laughed, hissing, inhuman laughter. The hairs on the back of my neck stood up, and a cold shudder glided gleefully up and down my spine.

"Well, Mister Dresden," she purred. "It would appear that Mavra was an able instructor, and my lessons well learned. We seem to be at something of a standoff. But there's one more piece I'd like to put on the board." She clapped her hands, and gestured to one side.

One of the vampires opened a door. Standing behind it, both hands on a stylish cane, stood a medium-sized man, dark of hair and coloring, brawny through the chest and shoulders. He wore a tailored suit of dark grey in an immaculate cut. He made me think of native South Americans, with a sturdy jaw and broad, strong features.

"Nice suit," I told him.

He looked me up and down. "Nice . . . ducks."

"Okay," I said, "I'll bite. Who's that?"

"My name," the man said, "is Ortega. Don Paolo Ortega, of the Red Court."

"Hiya, Don," I said. "I'd like to lodge a complaint."

He smiled, a show of broad, white teeth. "I'm sure you would, Mister Dresden. But I have been monitoring the situation here. And the Baroness," he nodded to Bianca, "has broken none of the

Accords. Nor has she violated the laws of hospitality, nor her own given word."

"Oh come on," I said. "She's broken the spirit of all of them!"

Ortega tsked. "Alas, that in the Accords it was agreed that there is no spirit of the law, between our kinds, Mister Dresden. Only its letter. And Baroness Bianca has strictly adhered to its letter. You have instigated multiple combats in her home, murdered her sworn bondsman, inflicted damage to her property and her reputation. And now you stand here prepared to continue your grievance with her, in a most unlawful and cavalier fashion. I believe that what you do is sometimes referred to as 'cowboy justice.'"

"If there's a point in here, somewhere," I said, "get to it."

Ortega's eyes glittered. "I am present as a witness to the Red King, and the Vampire Courts at large. That is all. I am merely a witness."

Bianca turned her eyes back to me. "A witness who will carry word of your treacherous attack and intrusion back to the Courts," she said. "It will mean war between our kindred and the White Council."

War.

Between the vampires and the White Council.

Son of a bitch. It was unthinkable. Such a conflict hadn't happened in millennia. Not in living memory—and some wizards live a damned long time.

I had to swallow, and hide the fact that I had just gulped. "Well. Since he isn't running off to tattle right this second, I can only assume that you're about to offer me a deal."

"I never thought you were slow on the uptake, Mister Dresden," Bianca said. "Will you hear my offer?"

I ached more with every moment that went by. My body was failing. I had ridden the rush of magic through the last several moments, but I had spent a lot of that power. It would come back, but I was running the batteries down—and the more I did it, the more I couldn't ignore my weakness, my dizziness.

Legally speaking, the vampires had me over a barrel. I needed a plan. I needed a plan in the worst way. I needed time.

"Sure," I said. "I'll hear you out."

Bianca curled her fingers through Susan's hair. "First. You shall be forgiven your . . . excesses of bad taste of the last few days. But for the two deaths, none of it is unworkable—and those two would have died shortly, in any case. I will forgive you, Mister Dresden."

"That's so kind."

"It gets better. You may take your equipment, your skull, and the White bastard's whore with you when you leave. Unharmed and free of future malice. All accounts will be called even."

I let the dry show in my tone. "How could I possibly say no."

She smiled. "You killed someone very dear to me, Mister Dresden—not directly, true, but your actions mandated her death. For that, too, I will forgive you."

I narrowed my eyes.

Bianca ran her hands over Susan's hair. "This one will stay with me. You stole away someone dear to me, Mister Dresden. And I am going to take away someone dear to you. After that, all will be equal." She gave Ortega a very small smile and then glanced at me and asked, "Well? What say you? If you prefer to remain with her, I'm sure a place could be made for you here. After suitable assurances of your loyalty, of course."

I remained silent for a moment, stunned.

"Well, wizard?" she snapped, harsher. "How do you answer? Accept my bargain. My *compromise.* Or it is war. And you will become its first casualty."

I looked at Susan. She stared blankly, her mouth partially open, caught in a trance of some kind. I could probably snap her out of it, provided a bunch of vampires didn't tear me limb from limb while I tried. I looked up at Bianca. At Ortega. At the hissing vampire cronies. They were drooling on the polished floor.

I hurt all over, and I felt so very damned tired.

"I love her," I said. I didn't say it very loud.

"What?" Bianca stared at me. "What did you say?"

"I said, I love her."

"She is already half mine."

"So? I still love her."

"She isn't even fully human any longer, Dresden. It won't be long before she is as a sister to me."

"Maybe. Maybe not," I said. "Get your hands off my girlfriend."

Bianca's eyes widened. "You are *mad,*" she said. "You would flirt with chaos, destruction—with war. For the sake of *this* one wounded soul?"

I smote my staff on the floor, reaching deep for power. Deeper than I've ever reached before. Outside, in the gathering morning, the air crackled with thunder.

Bianca, even Ortega, looked abruptly uncertain, looking up and around, before focusing on me again.

"For the sake of one soul. For one loved one. For one life." I called power into my blasting rod, and its tip glowed incandescent white. "The way I see it, there's nothing else worth fighting a war for."

Bianca's face distorted with fury. She lost it. She split apart her skin like some gruesome caterpillar, the black beast clawing its way out of her flesh mask, jaws gaping, black eyes burning with feral fury. "Kill him!" she shouted. "Kill him, kill him, kill him!"

The vampires came for me, across the floor, along the walls, scuttling like roaches or spiders—too fast for easy belief. Bianca gathered shadow into her hands and hurled it at me.

I fell back a pace, caught Bianca's strike with my staff, and parried it into one of her flunkies. The darkness enfolded the vampire, and it screamed from within. When the fog around it vanished, nothing remained but dust. I responded with another gout of fire from the rod, sweeping it like a scythe through the oncoming vampires, setting them aflame. They writhed and screamed.

Spittle sliced toward me from above and to one side, and I barely ducked away in time. The vampire clinging to the ceiling followed its venom down, but it met the end of my staff in its belly, the other end solidly planted against the floor. The vampire rebounded with a burping sound and landed hard on the floor. I lifted the staff and smote down on the thing's head, to the sound of more thunder outside. Power lashed down through the staff, and crushed the vampire's skull like an egg. Dust rained down from the ceiling, and the vampire's claws scratched a frantic staccato on the floor as it died.

I had done well for the moment—the vamps nearest me were falling back, teeth bared. But more were coming, from behind them. Bianca hurled another strike at me, and though I interposed both staff and shield, the deathly cold of it numbed my fingers.

I was running out of strength, panting, my weariness and weakness struggling to claim me. I fought off the dizziness, enough to send another flash of fire at an oncoming vampire, but it skittered aside, and all I did was plow a blazing furrow in the floorboards.

They fell back for a moment, separated from me by an expanse of flame, and I struggled to catch my breath.

They were coming. The vampires would be coming for me. My brain kept chattering at me, frantic, panicked. They're coming. Justine, Susan, and I might as well be dead. Dead like all the others. Dead like all their victims.

I leaned against the wall by the stairs, panting, fighting to hold on to some sense of clarity. Dead. Victims. The victims below. The dead.

I dropped the blasting rod. I fell to my knees.

With my staff, I scratched a circle around me, in the dust. It was enough. The circle closed with a thrum of power. Magic ran rampant in that house, the sea of supernatural energy stirred to froth.

I had no guide for this kind of spell. I had no focus, nothing to target, but that wasn't the kind of magic I was working with. I shoved my senses down, into the earth, like reaching fingers. I blanked out the burning hall, my enemies, Bianca's howling. I shut away the fire, the smoke, the pain, the nausea. I focused, and reached beneath me.

And I found them. I found the dead, the victims, the ones who had been taken. Not just the few piled below, like so much trash to be discarded. I found others. Dozens of others. Scores. Hundreds. Bones hidden away, never marked, never remembered. Restless shades, trapped in the earth, too weak to act, to take vengeance, to seek peace. Maybe on another night, or in another place, I couldn't have done it. But the way had been prepared for me, by Bianca and her people. They'd thought to weaken the border between life and death, to use the dead as a weapon against me.

But that blade can cut both ways.

I found those spirits, reached out and touched them, one by one.

"Memorium," I whispered. *"Memoratum. Memortius."*

Energy rushed out of me. I shoved it out as fast as it would go, and I gave it to them. To the lost ones. The seduced, the betrayed, the homeless, the helpless. All the people the vampires had preyed on, through the years, all the dead I could reach. I reached out into the turmoil Bianca and her allies had created, and I gave those wandering shades power.

The house began to shake.

From below, in the basement, there came a rumbling sound. It began as a moan. It rose to a wail. And then it became a screaming mob, a roar of sound that shattered the senses, that made my heart and my belly shiver with the sheer force of it.

The dead came. They erupted through the floor, and took forms of smoke and flame and cinder. I saw them as I swayed, weakened, finished by the effort of the spell. I saw their faces. I saw newsboys from the roaring twenties, and greaser street punks from the fifties. I saw delivery people and homeless transients and lost children rise up, deadly in their fury. The ghosts reached out with flaming hands to burn and sear; they shoved their smoky bodies into noses and throats. They howled their names and the names of their murderers, the names of their loved ones, and their vengeance shook that grand old house like a thunderstorm, like an earthquake.

The ceiling began to fall in. I saw vampires being dragged into the flames, down into the basement as burning sections of floor gave way. Some tried to flee, but the spirits of the dead knew no more pity than they had rest. They hammered at the vampires, raked at them, ghostly hands and bodies made nearly tangible by the power I'd channeled into them.

Vampires died. Ghosts swarmed and screamed everywhere, terrible and beautiful, heartbreaking and ridiculous as humanity itself. The sound banished any thought of speech, hammered upon my skin like physical blows.

I was more terrified than I had ever been in my life. I struggled to my feet and beckoned down the stairs. Justine stumbled up them, Bob's eyelights blazing bright orange, a beacon in the smoke. I grabbed her wrist and tried to make my way around the trembling house, the gaping hole in the floor that led down to an inferno.

I saw a spirit leap for Bianca with blazing hands reached out, and she smote it from the air with a blast of frozen black air. She seized Susan by the wrist and started dragging her toward the front door.

More spirits hurtled toward her, the eldest of the murderers of this house, fire and smoke and splinter—even one that had forged a body for itself out of the spent bullets laying upon the floor.

She fought them off. Talon and magic, she thrust her way through them, and toward the front door. Susan began to wake up, to look around her, her expression terrified.

"Susan!" I shouted. "Susan!"

She began to struggle against Bianca, who hissed, turning toward Susan. She fought to drag my girlfriend closer to the front door, but one of the ghosts clawed at the vampire's leg, setting it aflame.

Bianca screamed, berserk, out of control. She lifted one hand high, her claws glittering, dark, and swept it down at Susan's throat.

I sent my spell hurtling out along with Susan's name, the last strength of my body and mind.

I saw her rise. Rachel's ghost. She appeared, simple and translucent and pretty, and put herself between Bianca's claws and Susan's throat. Blood gouted from the ghost, scarlet and horrible. Susan tumbled limply to one side. Bianca started screaming, high enough to shatter glass, as the bloody ghost simply pressed against her, wrapping her arms around the monstrous black form.

My spell followed on the heels of Rachel's ghost, and took Bianca full in the face, a near-solid column of wind, which seized her, hurtled her up, and then smashed her down into the floor. The overstrained boards gave way beneath her with a creak and a roar, and flame washed up toward me in a wave of reeking black smoke. I felt my balance spin and I struggled to make it to the exit, but fell to the ground.

Spirits flooded after Bianca, fire and smoke, following the vampire sorceress down the hole. The house itself screamed, a sound of tortured wood and twisted beam, and began to fall.

I couldn't get my balance. I felt small, strong hands under one of my arms. And then I felt Susan beneath the other, powerful and terrified. She lifted me to my feet. Justine stayed by my other side, and together, we stumbled out of the old house.

We had gone no more than a dozen paces when it collapsed with a roar. We turned, and I saw the house drawing *in* upon itself, sucked down into the earth, into an inferno of flame. The fire department, later, called it some kind of inverted backblast, but I know what I saw. I saw the ghosts the dead had left behind settle the score.

"I love you," I said, or tried to say, to Susan. "I love you."

She pressed her mouth to mine. I think she was crying. "Hush," she said. "Harry. Hush. I love you, too."

It was done.

There was no more reason to hold on.

Chapter 39

I regard it as one last sadistic gibe of whatever power had decided to make my life a living hell that the burn ward was full, and I was given a room to share with Charity Carpenter. She had recovered in spirit, if not in body, and she started in on me the moment I awoke. The woman's tongue was sharper than any sword. Even *Amoracchius*. I smiled through most of it. Michael would have been proud.

The baby, I learned, had taken an abrupt turn for the better in the hours before dawn the morning Bianca's house had burned. I thought that maybe Kravos had taken a bite of the little guy, and I had gotten it back for him. Michael thought God had simply decreed the morning to be a day of good things. Whatever. The results were what counted.

"We've decided," Michael said, stretching a strong arm around Charity, "to name him Harry."

Charity glowered at me, but remained silent.

"Harry?" I asked. "Harry Carpenter? Michael, what did that poor kid ever do to you?"

But it made me feel good. And they kept the name.

Charity got out of the hospital three days before me. Michael or Father Forthill remained with me for the rest of my stay. No one ever said anything, but Michael had the sword with him, and Forthill kept a crucifix handy. Just in case I had some nasty visitors.

One night when I couldn't sleep, I mentioned to Michael that I was worried about the repercussions of my workings, the harmful magic I had dished out. I worried that it was going to come back to haunt me.

"I'm not a philosopher, Harry," he said. "But here's something for you to think about, at least. What goes around comes around. And sometimes you get what's coming around." He paused for a moment, frowning faintly, pursing his lips. "And sometimes you *are* what's coming around. You see what I mean?"

I did. I was able to get back to sleep.

Michael explained that he and Thomas had escaped the fight at the bridge only a few moments after it had begun. But time had stretched oddly, between the Nevernever and Chicago, and they hadn't emerged until two o'clock the following afternoon.

"Thomas brought us out into this flesh pit," Michael said.

"I'm not a wizard," Thomas pointed out. "I can only get in and out of the Nevernever at points close to my heart."

"A house of sin!" Michael said, his expression stern.

"A *gentlemen's* club," Thomas protested. "And one of the nicest ones in town."

I kept my mouth shut. Who says I never grow any wiser?

Murphy came out of the sleeping spell a couple days later. I had to go in a wheelchair, but I went to Kravos's funeral with her. She pushed me through a drizzling rain to the grave site. There was a city official there, who signed off on some papers and left. Then it was just us and the grave diggers, shovels whispering on earth.

Murphy watched the proceedings in complete silence, her eyes sunken, the blue faded out until they seemed almost grey. I didn't push, and she didn't talk until the hole was half filled in.

"I couldn't stop him," she said, then. "I tried."

"But we beat him. That's why we're here and he's there."

"*You* beat him," Murphy said. "A lot of good I did you."

"He sucker punched you. Even if you'd been a wizard, he'd have gotten to you—like he damn near did me." I shivered, remembered agony making the muscles of my belly tight. "Karrin, you can't blame yourself for that."

"I know," she said, but she didn't sound like she meant it. She was quiet for a long time, and I finally figured out that she wasn't talking because I'd hear the tears in her voice, the ones the rain hid from me. She didn't bow her head though, and she didn't look away from the grave.

I reached out and found her hand with mine. I squeezed. She squeezed back, silent and tight. We stayed there, in the rain, until the last bit of earth had been thrown over Kravos's coffin.

On the way out, Murphy stopped my wheelchair, frowning at

a white headstone next to a waiting plot. "He died doing the right thing," she read. She looked down at me.

I shrugged, and felt my mouth curl up on one side. "Not yet. Not today."

Michael and Forthill took care of Lydia for me. Her real name was Barbara something. They got her packed up and moved out of town. Apparently, the Church has some kind of equivalent of the Witness Protection Program, for getting people out of the reach of supernatural baddies. Forthill told me how the girl had fled the church because she'd been terrified that she would fall asleep, and gone out to find some uppers. The vampires had grabbed her while she was out, which was when I'd found them in that old building. She sent me a note that read, simply, "I'm sorry. Thank you for everything."

When I got out of the hospital, Thomas sent me a thank-you letter, for saving Justine. He sent it on a little note card attached to a bow, which was all Justine was wearing. I'll let you guess where the bow was. I took the note, but not the girl. There was too much of an ick factor in sharing girls with a sex vampire. Justine was pretty enough, and sweet enough, when she wasn't walking the razor's edge of an organic emotional instability—but I couldn't really hold that against her. Plenty of people have to take some kind of medication to keep stable. Lithium, supermodel sex vampires—whatever works, I guess.

I had woman problems of my own.

Susan sent me flowers and called me every day, in the hospital. But she didn't ever talk to me for long. And she didn't come to visit. When I got out, I went to her apartment. She didn't live there anymore. I tried to call her at work, and never managed to catch her. Finally, I had to resort to magic. I used some hair of hers left on a brush at my apartment, and tracked her down on a beach along Lake Michigan, on one of the last warm days of the year.

I found her laying in the sun wearing a white bikini that left maximum surface area bared to it. I sat down next to her, and her manner changed, subtly, a quiet tension that I didn't miss, though I couldn't see her eyes behind the sunglasses she wore.

"The sun helps," she said. "Sometimes it almost goes away for a while."

"I've been trying to find you," I said. "I wanted to talk to you."

"I know," she said. "Harry. Things have changed for me. In the daylight, it's not too bad. But at night." She shivered. "I have to lock myself inside. I don't trust myself around people, Harry."

"I know," I said. "You know what's happening?"

"I talked to Thomas," she said. "And Justine. They were nice enough, I guess. They explained things to me."

I grimaced. "Look," I said. "I'm going to help you. I'll find some way to get you out of this. We can find a cure." I reached out and took her hand. "Oh, Hell's bells, Susan. I'm no good at this." I just fumbled the ring onto it, clumsy as you please. "I don't want you far away. Marry me."

She sat up, and stared at her hand, at the dinky ring I'd been able to afford. Then she leaned close to me and gave me a slow, heated kiss, her mouth melting-warm. Our tongues touched. Mine went numb. I got a little dizzy, as the slow throb of pleasure that I'd felt before coursed through me, a drug I'd craved without realizing it.

She drew away from me slowly, her face expressionless behind the sunglasses. She said, "I can't. You already made me ache for you, Harry. I couldn't control myself, with you. I couldn't sort out the hungers." She pressed the ring into my hand and stood up, gathering her towel and a purse with her. "Don't come to me again. I'll call you."

And she left.

I'd bragged to Kravos, at the end, that I'd been trained to demolish nightmares when I was younger. And to a certain extent it was true. If something came into my head for a fight, I could put up a good one. But now I had nightmares that were all my own. A part of me. And they were always the same: darkness, trapped, with the vampires all around me, laughing their hissing laughter.

I'd wake up, screaming and crying. Mister, curled against my legs, would raise his head and rumble at me. But he wouldn't pad away. He'd just settle down again, purring like a snowmobile's engine. I found it a comfort. And I slept with a light always close.

"Harry," Bob said one night. "You haven't been working. You've barely left your apartment. The rent was due last week. And this vampire research is going nowhere fast."

"Shut up, Bob," I told him. "This unguent isn't right. If we can find a way to convert it to a liquid, maybe we can work it into a supplement of some kind—"

"*Harry,*" Bob said.

I looked up at the skull.

"Harry. The Council sent a notice to you today."

I stood up, slowly.

"The vampires. The Council's at war. I guess Paris and Berlin went into chaos almost a week ago. The Council is calling a meeting. Here."

"The White Council is coming to Chicago," I mused.

"Yeah. They're going to want to know what the hell happened."

I shrugged. "I sent them my report. I only did what was right," I said. "Or as close to it as I could manage. I couldn't let them have her, Bob. I couldn't."

The skull sighed. "I don't know if that will hold up with them, Harry."

"It has to," I said.

There was a knock at my door. I climbed up from the lab. Murphy and Michael had shown up at my door with a care package: soup and charcoal and kerosene for me, as the weather got colder. Groceries. Fruit. Michael had, rather pointedly, included a razor.

"How are you doing, Dresden?" Murphy asked me, her blue eyes serious.

I stared at her for a moment. Then at Michael.

"I could be worse," I said. "Come in."

Friends. They make it easier.

So, the vampires are out to get me, and every other wizard on the block. The little wizardlings of the city, the have-nots of magic, are making it a point not to go outside after dark. I don't order pizza for delivery anymore. Not after the first guy almost got me with a bomb.

The Council is going to be furious at me, but what else is new.

Susan doesn't call. Doesn't visit. But I got a card from her, on my birthday, Halloween. She only wrote three words.

I'll let you guess what three.

Jim Butcher is a ten-year student of martial arts, including Ryuku Kempo, Tae Kwan Do, Gojo Shorei Ryu, and a sprinkling of Kung Fu. He is a skilled rider and has worked as a summer camp horse wrangler and performed in front of large audiences in both drill riding and stunt riding exhibitions. He also enjoys fencing, singing, songwriting, and live-action gaming. He works as a computer support technician, although he has held a variety of jobs in the past, from fast-food management to door-to-door vacuum selling. Jim lives in Oklahoma with his wife and son and a houseful of computers.